2011 不求人文化

2009 懶鬼子英日語

我識出版集團
I'm Publishing Group
www.17buy.com.tw

2005 意識文化

2005 易富文化

2003 我識地球村

2001 我識出版社

2011 不求人文化

2009 懶鬼子英日語

我識出版集團
I'm Publishing Group
www.17buy.com.tw

2005 意識文化

2005 易富文化

2003 我識地球村

2001 我識出版社

神猜解多益聽力
TOEIC Listening

「攻略」＋「試題」＋「解析」一本搞定

〔攻略本〕

最清楚 的「解題分析」

本書獨創「黃金比例環狀圖」，分析每個題目所相對應的答案出現頻率。學會了這招，你就能勇闖多益測驗，變形考題也不怕！淺顯易懂的比例圖，不僅讓題目變得簡單易懂，節省作答時間之外，更幫助你在面對多益考試上不慌亂，穩穩答題、穩穩拿分！

主角 + 穿著 51%

動作 35%

地點 + 物品 14%

★ 黃金比例環狀圖

攻略 1 | 人與物品的關係

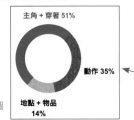

(A)　(B)　(C)　(D)

解題分析

主角 + 穿著 51%

動作 35%

地點 + 物品 14%

■ 主角 + 穿著 51% 推斷可能出現的主角主詞有 The woman、She、A lady……等。關於穿著，根據照片預測可能的字詞有 business suit、black jacket、white shirt、skirt。

■ 動作 35% 主角正在做的事情，可主動預測：standing、making a copy、operating a copy machine……等。

■ 地點 + 物品 14% 因為是在辦公場所，推斷的地點可能：in the office、conference room。而判斷物品可能出現的字詞包括 a white Xerox machine、a file cabinet。

最詳盡 的「解題技巧」

每個人都有自己獨特的個性，每道題也有自己專屬的解題方針。薛詠文老師於各題中詳細列出破解多益考試的解題技巧，一步一步分析該題要怎麼答題，掌握了技巧，就能掌握多益考試命題方向！

解題技巧 第一眼看到照片內容，可先自己在腦中預設可能會出現的關鍵字詞，預測的方式可分為「前景」與「背景」兩個部分：

【前景】

主角 看到前景是一位小姐，便可推斷可能出現的主詞會有：The woman、She、A lady 等。

穿著 這位小姐著較正式的裝扮，便可預測可能的字詞有：business suit、black jacket、white shirt、skirt 等。

動作 圖中主角正在做的事情，很明顯是在操作影印機，可主動預測：standing、making a copy、operating a copy machine 等。

【背景】

地點 此圖應可明確地看出是在辦公場所，所以可推斷的字有：in the office、conference room 等。

解題技巧 第一眼看到照片內容，可先自己在腦中預設可能會出現的關鍵字詞，預測的方式可分為「前景」與「背景」兩個部分：

的字詞包括：a white

輕鬆以對。

各選項解析

• 選項 (A) 內有「The woman is making a copy.」關鍵點正好描述照片內容，故正確。

• 選項 (B) 內的主角「The secretary（祕書）」是有可能沒錯，但動作「taking notes（寫筆記）」這部分不對，故不選。

最精闢 的「題目陷阱」

從小到大面臨的考試哪一個沒有陷阱？最專業的薛詠文老師將全新制多益測驗中每一種類型考題會出現的陷阱逐一點破，幫助你在正式上場時一眼看穿命題老師的詭計，並節省作答時間。也因為多益考試是活用的，所以老師也會隨機補充生活常見的單字或片語用法，讓你就算遇到再多陷阱也不害怕！

題目陷阱 ❶ 因為關鍵點是時間，因此，只要是選項沒有針對時間提供相關資訊，便算是沒有回答問題。就算是將題目中的關鍵字再唸一次也不能算有回答到題目。比方說：

➡ I'll turn in the report soon.（我會盡快交報告。）

此句似乎有提到「soon」，但是「很快」是多快呢？明天嗎？還是十天呢？因此，僅提到 soon 算是沒有精確地回答到 when 為首字的問題喔！

➡ Jerry has turned his report in.（傑瑞已將他的報告交出。）

此句內的關鍵字似乎很合理，此句裡的關鍵字為「has turned... report in」，但對象搞錯了喔！題目是在問對方「your report」，但回答變成在講另外一個人「Jerry」了，如此的答案就其他字都符合也不算是正確答案。

此外，說到「turn in」這個片語，在此題中是「呈交、交出」的意思。其實此片語還有其他的用法與意義，在多益考試中也常出現呢！現在就來整理在下方給同學參考：

❶ turn something in / turn in something (= hand in) 呈交、交出

題目陷阱 ❶ 因為關鍵點是時間，因此，只要是選項沒有針對時間提供相關資訊，便算是沒有回答問題。就算是將題目中的關鍵字再唸一次也不能算有回答到題目。比方說：

➡ I handed in the exam paper and left the classroom.
（我交出考卷後就離開教室。）

最道地 的「四國口音」

許多人在準備多益考試時，比較熟悉的是美國和英國口音。但別忘了世界上使用英文的人很多，所以也會有各種口音出現在多益考試中喔！除了大家較為熟悉的美、英口音，本書更邀請了澳、加口音的外國人來錄製，不僅提升考試的即戰力，在生活中遇到來自不同國家的外國人，也能應對自如！

★ 本書附贈 CD 內容音檔為 MP3 格式。
★ 攻略本的音檔依照頁數劃分成一頁一音軌，試題本的 2 回模擬試題音檔名為「Actual Test」。
★ 全書多益聽力題目完整收錄。

聽稿	(AU / W)	Hello. I'm Vicky Grand. I called three days ago to inform you that I hadn't received my book order and I'm calling again to let you know it still hasn't arrived.
英國口音	(UK / M)	Let me check the record for you please, Ms. Vicky Grand. Well, you ordered 4 books, and one book didn't arrive yet, so I couldn't send the whole package out until we'd received all four books.
澳洲口音	(AU / W)	Come on, how many more days do I need to wait anyway?
	(UK / M)	I'm truly sorry about this, Ms. Grand. I'll try my best to send the all four books out to you within two days.

聽稿	(US / W)	Hi, my name is Diane Brown. I need to cancel my checking account. Can you help me with that?
加拿大口音	(CA / M)	Ms. Brown, hi. Um... do you have a problem with your checking account?
美國口音	(US / W)	Well, I don't need two different accounts actually. I'd also like to transfer the money to my savings account.
	(CA / M)	All right, Ms. Brown. Please sign here and it'll take me around ten minutes to process your money transfer and account cancellation.

最準確 的「模擬試題」

本書 2 回擬真模擬試題由 6 次多益滿分補教名師「薛詠文」撰寫、全新制多益解題小組審訂，完全依照正式考試，讓你實戰體驗。命中率最高的題目、所備題型最多元、訓練答題速度，上考場絕不再手忙腳亂！

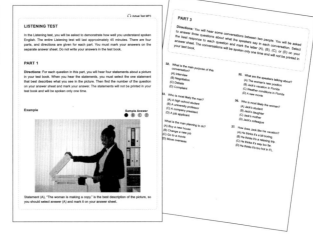

最完整 的「攻略 + 試題 + 解析」

玩遊戲有攻略，面對多益考試當然也要有！想要一次考過多益測驗，就要從攻略下手！並搭配試題、解析輔助，才能增加學習成效，也才能真正取得高分！本書深入聽力各類題考試重點，加上模擬試題和詳盡的解析，絕對能在考場上助你一臂之力！

★ 全新制題型：本書中若出現全新制的題目，則是以 🆕 的符號來標示，幫你快速掌握新制考題。

🆕 **Q3. Look at the table. Which meeting room will th**
　　(A) 7B　　　　　　　　　　　　　　(B
　　(C) 1S　　　　　　　　　　　　　　(D

🆕 **第三題**

在對話播放之前，應該要先大致讀一下印在題本上的題目這時就要在心中先做好準備，表格要搭配對話中的線索才可room will the speakers have the meeting in?」，主要考大議室開會。

根據對話中男子最後一句「I think the length of the mee meeting ends by noon...」的內容，可以得知會議有可能在表，就能得出此會議最有可能是在 5A 會議室舉辦的答案，

　　大多數台灣企業都會採取多益測驗當作錄取門檻，而多益題型變化多端，大家如何提高分數是一件重要的事。針對聽力測驗的新制題型，考生擔憂的不外乎是：對話篇幅加長；Part 3簡短對話題還新增了三人對話；甚至是一邊聽內容，還要一邊對照表格才可答題。

　　首先，我們應該要讓自己在準備多益測驗的同時，**也加強自身聽力能力**，今後在職場上使用英文時更可如魚得水。為了更符合職場情境而設計多樣化的聽力題目。例如在跨國公司開會，不可能只跟美國人講話，也會和有英國口音、澳洲口音、甚至是印度或新加坡口音的同事討論公事。再者，工作上本就會遇到多人開會討論，或一邊聽電話討論，一邊對照業績表的情況呀！

　　聽力考試並不是要考生「將全篇聽力內容聽懂」，考試的目的僅是測驗大家能合適地回答題目就好，考生要做的應是：**先掃瞄題目問些什麼，將注意力馬上聚焦到聽可以回答題目的相關資訊上**，然後在聽內容時一邊在選項中篩選出適合的答案。

　　比方說，先看到題目問「Who is the speaker?」，那麼心中打定主意要聽到「人名、職稱、關係」等字眼，以便回答「Who」問「人物」的相關問題。因此，應付聽力考試時不應使注意力無目標地發散到所有內容或每個單字上，而是應該先看題目，並將所有的注意力都集中到聽可回答題目的要點上即可！如此有意識地、有目標地聽，知道自己應將焦點擺在哪裡，就可以不受刻意設計的不相關內容影響。考生剛開始可能會不習慣「聚焦」的準備方式，但在練習本書內新題型的同時，也透過筆者一而再再而三地提醒「焦點放在哪」，考生將有機會扭轉注意力分散的壞習慣。

　　最後，除了設定多益聽力考高分的目標之外，最好也可以同時提升整體的聽力程度，若平時對英聽有興趣，想多聽英文廣播，那麼可以接觸以下幾種不同口音的新聞廣播節目：

VOA（美國）– https://www.voanews.com/

BBC（英國）– http://www.bbc.com/news

CBC（加拿大）– http://www.cbc.ca/

ABC Radio Australia（澳洲）– http://www.radioaustralia.net.au/international/

祝福所有考生都可以考得自己滿意的分數喔！

蔣詠文

2019.08

何謂 TOEIC 測驗？

TOEIC 是Test of English for International Communication（國際溝通英語測驗）的簡稱。TOEIC 是針對英語非母語之人士所設計的英語能力檢定測驗，測驗分數反映受測者在國際職場環境中，與他人以英語溝通的熟稔程度。測驗內容以日常使用之英語為主，因此參加本測驗毋需具備專業的詞彙。TOEIC是以職場為基準點的英語能力測驗中，世界最頂級的考試。全球有超過四千家企業使用多益測驗，每年有超過兩百萬人應試。

TOEIC 測驗會考的題型有哪些？

多益測驗屬於紙筆測驗，時間為兩小時，總共有二百題，全部為單選題，分成兩大部分：聽力與閱讀，兩者分開計時。

〔第一大類：聽力〕

總共有一百題，由錄音帶播放考題，共有四大題。考生會聽到各種各類英語的直述句、問句、短對話以及短獨白，然後根據所聽到的內容回答問題。聽力的考試時間大約為四十五分鐘。

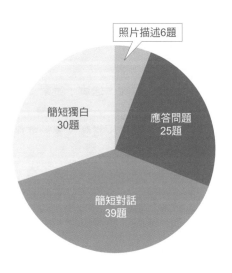

照片描述6題

簡短獨白 30題

應答問題 25題

簡短對話 39題

〔第一大題〕
照片描述 6 題／4選1

〔第二大題〕
應答問題 25 題／3選1

〔第三大題〕
簡短對話 39 題／4選1

〔第四大題〕
簡短獨白 30 題／4選1

〔第二大類：閱讀〕

總共有一百題，題目及選項都印在題本上。考生須閱讀多種題材的文章，然後回答相關問題。考試時間為七十五分鐘，考生可在時限內依自己能力調配閱讀及答題速度。

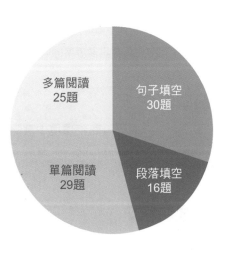

多篇閱讀 25題

句子填空 30題

單篇閱讀 29題

段落填空 16題

〔第五大題〕
句子填空 30 題／4選1

〔第六大題〕
段落填空 16 題／4選1

〔第七大題〕
單篇閱讀 29 題／4選1
多篇閱讀 25 題／4選1

TOEIC 測驗會考的內容有哪些？

TOEIC 的設計以職場的需求為主。測驗題的內容，從全世界各地職場的英文資料中蒐集而來，題材多元化，包含各種地點與狀況，舉例來說：

一般商務	契約、談判、行銷、銷售、商業企劃、會議
製造業	工廠管理、生產線、品管
金融／預算	銀行業務、投資、稅務、會計、帳單
企業發展	研究、產品研發
辦公室	董事會、委員會、信件、備忘錄、電話、傳真、電子郵件、辦公室器材與傢俱、辦公室流程
人事	招考、雇用、退休、薪資、升遷、應徵與廣告
採購	比價、訂貨、送貨、發票
技術層面	電子、科技、電腦、實驗室與相關器材、技術規格
房屋／公司地產	建築、規格、購買租賃、電力瓦斯服務
旅遊	火車、飛機、計程車、巴士、船隻、渡輪、票務、時刻表、車站、機場廣播、租車、飯店、預訂、脫班與取消
外食	商務／非正式午餐、宴會、招待會、餐廳訂位
娛樂	電影、劇場、音樂、藝術、媒體
保健	醫藥保險、看醫生、牙醫、診所、醫院

（雖然取材自這麼多領域，但考生毋需具備專業的商業與技術詞彙。）

TOEIC 測驗的適用範圍為何？

本測驗主要為測試英語非母語人士身處國際商務環境中實際運用英語的能力，為全球跨國企業所採用，其成績可作為評估訓練成果、遴選員工赴海外受訓、招聘員工、內部升遷等之標準；亦可作為個人入學及求職時之英語能力證明。

TOEIC 測驗的計分方式為何？

考生用鉛筆在電腦答案卷上作答。考試分數由答對題數決定，再將每一大類（聽力類、閱讀類）答對題數轉換成分數，範圍在5到495分之間。兩大類加起來即為總分，範圍在10到990分之間。答錯不倒扣。

TOEIC 台灣考試狀況為何？

根據ETS台灣官方統計，2015年度台灣參加多益測驗的人口約有376,706人，平均成績為532分（聽力平均293分／閱讀平均239分）。考生的年齡24歲以下居多，比例約佔77%；男女比例為1:1.30，女性應試者比男性應試者多出30個百分比。

台灣區多益測驗應試者分析：

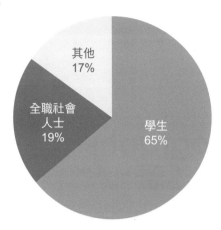

台灣區多益測驗考生成績分布：

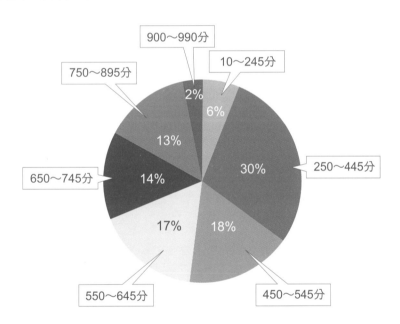

★以上參考數據來自ETS台灣區網站 http://www.toeic.com.tw/

哪裡可以取得更多TOEIC測驗之資訊？

TOEIC在台灣之考試資訊（考試報名、日期及考場等），更多考試訊息請上官網www.toeic.com.tw查詢。

|目錄| C O N T E N T S

PART 1. Photographs
照片描述題 **011**

PART 2. Question-Response
應答問題 **123**

PART 3. Conversations
簡短對話 **235**

PART 4. Talks
簡短獨白 365

100% 全新試題 + **100% 高命中率** + **100% 精闢解析**

=TOEIC多益滿分保證!!

LISTENING

PART

1

照片描述
Photographs

Introduction

當瀏覽照片時，可特別將注意力放在「前景」及「背景」。「前景」應注意「人物」及其「動作」、是否有明顯的「物品」和「交通工具」等；而「背景」應注意人物所在的「地點」、「景觀」和「氣候狀況」等。

分類解析

Unit 1 　一人獨照類
Unit 2 　多人共事類
Unit 3 　辦公情境類
Unit 4 　商旅出差類
Unit 5 　運動體育類
Unit 6 　餐廳飲食類
Unit 7 　建築施工類
Unit 8 　旅遊休閒類
Unit 9 　百貨購物類
Unit 10 　醫療看病類

綜合練習

Unit 1 一人獨照類

攻略 1 | 人與物品的關係

(A)　　(B)　　(C)　　(D)

解題分析

主角 + 穿著 51%

動作 35%

地點 + 物品 14%

■ **主角 + 穿著** 51%　推斷可能出現的主角主詞有 the woman、she、a lady……等。關於穿著，根據照片預測可能的字詞有 business suit、black jacket、white shirt、skirt。

■ **動作** 35%　主角正在做的事情，可主動預測：standing、making a copy、operating a copy machine……等。

■ **地點 + 物品** 14%　因為是在辦公場所，推斷的地點可能是：in the office、conference room。而判斷物品可能出現的字詞包括 a white Xerox machine、a file cabinet。

聽稿
（US / Ⓦ）

(A) The woman is making a copy.
(B) The secretary is taking notes.
(C) The copy machine is being repaired.
(D) The office is overcrowded.

中譯
（美 / 女）

答案：**(A)**
(A) 女子在影印。
(B) 祕書在記筆記。
(C) 影印機正在維修中。
(D) 辦公室非常擁擠。

解題技巧 第一眼看到照片內容，可先自己在腦中預設可能會出現的關鍵字詞，預測的方式可分為「前景」與「背景」兩個部分：

前景

主角 看到前景是一位小姐，便可推斷可能出現的主詞會有：the woman、she、a lady 等。

穿著 這位小姐著較正式的裝扮，便可預測可能的字詞有：business suit、black jacket、white shirt、skirt 等。

動作 圖中主角正在做的事情，很明顯是在操作影印機，可主動預測：standing、making a copy、operating a copy machine 等。

背景

地點 此圖應可明確地看出是在辦公場所，所以可推斷的字有：in the office、conference room 等。

物品 此圖內的物品除了影印機之外，還有檔案櫃，故可判斷可能出現的字詞包括：a white Xerox machine、a file cabinet 等。

在主動預期針對圖片內容可能出現的字詞與句子之後，再聽到題目內容就可輕鬆以對。

各選項解析

• 選項 (A) 內有「The woman is making a copy.」關鍵點正可描述照片內容，故正確。
• 選項 (B) 內的主角「the secretary（祕書）」是有可能沒錯，但動作「taking notes（寫筆記）」這部分不對，故不選。
• 選項 (C) 的「The copy machine（影印機）」在圖中是有出現沒錯，但其後的動作「being repaired（維修中）」並不正確，因自圖中看不出女子是在修影印機，故不選。
• 選項 (D) 內的關鍵字「the office」似乎是沒錯，但聽到其後「overcrowded（過度擁擠）」便可知跟圖片內容不符了，故不選。

題目陷阱 針對此人物照片的陷阱之處可能會是：

❶ 主要人物角色錯誤：A man is operating the copy machine.（男子在操作影印機。）

❷ 主角所進行的動作錯誤：The lady is talking on the phone.（女子正在講電話。）

❸ 主角使用之物品錯誤：The woman is using a laser printer.
　　　　　　　　　　　　（女子正在使用雷射印表機。）

❹ 主角穿著錯誤：The lady is wearing casual clothes.（女子穿著休閒的衣服。）

❺ 主角所在地點錯誤：The lady is standing on the beach.（女子站在沙灘上。）

關鍵字彙

secretary [ˈsɛkrəˌtɛrɪ] n 祕書
repair [rɪˈpɛr] v 修理
overcrowded [ˌovəˈkraʊdɪd] a 過度擁擠的

(A)　　(B)　　(C)　　(D)

解題分析

主角 + 動作 42%

地點 + 物品 35%

主角 + 穿著 23%

■ 主角 + 動作 42%　　由照片可以得知主角是一名女性，推測跟主角有關的主詞會有 the woman、she、a lady……等。圖中最明顯的是她正坐著寫東西，推測可以聽到 sitting、writing、studying 等動作。

■ 地點 + 物品 35%　　由桌上的書本、筆電跟身後的書架，可以清楚看出主角現在正在圖書館，推測地點相關詞為 in the library、studying area 等，而物品可能有 desk、a laptop、some bookshelves 等。

■ 主角 + 穿著 23%　　女子穿著雖無太特殊之處，但可以判斷她的穿著輕鬆隨意，可能聽到 casual attire。髮型為長髮，故可能有 wearing long hair 等詞句。

聽稿
（UK / M）

(A) The woman is doing exercise.
(B) The woman is waiting for the train.
(C) The woman is working on some documents.
(D) The woman is interacting with clients.

中譯
（英 / 男）

答案：(C)
(A) 此女子在運動。
(B) 此女子在等火車。
(C) 此女子在處理一些文件。
(D) 此女子在跟客戶討論。

解題技巧 在聽到題目之前，務必先把握幾秒的時間將圖片掃描，以便預測可能出現的關鍵用字。掃描時可將焦點放在前景與背景的人事物上。

前景

主角 看到前景裡有一位小姐，便可推斷可能出現的主詞會有：the woman、she、a lady……等。

穿著 這位小姐穿著輕鬆隨意的裝扮，便可預測可能的字詞有：casual attire，或此小姐是留長頭髮，便有可能會有 wearing long hair。

動作 圖中女主角正坐著寫東西，便可主動預測可能會聽到：sitting、writing、studying、reading、working on some documents……等。

背景

地點 此照片背景應可明確地看出是在圖書館，所以可推斷的字可能會有：in the library、studying area……等。

物品 此照片內的物品除了前景有桌子，上頭還有台筆記型電腦之外，背景還有書架，故可判斷可能出現的字詞包括：desk、a laptop、some bookshelves……等。

在心中早有預期的情況下，便可將選項中的字與預期的關鍵字比對，以判斷正確的描述。

各選項解析

- 選項 (A)「The woman is doing exercise.」中的 the woman 提到「女子」是沒錯，但動作「doing exercise」意指「在運動」卻與照片中行動不符，故不選。
- 選項 (B)「The woman is waiting for the train.」內關鍵點「waiting for the train」意指「在等火車」，但圖片中女子並非在火車站或月台，故不選。
- 選項 (C)「The woman is working on some documents.」內的關鍵點「working on some documents」意即「在處理一些文件」之意，的確有符合照片內女子的動作，故正確。
- 選項 (D)「The woman is interacting with clients.」內關鍵點「interacting with clients」意即「在跟客戶談話」，但照片中除了女子並無旁人或客戶，故錯誤。

題目陷阱 針對此人物照片的陷阱之處可能會是：

❶ 主要人物角色錯誤：A man is working on his laptop.
（男子正在使用他的筆記型電腦工作。）

❷ 主角所進行的動作錯誤：The lady is giving a presentation.（女子正在報告。）

❸ 主角使用之物品錯誤：The woman is holding a paintbrush.（女子正拿著一枝畫筆。）

❹ 主角穿著錯誤：The lady is wearing a baseball cap.（女子戴著棒球帽。）

❺ 主角所在地點錯誤：The lady is studying in her own room.
（女子正在她自己的房間內讀書。）

關鍵字彙

exercise [ˈɛksɚˌsaɪz] n 運動
wait for ph 等待
document [ˈdɑkjəmənt] n 文件

interact [ˌɪntɚˈrækt] v 互動
client [ˈklaɪənt] n 客戶

(A)　　(B)　　(C)　　(D)

解題分析

主角 + 穿著配件 46%

表情 43%

動作 11%

■ 主角 + 穿著配件 46%

■ 表情 43%

■ 動作 11%

可以明顯看出主角為一位小姐，相關的主詞為 the woman、she、a lady……等。主角的打扮輕鬆隨意，留著長髮，身上有許多配件，推測關鍵字詞可能有 backpack、earphone、smart-phone 或 a cup of coffee。

由於本題的圖片完全沒有背景，因此焦點完全放在人物本身。照片清楚拍到女子的臉部表情，看起來是輕鬆、高興的，推測可能出現 happy、smiling、delighted、relaxed 等形容心情的字。

主角是站著的，便預測可能會聽到：standing 等字眼。

聽稿
（CA / M）

(A) The woman is wearing a formal business suit.
(B) The professor is teaching theories.
(C) The student is doing her homework assignments.
(D) The lady seems happy and relaxed.

中譯
（加 / 男）

答案：(D)
(A) 此女子穿著正式商業套裝。
(B) 此教授在教理論。
(C) 此學生在寫回家作業。
(D) 此女子看起來很高興且放鬆。

解題技巧 在聽到所講的四個答案選項之前，可先掃過照片內容。像是此照片主要篇幅就是一女子，沒有背景的地點，那麼便要將焦點放在掃過此女主角身上的細節上，比方說：

前景

主角 看到前景是一位小姐，便可推斷可能出現的主詞會有：the woman、she、a lady……等。

穿著 這位小姐穿著輕鬆隨意的裝扮，便可預測可能會聽到的字詞有：casual attire、a sweater、jeans 等，或此小姐是留長頭髮，便有可能會有 wearing long hair。

物品 除了身上穿的衣物之外，此小姐還配戴了其他的物品，像是背包、手機、咖啡杯等，便可預期可能會聽到：backpack、earphone、smart-phone 或 a cup of coffee 等關鍵字。

動作 圖中女主角是站著的，便預測可能會聽到：standing 等字眼。

表情 此女主角的神情看起來是輕鬆高興的，故可判斷可能也會有：happy、smiling、delighted、relaxed 等形容心情或情緒的字眼。

各選項解析

- 選項 (A)「The woman is wearing a formal business suit.」內的關鍵人物「the woman」似乎是沒問題了，但另一關鍵點「wearing a business suit」提及「穿套裝」與照片中女子打扮不符，故不選。
- 選項 (B)「The professor is teaching theories.」內的關鍵人物「the professor」意即「教授」聽起來便有點問題了，又加上「teaching theories」提及在「教理論」，便確認與照片不符，故不選。
- 選項 (C)「The student is doing her homework assignments.」內的關鍵人物「the student」與關鍵動作「doing assignments」都沒在照片中出現，故不選。
- 選項 (D)「The lady seems happy and relaxed.」內的關鍵人物「the lady」提及「女子」與關鍵「happy and relaxed」正可以描述照片中女子所展現出來的表情，故選為最佳答案。

題目陷阱 針對此人物照片的陷阱之處可能會是：

❶ 主要人物角色錯誤：The doctor is making a call.（醫生正在打電話。）
❷ 主角所進行的動作錯誤：The woman is swimming.（女子正在游泳。）
❸ 主角使用之物品錯誤：The lady is holding an umbrella.（女子拿著一把傘。）
❹ 主角穿著錯誤：The lady is wearing Japanese costume.（女子穿著日式服飾。）
❺ 主角表情錯誤：The woman appears to be sad.（女子似乎有點難過。）

關鍵字彙

formal [`fɔrml] a 正式的
theory [`θiərɪ] n 理論
assignment [ə`saɪnmənt] n 指定作業、任務
relaxed [rɪ`lækst] a 放鬆的

(A)　　(B)　　(C)　　(D)

解題分析

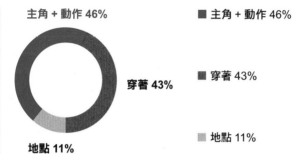

主角 + 動作 46%

穿著 43%

地點 11%

■ **主角 + 動作 46%**

■ **穿著 43%**

■ **地點 11%**

可以明顯看出主角為一名男性，相關的主詞為 the man、he 等。圖片中這位男子在做木工，故聯想到職業相關的字彙 carpenter。

男子身穿工作服，可能會有相關字詞 carpenter work apron 或是 tool apron，同時他也戴著護目鏡，可預測 wearing safety glasses 或 protective glasses 等詞彙。

工作的地點可能在一間裝潢中的廚房或房間，可預測出現：in a room、in the working area。

聽稿

（AU / Ｗ）

(A) The man is writing a report.

(B) The carpenter is working on a project.

(C) The janitor is cleaning the room.

(D) The boy is drawing a house.

中譯

（澳 / 女）

答案：**(B)**

(A) 此男子在寫報告。

(B) 此木匠在處理一建案。

(C) 此清潔員在打掃房間。

(D) 此男孩在畫一間房子。

解題技巧 　在四個答案選項播出之前會有幾秒時間可以先將照片內容看一下，以便在心中預測可能會聽到的關鍵用字。

前景

主角 　看到前景有一位男子，便可推斷可能出現的主詞會有 the man、he 等。且他又是在做木工，因此也有可能會唸出他的職業，比方說：carpenter 等。

穿著 　這位先生穿著工作服，便可預測可能的字詞有：carpenter work apron 或是 tool apron 等，或還戴著保護性質的眼鏡，便有可能會有 wearing safety glasses 或 protective glasses 等。

動作 　照片中男子正站著工作，便預測可能會聽到：standing、working on a project 等。

背景

地點 　此照片背景可能是房子內尚在裝潢的廚房或房間，因此可以推斷的字可能有：in a room、in the working area 等。

各選項解析

- 選項 (A)「The man is writing a report.」內的關鍵人物「the man」似乎沒問題，但在關鍵行動方面提到「writing a report」是在「寫報告」，這與照片中男子在做的事不符，故不選。
- 選項 (B)「The carpenter is working on a project.」內的關鍵人物「the carpenter」意即「木工」正是照片中的人物，且行動方面是「working on a project」也是與照片內容相符，故為最佳答案。
- 選項 (C)「The janitor is cleaning the room.」內的人物提到「the janitor」為「清潔工」，且關鍵動作是「cleaning the room」即「在清掃房間」，但這些都與照片內情景不符，故不選。
- 選項 (D)「The boy is drawing a house.」內提到「the boy」意為「男孩」，這照片中的是男子，且動作是「draw a house」，照片中男子也不是在「畫房子」，故不是答案。

題目陷阱 　針對此人物照片的陷阱之處可能會是：

❶ 主要人物角色錯誤：The professor is grading papers.（教授正在改作業。）

❷ 主角所進行的動作錯誤：The man is drawing flowers.（男子正在畫花。）

❸ 主角使用之物品錯誤：The gentleman is raising his hand.（男子舉起手。）

❹ 主角穿著錯誤：The old man is wearing a heavy jacket.（這位老人穿著厚重的外套。）

❺ 主角所在地點錯誤：The man is enjoying dinner in a restaurant.
（男子正在餐廳裡吃晚餐。）

關鍵字彙

carpenter [`karpəntɚ] n 木匠、木工
project [`pradʒɛkt] n 專案
janitor [`dʒænɪtɚ] n 清潔人員
draw [drɔ] v 畫畫、繪圖

(A)　　(B)　　(C)　　(D)

解題分析

主角 + 穿著 50%

動作 38%

地點、物品
12%

■ **主角 + 穿著** 50%　　圖片當中的主角是一位老先生，推測主詞有 the man、an old man、the grandfather…… 等。主角身穿毛衣、裝扮輕鬆，可能會出現 casual clothes、wearing a sweater 等，又戴著眼鏡，很有可能為老花眼鏡 reading glasses。

■ **動作** 38%　　主角在餐桌前，一手拿著報紙，一手拿著馬克杯，推測可能出現 sitting、reading newspapers、drinking coffee 等相關動作。

■ **地點、物品** 12%　　圖片的背景可以看出主角在家中的餐廳，可能聽到 in the dining room、in the kitchen 等字眼，桌上有相應的物品水果和點心，窗邊則擺放盆栽，故可能出現的字詞包括：desk、fruit、snacks、window、potted plants 等等。

聽稿

（CA / Ⓜ）

(A) The grandfather is playing with his grandsons.
(B) The man is reading newspapers.
(C) The physician is standing by the desk.
(D) The waiter is preparing coffee.

中譯

（加 / 男）

答案：**(B)**

(A) 此爺爺在跟他的孫子們玩。
(B) 此男子在看報紙。
(C) 此內科醫生站在桌旁。
(D) 此服務生在準備咖啡。

解題技巧 聽題目時眼神不應亂飄，而是應該將注意力放在看照片上，以便推論可能之關鍵用字。掃描照片時可注意前景的人物與背景的地點等。

前景

主角 看到前景是一位老先生，便可推斷可能出現的主詞會有：the man、an old man、the grandfather……等。

穿著 這位老先生穿著毛衣，便可預測可能會聽到：casual clothes、wearing a sweater……等，或還戴著老花眼鏡，便有可能會有 wearing reading glasses。

動作 照片中男主角正坐著看報紙，手上握著咖啡杯，便主動預測可能會聽到：sitting、reading newspapers、drinking coffee……等。

表情 此老先生的表情是歡笑愉快的，形容他的表情與心情的字可能會有：delighted、glad、smiling、contented 或 pleased。

背景

地點 此照片背景可明顯地看出是在家中的餐廳，因此推斷可能會聽到的字會有：in the dining room、in the kitchen 等。

物品 此照片內的物品除了前景有桌子，桌上還有水果和點心，故可判斷可能出現的字詞包括：desk、fruit、snacks 等。

裝潢 老人的背後還有窗戶，上面還有盆栽，因此可預期會聽到：window、potted plants 等。

各選項解析

- 選項 (A)「The grandfather is playing with his grandsons.」內的關鍵人物「the grandfather」似乎可以指照片中的老公公，但關鍵動作「playing with his grandsons」出現點問題，因照片中並沒看到「孫子」，故不選。
- 選項 (B)「The man is reading newspapers.」內的關鍵人物「the man」的確是在講照片中的男子，且動作方面是「reading newspapers」意即在「看報紙」，這的確是照片中男子在做的事，故為最佳答案。
- 選項 (C)「The physician is standing by the desk.」內的關鍵人物是「the physician」提及是「醫生」，且動作是「standing」意即「站著」，但照片中並沒有「醫生站在桌旁」，故不選。
- 選項 (D)「The waiter is preparing coffee.」內關鍵人物是「the waiter」意即「服務生」，且動作是「preparing coffee」意即「準備咖啡」，但這些都沒有在照片中出現，故不選。

題目陷阱 針對此人物照片的陷阱之處可能會是：

❶ 主要人物角色錯誤：The grandmother is taking care of a kid.
（這位奶奶正在照顧孩子。）

❷ 主角所進行的動作錯誤：The man is putting newspapers away.（男子把報紙歸位。）

❸ 主角使用之物品錯誤：The old man is holding an umbrella.（老先生正握著一把傘。）

❹ 主角穿著錯誤：The man is wearing swimming suit.（男子穿著泳裝。）

❺ 主角所在地點錯誤：The man is standing on the street.（男子正站在街上。）

關鍵字彙

physician [fɪ`zɪʃən] n 內科醫生

waiter [`wetɚ] n 服務生

prepare [prɪ`pɛr] v 準備

Unit 2 多人共事類

攻略 1 | 情境與人物

(A)　(B)　(C)　(D)

解題分析

主角＋穿著 36%

動作 36%

地點、物品 28%

■ 主角＋穿著 36%
圖片的前景出現兩個人，根據兩人的外表與互動可推測是爸爸和小女孩，所以可能出現 man、father、girl、daughter 等字詞。圖中兩人都穿著圍裙，因此可能會聽到 apron 這個字。

■ 動作 36%
兩人是站著正在切菜準備餐點，也許會聽到 standing、preparing food、cooking lunch、cutting fruit 等。兩個人臉部表情是愉快的，所以也有可能出現 smiling、joyful 之類的詞彙。

■ 地點、物品 28%
照片中的前景除了料理台外，還有蔬菜，也可能會出現許多廚房用具的詞彙，兩人的後方則有窗戶，櫥櫃與冰箱等，因此還可預期聽到的有 window、refrigerator、cabinet 等等。

聽稿
（US / Ⓦ）
(A) They're cleaning the carpet.
(B) They're preparing meals.
(C) They're having a party outdoors.
(D) They're fixing the refrigerator.

中譯
（美 / 女）
答案：**(B)**
(A) 他們正在清地毯。
(B) 他們正在準備餐點。
(C) 他們在參加戶外派對。
(D) 他們在修電冰箱。

解題技巧 利用短暫的時間將注意力放在掃過照片上，以便推論可能聽到之關鍵用字。

前景

主角 看到前景是一位爸爸與小女孩，便可推斷可能出現的主詞會有：man、father、girl、daughter……等。

穿著 兩人都穿著圍裙，自然可預測會聽到：an apron 的字眼。

動作 照片中兩人都站著在準備餐點與切水果，便主動預測可能會聽到：standing、preparing food、cooking lunch、cutting fruit……等。

表情 兩人的表情是歡笑愉快的，便預期可能會有相關字詞：smiling、joyful、enjoying their time together……等。

背景

地點 此照片背景可明顯地看出是在家中的廚房，因此推斷可能會聽到的字會有：in the kitchen。

物品 此照片內的物品除了前景有料理台，桌上還有蔬菜，故可判斷可能出現的字詞包括：countertop、vegetables……等。

裝潢 兩人的背後還有窗戶，廚櫃與冰箱等，因此還可預期會聽到：window、refrigerator、cabinet……等物品相關字詞。

各選項解析

- 選項 (A)「They're cleaning the carpet.」內的關鍵動作「cleaning the carpet」意即「清理地毯」，但這與照片中人物動作不符，故不選。
- 選項 (B)「They're preparing meals.」內的關鍵動作「preparing meals」意即「準備餐點」，照片內兩人是在處理食物、準備餐點沒錯，故正確。
- 選項 (C)「They're having a party outdoors.」內的動作「having a party」與關鍵地點「outdoors」都與照片內容不符，故不可選。
- 選項 (D)「They're fixing the refrigerator.」內提及一個物品的關鍵字「refrigerator」，的確照片背景有台冰箱，但兩人並沒有在「fixing」修理冰箱，故此選項也是故意使用混淆的字而已，不可選。

題目陷阱 針對此人物照片的陷阱之處可能會是：

❶ 主要人物角色錯誤：The doctor is giving the baby a checkup.（醫生正在幫嬰兒檢查。）

❷ 主角所進行的動作錯誤：They are doing homework assignments.
　（他們正在寫回家作業。）

❸ 主角使用之物品錯誤：Both of them are working on the computer.
　（他們兩人都在用電腦工作。）

❹ 主角穿著錯誤：Only the girl is wearing an apron.（只有女孩穿著圍裙。）

❺ 主角所在地點錯誤：They plan to buy a refrigerator in an electronic store.
　（他們計劃去電器行買冰箱。）

關鍵字彙

carpet [ˋkɑrpɪt] n. 地毯
refrigerator [rɪˋfrɪdʒəˌretə] n. 冰箱

攻略 2 | 多人討論

(A)　　(B)　　(C)　　(D)

解題分析

主角 + 穿著 44%

動作 36%

地點、物品 20%

■ 主角 + 穿著 44%　　圖片中有七個穿著套裝的人，可以合理推測是商業人士，推斷可能出現的主詞有 some workers、colleagues、employees……等。關於套裝也可能聽到 business suit、formal business attire、tie、shirts 等字眼。

■ 動作 36%　　七個人圍成一圈，坐著討論公事，或是也有可能在會議中，可能聽到相關動作 meeting、discussing、exchanging ideas、expressing opinions……等。

■ 地點、物品 20%　　照片中的地點可以明顯看出在會議室，故有機會出現的詞彙：in the office、in the conference room。桌上擺放著許多物品，如筆電、水杯、文件等，人物後方的背景擺放著小黑板和檔案櫃，這些辦公室用品都有可能在選項中出現。

聽稿
（AU / Ⓦ）

(A) People are having a picnic in the park.
(B) Students are listening to the lecture.
(C) Team members are discussing business issues.
(D) Managers are socializing on the golf course.

中譯
（澳 / 女）

答案：**(C)**
(A) 大夥在公園野餐。
(B) 學生們在聽課。
(C) 團隊同仁在討論商業議題。
(D) 經理們在高爾夫球場上社交。

解題技巧　很快地大略掃過一下照片，以便推論可能聽到之關鍵用字。再搭配看前景和背景的技巧，就能大概知曉答案。

前景

主角　看到前景是七位穿著商務套裝的員工，便可推斷可能出現的主詞會有：some workers、colleagues、employees、team members、representatives……等。

穿著	七人都穿著套裝，自然可預測會聽到：business suit、formal business attire、tie、shirts ……等字眼。
動作	照片中七人都圍坐著開會，便主動預測可能會聽到：sitting、round table、meeting、discussing、exchanging ideas、expressing opinions……等。
表情	由中間那幾位男子與女子的表情看來是愉快有笑容的，便預期可能會有相關字詞：smiling、light discussion、positive attitude……等。

背景

地點	此照片背景可明顯地看出是在公司會議室，因此推斷可能會聽到的字會有：in the office、in the conference room。
物品	此照片內的物品除了桌上有筆電、水杯和文件之外，背景還有檔案櫃與一個小黑板，故可判斷可能出現的字詞包括：laptops、glasses、documents、file cabinet 與 blackboard……等。

各選項解析

• 選項 (A)「People are having a picnic in the park.」內的關鍵行動「having a picnic」意即「野餐」與關鍵地點「in the park」意即「在公園」都不是照片內容所呈現的，故不選。

• 選項 (B)「Students are listening to the lecture.」內的關鍵人物點「students」就已經不對了，聽到「listening to the lecture」意即「在聽課」，這些與照片中的「商務人士在開會」場景不符，故不選。

• 選項 (C)「Team members are discussing business issues.」內聽到關鍵人物「team members」與關鍵動作「discussing issues」意即「同仁討論商業議題」的確有針對照片內容描述，故正確。

• 選項 (D)「Managers are socializing on the golf course.」內關鍵人物「managers」意即「經理人」似乎可以，但行動方面「socializing」與地點方面「on the golf course」提及「在高爾夫球場上社交」都與照片內容不符，故不選。

題目陷阱

針對此人物照片的陷阱之處可能會是：

❶ 主要人物角色錯誤：Some construction workers are having a discussion.
（一些建築工人正在討論。）

❷ 主角所進行的動作錯誤：All sales representatives are listening to an online speech.
（所有的業務代表都在聽線上演講。）

❸ 主角使用之物品錯誤：All of them are wearing glasses.（他們都戴著眼鏡。）

❹ 主角穿著錯誤：All workers are wearing T-shirts.（所有工人都穿著 T 恤。）

❺ 主角所在地點錯誤：They are listening to a presentation in a lecture hall.
（他們在演講廳裡聽一場報告。）

關鍵字彙

lecture [ˈlɛktʃɚ] n 授課、課程
member [ˈmɛmbɚ] n 成員、隊員
issue [ˈɪʃju] n 議題、事件

socialize [ˈsoʃəˌlaɪz] v 社交、交際、聯誼
golf course [ˈɡɑlf ˌkors] n 高爾夫球場

(A)　　(B)　　(C)　　(D)

解題分析

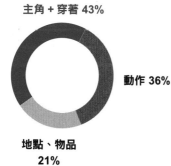

主角 + 穿著 43%

動作 36%

地點、物品 21%

■ 主角 + 穿著 43%　　圖中有一位老先生跟一位小男孩，有可能是祖孫關係，所以推測會聽到 the old man、grandfather、the child、boy 等主詞。兩人穿著輕鬆，較需注意的是小男孩的頭上戴著安全帽，可能出現 helmet 等字。

■ 動作 36%　　兩個人的動作不相同，小男孩在騎腳踏車，老先生則站在旁邊扶著，可能聽到 standing by the boy、riding a bike 等相關動作。兩人的表情是愉快的，推測有 smiling、enjoying 等可能性。

▨ 地點、物品 21%　　地點可以很明顯看出在戶外，由背景的樹林和草皮可以猜測他們在一座公園中，可主動推測會出現：in the park、outdoors 等字眼。

聽稿

（UK / Ⓜ ）

(A) The old man is wearing long hair.
(B) The child is standing right next to his mom.
(C) The teacher is giving a speech.
(D) The boy is learning to ride a bike.

中譯

（英 / 男 ）

答案：(D)

(A) 此老先生留長頭髮。
(B) 這個小孩站在他媽媽旁邊。
(C) 這個老師在演講。
(D) 這個小男孩在學騎腳踏車。

解題技巧	在聽到四個選項之前先把握時間，將注意力放在掃過大概的照片內容上，以便推論可能聽到之關鍵用字。

前景

主角 看到前景是一位老人與小孩子，便可推斷可能出現的主詞會有：the old man、grandfather、the child、boy……等。

穿著 兩人都穿著輕鬆的便服，自然可預測會聽到：casual clothes 等字眼。且小孩頭上還戴著安全帽，故有可能會聽到 helmet 等字。

動作 照片中老人是站著的，小孩是騎在腳踏車上，便主動預測可能會聽到：standing by the boy、riding a bike……等。

表情 兩人的表情是歡笑愉快的，便預期可能會有相關字詞：smiling、enjoying 或 pleased。

背景

地點 此照片背景可明顯地看出是戶外公園，因此推斷可能會聽到的字會有：in the park、outdoors 等。

物品 此照片內的地點除了看出是公園之外，背景還有些樹林，故可判斷可能出現的字詞包括：trees。

各選項解析

- 選項 (A)「The old man is wearing long hair.」內的關鍵人物「the old man」似乎沒錯，但其後「wearing long hair」意即「留長頭髮」便與照片內容不符了，故不選。
- 選項 (B)「The child is standing right next to his mom.」內的關鍵動作「standing」與位置「next to his mom」意即「站在媽媽旁邊」，但照片內容是「小孩在騎車」，並非站著，故不選。
- 選項 (C)「The teacher is giving a speech.」內的關鍵人物是「the teacher」與關鍵動作「giving a speech」意即「老師在講課」這些都與照片內容不符，故不選。
- 選項 (D)「The boy is learning to ride a bike.」內關鍵人物「the boy」與關鍵行動「learning to ride a bike」意即「小男孩在學騎車」，的確就是在學騎車，才會有大人在旁協助，有描述到照片內容，故正確。

題目陷阱 針對此人物照片的陷阱之處可能會是：

❶ 主要人物角色錯誤：The mother is teaching her girl how to swim.
（媽媽正在教女兒游泳。）

❷ 主角所進行的動作錯誤：They are enjoying their vacation on the beach.
（他們正在海灘上享受假期。）

❸ 主角使用之物品錯誤：The child is learning to ride a scooter.（小孩正在學騎機車。）

❹ 主角穿著錯誤：The grandfather is wearing a helmet.（爺爺戴著安全帽。）

❺ 主角所在地點錯誤：They are drinking in the bar.（他們正在酒吧裡喝酒。）

關鍵字彙

wear [wɛr] ⅴ 留（頭髮）
speech [spitʃ] ⅿ 演講
ride [raɪd] ⅴ 騎乘

(A)　　(B)　　(C)　　(D)

解題分析

主角 + 穿著 40%

動作 38%

地點、物品 22%

■ 主角 + 穿著 40%

■ 動作 38%

■ 地點、物品 22%

圖中有三個人，分別是兩女一男，推斷可能出現 two women、a man 等字詞。三人都穿著輕便襯衫，中間那名女子穿著圍裙，推測會聽見 shirts、apron 等衣著方面的詞彙。

照片中，三個人都在準備食物，主動預測可能會聽到：standing、preparing food、cooking lunch、meals⋯⋯等。

照片的地點為廚房，因此推斷可能會聽到的字會有：in the kitchen。照片內的物品除了前景有料理台，桌上還有蔬菜，故可判斷可能出現的字詞包括：countertop、vegetables 等。

聽稿
（AU /Ⓦ）

(A) They are preparing meals.
(B) They are having a serious discussion.
(C) They are enjoying their vacation.
(D) They are working on a term paper.

中譯
（澳 /女）

答案：(A)

(A) 他們在準備餐點。
(B) 他們在討論嚴肅的議題。
(C) 他們在享受假期。
(D) 他們在寫學期報告。

解題技巧

在聽到四個選項之前，可利用短暫的時間將照片很快地掃過一下，以便預測可能聽到之關鍵用字。一樣將照片分成前景和背景來解題。

前景

主角　看到前景是兩女一男，便可推斷可能出現的主詞會有：two women、a man 等字詞。

穿著 三人都穿輕便的襯衫，中間那位女子穿著圍裙，自然可預測會聽到：shirts、apron 等字眼。

動作 照片中三人都站著在準備食物，便主動預測可能會聽到：standing、preparing food、cooking lunch、meals……等。

表情 三人的表情是輕鬆愉快的，便預期可能會有相關字詞：easy、relaxing、looking pleased……等。

背景

地點 此照片背景可明顯地看出是在廚房中，因此推斷可能會聽到的字會有：in the kitchen。

物品 此照片內的物品除了前景有料理台，桌上還有蔬菜，故可判斷可能出現的字詞包括：countertop、vegetables……等。

裝潢 三人的背後還有類似像烤箱等烹煮設備，因此還可預期會聽到：microwave、oven 等物品相關字詞。

各選項解析

- 選項 (A)「They are preparing meals.」內有關鍵點「preparing meals」意指「準備餐點」，的確有針對照片內容描述，故正確。
- 選項 (B)「They are having a serious discussion.」內的關鍵行動點為「having a serious discussion」意指「嚴肅的討論」，但照片中人物看不出在討論什麼嚴肅的事，故不選。
- 選項 (C)「They are enjoying their vacation.」內的關鍵行動「enjoying their vacation」意即「享受假期」，但照片內人物是在煮東西，不是在度假，故不選。
- 選項 (D)「They are working on a term paper.」內關鍵行動「working on a term paper」意即在「寫學期報告」這與照片內容完全不符，故不選。

題目陷阱 針對此人物照片的陷阱之處可能會是：

❶ 主要人物角色錯誤：Nurses are taking care of their patients.（護士們正在照顧他們的病人。）

❷ 主角所進行的動作錯誤：They are taking an English exam.（他們正在考英文考試。）

❸ 主角使用之物品錯誤：The man is taking notes on his tablet.（男子在他的便箋本上寫筆記。）

❹ 主角穿著錯誤：All of them are wearing an apron.（他們都穿著圍裙。）

❺ 主角所在地點錯誤：They are doing a demo in a customer's office.（他們在客戶的辦公室裡進行展示。）

關鍵字彙

prepare [prɪ`pɛr] v 準備
serious [`sɪrɪəs] a 嚴肅的
discussion [dɪ`skʌʃən] n 討論
vacation [ve`keʃən] n 度假、假期
term paper [`tɝm ˌpepɚ] n 學期報告

(A)　　(B)　　(C)　　(D)

解題分析

動作 42%

地點、物品 38%

主角 + 穿著 20%

■ 動作 42%

照片中男子是站著，兩女子是坐著的，且在打電腦、討論事情，便主動預測可能會聽到：standing、sitting、working on the computer、having a discussion……等。

■ 地點、物品 38%

背景看起來可能是辦公室，判斷可能會聽到的字會有：in the office。此外，依據照片內的物品，故可判斷可能出現的字詞包括：tables and chairs、laptop computer、bookshelf、french window 等。

■ 主角 + 穿著 20%

看到前景是兩女子與一男子，便可推斷可能出現的主詞會有：two women、a man 等。三人都穿著輕便的服裝，便可預測會聽到：casual attire 等字眼。

聽稿
（UK / M）

(A) The professor is giving a lecture.
(B) Some people are having a discussion.
(C) The man is waving his hands.
(D) A woman is writing something on the board.

中譯
（英 / 男）

答案：**(B)**
(A) 教授在講課。
(B) 一些人在討論事情。
(C) 男子在揮手。
(D) 一女子在板子上寫東西。

解題技巧　利用短暫的時間將注意力放在掃過照片上，分為前景和背景來分析，以便推論可能聽到之關鍵用字。

前景

主角　看到前景是兩女子與一男子，便可推斷可能出現的主詞會有：two women、a man……等。

穿著　三人都穿著輕便的服裝，便可預測會聽到：casual attire 的字眼。

動作　照片中男子是站著，兩女子是坐著的，且在打電腦、討論事情，便主動預測可能會聽到：standing、sitting、working on the computer、having a discussion……等。

背景

地點　此照片背景看起來可能是辦公室、會議室、或是圖書館，因此可判斷可能會聽到的字會有：in the office、in the conference room 或 in the library 等。

物品　此照片內的物品除了桌椅之外，還包括電腦、書架、落地窗和兩盞吊燈，故可判斷可能出現的字詞包括：tables and chairs、laptop computer、bookshelf、french window 與 ceiling lamps……等。

各選項解析
- 選項 (A)「The professor is giving a lecture.」內關鍵人物「the professor」與關鍵行動「giving a lecture」意即「教授在講課」與照片內容不符，故不選。
- 選項 (B)「Some people are having a discussion.」內有關鍵行動「having a discussion」意即「在討論」，的確符合照片內人物的動作，故為正確答案。
- 選項 (C)「The man is waving his hands.」內僅提到「the man」與其動作「waving his hands」意即「男子揮手」，但照片中男子並沒有在揮手，故不選。
- 選項 (D)「A woman is writing something on the board.」內關鍵行動「writing something on the board」意即「在板子上寫東西」，但照片中三人在討論事情，且都在看著電腦，沒有人在板子上寫東西，故不選。

題目陷阱　針對此人物照片的陷阱之處可能會是：

❶ 主要人物角色錯誤：Some patients are waiting for the doctor.
（一些病人正在等待醫生。）

❷ 主角所進行的動作錯誤：They are having a lunch meeting.（他們正在進行午餐會議。）

❸ 主角使用之物品錯誤：They are looking at a large painting.
（他們正在看一幅巨大的畫作。）

❹ 主角穿著錯誤：All of them are wearing protective clothing.（他們都穿著防護衣。）

❺ 主角所在地點錯誤：They are chatting in a coffee shop.（他們在咖啡店裡聊天。）

關鍵字彙
professor [prəˋfɛsɚ] n 教授
lecture [ˋlɛktʃɚ] n 講課、授課
discussion [dɪˋskʌʃən] n 討論

wave [wev] v 揮動
board [bord] n 板子

攻略 1 | 公事討論

(A)　(B)　(C)　(D)

解題分析

地點 42%

表情、動作 38%

主角 + 穿著 20%

■ 地點 42%　　照片背景可明顯地看出是在辦公室或會議室內，可能會聽到的字會有：in the office、meeting、conference room 等。

■ 表情、動作 38%　　依據兩人的動作，可預測會聽到：sitting、looking at the computer screen、pointing to 等，而兩人的表情是嚴肅的，可能會有相關字詞：serious、businesslike 等。

■ 主角 + 穿著 20%　　前景是兩位商務人士，可能出現的主詞會有 two workers (colleagues) 等，服裝為襯衫，預測會聽到：business casual、shirts、wearing glasses 等。

聽稿
（US / W）

(A) Both men are pointing to the laptop.
(B) One of the men is taking notes.
(C) They both are looking at the screen.
(D) The man on the right is on the phone.

中譯
（美 / 女）

答案：(C)
(A) 兩個男子同時指著筆記型電腦。
(B) 其中一名男子在寫筆記。
(C) 兩人都看著螢幕。
(D) 右邊那位男子在講電話。

解題技巧　利用時間掃過照片的同時，也可以在腦中預測一下可能出現的關鍵用字，並將照片以前景和背景的模式來分析出答案。

前景

主角　看到前景是兩位商務人士，便可推斷可能出現的主詞會有：two men、two workers、two colleagues……等。

穿著　兩人都穿著簡單的上班襯衫，自然可預測會聽到：business casual、shirts 等字眼。且其中一男子還戴著眼鏡，故可能聽到 wearing glasses。

動作　照片中兩人都坐著，看著電腦螢幕，且其中一男子還指著電腦螢幕，便主動預測可能會聽到：sitting、discussing、looking at the computer screen、pointing to……等描述動作的字眼。

表情　兩人的表情是嚴肅的，便預期可能會有相關字詞：serious、businesslike 等。

背景

地點　此照片背景可明顯地看出是在辦公室或會議室內，因此推斷可能會聽到的字會有：in the office、meeting、conference room……等。

物品　此照片內的物品除了明顯的一個電腦螢幕之外，桌上還有另一台小的筆電和滑鼠等物，故可判斷可能出現的字詞包括：laptop computer、portable computer、mouse……等。

各選項解析

- 選項 (A)「Both men are pointing to the laptop.」聽到關鍵人物「both men」似乎合理，但關鍵行動「pointing to the laptop」意指「指著電腦」就有問題了。圖中一人指著電腦螢幕是沒錯，但並非兩個人都指著電腦，故不選。
- 選項 (B)「One of the men is taking notes.」內的關鍵動作為「taking notes」意指「記筆記」，但圖中並沒有其中一男子在寫筆記，故不選。
- 選項 (C)「They both are looking at the screen.」內關鍵動作「looking at the screen」意指「都在看著螢幕」的確有描述到照片內容，故正確。
- 選項 (D)「The man on the right is on the phone.」內關鍵人物「the man on the right」意指右邊的男子，關鍵動作是「on the phone」意指「在講電話」，但圖中右手邊的男子並沒有在講電話，故不選。

題目陷阱　針對此照片的陷阱之處可能會是：

❶ 主要人物角色錯誤：The woman is dealing with a difficult customer.
（女子正在與一位難纏的客戶交涉。）

❷ 主角所進行的動作錯誤：Both men are listening to music.（兩名男子都在聽音樂。）

❸ 主角使用之物品錯誤：One of the men is holding a fork.（其中一名男子拿著一隻叉子。）

❹ 主角穿著錯誤：They both are wearing gloves.（他們兩人都戴著手套。）

❺ 主角所在地點錯誤：They run into each other on the street.（他們在街上相遇。）

關鍵字彙

take notes ph 記筆記
screen [skrin] n 螢幕
on the phone ph 電話中

(A)   (B)   (C)   (D)

解題分析

表情、動作 44%

地點 36%

主角 + 穿著
20%

■ 表情、動作 44%　依據站立男子的動作，預測可能會聽到：making a presentation、participating in discussion 或 listening⋯⋯等。且他正在微笑，可能會有相關字詞：smiling、passionate 與 positive⋯⋯等。

■ 地點 36%　背景可看出是在辦公室、會議室內，因此推斷可能會聽到的字會有：in the office、meeting room、conference room、board room⋯⋯等。

■ 主角 + 穿著 20%　依據圖片內人物便可推測出現的詞會有：the man、his colleagues 等，且大家都穿著商業套裝，可預測會聽到：business suit、shirts、tie 等相關字眼。

聽稿
（CA / **M**）

(A) They are having a picnic outdoors.
(B) The man is sitting down.
(C) The man is standing and giving a presentation.
(D) One of the women is about to leave.

中譯
（加 / **男**）

答案：**(C)**
(A) 他們在戶外野餐。
(B) 此男子要坐下。
(C) 此男子站著做簡報。
(D) 其中一位女子正要離開。

解題技巧 ｜ 若是照片裡出現許多人，也無須害怕，照著前面教的方法，將照片分為前景和背景來分析，就能夠順利找出答案了。

前景

主角 看到前景是一位男子，另有其他四位同事，便可推斷可能出現的主詞會有：the man、his colleagues、audience members、coworkers……等。

穿著 所有人都穿著商業套裝，自然可預測會聽到：business suit、shirts、tie……等相關字眼。

動作 照片中主要男子站著做簡報，其他同事都坐著聽講，便主動預測可能會聽到：standing、presenting、making a presentation、participating in discussion 或 listening。

表情 主要男子的表情是正向、熱心、微笑的，便可預期可能會有相關字詞：smiling、passionate 與 positive……等。另外，男子手上還握著筆和記事本，便知可能會有holding a pen、a notebook 等字眼出現。

背景

地點 此照片背景可明顯地看出是在辦公室、會議室內，因此推斷可能會聽到的字會有：in the office、meeting room、conference room、board room……等。

物品 此照片內的物品便是桌上放了文件與玻璃杯，男子旁還有白板，因此可判斷可能出現的字詞包括：documents、several glasses of water 與 whiteboard……等。

裝潢 此照片內較明顯的背景還包括後面的窗簾，因此還可預期會聽到：window curtains 等相關字詞。

各選項解析

- 選項 (A)「They are having a picnic outdoors.」內的關鍵動作「having a picnic」與地點「outdoors」意指「在戶外野餐」，與照片內容不符，故不選。
- 選項 (B)「The man is sitting down.」內關鍵動作「sitting down」意為「坐下」，但照片中男子是站著的，非坐下，故不選。
- 選項 (C)「The man is standing and giving a presentation.」內出現的關鍵動作「standing and giving a presentation」意指「站著並做簡報」，與照片內容相符，故正確。
- 選項 (D)「One of the women is about to leave.」內關鍵人物「one woman」與關鍵動作「about to leave」意指「一位女子要離去了」，但照片中並沒看到女子起身要離開，故不選。

題目陷阱 ｜ 針對此照片的陷阱之處可能會是：

❶ 主要人物角色錯誤：The professor is grouping students.（教授正讓學生們分組。）

❷ 主角所進行的動作錯誤：The man in the middle is giving out materials.
（在中間的男子正在發資料。）

❸ 主角使用之物品錯誤：All listeners are using earphones.（所有聽眾都使用耳機。）

❹ 主角穿著錯誤：Ladies are wearing night gowns.（女子們穿著晚禮服。）

❺ 主角所在地點錯誤：They are talking in the hotel lobby.（他們在飯店大廳裡談話。）

關鍵字彙

presentation [ˌprizənˈteʃən] n 簡報

攻略 3 ｜ 研討會場景

(A)　(B)　(C)　(D)

解題分析

表情、動作 50%
地點 28%
主角 22%

■ 表情、動作 50%　　依據講者與聽眾的動作，預測可能會聽到：standing、presenting、looking at slides、giving a speech 等。

■ 地點 28%　　依據圖中地點，可推斷會聽到的字會有：in the conference room、lecture hall、board room 等。

■ 主角 22%　　主要為一位主講者在台前，另有很多聽眾坐著聽講，可能出現的主詞會有：the speaker、presenter、audience members、listeners、attendees……等。

聽稿
（US / Ⓦ）

(A) A conference is being held.
(B) The meeting room is empty.
(C) Some people are raising their hands.
(D) The meeting is about to adjourn.

中譯
（美 / Ⓦ）

答案：(A)

(A) 有一場研討會正在進行中。
(B) 此會議室是空的。
(C) 有些人舉起手。
(D) 此會議就要結束了。

解題技巧 | 很快地將照片內容掃過，並分成前景與背景來看，以便推論可能聽到之關鍵用字有哪些。

前景

主角 看到前景是一位主講者在台前，另有很多聽眾坐著聽講，便可推斷可能出現的主詞會有：the speaker、presenter、audience members、listeners、attendees 或是 participants。

穿著 主講者是穿著西裝的，自然可預測會聽到：business suit 等字眼。

動作 照片講者是站著的，且看著簡報內容在報告，其他聽眾都是坐著的，便主動預測可能會聽到：standing、presenting、looking at slides、giving a speech、listening to the presentation……等。

背景

地點 此照片背景可明顯地看出是在會議室或演講廳，因此推斷可能會聽到的字會有：in the conference room、lecture hall、board room……等。

物品 此會議類型照片內的物品當然都會與簡報會議相關，可能出現的字詞包括：powerpoint slides、microphone、projector……等。

裝潢 在左邊牆壁上還掛有海報與看板等，因此還可預期會聽到：posters 或 banners 等物品相關字詞。

各選項解析

- 選項 (A)「A conference is being held.」內關鍵點是「the conference」意指「研討會」與「being held」意為「進行中」，照片內容的確是一場進行中的研討會，故可為正確答案。
- 選項 (B)「The meeting room is empty.」內的關鍵點是「room is empty」意即「房內是空的」，但照片中會議室內很多人，並非是空的，故不選。
- 選項 (C)「Some people are raising their hands.」內關鍵點「people... raising... hands」意即「有些人舉手」，但照片中並沒有人舉起手來，故不選。
- 選項 (D)「The meeting is about to adjourn.」中的關鍵字「the meeting」似乎是沒問題，但「adjourn」是「休會、停止」之意，照片內的會議尚在進行中，還沒結束，故不選。

題目陷阱 | 針對此照片的陷阱之處可能會是：

❶ 主要人物角色錯誤：All pupils are feeling bored.（所有學生都覺得無聊。）

❷ 主角所進行的動作錯誤：All audience members are about to leave.
（所有觀眾即將離席。）

❸ 主角使用之物品錯誤：The speaker is writing something on the blackboard.
（講者在黑板上寫些東西。）

❹ 主角穿著錯誤：The performer is wearing Chinese costume.（表演者穿著中國服飾。）

❺ 主角所在地點錯誤：They are enjoying a film in the theater.
（他們正在電影院裡看電影。）

關鍵字彙

conference [`kɑnfərəns] n 會議	raise [rez] v 舉起、升起
empty [`ɛmptɪ] a 空的	adjourn [ə`dʒɝn] v 結束、休會

(A)　　(B)　　(C)　　(D)

解題分析

物品 55%

背景 45%

■ 物品 55%　　照片內有車輛與路樹，故可判斷可能出現的字詞包括：cars、vehicles、roadside trees……等。

■ 背景 45%　　照片中有道路和高樓，因此推斷可能會聽到的字會有：a modern city、business district、tall buildings、clean road 等。

聽稿

（UK / M）

(A) Some trees are blocking the road.

(B) The view of the business district is marvelous.

(C) Some buildings are for sale.

(D) This is a lovely apartment complex.

中譯

（英 / 男）

答案：(B)

(A) 一些路樹擋住道路了。

(B) 此商業區的街景看起來很壯觀。

(C) 有些大樓在拍賣。

(D) 此為一個漂亮的公寓住宅區。

解題技巧 很快地將照片內大致情形掃過，才有可能推論將會聽到之關鍵用字。此照片是一張都市街景，沒有主要人物出現，便將焦點放在背景上面即可。

背景

地點 此照片背景可明顯地看出是在一個發展的都市，有整齊的街道和林立的高樓，因此推斷可能會聽到的字會有：a well-developed city、modern city、business district、tall office buildings、clean road……等。

物品 此照片內的物品明顯的自然就是車輛與路樹了，故可判斷可能出現的字詞包括：traffic、cars、vehicles、roadside trees……等。

各選項解析

- 選項 (A)「Some trees are blocking the road.」內的關鍵點「trees... blocking... road」意為「樹擋住路了」，但照片中道路很通暢，沒有樹擋到，故不選。
- 選項 (B)「The view of the business district is marvelous.」內關鍵點「business district」為「商業區」且被形容為「marvelous」意為「非凡、壯觀」之意，的確，照片內的都市景象呈現出進步與不凡的榮景，故選為最佳答案。
- 選項 (C)「Some buildings are for sale.」內的關鍵點「some buildings」似乎沒問題，因照片中的確是有一些大樓，但後續關鍵字「for sale」說到「拍賣」就有問題的，照片中並看出不來有大樓要拍賣，故不選。
- 選項 (D)「This is a lovely apartment complex.」內的關鍵點「lovely apartment complex」為「漂亮的公寓住宅區」，但照片中其實是商業區，故與照片場景不符，不可選。

題目陷阱 針對此照片的陷阱之處可能會是：

❶ 主要人物角色錯誤：Travelers are waiting in the airport.（遊客在機場裡等待。）

❷ 主要場景地點錯誤：The mountain view is fantastic.（這山的景色非常棒。）

❸ 場景內氛圍錯誤：It's raining cats and dogs.（現在是傾盆大雨。）

關鍵字彙

block [blɑk] v 擋住、阻擋
business district [ˋbɪznɪs ˏdɪstrɪkt] n 商業區
marvelous [ˋmɑrvələs] a 令人驚豔的
for sale ph 拍賣
lovely [ˋlʌvlɪ] a 可愛的、美好的
apartment complex [əˋpɑrtmənt ˏkɑmplɛks] n 公寓大樓

(A)　　(B)　　(C)　　(D)

解題分析

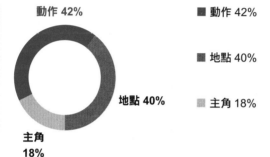

動作 42%

地點 40%

主角 18%

■ 動作 42%　　依據男子的動作，預測可能會聽到：sitting in front of the computer、looking at the screen……等字詞。

■ 地點 40%　　可能在男子辦公室或工作隔間區域，因此會聽到的字會有：in the office、in the working cubicle……等。

■ 主角 18%　　一位男子獨自坐著，便可推斷可能出現的主詞會有：the man、the worker……等。

聽稿

（CA / M）

(A) The man is wearing a headset.

(B) The man is fixing his car.

(C) The man is talking to his clients.

(D) The man is watching a TV program.

中譯

（加 / 男）

答案：**(A)**

(A) 此男子戴著耳機。

(B) 此男子在修車。

(C) 此男子在跟他的客戶交談。

(D) 此男子在看電視節目。

解題技巧 在選項播放之前，很快地將照片內容掃描一下，並且分辨出前景與背景，以便推論可能聽到之關鍵用字。

前景

主角 看到前景是一位男子獨自坐著，便可推斷可能出現的主詞會有：the man、the worker 等。

穿著 男子穿著襯衫，自然可預測會聽到：shirt 等字眼。

動作 照片中男子坐著聽耳機，看著電腦螢幕，手上還握著筆，便主動預測可能會聽到：sitting in front of the computer、looking at the screen、holding a pen、using headsets……等。

表情 由男子的表情看來是很認真專心的，便預期可能會有相關字詞：listening attentively、working diligently 等。

背景

地點 此照片背景可明顯地看出是在男子辦公室或工作隔間區域，因此推斷可能會聽到的字會有：in the office、in the working cubicle 等。

物品 此照片內的物品除了剛提到男子所戴的耳機之外，桌上還有眼鏡、鍵盤、滑鼠、盆栽等物品，故可判斷可能出現的字詞還包括：glasses、keyboard、mouse 與 potted plants。

裝潢 此男子的右手邊還有窗簾，因此還可預期會聽到：window curtains 等相關字詞。

各選項解析

- 選項 (A)「The man is wearing a headset.」內的關鍵點是「wearing a headset」意即「戴著耳機」的確有描述到照片內男子的配件，故正確。
- 選項 (B)「The man is fixing his car.」內的關鍵要點為「fixing his car」意指「在修車」，但照片中男子是在看電腦，並沒有在修車，故不選。
- 選項 (C)「The man is talking to his clients.」內關鍵行動是「talking to clients」意即「在跟客戶談話」，但照片中並沒看到有客戶，故不選。
- 選項 (D)「The man is watching a TV program.」內關鍵點是「watching a TV program」意為「在看電視節目」，但照片內男子是在看電腦，並非看電視，故不選。

題目陷阱 針對此照片的陷阱之處可能會是：

❶ 主要人物角色錯誤：The plumber is fixing pipes.（水電工正在修水管。）

❷ 主角所進行的動作錯誤：The man is giving a presentation.（男子正在報告。）

❸ 主角使用之物品錯誤：The man is using 3D glasses.（男子正使用 3D 眼鏡。）

❹ 主角穿著錯誤：The man is wearing a vest.（男子穿著背心。）

❺ 主角所在地點錯誤：The man is listening to music on the bed.（男子在床上聽音樂。）

關鍵字彙

headset [ˈhɛd͵sɛt] n 耳機
client [ˈklaɪənt] n 客戶

Unit 4 商旅出差類

(A)   (B)   (C)   (D)

解題分析

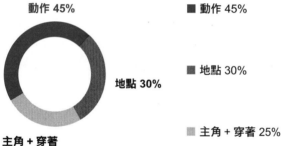

動作 45%

地點 30%

主角 + 穿著 25%

■ 動作 45%   兩人並肩行走與談話，預測可能會聽到：walking side by side、discussing、talking to each other 等動作的描述。

■ 地點 30%   雖不是很明顯可看出在哪裡，但依據男子手上的行李，可判斷可能是要去機場或火車站較為合理，因此會有：going to the airport、in the train station 等字眼。

■ 主角 + 穿著 25%   依據圖中的兩位男子，便可推斷可能出現的主詞會有：two men、colleagues、coworkers、associates 等。兩人都穿著商務套裝，可預測會聽到：business attire、wearing a tie 等字。

聽稿
（AU / Ⓦ）

(A) They are holding hands.
(B) One of the men is wearing a baseball cap.
(C) Two businessmen are walking side by side.
(D) They are signing a contract.

中譯
（澳 / 🚺）

答案：(C)
(A) 兩人手牽手。
(B) 其中一位男子戴著棒球帽。
(C) 兩位商務人士並肩而行。
(D) 他們在簽一張合約。

解題技巧 聽力題目播放出來之前，應利用時間將注意力放在掃描照片上，以便推論可能聽到之關鍵用字。

前景

主角 此照片內看到前景是兩位商務人士樣子的男子並肩行走著，便可推斷可能出現的主詞會有：two men、colleagues、coworkers、associates……等。

穿著 兩人都穿著商務套裝，自然可預測會聽到：business attire、wearing a tie、jacket……等字眼。其中一男子還戴著眼鏡，故可能會聽到 one of the men is wearing glasses 的相關描述。

動作 看到照片中兩人並肩行走與談話，便主動預測可能會聽到：walking side by side、discussing、talking to each other 等動作相關的描述。

背景

地點 此照片背景雖不是很明顯可看出在哪裡，但看左邊男子手上似乎還推著行李，因此可判斷可能是要去機場或火車站較為合理，因此推斷可能會聽到的字會有：going to the airport、in the train station……等。

各選項解析

- 選項 (A)「They are holding hands.」內的關鍵動作要點是「holding hands」意即「手牽手」，但照片內兩人並沒有牽手，故不選。
- 選項 (B)「One of the men is wearing a baseball cap.」內的關鍵點是「wearing a baseball cap」意為「戴著棒球帽」，但照片中男子並沒有戴棒球帽，故不選。
- 選項 (C)「Two businessmen are walking side by side.」內關鍵人物「two businessmen」意即「兩位商務人士」是沒問題，後續的關鍵動作點「walking side by side」意指「並肩行走」也的確描述到照片內容，故正確。
- 選項 (D)「They are signing a contract.」內的關鍵點是「signing a contract」意即「簽合約」，但照片中沒有在簽合約的線索，故不選。

題目陷阱 針對此照片的陷阱之處可能會是：

❶ 主要人物角色錯誤：Two women are sitting side by side.（兩名女子並肩坐著。）

❷ 主角所進行的動作錯誤：They are shaking hands.（他們正在握手。）

❸ 主角使用之物品錯誤：Both of them are wearing sunglasses.（他們兩人都戴著太陽眼鏡。）

❹ 主角穿著錯誤：Each of them is wearing a cloak.（他們都穿著斗篷。）

❺ 主角所在地點錯誤：They are sitting in a fastfood restaurant.（他們坐在速食店裡。）

關鍵字彙

cap [kæp] n 帽子
businessman [ˋbɪznɪsmən] n 生意人、商務人士
sign [saɪn] v 簽署
contract [ˋkɑntrækt] n 合約

(A)　(B)　(C)　(D)

解題分析

動作 50%

地點 40%

主角 10%

■ **動作** 50%　人們都站著排隊，手上都還推著行李，便預測可能會聽到：standing in a long line、waiting to board、holding luggage、holding suitcases……等。

■ **地點** 40%　背景可看出是在機場，因此推斷可能會聽到的字會有：in the airport、gate……等。

■ **主角** 10%　前景就是一群人，且背景看到飛機，可判斷這群人是旅客，便可推斷可能出現的主詞會有：many travelers、passengers 等。

聽稿

（CA / M）

(A) The airplane is about to land.
(B) Lots of shoppers are in the mall.
(C) People are going to attend a conference.
(D) The airport is full of passengers.

中譯

（加 / 男）

答案：**(D)**

(A) 飛機就快要降落。
(B) 購物中心內滿是人潮。
(C) 大家都要去參加一場研討會。
(D) 機場內滿是旅客。

解題技巧 就如同前面所學的，一看到照片，便很快地將照片內容大略掃描一下，以便主動掌握可能聽到之關鍵用字會有哪些。

前景

主角 此照片前景就是一群人，且背景看到飛機，可判斷這群人是旅客，便可推斷可能出現的主詞會有：many travelers、passengers、visitors……等。

動作 照片中的人都是站著在排隊的，且多數人手上都還推著行李，便主動預測可能會聽到：standing in a long line、waiting to board、holding luggage、holding suitcases 或 backpacks……等。

背景

地點 此照片背景可明顯地看出是在飛機場，因此推斷可能會聽到的字會有：in the airport、gate……等。

物品 此照片內的物品最明顯的就是那架飛機了，故可判斷可能出現的字詞包括：airplane、flight、taking off……等相關字詞。

各選項解析

- 選項 (A)「The airplane is about to land.」內關鍵點是「airplane... land」意即「飛機要著陸」，與照片內容不符，故不選。
- 選項 (B)「Lots of shoppers are in the mall.」內關鍵人物「shoppers」意即「購物者」與地點「in the mall」意即「在購物中心」都與照片內的機場場景不符，故不選。
- 選項 (C)「People are going to attend a conference.」內關鍵點是「attending a conference」意即「要去參加研討會」，但照片場景是在機場，非研討會會場，故不選。
- 選項 (D)「The airport is full of passengers.」內的關鍵字「the airport」與「passengers」都與照片內容相符，故選為正確答案。

題目陷阱 針對此照片的陷阱之處可能會是：

❶ 主要人物角色錯誤：Kids line up in front of the school.（孩子們在學校前排隊。）

❷ 主角所進行的動作錯誤：They are ready to enter the concert hall.
（他們準備進去演奏廳。）

❸ 主角使用之物品錯誤：All of them have a bottle of water on their hands.
（他們手上都拿著一瓶水。）

❹ 背景物品錯誤：The flight has landed safely.（這班機平安著陸。）

❺ 主角所在地點錯誤：They are standing in line in front of a post office.
（他們在郵局前面排隊。）

關鍵字彙

airplane [ˋɛrˏplen] n. 飛機	attend [əˋtɛnd] v. 出席
land [lænd] v. 著陸、降落	conference [ˋkɑnfərəns] n. 研討會
shopper [ˋʃɑpɚ] n. 購物者	passenger [ˋpæsṇdʒɚ] n. 旅客

(A)　　(B)　　(C)　　(D)

解題分析

動作 45%

主角、穿著 30%

地點、物品 25%

■ 動作 45%

■ 主角、穿著 30%

■ 地點、物品 25%

從男子動作，可能會聽到：standing in front of the counter 等。而依據服務人員的動作，便可能會聽到：sitting behind the counter、serving the client 等字眼。

依據圖中人員，可能出現的主詞會有：the man、two service representatives 等。

地點可能在飯店，也可能在接待處，推斷可能會聽到的字會有：check-in counter、hotel lobby、reception counter 等。而明顯的物品是櫃台與行李箱了，所以可判斷可能出現的字詞為：counter、suitcase、luggage⋯⋯等。

聽稿

（UK / M）

(A) The man is about to board the flight.

(B) They are having a job interview.

(C) Two service representatives are standing up.

(D) A businessman is standing in front of the counter.

中譯

（英 / 男）

答案：(D)

(A) 男子準備要登機了。

(B) 他們在進行面談。

(C) 兩位服務人員正站起來。

(D) 一位商務人士站在櫃台前。

解題技巧　多益考試的聽力部分，我們可以在內容播放之前，利用短暫的時間將注意力放在掃描照片上，以便推論可能聽到之關鍵用字。

前景

主角　看到前景是一位站著的男子與兩位坐在櫃台後的服務人員，便可推斷可能出現的主詞會有：the man、two service representatives 等。

穿著　主要男子穿著西裝，自然可預測會聽到：business attire、suit、wearing a tie……等字眼。

動作　照片中男子是站在櫃台前的，便主動預測可能會聽到：standing in front of the counter 等。另外兩位服務人員是坐在櫃台後的，且在提供客戶所需之服務，便可能會聽到：sitting behind the counter、serving the client……等相關字眼。

背景

地點　此照片背景可能是飯店櫃台，也有可能是公司的接待處，因此推斷可能會聽到的字會有：check-in counter、hotel lobby、reception area、reception counter……等。

物品　此照片內的物品較明顯的便是櫃台與男子的行李箱了，所以可判斷可能出現的字詞包括：counter、suitcase、luggage……等。

各選項解析

- 選項 (A)「The man is about to board the flight.」內關鍵動作是「board the flight」意即「要前往登機」，但照片內男子僅是站在櫃台前，並非要去登機，故不選。
- 選項 (B)「They are having a job interview.」內的關鍵點是「having a job interview」意即「在進行工作面談」，也與照片內容不符，故不選。
- 選項 (C)「Two service representatives are standing up.」內的關鍵人物是「two service representatives」意即「兩個服務人員」與關鍵行動是「standing up」意即「起身、站起來」，但照片中兩的服務人員是坐著的，故不選。
- 選項 (D)「A businessman is standing in front of the counter.」內關鍵人物「a businessman」的確就是照片中的主角，且其後關鍵動作「standing in front of the counter」意即「站在櫃台前」正確地描述到照片內容，故正確。

題目陷阱　針對此照片的陷阱之處可能會是：

❶ 主要人物角色錯誤：**All shoppers are standing in a long line.**
　　　　　　　　　　　（所有顧客都排在長長的隊伍裡。）

❷ 主角所進行的動作錯誤：**The man is sitting down.**（男子正坐下。）

❸ 主角使用之物品錯誤：**The man has three suitcases.**（男子有三個手提箱。）

❹ 主角穿著錯誤：**The man is wearing workout tights.**（男子穿著運動緊身褲。）

❺ 主角所在地點錯誤：**The man is resting in his hotel room.**（男子正在飯店房間內休息。）

關鍵字彙

board [bord] ⓥ 登、搭、乘
interview [ˈɪntɚˌvju] ⓝ 面談
representative [ˌrɛprɪˈzɛntətɪv] ⓝ 代表
counter [ˈkaʊntɚ] ⓝ 櫃台

(A)　　(B)　　(C)　　(D)

解題分析

動作、表情 40%

地點 35%

主角、穿著
25%

■ 動作、表情 40%　　依據男子動作，可預測會聽到：sitting、working on the laptop、thinking about issues 等。且他的表情較為嚴肅，可能會有相關字詞：deeply involved、immersed 等。

■ 地點 35%　　背景可看出是飛機內，推斷可能會聽到：cabin、passenger compartment 等。

■ 主角、穿著 25%　　主角為商務人士，推斷可能出現的主詞會有：the businessman、the worker……等。他穿著輕鬆的服飾，可預測會聽到：shirt、business casual、jeans 等字眼。

聽稿
（AU / Ⓦ）

(A) The man is talking to a flight attendant.
(B) The man is fastening his seatbelt.
(C) The man is working on his laptop.
(D) The man is sleeping on the plane.

中譯
（澳 / 女）

答案：(C)
(A) 此男子在跟空服員交談。
(B) 此男子正將安全帶繫緊。
(C) 此男子正用筆記型電腦工作。
(D) 此男子在飛機上睡覺。

解題技巧 在選項播放之前，很快地把握時間將注意力放在掃描照片上，並分出前景和背景，以便推論可能聽到之關鍵用字。

前景

主角 看到前景是一位商務人士，便推斷可能出現的主詞會有：the man、the businessman、the worker……等。

穿著 男子穿著輕鬆的襯衫與牛仔褲，自然可預測會聽到：shirt、business casual、jeans……等字眼。

動作 照片中男子坐著打電腦，並好似在思索公事，便主動預測可能會聽到：sitting、working on the laptop、thinking about issues……等。

表情 男子的表情是認真嚴肅的，便預期可能會有相關字詞：deeply involved、immersed、engaged……等。

背景

地點 此照片背景可明顯地看出是飛機機艙內，因此推斷可能會聽到的字會有：cabin、passenger compartment 等。

物品 此照片內的物品除了前景有筆記型電腦之外，男子旁邊還有一個窗戶，故可判斷可能出現的字詞包括：a laptop computer、a window 等。

各選項解析

- 選項 (A)「The man is talking to a flight attendant.」內的關鍵行動是「talking to a flight attendant」意即「跟空服員講話」，但照片中在機上的男子並沒有在跟空服員講話，故不選。
- 選項 (B)「The man is fastening his seatbelt.」內的要點是「fastening his seatbelt」意指「正在繫安全帶」，但自照片中也看不出此事，故不選。
- 選項 (C)「The man is working on his laptop.」內的關鍵行動點是「working on his laptop」意即「使用電腦並在工作中」的確描述到照片內男子的動作，故正確。
- 選項 (D)「The man is sleeping on the plane.」內的關鍵動作點是「sleeping on the plane」意即「在機上睡覺」，但照片中男子並沒有在睡覺，故不選。

題目陷阱 針對此照片的陷阱之處可能會是：

❶ 主要人物角色錯誤：The flight attendant is severing coffee.（空服員正端上咖啡。）

❷ 主角所進行的動作錯誤：The man is operating a huge machine.
（男子正在操作一台巨大的機器。）

❸ 主角使用之物品錯誤：The man is putting earphones on.（男子戴上耳機。）

❹ 主角穿著錯誤：The man is wearing shorts.（男子穿著短褲。）

❺ 主角所在地點錯誤：The boy is taking a computer lesson in the classroom.
（男孩正在教室裡上電腦課。）

關鍵字彙

flight attendant [ˋflaɪt əˋtɛndənt] n 空服員　　　seat belt [ˋsit ˏbɛlt] n 安全帶
fasten [ˋfæsn̩] v 繫緊　　　　　　　　　　　　　laptop [ˋlæptɑp] n 筆記型電腦

(A)　　(B)　　(C)　　(D)

解題分析

地點 42%

動作 38%

主角、穿著
20%

■ **地點 42%**　　背景看起來可能是在機場，因此聽到的字會有：at the airport、lobby、waiting area……等。

■ **動作 38%**　　依據兩人動作，可能會聽到：standing、looking at the screen 等，且男子還手指著螢幕，亦可能聽到 pointing to the screen 等字眼。

■ **主角、穿著 20%**　　依據主角服裝相似，其關係有可能是同事，可能出現的主詞有：two people、two colleagues 等。兩人都穿著商務套裝，可能會聽到：business suits、formal jacket 等字眼。

聽稿
（US / Ⓦ）

(A) They are shaking hands.
(B) The man is pointing at his colleague.
(C) Two business people are checking flight schedules.
(D) The woman is much taller than the man.

中譯
（美 / 女）

答案：(C)
(A) 兩人在握手。
(B) 男子指著他的同事。
(C) 兩位商務人士在看班機時刻表。
(D) 那女子長得比男子高很多。

解題技巧 把握未播放聽力內容前的時間，很快地將照片大略地掃描一下，以便推論可能聽到之關鍵用字。

前景

主角 看到前景是一位男子和一位女子，都穿著套裝，其關係有可能是同事，便可推斷可能出現的主詞會有：the man、the woman、two people、two colleagues、coworkers⋯⋯等。

穿著 兩人都穿著商務套裝，自然可預測會聽到：business suits、formal jacket 等字眼。且男子還背著提包，便可能會聽到 carrying a laptop bag 或 suitcase 等。

動作 照片中兩人都站著，且面對著螢幕在看時刻表，便主動預測可能會聽到：standing、looking at the big screen、checking⋯⋯等，且男子還手指著螢幕，便可能會聽到 pointing to the screen 的字眼。

背景

地點 此照片背景看起來可能是在機場，因此推斷可能會聽到的字會有：at the airport、lobby、waiting area⋯⋯等。

各選項解析

- 選項 (A)「They are shaking hands.」內的關鍵動作是「shaking hands」意即「在握手」，與照片內兩人的動作不符，故不選。
- 選項 (B)「The man is pointing at his colleague.」內關鍵點是「pointing at his colleague」意指「指著他的同事」，但照片內男子是手指著螢幕，並非指著同事，故不選。
- 選項 (C)「Two business people are checking flight schedules.」內關鍵人物是「two business people」意為「兩商務人士」，與其動作「checking flight schedules」意即「在看班機時刻」，的確都有正確地描述到照片內容，故選為最佳答案。
- 選項 (D)「The woman is much taller than the man.」內關鍵點是「woman... taller than... man」意即「女子比男子高」，但自照片中看出其實男子比較高，故不選。

題目陷阱 針對此照片的陷阱之處可能會是：

❶ 主要人物角色錯誤：A mother and her son are watching cartoon together.
（媽媽和兒子一起看著卡通。）

❷ 主角所進行的動作錯誤：They are talking to flight attendants.
（他們正在和空服員講話。）

❸ 主角使用之物品錯誤：Both of them are wearing hats.（他們兩人都戴著帽子。）

❹ 主角穿著錯誤：Only the man is wearing business suit.（只有男子穿著西裝。）

❺ 主角所在地點錯誤：They are looking at a painting in the museum.
（他們在博物館裡看畫。）

關鍵字彙

shake [ʃek] ☑ 握、搖動
colleague [ˋkɑlig] ☐ 同事
schedule [ˋskɛdʒul] ☐ 計畫表、事程表

Unit 5 運動體育類

攻略 1 │ 人物與穿著

(A)　　(B)　　(C)　　(D)

解題分析

主角、穿著 50%

動作、表情 30%

地點 20%

■ **主角、穿著 50%**　前景是一群在泳池的兒童，便可推斷可能出現的主詞會有：some children 等，大家都有泳裝配備等，可預測會聽到：swimming suit、swimming cap 等字。

■ **動作、表情 30%**　小孩都是站著的，預測會聽到：standing 等。小女孩的表情是開心的，可能有相關字詞：smiling、joyful、enjoying swimming……等。

■ **地點 20%**　背景可看出在游泳池，因此會聽到的字會有：in the swimming pool 等。

聽稿
（US / Ⓦ）

(A) Kids are learning how to swim.
(B) They are all professional basketball players.
(C) Children should learn math at school.
(D) A dance class is in session.

中譯
（美 / 女）

答案：**(A)**
(A) 小孩在上游泳課。
(B) 他們都是專業籃球員。
(C) 小孩在學校應學數學。
(D) 舞蹈課正在進行中。

解題技巧 | 很快地將照片掃描一下，看出前景與背景各有什麼明顯的人、事、物，以便推論可能聽到之關鍵用字。

前景

主角 看到前景是一群兒童，也有可能是游泳課的學生，便可推斷可能出現的主詞會有：some children、students、learners 等。

穿著 大家都穿著泳衣、戴泳帽與泳鏡等，自然可預測會聽到：swimming suit、swimming cap 與 goggles 等字眼。

動作 照片中小孩都是站著的，便主動預測可能會聽到：standing。

表情 小女孩的表情是歡笑愉快的，便預期可能會有相關字詞：smiling、joyful、enjoying swimming……等。

背景

地點 此照片背景可明顯地看出是在游泳池，因此推斷可能會聽到的字會有：in the swimming pool。

各選項解析

- 選項 (A)「Kids are learning how to swim.」內的關鍵人物點是「kids」的確是描述照片中的小孩子，且關鍵動作「learning... swim」也的確是在泳池中學游泳，故可選為最佳答案。
- 選項 (B)「They are all professional basketball players.」內聽到關鍵點「professional basketball players」意即「專業籃球員」便可知與照片內容不符了，故不選。
- 選項 (C)「Children should learn math at school.」內的要點人物「children」似乎是沒問題，但關鍵動作點「learn math at school」意即「在學校學數學」便與照片內的游泳池場景不符了，故不選。
- 選項 (D)「A dance class is in session.」內的關鍵點「dance class」意即「舞蹈課」，但這與照片內的「游泳」不符，故不選。

題目陷阱 | 針對此照片的陷阱之處可能會是：

❶ 主要人物角色錯誤：Parents are taking care of children.（父母在照顧著孩子。）
❷ 主角所進行的動作錯誤：Kids are playing games.（孩子們在玩遊戲。）
❸ 主角使用之物品錯誤：All of them are wearing sunglasses.（他們都戴著太陽眼鏡。）
❹ 主角穿著錯誤：All students are wearing uniforms.（所有學生都穿著制服。）
❺ 主角所在地點錯誤：They are being trained in the ocean.（他們在海上接受訓練。）

關鍵字彙

professional [prə`fɛʃənl] 形 專業的
in session 片 上課中、進行中

(A)　　(B)　　(C)　　(D)

解題分析

地點 42%

動作 38%

主角、穿著
20%

■ 地點 42%　可看出是在戶外公園,因此推斷可能會聽到的字會有:
in the park、outdoors……等。

■ 動作 38%　大家都在練習瑜伽,可預測會聽到:practicing yoga、
yoga poses、standing on the mat……等。

▨ 主角、穿著 20%　一群人在練瑜伽,可推斷出現的字詞有:all people、
some men and women 等。且大家都穿著瑜伽服裝,
可預測會聽到:yoga wear、yoga pants 等字眼。

聽稿
（UK / **M**）

(A) They are learning to stand straight.
(B) They are having a spinning class in the gym.
(C) They are practicing yoga outdoors.
(D) They are planting trees.

中譯
（英 / **男**）

答案:**(C)**
(A) 他們在學如何站直。
(B) 他們在健身房上飛輪課。
(C) 他們在戶外練習瑜伽。
(D) 他們在種樹。

解題技巧 利用短暫的時間將照片的大致內容掃描一下，看到此張照片有人物，就順便將其動作記下來，以便推論可能聽到之關鍵用字。

前景

主角 看到前景是一群人在練瑜伽，便可推斷可能出現的主詞會有：they、all people、some men and women……等。

穿著 大家都穿著瑜伽服裝，自然可預測會聽到：yoga wear、yoga pants……等字眼。

動作 照片中的人都在練習瑜伽動作，便主動預測可能會聽到：practicing yoga、yoga poses、standing on the mat……等。

背景

地點 此照片背景可明顯地看出是在戶外公園，因此推斷可能會聽到的字會有：in the park、outdoors……等。

物品 此照片內的物品除了背景有些樹之外，所有人都踩在自己的瑜伽墊上，故可判斷可能出現的字詞包括：some trees、yoga mat 等。

各選項解析

- 選項 (A)「They are learning to stand straight.」內的關鍵動作點是「learning to stand straight」意即「學習如何站直」，但照片中的人物是在做瑜伽，並非在學站直，故不選。
- 選項 (B)「They are having a spinning class in the gym.」的關鍵點是「having a spinning class」意即「上飛輪課」且關鍵地點是在「in the gym」意即「健身房」中，都與照片內容不符，故不選。
- 選項 (C)「They are practicing yoga outdoors.」內的關鍵動作是「practicing yoga」意即在「練瑜伽」且地點是「outdoors」意即「戶外」，的確都描述到照片內容，故選為最佳答案。
- 選項 (D)「They are planting trees.」內的關鍵動作是「planting trees」意即「種樹」，但照片內背景是有樹木沒錯，但人們並非在種樹，故不選。

題目陷阱 針對此照片的陷阱之處可能會是：

❶ 主要人物角色錯誤：Pedestrians are walking on the street.（行人在街上走著。）

❷ 主角所進行的動作錯誤：All of them are sitting on the mat.（他們都坐在墊子上。）

❸ 主角使用之物品錯誤：They are about to check in their luggage.
（他們將要去托運行李。）

❹ 主角穿著錯誤：All athletes are wearing sneakers.（所有運動員穿著運動鞋。）

❺ 主角所在地點錯誤：They are taking a lesson in a yoga studio.
（他們在瑜伽教室裡上課。）

關鍵字彙

straight [stret] a 直的、挺直的
spinning [`spɪnɪŋ] n 旋轉、飛輪（運動）
gym (= gymnasium) [dʒɪm] n 體育館
practice [`præktɪs] v 練習
outdoors [`aut`dorz] ad 在戶外、露天

(A)　　(B)　　(C)　　(D)

解題分析

表情、動作 40%

主角、穿著 35%

地點 25%

■ 表情、動作 40%　兩人都是在訓練慢跑的，可能會聽到：jogging、training 等。表情是愉快的，可能會有相關字詞：relaxing、enjoying their time together 等。

■ 主角、穿著 35%　依據圖中人物，推斷可能出現的主詞有：a man、a woman、the couple 等。兩人都穿著運動服裝，預測會聽到：sports attire、shorts、sneakers……等字眼。且女子長頭髮，也可能會有：wearing long hair 的字詞出現。

▨ 地點 25%　背景可看出是戶外小徑，可能會聽到的字會有：outdoors、along the trail 等。

聽稿

（AU / Ⓦ）

(A) They are discussing business strategies.
(B) The man is likely to win the competition.
(C) The woman is wearing a long dress.
(D) They are jogging along the trail.

中譯

（澳 / 女）

答案：(D)

(A) 他們在討論商業策略。
(B) 男子很有可能贏得比賽。
(C) 女子穿長洋裝。
(D) 他們沿著小徑慢跑。

解題技巧　利用短暫的時間很快地將照片大致內容掃描一下，並搭配前景和背景的分析技巧，以便推論可能聽到之關鍵用字。

前景

主角　看到前景是一位男子與一位女子，便可推斷可能出現的主詞會有：a man、a woman、the couple……等。

穿著　兩人都穿著運動服、短褲、T恤、與運動鞋，自然可預測會聽到：sports attire、shorts、T-shirts 與 sneakers……等字眼。且女子是留長頭髮，便也可能會有：wearing long hair 字詞出現的可能性。

動作　照片中兩人都是在訓練慢跑的，便主動預測可能會聽到：jogging、training……等。

表情　兩人的表情是歡笑愉快的，便預期可能會有相關字詞：relaxing、enjoying their time together……等。

背景

地點　此照片背景可明顯地看出是戶外小徑，因此推斷可能會聽到的字會有：outdoors、along the trail 等。

天氣　此照片內的氣氛看起來是晴天沒有下雨，判斷可能出現的字詞包括：sunny、good weather condition、comfortable……等。

各選項解析

- 選項 (A)「They are discussing business strategies.」內有關鍵動作點「discussing business strategies」意即「討論商業策略」，但照片中的人是在慢跑，沒有在開會討論策略，故不選。
- 選項 (B)「The man is likely to win the competition.」內提到「the man」，照片內是有一男子沒錯，但後續關鍵動作是「win the competition」意即「贏得比賽」，但照片中男子並沒有在進行競賽，也不會有所謂的輸贏之分了，故不選。
- 選項 (C)「The woman is wearing a long dress.」內關鍵人物是「the woman」，照片中是有一女子沒錯，但另一關鍵點「wearing a long dress」意即「穿長禮服」便不符照片內女子的穿著了，故不選。
- 選項 (D)「They are jogging along the trail.」內的關鍵動作「jogging along the trail」意即「沿著小徑慢跑」，的確有描述到照片內容，故正確。

題目陷阱　針對此照片的陷阱之處可能會是：

❶ 主要人物角色錯誤：**The father is holding his daughter.**（爸爸抱著女兒。）
❷ 主角所進行的動作錯誤：**The couple is doing household chores.**
　　　　　　　　　　　　　　（這對情侶正在做家事。）
❸ 主角使用之物品錯誤：**Each of them is carrying an umbrella.**（他們都拿著雨傘。）
❹ 主角穿著錯誤：**The woman is wearing high heels.**（女子穿著高跟鞋。）
❺ 主角所在地點錯誤：**They are doing exercise in the gym.**（他們在健身房裡運動。）

關鍵字彙

discuss [dɪ`skʌs] ☑ 討論
strategy [`strætədʒɪ] ⬛ 策略
competition [ˌkɑmpə`tɪʃən] ⬛ 競爭

jog [dʒɑg] ☑ 慢跑
trail [trel] ⬛ 小徑、足跡

(A)　　(B)　　(C)　　(D)

解題分析

表情、動作 45%

主角、穿著 30%

地點 25%

■ 表情、動作 45%

■ 主角、穿著 30%

■ 地點 25%

四人都是在玩足球，便主動預測可能會聽到：playing soccer 等。大家都是興奮的，便預期可能會有相關字詞：exciting、lively 與 active 等。

兩位大人與兩個小男孩，可能出現的主詞會有：four people、a man、two boys 等。四人都穿著輕便的服裝，可預測會聽到：casual clothes 等字眼。

可看出是在戶外草地，推斷會聽到的字會有：outdoors、on the grass 等。

聽稿
（CA / **M**）

(A) Boys are playing soccer.
(B) The man is about to hit the ball.
(C) One of the boys is falling down.
(D) These children are talented at math.

中譯
（加 / **男**）

答案：**(A)**
(A) 男孩在踢足球。
(B) 男子就要擊球了。
(C) 其中一個男孩快要跌倒。
(D) 這些小孩都很有數學天分。

解題技巧 很快地掃描一下照片，看出照片內容之前景與背景為何，以便推論可能聽到之關鍵用字。

前景

主角 看到前景是兩位大人與兩個小男孩，便可推斷可能出現的主詞會有：a man、a mother、two boys……等。

穿著 四人都穿著輕便的服裝，自然可預測會聽到：casual clothes 等字眼。

動作 照片中四人都是在玩足球，便主動預測可能會聽到：playing soccer 等。

表情 大家的表情是興奮的，便預期可能會有相關字詞：exciting、lively 與 active……等。

背景

地點 此照片背景可明顯地看出是在戶外草地，因此推斷可能會聽到的字會有：outdoors、on the grass……等。

各選項解析

- 選項 (A)「Boys are playing soccer.」的關鍵人物「boys」的確是提到照片中的男孩子，且關鍵動作為「playing soccer」意即「踢足球」也正確地描述到照片內的人物動作，故選為最佳答案。
- 選項 (B)「The man is about to hit the ball.」內的關鍵點是「about to hit the ball」意即「就要擊球了」，與照片中內容不符，故不選。
- 選項 (C)「One of the boys is falling down.」內提到的關鍵動作「falling down」意即「快跌倒」，但照片中並無男孩快跌倒，故不選。
- 選項 (D)「These children are talented at math.」內的關鍵人物「children」似乎可以是照片中的小孩，但其後的「talented at math」意即「有數學天分」，但自照片中看不出那些小孩數學是否優秀，故不選。

題目陷阱 針對此照片的陷阱之處可能會是：

❶ 主要人物角色錯誤：All girls are playing dolls.（女孩們玩著娃娃。）

❷ 主角所進行的動作錯誤：Boys are listening to the lecture attentively.
（男孩們聚精會神地聽課。）

❸ 主角使用之物品錯誤：The coach is holding a football.（教練手裡拿著美式足球。）

❹ 主角穿著錯誤：All of them are wearing shorts.（他們都穿著短褲。）

❺ 主角所在地點錯誤：Students are learning in the classroom.（學生們在教室裡學習。）

關鍵字彙

soccer [`sɑkɚ] n 足球
fall down ph 跌倒、跌落
talented [`tæləntɪd] a 聰明的、有才能的

(A)　　(B)　　(C)　　(D)

解題分析

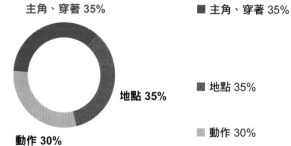

主角、穿著 35%

地點 35%

動作 30%

■ 主角、穿著 35%

■ 地點 35%

■ 動作 30%

主角是棒球員，可能出現的主詞會有：some baseball players、batter、catcher 等。大家都穿著棒球裝，可預測會聽到：baseball uniforms、baseball jerseys、baseball attire 等字。

圖中可看出是在棒球場，因此可能會聽到的字會有：baseball field、ball park 等。

圖中球員準備要擊球，便主動預測可能會聽到：about to hit the ball 等。

聽稿
（AU / Ⓦ）

(A) No one is wearing a helmet.
(B) All of them are sitting down.
(C) One of the men has won the race.
(D) A baseball game is taking place.

中譯
（澳 / 女）

答案：**(D)**
(A) 沒人戴著安全帽。
(B) 所有人都要坐下。
(C) 其中一位男子跑贏了比賽。
(D) 一場棒球賽正在進行中。

解題技巧 利用各題目間幾秒空檔的時間，將注意力放在掃描照片上，以便推論可能聽到之關鍵用字。

前景

主角 看到前景是一些棒球球員，便推論可能出現的主詞會有：some baseball players、batter、catcher……等。

穿著 數人都穿著棒球裝，自然可預測會聽到：baseball uniforms、baseball jerseys 或 baseball attire……等字眼。

動作 照片中打擊手準備要擊球，便主動預測可能會聽到：about to hit the ball。

背景

地點 此照片背景可明顯地看出是在棒球場，因此推斷可能會聽到的字會有：baseball field、ball park……等。

物品 此照片內的物品就是棒球員身上的裝備，包括：球棒、手套、保護頭盔與面罩等，故可判斷可能出現的字詞包括：baseball bat、baseball gloves、batting helmet 與 fielder's face guard……等。

各選項解析

- 選項 (A)「No one is wearing a helmet.」內的關鍵點「No one... wearing a helmet」意即「沒人戴安全帽」，但照片中每個人都有戴安全帽，故不選。
- 選項 (B)「All of them are sitting down.」內的關鍵動作點是「sitting down」，但照片中並沒有人要坐下，故不選。
- 選項 (C)「One of the men has won the race.」內的關鍵動作點「has won the race」意即「賽跑贏了」，但照片中人是在打棒球，並非在比賽跑步，故不選。
- 選項 (D)「A baseball game is taking place.」內的關鍵點「a baseball game」提及「棒球賽」進行中，的確與照片內容相符，故選為最佳答案。

題目陷阱 針對此照片的陷阱之處可能會是：

❶ 主要人物角色錯誤：Girls are doing exercises.（女孩們正在運動。）

❷ 主角所進行的動作錯誤：One of the men is about to kick the ball.
（其中一名男子即將要踢球。）

❸ 主角使用之物品錯誤：The man in the middle is holding a pen.
（中間的男子拿著一枝筆。）

❹ 主角穿著錯誤：They are wearing basketball jerseys.（他們都穿著籃球衣。）

❺ 主角所在地點錯誤：They are discussing strategies in the meeting room.
（他們在會議室裡討論策略。）

關鍵字彙

helmet [ˋhɛlmɪt] n 安全帽
race [res] n 賽跑、比速度
baseball game [ˋbes͵bɔl ˋgem] n 棒球賽
take place 進行、發生

Unit 6 餐廳飲食類

攻略 1 │ 人物、事件與地點

(A)　　(B)　　(C)　　(D)

解題分析

表情、動作 40%

地點、物品 35%

主角、穿著 25%

■ **表情、動作 40%**　大家都是坐著、自在地聊著天,預測可能會聽到:sitting、chatting、talking to each other、getting together……等。大家的表情是快樂的,預期可能會有:cheerful、pleasant、lively、happy……等。

■ **地點、物品 35%**　背景可看出是在家中餐廳,可能會聽到的字會有:in the dining room 等。照片內的物品除了桌上有水杯與點心,還有畫、窗戶,判斷可能出現的字詞包括:water glasses、snacks、portraits、pictures、windows……等。

■ **主角、穿著 25%**　共六人坐在桌子旁飲食聊天,推斷可能出現的字詞有:all people、friends、family members 等。大家都穿著便服,可預測會聽到:casual clothes、informal attire、easygoing clothes……等字。

聽稿
（UK / M ）

(A) They are playing cards.
(B) They are negotiating.
(C) They are enjoying a meal together.
(D) They are decorating the room.

中譯
（英 / 男）

答案:**(C)**
(A) 他們在玩牌。
(B) 他們在談判。
(C) 他們正一起吃飯。
(D) 他們正在裝潢房間。

解題技巧 在聽到四個答案選項之前，很快地利用短暫的時間，將注意力集中在掃描照片上，以便推論可能聽到之關鍵用字。

前景

主角 看到有男有女總共六人坐在同一桌子旁飲食聊天，便可推斷可能出現的主詞會有：all people、friends、family members、three men 與 three women……等。

穿著 眾人都穿著輕鬆的便服，便可預測會聽到：casual clothes、informal attire、easygoing clothes……等字眼。

動作 照片中六人都是坐著的，且自在地聊著天，便主動預測可能會聽到：sitting、chatting、talking to each other、getting together……等。

表情 六人的表情是快樂與投入的，便預期可能會有相關字詞：cheerful、pleasant、lively 或 happy……等。

背景

地點 此照片背景可明顯地看出是在家中的餐廳，因此推斷可能會聽到的字會有：in the dining room 等。

物品 此照片內的物品除了桌上有水杯與點心之外，背景還有畫掛在牆上，與窗戶，故可判斷可能出現的字詞包括：water glasses、snacks、portraits、pictures 與 windows……等。

各選項解析

- 選項 (A)「They are playing cards.」內的關鍵動作點是「playing cards」意即「在玩牌」，但照片中人物並沒有在玩牌，故不選。
- 選項 (B)「They are negotiating.」內的關鍵動作點是「negotiating」意即「在談判協商」，但照片中人物僅是開心地閒聊，沒有在商討嚴肅之事，故不選。
- 選項 (C)「They are enjoying a meal together.」內的關鍵動作點「enjoying a meal together」意即「一起用餐」，的確描述到照片內情景，故可選為最佳答案。
- 選項 (D)「They are decorating the room.」的關鍵點為「decorating the room」意即「裝飾房間」，但照片中人物都坐著飲食，沒有在裝潢房間，故不選。

題目陷阱 針對此照片的陷阱之處可能會是：

❶ 主要人物角色錯誤：Stockholders are having a serious meeting.
（股東們正嚴肅地開會。）

❷ 主角所進行的動作錯誤：All family members are arguing about something.
（所有家庭成員正在爭論一些事情。）

❸ 主角使用之物品錯誤：They are setting up the video-conferencing equipment.
（他們正在架設視訊會議的器材。）

❹ 主角穿著錯誤：All of them are wearing pajamas.（他們都穿著睡衣。）

❺ 主角所在地點錯誤：They are standing under the intense sun.
（他們在大太陽底下站著。）

關鍵字彙

play cards 玩撲克牌　　　　　　　　　　　decorate [ˋdɛkə͵ret] ⅴ 裝潢
negotiate [nɪˋgoʃ͵et] ⅴ 談判、協商

(A)　(B)　(C)　(D)

解題分析

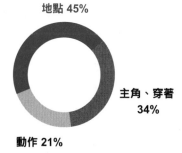

地點 45%

主角、穿著 34%

動作 21%

■ 地點 45%

背景可看出是在餐廳內，推斷可能會聽到的字有：in the restaurant、cafeteria、dining room 等。餐廳的風格是屬於現代感，因此還可能會聽到：modern 等字詞。

■ 主角、穿著 34%

主要有三人，可推斷出現的主詞有：two guests、customers、a lady、the waiter……等。依據圖中人物服裝，可預測會聽到：formal apparel、suit、dress、white shirt、uniform……等字。

■ 動作 21%

依據圖中人物動作，可預測聽到：sitting、standing、serving meals、serving dishes、supplying food……等字詞。

聽稿

（CA / **M**）

(A) The customers are complimenting the waiter.

(B) The waiter is serving food to customers.

(C) The waitress is sitting down.

(D) The chef is cooking Chinese food.

中譯

（加 / **男**）

答案：**(B)**

(A) 顧客在讚美服務生。

(B) 服務生為顧客送上餐點。

(C) 女服務生正要坐下。

(D) 廚師在煮中國菜。

解題技巧 在聽力內容播放之前，很快地利用幾秒的時間將照片掃描一次，以便推論可能聽到之關鍵用字。

前景

主角 看到前景是主要有三人，兩位客人坐著，與一位服務生站著，便可推斷可能出現的主詞會有：two guests、customers、a lady、the waiter……等。

穿著 兩位顧客穿的是正式的服裝，而服務生便是穿著制服，自然可預測會聽到：formal apparel、suit、dress、white shirt、uniform……等字眼。

動作 照片中兩位顧客是坐著的，服務生站著，且服務生在遞送餐點，便主動預測可能會聽到：sitting、standing、serving meals、serving dishes、supplying food……等。

背景

地點 此照片背景可明顯地看出是在餐廳內，因此推斷可能會聽到的字會有：in the restaurant、cafeteria 或 dining room 等。

裝潢 此餐廳的風格是屬於比較簡單現代的、且具風格的，因此還可預期會聽到：modern、stylish 或 new-fashioned……等相關字詞。

各選項解析

- 選項 (A)「The customers are complimenting the waiter.」內的關鍵人物「customers」意指「顧客」似乎是沒問題，但後續動作點「complimenting the waiter」意指「在讚賞服務生」，但自照片中並看不出此事，故不選。
- 選項 (B)「The waiter is serving food to customers.」內關鍵人物「the waiter」在講那位服務生，且後續動作「serving food to customers」意即「為顧客送餐」，的確有符合照片內容，故正確。
- 選項 (C)「The waitress is sitting down.」關鍵人物是「the waitress」意即「女服務生」，且動作「sitting down」意即「要坐下」，但照片中並非女服務生，也沒有要坐下，故不選。
- 選項 (D)「The chef is cooking Chinese food.」的關鍵人物「the chef」意即「廚師」，且關鍵動作是「cooking Chinese food」意即在「煮中國菜」，這些都沒在照片中出現，故不選。

題目陷阱 針對此照片的陷阱之處可能會是：

❶ 主要人物角色錯誤：**Three classmates are discussing math.**（三個同學討論著數學。）

❷ 主角所進行的動作錯誤：**The lady is paying by cash.**（女子以現金付款。）

❸ 主角使用之物品錯誤：**The waiter is holding menus on his hands.**
（服務生手裡拿著菜單。）

❹ 主角穿著錯誤：**The male customer is wearing a casual T-shirt.**
（這位男顧客穿著休閒 T 恤。）

❺ 主角所在地點錯誤：**They are having a picnic in the park.**（他們正在公園裡野餐。）

關鍵字彙

compliment [ˋkɑmpləmənt] ⓥ 讚美、激賞
serve [sɝv] ⓥ 服務
waitress [ˋwetrɪs] ⓝ 女服務生

(A)　　(B)　　(C)　　(D)

解題分析

表情、動作 40%

主角、穿著 35%

地點 25%

■ **表情、動作** 40%

廚師正在準備餐點，可能會聽到：preparing food、cooking lunch、serving meals……等。此廚師是專注的，可能會聽到：attentive、concentrating 等字眼。

■ **主角、穿著** 35%

前景是一位廚師，可能出現的主詞有：the chef、the cook 等。照片中廚師戴著廚師帽，稱為「chef's hat」、「toque」，而身上的衣服則稱為「chef's uniform」或「chef's whites」。

■ **地點** 25%

背景可看出是在餐廳廚房，推斷可能會聽到的字有：in the kitchen、in the restaurant 等。

聽稿
（UK / **M**）

(A) The chef is washing his hands.
(B) The chef is shopping for vegetables.
(C) The chef is serving customers.
(D) The chef is preparing meals.

中譯
（英 / **男**）

答案：**(D)**
(A) 主廚在洗手。
(B) 主廚在買蔬菜。
(C) 主廚在服務顧客。
(D) 主廚在準備餐點。

解題技巧 ｜ 很快地掃描照片內容，將注意力放在看前景中主要人物的動作上，以便推論可能聽到之關鍵用字。

前景

主角 看到前景是一位廚師，便可推斷可能出現的主詞會有：the chef、the cook 等。

穿著 照片中廚師戴著廚師帽，稱為「chef's hat」或「toque」，而身上穿的白色衣服則是「chef's uniform」或「chef's whites」。

動作 此廚師站著在準備餐點，便主動預測可能會聽到：standing、preparing food、cooking lunch、serving meals⋯⋯等。

表情 此廚師的表情是專注的，便可能會聽到：attentive、concentrating 或 on the job⋯⋯等形容專注神情的字眼。

背景

地點 此照片背景可明顯地看出是在餐廳廚房，因此推斷可能會聽到的字會有：in the kitchen、in the restaurant⋯⋯等。

各選項解析

- 選項 (A)「The chef is washing his hands.」內的關鍵人物「the chef」意指「主廚」似乎是沒問題了，但動作方面「washing his hands」意即「在洗手」這便與照片內容不符了，故不選。
- 選項 (B)「The chef is shopping for vegetables.」內的關鍵動作點「shopping for vegetables」意即「在選購蔬菜」，但這也非照片中男子的動作，故不選。
- 選項 (C)「The chef is serving customers.」內的關鍵動作點「serving customers」意即「在服務顧客」，但照片中除了廚師，並沒有看到其他顧客，故不選。
- 選項 (D)「The chef is preparing meals.」內關鍵點「preparing meals」意即「在準備餐點」，的確是照片內男子的動作，故可選為最佳答案。

題目陷阱 ｜ 針對此照片的陷阱之處可能會是：

❶ 主要人物角色錯誤：The customer is ordering food.（顧客正在點餐。）

❷ 主角所進行的動作錯誤：The chef is washing dishes.（廚師正在洗碗。）

❸ 主角使用之物品錯誤：The man is holding a pen.（男子手裡拿著筆。）

❹ 主角穿著錯誤：The gentleman is wearing business suit.（那名紳士穿著西裝。）

❺ 主角所在地點錯誤：The man is being interviewed on TV.（男子上電視受訪。）

關鍵字彙

chef [ʃɛf] n 廚師、主廚

(A)　　(B)　　(C)　　(D)

解題分析

表情、動作 67%

主角、穿著 33%

■ 表情、動作 67%　　兩人開心地吃著手中的披薩，預測可能會聽到：enjoying pizza、holding a pizza、eating pizza 等字。兩人的表情是愉快的，可見餐點是好吃的，預期可能會有字詞：delicious、tasty 等字。

■ 主角、穿著 33%　　前景是一男子與一女子，便可推斷可能出現的主詞會有：the man、the woman、a lady……等。

聽稿
（US / **W**）

(A) The man is getting his hair done.
(B) They are enjoying pizza.
(C) The woman appears to be sad.
(D) The man is cooking lunch for the woman.

中譯
（美 / **女**）

答案：**(B)**
(A) 男子在理髮。
(B) 他們在享用披薩。
(C) 女子看起來很悲傷。
(D) 男子在為女子準備午餐。

解題技巧 很快地掃描照片內的大概內容,此照片僅有前景沒有背景,便將注意力放在看主要角色或動作上,以便推論可能聽到之關鍵用字。

前景

主角 看到前景是一男子與一女子,便可推斷可能出現的主詞會有:the man、the woman、a lady……等。

穿著 兩人都穿著襯衫,自然可預測會聽到:shirts 等字眼。另外,女子是留長頭髮的,故可能會聽到 wearing long hair 等字眼。

動作 照片中兩人手上都拿著一塊披薩,並且很高興地吃著,便主動預測可能會聽到:enjoying pizza、holding a pizza 或 eating pizza 等關鍵字。

表情 兩人的表情是歡笑愉快的,便預期可能會有「食物很好吃」的相關字詞:delicious、appetizing、tasty 或 mouthwatering 等。

各選項解析

- 選項 (A)「The man is getting his hair done.」內關鍵動作「getting his hair done」意即「在剪頭髮」,但照片中男女並沒有在剪修頭髮,故不選。
- 選項 (B)「They are enjoying pizza.」關鍵動作點為「enjoying pizza」意即「在享用披薩」,的確描述到照片中男女的動作,故正確。
- 選項 (C)「The woman appears to be sad.」內的關鍵點「woman... sad」提及「女子傷心」,但照片中女子是開懷地笑著,故不選。
- 選項 (D)「The man is cooking lunch for the woman.」內關鍵點「man... cooking lunch」意即「男子在煮午餐」,但照片中男子並沒有在煮東西,故不選。

題目陷阱 針對此照片的陷阱之處可能會是:

❶ 主要人物角色錯誤:Two chefs are preparing Chinese food.
　　　　　　　　　　　　(兩位廚師正準備中式料理。)

❷ 主角所進行的動作錯誤:They are drinking coffee.(他們正在喝咖啡。)

❸ 主角使用之物品錯誤:The man is using chopsticks.(男子正在使用筷子。)

❹ 主角穿著錯誤:The woman is wearing a baseball cap.(女子戴著棒球帽。)

❺ 主角所在地點錯誤:They are in the airport.(他們在機場。)

關鍵字彙

pizza [ˋpitsə] n 披薩
appear [əˋpɪr] v 顯示出

攻略 5 | 人物的動作

(A)　　(B)　　(C)　　(D)

解題分析

表情、動作 45%
地點 22%
主角、穿著 33%

■ 表情、動作 45%

女子坐在窗邊並喝著手中飲料，便預測可能會聽到：sitting by the window、drinking coffee、holding a mug……等。女子表情是輕鬆的，可能會有：take it easy、relaxing、calm、feel at home……等字詞。

■ 主角、穿著 33%

前景是一位女子，可能出現的主詞有：the woman、the lady、the young woman……等。依據女子穿著，可預測會聽到：wearing a sweater、a dress 等字眼。

■ 地點 22%

背景較明顯的為坐在窗邊，推斷可能會有：by the window 等相關字眼。照片內的物品除了女子手上拿的馬克杯，還有些許植物，判斷可能出現的字詞為：mug、decorative plants 等。

聽稿
（AU / Ⓦ）

(A) The woman is washing dishes.
(B) The woman is planting flowers.
(C) The woman is standing by a car.
(D) The woman is sipping coffee.

中譯
（澳 / 女）

答案：**(D)**
(A) 女子在洗碗。
(B) 女子在種花。
(C) 女子站在車旁。
(D) 女子在啜飲咖啡。

解題技巧 很快地將照片內容大略地掃描一下，再看到照片有前景與背景之分，我們就可以大概推論可能聽到之關鍵用字。

前景

主角 看到前景是一位女子，便可推斷可能出現的主詞會有：the woman、the lady、the young woman……等。

穿著 此女子是穿著針織洋裝，自然可預測會聽到：wearing a sweater、a dress 等字眼。且女子是留長頭髮，也可能會聽到 wearing long hair 等相關字詞。

動作 照片中女子是坐在窗邊並拿著咖啡杯喝著飲料的，便主動預測可能會聽到：sitting by the window、drinking coffee 與 holding a mug……等。

表情 此女子的表情是輕鬆無慮的，便預期可能會有相關字詞：take it easy、relaxing、calm、feel at home……等。

背景

地點 此照片背景並沒有很明顯是在哪裡，較明顯的便是女子坐在窗邊了，因此推斷可能會聽到的字會有：by the window 等相關字眼。

物品 此照片內的物品除了女子手上拿的馬克杯之外，照片右方似乎還有裝飾用的植物，故可判斷可能出現的字詞包括：mug、decorative plants……等。

各選項解析

- 選項 (A)「The woman is washing dishes.」內的關鍵人物「the woman」似乎沒問題，但關鍵行動方面「washing dishes」意即「在洗碗盤」，與照片中女子動作不符，故不選。
- 選項 (B)「The woman is planting flowers.」內關鍵動作點是「planting flowers」意即「在種花」，但照片中女子並沒有在種花，故不選。
- 選項 (C)「The woman is standing by a car.」內關鍵動作是「standing by a car」意即「站在車旁」，但照片中女子是坐著的，故不選。
- 選項 (D)「The woman is sipping coffee.」內關鍵動作點「sipping coffee」意即「小口地喝著咖啡」，的確描述到照片中女子的動作，故正確。

題目陷阱 針對此照片的陷阱之處可能會是：

❶ 主要人物角色錯誤：The little girl is reading.（小女孩正在閱讀。）

❷ 主角所進行的動作錯誤：The woman is talking on the phone.（女子正在講電話。）

❸ 主角使用之物品錯誤：The lady is holding a flower on her hand.（女子手裡拿著花。）

❹ 主角穿著錯誤：The woman is wearing a swimming suit.（女子穿著泳衣。）

❺ 主角所在地點錯誤：The woman is standing by the door.（女子站在門旁邊。）

關鍵字彙

plant [plænt] v 種植
sip [sɪp] v 喝、飲

攻略 1 | 職稱、地點與動作

(A)　　(B)　　(C)　　(D)

解題分析

地點 42%

表情、動作 38%

主角、穿著 20%

■ 地點 42%　　背景可看出是在工地，推斷可能會聽到的字有：in the construction site 等。

■ 表情、動作 38%　　兩人都站著工作，預測可能會有：standing、working on something 等。

■ 主角、穿著 20%　　前景是兩位工人，出現的主詞可能會有：two men、two construction workers 等。兩人都穿著 T 恤和牛仔褲，可預測會聽到：T-shirts、jeans 等字眼。此外，兩人都有安全帽，可能會有 wearing helmets 等字詞。

聽稿
（CA / M）

(A) They are working in a construction site.
(B) They are having a meeting in the conference room.
(C) One of the men is taking notes.
(D) The man on the right is about to sit down.

中譯
（加 / 男）

答案：**(A)**
(A) 他們在工地工作。
(B) 他們在會議室內開會。
(C) 其中一名男子在記筆記。
(D) 右方男子即將坐下來。

解題技巧 很快地將照片大概內容掃描一下，看出前景人事物、與背景的地點，以便推論可能聽到之關鍵用字。

前景

主角 看到前景是兩位工人，便可推斷可能出現的主詞會有：two men、two construction workers 等。

穿著 兩人都穿著簡單 T 恤 和牛仔褲，自然可預測會聽到：T-shirts、jeans……等字眼。且兩人都有戴安全帽，便可預期會有 wearing helmets 等相關字詞。

動作 照片中兩人都站著並工作著，便主動預測可能會聽到：standing、working on something 等字詞。

背景

地點 此照片背景可明顯地看出是在施工工地，因此推斷可能會聽到的字會有：in the construction site。

物品 此照片背景內比較明顯的便是所搭起來的鷹架了，便判斷可能出現的字詞包括：scaffold 或 fence 等。

各選項解析

- 選項 (A)「They are working in a construction site.」內聽到關鍵動作點「working in a construction site」意即「在工地工作」，的確有描述到照片內容，故選為最佳答案。
- 選項 (B)「They are having a meeting in the conference room.」內的關鍵動作「having a meeting」意即「開會」，且關鍵地點是「in the conference room」意指「在會議室」，但照片中人物並非在會議室中開會，故不選。
- 選項 (C)「One of the men is taking notes.」內提到關鍵點「taking notes」意即其中一人在「記筆記」，但照片中兩人都在工作，沒有人在記筆記，故不選。
- 選項 (D)「The man on the right is about to sit down.」的關鍵人物「the man on the right」在指「右邊那位男子」，且關鍵動作是「to sit down」意即「要坐下」，但照片中男子沒有要坐下，故不選。

題目陷阱 針對此照片的陷阱之處可能會是：

❶ 主要人物角色錯誤：Two students are learning how to measure things.
（兩位學生正在學習如何測量事物。）

❷ 主角所進行的動作錯誤：Two construction workers are taking a break.
（兩名建築工人正在休息。）

❸ 主角使用之物品錯誤：Both of them are carrying heavy bags.
（他們兩人都提著很重的包包。）

❹ 主角穿著錯誤：They are both wearing ties.（他們兩人都有打領帶。）

❺ 主角所在地點錯誤：The man is waiting for the children in front of the school.
（這位男子在學校前等孩子們。）

關鍵字彙

construction [kən`strʌkʃən] n. 建造
site [saɪt] n. 地點

conference [`kɑnfərəns] n. 會議
take notes ph. 記筆記

(A)　　(B)　　(C)　　(D)

解題分析

地點、物品 38%

表情、動作 32%

主角、穿著 30%

■ 地點、物品 38% 　從圖中可看出是在工地，因此推斷可能會聽到的字會有：in the construction site 等。此照片內除了兩男子，還有一台怪手，判斷可能出現的字詞為：excavator 等。

■ 表情、動作 32% 　兩人站著討論著某個文件，預測可能會聽到：standing、looking at a document、talking about something……等。

■ 主角、穿著 30% 　主角為工人，推斷出現的主詞有：the men、construction workers 等。兩人穿著安全背心，戴著安全帽，可預測會聽到：safety vests、helmets 等字眼。

聽稿
（US / Ⓦ）

(A) Both of them are wearing a helmet.
(B) They are looking at a map.
(C) One of them is drinking coffee.
(D) They are discussing in the office.

中譯
（美 / 女）

答案：(A)
(A) 兩人都戴著安全帽。
(B) 他們在看地圖。
(C) 其中一人在喝咖啡。
(D) 他們在辦公室內討論事情。

解題技巧　利用短暫的時間將注意力放在掃描照片上，看出主要的前景與背景，以便推論可能聽到之關鍵用字。

前景

主角　看到前景是工人，便可推斷可能出現的主詞會有：the men、construction workers 等。

穿著　兩人都穿著安全背心，還戴著安全帽，自然可預測會聽到：safety vests、helmets 等字眼。

動作　照片中兩人都站著在看並討論某個文件，便主動預測可能會聽到：standing、looking at a document 與 talking about something……等。

背景

地點　此照片背景可明顯地看出是在工地中，因此推斷可能會聽到的字會有：in the construction site 等。

物品　此照片內的物品除了前景兩男子之外，遠處還有一台挖土機，故判斷可能出現的字詞包括：excavator 等。

各選項解析

- 選項 (A)「Both of them are wearing a helmet.」的關鍵要點是「wearing a helmet」意即兩人都有「戴安全帽」，的確描述到照片中男子的穿戴，故正確。
- 選項 (B)「They are looking at a map.」內的關鍵點「looking at a map」意即「在看地圖」，但自照片中看不出那份文件是否為地圖，故不選。
- 選項 (C)「One of them is drinking coffee.」內的關鍵行動點「drinking coffee」意即其中一男子在「喝咖啡」，完全與照片內容不符，故不選。
- 選項 (D)「They are discussing in the office.」內關鍵動作「discussing」與關鍵地點「in the office」意即「在辦公室內討論」，但照片中男子明明是「在戶外工作」，故不選。

題目陷阱　針對此照片的陷阱之處可能會是：

❶ 主要人物角色錯誤：**The two managers are discussing sales strategies.**
（兩位經理正在討論銷售策略。）

❷ 主角所進行的動作錯誤：**The man on the right is sitting down.**（右邊的男子正坐下。）

❸ 主角使用之物品錯誤：**Both of them are holding a cup of coffee.**
（他們兩人手中都有咖啡。）

❹ 主角穿著錯誤：**Only the man on the left is wearing a helmet.**
（只有左邊的男子戴著安全帽。）

❺ 主角所在地點錯誤：**The two workers are discussing inside the car.**
（兩名工人在車子裡討論著。）

關鍵字彙

helmet [ˋhɛlmɪt] n 安全帽、頭盔	drink [drɪŋk] v 喝
map [mæp] n 地圖	discuss [dɪˋskʌs] v 討論

(A)　　(B)　　(C)　　(D)

解題分析

動作 55%

地點、物品 27%

主角、穿著 18%

■ 動作 55%

■ 地點、物品 27%

■ 主角、穿著 18%

男子是蹲在地上修剪樹木的，可預測聽到：crouching down、trimming、working in the garden、planting 等。

背景看出是在花園內，推斷可能聽到：in the garden。男子手上握有修剪刀，故可能的字詞還有：shears。

前景是一位園丁，推斷出現的主詞有：the man、the gardener 等。男子穿著工作圍裙、戴著帽子、眼鏡與手套，可預測會聽到：working apron、cap、glasses、gloves……等。

聽稿
（US / Ⓦ）

(A) The man is taking off his cap.
(B) The man is working in the garden.
(C) The man is cutting some papers.
(D) The man is standing by the trees.

中譯
（美 / Ⓩ）

答案：**(B)**
(A) 此男子將帽子拿下。
(B) 此男子在花園中作業。
(C) 此男子在剪紙。
(D) 此男子站在樹旁。

解題技巧 在聽力選項播放出來之前，很快地掃描一下照片內容，以便推論可能聽到之關鍵用字。

前景

主角 看到前景出現一位園丁，便可推斷可能出現的主詞會有：the man、the gardener 等。

穿著 照片中男子穿著工作圍裙，自然可預測會聽到：working apron 等字眼。另外此男子也戴著帽子、眼鏡與手套，便也可預期可能會聽到 cap、glasses、gloves……等字眼。

動作 照片中男子蹲在地上修剪樹木，便主動預測可能會聽到：crouching down、trimming、working in the garden、planting……等。

背景

地點 此照片背景可明顯地看出是在花園內，因此推斷可能會聽到的字會有：in the garden 等。

物品 此照片內的物品還有男子手上握的修剪刀，故可能出現的字詞還包括：shears。

各選項解析

- 選項 (A)「The man is taking off his cap.」內的關鍵動作點是「taking off his cap」意即「將帽子取下」，但照片中男子是戴著帽子的，沒有要取下的動作，故不選。
- 選項 (B)「The man is working in the garden.」內的關鍵動作與地點為「working in the garden」意即「在花園中工作」，的確有針對照片描述，故正確。
- 選項 (C)「The man is cutting some papers.」內的關鍵點是「cutting papers」意即在「剪紙」，與照片中男子動作不符，故不選。
- 選項 (D)「The man is standing by the trees.」內的關鍵點是「standing by the trees」意即「站在樹旁邊」，但照片中男子是蹲著，並非站著，故不選。

題目陷阱 針對此照片的陷阱之處可能會是：

❶ 主要人物角色錯誤：The farmer is growing rice.（農夫在種稻。）

❷ 主角所進行的動作錯誤：The man is doing laundry.（男子正在洗衣服。）

❸ 主角使用之物品錯誤：The boy is typing a letter on the computer.
（男孩正在電腦上寫信。）

❹ 主角穿著錯誤：The gardener is wearing a heavy jacket.（園丁穿著厚重的外套。）

❺ 主角所在地點錯誤：The man is serving customers in the restaurant.
（男子正在餐廳裡服務客人。）

關鍵字彙

take off 起飛、高升
cap [kæp] 棒球帽
garden ['ɡɑrdṇ] 花園

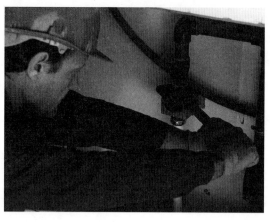

(A)　　(B)　　(C)　　(D)

解題分析

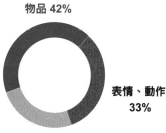

物品 42%

表情、動作
33%

主角、穿著
25%

■ 物品 42%

■ 表情、動作 33%

■ 主角、穿著 25%

除此之外，工人手上有鉗子，故可判斷可能出現的字詞包括：pliers 等。

男子很明顯地在修水管，預測可能會聽到：fixing the pipes、adjusting plumbing……等。

依據圖片中的主角，可推斷出現的主詞有：the man、the plumber 等。男子穿著制服，戴著手套和安全帽，可預測聽到：uniform、gloves、helmet……等字。

聽稿

（AU / Ｗ）

(A) The technician is repairing a printer.
(B) The man is doing exercise.
(C) The father is taking care of his baby.
(D) The plumber is fixing the pipe.

中譯

（澳 / 女）

答案：(D)
(A) 此技工在修印表機。
(B) 此男子在做運動。
(C) 此爸爸在顧小孩。
(D) 此水電工在修水管。

解題技巧 很快地將照片內容掃描一下，看看有哪些明顯的人事物，以便推論可能聽到之關鍵用字。這一題因為背景不明顯，所以單就前景來推測出最適合的答案。

前景

主角 看到前景是一位男子技工，便可推斷可能出現的主詞會有：the man、the plumber、the technician……等。

穿著 照片中男子穿著制服，還戴著手套和安全帽，自然可預測會聽到：uniform、gloves 與 helmet 等字眼。

動作 男子很明顯是在修水管，我們便可主動預測可能會聽到：fixing the pipes、adjusting plumbing……等。

物品 此照片內的物品還有工人手上的鉗子，故可判斷可能出現的字詞包括：pliers。

各選項解析

- 選項 (A)「The technician is repairing a printer.」聽到關鍵人物與行動為「the the technician is repairing...」意即「技術人員在修理…」似乎沒問題，但關鍵物品「a printer」意指「印表機」便錯了，照片中並沒看到印表機，故不選。
- 選項 (B)「The man is doing exercise.」內的關鍵點是「doing exercise」意即「在做運動」，與照片中男子動作不符，故不選。
- 選項 (C)「The father is taking care of his baby.」內的關鍵點「father... taking care... baby」意即「爸爸在照顧小孩」，這完全沒在照片中出現，故不選。
- 選項 (D)「The plumber is fixing the pipe.」內的關鍵人物「the plumber」意即「水電工」與關鍵動作「fixing the pipe」意即「修理水管」，完全描述到照片內的人物與動作，故選為最佳答案。

題目陷阱 針對此照片的陷阱之處可能會是：

❶ 主要人物角色錯誤：The professor is doing a demonstration.（教授正在進行展示。）

❷ 主角所進行的動作錯誤：The man is paving the road.（男子正在鋪路。）

❸ 主角使用之物品錯誤：The technician is holding a power meter.（技工拿著電表。）

❹ 主角穿著錯誤：The man is wearing sunglasses.（男子戴著太陽眼鏡。）

❺ 主角所在地點錯誤：The worker is fixing the projector in the conference room.
（工人正在會議室裡修理投影機。）

關鍵字彙

technician [tɛkˋnɪʃən] **n** 技術人員
repair [rɪˋpɛr] **v** 修理
printer [ˋprɪntɚ] **n** 印表機
exercise [ˋɛksɚˌsaɪz] **n** 運動
take care **ph** 照顧
plumber [ˋplʌmɚ] **n** 水電工
pipe [paɪp] **n** 水管

(A)　　(B)　　(C)　　(D)

解題分析

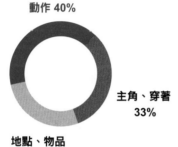

動作 40%

主角、穿著 33%

地點、物品 27%

■ 動作 40%　兩人站著在看文件，且男子手上還有其他文件，預測可能會有：standing、looking at a document、holding a paper on his hand……等。

■ 主角、穿著 33%　依據圖片，便可推斷可能出現的主詞會有：the coworkers、two construction workers…… 等。 且圖中兩人都穿著安全背心、戴安全帽，可預測會聽到：safety vests、wearing a helmet 等字。

■ 地點、物品 27%　背景可看出是在工地，推斷可能會聽到的字有：in the construction site 等。此照片內較明顯的物品為起重機，故判斷可能的字詞包括：the crane 等。

聽稿
（UK / M ）

(A) They are looking at a map.
(B) They are working in a construction site.
(C) They are having a conference call.
(D) They are climbing to the top of the crane.

中譯
（英 / 男 ）

答案：(B)
(A) 他們在看地圖。
(B) 他們在工地作業。
(C) 他們在打會議電話。
(D) 他們要爬上起重機。

解題技巧　很快地將照片內容大略地掃描一下，看到前景與背景，以便推論可能聽到之關鍵用字。

前景

主角　看到前景是一男一女，便可推斷可能出現的主詞會有：the man、the woman、the coworkers、two construction workers……等。

穿著　兩人都穿著安全背心，自然可預測會聽到：safety vests 等字眼。且兩人都戴安全帽，也可能聽到 wearing a helmet 的相關字詞。

動作　照片中兩人都站著在看文件，且男子手上還握著其他文件，便主動預測可能會聽到：standing、looking at a document、discussing the project 與 holding a paper on his hand……等。

背景

地點　此照片背景可明顯地看出是在工地，因此推斷可能會聽到的字會有：in the construction site。

物品　此照片內較明顯的物品是後方的起重機，故判斷可能出現的字詞包括：the crane。

各選項解析

- 選項 (A)「They are looking at a map.」內關鍵動作為「looking at a map」意即「在看地圖」，但照片中看不出兩人是在看地圖，故不選。
- 選項 (B)「They are working in a construction site.」內關鍵動作點為「working in a construction site」提及是「在工地工作」，的確描述到照片內的場景，故可選為最佳答案。
- 選項 (C)「They are having a conference call.」內的關鍵點是「having a conference call」意即「在打會議電話」，但照片中兩人並非透過電話開會，故不選。
- 選項 (D)「They are climbing to the top of the crane.」內關鍵動作「climbing to the top」與關鍵物品「the crane」組合在一起意即「爬到起重機的頂端」，這完全與照片內人物的動作不符，故不選。

題目陷阱　針對此照片的陷阱之處可能會是：

❶ 主要人物角色錯誤：The accountant is working on numbers.（會計正在處理數字。）

❷ 主角所進行的動作錯誤：Two workers are moving machines.
（兩名工人正在搬運機器。）

❸ 主角使用之物品錯誤：The man is taking his helmet off.（男子拿下他的安全帽。）

❹ 主角穿著錯誤：Both of them are wearing a sweater.（他們兩人都穿著毛衣。）

❺ 主角所在地點錯誤：They are discussing in the man's office.
（他們在男子的辦公室裡進行討論。）

關鍵字彙

construction [kənˋstrʌkʃən] n 修築、建造
site [saɪt] n 場地、工地
conference call [ˋkɑnfərəns ˏkɔl] n 電話會議
climb [klaɪm] v 攀爬
crane [kren] n 起重機、吊車

攻略 1 | 物品與人物穿著

(A)　(B)　(C)　(D)

解題分析

地點、物品 42%

表情、動作 38%

主角、穿著 20%

■ 地點、物品 42%

圖中背景可看出是在戶外或是都市景觀等，因此可能會聽到的字有：outdoors、visiting tourist attractions 等。此照片內的物品除了男子身上的照相機，後面還有類似古蹟的房子，故判斷可能出現的字詞有：camera、historical buildings 等。

■ 表情、動作 38%

兩人都站著，且依據他們的動作，便主動預測可能會聽到：standing、looking at the map、pointing at something 等。兩人的表情都是輕鬆的，便預期可能會有相關字詞：pleasant、exciting……等。

■ 主角、穿著 20%

圖中為一對男女，可推斷出現的主詞有：a man、a woman、the couple 等。兩人都穿著便服、戴太陽眼鏡，可預測會聽到：casual attire、sunglasses 等字眼。

聽稿

（CA / M）

(A) The woman is asking someone for directions.
(B) The man is holding a map on his hands.
(C) The man is pointing at the skyscraper.
(D) The woman is making a hotel reservation.

中譯

（加 / 男）

答案：**(B)**

(A) 女子在向路人問路。
(B) 男子手上拿著地圖。
(C) 男子手指著大樓。
(D) 女子在訂飯店。

解題技巧 很快地利用短暫的時間,將注意力放在掃描照片上,看一下前景與背景內的元素,以便推論可能聽到之關鍵用字。

前景

主角 看到前景是一男一女,便可推斷可能出現的主詞會有:a man、a woman 或 the couple 等。

穿著 兩人都穿著輕鬆便服,自然可預測會聽到:casual attire 的字眼。另外男子有戴帽子,兩人皆有戴太陽眼鏡,故可推斷可能會聽到:wearing a hat、sunglasses 等字詞。

動作 照片中兩人都站著,且男子在看地圖,女子手指著遠方,便主動預測可能會聽到:standing、looking at the map 或 pointing at something⋯⋯等。

表情 兩人的表情是快樂輕鬆的,並且很有可能是在度假中,便預期可能會有相關字詞:pleasant、exciting 或 enjoying their vacation⋯⋯等。

背景

地點 此照片背景可明顯地看出是在戶外,要去看都市景觀等,因此推斷可能會聽到的字會有:outdoors、visiting tourist attractions⋯⋯等。

物品 此照片內的物品除了男子身上的照相機之外,後面還有看似像是古蹟的房子,故可判斷可能出現的字詞包括:camera、historical buildings⋯⋯等。

各選項解析

- 選項 (A)「The woman is asking someone for directions.」內的關鍵點是「asking for directions」意即「問路」,但照片中女子並非在向陌生人問路,故不選。
- 選項 (B)「The man is holding a map on his hands.」內關鍵點是「holding a map on his hands」意即「手中握有地圖」的確有描述到男子的動作,故為正確答案。
- 選項 (C)「The man is pointing at the skyscraper.」內關鍵動作「pointing at」與關鍵物品「the skyscraper」意指「指著摩天大樓」,但照片中男子並沒有指著任何大樓,故不選。
- 選項 (D)「The woman is making a hotel reservation.」內的關鍵要點「making a hotel reservation」意即「在預約飯店」,與照片內容不符,故不選。

題目陷阱 針對此照片的陷阱之處可能會是:

❶ 主要人物角色錯誤:Sales representatives are preparing quotations.(業務代表們正準備報價單。)

❷ 主角所進行的動作錯誤:The couple is driving the wrong way.(兩人開錯了路。)

❸ 主角使用之物品錯誤:The woman is holding a camera.(女子拿著相機。)

❹ 主角穿著錯誤:Both of them are wearing raincoats.(他們兩人都穿著雨衣。)

❺ 主角所在地點錯誤:They are working on the farm.(他們在農場裡工作。)

❻ 主角心情描述錯誤:The woman is complaining to the man.(女子正在向男子抱怨。)

關鍵字彙

ask for directions 問路
map [mæp] 地圖
skyscraper [ˋskaɪˏskrepɚ] 摩天大樓
reservation [ˏrɛzɚˋveʃən] 預約、預訂

(A)　　(B)　　(C)　　(D)

解題分析

地點、物品 42%

表情、動作 38%

主角、穿著 20%

■ 地點、物品 42%　　背景可看出是在山上滑雪，推斷可能會聽到的字有：on the mountain、ski area、ski resort 等。此照片內的物品還有滑雪用具等，故判斷可能出現的字詞有：ski、ski pole 等。

■ 表情、動作 38%　　依據照片中人物的坐姿，預測可能會聽到：sitting in the front、standing behind 等字詞。大家的表情是興奮的，預期可能會有相關字詞：extremely happy、enjoying skiing……等。

■ 主角、穿著 20%　　前景為一個家庭，便可推斷可能出現的主詞會有：the family、parents、children 等。大家都穿著厚外套，戴帽子與太陽眼鏡，可預測會聽到：wearing heavy jackets、ski wear、ski glasses……等字。

聽稿
（US / Ｗ）

(A) They don't like outdoor activities that much.
(B) They are wearing swimming suits.
(C) They consider learning math great fun.
(D) They are enjoying skiing in the winter.

中譯
（美 / 女）

答案：**(D)**

(A) 他們並不是很喜歡戶外活動。
(B) 他們穿著泳衣。
(C) 他們覺得學數學很有趣。
(D) 他們享受在冬天滑雪。

解題技巧　很快地將照片內容掃描一下，大概了解前景有什麼與背景為何，以便推論可能聽到之關鍵用字。

前景

主角　看到前景是一個家庭，有爸媽與小孩，便可推斷可能出現的主詞會有：the family、parents、children……等。

穿著　大家都穿著厚外套，並戴帽子與太陽眼鏡，自然可預測會聽到：wearing heavy jackets、ski wear、hats 或 ski glasses 等字眼。還穿著滑雪靴，那便是 ski boots。

動作　照片中有些人坐在前面，一位小孩站在後面，便主動預測可能會聽到：sitting in the front 或 standing behind 等相關字詞。

表情　所有人的表情是興奮的，便預期可能會有相關字詞：extremely happy、exciting、enjoying skiing、taking a vacation……等。

背景

地點　此照片背景可明顯地看出是在山上滑雪之處，因此推斷可能會聽到的字會有：on the mountain、ski area、ski resort……等。

物品　此照片內的物品還包括滑雪板，滑雪杖等，故可判斷可能出現的字詞包括：ski、ski pole……等。

各選項解析

- 選項 (A)「They don't like outdoor activities that much.」內的關鍵點是「don't like outdoor activities...」意即「不喜歡戶外活動」，但根據照片內容，他們的表情都是很愉快的，並沒有「不喜歡」的樣子，故不選。
- 選項 (B)「They are wearing swimming suits.」內的關鍵點「wearing swimming suits」提及「穿泳衣」，與照片內人物都穿著外套不符，故不選。
- 選項 (C)「They consider learning math great fun.」內的關鍵點是「consider learning math fun」意即「認為學數學很好玩」，但照片中的人是在滑雪的場景，沒有在學數學，故不選。
- 選項 (D)「They are enjoying skiing in the winter.」內的關鍵點「enjoying skiing in the winter」意即「喜歡在冬天滑雪」，的確描述到場景是冬天，且人物是在滑雪的裝扮，故正確。

題目陷阱　針對此照片的陷阱之處可能會是：

❶ 主要人物角色錯誤：Executives are having a serious discussion.
（主管們正嚴肅地討論著。）

❷ 主角所進行的動作錯誤：They are painting the room white.
（他們正在將房間漆成白色。）

❸ 主角使用之物品錯誤：None of them is wearing sunglasses.
（他們沒有人戴著太陽眼鏡。）

❹ 主角穿著錯誤：All of them are wearing high heels.（他們都穿著高跟鞋。）

❺ 主角所在地點錯誤：Kids are studying in the classroom.（孩子們在教室裡學習。）

❻ 主角表情錯誤：Some of them don't enjoy skiing at all.（有些人並不喜歡滑雪。）

關鍵字彙

outdoor [ˋaʊt͵dor] a 戶外的、露天的	consider [kənˋsɪdɚ] v 認為
activity [ækˋtɪvətɪ] n 活動	ski [ski] v 滑雪
swimming suit [ˋswɪmɪŋ ͵sut] n 泳衣、泳裝	

攻略 3 ｜ 度假地點與物品

(A)　　(B)　　(C)　　(D)

解題分析

地點 42%

表情、動作 30%

主角 28%

■ 地點 42%　　背景可看出是在海灘，因此推斷可能會聽到的字會有：on the beach。

■ 表情、動作 30%　　兩人都坐在躺椅上享受陽光，其中左邊那位還戴著帽子，便可預測會聽到：sitting on the beach chair、wearing a hat、enjoying sunshine 等。

■ 主角 28%　　看到前景是有度假者，可推斷出現的主詞會有：two people、the couple 等。

聽稿

（AU / Ⓦ）

(A) Both of them are wearing a hat.

(B) They are enjoying sunshine on the beach.

(C) Workers are having a meeting in the office.

(D) Children are running around the house.

中譯

（澳 / 女）

答案：**(B)**

(A) 兩人都戴著帽子。

(B) 他們在海灘上享受陽光。

(C) 員工在辦公室裡開會。

(D) 小孩在家裡跑來跑去。

解題技巧 利用聽力內容播放前短暫的時間將注意力放在掃描照片上，以便推論可能聽到之關鍵用字。

前景

主角 看到前景是有兩位度假者，便可推斷可能出現的主詞會有：two people、the couple 等。

動作 照片中兩人都坐在躺椅上享受陽光，其中左邊那位還戴著帽子，便主動預測可能會聽到：sitting on the beach chair、wearing a hat 與 enjoying sunshine 等。

背景

地點 此照片背景可明顯地看出是在海灘，因此推斷可能會聽到的字會有：on the beach 等。

各選項解析

- 選項 (A)「Both of them are wearing a hat.」內的關鍵點是「both... wearing a hat」提及「兩人都戴帽子」，但照片中僅一人有戴帽子，並非兩人，故不選。
- 選項 (B)「They are enjoying sunshine on the beach.」內的關鍵動作「enjoying sunshine」與關鍵地點「on the beach」意即「在海灘上享受陽光」，的確針對照片中情景描述，故正確。
- 選項 (C)「Workers are having a meeting in the office.」內的關鍵點「workers」和關鍵行動「meeting in the office」提及「員工在公司開會」，與照片內海灘的情景都不合，故不選。
- 選項 (D)「Children are running around the house.」內的關鍵人物「children」聽起來就有點問題了，且行動點「running around the house」意即「在屋內跑來跑去」，這些都是在照片內沒有的情景，故不選。

題目陷阱 針對此照片的陷阱之處可能會是：

❶ 主要人物角色錯誤：The students are learning swimming.（學生們正在學游泳。）

❷ 主角所進行的動作錯誤：They are fixing the chairs.（他們在修理椅子。）

❸ 主角使用之物品錯誤：The man's hat is bigger than the woman's.
（男子的帽子比女子的大。）

❹ 主角所在地點錯誤：They are enjoying a great film in the theater.
（他們在電影院裡享受一部很棒的電影。）

關鍵字彙

hat [hæt] n 帽子
sunshine [ˈsʌnˌʃaɪn] n 陽光
run around ph 東奔西跑

(A)　　(B)　　(C)　　(D)

解題分析

動作 40%

地點 40%

主角、穿著
20%

■ 動作 40%　　兩人手牽手並散步遛狗，便預測可能會聽到：walking the dog、holding hands 等。

■ 地點 40%　　照片背景可看出是郊外，推斷可能會聽到的字有：in the countryside、outskirts、suburb 等。

▨ 主角、穿著 20%　　前景的男女，牽了一隻狗，便推斷出現的主詞會有：the man、the woman、the couple、a dog 等。此外，兩人都穿著厚的衣著，可預測會聽到：heavy coats、jeans 等字。

聽稿

（CA / Ⓜ）

(A) They are going sightseeing.
(B) They are having a picnic.
(C) They are climbing high mountains.
(D) They are walking the dog.

中譯

（加 / 男）

答案：**(D)**
(A) 他們要去觀光。
(B) 他們在野餐。
(C) 他們在登高山。
(D) 他們在遛狗。

解題技巧 | 處理照片題最好是可以在題目播放出來之前，很快地掃描照片內之前景與背景內容，以便推論可能聽到之關鍵用字。

前景

主角 看到前景是一男一女，還牽了一隻狗，便可推斷可能出現的主詞會有：the man、the woman、the couple、a dog……等。

穿著 兩人都穿著厚外套和牛仔褲，自然可預測會聽到：heavy coats 或 jeans 等字眼。

動作 照片中兩人是在散步遛狗，且兩人還牽著手，便主動預測可能會聽到：walking the dog、holding hands……等。

背景

地點 此照片背景可明顯地看出是郊外，因此推斷可能會聽到的字會有：in the countryside、outskirts 與 suburb……等。

各選項解析

- 選項 (A)「They are going sightseeing.」內的關鍵行動是「going sightseeing」意即「去觀光」，但照片內兩人牽著狗在草原上散步，並非觀光，故不選。
- 選項 (B)「They are having a picnic.」內的關鍵點「having a picnic」意即「在野餐」也不符照片內人物的動作，故不選。
- 選項 (C)「They are climbing high mountains.」內的關鍵點「climbing high mountains」意即「在登高山」，但照片內兩人僅是在悠閒地走路，不是在登高山，故不選。
- 選項 (D)「They are walking the dog.」內的要點是「walking the dog」意即「在遛狗」，的確有針對照片內情景描述，故正確。

題目陷阱 | 針對此照片的陷阱之處可能會是：

❶ 主要人物角色錯誤：The girl is learning how to walk.（女孩正在學走路。）

❷ 主角所進行的動作錯誤：The couple is going camping.（情侶要去露營。）

❸ 主角使用之物品錯誤：The man is carrying a cat.（男子抱著一隻貓。）

❹ 主角穿著錯誤：The woman is wearing a long skirt.（女子穿著長裙。）

❺ 主角所在地點錯誤：The couple is waiting for the bus.（兩人正在等公車。）

關鍵字彙

sightseeing [ˋsaɪt͵siɪŋ] n 觀光、遊覽
picnic [ˋpɪknɪk] n 野餐
climb [klaɪm] v 爬升、攀登
mountain [ˋmaʊntn̩] n 山脈

(A)　　(B)　　(C)　　(D)

解題分析

表情、動作 55%

主角、穿著 45%

■ 表情、動作 55% 　兩人都站著，女子在看地圖，男子在照相，便主動預測可能聽到：standing、looking at the map、taking photos 等。兩人的表情是感覺很投入，預期可能會有相關字詞：passionate、enjoying their time together……等。

■ 主角、穿著 45% 　圖片中有穿著像是遊客的男女，故可推斷出現的主詞會有：the couple、two travelers、tourists 等。兩人都穿著輕便的服裝，可預測會聽到：casual clothes 等字眼。

聽稿
（US / Ⓦ）

(A) They are sitting beside the river.
(B) They are going swimming.
(C) The man is taking photos.
(D) The woman is mopping the floor.

中譯
（美 / 女）

答案：(C)
(A) 他們坐在河邊。
(B) 他們要去游泳。
(C) 男子在照相。
(D) 女子在拖地板。

解題技巧 很快地將照片內容掃描一下，看出前景人物的主要動作，以及他們手上拿的物品之後，以便推論可能聽到之關鍵用字。

前景

主角 看到前景是有一男一女，看似是遊客，便可推斷可能出現的主詞會有：a man、a woman、the couple、two travelers、tourists……等。

穿著 兩人都穿著輕便的服裝，自然可預測會聽到：casual clothes 等字眼。兩人都戴著墨鏡、背著背包，都有戴手錶，且女子還戴著帽子，便可預期會聽到：wearing sunglasses、backpacks、a watch 或 a hat。

動作 照片中兩人都站著，女子在看地圖，男子在照相，便主動預測可能會聽到：standing、looking at the map、taking photos……等。

表情 兩人的表情是感覺投入的，便預期可能會有相關字詞：passionate、enjoying their time together 或 enjoying their vacation。

各選項解析

- 選項 (A)「They are sitting beside the river.」內的關鍵行動點是「sitting beside the river」意即「坐在河邊」，但照片內並沒有看到河流，故不選。
- 選項 (B)「They are going swimming.」內的關鍵點是「going swimming」意即「要去游泳」，但照片中兩人也沒有穿游泳衣要去游泳的跡象，故不選。
- 選項 (C)「The man is taking photos.」內關鍵點「man... taking photos」提及「男子在照相」，正確地描述到照片內男子的動作，故正確。
- 選項 (D)「The woman is mopping the floor.」內的關鍵點是「mopping the floor」意即「在拖地」，但照片中女子並沒有在拖地，故不選。

題目陷阱 針對此照片的陷阱之處可能會是：

❶ 主要人物角色錯誤：These game rangers are feeding animals.
（這些動物管理員正在餵食動物。）

❷ 主角所進行的動作錯誤：They are asking for directions.（他們正在問路。）

❸ 主角使用之物品錯誤：The woman is carrying a computer.（女子抱著一台電腦。）

❹ 主角穿著錯誤：None of them is wearing a watch.（他們都沒有戴手錶。）

❺ 主角所在地點錯誤：They are standing in front of a skyscraper.（他們在高樓前站著。）

關鍵字彙

beside [bɪˈsaɪd] prep 在～旁邊
photo [ˈfoto] n 照片
mop [mɑp] v 用拖把拖地

攻略 1 │ 選購衣物

(A)   (B)   (C)   (D)

解題分析

表情 42%

動作 38%

主角、穿著 20%

■ 表情 42%　　　兩人的表情是愉快的，便可能會有相關字詞：smiling、easy、enjoying shopping 等。

■ 動作 38%　　　照片中兩人都站著並在選購 T 恤，便可預測聽到：standing、shopping for clothes 等。

■ 主角、穿著 20%　　圖片中為一男一女，可推斷出現的主詞會有：a man、a woman、the couple 等。兩人都穿著輕鬆的衣物，可預測會聽到：casual attire、jacket 等字眼。

聽稿
（UK / M ）

(A) They are picking fruit.
(B) They are furniture designers.
(C) They are shopping for clothes.
(D) They are good at sewing.

中譯
（英 / 男 ）

答案：(C)
(A) 他們在摘水果。
(B) 他們是傢俱設計師。
(C) 他們在選購衣服。
(D) 他們精通縫紉。

解題技巧　很快地將照片掃描一下，大概了解一下前景與背景的內容，以便推論可能聽到之關鍵用字。

前景

主角　看到前景是一男一女，便可推斷可能出現的主詞會有：a man、a woman、they、the couple⋯⋯等。

穿著　兩人都穿著輕鬆的衣物，自然可預測會聽到：casual attire、jacket 等字眼。

動作　照片中兩人都站著並在選購 T 恤，便主動預測可能會聽到：standing、shopping for clothes 等。

表情　兩人的表情是歡笑愉快的，便預期可能會有相關字詞：smiling、easy、enjoying shopping⋯⋯等。

背景

地點　此照片背景可明顯地看出是在購物中心或服飾店，因此推斷可能會聽到的字會有：in the shopping mall、apparel store、fashion store⋯⋯等。

各選項解析

- 選項 (A)「They are picking fruit.」內的關鍵點是「picking fruit」意即「在摘水果」，但照片中兩人是在選購衣服，故不選。
- 選項 (B)「They are furniture designers.」內提到兩人是「furniture designers」意即「傢俱設計師」，但自照片中並看不出兩人的職業，故不選。
- 選項 (C)「They are shopping for clothes.」內的關鍵點是「shopping for clothes」意即「選購衣服」，符合照片內的情景，故正確。
- 選項 (D)「They are good at sewing.」內的要點是「good at sewing」意即「善於裁縫」，但照片中兩人是在買衣服，看不出是否會裁縫，故不選。

題目陷阱　針對此照片的陷阱之處可能會是：

❶ 主要人物角色錯誤：The father is doing laundry.（爸爸正在洗衣服。）

❷ 主角所進行的動作錯誤：The couple is cooking dinner.（兩人正在煮晚餐。）

❸ 主角使用之物品錯誤：The woman is shopping for jeans.（女子在買牛仔褲。）

❹ 主角穿著錯誤：Both of them are wearing sunglasses.（他們兩人都戴著太陽眼鏡。）

❺ 主角所在地點錯誤：Two people plan to camp beside the river.
（他們兩人計劃去河邊露營。）

關鍵字彙

furniture [ˋfɝnɪtʃɚ] n 傢俱
designer [dɪˋzaɪnɚ] n 設計師
sew [so] v 裁縫

(A)　(B)　(C)　(D)

解題分析

動作 45%

地點、物品 40%

主角、穿著 15%

■ **動作** 45%　　照片中女子是站著選口紅，主動預測可能會聽到 standing、shopping for makeups、lipsticks……等。

■ **地點、物品** 40%　此照片背景可看出是在購物中心，推斷可能會聽到的字有：in the shopping mall、a cosmetics shop 等。此照片中主要是各式各樣的化妝品，可判斷可能出現的字詞為化妝品的名稱：lipsticks、facial creams、lotions、blush 等。

■ **主角、穿著** 15%　看到前景是一位女顧客，便可推斷可能出現的主詞會有：the lady、the woman、the customer……等。她穿著厚外套，可預測聽到：wearing a heavy coat 等字。

聽稿
（US / Ⓦ）

(A) A consumer is complaining about lousy services.
(B) The woman cannot decide which T-shirt to purchase.
(C) A lady is selecting cosmetics.
(D) The service representative is assisting customers.

中譯
（美 / 女）

答案：(C)
(A) 一位消費者抱怨服務不佳。
(B) 那女子無法決定要買哪件 T 恤。
(C) 一位女子在選購化妝品。
(D) 那客服專員在協助客戶。

解題技巧 | 很快地將照片的前景人物動作與背景的地點看過一遍，以便推論可能聽到之關鍵用字。

前景

主角 看到前景是一位女顧客，便可推斷可能出現的主詞會有：the lady、the woman、she、the customer⋯⋯等。

穿著 照片中女子穿著厚外套，自然可預測會聽到：wearing a heavy coat 的字眼。

動作 照片中女子是站著的，且在化妝品櫃台之前選口紅，便主動預測可能會聽到：standing、shopping for makeups、cosmetics 或 lipsticks。

背景

地點 此照片背景可明顯地看出是在購物中心，因此推斷可能會聽到的字會有：in the shopping mall、a cosmetics shop 等。

物品 此照片內容主要是各式各樣的化妝品，故可判斷可能出現的字詞包括一些化妝品的名稱：lipsticks、facial creams、lotions、blush 與 powder⋯⋯等。

各選項解析

- 選項 (A)「A consumer is complaining about lousy services.」內的關鍵動作點「complaining about lousy services」意即「在抱怨服務不佳」，但照片中的客戶並沒有顯示出在抱怨的樣子，故不選。
- 選項 (B)「The woman cannot decide which T-shirt to purchase.」內的關鍵點「cannot decide... T-shirt...」意即「不知該買哪件 T 恤」，但照片中的女子是在買化妝品，故不選。
- 選項 (C)「A lady is selecting cosmetics.」內的關鍵動作點「selecting cosmetics」意即「在選購化妝品」，的確有描述到照片內的情景，故正確。
- 選項 (D)「The service representative is assisting customers.」內提到「service representative」意即「客服人員」，且關鍵動作「assisting customers」意即「協助客戶」，但照片內並沒有看到客服人員在協助女子，故不選。

題目陷阱 | 針對此照片的陷阱之處可能會是：

❶ 主要人物角色錯誤：The secretary is taking notes.（祕書正在做筆記。）

❷ 主角所進行的動作錯誤：The lady is washing her face.（女子在洗臉。）

❸ 主角使用之物品錯誤：The girl's backpack seems to be heavy.
（女孩的背包似乎很重。）

❹ 主角穿著錯誤：The woman is wearing a head scarf.（女子戴著頭巾。）

❺ 主角所在地點錯誤：The woman is waiting outside the operating room.
（女子在手術室外面等待。）

關鍵字彙

consumer [kən`sjumə] n 消費者	purchase [`pɝtʃəs] v 購買
complain [kəm`plen] v 抱怨	select [sə`lɛkt] v 選擇
lousy [`lauzɪ] a 惡劣的	cosmetics [kɑz`mɛtɪks] n 化妝品
decide [dɪ`saɪd] v 決定	assist [ə`sɪst] v 協助

攻略 3 | 購物地點與商品

(A)　(B)　(C)　(D)

解題分析

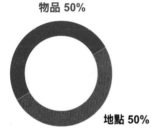

物品 50%

地點 50%

■ 物品 50%

■ 地點 50%

此照片主要為衣物,可判斷可能會聽到:apparel、attire、shirts、on display 等相關字詞。

此照片背景可看出是在購物中心或服飾店,推斷可能會聽到的字有:in the shopping mall、department store……等。店內擺設很整齊,因此還可預期會聽到:well-organized 等相關字詞。

聽稿

(CA / **M**)

(A) The station is full of passengers.
(B) Some shoppers are trying clothes on.
(C) Clothes are on display.
(D) The store manager is talking to customers.

中譯

(加 / **男**)

答案:(C)

(A) 火車站滿是旅客。
(B) 一些購物者在試穿衣服。
(C) 店內展示著衣物商品。
(D) 店經理在跟客戶講話。

解題技巧　此照片內沒有人物，主要是衣物的展示，可先推論可能聽到之關鍵用字。

前景

物品　此照片內最明顯的物品就是衣物了，故可判斷可能會聽到包括：apparel、attire、shirts、T-shirts 或 on display 等相關字詞。

背景

地點　此照片背景可明顯地看出是在購物中心或服飾店，因此推斷可能會聽到的字會有：in the shopping mall、department store、apparel shop……等。

裝潢　此店內擺設很整齊，因此還可預期會聽到：neat and clean、well-organized 等相關字詞。

各選項解析

- 選項 (A)「The station is full of passengers.」內的關鍵點是「station」與「full of passengers」意即「火車站滿是旅客」，但照片中是服飾店，且也沒旅客，故不選。
- 選項 (B)「Some shoppers are trying clothes on.」內的關鍵人物是「shoppers」，且行動關鍵點是「trying clothes on」意即「在試穿衣服」，但照片中並沒有看到人，故不選。
- 選項 (C)「Clothes are on display.」提及「衣物展示」，的確是照片內的情景，故正確。
- 選項 (D)「The store manager is talking to customers.」內的關鍵人物是「manager」與行動「talking to customers」意即「店經理在跟客戶交談」，但店內並沒有看到經理與客戶，故不選。

題目陷阱　針對此照片的陷阱之處可能會是：

❶ 主要人物角色錯誤：Some tourists are coming in.（一些遊客們走了進來。）
❷ 主角所進行的動作錯誤：A lady is mopping the floor.（女子正在拖地。）
❸ 主角使用之物品錯誤：Shoppers are trying shirts on.（消費者正在試穿衣服。）
❹ 主角所在地點錯誤：The supermarket is full of people.（超市裡擠滿了人。）

關鍵字彙

station [`steʃən] n 車站
passenger [`pæsn̩dʒɚ] n 旅客、乘客
shopper [`ʃɑpɚ] n 購物者
try something on ph 試穿
on display ph 展示
manager [`mænɪdʒɚ] n 經理
customer [`kʌstəmɚ] n 客戶、主顧

(A)　　(B)　　(C)　　(D)

解題分析

表情、動作 40%

主角、穿著 35%

地點 25%

■ 表情、動作 40%

■ 主角、穿著 35%

■ 地點 25%

男子是站著的，並在試穿衣物，可預測會聽到：standing、trying jackets on 等。

照片中是一位男士，便可推斷可能出現的主詞會有：a man、the customer、the male shopper 等。男子在試穿外套，自然可預測會聽到：jacket 的字眼。

此照片背景可看出是百貨公司或服飾店，推斷可能會聽到的字會有：in the department store、apparel store、boutique 等。

聽稿
（AU / Ⓦ）

(A) The father is folding blankets.
(B) The CEO is taking his suit off.
(C) The man is trying jackets on.
(D) The sales rep is selling women's apparel.

中譯
（澳 / 女）

答案：**(C)**
(A) 爸爸在摺毯子。
(B) 執行長正要把西裝脫掉。
(C) 此男子在試穿外套。
(D) 此業務代表在賣女裝。

解題技巧 很快地利用播放聽力內容前短暫的時間將照片看一遍，並試著分析前景和背景，以便推論可能聽到之關鍵用字。

前景

主角 看到前景是一位男子，便可推斷可能出現的主詞會有：a man、the gentleman、the customer、the male shopper……等。

穿著 男子在試穿外套，自然可預測會聽到：jacket、pants 等字眼。

動作 照片中男子是站著的，並在試穿衣物，便主動預測可能會聽到：standing、trying jackets on、doing the button up……等。

背景

地點 此照片背景可明顯地看出是百貨公司或服飾店，因此推斷可能會聽到的字會有：in the department store、shopping mall、apparel store、boutique……等。

各選項解析

- 選項 (A)「The father is folding blankets.」內的關鍵人物是「father」且動作是「folding blankets」意即「爸爸在摺毯子」，但照片中男子是在試穿外套，並非摺毯子，故不選。
- 選項 (B)「The CEO is taking his suit off.」內的關鍵要點是「taking suit off」意即「脫掉西裝」，但照片中男子的動作剛好相反，是在試穿外套，故不選。
- 選項 (C)「The man is trying jackets on.」內的關鍵動作點「trying jackets on」意即「在試穿外套」，正符合照片中男子的動作，故正確。
- 選項 (D)「The sales rep is selling women's apparel.」內的關鍵點是「selling women's apparel」意即「在賣女裝」，但照片中男子是在男裝部，故不選。

題目陷阱 針對此照片的陷阱之處可能會是：

❶ 主要人物角色錯誤：The tailor is talking to his customers.
　　　　　　　　　（這位裁縫師正在和顧客說話。）

❷ 主角所進行的動作錯誤：The man is fixing a sewing machine.（男子正在修理縫紉機。）

❸ 主角使用之物品錯誤：The man is wearing a black tie.（男子戴著黑色領帶。）

❹ 主角穿著錯誤：The young man is taking off his uniform.
　　　　　　　　（這名年輕的男子正脫下他的制服。）

❺ 主角所在地點錯誤：The old man is standing in a cloakroom.（老先生站在盥洗室裡。）

關鍵字彙

fold [fold] **v** 摺疊
blanket [`blæŋkɪt] **n** 毛毯、被子
take off **ph** 脫下、取下
suit [sut] **n** 套裝
try on **ph** 試穿
apparel [ə`pærəl] **n** 衣服、服裝

(A)　　(B)　　(C)　　(D)

解題分析

表情、動作 40%

主角、穿著 33%

地點 27%

■ 表情、動作 40%

■ 主角、穿著 33%

■ 地點 27%

女子是站著選購食物,故預測會聽到:standing、shopping for fruits and vegetables 等。另外,女子手上提著菜籃,也可能會聽到:carrying a basket on her arm 等。

看到前景是一位女子,可能出現的主詞會有:a woman、the lady、the shopper 等。照片內女子穿著風衣與長褲,可預測會聽到:trench coat、trousers 等字眼。

此照片背景地看出是在超級市場,因此推斷可能會聽到的字會有:in the supermarket、grocery store 等。

聽稿
(UK / M)

(A) The mother is cooking dinner.
(B) The woman is shopping for food.
(C) The lady is wearing a long dress.
(D) The girl is carrying a backpack.

中譯
(英 / 男)

答案:(B)
(A) 這位媽媽在煮晚餐。
(B) 此女子在購買食物。
(C) 這位淑女穿著長洋裝。
(D) 此女孩背著一個後背包。

解題技巧 把握住聽力內容播放前的幾秒鐘，很快地掃描照片，期望看到前景與背景內的要點，以便推論可能聽到之關鍵用字。

前景

主角 看到前景是一位女子，可推斷可能出現的主詞會有：a woman、the lady、she、the shopper……等。

穿著 照片內女子穿著風衣與長褲，自然可預測會聽到：trench coat、trousers 或 pants 等字眼。且她還留著長髮，故也有可能聽到 wearing long hair 等字。

動作 照片中女子是站著，且在選購食物，便主動預測可能會聽到：standing、shopping for fruits and vegetables……等。另外，女子手上還提著菜籃，便預期可能會聽到：carrying a basket on her arm。

背景

地點 此照片背景可明顯地看出是在超級市場，因此推斷可能會聽到的字會有：in the supermarket、grocery store……等。

各選項解析

- 選項 (A)「The mother is cooking dinner.」內的關鍵動作點是「cooking dinner」意即「在煮晚餐」，但照片中女子是在買菜而已，沒在煮晚餐，故不選。
- 選項 (B)「The woman is shopping for food.」內關鍵點是「shopping for food」意即在「購買食物」，的確符合照片中女子的動作，故正確。
- 選項 (C)「The lady is wearing a long dress.」內的關鍵點是「wearing a long dress」意即「穿長洋裝」，但照片中女子並非穿長洋裝，故不選。
- 選項 (D)「The girl is carrying a backpack.」內的關鍵點是「carrying a backpack」意即「背著後背包」，但照片中女子是提菜籃，不是背後背包，故不選。

題目陷阱 針對此照片的陷阱之處可能會是：

❶ 主要人物角色錯誤：The man is planting vegetables.（男子正在種植物。）
❷ 主角所進行的動作錯誤：The woman is trying the jacket on.（女子正在試穿外套。）
❸ 主角使用之物品錯誤：The lady is carrying her baby.（女子抱著嬰兒。）
❹ 主角穿著錯誤：The woman is wearing a long scarf.（女子戴著長圍巾。）
❺ 主角所在地點錯誤：The lady is shopping in a mall.（女子正在商場裡購物。）

關鍵字彙

lady [ˋledɪ] n 淑女、女子
carry [ˋkærɪ] v 提著、背著
backpack [ˋbæk͵pæk] n 背包、雙肩後背包

Unit 10 醫療看病類

攻略 1 | 人物職業與動作

(A)　　(B)　　(C)　　(D)

解題分析

地點、物品 42%

表情、動作
38%

主角、穿著
20%

■ 地點、物品 42% ── 照片背景可看出是在醫院或診所，因此可能會聽到的字會有：in the hospital、clinic 等。此外，照片內的物品較明顯的為聽診器，故可判斷可能出現的字還包括：stethoscope 等。

■ 表情、動作 38% ── 兩人都是坐著的，且在談話，故預測可能會聽到：sitting、talking、discussing、informing the patient 等。另外，醫生手上還握著文件，因此也可能有 hold a piece of paper 等字詞。

■ 主角、穿著 20% ── 前景是一位醫生與老人，可推斷可能出現的主詞會有：the doctor、an old man 等。依據醫生與老人的穿著，可預測會聽到：doctor's coat、doctor's overall、casual attire、vest 等字。

聽稿
（CA / Ⓜ）

(A) The patient is operating a machine.
(B) The doctor is talking to his patient.
(C) The old man is lying down.
(D) A nurse is coming into the room.

中譯
（加 / 男）

答案：**(B)**
(A) 病人在操作機器。
(B) 醫生在跟他的病人談話。
(C) 那老人要躺下來。
(D) 一位護理師正要進房間。

解題技巧 | 利用短暫的時間將注意力放在掃描照片的前景與背景上，以便推論可能聽到之關鍵用字。

前景

主角 看到前景是一位醫生與老人，便可推斷可能出現的主詞會有：the doctor、an old man 或 patient 等。

穿著 醫生是穿著醫生袍，老人穿便服與背心，自然可預測會聽到：doctor's coat、doctor's overall、casual attire、vest……等字眼。

動作 照片中兩人都是坐著的，並在談話，便主動預測可能會聽到：sitting、talking、discussing、informing the patient……等。另外，醫生手上還拿著文件，因此也可能有 hold a piece of paper、document 等字詞。

背景

地點 此照片背景可明顯地看出是在醫院或診所，因此推斷可能會聽到的字會有：in the hospital、clinic、doctor's office 等。

物品 此照片內的物品較明顯的就是醫生的聽診器了，故可判斷可能出現的字還包括：stethoscope。

各選項解析

- 選項 (A)「The patient is operating a machine.」內的關鍵人物提到「patient」意即「病人」，且提到其動作是「operating a machine」意即「操作機器」，但照片中的病人僅在談話，沒在操作機器，故不選。
- 選項 (B)「The doctor is talking to his patient.」內主要關鍵人物是「the doctor」有對應到照片中的醫生，另外其關鍵動作為「talking to his patient」意為「在跟他的病人談話」的確有針對照片內容描述，故正確。
- 選項 (C)「The old man is lying down.」內的關鍵動作點是「lying down」意為「要躺下」，但照片中老人並沒有要躺下的樣子，故不選。
- 選項 (D)「A nurse is coming into the room.」內的關鍵人物「the nurse」與關鍵動作「coming into the room」意為「護理師正要進來」，但照片中並沒有護理師出現，故不選。

題目陷阱 | 針對此照片的陷阱之處可能會是：

❶ 主要人物角色錯誤：The father is reading to his son.（爸爸正在講故事給他的兒子聽。）

❷ 主角所進行的動作錯誤：They are signing a contract.（他們正在簽合約。）

❸ 主角使用之物品錯誤：The old man is working on his computer.
（老先生正在用電腦工作。）

❹ 主角穿著錯誤：The doctor is taking off his vest.（醫生正脫下他的背心。）

❺ 主角所在地點錯誤：They are sitting on the platform.（他們坐在月台上。）

關鍵字彙

patient [`peʃənt] n 病患
operate [`ɑpə͵ret] v 操作
machine [mə`ʃin] n 機器
nurse [nɝs] n 護理師

攻略 2 ｜ 人物表情與動作

(A)　　(B)　　(C)　　(D)

解題分析

表情、動作 45%
地點、物品 30%
主角、穿著 25%

■ **表情、動作** 45%

女子是躺在沙發上的，便主動預測可能會聽到：lying on the sofa、taking a rest 等。她的表情是看起來有點頭暈、感到不舒服，故可能會有相關字詞：headache、uncomfortable、feeling pain 等。

■ **地點、物品** 30%

背景看出是在家中客廳，故推斷可能會聽到的字會有：in the living room 等。照片內較明顯的物品為窗戶和架子了，故可判斷可能出現的字詞包括：windows、shelves 等。

■ **主角、穿著** 25%

照片中是一位女子，故可推斷可能出現的主詞有：the woman、the lady、she 等。因為女子穿著襯衫，可預測會聽到：shirt 等字眼。且她留著長頭髮，故可能有 long hair 等字。

聽稿
（US / W）

(A) The woman is making a phone call.
(B) The woman is brewing coffee.
(C) The woman is doing household chores.
(D) The woman is not feeling well.

中譯
（美 / 女）

答案：**(D)**
(A) 女子在打電話。
(B) 女子在煮咖啡。
(C) 女子在做家事。
(D) 女子感覺不舒服。

解題技巧 很快地將照片主要前景與背景掃描一下，如此一來，我們就可以在腦中事先推論可能聽到之關鍵用字。

前景

主角 看到前景是一位女子，便可推斷可能出現的主詞會有：the woman、the lady、the mother、she……等。

穿著 照片中女子穿著襯衫，自然可預測會聽到：shirt 等字眼。且她留著長頭髮，故可能有 long hair 等字詞。

動作 照片中女子是躺在沙發上的，便主動預測可能會聽到：lying on the sofa、taking a rest……等。

表情 女子的表情是好像頭暈、感到不舒服的，便預期可能會有相關字詞：headache、dizzy、uncomfortable 或 feeling pain。

背景

地點 此照片背景可明顯地看出是在家中客廳，因此推斷可能會聽到的字會有：in the living room。

物品 此照片內較明顯的物品便是後面的窗戶和架子了，故可判斷可能出現的字詞包括：windows、shelves。

各選項解析

- 選項 (A)「The woman is making a phone call.」內的關鍵點「making a phone call」意即「打電話」，但照片中女子並非在打電話，故不選。
- 選項 (B)「The woman is brewing coffee.」內的關鍵點「brewing coffee」意即「煮咖啡」，也不與照片中女子動作相符，故不選。
- 選項 (C)「The woman is doing household chores.」內的關鍵點「doing household chores」意為「做家事」，但照片中女子也不是在做家事，故不選。
- 選項 (D)「The woman is not feeling well.」內關鍵點「not feeling well」意即「感覺不適」，的確描述到照片中女子的感覺，故選為最佳答案。

題目陷阱 針對此照片的陷阱之處可能會是：

❶ 主要人物角色錯誤：The manager is hosting a meeting.（經理正在主持一場會議。）

❷ 主角所進行的動作錯誤：The lady is combing her hair.（女子正在梳頭髮。）

❸ 主角使用之物品錯誤：The woman is leaning on the door.（女子正靠著門。）

❹ 主角穿著錯誤：The woman is wearing bracelets.（女子戴著手環。）

❺ 主角所在地點錯誤：The lady is lying on the floor.（女子正躺在地板上。）

❻ 主角之心理狀況錯誤：The woman appears to be very happy.（女子似乎非常開心。）

關鍵字彙

brew [bru] v 泡（茶）、煮（咖啡）、釀造

household [`haus͵hold] a 家庭的、日常的

chore [tʃor] n 雜務、零星工作

feel [fil] v 感覺

(A)　　(B)　　(C)　　(D)

解題分析

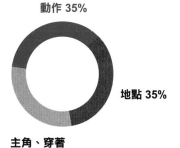

動作 35%

地點 35%

主角、穿著 30%

■ **動作** 35%

照片中女子在看顯微鏡，可預測聽到：using a microscope、examining something under microscope 等相關詞。

■ **地點** 35%

依據照片背景可看出是實驗室，推斷可能會聽到的字有：in a laboratory、lab 等。

■ **主角、穿著** 30%

照片中是一位女子，可能是研究人員或科學家，故可推斷可能出現的主詞會有：the woman、she、the lady、researcher、scientist……等。女子穿著外套，還戴著護目鏡和手套，故可預測會聽到：jacket、protective glasses、protective gloves……等。

聽稿

（AU / Ⓦ）

(A) The support engineer is fixing a steam engine.

(B) The professor is correcting papers.

(C) The scientist is using a microscope.

(D) The woman is buying sunglasses.

中譯

（澳 / Ⓦ）

答案：(C)

(A) 支援工程師在修蒸氣機。

(B) 教授在修改報告。

(C) 科學家在使用顯微鏡。

(D) 女子在買太陽眼鏡。

解題技巧 一看到照片，我們應該先將照片內容分為「前景」和「背景」來分析，並且推論可能聽到之關鍵用字。

前景

主角 看到前景是一位女子，看起來可能是研究人員或科學家的穿著，便可推斷可能出現的主詞會有：the woman、she、the lady、researcher、scientist、lab assistant⋯⋯等。

穿著 女子都穿著外套還戴著護目鏡和手套，自然可預測會聽到：jacket、protective glasses 或 protective gloves 等字眼。

動作 照片中女子在看顯微鏡，便主動預測可能會聽到：using a microscope 或 examining something under microscope、equipment 等。

背景

地點 此照片背景可明顯地看出是實驗室，因此推斷可能會聽到的字會有：in a laboratory 或 lab 等相關字詞。

各選項解析

- 選項 (A)「The support engineer is fixing a steam engine.」內關鍵動作是「fixing a steam engine」意為「修理蒸氣機」，但照片中並沒看到蒸氣機，故不選。
- 選項 (B)「The professor is correcting papers.」內關鍵人物「the professor」和其動作「correcting papers」意即「教授在修改報告」，但照片中女子是在看顯微鏡，故不選。
- 選項 (C)「The scientist is using a microscope.」內的關鍵點是「using a microscope」意為「使用顯微鏡」，的確是照片中女子在做之事，故正確。
- 選項 (D)「The woman is buying sunglasses.」內關鍵動作點是「buying sunglasses」意即「在買太陽眼鏡」，與照片中女子動作不符，故不選。

題目陷阱 針對此照片的陷阱之處可能會是：

❶ 主要人物角色錯誤：The mother is teaching her son math.（媽媽正在教兒子數學。）

❷ 主角所進行的動作錯誤：The scientist is presenting her research results.
（科學家正在報告她的研究成果。）

❸ 主角使用之物品錯誤：The scientist is gazing at stars.（科學家正在觀測星星。）

❹ 主角穿著錯誤：The woman is wearing a night gown.（女子穿著晚禮服。）

❺ 主角所在地點錯誤：The lady is waiting for someone in the bus station.
（女子在公車站等人。）

關鍵字彙

support [sə`port] n 支援、支持
engineer [ˌɛndʒə`nɪr] n 工程師
steam [stim] n 蒸氣、水氣
engine [`ɛndʒən] n 引擎
professor [prə`fɛsə] n 教授

correct [kə`rɛkt] v 訂正、修改
scientist [`saɪəntɪst] n 科學家
microscope [`maɪkrəˌskop] n 顯微鏡
sunglasses [`sʌnˌglæsɪz] n 太陽眼鏡

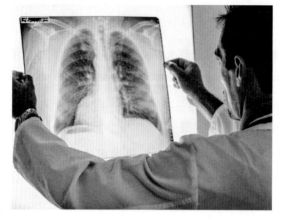

(A)　　(B)　　(C)　　(D)

解題分析

動作 58%

■ **動作 58%**

■ **主角、穿著 42%**

主角、穿著
42%

照片中男子在看 X 光片，便主動預測可能會聽到：looking at an X-Ray film 的字眼。

看到前景是一位醫生，便可推斷可能出現的主詞會有：the man、a doctor 或 he 等。男子穿著醫生袍，自然可預測會聽到：doctor's coat 等字眼。

聽稿
（UK / Ⓜ）

(A) The doctor is holding a book.
(B) The doctor is talking to a nurse.
(C) The doctor is having an operation.
(D) The doctor is looking at an X-Ray film.

中譯
（英 / 男）

答案：**(D)**
(A) 醫生拿著一本書。
(B) 醫生在跟護理師談話。
(C) 醫生在動手術。
(D) 醫生在看 X 光片。

解題技巧 很快地掃描一下此照片內容，發現此張照片僅有前景的人物與動作，便可能先推論可能聽到之關鍵用字。

前景

主角 看到前景是一位男性醫生，便可推斷可能出現的主詞會有：the man、a doctor 或 he。

穿著 男子穿著醫生袍，自然可預測會聽到：doctor's coat 等字眼。

動作 照片中男子在看 X 光片，便主動預測可能會聽到：looking at an X-Ray film 等。

各選項解析

- 選項 (A)「The doctor is holding a book.」內的關鍵人物「the doctor」是在指照片中的醫生，但其後的關鍵動作卻說是「holding a book」，便沒有與照片中人物的動作相符，故不選。
- 選項 (B)「The doctor is talking to a nurse.」內的關鍵動作點是「talking to a nurse」意即「在與護理師談話」，但照片中並沒看到護理師，故不選。
- 選項 (C)「The doctor is having an operation.」內關鍵點是「having an operation」意即「動手術」，也與照片中男子的動作不符，故不選。
- 選項 (D)「The doctor is looking at an X-Ray film.」內的關鍵動作是「looking at an X-Ray film」意即「在看 X 光片」，的確有針對照片內人物描述，故正確。

題目陷阱 針對此照片的陷阱之處可能會是：

❶ 主要人物角色錯誤：The old lady is having her lungs checked.
（這位老太太正在做肺部檢查。）

❷ 主角所進行的動作錯誤：The doctor is developing films.（醫生正在洗照片。）

❸ 主角使用之物品錯誤：The doctor is using a stethoscope.（醫生正在用聽診器。）

❹ 主角穿著錯誤：The doctor is taking off his watch.（醫生正拿下他的手錶。）

關鍵字彙

nurse [nɝs] n 護理師
operation [ˌɑpəˈreʃən] n 手術
X-Ray [ˈɛksˈre] n X 光
film [fɪlm] n 底片

(A)   (B)   (C)   (D)

解題分析

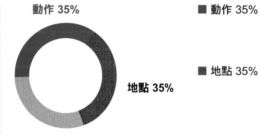

動作 35%

地點 35%

主角、穿著 30%

■ 動作 35%

■ 地點 35%

■ 主角、穿著 30%

照片中兩人應是在討論，可主動預測能會聽到：discussing issues with the patient、explaining something 等。

照片背景可看出是在牙科診所，推斷可能會聽到的字會有：in the dentist office、clinic 等。照片內的物品有一些設備，亦可判斷可能出現的字詞包括：dental equipment。

照片中為牙醫與女子，可推斷可能的主詞會有：the man、the dentist、a woman、a patient 等。牙醫戴著眼鏡和手套，便預測會聽到：casual coat、wearing glasses、protective gloves 等字。

聽稿
（CA / M ）

(A) The waiter is serving customers.

(B) The dentist is discussing with the patient.

(C) The man is brushing his teeth.

(D) The woman is standing up.

中譯
（加 / 男 ）

答案：**(B)**

(A) 那服務生在服務顧客。

(B) 牙醫在與病人討論。

(C) 男子在刷牙。

(D) 女子正要站起來。

解題技巧

大家千萬要把握住多益考試中最好拿分的照片題，一看到照片，先很快地將照片內容大概掃描一下，以便推論可能聽到之關鍵用字。

前景

主角 看到前景是一位牙醫與女子，便可推斷可能出現的主詞會有：the man、the dentist、a woman、a patient……等。

穿著 照片中女子穿著輕便外套，還留著長頭髮，自然可預測會聽到：casual coat、long hair 等字眼。且牙醫戴著眼鏡和手套，便可預期聽到 wearing glasses、protective gloves 等。

動作 照片中兩人應是在討論病情的，便主動預測可能會聽到：discussing issues with the patient、explaining something……等。

背景

地點 此照片背景可明顯地看出是在牙科診所，因此推斷可能會聽到的字會有：in the dentist office、clinic 等。

物品 此照片內的物品尚有背景的一些設備和物品，便可判斷可能出現的字詞包括：dental equipment 等。

各選項解析

- 選項 (A)「The waiter is serving customers.」內的關鍵人物是「the waiter」意即「服務生」，便有點問題了，且其後的動作「serving customers」意即在「服務顧客」，這些都與照片內牙醫的情景不符，故不選。
- 選項 (B)「The dentist is discussing with the patient.」內的關鍵點「discussing with the patient」意即牙醫「在與病人討論」，的確是照片中人物的情景，故正確。
- 選項 (C)「The man is brushing his teeth.」內的關鍵點是「brushing his teeth」意即「在刷牙」，但照片中的牙醫並非在刷牙，故不選。
- 選項 (D)「The woman is standing up.」中的關鍵點是「standing up」意即「要站起」，但照片中女子明明是坐著的，故不選。

題目陷阱

針對此照片的陷阱之處可能會是：

❶ 主要人物角色錯誤：The teacher is talking to his pupils.（老師正在和學生們說話。）

❷ 主角所進行的動作錯誤：The dentist is talking on the phone.（牙醫正在講電話。）

❸ 主角使用之物品錯誤：The patient is holding a toothbrush on her hand.
（病患手裡拿著牙刷。）

❹ 主角穿著錯誤：The dentist is wearing sunglasses.（牙醫戴著太陽眼鏡。）

❺ 主角所在地點錯誤：They are having a meeting in a conference room.
（他們在會議室裡開會。）

關鍵字彙

serve [sɝv] v 服務
dentist [ˋdɛntɪst] n 牙醫
discuss [dɪˋskʌs] v 討論
patient [ˋpeʃənt] n 病人
brush [brʌʃ] v 刷

綜合練習

(A)　　　(B)　　　(C)　　　(D)

聽稿
（US / Ⓦ）

(A) The man is riding a horse.
(B) The man is driving a car.
(C) The man is waiting for the bus.
(D) The man looks a bit down.

中譯
（美 / 女）

答案：(B)
(A) 男子在騎馬。
(B) 男子在開車。
(C) 男子在等公車。
(D) 男子看來有點失落。

解析

先很快地掃描一下圖片，看到主要影像是男子在開車，心中有底要聽到「man / driving」等相關字詞才有可能是答案。

依據照片中可看出男子正在開車，因此判斷可能出現的字詞有：a man、a gentleman 等。他穿著隨興的套裝，故可能聽到的字詞也會有：casual suit 等字詞。且由照片中可得知，男子正在開車，因此可能聽到：driving、in the car 等字詞。

各選項解析

- 選項 (A)「The man is riding a horse.」內關鍵點提到「騎馬」，與照片內容不符。
- 選項 (B)「The man is driving a car.」便知與圖片內容配合，故正確。
- 選項 (C)「The man is waiting for the bus.」關鍵點是「等公車」，也與照片內容不符。
- 選項 (D)「The man looks a bit down.」內提到男子看起來失落，但圖片中男子是笑得很開懷，故此選項也與照片內容不相符，不選。

關鍵字彙

ride [raɪd] ☑ 騎乘
drive [draɪv] ☑ 駕駛、開車
down [daʊn] ⓐ 沮喪的、心情低落的

練習 2 | 多人共事類

(A)　　(B)　　(C)　　(D)

| 聽稿
（UK / M） | (A) Both of them are enjoying playing guitar.
(B) The man is teaching the girl geometry.
(C) They are about to leave the room.
(D) The father is preparing dinner for the girl. | 中譯
（英 / 男） | 答案：(A)
(A) 兩人都很喜愛彈吉他。
(B) 男子在教女孩幾何學。
(C) 他們即將離開房間了。
(D) 那位爸爸在為女孩準備晚餐。 |

解析

把握時間將照片很快地掃描一次，我們可以看到主要人物是一名男子和一位女孩，但不確定是否為父女，兩人正在開懷地彈吉他，腦中便可能浮現「guitar」等關鍵字。

依據照片可推測，男子跟女孩可能是家人，正在一起練習吉他，因此可能聽到的字詞有：the man、the girl、the father、the daughter、the family……等字語。而他們的動作和表情，可以從照片中可看出，他們兩個人的情緒是開心愉快的，因此可以出現的字詞有：enjoy、happy 等字詞。並且他們彈著吉他，因此也有可能聽到 guitar 這個關鍵字。

各選項解析

- 選項 (A)「Both of them are enjoying playing guitar.」內的關鍵人物、行動、與物品都與照片內的相符，故選為答案。
- 選項 (B)「The man is teaching the girl geometry.」內的人物「the man」與「the girl」符合照片，但行動「teaching geometry」意指「教她幾何學」便與照片內容不符了，故不選。
- 選項 (C)「They are about to leave the room.」內的關鍵點「leave the room」意指兩人正要「離開房間」，與照片內容不符，故非答案。
- 選項 (D)「The father is preparing dinner for the girl.」內的人物「the father」與「the girl」似乎合理，但動作「preparing dinner」意指在「準備晚餐」，與照片內容不符，故不選。

關鍵字彙

guitar [gɪˋtɑr] n 吉他
geometry [dʒɪˋɑmətrɪ] n 幾何學
prepare [prɪˋpɛr] v 準備

(A)　　　(B)　　　(C)　　　(D)

| 聽稿
（AU / Ⓦ） | (A) Some files are piled up on the desk.
(B) The man is working on the computer.
(C) The manager is bringing books into line.
(D) The service rep is helping clients. | 中譯
（澳 / 女） | 答案：(A)
(A) 一些檔案堆在桌上。
(B) 男子用電腦工作。
(C) 經理正在將書本排整齊。
(D) 服務人員在協助客戶。 |

解析　很快地掃描一下照片內容，主要影像是一位穿著西裝的男子坐在文件堆中，那麼腦中可能浮現的單字會有「the businessman」或「files」等關鍵字。

從照片中可看出，一個男人可能是在上班，因此腦中浮現的單字可能為：the businessman。再來從男人表情中可看出他十分地疲累，因此可能可以聽到：exhausting、pretty tired 等字語。至於地點，我們可以從照片中可推測他可能是在辦公室中，故推測可能聽到：in the office 等字語。

各選項解析

- 選項 (A)「Some files are piled up on the desk.」內的關鍵點為「files are piled up...」意指「堆滿文件」之意，的確與照片內容相符，故正確。
- 選項 (B)「The man is working on the computer.」內的關鍵點「the man is working...」符合照片，但物件「computer」卻是沒在照片中出現的，故不選。
- 選項 (C)「The manager is bringing books into line.」內人物關鍵點「the manager」好像符合照片，但是句中關鍵片語「bring something into line」是「將某物排整齊」之意，但照片中男子並沒有在「將書排整齊」，故不選。
- 選項 (D)「The service rep is helping clients.」內的人物「the service rep」為「服務人員」與行動「help clients」為「協助客戶」都與照片內容不符，故不選。

關鍵字彙

pile up ph. 堆、疊
bring something into line ph. 保持一致、使齊頭
rep (= representative) [rɛp] n. 代表
client [`klaɪənt] n. 客戶

練習 4 ｜百貨購物類

(A)　　(B)　　(C)　　(D)

聽稿
（CA / **M**）

(A) The woman is shopping for fruit.
(B) The woman is stacking shelves.
(C) The woman is paying by cash.
(D) The woman is planting vegetables.

中譯
（加 / **男**）

答案：(A)
(A) 女子在買水果。
(B) 女子將商品擺到架上。
(C) 女子要用現金付款。
(D) 女子在種蔬菜。

解析　利用各題間幾秒空檔的時間，將照片大略掃描一下，以預測可能出現的單字。此照片很明顯是一女子在超市買水果，便預期可能有「the woman」、「fruit」，或「supermarket」等關鍵字。

從照片中可得知，主角為一個女子或是主婦，因此可推測可能聽到：the woman、the housewife 等字詞。再者，由照片中可看出女子正在挑選蔬果，因此可能會聽到：picking up the fruits and vegetables 等字語。接著，因為女子正在超市裡面，故可能聽到：in the supermarket、the grocery shop 等字語。

各選項解析

- 選項 (A)「The woman is shopping for fruit.」內的人物「the woman」與行動「shopping for fruit」都與照片內容相符，故正確。
- 選項 (B)「The woman is stacking shelves.」內的關鍵動作「stacking shelves」意即「將商品排到架上」之意，與照片內容不符，故不選。
- 選項 (C)「The woman is paying by cash.」內的關鍵動作「paying by cash」意即「以現金付款」之意，但自照片內容並看不出女子是要以何方式付款，故不選。
- 選項 (D)「The woman is planting vegetables.」內的關鍵動作「planting vegetables」為「種蔬菜」之意，但照片中女子並非在種菜，故不選。

關鍵字彙

stack [stæk] **v** 堆疊
shelf [ʃɛlf] **n** 架子
vegetable [ˋvɛdʒətəbl] **n** 蔬菜

(A)　　(B)　　(C)　　(D)

| 聽稿
（US / W） | (A) The conductor is standing on the stage.
(B) The supervisor is announcing company directions.
(C) The woman is teaching the pupil music.
(D) The musician is playing the violin. | 中譯
（美 / 女） | 答案：(D)
(A) 指揮正站在台上。
(B) 老闆在宣布公司未來方向。
(C) 女子在教小學生音樂。
(D) 音樂家在演奏小提琴。 |

解析

很快地掃描一下照片內容，看到的是一女子在演奏小提琴，腦中便浮現可能會出現的字是「the violin」等。

從照片中可看出一個女子正在拉小提琴，因此可以預測可能聽到：the woman、the violinist 等字詞。至於女子的動作，從照片中我們可看到女子專注地在拉小提琴，顯現出她很專業的樣子，因此也有可能聽到：playing the violin professionally 等字詞。

各選項解析

- 選項 (A)「The conductor is standing on the stage.」內關鍵人物「the conductor」意為「指揮」，與動作「standing on the stage」意為「站在舞台上」，都與照片內容不符，故不選。
- 選項 (B)「The supervisor is announcing company directions.」內的關鍵人物是「the supervisor」與動作「announcing directions」都與照片主要影像「女子拉小提琴」無關，故不選。
- 選項 (C)「The woman is teaching the pupil music.」內的關鍵人物「the woman」似乎可能接受，但關鍵動作「teaching the pupil music」意指「在教小學生音樂」，但照片中並沒看到小學生，故不選。
- 選項 (D)「The musician is playing the violin.」內的關鍵人物是「the musician」意指「音樂家」與關鍵動作「playing the violin」意指「拉小提琴」都與照片內容相符，故正確。

關鍵字彙

conductor [kənˋdʌktɚ] n 車掌、指揮　　　direction [dəˋrɛkʃən] n 方向
stage [stedʒ] n 舞台　　　pupil [ˋpjupḷ] n 小學生
supervisor [ˌsupɚˋvaɪzɚ] n 老闆、領班　　　musician [mjuˋzɪʃən] n 音樂家
announce [əˋnaʊns] v 宣布、公告　　　violin [ˌvaɪəˋlɪn] n 小提琴

練習 6 | 商旅出差類

(A)　　(B)　　(C)　　(D)

聽稿
（AU / Ⓦ）

(A) The businessman is giving a speech.
(B) The businessman is negotiating a deal.
(C) The businessman is making a phone call.
(D) The businessman is standing by the counter.

中譯
（澳 / 女）

答案：(D)
(A) 那商務人士在演講。
(B) 那商務人士在談一樁生意。
(C) 那商務人士在打電話。
(D) 那商務人士站在櫃台旁。

解析

先利用時間將照片內容約略地掃描一下，可看出此照片的主要影像是一名商務男子站在某一櫃台前面。那麼心中可能浮現「the businessman（商務人士）」與「counter（櫃台）」等關鍵字。

從照片中可看出，一個商務人士穿著體面，因此可推測可能聽到的單字為：the businessman、the suit 等字詞。至於圖片中的地點，從照片中可看出男子站在櫃台旁邊，因此可以推測可能聽到：counter 等字語。

各選項解析

- 選項 (A)「The businessman is giving a speech.」內的關鍵動作是「giving a speech」意即「在演講」之意，與照片內容不符，故不選。
- 選項 (B)「The businessman is negotiating a deal.」內的關鍵動作是「negotiating a deal」意即「在談生意」之意，與照片內容不符，故不選。
- 選項 (C)「The businessman is making a phone call.」內的關鍵動作是「making a phone call」意即「在打電話」之意，但照片中男子並沒有在打電話，故不選。
- 選項 (D)「The businessman is standing by the counter.」內的關鍵點「standing by the counter」意即「站在櫃台前」，的確符合照片內容，故為最佳答案。

關鍵字彙

businessman [ˋbɪznɪsmən] n 商人、業務人士
speech [spitʃ] n 演講、演說
negotiate [nɪˋgoʃɪet] v 協商、談判
counter [ˋkaʊntɚ] n 櫃台

(A)　　(B)　　(C)　　(D)

聽稿
（UK / Ⓜ）

(A) Both of them are wearing glasses.
(B) One of them is picking apples.
(C) Two farmers are planting rice.
(D) Two girls are working in the garden.

中譯
（英 / 男）

答案：(D)
(A) 兩人都戴者眼鏡。
(B) 其中一人在摘蘋果。
(C) 兩個農夫在種稻米。
(D) 兩個女孩在花園中工作。

解析

先掃描一下照片內容，可看出主要影像是兩個女孩蹲在花園裡。從照片中可看出兩個女子正在種植植物，因此可以推測出：the two girls、friends 等字詞。再來，從照片中可以看出她們兩個人正開心地一起在花園中工作，故可以推測出可能會聽到：planting the plants happliy 等字詞。

各選項解析

- 選項 (A)「Both of them are wearing glasses.」內的關鍵點是「both... wearing glasses」意即兩人都戴眼鏡，但根據照片內容，僅一人戴眼鏡，並非兩人都戴，故不選。
- 選項 (B)「One of them is picking apples.」內的關鍵點是「picking apples」意即「在摘蘋果」之意，與照片內容不符，故不選。
- 選項 (C)「Two farmers are planting rice.」中的關鍵點「two farmers」意即「兩個農夫」，與行動「planting rice」意即「在種稻米」，都與照片內容不符，故不選。
- 選項 (D)「Two girls are working in the garden.」內的關鍵點「two girls」與「working in the garden」都與照片內容相符，故正確。

關鍵字彙

glasses [ˋglæsɪz] n 眼鏡
pick [pɪk] v 摘取、摘下
farmer [ˋfɑrmɚ] n 農夫
plant [plænt] v 種植
garden [ˋgɑrdn̩] n 花園

練習 8 | 醫療看病類

(A)　　(B)　　(C)　　(D)

聽稿
（US / Ⓦ）

(A) The woman is giving the man a checkup.
(B) The man is filling out a job application.
(C) The doctor is explaining something to the man.
(D) The man is having an interview with the woman.

中譯
（美 / 女）

答案：(C)

(A) 女子在幫男子做健康檢查。
(B) 男子在填求職申請表。
(C) 那醫生在跟男子解釋事情。
(D) 那男子在跟女子面談。

解析

很快地掃描一下照片內容，看到的是一女醫生手拿文件在與男子解釋著某事，那麼腦中可能浮現「the woman」、「the man」、「document」或「explain」等關鍵字。

從照片中人物的表情與動作可以得知，女醫生似乎在與男子討論文件，因此可能可以聽到：discussing the document 等字詞。

各選項解析

- 選項 (A)「The woman is giving the man a checkup.」內的關鍵點是「giving a checkup」意即「在健檢」，但照片內容並非在做健檢，故不選。
- 選項 (B)「The man is filling out a job application.」內關鍵點是「filling... job application」意即在「填求職申請表」，這也與照片內容無關，故不選。
- 選項 (C)「The doctor is explaining something to the man.」內聽到關鍵人物「the doctor」與行動「explaining something」都與照片內容相符，故選為最佳答案。
- 選項 (D)「The man is having an interview with the woman.」內的關鍵人物「the man」與「the woman」聽起來都還可以接受，但關鍵行動「having an interview」意指在「面談」便與照片內容不符了，故不選。

關鍵字彙

checkup [ˋtʃɛkˌʌp] ⓝ 健康檢查
fill out ⓟʰ 填寫、填入
application [ˌæpləˋkeʃən] ⓝ 申請書、申請
explain [ɪkˋsplen] ⓥ 解釋
interview [ˋɪntɚˌvju] ⓝ 面談

練習 9 | 運動體育類

(A)　　(B)　　(C)　　(D)

聽稿
（AU / Ｗ）

(A) None of them is wearing a coat.
(B) They are enjoying skiing.
(C) All trees have been covered with snow.
(D) The child is learning figure skating.

中譯
（澳 / 女）

答案：(B)

(A) 他們都沒有穿外套。
(B) 他們喜愛滑雪。
(C) 所有樹都被雪覆蓋。
(D) 那小孩在學花式溜冰。

解析

先掃描此照片，很明顯地是一對父母帶小孩在滑雪，那麼便可預期會聽到「parents」、「the kid」或是「skiing」等關鍵字。人物的穿著也有可能會出現關鍵字，像是「coat」或者是「jeans」。至於照片地點，有可能會出現與天氣相關的字詞，例如：snow、cold、weather。

各選項解析

- 選項 (A)「None of them is wearing a coat.」內關鍵點是「none... wearing a coat」意即「沒人穿外套」，但照片中是每個人都穿著外套，故不選。
- 選項 (B)「They are enjoying skiing.」內關鍵點「enjoying skiing」意即「享受滑雪樂趣」的確與照片內容相符，故正確。
- 選項 (C)「All trees have been covered with snow.」內關鍵點「trees... covered with snow」意即「樹上都覆蓋著雪」之意，但看不出樹上有無覆蓋著雪，故不選。
- 選項 (D)「The child is learning figure skating.」內關鍵點是「learning figure skating」意即「學花式溜冰」之意，但照片中小孩並非在訓練「花式溜冰」，故不選。

關鍵字彙

cover [ˋkʌvɚ] ⓥ 覆蓋
figure skating ⓟⓗ 花式溜冰

練習 10 | 運動體育類

(A)   (B)   (C)   (D)

聽稿
（UK / Ⓜ）

(A) The performer is wearing Japanese costume.
(B) The singer is performing on the stage.
(C) The woman appears to be in a bad mood.
(D) The dancer is performing elegantly.

中譯
（英 / 男）

答案：(D)
(A) 那表演者穿著日式服裝。
(B) 歌手在台上表演。
(C) 那女子似乎心情不好。
(D) 那舞者優雅地表演。

解析

先掃描照片內容以便可預期可能之關鍵字；從照片中可得知，一個女舞者正在跳芭蕾，因此可以推測可能聽到：the woman、the girl、the dancer、she 等字詞。至於人物的動作，我們從照片中可得知，女芭蕾舞者的動作十分地優雅，因此可能聽到：performance、elegantly 等字詞。

各選項解析

- 選項 (A)「The performer is wearing Japanese costume.」內關鍵點是「wearing Japanese costume」意為「穿著日本服飾」，但與照片內容不符，故不選。
- 選項 (B)「The singer is performing on the stage.」內的關鍵人物是「the singer」意即「歌手」，與照片內人物不同，故不選。
- 選項 (C)「The woman appears to be in a bad mood.」內的關鍵人物「the woman」似乎沒錯，但關鍵行動「to be in a bad mood」意即「心情不好」，這與照片內容不符，故不選。
- 選項 (D)「The dancer is performing elegantly.」內關鍵人物「the dancer」意即「舞者」與行動「performing elegantly」意即「優雅地表演」都正確地描述到照片的內容了，故為正確答案。

關鍵字彙

performer [pɚˋfɔrmɚ] n 表演者
costume [ˋkɑstjum] n 戲服
singer [ˋsɪŋɚ] n 歌手
stage [stedʒ] n 講台、舞台
appear [əˋpɪr] v 顯示
mood [mud] n 心情
elegantly [ˋɛləgəntlɪ] ad 優雅地

應試策略總整理

多益測驗中照片敘述題所考的句子頗為簡短，對台灣考生來說並不是很困難的題型，若可以掌握考試中常出現的單字，聽到單字後可以馬上對應到照片內的人物與動作，要將這六題照片描述都答對是輕而易舉之事。

針對照片描述題，在試題四個答案選項尚未播放之前，會有幾秒的空檔，考生務必把握這簡短的空檔，很快地瀏覽照片，以大概了解照片內的布局，並自己先預測有可能出現的單字。

當考生在瀏覽照片內容時，可特別將注意力放在看「前景」及「背景」兩大部分。看「前景」便是應注意「人物」及其「動作」、是否有明顯的「物品」和所搭乘的「交通工具」等，而「背景」就是應該注意人物所在的「地點」、「景觀」和「氣候狀況」等。

看到一張前景有「人物」的圖片時，就可以先在腦中想像：這些人在做什麼？人物所在的地點？這些是什麼職業的人？是否可從制服或行動上看出職業？這些人物之特徵為何？是否有戴眼鏡或帽子？試著從人物的表情中看出他們是否感到高興、悲傷、興奮、無聊……等。

若看到的是「物件」，則可以大約自己描述一下：這是什麼物品？這物品是什麼材質做成的？這物品所擺設之位置？

若看到的是一張風景的照片，而前景沒有「人物」或「物品」，則應注意其「背景」之描述。可以問自己：地點是在哪裡？（例如：海邊、山上、購物中心……等）有無特殊之事物？（大太陽、樹木、或動物等）與照片中是否有交通工具、花草、或擺飾……等。

Part 1 照片描述題的答案選項是四選一，且通常會有一到兩個答案有「明顯的」錯誤，可使用「消去法」將答案縮小範圍至兩個選一個。比方說，若照片明明是一張海灘的場景，答案選項內卻出現「trade fairs（展覽）」或「skiing（滑雪）」等不相關之字，那個選項便不會是答案了。若聽到有數個聽起來都很「正確」的答案，卻不一定是與照片內場景最吻合，則應該選擇的是「最接近的答案」。

最後，圖片題中的陷阱通常有「字義混淆」及「相似音混淆」兩種，例如：walk 與 work、sheep 與 ship、flute 與 fruit、或 test 與 taste 等，需特別注意區分喔！

LISTENING
PART
2

應答問題
Question-Response

Introduction

此大題屬於日常生活的基本對話。但此類試題的主要問題在於：正因為題目不長，且僅播放一次，若沒立即抓到問題的「關鍵點」，在選擇答案上就會發生困難。應集中注意力在「題目關鍵字」上，專心地聽相對應的答案即可。

分類解析

Unit 1 以 Who 為首的題型
Unit 2 以 Where 為首的題型
Unit 3 以 When 為首的題型
Unit 4 以 What 為首的題型
Unit 5 以 Why 為首的題型
Unit 6 以 How 為首的題型
Unit 7 問 Yes / No 的題型
Unit 8 附加問句題型
Unit 9 選擇問句題型
Unit 10 直述句題型

綜合練習

Unit 1 以 Who 為首的題型

攻略 1 │ 人、物品與動作

Mark your answer on your answer sheet.
(A)　　(B)　　(C)

解題分析

人名、人物 55%
動作 32%
物品 13%

■ 人名、人物 55%　　因為是 who 開頭的問題，所以預期會出現的答案有可能是「人名」、「人物」或是「人稱代名詞」。

■ 動作 32%　　「Who」開頭的問句，主要先注意的是「人物」；其次，要留意的是「動作」，題目中敘述的動作，若是選項有出現相呼應的動作，便是答案。

■ 物品 13%　　因為題目是詢問和人物有關的問題，所以人物使用或是得到的物品，都有可能成為影響答案的因素。

聽稿
（US / Ⓦ）

Who assisted you to finish this project?
(A) Well, I don't think Mr. Chen will give us a hand.
(B) I dealt with this case all by myself.
(C) Yes, I installed it already.

中譯
（美 / 女）

誰協助你完成此專案的？（答案：B）
(A) 嗯，我不認為陳先生會願意幫我們。
(B) 我都是靠自己完成此案子的。
(C) 有的，我已安裝好了。

解題技巧　　聽到此問句，應馬上將注意力放在首字關鍵點上，此題「Who assisted you to finish this project?」的關鍵點很明確是在第一個字「who」上面。在三個答案選項播出之前，可利用一兩秒時間在腦中預設個答案目標，也就是要聽到跟「人物」相關的答案才合理。而此「人物」的關鍵點，在聽力的考題中，自然也會以重音來加以強調了。本題的重音在於：「Who assisted you to finish this project?」。因此，本題的要點是在「誰協助完成」上面。

各選項解析

- 選項 (A)「Well, I don't think Mr. Chen will give us a hand.」中雖然說出現了「人物（Mr. Chen）」，但句型「I don't think (someone) will give us a hand.」，其中的「give (someone) a hand」為片語，是「提供協助」之意，並沒有針對此問題回答，故不選。
- 選項 (B)「I dealt with this case all by myself.」中的「人物」相關回答便是「myself」，此選項意即「沒人幫我，是我自己完成的。」，有針對本問題做回應，故正確。另外要提醒大家的是，若是答案提到「某人協助我」的話，可能的答案會有「Mary assisted me to do it.」、「Mary lent me a hand.」或是「I leaned on Mary for support.」等說法。
- 選項 (C)「Yes, I installed it already.」其中的「install」為「安裝」之意，沒有回答到「人物」相關的問題，故不選。

題目陷阱 考試時如果可以馬上聽到問句的關鍵字最好，但若剛好首字沒聽清楚，也可以使用刪去法，以便增加選到正確答案的機會。而此題陷阱之處可能是：

❶ 答案內仍有提到「人物」關鍵字，但內容卻與問題無關：

➡ Mr. Chen is our VP of Marketing.
（陳先生是我們的行銷副總。）

➡ My uncle and aunt live in Japan.
（我舅舅和舅媽住在日本。）

➡ Jerry helped me move those heavy boxes.
（傑瑞幫我搬那些很重的箱子。）

❷ 若答案僅是將題目內的某個字重複一次，也不會是正確答案：

➡ Jerry asked us to finish the project as soon as possible.
（傑瑞要我們盡快完成專案。）

➡ Yes, this indeed is an ambitious project.
（是的，這真是個大案子。）

➡ Okay, I'll assist you.
（好的，我會協助你。）

關鍵字彙

assist [ə`sɪst] ☑ 協助
give someone a hand 🔤 提供協助
deal with 🔤 處理
install [ɪn`stɔl] ☑ 安裝

Mark your answer on your answer sheet.

(A)　　(B)　　(C)

解題分析

人物、人名 56%

動作 44%

■ 人物、人名 56%

■ 動作 44%

問題關鍵點是「who」，極大可能是跟「人物」相關的回答。無論是人名或是職稱，都是代表著「人物」。

題目中 who 後面接的訊息也是很關鍵的，這一題 who 後面是接動作。所以如果答案選項中的動作與題目的動作不一致，便不會是正確答案。

聽稿

（UK / Ⓜ ）

Who can fix this laser printer?
(A) I think John can do it.
(B) You've got to check with your mom first.
(C) Yeah, it's a no-brainer.

中譯

（英 / 男 ）

誰會修這台雷射印表機？（答案：A）
(A) 我想約翰應該會。
(B) 你要先跟你媽媽確認一下。
(C) 是呀，用膝蓋想也知道。

解題技巧

在聽到問題的同時，馬上將注意力放在聽問題的關鍵點上，此句「Who can fix this laser printer?」的問題關鍵點是「who」，隨後馬上利用一到兩秒的時間，在腦中勾勒出可能聽到的答案，極有可能是跟「人物」相關的回答。

在聽問題時，應注意題目中特別加強重音之處，因為那極有可能是問題的要點。而本題的重音在於：「Who can fix this laser printer?」，那麼此題的要點便是在「誰修印表機」上面。

各選項解析

- 選項 (A)「I think John can do it.」當中的確有清楚地提到「John」這個人物關鍵字，且說明「John can do it.」，意即約翰會修印表機，有針對問題回答，故推論為正確答案。
- 選項 (B)「You've got to check with your mom first.」，這與題目「誰會修印表機」並沒有直接關係，完全沒有針對問題回答，故不選。
- 選項 (C)「Yeah, it's a no-brainer.」其中的「no-brainer」意為「極為簡單、想都不用想可知之事」，沒有針對「who」來回答，故也不選。

題目陷阱 此題可能出現的陷阱會是有提到人物，或提到題目中的關鍵字，以混淆考生，但內容卻是跟題目無關的，比方說：

➡ John is standing right next to the laser printer.
（約翰就站在雷射印表機旁。）

➡ That laser printer is out of paper.
（那台雷射印表機沒紙了。）

➡ Wilson is the maintenance manager.
（威爾森是維修部經理。）

不論答案選項內故意出現的混淆因子為何，考生都應盡量將注意力放在焦點「who」上面，以求精準地選到可回答題目的答案。

另外，除了 laser printer（雷射印表機）之外，常會出現在工作場所、或出現在聽力問題內的辦公用品還可能有：

➡ calculator 計算機

➡ fax machine 傳真機

➡ hole punch 打洞機

➡ scanner 掃描機

➡ interactive whiteboard 互動式白板

➡ paper shredder 碎紙機

➡ pencil sharpener 削鉛筆機

➡ personal computer 個人電腦

➡ photocopier (Xerox Machine) 影印機

➡ typewriter 打字機

➡ projector 投影機

➡ laptop computer 筆記型電腦

➡ telephone 電話

➡ coffee maker 咖啡機

關鍵字彙

fix [fɪks] ✔ 修理
no-brainer [noˋbrenɚ] ⓝ 不用想也知道之事

Mark your answer on your answer sheet.

(A)　　(B)　　(C)

解題分析

人物、人名 70%

人物的身分 30%

■ 人物、人名 70%　因為是 who 開頭的問句，所以選項內出現人名、代名詞……等的回應成為正確答案的機率很高。

■ 人物的身分 30%　這一題的題目關鍵字中出現了人物的身分，所以選項中若以與「行銷副總」同義字來重複問題，也有很大的可能是答案。

聽稿

（AU / Ⓦ）

Who is the new VP of Marketing?

(A) Jerry is our senior engineer.

(B) All right, let's discuss marketing campaigns.

(C) That's Ms. Ellen Johnson.

中譯

（澳 / Ⓕ）

新的行銷副總是誰呀？（答案：C）

(A) 傑瑞是資深工程師。

(B) 好，讓我們來討論行銷活動吧。

(C) 是艾倫・強森小姐。

解題技巧

聽到問題的同時，將注意力集中到聽關鍵問題點上，此問題「Who is the new VP of Marketing?」，其中的關鍵問題點在「who」上面，故可預期在三個答案選項內，必須要選一個有提及「人物」相關內容的選項，才可考慮當答案。此問題點的關鍵之處，自然會以加強重音的方式呈現：「Who is the new VP of Marketing?」，「Who」和「VP」是這一題的關鍵問題點。因此，聽到答案之前可在心裡設定好要聽到「人名」的答案較為合理。

各選項解析

- 選項 (A)「Jerry is our senior engineer.」內雖說有提到人名「Jerry」，但他的職稱是「senior engineer（資深工程師）」，並非題目問的「VP of Marketing（行銷副總）」，故不選。
- 選項 (B)「All right, let's discuss marketing campaigns.」中並沒有提到人物相關的詞，而且故意將題目內的「marketing」一字重複在答案中，混淆視聽，卻沒針對問題回答，故不選。
- 選項 (C)「That's Ms. Ellen Johnson.」內容的確提到「Ms. Ellen Johnson」的關鍵人物人名，有針對問題回答，所以是正確答案。

題目陷阱 此類問人物職稱的問題陷阱，最常是有提到人名，卻故意提及與題目所問的無關之資訊，例如：

➡ Mr. Chen is my supervisor.
（陳先生是我老闆。）

➡ Jenny has been working here for 2 years.
（珍妮已經在此工作兩年了。）

➡ The VP of Marketing will give a speech.
（行銷副總要演講。）

這些答案的設計都沒有針對題目回答，在沒聽清楚關鍵點之情況下，也可用消去法以增加選對答案之機會。

另外，在企業內常見、新制多益也常考的職稱還包括：

➡ Chief Executive Officer (CEO) 執行長
➡ Vice President of Operation 營運副總
➡ General Manager 總經理
➡ Marketing Director 行銷處長
➡ Controller（財務）主計長
➡ Accountant 會計師
➡ Sales Representative 業務代表
➡ Marketing Specialist 行銷專員
➡ Technical Support Engineer 技術支援工程師
➡ Receptionist 接待員
➡ Customer Service Staff 客戶服務人員
➡ Director of Human Resources 人資主管

關鍵字彙

VP (= Vice President) n 副總
senior [ˈsinjɚ] a 資深的
discuss [dɪˈskʌs] v 討論
campaign [kæmˈpen] n 活動、戰役

Mark your answer on your answer sheet.

(A)　　(B)　　(C)

解題分析

人物、人名 71%

事件、情境 29%

■ 人物、人名 71%　因為本題是問「誰會來參加」，所以必須選擇出現人名、代名詞、職稱……等的選項為正確答案。

■ 事件、情境 29%　有時候 who 開頭的問題會提出人物參與的事件或情境，這時候就要選擇選項中出現與題目相符合的事件、情境。

聽稿

（CA / Ⓜ）

Who will join our dinner party tonight?
(A) How many wedding attendees can we expect?
(B) That's a brilliant idea.
(C) Well, I invited Linda and her husband.

中譯

（加 / 男）

今晚誰會來參加晚宴？（答案：C）
(A) 我們預期幾個來賓會來參加婚禮？
(B) 那真是個好主意。
(C) 嗯，我邀請了琳達和她先生了。

解題技巧

聽到問題，試著將注意力放在關鍵問題點上，此題問題的是「Who will join our dinner party tonight?」，可聽出問的是「who」問題，故可預期答案要有「人物、人名」關鍵字來回答較為合理。題目的關鍵點自然會被加以強調，並以加強重音的方式來吸引聽者的注意：「Who **will** join **our** dinner party **tonight**?」因此，心中可以先預設要聽到選項中出現「誰參加派對」的關鍵字才可以選擇。

各選項解析

• 選項 (A)「How many wedding attendees can we expect?」內容提到「wedding attendees」是在講「婚禮來賓」，且問「How many」是在問「有幾位」，這反問句完全與題目無關，故不選。
• 選項 (B)「That's a brilliant idea.」內關鍵點「a brilliant idea」意思為「是個好點子」，也沒針對題目問的「人物」回答，故不選。
• 選項 (C)「Well, I invited Linda and her husband.」內的確有很明確的「人物」關鍵點，也就是「Linda and her husband」有受邀來參加派對，有回答到問題，故為正確答案。

題目陷阱

❶ 針對此題可能設計的陷阱，可能是有提到人名，但並不是在回答「受邀派對」一事，例如：

➡ Yes, <u>Linda</u> is one of my team members.
（是的，琳達是我的同事之一。）

➡ I don't know why <u>Linda</u> is not invited.
（我不知琳達為何沒受邀。）

➡ <u>Linda</u> is too busy to attend the meeting.
（琳達太忙以致無法參加會議。）

❷ 或是將「party（派對）」故意改為其他活動，像是：

➡ I've invited Linda to join our <u>discussion</u>.
（我邀請琳達來參與討論。）

➡ I'm sure Linda will <u>win the case</u>.
（我相信琳達會贏得案子的。）

了解其他錯誤答案設計的可能性之後，在聽答案選項時，就更應該將注意力集中在考點上，不要被錯誤答案影響而分心。

另外，除了大家常聽到的「party（派對）」之外，企業界也常會因為不同目的舉辦不同性質的聚餐、活動，比方說：

➡ happy hours　點心時間
➡ company picnic　公司野餐
➡ fundraising event　募款活動
➡ luncheon meeting　午餐會議
➡ reception　接待會
➡ farewell party　歡送會、惜別會
➡ gala dinner　正式社交晚宴
➡ award ceremony　頒獎典禮
➡ press conference　記者會
➡ product launch campaign　產品上市活動

關鍵字彙

attendee [ə`tɛndi] n 與會者、出席來賓
expect [ɪk`spɛkt] v 預期
brilliant [`brɪljənt] a 聰明的、睿智的
invite [ɪn`vaɪt] v 邀請

攻略 5 | 人物與動作

Mark your answer on your answer sheet.

(A)　　(B)　　(C)

解題分析

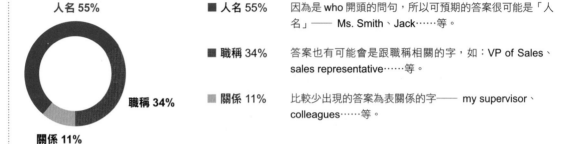

■ 人名 55%　因為是 who 開頭的問句，所以可預期的答案很可能是「人名」── Ms. Smith、Jack……等。

■ 職稱 34%　答案也有可能會是跟職稱相關的字，如：VP of Sales、sales representative……等。

■ 關係 11%　比較少出現的答案為表關係的字── my supervisor、colleagues……等。

聽稿
（UK / M）

Who else wants a copy of the agenda?
(A) Don't copy my style.
(B) It's illegal to sell scalped tickets.
(C) Please also make Mr. Ted a copy.

中譯
（英 / 男）

還有誰需要一份議程呢？（答案：C）
(A) 不要學我的風格。
(B) 賣黃牛票是違法的。
(C) 請印一份給泰德先生。

解題技巧

在面對新制多益 Part 2 考題時，注意力務必要放在聽問句的「首字」關鍵點上，像此題是問「who」，所以答案會是跟「人」有關的字詞。像是人名、職稱、人與人之間的關係……等，都是有可能會出現的答案。

接下來還可以注意一下次要資訊，比方說動作、物品等。而這些主要問題資訊和次要資訊，通常會使用「重音」來強調。就拿這一題的問句來說，重點是在 Who 與 wants a copy 上，至於「要什麼文件的影本」，相對而言便不是那麼重要了。

各選項解析

- 選項 (A)「Don't copy my style.」僅是重複「copy」一字而已，並沒有出現「人物」相關答案，故不選。
- 選項 (B)「It's illegal to sell scalped tickets.」內故意以考生可能不甚熟悉的「scalped tickets（黃牛票）」來混淆考生，但也沒聽到「人物」相關回答，故不選。
- 選項 (C)「... make Mr. Ted a copy...」，的確有提及人名 Mr. Ted，且動作「make a copy」也相符，故選 (C) 為答案。

題目陷阱 考試時如果可以馬上聽到問句的關鍵字是最好，但若剛好首字沒聽清楚，也可以使用刪去法，以便增加選到正確答案的機會。

❶ 而此題陷阱之處可能是答案有提及「人物」，但動作錯誤：

➡ Mr. Lin is taking meeting minutes.
（林先生在做會議記錄。）

➡ Ms. Wilson is adjusting the projector.
（威爾森小姐在調整投影機。）

❷ 或是選項內容僅重複問句中某字而已：

➡ This is the most important item on the agenda.
（這是議程上最重要的議題。）

➡ What's on the agenda this afternoon?
（今天下午要討論的事項有哪些？）

➡ What's wrong with the copy machine?
（這印表機有什麼問題？）

❸ 選項與問題內容完全無關：

➡ Thank you for returning my call.
（謝謝你回電給我。）

另外，在真正工作場合的會議中，主持人在說明議程時，也可能會說到以下這些實用語句：

➡ Have you all received a copy of the agenda?
（每個人都拿到議程了嗎？）

➡ As you can see, there are five items on the agenda.
（大家可以看到，議程上有五個項目要討論。）

➡ Then let's take the points in this order, okay?
（那麼我們就照此順序討論了，可以嗎？）

➡ If you don't mind, I'd like to discuss item 2 first.
（可以的話，我想先討論第二點。）

➡ I suggest we skip item 1 and move on to item 2.
（我建議先跳過第一點，並直接討論第二點。）

關鍵字彙

agenda [ə`dʒɛndə] n 議程
style [staɪl] v 風格
illegal [ɪ`lig!] a 非法的
scalped ticket [skælpt`tɪkɪt] ph 黃牛票

攻略 1 │ 地點與動作

Mark your answer on your answer sheet.

(A)　　(B)　　(C)

解題分析

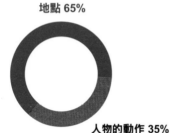

地點 65%

人物的動作 35%

■ 地點 65%

因為是 where 開頭的問句，所以可預期的答案很可能是地點、地名、位置……等。

■ 人物的動作 35%

選項中若是出現和題目中不一致的動作或是情境，就不會是正確選項。

聽稿

（CA / **M**）

Where are you meeting your friends?

(A) No, I won't be able to join the meeting.

(B) In front of the station entrance.

(C) Tom is a considerate friend.

中譯

（加 / **男**）

你跟你朋友會在哪裡碰面？（答案：B）

(A) 不，我無法參加會議。

(B) 在火車站入口前面。

(C) 湯姆是個善解人意的朋友。

解題技巧

首先要將注意力集中到聽「關鍵問題點」之上，否則很難判斷答案的方向。此題問的是「Where are you meeting your friends?」，關鍵問題點則是在「where」上面，那麼心中便有個底，預設要聽到「地點、位置」相關的答案才合理。

而關鍵問題點通常會以加強重音來呈現，本題的關鍵問題點在於：「Where **are you** meeting your friends?」。如此一來先聽出問題要點，掌握了關鍵問題點，才可預期可能的答案。

各選項解析

- 選項 (A)「No, I won't be able to join the meeting.」內只有說無法參加會議，但沒有提到「地點、位置」的資訊可以回答到本題，故不選。

- 選項 (B)「In front of the station entrance.」提到「車站門口前」，的確是針對「地點、位置」來回答的答案，故為正確答案。

- 選項 (C)「Tom is a considerate friend.」內容與問「where」的問題無關，選項中完全沒有提到任何地點的資訊，故不選。

題目陷阱

❶ 此題錯誤答案的設計也有可能是講「地點、位置」的答案，但答案針對題目的內容卻是不合理的，比方說：

Q: Where are you meeting your friends?（你和朋友會在哪裡會合？）

A: In North America.（在北美。）

此答案雖然也是提到「地點」，但和朋友在「北美」會合，這範圍太大了，無法很精確地回答到「集合地點」的問題。

又另一個例子是：

Q: Where are you meeting your friends?（你和朋友會在哪裡會合？）

A: In Mr. Jackson's office.（在傑克森先生的辦公室。）

此答案也是有提到「地點」，但和朋友約在「傑克森先生的辦公室」會合，感覺並不是非常合理的回答。

新制多益題目內容都是一般生活化的取材，不是為了難倒考生而出一些刁鑽的題目。因此，考試時應專注在選擇最佳、最合理的答案即可。

❷ 另外，陷阱也有可能是出現在答案僅將題目內的文字重複唸一次而已，比方說：

➡ I meet my friends once a week.（我一週和朋友碰面一次。）

➡ Jerry is one of my best friends.（傑瑞是我好友之一。）

➡ The meeting will be held at 4.（會議在四點開始。）

這些範例都僅將題目中有的單字覆述一次而已，並沒有針對「where」的題目作回答。

最後，除了此題的「station entrance（車站門口）」會是和朋友碰面的可能地點之外，以下為新制多益聽力題常出現的其他地點或可能的答案。

➡ We'll meet outside the cinema.（我們會在電影院外碰面。）

➡ Linda and Tim will go to the restaurant directly.（琳達和提姆會直接去餐廳。）

➡ Sherry will come to my home and pick me up.（雪莉會來我家接我。）

➡ I'll meet Joe in the library.（我和喬會在圖書館碰面。）

➡ We'll meet up with John in the shopping mall.（我們和約翰會在購物中心碰面。）

而上述這些語句也都是在日常生活中可以派上用場的，如果學起來，會十分實用喔！

關鍵字彙

entrance ['ɛntrəns] n 出入口
considerate [kən'sɪdərɪt] a 善解人意的、為人著想的

Mark your answer on your answer sheet.

(A)　　(B)　　(C)

解題分析

地點 63%

位置、距離 37%

■ 地點 63%

■ 位置、距離 37%

因為是 where 開頭的問句，所以可預期的答案很可能是「地點」── bookstore、train station……等。

答案也有可能會是跟位置相關的字眼，如：in front of、near、along the street……等。

聽稿

（AU / Ｗ）

Where is the nearest bus stop please?

(A) Let me introduce you to Ms. Terry please.

(B) You can go by bus.

(C) The New Street stop is just one block away.

中譯

（澳 / 女）

請問離這裡最近的公車站是哪裡？（答案：C）

(A) 就讓我幫你介紹跟泰瑞小姐認識一下。

(B) 你可以搭公車去。

(C) 新街站就在下個路口而已。

解題技巧

在題目播放的同時，應馬上將注意力集中在聽關鍵問題點上。此題問的是「Where is the nearest bus stop please?」，既然是問「where」，那麼自己可以先預設會聽到位置、方位等相關答案較為合理。而此題目的關鍵點便是重點部分：「Where is the nearest bus stop please?」。透過了解到題目的關鍵點是在問「最近的車站在哪？」，那麼便可在心中先規劃出要注意的答案關鍵點了。

各選項解析

- 選項 (A)「Let me introduce you to Ms. Terry please.」內容的關鍵點是「Ms. Terry（人名）」，並無法回答「where」這樣關於地點的問題，故不選。
- 選項 (B)「You can go by bus.」中提到可以搭公車去，但這比較偏向回答「how」這類如何前往的問題了，並非回答「where」地點的問題，故不選。
- 選項 (C)「The New Street stop is just one block away.」內有關鍵點「New Street stop（車站名）」和「one block away（下一條街）」，的確有針對 where 開頭的問題回答，所以為正確答案。

題目陷阱 針對此題的設計陷阱有可能是將題目內的字詞重複唸一次，但意義卻不盡相同，比方說：

➡ The boy couldn't <u>stop</u> crying.（那男孩無法停止哭泣。）

這一個選項僅是將 stop 一字重複唸一次，但要小心的是，此處的 stop 並非「車站」之意，而是作為動詞「停止」之意。

➡ The <u>nearest</u> coffee <u>shop</u> is on Cedar Lane.（最近的咖啡廳在西得街上。）

此句內容是將 nearest 重唸一次，且故意以和「stop」音相近的「shop」來混淆考生，卻沒針對問題來回答。

➡ This <u>bus</u> goes to the <u>City Hall</u>.（此公車開到市政府。）

此句內容是將 bus 一字放入句子重複一次而已，但沒有回答到問題。另外，雖說此句內也有提到 City Hall 的地點關鍵字，但是整句話的語意為「公車開往的地點」，並非題目問的「公車站牌的地點」，故也沒有針對問題回答。

問路類型的問題不但在多益聽力題目內常考，在日常生活中更是有機會碰到。因此，多準備一些「問路」或「指引方向」的實用語句是非常有幫助的。

❶ 在日常生活中可能會聽到的問路問題：

➡ How can I get to the City Hall?（我要如何前往市政府呢？）

➡ Where is the closest convenience store please?（請問最近的便利商店在哪裡？）

➡ Could you please tell me where the City Hall is?（請問市政府在哪裡呢？）

➡ I'm going to the City Hall, but I'm a bit lost.（我要去市政府，但有點迷路了。）

❷ 而這時可以給他人指引時使用的實用語句：

➡ Just go down (right / left / up / through) this street and it's on your right.
（就朝這條街走，就會看到它在右手邊。）

➡ Stay on Madison Avenue for a mile and you'll see it.
（沿麥得遜街走一英里就會看到了。）

➡ The quickest way is to take Wilson Road.（最快的方式是走威森路。）

➡ It's just around the corner.（就在街角不遠處。）

➡ It's a 10-minute walk from here.（從這大約要走十分鐘。）

➡ Do you want me to draw you a map?（你要我畫張地圖給你嗎？）

❸ 若是遇到他人問路，但自己對那地區也不熟悉的話，也可使用這些實用語句：

➡ I'm sorry, but I'm not a local person.（不好意思，我不是本地人。）

➡ I'm afraid I can't help you.（恐怕我無法幫到你。）

➡ Why don't you ask the bus driver?（你何不問公車司機呢？）

➡ Maybe you should ask the police officer.（你可能要問警察了。）

關鍵字彙

introduce [ˌɪntrəˈdjus] ⓥ 介紹、引見
block [blɑk] ⓝ 街道、街區

Mark your answer on your answer sheet.

(A)　　(B)　　(C)

解題分析

地點 63%

事件、情境 37%

■ 地點 63%　　Where 開頭的問句，答案裡應該要出現與「地點」相關的詞彙，如：company、train station……等。

■ 事件、情境 37%　　因為這一題是問「在哪裡上班」，所以選項內容要包含公司、產業才可能是適合的答案。

聽稿
（US / Ⓦ）

Where does your brother work?
(A) He works at a software company in Singapore.
(B) He doesn't like to work overtime.
(C) My brother is one year younger than me.

中譯
（美 / 女）

你弟弟在哪裡上班？（答案：A）
(A) 他在新加坡的一間軟體公司工作。
(B) 他不喜歡加班。
(C) 我弟弟小我一歲。

解題技巧

在聽題目的同時就應將注意力集中到聽關鍵問題點上面，以便在聽答案選項的時候才可知可能之方向。此題問的是「Where does your brother work?」，那麼關鍵點會落在「Where」和「work」上面。既然是問「在哪裡工作」，那麼可預期的答案內容要包括公司、產業等相關答案來回答較為合理。

各選項解析

• 選項 (A)「He works at a software company in Singapore.」的內容明確地提到「a software company in Singapore」是在新加坡的軟體公司，的確有針對 where 的題目回答，故為最佳答案。

• 選項 (B)「He doesn't like to work overtime.」提到不加班，但句子內並無提到公司、產業相關內容來回答，因此不選。

• 選項 (C)「My brother is one year younger than me.」內容中提到年紀，但題目並非問「how old」類型的問題，故不選。

題目陷阱

❶ 此題目所設計的陷阱可能選項中也有提到與「工作」相關的字眼，但仍然沒有很精準地針對問題「where」回應。以下舉出幾個例子做說明：

Q: Where does your brother work?（你弟弟在哪裡工作？）

A: He is a sales representative.（他是當業務。）

此回應雖說也是與「工作」相關的，但卻沒精準地回答到 where 的問題。

另一例子是：

Q: Where does your brother work?（你弟弟在哪裡工作？）

A: He's been working in the same company for 2 years.
（他在同一家公司工作兩年了。）

此回應也是有提到與「工作」相關內容，但此回應的要點跑到「for 2 years（時間點）」上面了。可是題目並非問「for how long」的問題，故也沒有針對題目回答。

❷ 另外，也有可能是答案有提到「地點」，但與「工作」無關的，比方說：

Q: Where does your brother work?（你弟弟在哪裡工作？）

A: My brother is in the U.S. now.（我弟弟人現在美國。）

此回應是有提到「in the U.S.」地點之資訊，但在美國也有可能是去留學或度假。沒提到 work 相關資訊，並沒有直接地回答到問題。

最後，多益考題內容偏向辦公環境內會使用到的英文，因此問及工作相關的問題自然是不會少，且在正常的辦公場合內也是有多種機會聊到自己的工作的，故應多熟悉以下論及工作的實用語句：

➡ I used to work at Dell.（我曾在戴爾公司工作。）

➡ I work for Summit Bank.（我在高峰銀行上班。）

➡ Jerry works in a factory.（傑瑞在工廠工作。）

➡ My sister works as a teacher in Canada.（我姐姐在加拿大當老師。）

➡ Mr. Smith works in the Engineering Department.（史密斯先生在工程部門工作。）

➡ I work in the software industry.（我在軟體產業服務。）

➡ She works with children of special needs.（她工作和兒童特教有關。）

➡ Mary is in charge of marketing.（瑪莉負責行銷。）

➡ My father is self-employed.（我爸爸自己當老闆。）

➡ I will start my own business.（我會自己創業。）

若是目前沒有在工作或是待業中，則可使用以下說法：

➡ I'm currently unemployed.（我目前沒工作。）

➡ I'm in between jobs at the moment.（我現在待業中。）

➡ I'm looking for work in sales.（我在找業務的工作。）

關鍵字彙

work overtime ph. 加班、超時工作

Mark your answer on your answer sheet.

(A)　　(B)　　(C)

解題分析

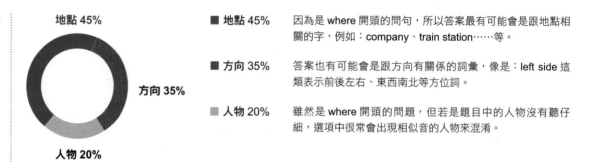

地點 45%

方向 35%

人物 20%

■ 地點 45%　因為是 where 開頭的問句,所以答案最有可能會是跟地點相關的字,例如:company、train station……等。

■ 方向 35%　答案也有可能會是跟方向有關係的詞彙,像是:left side 這類表示前後左右、東西南北等方位詞。

■ 人物 20%　雖然是 where 開頭的問題,但若是題目中的人物沒有聽仔細,選項中很常會出現相似音的人物來混淆。

聽稿

(UK / M)

Where should I be waiting?

(A) I've been waiting for a long time.

(B) In the lobby please.

(C) How about spending a week in Florida?

中譯

(英 / 男)

我該在哪裡等你?(答案:B)

(A) 我已經等很久了。

(B) 請在大廳等。

(C) 何不去佛羅里達州待上一週?

解題技巧　聽題目的同時也應盡力地將注意力集中到該聽的關鍵問句上,以期望可以預測答案的方向。像此句問的是「Where should I be waiting?」,其中的問題關鍵點自然會落在「where」上面。故可預期可能的答案要包括「地點」、「位置」的內容來回答較為合理。而整句的要點在唸出時會以重音的方式呈現:「Where should I be waiting?」。

各選項解析

- 選項 (A)「I've been waiting for a long time.」內提到的要點是「for a long time」是時間,並無法回答「地點」的問題,故不選。
- 選項 (B)「In the lobby please.」內有關鍵字「lobby」說明是要在大廳等,這個選項內容可以回答到問地點的問題,故選為最佳答案。
- 選項 (C)「How about spending a week in Florida?」,內容雖然有地點「in Florida」,但並非針對題目問的「在哪等」的答案,反而是偏向「度假地點」了,故不選。

題目陷阱 此題的可能變化陷阱，可能是有提到問句中的關鍵字，但意義卻不盡相同，比方說：

➡ The waiter is standing over there.
（服務生就站在那邊。）
故意使用「waiter」一字來讓考生與「waiting（等待）」一字混淆。

➡ Students are waiting to enter the hall.
（學生都等著要進大廳。）
此句僅故意將「waiting」一字重複唸一次而已，卻沒有真正地回答到題目所問。

最後，針對此題問等待地點的情境，另有可能的回答包括：

➡ Please wait for me at the corner.
（請在街角等我。）

➡ I'll go downstairs in a minute.
（我一分鐘後下樓去。）

➡ Let's meet in front of Gate 5 in 20 minutes.
（我們二十分鐘後在五號登機口見。）

➡ Please wait in hotel lobby. I'll be right down.
（請在飯店大廳等一下，我馬上下去。）

➡ You can stay in the car. I'll go find you.
（你可以待在車上，我會去找你。）

關鍵字彙

lobby [ˋlɑbɪ] n（飯店的）迎賓大廳

Mark your answer on your answer sheet.

(A)　　(B)　　(C)

解題分析

地點 64%

人物 25%

事件、情境 11%

■ 地點 64%

■ 人物 25%

■ 事件、情境 11%

因為這一題是以 where 開頭的問句，問對方購買地點，所以答案應該會是可以買東西的地點，例如：department store。

雖然是 where 開頭的問句，但經常會有與題目詞彙發音相似的人名混入選項中，需要小心辨認。

除了地點之外，選項中所提到的事件也要與題目相符，才是正確的答案。

聽稿

（US / Ⓦ）

Where did you buy that new jacket?

(A) You like my new jacket, don't you?

(B) I need to buy something for Jackie's birthday.

(C) I bought it in an online store.

中譯

（美 / 女）

那件新外套你是在哪裡買的？（答案：C）

(A) 你喜歡我的新外套，對吧？

(B) 傑克生日我要買禮物送他。

(C) 我是在線上商店訂購的。

解題技巧

聽到此問題「Where did you buy that new jacket?」的同時，應該馬上就要判斷關鍵問題點是在 where 上面。那麼既然是問「外套在哪裡買的」，自然就要以聽到有購買地點的答案來回答較為合理。而題目在唸出的時候，句子的要點自然會以加強重音來呈現：「Where **did** you **buy** **that** new jacket?」。如此一來，將焦點放在聽出哪裡買的資訊上即可，比試圖想聽到所有資訊簡單得多了。

各選項解析

- 選項 (A)「You like my new jacket, don't you?」內容問到是否喜歡夾克？但是沒回答到「where 哪裡買」的問題，故不選。
- 選項 (B)「I need to buy something for Jackie's birthday.」中的內容故意將發音類似的 Jackie 和 jacket 來混淆考生，卻沒有提及地點的資訊，故不選。
- 選項 (C)「I bought it in an online store.」內容關鍵點是「an online store」說明了是在線上商店購買的，有回答到 where 開頭的問題，故選為最佳答案。

題目陷阱　針對此題的陷阱可能設計為：有提到地點、也重複句子中的關鍵字，但卻不是針對問題來回答的。比方說：

➡ <u>Jackie</u> is from Germany.
（傑克是德國人。）

此句內故意唸與 jacket 發音相似的 Jackie，還提到了地點 Germany，但整句話的內容並非針對問題回答。

➡ The VP of Marketing just <u>bought</u> a new Beemer.
（行銷副總剛買了台新的寶馬汽車。）

此句內容也是提到「購買了某物」，但並非題目中的 jacket，也沒提到購買地點。

➡ I <u>bought</u> this lipstick in the shopping mall.
（我這口紅是在購物中心買的。）

此句內是有提到 shopping mall，是地點沒錯，但並非題目中討論的 jacket，而是其他物品 lipstick，因此也算是沒有針對題目回答。

最後，針對購買商品的地點、商店，日常生活中還有一些常見、或多益考試也常考的銷售管道補充如下：

➡ shopping channel 購物頻道
➡ wholesaler 大盤商
➡ retailer 零售商
➡ outlet 經銷點、暢貨中心
➡ online marketplace 線上市集
➡ catalog 郵購目錄
➡ department store 百貨公司
➡ distributor 經銷商
➡ franchiser 加盟店
➡ convenience store 便利商店
➡ hypermarket 大賣場
➡ auction 拍賣會

關鍵字彙

jacket [ˋdʒækɪt] n 外套
online [ˋɑnˌlaɪn] a （網路）線上的

Unit 3 以 When 為首的題型

攻略 1 | 時間與事件

Mark your answer on your answer sheet.
(A)   (B)   (C)

解題分析

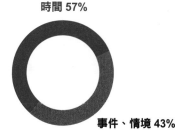

時間 57%

事件、情境 43%

■ 時間 57%

■ 事件、情境 43%

When 開頭的問句,答案裡出現「時間」相關的詞彙才是合理的,而且通常都會是某個特定的時間點,如:12 noon、11:00……等。

因為題目中問了「何時吃午餐」,所以答案的選項中除了提到時間之外,還必須強調吃午餐這個事件。如果選項的重點與題目不一樣,就不是正確答案。

聽稿
（UK / M ）

When do you usually have lunch?
(A) Well, around 12 noon.
(B) I usually have a sandwich for lunch.
(C) He lapsed into food coma after lunch.

中譯
（英 / 男 ）

你通常是何時吃午餐?（答案:A）
(A) 嗯,大約中午十二點吧。
(B) 我午餐通常是吃三明治。
(C) 他午餐吃太飽想睡了。

解題技巧

在聽到題目播放的同時,將注意力集中在聽關鍵問題點上,此題「When do you usually have lunch?」的關鍵問題點就在 when 一字上,因此就可以馬上判斷要聽到關於時間的答案較為合理。題目唸出的同時,考生要特別注意之處通常會以加強重音來呈現:「When do you usually have lunch?」,When 和 lunch 都是本題需要特別注意的地方。根據這樣的關鍵點,可預測必須聽到可以回答「吃午餐之時間」的答案才合理。

各選項解析

• 選項 (A)「Well, around 12 noon.」內很明確地有時間點「12 noon」,說明是中午十二點吃午餐的,因此有針對題目回答,故正確。

• 選項 (B)「I usually have a sandwich for lunch.」內僅將題目中 usually 和 lunch 兩字重複再唸一次罷了,完全沒有提到時間點的內容,故不選。

• 選項 (C)「He lapsed into food coma after lunch.」內的 lapse into food coma 是「因吃太飽而想昏睡」之意,反而沒有針對時間回答,故不選。

題目陷阱 針對此題的陷阱通常會設計成有將題目中的關鍵點重複唸出，但答案方向卻不是針對時間點在做回應的。比方說：

➡ I usually <u>have</u> burgers for <u>lunch</u>.（我通常吃漢堡當午餐。）

此句內雖有提到題目中的 lunch 一字，但要點卻是在 burgers 上面，提到「午餐吃什麼」，而沒有針對題目問的「何時吃」來回應。

➡ I will meet a client <u>at 11:30</u>.（我十一點半要跟一個客戶碰面。）

此句內有提到時間 11:30，但內容要點是「meet a client（與客戶碰面的時間）」，並非題目問的「吃午餐的時間」。

➡ Let's discuss the project issue over <u>lunch</u>.（我們午餐時順便討論此案子吧。）

此句內雖然也有提到關鍵字 lunch，但是這句話的主旨為邀請某人午餐時順便討論公事，內容並沒有時間點在內。

另外，值得補充的是，一般商務場合會有一邊吃午餐、一邊討論公事的午餐會議「lunch meeting」，較正式一點的午餐會議便稱做「luncheon」。不論是一般的 lunch meeting 或正式的 luncheon，也不能因為氣氛輕鬆就亂聊，通常也有以下幾個要點要遵守：

❶ Stick to clear agenda and objectives.（要有清楚明確的議程與目的。）

❷ It's all about business, nothing personal.（談的內容都是公事，沒有私事。）

午餐會議的用餐氛圍自然會比在會議室內來得輕鬆愉快沒錯，但就算是午餐會議，討論的也應與公事有關。因此應避免提到個人私事、親戚關係、休閒生活等與公司業務無直接相關之話題。

❸ Encourage attendees to talk.（鼓勵出席者發言。）

很多老闆約午餐會議就是要參與的人坐著聽他一人唱獨角戲，殊不知約午餐會議的目的是為了讓參與者在較為輕鬆的氣氛之下，可以產生出更有創意或具建設性的點子。因此約午餐會議的領導人，應多鼓勵共同參與者多發表意見。

❹ No alcohol.（沒有酒精。）

用餐時想搭配點酒類也是無可厚非的事，但午餐會議的重點不是「用餐」，而是在於「會議」。故應將焦點放在討論，而非飲酒作樂上面。

關鍵字彙

sandwich [`sændwɪtʃ] ⓝ 三明治
lapse [læps] ⓥ 陷入
coma [`komə] ⓝ 昏迷

攻略 2 │ 時間與情境

Mark your answer on your answer sheet.

(A)   (B)   (C)

解題分析

時間 68%

事件、情境 32%

■ 時間 68%

■ 事件、情境 32%

因為是 when 開頭的問句,所以回答的內容應該要提到「時間」,例如:10:00、1994、ten minutes ago、in five minutes……等。

注意「時間」的同時,也要仔細確認選項中敘述的事件有沒有與題目符合,以免落入設計好的陷阱當中。

聽稿

(AU / **W**)

When will the train arrive?
(A) Right, let's go to the information booth.
(B) The train station looks fantastic.
(C) Maybe in ten minutes.

中譯

(澳 / **女**)

火車何時會抵達呢?(答案:**C**)
(A) 是的,我們去服務台問問看。
(B) 這個火車站看起來很讚。
(C) 可能再十分鐘會到。

解題技巧

想要精準地預期答案之方向,就要在聽題目的同時,將注意力放在首字問題關鍵點上。此題問的是「When will the train arrive?」,那麼關鍵點便是在 when 一字上面,可預期要聽到關於時間點的回應當答案較為合理。題目的關鍵點通常會以加強重音來呈現,而本題的關鍵點在於「When **will** the train arrive?」。接下來就只要注意聽有出現時間點的答案即可。

各選項解析

- 選項 (A)「Right, let's go to the information booth.」內提到地點,也就是 information booth,但題目並非問「where」,而是問「when」,故此回應並沒有針對問題回應,所以不可選。
- 選項 (B)「The train station looks fantastic.」的內容描述車站看起來壯觀,不過卻沒有回答到時間「when」的問題,故不選。
- 選項 (C)「Maybe in ten minutes.」中提到「in ten minutes」,意謂著「再過十分鐘火車就會來」之意,有針對問題回答,故選為最佳答案。

題目陷阱

因為此題的問題要點是「when」，因此只要在腦中輸入「沒有回答到時間點的答案都不可選」的想法，這樣一來，便可以過濾掉不重要的訊息。其中有可能僅是將題中關鍵字重複一次的，或以答非所問的方式呈現。下列將舉出多個例子讓各位多加練習：

➡ The <u>train</u> goes to Newark.（此火車開往紐華克。）

句中只是將關鍵字 train 重複一次而已，但句中沒提到時間點，且題目也不是在問 where，因此就算此句表明 Newark 這個地點也無法回答問題。

➡ This line has been operating since <u>2004</u>.（此線自二〇〇四年就開始營運了。）

此句內刻意地提到時間點，也就是 2004；但問題問的是「火車到站之時間」，並非此句中提到的「開始營運之時間」。故要注意就算是提及時間，也要符合題目內容才行。

➡ The bus left <u>five minutes ago</u>.（公車五分鐘前開走了。）

此句內也有提到時間點，但是 bus 與題目設定的 train 不符，句中的 leave 也與題目設定的 arrive 完全相反，就只是故意混淆考生罷了。

此題提到了 train（火車），世界各地的旅遊都少不了以火車當交通工具。而在日常生活中常會聽到的，且也會在英文測驗聽力題目聽到的火車類型有：

➡ steam locomotive 蒸氣火車

➡ diesel rail car 柴油客車

➡ diesel-electric locomotive 柴電火車

➡ electric locomotive 電動火車

➡ passenger car 客車

➡ freight car 貨車

➡ high speed rail 高速鐵路

➡ maglev 磁浮火車

➡ monorail 單軌火車

➡ tram 纜車

關鍵字彙

arrive [ə`raɪv] V 抵達、到達
booth [buθ] n 攤位、崗亭
fantastic [fæn`tæstɪk] a 極好的

Mark your answer on your answer sheet.

(A)　　(B)　　(C)

解題分析

時間 65%

■ 時間 65%

■ 人物的動作 35%

人物的動作 35%

聽見 when 開頭的問句,答案應該會跟「時間」相關,挑出有提到時間的選項,極有可能是正確答案。

題目中除了 when 這個時間關鍵字外,還提到了「前往芝加哥」這個動作。答案所提到的動作,也必須與題目一致。

聽稿

（CA / **M**）

When are you leaving for Chicago?
(A) I'm not sure why Jack wants to leave.
(B) Tomorrow afternoon at 4. Why?
(C) I used to live in Chicago.

中譯

（加 / **男**）

你何時要前往芝加哥呢?(答案:B)
(A) 我不確定傑克為何想離開。
(B) 明天下午四點,怎麼了嗎?
(C) 我之前住在芝加哥過。

解題技巧

與其想要每個字都聽懂,還不如將注意力集中在真正會發揮作用的關鍵字詞上。此題問的是「When are you leaving for Chicago?」,那麼可聽出主要問題點是在 when 上面,所以可預期要聽到以時間點來回答題目較為合理。而此題的關鍵問題點為:When **are you** leaving **for** Chicago?

各選項解析

• 選項 (A)「I'm not sure why Jack wants to leave.」內的要點在於討論「not sure why」,但本題目問的是 when 時間相關之問題,並非討論傑克離開的原因,沒有針對問題回應,故不選。
• 選項 (B)「Tomorrow afternoon at 4. Why?」內有明確地提到時間「tomorrow afternoon at 4」,意即「明天下午四點班機前往芝加哥」,有針對 when 開頭的問題回答,故正確。
• 選項 (C)「I used to live in Chicago.」內僅是故意將題目中有的關鍵字「Chicago」重複唸一次而已,但題目並非問「住哪裡」的問題,所以沒有針對問題回答,故不選。

題目陷阱

此題既然是問「when」時間點的問題,那麼選項若是出現與回答時間無關的內容,其正確率自然會降低,且題目中尚會出現故意混淆考生的不相關答案,例如:

➡ I came to Chicago two years ago.(我兩年前來到芝加哥的。)

此句內容雖將題目中的關鍵字「Chicago」重複唸一次,且句內也有時間點「two years ago」,但這種時間點並沒辦法回答「何時出發」的問題點。

➡ I'm looking forward to visiting the Prairie State.（我很期待去草原州旅遊。）

此句內有一個頗有趣之處，就是「The Prairie State（草原州）」，草原州是 Illinois（伊利諾州）的小名。但因此句內容沒有提及時間點，故也沒有針對問題回應。

說到美國的各個州名，都有相對應的小名，以下列出給大家參考：

州名	中文	暱稱	中文
Alabama	阿拉巴馬州	The Yellowhammer State	金色啄木鳥之州
Alaska	阿拉斯加州	The Last Frontier	最後邊疆
Arizona	亞利桑那州	The Grand Canyon State	大峽谷之州
Arkansas	阿肯色州	The Natural State	自然之州
California	加利福尼亞州	The Golden State	黃金之州
Colorado	科羅拉多州	The Centennial State	百年之州
Connecticut	康乃狄克州	The Constitution State	憲法之州
Delaware	德拉瓦州	The First State	第一州
Florida	佛羅里達州	The Sunshine State	陽光之州
Georgia	喬治亞州	The Peach State	桃子州
Hawaii	夏威夷州	The Aloha State	阿羅哈州
Idaho	愛達荷州	The Gem State	寶石之州
Illinois	伊利諾州	The Prairie State	草原之州
Indiana	印第安那州	The Hoosier State	胡希爾之州
Iowa	愛荷華州	The Hawkeye State	鷹眼之州
Kansas	堪薩斯州	The Sunflower State	向日葵之州
Kentucky	肯塔基州	The Bluegrass State	藍草之州
Louisiana	路易西安那州	The Pelican State	鵜鶘之州
Maine	緬因州	The Pine Tree State	松樹之州
Maryland	馬里蘭州	The Old Line State	戰線之州
Massachusetts	麻州	The Bay State	灣州
Michigan	密西根州	The Great Lakes State	大湖之州
Minnesota	明尼蘇達州	The North Star State	北星之州
Mississippi	密西西比州	The Magnolia State	木蘭之州
Missouri	密蘇里州	The Show Me State	索證之州
Montana	蒙大拿州	The Treasure State	財富之州
Nebraska	內布拉斯加州	The Beef State	牛肉之州
Nevada	內華達州	The Silver State	銀之州
New Hampshire	新罕布夏州	The Granite State	花崗岩之州
New Jersey	新澤西州	The Garden State	花園之州
New Mexico	新墨西哥州	The Land of Enchantment	迷人之地
New York	紐約州	The Empire State	帝國州
North Carolina	北卡羅萊納州	The Tar Heel State	焦油鞋跟州
North Dakota	北達科他州	The Peace Garden State	和平花園之州
Ohio	俄亥俄州	The Buckeye State	七葉果之州
Oklahoma	奧克拉荷馬州	The Sooner State	捷足之州
Oregon	奧勒岡州	The Beaver State	海狸之州
Pennsylvania	賓州	The Keystone State	拱心石之州
Rhode Island	羅德島州	The Ocean State	海洋之州
South Carolina	南卡羅萊納州	The Palmetto State	玲瓏棕櫚州
South Dakota	南達科他州	Mount Rushmore State	羅思摩爾山之州
Tennessee	田納西州	The Volunteer State	自願者之州
Texas	德州	The Lone Star State	孤星之州
Utah	猶他州	The Beehive State	蜂巢之州
Vermont	佛蒙特州	The Green Mountain State	綠山之州
Virginia	維吉尼亞州	The Old Dominion State	老自治州
Washington	華盛頓州	The Evergreen State	長青之州
West Virginia	西維吉尼亞州	The Mountain State	山脈之州
Wisconsin	威斯康辛州	The Badger State	獾州
Wyoming	懷俄明州	The Cowboy State	牛仔之州

關鍵字彙

leave for somewhere 片 出發前往～某處

Mark your answer on your answer sheet.

(A)　　(B)　　(C)

解題分析

時間 59%

■ 時間 59%

■ 事件、情境 41%

事件、情境 41%

以 when 開頭的問句，第一個聯想到的是「時間」，答案的選項如果沒有提到時間，是正解的可能性則非常低。

本題除了問時間以外，還提到會員資格「到期」這樣的「事件」，有時答案雖然會提到時間，卻以完全不相干的事來混淆，必須聽清楚題目的關鍵，小心選擇答案。

聽稿

（UK / M ）

When will my membership expire?

(A) Well, it's valid up to the end of this year.

(B) Sorry, but our reservation system is down.

(C) Mine expired two years ago.

中譯

（英 / 男 ）

我的會員資格何時到期呢？（答案：A ）

(A) 嗯，有效期限到今年底。

(B) 不好意思，我們的預約系統壞了。

(C) 我的兩年前就到期了。

解題技巧

聽題目時應將注意力集中到聽關鍵問題點上，此題問的是「When will my membership expire?」，便要可以判斷關鍵點落在 when 一字上頭，如此一來才可判斷要注意聽與時間相關的答案以便回答。再者，要提到的是整句的重音落在關鍵點「When」和「expire」上面。先聽出題目的關鍵點所在，也才能準確地判斷適合的答案，針對此題要將注意力放在聽「會員到期日」即可。

各選項解析

• 選項 (A)「Well, it's valid up to the end of this year.」可判斷內容有關於時間的關鍵點，也就是「the end of this year」，意思為「會員至年底到期」，有針對問此題目回答，故正確。

• 選項 (B)「Sorry, but our reservation system is down.」內的要點提到「system is down」，意即「系統壞掉」，可是並沒有提到與時間相關的內容以回答 when 的問題，故不選。

• 選項 (C)「Mine expired two years ago.」內的陷阱是，故意重複提及問句中的關鍵字「expire」，也提及「two years ago」的時間關鍵點，但是「對象」搞錯了，故不選。

題目陷阱

此題問「when」的問題常見設計的陷阱便是：選項內容與回答時間點無關，或僅是重複題目內有提到的關鍵字，卻無法回答題目者。舉例來說：

➡ Your <u>membership</u> is still valid.（你的會員還是有效。）

　此答案內容提及「membership」，也說還在期限內。乍聽之下好像合理，但是題目並不是在問「會員有效否」，而是問「到期日」喔。所以，還是要選擇較為接近問題的精準回答。

➡ My old passport has <u>expired</u>.（我舊護照已經到期了。）

　此句內雖然提到題目出現的關鍵字「expired」，講的主體卻是「passport」，而非題目問的「membership」，因此就算有提到相同字眼也不能算正確。

再者來進階學習更多實用用法，在日常生活中常見且多益也常會聽到的 membership types（會員類型）列舉如以下，若聽到時便可以馬上了解：

➡ Individual membership 個人會員

➡ Student membership 學生會員

➡ Retiree membership 退休會員

➡ Enterprise membership 企業會員

➡ Senior membership 年長者會員

➡ Group membership 團體會員

➡ Honor membership 榮譽會員

➡ Lifelong membership 永久會員

➡ Short-term membership 短期會員

➡ Family membership 家庭會員

關鍵字彙

membership [`mɛmbɚˌʃɪp] n 會員資格
expire [ɪk`spaɪr] v 到期
valid [`vælɪd] a 有效的
reservation [ˌrɛzɚ`veʃən] n 預約

Mark your answer on your answer sheet.

(A)　　(B)　　(C)

解題分析

時間 66%

動作 34%

■ 時間 66%

■ 動作 34%

因為是 when 開頭的問題，所以預期會出現的答案最有可能是「時間」。

聽到 when 開頭的問句，最重要的是注意答案中的「時間」，再來要留意的是「人物的動作」。以本題為例，因為問題有提到「交出」這個關鍵動作，所以答案的選項必須與之相符。

聽稿
（US / Ⓦ）

When can you turn in the report?
(A) Yes, I'll drive you to the airport.
(B) That's a market research report.
(C) By the end of this week, I guarantee.

中譯
（美 / 女）

你何時可以將報告交上來呢？（答案：C）
(A) 是的，我可以載你去機場。
(B) 那是份關於市場調查的報告。
(C) 本週內，我保證。

解題技巧

此題問的是「When can you turn in the report?」，便可預期關鍵問題點在開頭字「when」上面。首先須將注意力放在聽首字關鍵問題點上，以便預設可能的答案。當心中打定主意要聽到時間點的答案後，就需要選擇有回答關鍵字的選項，才較為合理。且問題關鍵之處會以加強重音來呈現，而這一句的重音在：「When **can you** turn in **the report**?」。因此便可將注意力放在聽「何時交出」的關鍵點上即可。

各選項解析

- 選項 (A)「Yes, I'll drive you to the airport.」內容提到「我載你去機場」，但並沒有以時間為主的關鍵點以回答題目所問的 when；且另一陷阱是以和「report」有點類似的「airport」發音混淆考生，沒有針對問題回答，故不選。
- 選項 (B)「That's a market research report.」內也僅是故意重複唸題目內的「report」一字罷了，也沒有回答到以 when 開頭的時間問題，故不選。
- 選項 (C)「By the end of this week, I guarantee.」內有時間的關鍵點「the end of the week」，即為「報告會在本週內交出」之意，有針對問題回答，故選為最佳答案。

題目陷阱 因為關鍵點是時間，因此，只要是選項沒有針對時間提供相關資訊，便算是沒有回答問題。就算是將題目中的關鍵字再唸一次也不能算有回答到題目。比方說：

➡ I'll turn in the report <u>soon</u>.（我會盡快交報告。）

此句似乎有提到「soon」，但是，「很快」是多快呢？明天嗎？還是十天呢？因此，僅提到 soon 算是沒有精準地回答到 when 為首字的問題喔！

➡ Jerry has <u>turned his report in</u>.（傑瑞已將他的報告交出。）

此句內的關鍵字似乎都很合理，此句裡的關鍵字為「has turned... report in」，但對象搞錯了喔！題目是在問對方「your report」，但回答變成在講另外一個人「Jerry」了，如此的答案就算其他字都符合也不算是正確答案。

此外，說到「turn in」這個片語，在此題中是「呈交、交出」的意思。其實此片語還有其他的用法與意義，在多益考試中也常出現呢！現在就整理在下方給同學參考：

❶ turn something in / turn in something (= hand in) 呈交、交出

➡ You've got another day to <u>turn in</u> the report.
（你還有一天的時間就要將報告交出了。）

➡ He found a wallet and he didn't want to <u>turn</u> it <u>in</u> to the police.
（他發現一只皮夾，但他不想交給警察。）

➡ I <u>handed in</u> the exam paper and left the classroom.
（我交出考卷後就離開教室。）

❷ turn in 去睡覺、就寢

➡ I'm sleepy. I'm gonna <u>turn in</u>.（我好睏，我要去睡了。）

➡ Good night. It's time to <u>turn in</u>.（晚安，睡覺時間到了。）

❸ turn someone in 檢舉某人

➡ The accountant <u>turned</u> his colleague <u>in</u> for cooking the books.
（會計師發現他同事做假帳，便去告發他。）

❹ turn myself / herself / himself in 自首

➡ The thief found that the police officer was looking for him and <u>turned himself in</u>.
（那小偷發現警察在找他，他便去自首了。）

關鍵字彙

turn in ph. 送交、交出
market research ph. 市場調查
guarantee [ˌɡærən`ti] v. 保證

攻略 1 | 活動、時間與人物

Mark your answer on your answer sheet.

(A)　　(B)　　(C)

解題分析

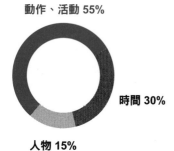

動作、活動 55%

時間 30%

人物 15%

■ 動作、活動 55%　在問題當中聽到 what 之後，必須在問題的後面找出關鍵線索，通常會出現一些與動作、活動有關的敘述，例如本題詢問了「做些什麼活動」，因此選項中如果有提到活動，該選項是正確答案的可能就非常高。

■ 時間 30%　在問題中，也有提到特定時間，此時就要注意選項中的時間是否跟題目吻合，有些選項會設下陷阱，雖然出現了動作的關鍵字，時間卻跟題目毫無關聯。

■ 人物 15%　也要小心題目雖然提到「做什麼活動」，人物卻不符合的陷阱。

聽稿
（US / W）

What are you doing after work this evening?
(A) I'll go swimming this weekend.
(B) I can't work with you breathing down my neck.
(C) I need to do some house chores.

中譯
（美 / 女）

你今晚下班後要做什麼？（答案：C）
(A) 我本週末要去游泳。
(B) 你在我背後東窺西探的，我無法工作。
(C) 我要整理家務。

解題技巧　在應對多益聽力部分 Part 2 時，應將注意力集中到聽問題關鍵字上，才有辦法判斷可能的答案方向。那麼此句問的是「What are you doing after work this evening?」，既然問的是下班後的活動，便可預期要聽到活動和做些什麼等相關的答案較為合理。此問題的焦點部分標示如下：「What **are you** doing after work **this evening**?」如此一來，心中便有個底要聽到「下班後活動」的答案才可選擇。

各選項解析

- 選項 (A)「I'll go swimming this weekend.」內容雖有「go swimming（去游泳）」的活動，但句末的時間點「this weekend」並不是題目問的「this evening」，故不選。
- 選項 (B)「I can't work with you breathing down my neck.」內使用一個慣用語來混淆考生──「breathe down someone's neck」，意思是「在某人背後東窺西探」，但與題目問的下班活動無關，故不選。
- 選項 (C)「I need to do some house chores.」內提到活動「do house chores（做家務）」的確是下班回到家後可能會做的事，故選為最佳答案。

題目陷阱 此題可能設計的陷阱會是有提到「做什麼活動」相關的事，但時間或人物與題目不符合，例如：

➡ My children do homework assignments after school.

（我小孩放學後就寫回家作業。）

此句子內容雖說有提到「do homework assignments」的活動，但人物是「children」，時間是「after school」，皆與題目的設計不符。

➡ Let's arrange a meeting to discuss this project.

（讓我們安排個會議來討論此案子。）

此句有提到「discuss this project」的活動，但似乎不應該是「after work（下班後）」還在做的事，語意邏輯上不符，也沒有針對題目回應。

➡ I don't have a plan yet. Going to Florida might be a good choice.

（我還沒規劃。去佛羅里達玩可能是個好主意。）

此句聽到前半部「I don't have a plan yet.」似乎是可以回答下班做什麼的問題，但後半段「Going to Florida...」便可聽出這句話比較像是在規劃「度假」活動，而非題目所問的下班後活動的範圍了。

另外，若被問到下班後的活動，可能的答案，或在日常生活中也是很常與同事交流的話題，還包括：

➡ I usually read for at least 40 minutes in the evening.

（我晚上通常會閱讀四十分鐘以上。）

➡ I just switch off all my electronic devices and relax.

（我會把所有電子用品關掉，並放鬆。）

➡ My wife and I are going shopping after dinner.

（我太太和我晚餐之後要去購物。）

➡ I have to rush home and cook.（我要趕回家煮飯。）

➡ I do some exercises to stay fit.（我做些運動以維持身材。）

➡ I've got a Japanese class to attend.（我要去上日文課。）

關鍵字彙

breathe down someone's neck 📙 東窺西探
chore [tʃor] 🔳 家庭雜務

Mark your answer on your answer sheet.

(A)　　(B)　　(C)

解題分析

事件、原因 89%

物品 11%

■ 事件、原因 89%

■ 物品 11%

除了 what 以外，還需要注意與其相對應的關鍵字，在本題中出現的 happen 就是解題關鍵，透過這個方法可以了解到，本題在詢問的是印表機所「發生的問題」。因此，在答案中找出相符的原因便是解題關鍵。

有時，題目中出現的物品，會跟答案選項中的物品或事件有關聯，例如此題出現了「印表機」，答案必須與它相關，例如故障、沒墨水等等才是正確的。

聽稿
（UK / Ⓜ）

What happened to the printer?
(A) It's out of ink.
(B) Please call Peter immediately.
(C) Everything happens for a reason.

中譯
（英 / 男）

印表機怎麼了？（答案：A）
(A) 沒墨水了。
(B) 請馬上打電話給彼得。
(C) 任何事發生都有原因的。

解題技巧

在聽題目的同時，務必將注意放在聽首字問題關鍵點上，若錯過的話，之後便難以判斷答案的方向了。此題問的是「What happened to the printer?」可聽出關鍵點是「what」，那麼便要仔細聽到有回答到關鍵點的答案來回應較為合理。因此，此句的重音呈現便會是：「What」和「happened」。心中有個底之後，將焦點集中在聽可以回答「what」的問題點上即可。

各選項解析

- 選項 (A)「It's out of ink.」內的關鍵點「out of ink」意即「沒有墨水」，的確有回答到本題「what happened」的問題點，故為最佳答案。
- 選項 (B)「Please call Peter immediately.」內提到「call peter」，但是回答「打電話給彼得」並沒有回答到題目中印表機的問題，故不選。
- 選項 (C)「Everything happens for a reason.」提及「所有發生之事都有原因」，但也只是提到「reason」一字而已，而沒有說明是「什麼原因」，故無法回答 what 開頭的問題，也不選。

題目陷阱

此題既然是問「印表機的問題」,那麼答案內容設計與「問題」無關的,自然不會是正確選項了。若僅是將題目內的文字重複唸一次,也不是針對問題回答。比方説。

➡ <u>What happened</u> to Peter? He looks a bit down.
（彼得怎麼了?看起來心情太不好。）

此句僅是將「what happened」再唸一次而已,但對象是在講「Peter」,與原問題並無關連。

➡ Yes, <u>that printer</u> is new.（是,那台印表機是新的。）

雖然也有提到「printer」一字,但題目並非在問新或舊的問題,而是在講印表機的問題點,故此句也不算是針對問題回答。

另外,關於「印表機故障」的問題,也是多益考試中常見的考點。那麼,印表機常見的故障,也就可能是選項內的答案,包括下列幾種情況:

➡ It's out of paper.（沒紙了。）

➡ It's not connected to the network.（印表機沒連上網路。）

➡ Maybe the drivier is not installed.（可能是沒裝驅動程式。）

➡ It's out of toner.（碳粉沒了。）

➡ We should remove those jammed papers first.（我們要先將卡住的紙移除。）

➡ Try to update your printer driver.（試著更新印表機程式看看。）

➡ Are you sure it's plugged in?（你確定印表機有插上電源嗎?）

➡ Some paper clips have fallen into the input tray.（有些迴紋針掉到送紙匣內了。）

➡ Why don't you reset the machine?（你何不重開機看看?）

➡ Let's clear the jam first.（讓我們先排除卡紙問題。）

關鍵字彙

out of something **ph** 缺乏、短少（某物）
ink [ɪŋk] **n** 墨水
immediately [ɪˋmidɪɪtlɪ] **ad** 立即地、馬上地
reason [ˋrizn̩] **n** 原因、理由

Mark your answer on your answer sheet.

(A)　　(B)　　(C)

解題分析

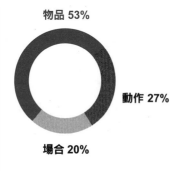

物品 53%

動作 27%

場合 20%

■ 物品 53%　What 開頭的問句，聽到的時候心裡大概就要有個底，題目是在詢問某樣物品，搭配問句中的另一個關鍵字：wear，便可以知道答案跟穿衣類型有很大的關聯。

■ 動作 27%　題目中提到的動作也要注意，像本題中的 wear 便是一個關鍵，將答案範圍縮小至「穿衣」類型。也有可能出現一些陷阱題，雖然提及的物品與題目有關聯，動作卻與題目不相干，需小心留意。

■ 場合 20%　題目中提到了「派對」這個「場合」，答案的選項就必須回答出與該場合相關的服裝，若是選項中有服裝，卻不是跟派對有關，等於是沒有準確回答到問題。

聽稿
（AU / Ⓦ）

What are you gonna wear to the party?
(A) Is it really necessary?
(B) My new red dress, of course.
(C) Okay, I'll bring some wine.

中譯
（澳 / 女）

你要穿什麼去參加派對？（答案：B）
(A) 真的必要嗎？
(B) 當然是我的新紅色洋裝呀。
(C) 好的，我會帶些酒去。

解題技巧　聽到題目播放出來的同時，便要將注意力集中在聽關鍵問題點的地方。此題問的是「What are you gonna wear to the party?」，而本題關鍵問題點是「what」，那麼便可預設要聽到「穿什麼」、「服裝」等類型答案以回答 what 的問題。另外，此題的問題重音則是落在：「What」和「wear」上。了解問題點是在問「穿什麼」之後，便可仔細聽「穿衣類型」的答案以便回答。

各選項解析

- 選項 (A)「Is it really necessary?」，這個選項是反問：「有必要嗎？」，但沒提到「穿什麼」的相關內容以回答 what 開頭的題目，故不選。
- 選項 (B)「My new red dress, of course.」內有關鍵詞「red dress」，整句話為「要穿那套紅色洋裝」，的確有針對「what to wear」的問題，故正確。
- 選項 (C)「Okay, I'll bring some wine.」內的關鍵詞「bring wine」，意即「要帶酒去」，並非回答本問題「要穿什麼」合適的答案，故不選。

題目陷阱 此題既然是問「要穿什麼衣服」的問題，答案自然要回答與服裝類型相關的答案才合理。若選項內都提及與服裝無關的字眼，自然不會是答案。若是故意重複問題中的字詞，卻與題目中設定的場合「party」無關的話，也不會是合理的答案。以下舉出數個考題陷阱的範例以供參考：

➡ I really need to buy a raincoat.（我真的要買件雨衣。）

　　雖然此回應中有提到「raincoat（雨衣）」，但卻不是可以穿著出席派對的服裝。因此，就算有提到服裝類型的答案也不合理。

➡ The party will begin at 5 p.m.（派對下午五點會開始。）

　　此句內提到關鍵字「party」，但描述的主體是「時間」，沒提到「穿什麼服裝」的資訊，因此也是陷阱句。

另外，此題討論到「服裝類型」，那麼日常生活中與多益常考的服裝相關語詞可以多認識一些，以便聽到時馬上可以了解。

➡ designer clothes 設計師服飾

➡ tailor-made clothes 訂製服飾

➡ handmade clothes 手工製服飾

➡ ready-made clothes 成衣

➡ trench coat 風衣

➡ business attire 商務套裝

➡ cocktail dress 酒會禮服

➡ low-cut dress 低胸禮服

➡ evening gown 晚宴禮服

➡ tuxedo（男士）晚禮服

➡ tail coat 燕尾服

➡ black tie / white tie 黑領結、白領結（皆為正式服裝）

關鍵字彙

necessary [ˋnɛsəˌsɛrɪ] a 必要的
dress [drɛs] n 洋裝
wine [waɪn] n 酒

攻略 4 │ 動作與食物

Mark your answer on your answer sheet.

(A)　　(B)　　(C)

解題分析

食物名稱 77%

動作 23%

■ **食物名稱** 77%

■ **動作** 23%

因為是 what 開頭的問句，所以預期答案會出現物品，而且問句中還提到了「晚餐」這個關鍵線索，可由此推斷正確解答是某種食物的名稱或選擇。

有些選項為了混淆考生，會重複題目相關的動作，卻沒有精準回答到問題本身，要仔細辨別。

聽稿

（CA / M ）

What do you want for dinner?

(A) How about chicken soup and salad?

(B) Is that what you really want?

(C) Yes, let's go out for dinner.

中譯

（加 / 男 ）

你晚餐想吃什麼？（答案：**A**）

(A) 雞湯和沙拉如何？

(B) 那真的是你想要的嗎？

(C) 好的，我們出去吃晚餐。

解題技巧

聽到題目播放的同時，要將注意力放在聽關鍵問題點的字上面，以預期可能的答案。此題問的是「What do you want for dinner?」，那麼關鍵問題點自然是在「what」一字上面，心中有個底之後便可預期以要聽到「吃什麼」的答案才合理。且問句的關鍵之處會以加強重音來呈現：「What do you want for dinner?」。知道關鍵處後，這時候就想著要聽到晚餐所吃的食物名稱來當答案較為合理。

各選項解析

- 選項 (A)「How about chicken soup and salad?」內的關鍵點是「chicken soup and salad」都是食物的名稱，的確可以回答到 what 開頭的問句──「晚餐要吃什麼」的問題，故為正確答案。
- 選項 (B)「Is that what you really want?」為反問「這真是你想要的嗎？」，但實際上並非可以回答「what to eat」的關鍵答案，故不選。
- 選項 (C)「Yes, let's go out for dinner.」內故意將題目中提到的「dinner」一字重複一次，且「let's go out for dinner」是說要外出用餐的意思，並沒有提到本題「what ──要吃什麼」的關鍵答案，故也不能選。

題目陷阱 此題既然是問「晚餐」想吃什麼，那麼若提到與晚餐食物無關的字眼，自然就不會是答案。且若僅是將題目中有的字詞重唸一次，卻沒有針對問題回答的句子，也不合理，舉例如下：

➡ Let's have <u>dinner</u> together.（我們共進晚餐吧！）

　句中雖有將題目關鍵字「dinner」重複一次，但並沒有真正地提到晚餐內容，因此不算是合理的回應。

➡ I really want a <u>pie</u> for dessert.（我真的很想吃塊派來當點心。）

　此句內雖然提到食物的名稱「pie」，但屬性卻是「點心」，而不是晚餐所要吃的，故也沒有針對題目做正確的回應。

因為多益考試常出現的場景自然是商務場合，因此就算是接待客戶、或參加晚宴等，有需要邀請他人共進晚餐的機會也是不少的。因此對幾個主要國家的食物可以多加了解一下，以便在生活上或是考試上有所幫助。

➡ Italian food: pasta and pizza
　義式料理：義大利麵和披薩

➡ Chinese food: rice and noodles
　中式料理：飯和麵食

➡ American food: hot dogs, burgers, French fries, steaks
　美式料理：熱狗、漢堡、薯條、牛排

➡ Japanese food: Sushi and ramen
　日式料理：壽司和拉麵

➡ Indian: hot curries, rice and seafood
　印度料理：咖哩、飯、海鮮

➡ English: fish and chips, pies and stews
　英式料理：炸魚和薯條、派餅和燉湯

➡ German: sausages and sauerkraut
　德國料理：香腸和德國酸菜

➡ Scandinavian: potatoes and minced meat
　北歐料理：馬鈴薯和絞肉丸

關鍵字彙

chicken soup 🔢 雞湯

Mark your answer on your answer sheet.

(A)　　(B)　　(C)

解題分析

討論的話題 61%

事件、情境 39%

■ 討論的話題 61%

■ 事件、情境 39%

What 是本題的關鍵詞，搭配另一個重要的關鍵「討論」，可以得知題目是在問討論了「什麼」話題，因此答案選項可將範圍縮小為某種話題或主題。

從題目也可以了解到，本題的答案選項與「會議」有關聯，答案或許不會重複題目的關鍵字，但是一定要回答出與會議相關的內容，以符合本題的情境。

聽稿

（US / Ⓦ）

What will we discuss at the meeting?

(A) I hope to end the meeting by 3.

(B) Just perform your best, okay?

(C) We need to finalize the budget plan.

中譯

（美 / 女）

我們開會要討論什麼？（答案：C）

(A) 我希望可以在三點前結束會議。

(B) 你就好好表現，可以嗎？

(C) 我們要確認預算規劃了。

解題技巧

在聽到題目播放出的同時，也要記得將聽力焦點放在首字關鍵問題點上，以掌握可能的答案方向。此題問的是「What will we discuss at the meeting?」，那麼關鍵問題字自然是落在「what」上面了。因此可以預期要聽到「討論什麼話題」的答案內容才合理。

務必要記住的是：問句的關鍵點出現之處會以加強重音來呈現。因此，只要特別留意重音的地方，答題就會順利多了。

此題的關鍵問題點落在：「What **will** we **discss** at the meeting?」。掌握到問題的關鍵點，如此一來便可預期要聽到討論「什麼主題」的選項才會是最佳答案。

各選項解析

• 選項 (A)「I hope to end the meeting by 3.」內的關鍵點是「end... by 3」，意謂著會議要三點前結束。但題目並不是在問以 when 開頭的時間性問題，故不能選。

• 選項 (B)「Just perform your best, okay?」內的關鍵點提到「perform... best」，意謂著要「好好表現」，但這個選項也無法回答到問「開會要討論什麼」的問題，故不選。

• 選項 (C)「We need to finalize the budget plan.」內的關鍵點是「finalize the budget plan」，意即「開會要討論預算的規劃」一事。此選項確實有針對問題回答，故選為最佳答案。

題目陷阱 此題問的是會議要討論「什麼內容」，那麼自然地選項內容與會議話題無關的，或僅是將文字再唸一次，卻沒有提到「會議討論話題」的答案都會是陷阱所在，都是不能選的答案。舉例來說：

➡ Let's arrange a meeting and discuss it.
　（讓我們安排個會議來討論此事吧。）

　此句內重複唸了兩個關鍵字「meeting」和「discuss」，但僅是說要開會討論，也沒講出要討論什麼議題，如此的答案並沒有針對問題回答。

➡ The meeting will be held next Wednesday.
　（會議是下週三舉行。）

　此句內也是提到關鍵字「meeting」，但此句說的是時間點「next Wednesday」，無法回答到問 what 的問題喔。

另外，商務會議上常討論的，也有可能是多益考試中常考的，除了像此題答案說要討論「budget plan」之外，還有可能會出現以下幾種討論的商業主題。若可以事先預習並了解，當你在考試時聽到關鍵字，自然可以馬上辨識出正確答案了。

➡ We are meeting today to talk about the market expansion plan.
　（我們今天開會要討論市場拓展計劃。）

➡ Our objective today is to come up with effective sales strategies.
　（我們今天的目標是要想出有效的業務策略。）

➡ We'll be discussing the customer service issue today.
　（今天我們會討論客戶服務議題。）

➡ Jimmy will present an analysis of our customer base.
　（吉米會針對我們客戶群的分析跟大家做簡報。）

➡ Mr. Lee will give us an overview of the product launch campaign.
　（李先生會給我們一個產品上市活動的概要。）

➡ Linda will propose some solutions to this problem.
　（琳達會針對此問題提出幾個解決方案。）

關鍵字彙

end [ɛnd] v 終止、結束
perform [pəˋfɔrm] v 表現
finalize [ˋfaɪn‚laɪz] v 定稿、定案
budget [ˋbʌdʒɪt] n 預算

Unit 5　以 Why 為首的題型

攻略 1 ｜ 原因與情境

Mark your answer on your answer sheet.
(A)　　(B)　　(C)

解題分析

原因 71%

事件、情境 29%

■ 原因 71%

■ 事件、情境 29%

Why 開頭的問句，有很大的機率都是詢問原因、理由，搭配題目其他的線索可以得知是在問「很累」的原因，如果答案提到了某個原因或理由，很有可能就是正確答案。

題目所描述的情境，也要小心的解讀與判斷，在答案中找到關聯性最高的選項。像本題詢問很累的原因，就要給予相關的回答，如：沒睡好、工作很忙等等。

聽稿
（AU／Ⓦ）

Why do you look so exhausted?
(A) Thank you for reminding.
(B) I didn't sleep well last night.
(C) The war never ends.

中譯
（澳／女）

你為何看起來很累？（答案：B）
(A) 謝謝你提醒我。
(B) 我昨晚沒睡好。
(C) 戰爭永不停歇。

解題技巧　若沒有聽到問題關鍵點，等於是後續完全無法得知該專注在聽什麼答案了。因此，為了要順利地聽到合理答案，注意力務必放在聽問題關鍵點上。此題問的是：「Why do you look so exhausted?」，其關鍵點便是落在「why」一字上，那麼可判斷答案要聽到有描述「很累的原因」之答案才合理。另外，此句的重點會以加強重音來強調：「Why do you look so exhausted?」。

各選項解析

- 選項 (A)「Thank you for reminding.」內提及「謝謝你的提醒」，但並沒有針對問題回答「why —— 看起來很累的原因」，故不選。
- 選項 (B)「I didn't sleep well last night.」內的關鍵點為「didn't sleep well」，即為「沒睡好」之意，的確是針對問題「為何看來很累的原因」，有針對問題回答，故為正確答案。
- 選項 (C)「The war never ends.」的回答內容完全與題目問的「看起來很累之原因」無關，故不選。

題目陷阱

既然此題要找的答案是很累的原因，那麼，只要選項內容出現跟「為何會累」無關的字眼，通常都不會是答案。除此之外，僅將問句內關鍵字重複提及，卻沒有回答到 why 問題的選項也會是陷阱所在。舉例來說：

➡ <u>Because</u> I really enjoy my job.（因為我很喜歡我的工作。）

此回答乍聽之下有「because」好像是可以回答「why」的答案，其內容「enjoy my job」提到的是「喜歡工作內容」，但一個人喜歡工作內容就等於看起來很累嗎？這兩者間關聯性並沒有很強，故不算有針對問題回答。

➡ If you want to be a leader, you'd better <u>look</u> the part.
（你如果想當老闆，看起來要名符其實。）

此句內有個英文慣用語「look the part」為「看來很適任～（某職位）」之意，但這個慣用語只是為了用來跟題目中的「look」一字混淆，也沒有回答到「為何看起來累」。

除了題目中所提及的「感覺到累」是「exhausted」之外，在英文裡，另外還有以下十種說法：

➡ I'm beat.（我累癱了。）

➡ I'm totally worn out.（我累壞了。）

➡ I'm like dog-tired. (= I'm as tired as a dog.)（我累得跟狗一樣。）

➡ I'm drained.（我精疲力盡了。）

➡ I'm completely knocked out.（我徹底累壞了。）

➡ I'm bushed.（我疲憊不堪。）

➡ I'm out of breath.（我上氣不接下氣的。）

➡ I'm fried.（我累壞了。）

➡ I'm ready to drop.（我極度疲憊。）

➡ I'm dead tired.（我累死了。）

關鍵字彙

exhausted [ɪgˋzɔstɪd] a 疲憊的

Mark your answer on your answer sheet.

(A)　　(B)　　(C)

解題分析

原因 67%

事件、情境 33%

■ 原因 67%

■ 事件、情境 33%

因為本題是 why 開頭的問句，有最大的機率為詢問事情發生的原因及理由，此時要配合題目其他的關鍵字，找到選項中最切中問題的答案。

在題目的關鍵字 why 之後會出現某個事件、情境，例如本題的重點為「離開公司」的原因，這時候就要選擇選項中符合上述事件或情境的，才是最佳解答。

聽稿
（UK / M ）

Why did Mr. Terry leave the company?
(A) He's got a better offer from our competitor.
(B) He left early today for his dentist appointment.
(C) Terry joined the company in 2013.

中譯
（英 / 男 ）

泰瑞先生為何會離開公司呢？（答案：A）
(A) 我們的競爭廠商提供更高的薪水把他挖走了。
(B) 他要去看牙醫所以提早離開。
(C) 泰瑞是在二〇一三年進公司的。

解題技巧

聽題目的同時，就應該有意識地將焦點放在聽問題關鍵點之處，以利於答案的預設。此題問的是「Why did Mr. Terry leave the company?」，聽完之後便可判斷要點會是「why」一字，故要聽到可以描述「原因」的答案才合理。且重點字在句子中通常會以加強重音來呈現：「Why did Mr. Terry leave the company?」，標記的地方即是問題的重點之處。在了解關鍵問題點之後，便可以更有信心地去聽可回答 why 開頭問句的可能答案了。

各選項解析

- 選項 (A)「He's got a better offer from our competitor.」內的關鍵點「got a better offer」，意即為「得到更好的工作」，的確可以回答到「why ——離開公司之原因」的問題，故選為最佳答案。
- 選項 (B)「He left early today for his dentist appointment.」的陷阱在於好似有提到原因，也就是「for dentist appointment」，也有提及「left（leave 的過去式）」關鍵字，但問題在於題目所問的「leave the company」是「自公司離職了」之意，並非「僅某日提早離開」而已，故不算針對本問題回答，故不選。
- 選項 (C)「Terry joined the company in 2013.」內的關鍵點是「二〇一三年加入公司」，但題目並不是在問「加入公司的年分」，而是問「離開公司的原因」，因此，這個選項沒有針對問題回答，不選。

題目陷阱

此題問的是 why ——原因題，若選項內容無法回答「Mr. Terry 離開公司的原因」的話，便不會是答案。另一點必須一再強調的是，若僅是將題目中的關鍵字再唸一次的話，卻沒有講出「原因」，一樣是不能當答案的。例如：

➡ Mr. Terry plans to leave the company.
（泰瑞先生計劃要離開公司。）

此句內僅是將「leave the company」關鍵點重述一次，但沒說明「原因」，故不能當答案。

➡ Why did Mr. Terry make such a decision?
（泰瑞先生怎麼會下這種決定呢？）

此句故意又以「Why did Mr. Terry...」開頭來混淆考生，但問句內的「why」都尚未得到解答，又再問一次 why 開頭的問題似乎不是很合理，故這也是陷阱之一。

在真實的商業環境中，公司員工來來去去也是自然的狀況，在現今競爭激烈的職場上，很少看到像三十年前一般，找到一個工作可以做二十五年的情況。因此，有關於討論離職原因，在多益考試內會是一個考題之外，在就業面談時也是可以應用的，此將常見的離職理由列如以下供參考：

➡ The competitor tries to poach our company's best employees.
（競爭對手想挖角我們公司最優秀的員工。）

➡ There is no room for me to advance in this company.
（我在此公司沒有再晉升的空間了。）

➡ Jack is going to pursue advanced education.
（傑克打算回學校進修。）

➡ My supervisor left, and I thought it was time for me to move on and look for other challenges.（我老闆離開了，我想也是我該繼續迎接其他挑戰的時候了。）

➡ Linda left the job in order to take care of her family issue.
（琳達離職是為了處理家庭事務。）

➡ Ms. Chen's position was eliminated and she was let go.
（陳小姐的職位被撤銷了，於是她被解僱。）

➡ I re-evaluated my career goals and am looking for something even more challenging.（我重新評估了我的職涯目標，並找尋其他更具挑戰的機會。）

➡ Jerry was offered a position with another company and he accepted.
（別的公司給傑瑞工作機會，他接受了。）

關鍵字彙

offer [`ɔfɚ] ☑ 提供
competitor [kəm`pɛtətɚ] ⋒ 競爭對手
dentist [`dɛntɪst] ⋒ 牙醫
appointment [ə`pɔɪntmənt] ⋒ 約定、會議

攻略 3 | 原因與交通

> **Mark your answer on your answer sheet.**
> (A)　　(B)　　(C)

解題分析

原因 65%

事件、情境 35%

■ 原因 65%

■ 事件、情境 35%

問句是 why 開頭，可以預期答案會是某件事發生的「原因、理由」，如果選項無法提供明確的解釋，就不會是正確答案。

如果選項有提到原因和理由，卻跟題目的情境毫不相干，或是重複了題目的關鍵字，看似符合情境，卻並未針對事件發生的原因回答，這樣的選項可能只是為了混淆考生。

聽稿
（US / Ⓦ）

Why has the flight been delayed?
(A) Fred just wants to be a free-rider.
(B) Because the weather conditions are too bad.
(C) I'm too tired to walk another step.

中譯
（美 / Ⓦ）

飛機為何會延誤呢？（答案：B）
(A) 佛瑞得只想搭順風車（坐享其成）。
(B) 因為天氣狀況太糟了。
(C) 我累到都走不動了。

解題技巧

聽到問題句播放出來的同時，也應立即將焦點放在聽關鍵問題點上。此題問的是「Why has the flight been delayed?」，其關鍵字自然是落在「why」一字上面。聽到關鍵字後，便可判斷這一題要選擇的是：可以解釋飛機延誤的原因或理由，才可當答案。且問句關鍵點之處，通常會以加強重音來凸顯：「Why has the flight been delayed?」，要抓住關鍵點，聽到重音就對了。了解句中的關鍵要點之後，便可仔細地找尋選項中有無解釋原因的答案了。

各選項解析

- 選項 (A)「Fred just wants to be a free-rider.」內的關鍵點提到的「free-rider」為「想不勞而獲之人」，完全無法回答班機為什麼延誤的問題，故不選。
- 選項 (B)「Because the weather conditions are too bad.」中的關鍵點是「weather... too bad」，意即「天候太糟」。此關鍵點的確可以當作說明班機延誤之原因，故選為最佳答案。
- 選項 (C)「I'm too tired to walk another step.」內有「too... to...」句型，此句型為「太～以至於不～」的用法，整句話的意思是「太累而走不動」。雖然是一個具有因果關係的句子，但是完全沒有針對班機延誤的原因來回答，故不選。

題目陷阱 此題問的是班機延誤的「原因」，若是答案選項內容沒有說明「原因」的，自然就不是合理的回應。且若僅是將關鍵字重唸一次，內容卻與問題無直接關係的話，也是不能當答案的。比方說：

➡ This <u>flight</u> is heading to Chicago.
（此班機將要前往芝加哥。）

此句內僅是將關鍵字「flight」重複一次罷了，內容要點卻提到了「地點」，但是此題並非是 where 開頭的題型，而是在問「why 原因題」，故沒針對問題回答。

➡ The <u>flight</u> was <u>delayed</u> for about three hours.
（班機被延誤了大約三小時之久。）

此句內故意重複唸了 flight 和 delay 兩個關鍵字，但是整句要點卻是在時間—— three hours 上頭。題目並非問「how long」的題型喔。故此答案無法回答「原因」類型之題目。

隨著出差、旅遊的頻率增加，人們前往機場搭飛機並經歷班機的等待、延誤、改期等機會也是免不了的。通常班機的延誤原因，不但是多益考試聽力內常出題的情境，在商務出差或日常旅遊中，也是常會有機會討論到的話題，常見的班機延遲原因如下：

➡ The flight was delayed because of a significant mechanical problem.
（班機延誤是因為有重大的機械問題。）

➡ It seems like the air traffic is extremely busy.
（看起來是空中交通太繁忙了。）

➡ We can't depart due to the thick fog.
（我們無法起飛因為霧太濃了。）

➡ We're waiting for the last five passengers to show up.
（我們在等最後五位乘客登機。）

➡ It's simply because the previous flight arrived late.
（純粹是因為上一班飛機晚到了。）

關鍵字彙

flight [flaɪt] n 班機、飛機
delay [dɪ`le] v 耽誤、延遲
free-rider [fri`raɪdɚ] n 坐享其成之人
condition [kən`dɪʃən] n 狀況

Mark your answer on your answer sheet.

(A)　　　(B)　　　(C)

解題分析

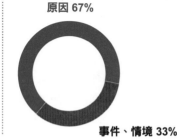

原因 67%

事件、情境 33%

■ 原因 67%

■ 事件、情境 33%

聽到以 Why 為首的問句，要先鎖定表示「原因、理由」的回答，並且搭配題目的關鍵詞，選出與之相關的答案，有很高的機率是正確的。

回答必須針對問題的情境，若是不能肯定，可以使用刪去法，先將完全不符合的答案剔除。而本題是問「會議改期」的「原因」，回答「不確定」雖然並不是直接說出改期的理由，卻還是與題目詢問的事件相關。

聽稿

（CA / **M**）

Why was the meeting rescheduled?

(A) I'm not sure, but I'll call Maggie to find out.

(B) All sales reps are required to attend, right?

(C) Okay, let's call it a day.

中譯

（加 / **男**）

會議為何會改期呢？（答案：A）

(A) 我不確定，但我會打電話給梅姬確認一下。

(B) 所有業務代表都被要求參加，對嗎？

(B) 好的，那我們今天就到這裡結束。

解題技巧

在聽這類題型的時候，一再強調的是：聽到題目播放出來的同時，一定要將注意力放在問題的關鍵點上，以便判斷接下來要聽的答案方向。而此題問的是：「Why was the meeting rescheduled?」。在回答這類型的題目時，只要聽懂第一個字，基本上就不會有太大的問題。因此，本題的關鍵點自然是落在「why」一字上面，也就是說，我們要聽到可以解釋會議改期之原因或是理由的答案才是合理。且問題的關鍵之處：「Why was the meeting rescheduled?」，標示的地方即為問題的核心。聽到題目所要強調的重音之後，便可預期要聽到有「解釋原因」的選項，才會是正確答案。

各選項解析

- 選項 (A)「I'm not sure, but I'll call Maggie to find out.」內有關鍵字「not sure」，是表示「不是很確定」的意思，但回應這句話的人表示會「find out」，意即「還是會找出原因」。那麼針對問「會議改期的原因」之問題，回應者雖然回答不是很確定，但他還是會去問他人，某種程度上是有針對問題回答，故選為最佳答案。

- 選項 (B)「All sales reps are required to attend, right?」的關鍵點是「reps... required... attend」，是「業務都要參加」的意思。但題目並非為問「誰要參加會議」之問題，故不選。

- 選項 (C)「Okay, let's call it a day.」內的關鍵點是「call it a day」，即「收工、結束了」之意，這個選項無法回答「為什麼會議改期」的問題，有點牛頭不對馬嘴的意味，故不能選。

題目陷阱 此題問的是會議改期的原因，那麼選項內容若是沒有提到原因的答案自然便無法針對問 why 的問題做出說明了。且若僅是將題目內的關鍵字重述一次，本身並沒有回答到原因的話，通常會是命題的陷阱，不會是答案。舉例來說：

➡ Let's <u>reschedule the meeting</u> to next Wednesday.

（我們將會議改期到下週三。）

此句內重複唸到題目中的關鍵字「reschedule」和「meeting」，但此句話的要點卻是在「next Wednesday」上面，也就是專注在回答 when 開頭的問時間問題，並非說明原因，因此不會是答案。

➡ Linda arranged this <u>meeting</u>.（琳達安排此會議。）

此句內要點變成是在回答 who 開頭的問題了。因為選項出現了「Linda arranged...」的內容。但是，這一道題目是在詢問原因；故此句也僅是故意以「meeting」一字來混淆考生罷了。

現在職場業務繁忙，原本約好的會議因事改期也是常有的事。因此此類相關會議改期的話題，不但是多益的聽力測驗內經常會聽到的情境，在日常辦公環境內也是會應用到的。現在便將要求會議改期的說法整理如下：

➡ I'm afraid I can't make it. Is it okay if we put off the meeting?

（我恐怕無法參與，若我們將會議延後方便嗎？）

➡ Let's rearrange the appointment please.

（讓我們重新安排會議時間。）

➡ The brainstorm session has been postponed till tomorrow.

（腦力激盪會議被延期到明天舉行。）

➡ Something urgent just came up. Can we adjourn the discussion early?

（我有緊急的事要先處理。今天的討論可以提早結束嗎？）

➡ We need to organize a conference next month.

（我們要安排一場下個月的研討會。）

關鍵字彙

reschedule [ri`skɛdʒul] v 改期、重新定時間
find out ph 發現、找出
rep (= representative) [rɛp] n 代表
require [ri`kwair] v 要求
attend [ə`tɛnd] v 出席
call it a day ph 收工、今天就到此為止

Mark your answer on your answer sheet.

(A)   (B)   (C)

解題分析

原因、理由 79%

事件、情境 21%

■ 原因、理由 79%　問題為 Why 開頭，最有可能的答案就是「原因、理由」，從句子中的 can't 可理解題目在問的是「為何不」參與討論的原因，回答必須有關聯才行。

■ 事件、情境 21%　抓住題目的關鍵字，便可預期答案要聽到解釋「不參與討論」的原因、理由，正確的選項除了是一個理由之外，更要緊扣問題的情境。

聽稿

（UK / M）

Why can't you join our discussion?
(A) I need to get back on my own feet.
(B) Let's exchange some creative ideas.
(C) Well, my clients are down in the lobby waiting for me.

中譯

（英 / 男）

你為何無法參與討論？（答案：C）
(A) 我要靠自己重新振作起來。
(B) 我們來交換有創意的點子。
(C) 嗯，我客戶在樓下大廳等著我呀。

解題技巧

聽到題目時，應立即將注意力集中在聽關鍵問題字上，才能有效地預測可能的答案。此題問的是「Why can't you join our discussion?」，那麼關鍵問題點就是在 why not 上頭了。如此一來，我們便可以預期要聽到可以解釋不參與討論的原因、理由的答案較為合適；且問句的關鍵所在，通常會以加強重音來強調：「Why can't you join our discussion?」。經由前述的解說後，我們判斷正確答案的方向應是在解釋的原因之上。

各選項解析

- 選項 (A)「I need to get back on my own feet.」內提到的關鍵主旨「get back on someone's own feet（靠某人的腳站起來）」，為「重新振作」之意，跟這一題要問的「不參與討論的原因」毫無相關性，無法回答此問題，故不能選。
- 選項 (B)「Let's exchange some creative ideas.」內容的主旨為「exchange ideas」，意即「交換意見」。但問題問的是為何不參與討論，這個選項直接說來交換意見，沒有針對問題回答，故不選。
- 選項 (C)「Well, my clients are down in the lobby waiting for me.」內提到的是「客戶已在樓下等我了」，這的確有可能是現在無法參與討論的原因，因此選為最佳答案。

題目陷阱 此題是以 why 開頭的問題，問的內容是「無法參加討論會的原因」，那麼意思就是若內容不是在說明原因的選項，就不會是正確的選項。另有可能會陷阱是僅將題目內的關鍵字重唸一次，卻沒有真正說明原因的。這樣的選項也不正確。請看以下例子：

➡ I'd love to join, but I can't.（我很想參加，但沒辦法。）

此句內僅是重複關鍵字「join」和「can't」，但僅說「不能參加」，卻沒回答到無法參加討論會的原因，故不能回答問題。

➡ Who else is going to join the discussion?（還有誰會加入討論？）

此為另外拋出一個問題，但此問題要點是問誰會參加，另外再拋出一個疑問並沒有回答到原問題，故也是混淆視聽的陷阱選項。

在多益測驗內，常討論到的「無法參加會議的原因」還可能包括以下情形：

➡ I won't be able to attend due to a schedule conflict.
（我因行程衝突而無法參與。）

➡ I need to deal with an urgent issue.
（我需要處理一件緊急的事情。）

➡ Let me return an important phone call and I'll be a bit late for the meeting.
（我先回個重要的電話，開會可能會晚點到。）

➡ Sorry, but I'm supposed to send out the quotation before noon.
（不好意思，我今天中午前一定要將報價單送出去。）

➡ I'm in the middle of something. Why don't you just start and I'll join you later.
（我正在處理些事情，你們先開始，我等會兒再加入。）

關鍵字彙

discussion [dɪ`skʌʃən] n 討論
get back on someone's feet ph 重新振作
exchange [ɪks`tʃendʒ] v 交換
creative [krɪ`etɪv] a 有創意的
client [`klaɪənt] n 客戶

攻略 1 | 人數與狀態

Mark your answer on your answer sheet.
(A)　　(B)　　(C)

解題分析

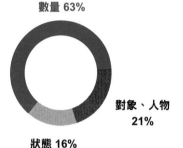

■ **數量** 63%

因為問句是 how many 開頭，很明顯就是在詢問物品的數量或是人數，接著就要把注意力放到後面的關鍵字上，弄清楚題目所詢問數量的對象為何。

■ **對象、人物** 21%

由題目的重音可以判斷本題關鍵為詢問「研討會參與者」的人數，如果選項所敘述的對象與之相符，有很大的機率是正確答案。

■ **狀態** 16%

因為 how 有許多的用法，其中一種是詢問事物的狀態，所以有些選項會藉此設下陷阱。要分辨清楚本題的開頭是 how many，只有「數量、人數」的回答才可能是正確的。

聽稿
（CA / **M**）

How many attendees were at the conference?
(A) Yes, the attendees all enjoyed the wedding.
(B) There were fifty approximately.
(C) The conference was held in Tokyo.

中譯
（加 / **男**）

有多少人來參加研討會呢？（答案：**B**）
(A) 是的，婚禮來賓都玩得很愉快。
(B) 大約五十位吧。
(C) 會議在東京舉辦。

解題技巧

做聽力的題目要訓練到一聽到題目，能馬上有意識地將注意力放到聽首字關鍵問題點上，藉此判斷答案的可能方向。此題問的是「How many attendees were at the conference?」，關鍵點便是在 how many 上頭了。如此便可預期要聽到與「數字」相關答案才會合理。且問句的關鍵字詞通常會以加強重音來呈現：「How many attendees **were at the conference**?」，有了焦點之後，自然可以將注意力放在聽「幾位來賓」的數字上面即可。

各選項解析

- 選項 (A)「Yes, the attendees all enjoyed the wedding.」內的主旨是「enjoyed... wedding」，意思是「大家都玩得很盡興」，但這並無法回答此題 how many 開頭問數量的問題，而是在敘說參與者的狀態，故不能選為正確答案。
- 選項 (B)「There were fifty approximately.」內的關鍵點提到了「fifty」，這個選項是在說「大約五十人參與會議」，的確可以拿來回答問 how many 的問題，故正確。
- 選項 (C)「The conference was held in Tokyo.」內的關鍵點是「held in Tokyo」，並提到會議是在東京舉辦，此選項回應的是會議舉辦的地點，並非題目問的數量問題，所以也不能選。

題目陷阱

此題既然是 how many 開頭的問句，便可預期若不是回答「數量」的選項，便不會是正確答案。或是選項中僅將問句內的關鍵字重述一次，沒有針對數量來回答者，也不可選擇當作答案。甚至是有時候答案內確實提到了數量，但句子主旨卻與問句無關的選項，也不正確。用以下句子來舉例：

➡ There were around <u>20 students</u> in that class.
（那個班上大約有二十位同學。）

此句雖然有特別點出「人數」，也就是「20 students」，但是題目是在問「conference attendees」，即「會議出席者」的人數，並非在問學生人數，故此句就算有出現數量的詞，也不能算是有針對問題回應。

➡ <u>Two speakers</u> will present <u>at the conference</u>.
（兩位演講者將會在研討會上報告。）

此句內刻意以「two speakers」和「conference」來混淆視聽，但選項內容卻不是回答「與會者的人數」，僅是將關鍵字重複的選項是無法當答案的。

順帶一提，此題內所出現的「conference」一字，在商務往來與多益考試中出現頻率極高，這個英文字也就是「會議、研討會」之意。那麼會議除了最簡單的「meeting」和「conference」之外，英文裡面還有其他研討會類型，貼心地幫大家整理如下：

➡ press conference 記者會
➡ seminar 研討會
➡ information session 說明會
➡ webinar 線上研討會
➡ summit 高峰會
➡ conference call 電話會議
➡ video conference 視訊會議
➡ hearing 聽證會
➡ symposium 大型研討會
➡ convention 會議
➡ forum 論壇
➡ round table 圓桌會議
➡ workshop 工作坊
➡ group discussion 團體討論
➡ gathering 聚會
➡ powwow 集會、舉行祈禱儀式

關鍵字彙

attendee [ə`tɛndi] n 出席人、與會者
conference [`kɑnfərəns] n 會議、研討會
wedding [`wɛdɪŋ] n 婚禮
approximately [ə`prɑksəmɪtlɪ] ad 約略地

Mark your answer on your answer sheet.

(A)   (B)   (C)

解題分析

頻率 72%

對象、人物 28%

■ 頻率 72%

■ 對象、人物 28%

How often 出現在問句句首，最高的機率是在詢問一件事情發生的「頻率」，此時要配合句子裡的其他線索找出答案。

本題主要是詢問「拜訪父母」的頻率，答案選項必須針對問題回答，如果有提到頻率，但是指稱的對象毫無關聯，這樣的選項是專門混淆考生的陷阱，要小心辨認。

聽稿

（US / Ｗ）

How often do you visit your parents?
(A) Well, once every two weeks.
(B) Maybe in July.
(C) The bus leaves every hour on the hour.

中譯

（美 / 女）

你多久去看父母一次？（答案：A）
(A) 嗯，每兩週一次吧。
(B) 可能要七月了。
(C) 那公車整點發車。

解題技巧

聽到題目前切勿放空且被動地聽，而是要主動地預測答案可能性。聽到題目是「How often do you visit your parents?」這樣的問句，就可將焦點放在 how often 上面。並預設要聽到「多久一次」與頻率相關的答案才會合理。此問句的要點加強重音呈現如下：「How often do you visit your parents?」。如此便可預期要聽到可以回答「多久去拜訪一次」的答案即可。

各選項解析

- 選項 (A)「Well, once every two weeks.」，可以發現，其中有可以回答多久一次的關鍵點，也就是「every two weeks」，中文意思就是「每兩週回家看父母一次」。有針對問題回答，故為正確答案。
- 選項 (B)「Maybe in July.」內重要訊息是「in July」，但題目並非是在問 when 類型的問題，而是在問頻率的問題，回答方向錯誤，故此選項無法針對題目回答。
- 選項 (C)「The bus leaves every hour on the hour.」內故意使用混淆點「every hour on the hour」，意即「每小時整點之時」，雖然說和題目的頻率問題同樣也是時間間隔的類型，或許在其他題可以用來回答 how often 的問題，但是卻和題目問的主題「visit parents」不相關，題目並非在問「bus schedule（公車時刻表）」喔！因此，也不算是有針對問題回答到，所以不能選。

題目陷阱 此題問的是 how often 頻率問題，自然可以在腦中先預設若非回答「頻率、多久一次」的答案，便不算是有針對問題回答。且若僅是將題目中有的關鍵字詞重提一次，而沒有回答到題目，絕對也不會是正確的回應。請參考以下陷阱的例句：

➡ <u>My parents</u> go to the gym once a week.
（我爸媽一週去健身房一次。）

此句內刻意地提到「my parents」這個題目中出現的對象，也有出現「once a week」來回答此題頻率的關鍵字。可是，要小心的是，這個回應是在說「去健身房的次數」，與題目不符，故這些相關資訊僅是混淆大家的陷阱。

➡ I <u>visit</u> clients in Korea at least twice a quarter.
（我一季至少去拜訪韓國的客戶兩次。）

此句子內一樣也有出現「visit」和「twice a quarter」等陷阱誘惑考生選擇，但要注意的是，題目是在討論「visit parents」，而非「clients」喔！拜訪的對象錯了，就算出現頻率正確的字眼，也不會是正確答案。因此要仔細分辨，不要被陷阱拉走了。

此題是問「how often」頻率的問題，不只在多益考試中的聽力部分，其他的題型，像是閱讀長篇文章的題型內也常出現變化題型。舉例來說，看到訂雜誌的廣告，若廣告中寫「52 issues / year」，那麼，題目有可能會問：「How often does the magazine come out?」。既然一年有五十二本雜誌，那便是一週一本的週刊（weekly magazine）了。現在，我們將各種頻率的變化列出來：

➡ 52 issues a year = every week = weekly
➡ 26 issues a year = every other week = twice a month = bi-weekly
➡ 12 issues a year = every month = monthly
➡ 6 issues a year = every other month = bi-monthly
➡ Twice a year = once every six month = biannually
➡ Once a year = annually = yearly
➡ Once a day = every day = daily
➡ Once every two days = every other day

關鍵字彙

every hour on the hour 整點（「on the hour」是「某整點」的意思）

Mark your answer on your answer sheet.

(A)　　(B)　　(C)

解題分析

方法、方式 72%

動作 28%

■ **方法、方式 72%**

問句是 how 開頭，可以判別本題的方向是詢問做某一件事情的「方法」，因此，要多留意選項中是否有出現相關的方法，如果有的話，有很高的機率是解答。

■ **動作 28%**

題目所出現的動作是答案選項的依據，透過本題的關鍵詞，可得知題目的主旨是在問「聯絡」的方式。

聽稿

（UK／M）

How can I get in touch with you?
(A) All right, I'll call Josh to confirm.
(B) I'll send you a sample package, okay?
(C) Here is my business card with my numbers.

中譯

（英／男）

我要如何跟你聯絡呢？（答案：C）
(A) 好的，我會打電話跟喬許確認。
(B) 我會將試用包寄給你，好嗎？
(C) 這是我的名片，上面有我的電話。

解題技巧

聽到題目播放出來的同時，可將注意力放到聽首字的關鍵問題點上，目的是要可以更精準地預測答案方向。此題問的是「How can I get in touch with you?」，便可判斷問題要點是在「how」上面。知道了關鍵的問題點之後，想要選擇合理的答案，就要專注去聽有沒有提到「方式、方法」的選項。且此句的重音呈現會是：「**How** can I get in **touch** with **you**?」。了解關鍵要點以及知道問題的主題之後，便可以在心裡想著要聽到「聯絡方式」的答案即可。

各選項解析

- 選項 (A)「All right, I'll call Josh to confirm.」內主要的關鍵點是「call Josh」，但是跟此問題想要問的對象不同，問題要問的是「you」，這個選項卻是回應「call Josh」，沒有針對問題回答，故不選。
- 選項 (B)「I'll send you a sample package, okay?」內的主旨是「send a sample package」，即要「寄試用品包裹」，但題目問的是「要怎麼聯絡到你」，選項 (B) 雖然有提到聯絡的其中一項方式：寄送，但主旨和題目不符，無法回答題目，故不選。
- 選項 (C)「Here is my business card with my numbers.」內關鍵點為「business card」與「numbers」；因為提到給名片，並且名片上面有聯絡電話的號碼，的確可以回答到此題問如何聯絡的問題，故為正確答案。

題目陷阱

此題是以 how 開頭的題目，問的是「保持聯繫的方式」為何。那麼，若沒有回答到如何聯絡的答案，或是僅故意重複唸某關鍵字，卻沒有回答到 how 開頭問題的答案，都不會是正確的。例如：

➡ Sure, let's keep in touch.（當然，我們保持聯絡。）

此句內關於聯絡的字詞就是「keep in touch」一詞，雖然和聯絡有相關性，卻沒提到是如何聯絡，或是用什麼方式聯絡，故沒回答到問題。

➡ Can you tell me how I can get to the airport?
（你可以告訴我如何前往機場嗎？）

此句只是將關鍵點「how I can get...」故意重複一次罷了，雖然和題目一樣都是 how 開頭，但這個回應主要討論的是「前往機場」，並非「如何聯絡」，回應的方向錯誤，故沒有針對問題回答。

在商務場合上，不論是開完會、或是社交活動結束後，大家不免會互道再見，或互留資訊以便日後聯絡。因此，在這樣的場合下，有一些實用語句可以派上用場：

➡ Thank you for coming. We've had a wonderful time.
（謝謝你來訪，我們共度了快樂的時光。）

➡ I hope we'll see you again soon.（我希望我們很快再見到你。）

➡ I'm sure we'll meet each other again soon.
（我很確定我們很快會再見面。）

➡ I'm looking forward to seeing you in the conference.
（我很期待在研討會上再見到你。）

➡ Give me a call when you visit Taipei next time.
（下次你再到台北來時請再打電話給我。）

➡ Let me give you my business card.（讓我給你我的名片吧。）

➡ Call me. You know my number.（打電話給我，你有我的號碼吧。）

➡ Can I give you my e-mail address?（我可以給你我的電郵地址嗎？）

➡ Write or give me a ring anytime.（任何時間都可以寫信或打電話給我。）

➡ Let's keep in contact.（我們保持聯絡喔。）

關鍵字彙

get in touch with **ph** 與～聯絡
confirm [kən`fɜm] **v** 確認
sample package [`sæmpḷ ˌpækɪdʒ] **n** 試用包
business card [`bɪznɪs ˌkɑrd] **n** 名片

Mark your answer on your answer sheet.

(A)　　(B)　　(C)

解題分析

年齡 68%

人物、對象 22%

數字 10%

■ **年齡 68%**

一聽到問句的關鍵字 how old，馬上就可以聯想到年齡、年紀，不過，選項必須清楚答出歲數才算針對問題回答。

■ **人物、對象 22%**

題目中提到的對象是很重要的，本題是問「孩子們」的年齡，就算有回答年紀，如果主角與問題的人物毫不相干，如：my grandmother、his neighbor 等等，就不是答案。

■ **數字 10%**

若是詢問年齡，一定要清楚回答，不能只回答「年紀很大」或「年紀小」，以數字回答是較好的方式。然而，有些答案選項有提到數字，卻不是在表達人物的年紀，也不是正解。

聽稿

（AU／Ⓦ）

How old are your children now?

(A) Work hard if you want to one-up others.

(B) They are 9 and 11 this year.

(C) Your children are still very young, aren't they?

中譯

（澳／👩）

你小孩現在幾歲了？（答案：B）

(A) 你要勝人一籌就要努力工作。

(B) 他們今年分別是九和十一歲了。

(C) 你的小孩都還很小，不是嗎？

解題技巧

在聽這類題目時，專心聽問句的同時，也要聽到關鍵的問題點，才可以有效地預測可能的答案方向，而不會發生聽到三個選項卻毫無頭緒的情況。此題問的是：「How old are your children now?」，那麼非常明顯地，問題關鍵點是在「how old（幾歲）」上面，如此便可預期要聽到關於年紀、幾歲的答案才合理。且問題的關鍵之處會以加強重音來強調：「How old **are** your children now?」。聽到了要點之處，也了解問題要問的是什麼之後，可以知道要聽到「小孩幾歲」的選項才能選擇來當正確答案。

各選項解析

- 選項 (A)「Work hard if you want to one-up others.」內有跟數字有關的字詞，「one-up」為「略勝一籌」之意，雖然跟數字有相關性，但根本不是在表達年紀，無法回答「how old」的問題，故不選。
- 選項 (B)「They are 9 and 11 this year.」內有明確的關鍵點可以回答此年紀的問題，也就是「9 and 11」，這個選項的中文意思是「他們今年分別是九歲和十一歲」，完全針對問 how old 的問題做出正確的回應，故為正確答案。
- 選項 (C)「Your children are still very young, aren't they?」的內容是在反問「小孩是否還小？」但並沒有直接回答到 how old 的年紀相關問題，故不選。

題目陷阱

既然此題問的是 how old 的問句，那麼若沒有回答到「年紀」的選項，或是僅重複唸題中的關鍵字，卻沒有針對「幾歲」來做回答者，都不會是答案，可以刪去法來做這道題。另有可能的陷阱，是有回答到年紀，但主角卻不是題目中所提及的「children」，也算是錯誤的答案。以下舉出幾個陷阱選項：

➡ My grandmother is <u>87 years old</u> already.（我祖母已經八十七歲了。）

此句內雖然說有提到年齡可以回答 how old 的問題，但是本題中主角是要討論 children，而非 grandmother 喔！因為這個選項的主角和題目不相符，所以不能算是有針對題目給出正確的回應。

➡ <u>My kids</u> are still very young.（我小孩還很小。）

首先，此句主角「kids」是「children」的同義字，都是「小孩」的意思。但此句的關鍵點「very young」卻沒有明確地說出是幾歲，因此就不會是答案了。

針對此題的問題情境，比較屬於在社交場合上會提及的話題。當然，在日常辦公環境中，也不會是完全都在講公事，會有休息時間或午餐時間，這當中不免也會聊到家庭、小孩、生活瑣事等話題，以此與同事拉近彼此距離。那麼除了聊小孩話題之外，一般社交情境可聊的話題還包括：

❶ Family and relationships 討論家庭與關係

➡ I've got two sisters, and they both are working in New York.
（我有兩個姐姐，她們都在紐約工作。）

➡ Bob is Mr. Smith's brother. No wonder he could work banker's hours.
（鮑伯是史密斯先生的弟弟，難怪他可以早早就下班。）

❷ Interests and sport 討論興趣和運動

➡ I'm interested in photography.（我對攝影有興趣。）

➡ I play table tennis. Do you play any ball sports?
（我會打乒乓球，你有玩什麼球類運動嗎？）

❸ Movies and stage shows 討論電影

➡ Jack Nilson is a wonderful actor. He just won an Oscar for best supporting actor.（傑克尼爾森是個很棒的演員，他剛得了奧斯卡最佳男配角獎。）

❹ Vacations 討論度假活動

➡ Every year I like to get away and enjoy sunshine on the beach.
（每年我都要休息一下，並到海邊享受陽光。）

關鍵字彙

one-up [wʌnˋʌp] ⅴ 略勝一籌

Mark your answer on your answer sheet.

(A)　　(B)　　(C)

解題分析

喜好、觀感 64%

對象 36%

■ **喜好、觀感** 64%　How do you like 是詢問對方「喜好」的句型，回應必須針對主題，說出相關的「觀感」或是給予「評論」。

■ **對象** 36%　問句的主題圍繞在對「台北」的喜好，選項中即便有提到喜好和觀感，也要注意指稱的對象是否正確。

聽稿
（US / Ⓦ）

How do you like Taipei?
(A) I think it's a charming city.
(B) Well, I prefer not to answer personal questions.
(C) My parents are flying to Taipei next week.

中譯
（美 / Ⓦ）

你喜歡台北嗎？（答案：A）
(A) 我覺得台北是個迷人的都市。
(B) 嗯，我不想回答私人問題。
(C) 我父母下週會搭機前往台北。

解題技巧

想要預料可能的答案，在聽到題目播放出的同時，將焦點放在聽關鍵問題點上面就可以了。此題問的是「How do you like Taipei?」，在這裡介紹一下，這其中有個很實用的句型：「How do you like (something)？」，意思即「你喜歡（某事物）嗎？」。

例如：「How do you like Chinese food?（你喜歡中式菜餚嗎？）」，或「How do you like Mr. Williams?（你覺得威廉先生如何？）」，那麼可預期的答案方向會是「說明對（某事物）的喜好」。而此句的重音呈現會是：「How do you like Taipei?」，由上面的論點可猜想答案內可能會出現對 Taipei 的觀感與評論。

各選項解析

- 選項 (A)「I think it's a charming city.」內關鍵點「a charming city」提到「它是一個迷人的都市」，的確可以針對此題問對台北的觀感做回應，故選為最佳答案。
- 選項 (B)「Well, I prefer not to answer personal questions.」內的重要訊息是「not to answer...」，提到的是「不想回答私人問題」，雖然題目是問對台北的觀感，但是這類的問題也不太算是私人的問題，所以此回應沒有針對題目回答，因此不選。
- 選項 (C)「My parents are flying to Taipei next week.」內的關鍵詞句「flying to Taipei」，僅是將題目中提到的地點「Taipei」一字重複唸一次罷了。細看選項內容的話，可以發現選項主題和題目並沒有連結在一起，所以也不能選。

此題要問的是對台北的觀感，若非回答「對台北的印象」之選項，便不會是答案。且若僅是將題目中的關鍵字詞重複唸一次者，卻迂迴地沒有針對問題回應，也可以刪去喔！例如：

➡ I've been to Taipei twice.（我來過台北兩次。）

此句的要點變成是在討論「次數」了，但本題目並不是問「how many times」的問題，方向和題目問的完全不一樣，因此不算是針對問題回答。

➡ I think Tokyo is a highly developed city.（我認為東京是個高度發展的都市。）

此句是有描述到對都市的印象了，但描述的都市錯了，題目是在討論「Taipei」，而非「Tokyo」。因此這個選項是為了故意混淆考生注意力而設下的陷阱。

在工作場合需要出差、拜訪客戶、參展的機會很多，到某個新的都市前，可以先針對那個都市做點功課，了解一下當地的人文風情，以便到時被問到「How do you like (city name)?」時，有話題能和廠商或客戶聊。比方說：

➡ I never see a trash can on the street, but Tokyo is really clean.
（我在路上都沒看到垃圾桶，但東京真的好乾淨。）

➡ I'm pretty amazed by the Camp Nou football stadium in Barcelona.
（我對巴塞隆納的諾坎普體育場感到驚豔。）

➡ The Statue of Christ in Rio is really fantastic.
（里約的基督像真的很壯觀。）

➡ I can't wait to try the local cuisine in Colombo.
（我等不及要試試可倫坡的當地美食了。）

➡ Chicago is definitely a wonderful city I would like to visit again.
（芝加哥的確是我還會想造訪的美好都市。）

關鍵字彙

charming [ˈtʃɑrmɪŋ] a 迷人的
personal [ˈpɝsn̩l] a 私人的

攻略 1 │ 動作與是或否

Mark your answer on your answer sheet.
(A)　　(B)　　(C)

解題分析

是或否 65%

動作 35%

■ 是或否 65%

Has 或 have 開頭的問句，通常為「是或否」的問題，答案大部分都會有明確的 yes 或 no，考生可以先針對此特點使用刪去法。

■ 動作 35%

問題為 Has 開頭，有很大的機率是問某一個動作或某一件事情「是否完成」，本題又是「Has... yet」的句子，幾乎已經可以肯定了。除了答案要有「是 / 否」之外，也須注意選項中的動作是否與題目一致。

聽稿
（UK / **M**）

Has the order arrived yet?
(A) Yes, I received your e-mail yesterday.
(B) No, not yet. But I'll check with the vendor. Don't worry.
(C) The client ordered two installation guides.

中譯
（英 / **男**）

訂的貨寄到了嗎？（答案：B）
(A) 是的，我昨天收到你的電郵了。
(B) 還沒耶，但我會向廠商查詢看看，別擔心。
(C) 客戶訂了兩本安裝手冊。

解題技巧

先聽到題目的同時，就應該將注意力集中到聽問題關鍵點上，以方便預期可能的答案。此題問的是：「Has the order arrived yet?」，那麼應立即判斷要點會落在「Has... yet?」上面；既然是問「是否」的問題，可預期回答的答案會有 yes 或 no 等可能性。另外，此問句的關鍵點會以加強重音來處理：「Has the order arrived yet?」。知道問題的關鍵點後，便可預期要聽到「貨收到與否」的相關答案才會正確。

各選項解析

- 選項 (A)「Yes, I received your e-mail yesterday.」內出現了疑似關鍵字眼的內容：「Yes, I received...」，提及「已收到」。但是，題目問的是「是否收到所訂的貨」，並不是問「是否收到電郵」喔！此回應和問題不相關，因此不選。
- 選項 (B)「No, not yet. But I'll check with the vendor. Don't worry.」內第一個關鍵點是「not yet」，意謂「尚未收到」，且後續又說「check with the vendor」，即為「要跟廠商詢問」的意思。的確有針對題目做出正確的回應，故選為最佳答案。
- 選項 (C)「The client ordered two installation guides.」內僅是重複唸題目中有出現的「order」一字罷了，但選項 (C) 內的「order」是動詞，表示「訂購」之意，沒有針對題目回應，故不選。

題目陷阱

這一題要問的是「貨是否到了」，那麼若非是回答「是」或「否」的答案，或僅是將原句內出現的字詞重複一次者，都可能是陷阱所在。舉例來說：

➡ Yes, <u>the order</u> has been sent.（是的，貨已經寄出了。）

此句子重複了 the order 一字，卻提到「sent（寄出）」，而非題目中的「arrive（送達）」，與題目的關鍵點不一致，故不算是回答到題目。

➡ Mr. Chen will <u>arrive</u> at around 5:30.（陳先生大約五點半會抵達。）

此句內重複了題目的關鍵字「arrive」，但這個回應中的主角卻是在講「Mr. Chen」，而非題目的「the order」。由於主角和問題的不同，故也沒針對問題回答。

討論到「order（訂單）」，在辦公環境是不可避免的主題之一，任何企業老闆最關心的事之一，大概就是業務員幫公司贏得多少訂單了。因此，一些討論到「訂單、下訂」等基本用語，應該先熟悉，以便在工作場合，或在多益聽力考題內聽到時，都能夠運用自如：

➡ I'd like to place an order for three of your database software packages.
（我想購買您的三套資料庫軟體。）

➡ We are considering the purchase of three file cabinets.
（我們想要購買三個檔案櫃。）

➡ Your order is being processed. We expect to have your order ready for shipment by July 7th.（您的訂單已在處理中了。我們預計您的貨會在七月七日之前寄出。）

➡ Your goods will be dispatched within three days.
（您的貨會在三天內寄出。）

➡ We are sorry to inform you that the products you order are out of stock, so we'll have to cancel your order.
（我們很抱歉要告知您：因為您訂的產品沒貨了，所以我們會取消您的訂單。）

關鍵字彙

order [ˋɔrdɚ] n 訂單、貨物 v 訂購
arrive [əˋraɪv] v 抵達
receive [rɪˋsiv] v 接收、收到
vendor [ˋvɛndɚ] n 廠商、賣主
installation [͵ɪnstəˋleʃən] n 安裝
guide [gaɪd] n 手冊

Mark your answer on your answer sheet.

(A)　　(B)　　(C)

解題分析

是或否 75%

物品 11%　　動作 14%

■ 是或否 75%

■ 動作 14%

■ 物品 11%

因為是 do 開頭的問題,所以預期會出現的答案基本上就是「是」與「否」這兩種,第一個字是最重要的關鍵,除此之外,也要仔細聽問題後面的線索。

聽到 do 開頭的問句,首先可以判斷答案會是「是 / 否」兩種形式,do 之後的關鍵字 have 是個很重要的動作,藉此縮小正確選項範圍為「我有」以及「我沒有」。

有時答案的選項會重複題目出現過的物品,但是,如果情境和動作與題目完全無關聯,或是沒有回答「是 / 否」,都不是正解。

聽稿

（US / Ⓦ）

Do you have my business card?

(A) Good. Then I'll see you in New York.

(B) You can call my assistant to arrange a meeting.

(C) Well, let me see. Yes, right here.

中譯

（美 / 女）

你有我的名片嗎?（答案:C）

(A) 很好,那我們就紐約見了。

(B) 你可以打電話給我助理約個會議。

(C) 嗯,讓我看一下,有,在這裡。

解題技巧

想掌握要回答什麼方向的答案,那就要在聽題目的同時,也將注意力放在首字問題關鍵點上。換句話說,問題的第一個字是最重要的關鍵點,千萬不要忽略了!此題問的是「Do you have my business card?」,既然開頭是「Do you have...?」的問題,那麼可預期的答案不外乎就是「是的,我有」,不然就是「我沒有」這兩種可能性了。且此問句的要點會以加強重音來強調,重音標示如:「Do you have my business card?」。

各選項解析

• 選項 (A)「Good. Then I'll see you in New York.」內的關鍵點是「see you in New York」,提到「要在紐約見」;但題目問的是「是否有名片」,選項 (A) 完全沒有提及跟題目相關的回應,因此不能選。

• 選項 (B)「You can call my assistant to arrange a meeting.」內主題是「call my assistant...」,但題目並不是在問「如何跟你約會議時間」之事,所以選項 (B) 的回答方向完全相反了,也不能選。

• 選項 (C)「Well, let me see. Yes, right here.」內的關鍵點在後半段「Yes, right here.」,意即「有,名片在這裡」。可以看出有針對問題回答,可選為最佳答案。

題目陷阱 此問題問的是：「是否有我的名片」，那麼若不是回答「有」或「沒有」的答案，或僅是故意將題目內字詞重複唸一次的選項，都可能是命題的陷阱。舉例如下：

➡ Here is my business card.（這是我的名片。）

此句內重複題目中有出現的關鍵字「business card」，這個選項回答的是自己的名片，但卻沒回答到「是否」有對方的名片，沒有直接回答問題，故為陷阱。

➡ Thank you for doing business with us.（感謝你跟我們做生意。）

此句內僅重複 business 一字，不但完全沒有提到題目中的關鍵字「名片」，也沒有回答到「是否」的問題。沒有正面回應本問題，故也不能選為正確答案。

相信有在職場工作經驗的朋友都知道，廠商、客戶、合作對象第一次來到公司開會時，初次見面都是以交換名片來開啟話題，如此一來也才能很快地知道對方要如何稱呼、職位為何、和職責所在等資訊。那麼在交換名片的同時，也不會就閉著嘴巴安靜地不講話，還是會順帶地講一下初次會面的暖場話。例如：

➡ Hello, my name is Linda Chen. It's my pleasure to meet you.
（您好，我是陳琳達，很高興認識您。）

➡ How do you do, Mr. Smith. Welcome to Taipei.
（您好，史密斯先生，歡迎來到台北。）

➡ Ms. Liang, may I introduce you to our VP of Marketing?
（梁小姐，我能為您介紹我們的行銷副總嗎？）

➡ So you are based in Perth. How's the weather there?
（所以您在伯斯工作，那裡的天氣如何呢？）

➡ Nice to meet you, Ms. Nilson. My name is Lili-Anna. Please just call me Lili.
（尼爾森小姐，很高興認識您。我是莉莉安娜，請叫我莉莉就可以了。）

➡ When did you arrive?（您何時抵達的？）

➡ Did you have a good journey?（您旅途還順利嗎？）

➡ Can I get you something to drink? I've got the best Taiwanese tea.
（您要喝點什麼嗎？我們有上等的台灣茶。）

關鍵字彙

assistant [ə`sɪstənt] n 助理
arrange [ə`rendʒ] v 安排

攻略 3 ｜ 是或否與事件

Mark your answer on your answer sheet.

(A)　　(B)　　(C)

解題分析

是或否 59%

動作 41%

■ 是或否 59%

■ 動作 41%

問句開頭的關鍵字是 did，跟 do 一樣主要為「是」與「否」兩種回答，只差在是過去發生的事，除此之外，答案選項也必須跟問題的主題相符才行。

本題的三個選項，都是以 yes / no 為開頭，這時候就要根據選項和題目的動作是否有關來判斷，避免掉進陷阱裡。

聽稿

（CA /　M ）

Did you receive the agreement I sent you?

(A) Yes, I did. Thank you.

(B) Yes, I just arrived.

(C) Yes, I completely agree with you.

中譯

（加 /　男 ）

你有收到我寄給你的合約嗎？（答案：A）

(A) 有的，收到了，謝謝。

(B) 是的，我剛抵達。

(C) 是的，我完全同意你的意見。

解題技巧

在題目播放前，考生便要有自覺必須聽到最關鍵的問題點才行，這樣隨後即可預期答案的可能性。此題問的是：「Did you receive the agreement I sent you?」，那麼關鍵問題點便會是開頭的「did you receive」了，答案的可能性便會是「yes」或「no」。另外，外國人在談話時，若是有想要強調的重點，會加重音來呈現。而此問題的重音點：「Did」和「receive」，就是這一題的關鍵之處了。了解關鍵問題點之後，便可專注在聽能夠回答「是否收到合約」的答案上。

各選項解析

- 選項 (A)「Yes, I did. Thank you.」內的關鍵點是「Yes, I did.」，此回應代表「是的，有收到合約了」之意，的確有針對問題回答，故為正確答案。
- 選項 (B)「Yes, I just arrived.」內的重要訊息「I arrived.」為「我到了」之意；但題目問的是「合約是否寄到」一事，故此選項無法針對題目回答。
- 選項 (C)「Yes, I completely agree with you.」內的關鍵點是「agree with you」，提到的是「同意對方看法」，但也沒有正面回答到是否收到合約一事，故不選。

題目陷阱 此題既然是問「是否收到」，那麼陷阱設計便會是與「是 / 否」無關的答案選項；或是可能僅將問句內容重複一次，卻沒有針對「是 / 否」來回應的選項，也都不會是正確答案。比方說：

➡ Please sign the <u>agreement</u> and send it back to me.
（請簽合約並寄回給我。）

此句內有重複題目出現過的關鍵字「agreement」，但卻是指示對方簽名，不是針對問題「是否收到」來回應，故不可算正確答案。

➡ The package you sent <u>arrived</u> yesterday.
（你之前寄的包裹昨天收到了。）

此句回應收到 package 了，有回應到「是否收到」，但別忘記題目是問有沒有收到「agreement」，所以這個選項的主題和題目的不一致，故也算是一個故意混淆的選項。

在商業環境中，與同事、廠商、客戶等人討論議題或交換意見的機會必定不少，若大家意見一致，那便是「reach an agreement（達成共識）」了，隨後可能就是會將大家同意的事項以白紙黑字寫在「agreement」上，並且交由雙方簽名確認。

那麼，在表達「同意」與「持相反意見」的用語上，有數種說法，若這些實用說法都熟練到可自然地表達，不但可以在職場上應用，在多益聽力題目內聽到的話，更是可以馬上分辨出喔。

❶ 表達同意：

➡ I couldn't agree with you more.（我非常同意你。）

➡ That's exactly how I feel.（那正是我想的。）

➡ Exactly. No doubt about it at all.（的確，正是如此。）

➡ Definitely. That's for sure.（真的，那是必然的。）

➡ I 100% agree with James.（我百分之百同意詹姆士所說的。）

➡ Yeah, tell me about it.（是的，那還用說嗎。）

❷ 表達反對：

➡ Well, I don't think it's a brilliant idea.（我不認為那是明智的作法。）

➡ That's not always the case.（並不一定是這樣吧。）

➡ I think your idea is just halfway correct.（我認為你的點子不是很周全。）

➡ Not necessarily.（不一定是這樣。）

➡ I'm afraid I can't agree with you.（我恐怕無法同意你的意見。）

➡ No way.（不可能。）

關鍵字彙

agreement [ə`grimənt] n 合約
completely [kəm`plitlɪ] ad 完全地

Mark your answer on your answer sheet.

(A)　　(B)　　(C)

解題分析

是或否 58%

動作 42%

■ 是或否 58%

■ 動作 42%

聽到 will 開頭的問句，答案的選項也只有「是或否」的可能，要先把沒有回答到是或否的選項刪除，再選出與問題關鍵字最相符的，便是正確解答。

繼續往下看，問題主要是圍繞在是否「討論預算」，平時就要熟記商業相關的單字，才能準確抓住問題的核心。

聽稿

（AU / Ⓦ）

Will we discuss the budget issue at today's meeting?
(A) No, not me. Mr. Chen will take the chair.
(B) Yes, it has to be finalized today.
(C) Yes, I'm sending you the quotation now.

中譯

（澳 / 女）

我們今天開會會討論到預算問題嗎？（答案：B）
(A) 不，不是我，陳先生才是主席。
(B) 會呀，預算今天一定要確認。
(C) 是的，我現在馬上將報價單寄給你。

解題技巧

聽到題目的同時要將注意力放在聽關鍵問題點上，以便預設可能的答案。此題問的是「Will we discuss the budget issue at today's meeting?」，關鍵點便會是在開頭的「Will... discuss...」上面。既然是問「是否會討論到～」，那麼可能的答案便會有「會討論」或「不會討論到」這兩種可能性。而此問句內的關鍵點會以加強重音來強調：「Will we discuss the budget issue at today's meeting?」。了解問題的關鍵點是「是否討論預算」之後，也才能將注意力放在聽正確的答案上。

各選項解析

- 選項 (A)「No, not me. Mr. Chen will take the chair.」內有個大家可能比較不熟悉的片語「take the chair」，即「主持會議」之意，故整句的主要訊息是「陳先生是主持人」，但這樣的內容是在回應「who」的題目，但本題是在詢問是否討論預算，回應與題目不符，所以不選。

- 選項 (B)「Yes, it has to be finalized today.」內關鍵訊息「Yes, it... finalized...」，其中的「it」是指題目中提到的「budget」，整句話的意思便是「預算一事今開會討論後就會確定下來」，有針對問題回答，故選為最佳答案。

- 選項 (C)「Yes, I'm sending you the quotation now.」內要點提到「寄報價單」，但是，題目並沒有提到什麼報價單，這個選項完全與題目不相關，所以也不會是正確答案。

題目陷阱 此題既然是問到「是否會討論到」，那麼只要是與「是／否」無關的答案，或是僅重複唸出題目關鍵字，卻沒回答到「是／否」的選項，都會是陷阱的答案。比方說：

➡ We'll discuss many topics at the meeting.
（我們在會議中會討論很多主題。）

此句內有關鍵字「discuss」和「at the meeting」都是在題目中有出現的，但這個回應卻沒針對要點「budget」一事做出回應。此回應說會討論數個主題，那是有包括預算主題嗎？此句並沒有直接回答問題，故不會是答案。

➡ Yes, we'll talk about marketing strategies.
（是的，我們會討論行銷策略。）

此題雖說以 yes 為開頭，其後面的內容卻說要討論「marketing strategies」。但別忘了題目是問是否討論「預算」，並非「行銷策略」，討論的主題與題目不合，故也算是故意混淆考生視聽的答案。

討論到「budget（預算）」一事，多數企業自然是想以最少的投資，來換取最大的利潤和產生出最大的效能。經常在討論「budget issue」的時候，老闆們可能會想知道如何幫公司節省支出的方法，那麼在參與討論時，可以運用以下的實用語句來表達喔：

➡ I suggest you cut the costs of advertising.
（我建議你降低廣告的花費。）

➡ I think we should reduce expenses on electricity.
（我認為我們應該降低電費的花費。）

➡ Can we consider relocating the office to a more affordable area?
（我們可以考慮將辦公室搬到租金較低的地區嗎？）

➡ Let's control the costs of office supplies.
（讓我們控制辦公用品的花費。）

➡ Some managers would like to reduce costs by cutting out the dead woods.
（一些經理想藉由刪減人事來降低成本。）

➡ Let's trim the fat by cutting some job positions.
（讓我們裁撤掉一些工作職位以節省花費。）

➡ Shouldn't we minimize the number of service reps?
（我們不該減少服務人員的數量嗎？）

➡ Let's reduce spending on marketing activities.
（讓我們降低行銷活動的花費。）

關鍵字彙

budget [ˈbʌdʒɪt] n 預算
issue [ˈɪʃju] n 事項、議題
take the chair ph 主持會議
finalize [ˈfaɪn̩ˌaɪz] v 定稿、最終確認
quotation [kwoˈteʃən] n 報價單

Mark your answer on your answer sheet.

(A)　　(B)　　(C)

解題分析

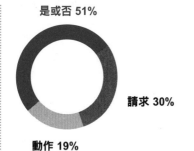

是或否 51%

請求 30%

動作 19%

■ 是或否 51%　Can 開頭的問句，同樣一定要回答「是」與「否」其中一種答案，如果選項中沒有提到 yes / no 就不能選擇。

■ 請求 30%　也許 Can 開頭的句子有幾種不同意思，但看到「Can you... please?」句型，馬上就要想到這是「請求」對方同意協助的用法。答案必須是表達同意或否定請求才算回答到問題。

■ 動作 19%　如果答案選項有回答 yes / no，並且是跟答應請求相關，雖然答對的機率很高，但是也要仔細聽回答的動作是否與題目相符。例如本題是問「可否載去機場」，答覆就必須針對問題，如果有提到機場相關詞彙，動作卻不一致，也不能選。

聽稿

（UK / M）

Can you take me to the airport please?

(A) All right, I hope to see you in the near future.

(B) Thank you for inviting, but I can't.

(C) Sure, let me take my keys.

中譯

（英 / 男）

你可以載我去機場嗎？（答案：C）

(A) 好的，我希望很快能再與你見面。

(B) 謝謝你邀請我，但我沒辦法去。

(C) 當然，等我拿個鑰匙。

解題技巧　想要在回答這類問題時能順利地找到正確答案，那就要在聽題目的同時，將注意力放在關鍵問題點上，如此才能掌握答案的回答方向。此題問的是「Can you take me to the airport please?」，那麼關鍵點便是在「can you... please」上面了。可預期的答案便會是「yes，可以」或是「no，沒辦法」等。另外，問題的關鍵點通常會以加強重音的方式來強調：「Can you take me to the airport please?」。在知道如何回答問題的方向之後，便可將注意力放在聽相對應的答案上了。

各選項解析

• 選項 (A)「All right, I hope to see you in the near future.」內的關鍵訊息是「see you in the future」，意即「很快再相見」；另外，「in the future」是指「很快就會來臨的將來」。雖然選項 (A) 的一開始提到了同樣也是「同意」意思的「all right」，但後續的回應並沒有針對題目來回答所問的「是否可載我去機場」，因此不會是正確答案。

• 選項 (B)「Thank you for inviting, but I can't.」內關鍵點提到「謝謝邀請」，但題目並非在問相關邀請出席活動，此選項沒有針對問題回答，因此也不選。

• 選項 (C)「Sure, let me take my keys.」內關鍵點有「sure」，可初步判斷是對於「可以載你去機場」的回應了；後來又聽到了「take my keys」，可得知可能是要「拿鑰匙去開車」。因此，有針對問題做回應，可選為最佳答案。

題目陷阱

此句既然是問「可否載去機場」，那麼只要是回答與「是 / 否」無關的答案；或僅是將關鍵字重複唸，卻沒回答到「yes / no」的答案排除。舉例來說：

➡ The <u>airport</u> is pretty far away from here.（機場離此處很遠。）

此句僅將題目中的地點「airport」再重述一次，卻沒回答「可以載」或「無法載」的問題，因此便不會是答案。

➡ <u>I can give you a ride</u> home if you'd like.（若你要的話，我可以載你回家。）

此句雖然有提到同樣也是載人回家的片語「give (someone) a ride」，但要特別注意的是，題目問的可否載到機場「to the airport」，這個回應則是說可以載回家「go home」，回應的地點和題目的不相符，故此句內容也是刻意混淆考生罷了。

公司內同事間通常不會是單打獨鬥，有時也會需要請求他人的協助。想要尋求他人協助，除了本題的「Can you... (do something) please?」句型之外，還可以使用以下幾種有禮貌的句型：

➡ Could you do me a favor please?（你可以幫我個忙嗎？）

➡ Could you please take me to work?（你可以送我去上班嗎？）

➡ Could you possibly give me a lift back home?（你可以讓我搭個便車回家嗎？）

➡ Would you mind driving me to the station?（你介意送我去車站嗎？）

➡ Would it be too much trouble for you to pick me up at the airport?
（請你來機場接我會不會太麻煩呢？）

另外，要回應的話，也有幾種情況：

➡ No problem at all.（沒問題。）

➡ I'd be glad to help out.（我很樂意幫忙。）

➡ It's my pleasure to assist.（協助你是我的榮幸。）

➡ I'm afraid I can't.（我恐怕沒辦法耶。）

➡ Sorry, but I'm unable to do that.（不好意思，我沒辦法。）

➡ Unfortunately, I don't have time then.（真不巧，我那天沒空。）

關鍵字彙

airport [ˈɛrˌport] n 機場
future [ˈfjutʃɚ] n 未來
invite [ɪnˈvaɪt] v 邀請

Unit 8 附加問句題型

攻略 1 | 事件與是或否

Mark your answer on your answer sheet.

(A)　　(B)　　(C)

解題分析

是或否 51%

動作 49%

■ **是或否** 51%　　本題是附加問句的形式,在敘述之後以問句確認前面的內容。這樣的題目,答案也是分成「是」與「否」兩種可能。

■ **動作** 49%　　因為只是再次確認,附加問句的重點還是要放在句子前面敘述的主題,例如本題的關鍵是「英語講得好」,所以就要選與主題方向相符的選項。

聽稿
(UK / M)

Mr. Chen speaks good English, doesn't he?
(A) Yes, he speaks a little English.
(B) Yes, his English is not that good.
(C) Yes, he speaks fluent English.

中譯
(英 / 男)

陳先生英語講得不錯,對吧?(答案:C)
(A) 是的,他會講一點英語。
(B) 是的,他英語不是很好。
(C) 是的,他會講流利的英語。

解題技巧

雖然這一題主要問的是附加問句,但也跟前面的題目一樣,都要注意題目的關鍵字,目的是為了可以更精準地預測可能的答案方向。此題講述的是「Mr. Chen speaks good English, doesn't he?」,雖然說句尾有「doesn't he?」,但重點其實還是落在「speaks good English」上面。因此,考生無需受到附加問句的影響喔!應將要點放在前面的描述上。可預期的答案便可能有肯定的回應「同意,他英語好」或是否定的回應「不同意,他英語不太好」等可能性。另外,此描述句的重音會落在:「**Mr. Chen** speaks good Enlgish, doesn't he?」。了解題目所要強調的要點後,也才有辦法將注意力放在該有的回應上。

各選項解析

• 選項 (A)「Yes, he speaks a little English.」關鍵點是「a little」,整句話的意思是「僅會講一點英語」。可是原問題是說「英語講得很好」,若要回答「同意」的話,應是同意「英語講得好」一事,而不會是變成「僅會講一點」,這個選項和題目有點不適合,故不選。

• 選項 (B)「Yes, his English is not that good.」內的主要訊息在「not that good」上,那麼跟上述選項 (A) 的理由一樣,選項 (B) 和題目表達的不同,因此也不會是最佳答案。

• 選項 (C)「Yes, he speaks fluent English.」內的關鍵點很明確是「Yes... fluent English」上面,意即「同意他英語講得好」一事,可對應到題目所問的,故為正確答案。

題目陷阱 此句既是在討論「英語是否講得好」，若是回應與「好或不好」無關，或僅是將關鍵字再唸一次，卻沒針對英語好壞一事回應的選項，自然就不會是正確的答案。舉例來說：

➡ Mr. Chen speaks excellent Japanese.（陳先生日文極棒。）

此句幾乎重複了題目中出現的每個字「Mr. Chen speaks good...」，但本問題關鍵點是在討論「Enlgish」，而非「Japanese」喔！主要的訊息和題目的沒有吻合，故不算是有針對問題回答。

➡ Yes, English is an international language.（是的，英語是國際語言。）

此句僅重複了「English」一字，但沒有針對問題正面回應「陳先生的英語程度」一事，故也是混淆視聽的陷阱。

要描述某人的語言程度、或其他技能時，除了像句中的「someone speaks good Eglish」的句型之外，還有其他很生動活潑的說法，以下列出幾個實用的句型：

➡ James has a flair for languages.（詹姆士有語言天分。）

➡ Ms. Jones is very skillful at presentation.（瓊斯小姐很擅長做簡報。）

➡ My brother has a genius for solving math problems.
（我弟弟是解數學題的天才。）

➡ Jenny is a past master at arranging marketing campaigns.
（珍妮是安排行銷活動的老手了。）

➡ I've done the same drawing so many times I could do it in my sleep now.
（我已經畫過一樣的圖太多次了，閉著眼睛也會畫了。）

➡ Jones has a real knock for the piano.
（瓊斯在琴藝方面精進。）

➡ My mother seems to have a magic touch with kids.
（我媽媽對小孩很有一套。）

➡ I use English to communicate in the office, and I have to keep in practice.
（在辦公室我都使用英語溝通，因此要時時精進。）

關鍵字彙

fluent ['fluənt] a 流利的

Mark your answer on your answer sheet.

(A)　　(B)　　(C)

解題分析

是或否 62%

事件、狀態 38%

■ 是或否 62%

■ 事件、狀態 38%

本題為附加問句的句型，在直述句後面加一個問題，為了確認前面敘述的主題，而答案通常是「yes」和「no」兩種。要特別注意，中文跟英文回答是否的方式有些不同，要小心別混淆了。

答案選項必須符合問題描述的方向，例如本題的意思是在問「是否下雨」，答案就要針對問題，也就是天氣做出回應。

聽稿
（US / W）

It's not raining outside, is it?
(A) Yes, I'll bring my books.
(B) Yes, it's not snowing.
(C) No, it's not. The weather is rather good.

中譯
（美 / 女）

外面沒在下雨吧，有嗎？（答案：C）
(A) 是的，我會帶書。
(B) 是的，沒下雪。
(C) 沒有，沒下雨，天氣還算滿好的。

解題技巧

聽到題目的同時，也應該可以聽出關鍵問題點，才可能精準地預測到可能的答案方向。此題問的是「It's not raining outside, is it?」，可聽出問題點在於講者認為「沒下雨」，那麼可預期的答案便縮小到剩下兩種可能了，一個是「的確沒下雨」的可能性，另一個則是「其實有下雨」的方向。此句的要點會以加強重音來呈現，且其後的「is it?」語氣會上揚，本題的重音會在：「not raining」和「is it?」上面。

各選項解析

- 選項 (A)「Yes, I'll bring my books.」內關鍵訊息「bring books」，意即「會帶書」，但這與題目問的「是否下雨」無關，故不選。
- 選項 (B)「Yes, it's not snowing.」內關鍵訊息是「not snowing」提到沒下雪，但題目問的是「是否下雨」，此回應與題目問的方向不同，故不選。
- 選項 (C)「No, it's not. The weather is rather good.」先有關鍵點「it's not」便可聽出是「沒下雨」之意了，接著又聽到「weather... good」，整句話的意思連接起來就是「沒下雨，天氣好」。有針對題目做出正確的回應，故為正確答案。

題目陷阱

此題「It's not raining outside, is it?」的要點為附加問句，也就是在簡單直述句之後加了用以徵求對方同意的簡單問題。若直述句是肯定的，那麼附加問句便是否定的；相反地，若直述句是否定的，附加問句便是肯定的。至於此類問題的陷阱，更是一般台灣學生會混淆之處，也就是被「yes / no」搞混。比方說：

Q: He is still a student, isn't he?（他還是學生，對吧？）
　　——此句的意思是「他還是個學生，難道不是嗎？」

A: Yes, he is a student.（是的，他還是學生。）
　　——此句以肯定的 yes 開頭，那麼其後就也要肯定句，不可以是否定。

A: No, he is not a student. He is working now.（不，他不是學生，他在工作了。）
　　——此句是以否定的 no 開頭，其後也要接否定句，要有一致性。

問題就出現於大家都會想說「isn't he?」是否定的句子，那麼要表達「你想錯了」的感覺，便講出了以下這樣的回答：

Q: He is still a student, isn't he?
A: No, he is a student. (X)

或是：

Q: He is not a student, is he?
A: Yes, he is not a student. (X)

這些回應都不會是正確的喔！

更多例子請看以下：

Q: Mr. Smith doesn't speak Japanese, does he?（史密斯先生不會講日文，沒錯吧？）
A: No, he doesn't.（不，他不會講。）
A: Yes, he doesn't.（對，他不會講。）(X)

Q: Judy will be promoted, won't she?（茱蒂會被升官，不會嗎？）
A: Yes, she will.（是的，她會升官。）
A: No, she will.（錯了，她其實會升官。）(X)

Q: It is not snowing outside, is it?（外面沒下雪吧？）
A: No, it's not snowing now.（沒有，現在沒下雪。）
A: Yes, it's not snowing now.（對，現在沒下雪。）(X)

總之，請大家要記得，若回答是「yes」的話，那麼其後就接「肯定」的答案；相反地，若回答是「no」的話，其後就接「否定」的答案。

關鍵字彙

umbrella [ʌm`brɛlə] n. 雨傘
rather [`ræðɚ] adv. 相當、有點

Mark your answer on your answer sheet.

(A)　　(B)　　(C)

解題分析

徵求同意 86%

形容 14%

■ 徵求同意 86%

■ 形容 14%

本題也是在直述句後反問的附加問句，前面句子是關鍵，描述「風景很美」，後面的 isn't it 為徵求對方同意自己的看法，因此答案要圍繞在同意風景很美這件事上。

本題答案必須表達對風景的看法，所以要注意選項中的形容詞是否適合形容風景優美，如果跟風景完全無關，就不是正確答案。

聽稿

（CA / M）

It's a beautiful view, isn't it?
(A) I'm afraid I can't.
(B) It's certainly breathtaking.
(C) Okay, I'll make sure first.

中譯

（加 / 男）

這風景真好看，不是嗎？（答案：B）
(A) 我恐怕不行耶。
(B) 真的是令人屏息。
(C) 好的，我會先確認一下。

解題技巧

此題要問的是「It's a beautiful view, isn't it?」，要點落在講者認為風景「beautiful」上面。其後的附加問句「isn't it?」有加強說明「難道不是嗎」的意味；因此可聽出講者是希望回應的人也同意其說法。而此句重點部分會以加重音來強調，那麼此句的重音便會落在：「It's a beautiful view, isn't it?」。在了解題目想問的關鍵點後，便可將注意力放在聽「風景的確很美」的可能回應上。

各選項解析

- 選項 (A)「I'm afraid I can't.」內關鍵訊息提到的是「我沒辦法」，但這與題目提到的「風景好看」完全無關，故不選。
- 選項 (B)「It's certainly breathtaking.」內的關鍵字為「breathtaking」，意即「壯觀的、令人讚嘆的」，的確是在形容風景好，有針對問題做出適當的回應，所以選為正確答案。
- 選項 (C)「Okay, I'll make sure first.」內提到的重要訊息「make sure」說的是「要先確認」，但是，看風景為何要先確認？要確認什麼樣的事呢？此回應與題目不相關，故也不能選。

題目陷阱 此句講者既然是表達風景很美之意，其後面的「isn't it?」有徵求對方同意的意味。那麼若是答案與「表達對風景之看法」無關的，或僅是將題中關鍵字再重複一次，卻沒提到「風景美不美」相關回應者，都不會是答案。比方說：

➡ Jenny's daughter is beautiful.（珍妮的女兒很漂亮。）

此句僅重複關鍵字「beautiful」，是在形容「daughter」，但題目的 beautiful 是在討論「view」。形容的主體和題目不一致，所以不會是正確答案。

➡ I understand your point of view.（我了解你的觀點。）

此句內以「point of view（觀點、看法）」片語來混淆考生。雖然有出現「view」，卻不是題中所提及的「風景」之意，意思和題目的不相符，故此選項僅是陷阱。

在旅遊時看到美麗的風景，我們通常會以中文意思直接聯想到「beautiful」一字來形容。但是除了這個字之外，還有更多的說法，不只可以在日常生活中應用到，在多益聽力測驗內更是會經常聽到的：

➡ Wow, that's a picturesque village.
（哇，那真是如畫般的美麗村莊。）

➡ My trip to Grand Canyon was incredible.
（我的大峽谷之旅真令我難忘。）

➡ It was a such a breathtaking adventure.
（那真是個令人驚艷不已的冒險。）

➡ I was totally amazed by the force of nature.
（我被自然的力量震撼住了。）

➡ The ocean view was absolutely tremendous.
（海洋景觀的確令人咋舌。）

➡ We had a terrific vacation in Florida.
（我們在佛羅里達度過一個很棒的假期。）

關鍵字彙

afraid [ə`fred] a 害怕的
breathtaking [`brɛθˌtekɪŋ] a 令人屏息的

Mark your answer on your answer sheet.

(A)　　(B)　　(C)

解題分析

是或否 57%

動作 43%

■ 是或否 57%

■ 動作 43%

本題也是附加問句的題目，此類句型都是以後面的問句強調前面的敘述，大部分的回答為「是」跟「否」兩種。

附加問句前面的敘述非常重要，要仔細聽才不會錯過問題的關鍵。例如本題是在尋求對方同意「協助關門」，所以本題的動作需要針對動作，回答「可以幫忙關門」或是「不能幫忙關門」兩種，動作不符合前面敘述的關鍵的就不是答案。

聽稿

（AU / Ⓦ）

Please close the door, would you?
(A) Sure, no problem.
(B) No, I don't mind at all.
(C) Yes, please come in.

中譯

（澳 / Ⓩ）

你可以將門關起來嗎，拜託？（答案：A）
(A) 好的，沒問題。
(B) 不，我完全不介意。
(C) 是的，請進來。

解題技巧　若遇到附加問句的題目，要注意的是：附加問句前的訊息很重要，務必聽清楚。此題問的是「Please close the door, would you?」，那麼關鍵問題點便落在「close the door」上面，可以預設答案的最大可能性會落在「好的，我幫忙關門」上。另外，整個問題的關鍵之處也會以加強重音來呈現，分別是「close」和「door」。準確地抓到問題點是選取正確答案的第一步。那麼根據問題點，便可預期此題的合理回應便要與「協助關上門」符合。

> 各選項解析

- 選項 (A)「Sure, no problem.」的重要訊息很明顯是「沒問題」，是個可以針對問題的適當回應，故為正確答案。
- 選項 (B)「No, I don't mind at all.」內提到了「不介意」，卻沒有提到是不是不介意「可以幫忙關門」一事，沒有直接針對問題回答，故不能選。
- 選項 (C)「Yes, please come in.」內的有個關鍵字，提到了「請進」，這並非針對題目問的「可否幫忙關門」應有的回應，故不選。

題目陷阱 此題問的是「是否可幫忙關門」，那麼若不是「可以」或「不行」等相關答案者，或是僅將題目中的關鍵字重複唸一次，而沒提到「關門」一事者，都可能僅是陷阱，絕對不是針對題目回應的答案。舉例來說：

➡ Please open the door and let fresh air in.（請將門打開，讓空氣流通。）

此句內雖然重複了關鍵字「door」，但這句話並沒有直接回應到題目所問的「請幫忙關門」之要求，反而是又提出了一個相反的要求，要求把門打開，完全與題目不相符，是一個明顯的陷阱。

➡ Let's close the deal today.（我們今天就要結案。）

此句內故意以「close」一字來混淆考生。仔細一看可以發現：「close the deal」這個片語為「結案」之意，與題目中的「close」雖然同字，但意思不相同，所以也不能選為答案。

此題內所提及的「close the door」在其他的前後文中也有不同的意思喔，請看例句：

➡ The manager closed the door on future negotiations.
（經理斷絕了未來協商的可能性。）

此處「close the door on something」片語如同表面意思「關上大門」一般，意即「斷絕可能性」之意。

另外，若 close 與其他字搭配，會產生不同的意思，比方說：

❶ close the books（公司）關帳、結束一個任務

➡ I'm glad to close the books on this case.（我很高興此案子告一段落了。）

❷ close down（生意）收攤、關閉

➡ The recession has closed many business down.
（很多公司在不景氣中都關門大吉了。）

❸ close eyes to something 對～視而不見、刻意迴避

➡ You can't just close your eyes to your problem. Stand up and deal with it.
（你不能對你的問題視而不見，起身處理吧。）

❹ too close to call 難分伯仲

➡ The competition is actually too close to call.（這場比賽真是難分伯仲呀！）

❺ close, but no cigar 很接近，但差一點就能成功

➡ The ball was close but no cigar.（那球差點就進了，但最後還是沒成功。）

關鍵字彙

mind [maɪnd] v 介意

Mark your answer on your answer sheet.

(A)　　(B)　　(C)

解題分析

是或否 55%

動作 32%

地點 13%

■ 是或否 55%　聽到附加問句，必須將注意集中在前面直述句的關鍵詞上，答案必須與題目的關鍵相符，而且大多都是「是 / 否」的回答。

■ 動作 32%　答案必須針對問題的關鍵回應，像本題是詢問「是否去過日本」，答案一定要是「有去過」或「沒去過」其中一種。有些選項會重複題目中出現的字混淆考生，這時候絕不能上當，一定要選動作與問題完全符合的答案。

■ 地點 13%　因為問題有出現「日本」這個地點，聽答案時一定要留意選項中的地名是否與此符合，平常也要多熟記不同國家、不同地區的英文地名，對於回答題目會更有利。

聽稿

（UK / M ）

Ms. Wilson has been to Japan, hasn't she?

(A) Yes, Ms. Wilson lives in New York.

(B) Yes, she's been there several times.

(C) No, William is not from Japan.

中譯

（英 / 男 ）

威爾森小姐有去過日本，沒有嗎？（答案：B）

(A) 是的，威爾森小姐住紐約。

(B) 是的，她去過數次了。

(C) 不是，威廉不是日本人。

解題技巧

聽到題目的同時，馬上應將注意力集中到聽關鍵問題字上，以便判斷可能的答案。此題問的是：「Ms. Wilson has been to Japan, hasn't she?」，要點便落在「has been to Japan」上，可以聽出講者認為 Ms. Wilson 是去過日本的。聽出關鍵點後，那麼可預期的答案便可能會出現「是，她的確去過」，或是「不，她沒有去過」等可能性。另外，此題目的重音在「been to Japan」上，也就是題目的關鍵之處。知道這一題要問的是什麼之後，便可仔細地聽三個選項中有沒有出現「有去過」或「沒去過」的可能答案上。

各選項解析

- 選項 (A)「Yes, Ms. Wilson lives in New York.」內提到了正確的人名和地點，要小心的是，選項 (A) 裡的地點是「in New York」，但題目問的是「Japan」。因此，此回應沒有針對題目的地點做出正確回答，故不選。
- 選項 (B)「Yes, she's been there several times.」內關鍵點有「yes」，和相關的訊息「several times」，這個選項意思為「是的，她已去過日本好幾次」。有針對題目回答，故為正確答案。
- 選項 (C)「No, William is not from Japan.」內的重要訊息是「not from Japan」，即為「不是從日本來的，不是日本人」之意，雖說有重複唸到 Japan 一字，但此選項的人名錯誤，回應內容也與題目無直接關係，故不選。

題目陷阱 此題講者主要認為「Ms. Wilson 有去過日本」，那麼若非是回應「是」或「否」，亦或是僅將題中關鍵字重唸一次，卻無針對問題回應的答案，都是陷阱所在喔！比方説：

➡ Yes, she's been working for two years.（是的，她已工作兩年了。）

此句內刻意地提到「yes」，還將「she has been」提了一次，但整句話卻沒有提及「Japan」，也跟日本毫無關係，故僅算是重複關鍵字的陷阱。

➡ No, I don't understand Japanese at all.（不，我完全不懂日文。）

此句內刻意地提及「Japanese」，目的是想讓考生將之與「Japan」聯想在一起。但別忘了題目是在討論有沒有去過日本，並非討論懂不懂日文，兩者討論的主題不同，故此選項為陷阱。

此處題目中提到了「Japan（日本）」，便可以猜想選項中可能以「Japanese（日文）」來混淆視聽。除了此字之外，我們也整理出幾個比較常考的國家名稱，還有其名詞和形容詞。

國家	名詞	形容詞
The United States of America 美國	American 美國人	American 美國的
Asia 亞洲	Asian 亞洲人	Asian 亞洲的
Australia 澳大利亞、澳洲	Australian 澳洲人	Australian 澳洲的
Canada 加拿大	Canadian 加拿大人	Canadian 加拿大的
China 中國	Chinese 中國人	Chinese 中國的
Denmark 丹麥	Dane 丹麥人	Danish 丹麥的
Europe 歐洲	European 歐洲人	European 歐洲的
Germany 德國	German 德國人	German 德國的
Italy 義大利	Italian 義大利人	Italian 義大利的
Korea 韓國	Korean 韓國人	Korean 韓國的
The Netherlands 荷蘭	The Dutch 荷蘭人	Dutch 荷蘭的
The Philippines 菲律賓	Filipino 菲律賓人	Filipino 菲律賓的
Sweden 瑞典	Swede 瑞典人	Swedish 瑞典的
Switzerland 瑞士	Swiss 瑞士人	Swiss 瑞士的
Thailand 泰國	Thai 泰國人	Thai 泰國的

請看以下以 Denmark 為例的例句。若是換成其他國家、名詞、形容詞，皆可代入類推：

➡ Copenhagen is the capital of Denmark.
（哥本哈根是丹麥的首都。）

➡ The Danes are the happiest people on the planet.
（丹麥人是世界上最快樂的民族。）

➡ Some people think that Danish language is very difficult to learn.
（有些人認為丹麥語很難學。）

關鍵字彙

several [ˋsɛvərəl] a 數個、一些、若干

Unit 9 選擇問句題型

Mark your answer on your answer sheet.
(A)　　(B)　　(C)

解題分析

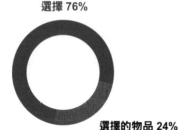

選擇 76%

選擇的物品 24%

■ 選擇 76%

■ 選擇的物品 24%

Which 開頭的問句，非常有可能跟「選擇」有關，但是這類的題目光看句首並不能掌握問題的全貌，像本題後面的 tea 跟 coffee 也是關鍵，幫助將選擇的範圍明確規範為咖啡跟茶的「二擇一」。

因為問題有明確指出選擇範圍，所以選擇的物品一定要符合題目中所列出來的，例如本題就必須選擇咖啡或茶其中一個，或是可以選擇兩個都不要，但絕對不能與問題毫無關聯。

聽稿
（AU / W）

Which do you prefer, tea or coffee?
(A) Why can't I have both?
(B) Tea sounds wonderful, thank you.
(C) Okay, let me mull it over.

中譯
（澳 / 女）

你想喝什麼，茶或咖啡？（答案：B）
(A) 為何我不能兩種都喝？
(B) 茶聽起來不錯，謝謝。
(C) 好的，讓我仔細想想。

解題技巧　遇到這類題目，光是聽問題的第一個字是不夠的，會發生資訊不足的狀況。聽到題目的同時，也應將注意力放在聽問題關鍵點上，以便判斷可能的答案方向。此題問的「Which do you prefer, tea or coffee?」，很明確地是詢問在「tea」和「coffee」兩者中選一。那麼可能的答案會是選 tea 或選 coffee；當然也有可能想選其他的，比方說選「water」的答案。另外，這個問題的重要訊息會以加重音的方式呈現，此問句的重音呈現如：「Which **do** you **prefer**, **tea** or **coffee**?」。在了解問題想要詢問的點後，接下來要將注意力放在聽有沒有二擇一的選項上。

各選項解析

- 選項 (A)「Why can't I have both?」內關鍵點提到「both」，整句乍聽之下似乎也沒錯，但人在一般狀況之下，應該不會將茶和咖啡同時混在一起喝吧，因此此答案並非最佳選擇。
- 選項 (B)「Tea sounds wonderful, thank you.」內關鍵訊息很明顯是「tea... thank you」，隱藏的意思其實是「給我茶，謝謝」，有針對問題回答，故為正確答案。
- 選項 (C)「Okay, let me mull it over.」內有個大家比較不熟悉的片語「mull over」，為「仔細琢磨、反覆思量」之意，但只是咖啡和茶在選擇的情境，正常來說，不需要經過很久的思考才對，故此選項也非最佳答案。

題目陷阱 此題問的是在「coffee」和「tea」之間二選一，那麼若非「兩者選一」者，或是僅刻意地提及題中關鍵字，卻沒針對問題回答者，都可能是陷阱。請看以下例句：

➡ Well, <u>neither</u>. I actually like that red jacket.
（嗯，兩個都不要，我其實喜歡那件紅夾克。）

此句說「neither」，當然在 coffee 和 tea 之間的選擇也是有可能兩個都不要，若是回應說想要喝「juice（果汁）」也是合理的。但此句卻說了「that red jacket」，變成在討論「紅色外套」了！完全偏離掉題目所問的了，故為陷阱。

➡ Well, he is not my cup of <u>tea</u>.（嗯，他不是我的菜。）

此句雖然有提到和題目相同的關鍵字「tea」，但此回應使用到的慣用語「not my cup of tea」卻有完全不同的意思，這個慣用語的意思為「不是我喜歡的類型」，沒有針對問題做出適當的回應。

此題內提到的「coffee（咖啡）」和「tea（茶）」，相信大家一定都知道這兩個字。但是，當老闆說「Your proposal is rather weak tea.」是什麼意思呢？以下為「coffee（咖啡）」和「tea（茶）」常見的慣用語，學起來後就能聽懂更道地的英文喔！

❶ not someone's cup of tea 不是～喜歡的類型、不是某人的菜
➡ This novel is <u>not my cup of tea</u>.
（這本小說不是我喜歡看的類型。）

❷ weak tea 索然無味、平淡無奇
➡ Well, this proposal for reducing the number of employees is rather <u>weak tea</u>.
（嗯，此份提及要裁員的計畫案了無新意。）

❸ all the tea in China 天大的好處、無價的事物
➡ I wound't get married for <u>all the tea in China</u>.
（就算給我天大的好處我都不想結婚。）

❹ wake up and smell the coffee 腦筋放清醒點
➡ Jerry, <u>wake up and smell the coffee</u>! We start to lose our customer base.
（傑瑞，清醒點，趕緊做點事吧！我們開始流失客群了。）

關鍵字彙

prefer [prɪ`fɜ] ⓥ 寧願、較喜歡
sound [saʊnd] ⓥ 聽起來
wonderful [`wʌndɚfəl] ⓐ 很棒的
mull over ⓟ 仔細思考

Mark your answer on your answer sheet.

(A)　　(B)　　(C)

解題分析

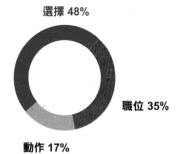

選擇 48%

職位 35%

動作 17%

■ 選擇 48%　本題的開頭 would you rather be 是一種詢問選擇的句型，關鍵字為 rather，因此回答必須從題目所列出的選項挑選出一個，才是正確的。

■ 職位 35%　題目是詢問「業務代表」跟「行銷專員」當中，要選哪一個，此時具備相關單字的知識是非常重要的，如果不知道這些職務跟領域的英文是什麼，可能就聽不懂題目了。而且，答案可能不會僅重複題目的名詞，也許會換一種說法，要小心不要混淆。

■ 動作 17%　要注意答案選項的動作有沒有跟題目的方向相符，有些選項會重複題目的關鍵字，例如 sales rep 或 marketing specialist，但是如果沒有針對題目回答，就可能是混淆考生的陷阱。

聽稿
（UK / M）

Would you rather be a sales rep or marketing specialist?
(A) Well, I used to work as a sales rep.
(B) Our products sell like hot cakes.
(C) I'm passionate about marketing.

中譯
（英 / 男）

你比較想當業務代表還是行銷專員？（答案：C）
(A) 嗯，我之前當過業務代表。
(B) 我們產品很熱賣。
(C) 我對行銷抱持熱情。

解題技巧

聽到題目且要選到相配合的答案，便務必要先了解題目的關鍵問題點，才有可能針對其問題點回應。此題問的是「Would you rather be a sales rep or marketing specialist?」，關鍵問題點便會是在「sales rep」和「marketing specialist」兩者中二選一了。那麼可預期的答案便會是在兩者中擇一，或甚至會有還想當「其他職位」的可能。此題的關鍵點會以加強重音來呈現：「Would you rather be a sales rep or marketing specialist?」，「rather」、「sales rep」、「specialist」則是這一題的關鍵點。在知道了此題想問的關鍵之後，便可將注意力放在聽「rep」和「specialist」二選一的可能答案上了。

各選項解析

• 選項 (A)「Well, I used to work as a sales rep.」內容雖然說有提到關鍵字「sales rep」，但其實「used to work...」意即「一度、曾經當過」，所以現在並不是業務了。但因為此題問的是想當哪一個，因此這個選項沒有針對問題做出適當的回應，故不選。

• 選項 (B)「Our products sell like hot cakes.」內有一個頗有趣的慣用語「sell like hot cakes」，即為「熱賣商品」的意思。可以想像商品好似剛出爐的蛋糕，一推出就被買光的感覺。雖然這個選項中出現與題目關鍵點有關的「product」，但是並沒有針對此二擇一的問題來回應，僅是敘述情況而已，所以也不選。

• 選項 (C)「I'm passionate about marketing.」內有一個片語「be passionate about something」，是「對某事有熱誠」的涵義，後續又提到「marketing」，的確有在 sales 和 marketing 之中二選一，因此有針對問題回答，故選為正確答案。

題目陷阱 此題明顯是問在「sales rep」和「marketing specialist」兩者當中擇一。那麼若非「二選一」；或僅是重複唸題目關鍵字,卻沒有針對問題回答者,都可能是陷阱而非答案。舉例來說:

➡ I'm looking forward to the annual <u>marketing</u> conference.
（我期待參加年度行銷會議。）

此句內重複題目中的關鍵字「marketing」,乍聽之下很像是正確答案,但仔細聽後面的訊息就會發現:這裡的「marketing」是在說「行銷研討會」,而非指想當「行銷專員」。雖然都是「marketing」,但指的事物或事件不同,因此不會是正確答案。

➡ I need to talk to one of your <u>sales representatives</u>.
（我要跟你們業務代表談談。）

此句內提到「sales representative」,但題目並非問「要與誰談」的 who 開頭類問題,而是在問「要選哪個職位」,故此選項也沒有針對問題回答。

此題句型為「Would you rather be...」。有時候常常會聽到同學說「I would rather to be a teacher.」,但是請注意,有一些片語之後的「to」應該要省略喔!例如:had rather（寧願）、would rather（寧願）、had better（最好）、do nothing but（只是）等字詞後面的「to」要記得省略。

➡ I would rather go out to work than stay home all day.
（我寧願出去工作也不願整天待在家裡。）
➡ You had better depend on yourself.（你最好靠自己吧。）
➡ The old man did nothing but sleep all day long.
（那老人整天什麼都沒做只顧睡覺。）

另外,此題目的回應句也可套用到下列不同的句型來表達:

I <u>prefer to</u> be a sales representative <u>rather than</u> work as a marketing specialist.

= I <u>prefer</u> working as a sales representative <u>to</u> being a marketing specialist.

= I <u>would</u> work as a sales representative <u>rather than</u> work as a marketing specialist.

= I <u>would rather</u> work as a sales representative <u>than</u> work as a marketing specialist.

（我比較想當業務代表,而不想當行銷專員。）

關鍵字彙

specialist [ˋspɛʃəlɪst] n. 專員、專門人才
sell like hot cakes ph. 熱銷
passionate [ˋpæʃənɪt] a. 有熱忱的

Mark your answer on your answer sheet.

(A)　　(B)　　(C)

解題分析

選擇 74%

地點 26%

■ 選擇 74%　本題的關鍵字是 prefer，目的在詢問對方的選擇。大部分的答案會針對問題的選項擇一，但是也可以像本題一樣選擇兩個都不要。

■ 地點 26%　由於題目是詢問會面的「地點」，不管是選本題的 Gate 4、Gate 6，或是兩個都不要，提出另外的選項，都必須回答到「地點」才算符合題目的方向。

聽稿
（US / Ⓦ）

Would you prefer to meet at Gate 4 or Gate 6?
(A) Well, how about meeting at Gate 8?
(B) I like both actually.
(C) My flight departs at 4.

中譯
（美 / 女）

你想在四號還是六號登機口碰面？（答案：A）
(A) 嗯，那在八號登機口碰面好嗎？
(B) 我其實兩個都喜歡。
(C) 我那班飛機四點起飛。

解題技巧

在作答 Part 2 題目的同時，務必有意識地將焦點放在聽問題關鍵點上，以期可以判斷答案的可能方向。此題問的是「Would you prefer to meet at Gate 4 or Gate 6?」，很明顯可以判斷是在問會面的地點，並且是「Gate 4」和「Gate 6」當中二選一。要注意的一點是，可能出現的答案包括「Gate 4」或「Gate 6」，甚至於可能是「其他閘門」等選項。另外，此句想加強的要點重音會落在：「Would you prefer to meet at Gate 4 or Gate 6?」。在了解題目的問題點之後，便可將注意力放在聽可相符的答案上了。

各選項解析

- 選項 (A)「Well, how about meeting at Gate 8?」內的關鍵點「how about... Gate 8」可聽出是提出第三個選項，也就是「在八號登機口碰面」之意，的確也是針對題目可能會出現的回應沒錯，所以為正確答案。
- 選項 (B)「I like both actually.」內的重要訊息是「both」，提到兩個都要。但正常來說，和對方約會面的地點，不太可能同時出現在 Gate 4，又出現在 Gate 6！因此這個選項不是很合理、不合邏輯，所以不能選來當作答案。
- 選項 (C)「My flight departs at 4.」內的主要訊息為「時間」，此選項提到班機四點起飛，但無法回應題目所問，是為答非所問的選項，故也不選。

題目陷阱 　此題既然是要在 Gate 4 與 Gate 6 兩個登機門中擇一，若非是回答其中一個、或其他選擇或是僅重複題目出現過的字，卻沒提到與登機門相關答案者，都可能是陷阱。例如：

➡ The duty free shop is right next to <u>Gate 1</u>.（免稅商店就在一號登機口旁邊。）

　此句雖然有提到 Gate 1 這個與題目關鍵訊息相關的選擇，但此回應卻是在講免稅店的位置，而非會面的位置，地點與題目不符，故不會是正確選項。

➡ <u>Gate 4</u> is really far away from here.（四號登機口離此處很遠。）

　此句內關鍵點的確有提到 Gate 4，這句回應卻比較偏向在講距離遠近。但不管登機口距離遠近，要搭機的話就是要前往呀！因此，此句沒有做出適當的回應，不能算是有針對問題回應。

➡ I'm looking forward to <u>meeting</u> you on May 4th.（我期望在五月四日與你見面。）

　此句重複題目關鍵字「meet」，且還刻意以「4th」混淆視聽，儘管如此，這個選項並沒有針對在問位置的問題回應，因此也不會是正確選項。

另外，上面提到的「I'm looking forward to meeting you on May 4th.」一句中有片語「look forward to」，此片語和下列常考片語中的「to」都是當介系詞用，後面應該要接 V-ing 動名詞做為受詞，而非接原形動詞喔！

❶ admit to 承認

➡ The boy <u>admitted to</u> stealing the money.（小男孩承認偷了那筆錢。）

❷ be addicted to 沉溺於

➡ Young people nowadays <u>are addicted to</u> playing online games.
（現在年輕人都沉溺於玩線上遊戲。）

❸ object to 拒絕

➡ I <u>object to</u> obeying unreasonable rules.（我拒絕遵從不合理的規定。）

❹ be accustomed to 習慣於

➡ I'<u>m accustomed to</u> working the graveyard shift.（我已習慣上大夜班了。）

❺ be dedicated to 致力於

➡ The teacher <u>is dedicated to</u> enhancing students' language ability.
（那老師致力於加強學生的語言能力。）

關鍵字彙

actually [ˋæktʃʊəlɪ] ad 事實上、實際地
depart [dɪˋpɑrt] v 啟程、出發、起飛

Mark your answer on your answer sheet.

(A)　　　(B)　　　(C)

解題分析

選擇 73%

物品 27%

- ■ 選擇 73%　本題的題目雖然較長，但仍然可清楚聽出重點是在「藍色上衣」與「紅色上衣」之間做出「選擇」，因此選項中有明確選出上述物品的，有很高的機率是正確解答。

- ■ 物品 27%　答案的方向必須與題目符合，有時會重複題目中出現的字詞來混淆考生，例如本題選項 (A) 雖然提到了一件衣物，但卻不是問題所問的「上衣」，要仔細分辨句子裡所指的物品是否前後一致，才不會上當。

聽稿

（CA / M）

Do you think I should buy this blue shirt or that red one?
(A) I prefer to buy that black jacket.
(B) I don't have the budget for both.
(C) Well, the red one looks better.

中譯

（加 / 男）

你認為我應該買藍色上衣還是紅色那件？（答案：C）
(A) 我想買那件黑色夾克。
(B) 我沒有預算兩件都買。
(C) 嗯，紅色那件看起來較好。

解題技巧

馬上將注意力放在聽問題關鍵點上，是作答這類題目最主要的關鍵，如此一來才能選到最正確、最適當的答案。此題問的是：「Do you think I should buy this blue shirt or that red one?」，雖然說問題的句子有點長，但焦點非常明顯，就是要在「blue shirt」和「red one」兩者之中選一個。那麼可預期的答案會是兩者中的一個，或甚至有「兩件都買」或「兩色都不要，選其他顏色」等其他可能性。接著來注意本題的關鍵點，重音會是在：「Do you think I should buy this blue shirt or that red one?」。也唯有在知曉問題的關鍵點之後，才有可能預測答案的可能方向。

各選項解析

- 選項 (A)「I prefer to buy that black jacket.」內提到「要買那件黑色夾克」，但題目是「紅色和藍色上衣」在做選擇，因此，此選項回答的方向和題目不同，故不選。
- 選項 (B)「I don't have budget for both.」內的主要訊息是「don't have budget」，即為「沒預算」的意思。但題目並非在問錢夠不夠的問題，選項回答的與題目走向不合，故此選項也並非最佳答案。
- 選項 (C)「Well, the red one looks better.」內的關鍵點「red... better」，意即「紅色較好看」，的確有針對問題做出適當的回應，故為正確答案。

題目陷阱 此題是在「blue shirt」和「red shirt」之間二擇一，那麼，若非回答「二選一」，或是重複了關鍵字，卻不見得是在回答問題的選項，都不算是答案。比方說：

➡ I think the blue car is pretty awesome.（我認為那藍色的車很奇特。）

此處雖然提到關鍵點「blue」，討論的主體卻是「car」，而非題目所問的「shirt」，故「blue」僅是一個混淆因子。

➡ Well, I think you should buy just one.（我認為你應買一件就好。）

此句內重複「buy（ 購買）」一字，但回應的要點卻是放在「買幾件」上面，提及說要「買一件」，仍然沒回答是「哪一件」，故也是陷阱。

此題提到了顏色「red」與「blue」，其實許多使用在商業活動上、或是多益題目也常考的用語，都跟顏色有關喔！請參考以下常見顏色的商業用語：

❶ in the red 赤字、負債、虧損

➡ The company has been in the red for five years.
（公司已經連續虧損五年了。）

❷ black and white 白紙黑字

➡ I won't believe we've won the agreement until I see it down black and white.
（我要看到白紙黑字寫下來，我才會相信我們贏得合約了。）

❸ red carpet 紅地毯、隆重接待

➡ We have to roll out the red carpet for that important client.
（我們要特別禮遇那個重要的客戶。）

❹ in the black 賺錢、有盈餘

➡ Our company is finally back in the black.
（我們公司終於轉虧為盈了。）

❺ out of the blue 突如其來地

➡ Then out of the blue, he offered me pay increase.
（他突然給我加薪，超乎我意料之外。）

關鍵字彙

prefer [prɪˋfɝ] v 寧願、較喜歡
budget [ˋbʌdʒɪt] n 預算

Mark your answer on your answer sheet.

(A)　　(B)　　(C)

解題分析

選擇 79%

職位 21%

■ 選擇 79%

■ 職位 21%

本題的重點是問「陳先生」跟「林小姐」哪一位會在會議中當主席，答案有可能為兩個選項中擇一，或是兩個都不選的第三個選項。但要注意，不管是選哪一個人，其職位一定要符合題目的方向才正確。

對於人名，應該較不容易聽錯，但是如果答案選項的人名符合，職位或工作內容卻與題目不相關，就很容易不小心選錯，因此要熟記相關的詞彙，才不會掉進陷阱裡。

聽稿

（CA / M）

Will Mr. Chen or Ms. Lin take the chair?
(A) Mr. Chen is in charge of marketing.
(B) I think Ms. Lin will.
(C) They're both good managers.

中譯

（加 / 男）

是陳先生還是林小姐會當主席？（答案：**B**）
(A) 陳先生負責行銷。
(B) 我想是林小姐吧。
(C) 他們兩個都是好經理。

解題技巧

此句問的是：「Will Mr. Chen or Ms. Lin take the chair?」，便可判斷關鍵點即為要在「Mr. Chen」和「Ms. Lin」兩者中擇一；另外，題目中出現的「take the chair」是在會議中「主持會議」之意。那麼，我們就可以預期答案會有「陳先生」、「林小姐」或「另有他人」等可能。且此句的關鍵要點「Mr. Chen」和「Ms. Lin」會以加強重音來強調。在聽到題目想問的關鍵點後，便可將注意力放在聽有自兩人中選一人的選項上來當作答案。

各選項解析

- 選項 (A)「Mr. Chen is in charge of marketing.」內雖說有提到「Mr. Chen」沒錯，但後面的訊息提到的「in charge of marketing」為「負責行銷」之意，如此並沒有針對「誰主持會議」的問題回答，故不能選。
- 選項 (B)「I think Ms. Lin will.」內的關鍵點是「Ms. Lin will」，即「林小姐會主持會議」之意，有針對問題回答，故為正確答案。
- 選項 (C)「They're both good managers.」提到「both good managers」，意即「兩個都是好經理」；但題目並非問「哪個好」，因此此回應的回答方向與題目需要的不符，故不能選。

題目陷阱 此題很明顯是要在「Mr. Chen」和「Ms. Lin」二者當中擇一的題目。若是選項中不是二選一，或僅是故意將關鍵字重唸一次，而完全沒有針對題目回答者，都可能是陷阱。請看以下例子：

➡ Mr. Chen will talk about sales progress.（陳先生會討論業務進度。）

雖然這個回應中有出現「Mr. Chen」的關鍵字，但其後卻是「討論業務」，而非題目所問的「take the chair（當主席）」。雖然主詞有符合題目，但事件和題目的不符，因此根本不算有針對問題回答。

➡ Please don't move the chair.（請不要移動椅子。）

此句刻意提及關鍵字「the chair」，但題目中的「take the chair」是在會議中「主持會議」的意思，並不是真的「搬椅子」。所以，「the chair」很明顯是混淆因子罷了。

此題目中使用「take the chair」一詞，是為「當主席、主持會議」之意，事實上在商業會議中，還會使用到很多類似的慣用語，常見與常考的將列在下方：

➡ adjourn the meeting 結束會議

➡ call a meeting to order 開始會議

➡ call on (someone) to speak 請（某人）發言

➡ carry a motion 提出動議

➡ circulate the agenda 將議程傳下去

➡ conduct a meeting 主持會議

➡ hold the floor 有發言權

➡ lay (something) on the table 提出討論議題

➡ bring (ideas) to the table 展現出、搬到檯面上

➡ take meeting minutes 做會議記錄

關鍵字彙

take the chair ph 主持會議
in charge of ph 負責、承擔～責任

Unit 10 直述句題型

攻略 1 │ 建議與附和

Mark your answer on your answer sheet.
(A)　　(B)　　(C)

解題分析

附和 83%

建議 17%

■ 附和 83%

回答本題之前須掌握題目的意思，在這個直述句當中，說明會議不只冗長還持續了三個小時，很明顯為抱怨，可能的回答方向就是順著說話者的意思附和，表示這個會議真的很長、很累人等等。

■ 建議 17%

既然題目是抱怨，回應也有可能是針對說話者的困擾提出解決的建議，但是要確定此建議是否有回答到題目的關鍵，如果回應不相干或不合理，是正確答案的機率很低。

聽稿
（US / **W**）

The long meeting lasted three hours.
(A) Really? You must be exhausted.
(B) Okay, good to hear that.
(C) Why don't you take a vacation?

中譯
（美 / **女**）

那冗長的會議開了三個小時。（答案：**A**）
(A) 真的嗎？你們一定很累吧。
(B) 好的，很高興聽到此事。
(C) 你何不去度個假呢？

解題技巧

在作答多益測驗 Part 2 時，播放題目的同時，考生應該立即將注意力集中到聽問題的關鍵點上。此直述句描述的是：「The long meeting lasted three hours.」，可聽出最關鍵的訊息是在抱怨「冗長會議開了三個小時」。那麼有機會成為正確選項的答案可能是「附和三個小時的會議真的很久、又很累人」等。另外，句中要點之處會以加強重音來強調：「The long meeting lasted three hours.」。在聽出關鍵點之後，才有可能知道要將注意力放在什麼樣的回應上頭。

各選項解析

- 選項 (A)「Really? You must be exhausted.」內關鍵點為「must be exhausted」，提及「那一定很累吧」，的確是可能出現在開了冗長三個小時的會議之後的反應，可以看出這個選項有針對問題回應，故選為最佳答案。
- 選項 (B)「Okay, good to hear that.」內提到「很高興聽到此消息」這樣的回答，針對一個包含抱怨成分在內的句子來說，這個選項顯得不是很合理，不是一個適當的回應，所以以不能選。
- 選項 (C)「Why don't you take a vacation?」內建議到「take a vacation」，說要去度假，一般企業上班族的 vacation 通常會是在夏天或年底假期時做妥善的規劃和安排，通常不會是只因為開了一個很久的會議之後就來個度假的，故此選項也不是很合理。

題目陷阱 此直述句在描述的是「三小時的冗長會議」，若非針對此事做出合宜的回應，或僅是重複唸出關鍵字，內容卻與冗長會議無關者，都可以是被歸類為陷阱之處。以下舉出數個例子：

➡ Three hours of sleep is not enough for an adult.
（三小時的睡眠對成人來說是不夠的。）

此句是有提及 three hours 關鍵之處，但卻是在描述「sleep」，而非題目中的「meeting」。由於敘述的主體不同於題目所表達的，故不會是答案。

➡ I didn't join the meeing last night.（我沒參加昨晚的會議。）

此句有提到「meeting」，但刻意以「last night」來與題中的「last（持續）」混淆，題目中也並非在問「是否參與昨晚會議」一事，回答的方向不同於題目，故也不會是正確答案。

此題內關鍵點之一為「冗長」一事，在英文中除了用「last long」來代表「持續很久」之外，還可能有以下幾種表達方式，這些在職場上或多益聽力測驗內都是經常出現的喔！

❶ forever and a day 很久很久（直譯為「比永遠多一天」）

➡ Hi, Jim. It's been forever and a day since I last saw you.
（嗨，吉姆，距離我上次看到你已經超久了啊！）

❷ a month of Sundays 很久

➡ The little girl hadn't seen her family in a month of Sundays.
（那小女孩好久都沒見到她家人了。）

❸ days / weeks / months / years on end 經過很久時間

➡ We don't see each other for weeks on end, but we're still best friends.
（我們好久都沒見面，但還是最好的朋友。）

❹ a dog's age 很久的時間

➡ It's been a dog's age since I raised children.
（我養育小孩已經是好久以前之事了。）

❺ ages 久遠

➡ Hey, Jerry. I haven't seen you for ages. How's everything?
（嘿，傑瑞，好久沒看到你了，你還好嗎？）

關鍵字彙

last [læst] v 持續、維持
exhausted [ɪgˈzɔstɪd] a 極累的、累壞的
vacation [veˈkeʃən] n 假期、度假

攻略 2 | 說服與事件

Mark your answer on your answer sheet.

(A)　　(B)　　(C)

解題分析

同意、附和 44%

說服 31%

事件、情境 25%

■ **同意、附和 44%** 　本題的關鍵是開頭的 I can't believe，傳達出無法置信的語氣，所以其中一個回答方式可以是附和意見。

■ **說服 31%** 　除了順著他人的語氣附和外，也有可能以「沒辦法、就接受吧」這種說法說服對方，不過要注意回答的內容要針對題目的敘述回應。

■ **事件、情境 25%** 　題目的主題是在談論「產品的保固期」只有三個月，所以回答時必須針對題目的方向，也就是保固期很短這件事做出回應。

聽稿

（UK / **M**）

I can't believe the product warranty is only valid for three months.
(A) You should bring a valid passport with you.
(B) No way. It should be at least a year, right?
(C) I think the price is reasonable enough.

中譯

（英 / **男**）

我無法相信這產品保固期僅三個月。（答案：B）
(A) 你應該隨身攜帶有效的護照。
(B) 不會吧，至少要有一年吧，對嗎？
(C) 我認為價格算合理了。

解題技巧　聽到題目的同時，馬上將焦點放在句子的關鍵點上，以便預期可能的答案。此題目問的是：「I can't believe the product warranty is only valid for three months.」，而句子當中「I can't believe...」的句型有「驚嘆、無法置信」的語氣在內，判斷可能的答案方向會是「同意、真難以相信」或「沒辦法、就接受吧」等方向。而此句的關鍵點會以加強重音來呈現：「I can't believe the product warranty is only valid for three months.」。了解此句的關鍵所在之後，才有可能將注意力放在可能的回應上。

各選項解析

- 選項 (A)「You should bring a valid passport with you.」內的關鍵點是「bring... passport」，即要人家「帶護照」之意，但這與題目中提到的「產品保固期限」一事無直接關係，沒有針對題目回答，故不能選。
- 選項 (B)「No way. It should be at least a year, right?」內的關鍵點「No way」有「不會吧」表達不相信之意，而且其後又提到「should be a year」意即「至少要一年」，有針對題目所說的保固三個月太短一事做出回應，所以選為最佳答案。
- 選項 (C)「I think the price is reasonable enough.」內最重要的訊息就是「price... reasonable」，提及「價格合理」之意，但題目是在講「保固期」，並不是在討論價格是否合理，此選項與題目所問無法相對應，故不選。

題目陷阱 此直述句既然是在描述「產品保固期」，那麼與此話題無關，或僅是重複提到關鍵字者，都有可能是陷阱所在之處。舉例來說：

➡ Yeah, I purchased this <u>product three months</u> ago.
（是呀，我三個月前買這產品的。）

此句內雖然重複關鍵字「product」和「three months」，但與題目所問的不一樣，題目不是在問何時買產品，故此句沒有針對題目的設定做出適當的回應。

➡ <u>I can't believe</u> it's snowing now either.
（我也無法相信現在在下雪耶。）

此句刻意地重複關鍵點「I can't believe...」一詞，但其後面的敘述卻是在討論下雪，與題目所提的產品保固期無關，因此也是陷阱選項。

此描述以「I can't believe...」開頭來表達「我簡直無法相信～」之意，句子本身已有「很驚訝」的成分在內，因此在給出回應時，也有可能以「不會吧！」或是「真的呀！簡直難以置信！」的用語來回應。現在請參考以下針對此句、或日常生活中表達驚訝的可能回應：

➡ Really? Are you sure?（真的嗎？你確定？）

➡ Are you kidding me?（你在開玩笑吧？）

➡ No way.（不可能吧。）

➡ Get out of here.（不會吧。）

➡ You are joking, aren't you?（你在開玩笑吧？）

➡ Wow, it's unbelievable.（哇，真不敢相信。）

➡ It's hard to imagine, isn't it?（真難想像，對吧？）

➡ For sure? Oh, no!（真假？不會吧！）

關鍵字彙

warranty [`wɔrəntɪ] n 保證、擔保
valid [`vælɪd] a 有效的
at least ph 至少
reasonable [`riznəbl] a 合理的
enough [ə`nʌf] a 足夠的、充足的

Mark your answer on your answer sheet.

(A)　　(B)　　(C)

解題分析

可能的位置 79%

建議 21%

■ 可能的位置 79%

■ 建議 21%

回答本題之前要先抓出關鍵字，本題的重點在於 forget where 跟 reports，可以得知說話者忘了報告的位置，這時候回答可能有幾個方向，可能知道物品的位置或是表示不知道，要找找看等等。

當有人忘了東西放在哪裡，回答「可以到某處看看」或是「某地方找過了嗎」是合理的，但是回答的物品要跟題目的一致，否則就是答非所問。

聽稿

（CA / M）

I forgot where I put my marketing reports.

(A) Oh, that's a wonderful suggestion.

(B) Oh, they are on my desk.

(C) Oh, I totally forgot about it.

中譯

（加 / 男）

我忘記我把行銷報告放哪去了。（答案：B）

(A) 喔，那是個很棒的建議。

(B) 喔，報告在我桌上。

(C) 喔，我完全忘了這回事。

解題技巧

想要正確答題，就要先判斷可能的答案方向，必須先注意到題目的關鍵訊息，此題描述的是「I forgot where I put my marketing reports.」，要點在於「forgot... reports」，即為「忘掉將報告擺到哪去了」之意，那麼心中要先有個底需要聽到「可能在某處」或「不知道，要找找」等可能的答案。此句的要點自然也會以加強重音來呈現，這一句要將注意力放在：「forgot where」、「reports」上面。

各選項解析

- 選項 (A)「Oh, that's a wonderful suggestion.」內主要需要注意的訊息是「a wonderful suggestion」，就是「很好的建議」的意思。這個選項很明顯地無法和題目做出有邏輯的回應，因此不能選。
- 選項 (B)「Oh, they are on my desk.」內的關鍵點「on my desk」有提醒對方的意味，即為「報告在我桌上」之意，有和題目的敘述句連結到，所以為最佳答案。
- 選項 (C)「Oh, I totally forgot about it.」中最主要的訊息是「forgot about it」，但這個選項的回應僅是將題目中的「forgot」一字重複唸一次而已，沒有針對問題做出適當的回應，故不選。

題目陷阱

此題句子既然是討論到「忘了報告放哪裡」，那麼答案若非提及「可能的位置」，就不會是答案了。很多時候會聽到選項中有出現與題目重複的字眼，卻沒有針對「報告放哪」一事來回應的話，也不可能是答案。以下將列舉出常見的陷阱選項，以利各位避免選到錯誤的答案：

➡ Yeah, that 100-page report is a bit dry.（是呀，那份一百頁的報告有點枯燥。）

這一個回應內重複唸了關鍵字與題目相同的「report」，要點卻是在「dry」上面，整句話的意思是「冗長的報告很乏味」，但沒有針對「可能在哪」的要點訊息回應，故為陷阱選項。

➡ Did you check the kitchen?（你有去廚房找過了嗎？）

此回應陷阱之處在於：當有人提到「我忘了某物放哪去了」時，回答「那你去某處找過了嗎」其實是合理的，但問題就是在於題目句是說「marketing reports」，與回應句的「kitchen（廚房）」間並沒有直接的關聯性，故也是陷阱。

另外，此句內的關鍵字之一「forget」，其後可接動名詞或不定詞當受詞。也還有其他的動詞，同樣也是接動名詞或不定詞，但是接動名詞和接不定詞會有些許差異，請看下列範例：

❶ remember

➡ remember + to V 都會記得執行某個任務之意

Jones always remembers to lock the door.（瓊斯都會記得鎖門。）

➡ remember + V-ing 記得過去有發生過的事

Jones remembered locking the door.（瓊斯記得他明明有鎖門。）

❷ forget

➡ forget + to V 忘記執行某個任務之意

Linda sometimes forgets to turn off the lights.（琳達有時候會忘記關燈。）

➡ forget + V-ing 忘記過去有發生過的事

Linda forgot sending out that e-mail.（琳達忘掉自己有將電郵寄出。）

❸ regret

➡ regret + to V 為～抱歉

I regret to inform you that I need to let you go.
（我很抱歉要通知你，我要請你走路了。）

➡ regret + V-ing 後悔過去做過某事之意

I regret considering you my best friend.（我很後悔把你當成最好的朋友。）

❹ stop

➡ stop + to V 停下來、開始做某事

We should stop to take a break.（我們應該停下來，休息一下。）

➡ stop + V-ing 停止做某事

Please stop talking.（請停止講話。）

關鍵字彙

marketing [ˈmɑrkɪtɪŋ] n 行銷
wonderful [ˈwʌndɚfəl] a 很棒的、極佳的
suggestion [səˈdʒɛstʃən] n 建議、提議
totally [ˈtotl̩ɪ] ad 完全地、全部地

攻略 4 ｜ 同意與意見

Mark your answer on your answer sheet.

(A)   (B)   (C)

解題分析

同意 50%

相反意見 50%

■ 同意 50%

■ 相反意見 50%

聽到題目是一個直述句，就必須先抓住關鍵點，猜測可能的回答方向。例如本題是說「喜歡吃美式食物」，其中一種可能就是回答「我也喜歡」表示同意，並且針對特定的食物種類做出描述。

回答也有可能與題目的敘述站在相反立場，表示「喜歡別的食物」，但要注意回應必須要圍繞在食物的主題，才算是針對問題回答。

聽稿
（AU / Ｗ）

I love American food very much.
(A) What kind of food do you like?
(B) Right, American people are always direct.
(C) Me too. I especially love steaks.

中譯
（澳 / 女）

我很喜歡吃美式食物。（答案：C）
(A) 你喜歡何種食物？
(B) 是的，美國人都很直接。
(C) 我也是，我特別喜歡吃牛排。

解題技巧

聽力題目播放出來的同時，就應該在心中設定好要聽關鍵問題點，以判斷答案的方向。此直述句提到「I love American food very much.」，那麼我們便可以預期可能會出現的答案包括「同意，我也喜歡」，或是持相反意見——「我喜歡別的食物」等。另外，一定要記住的是，句子的要點通常會以加強重音來描述：「I love American food **very much.**」。當聽出了本題目的重要的訊息之後，心中便有了底要聽到與「討論食物」相關的答案才合理。

> **各選項解析**

- 選項 (A)「What kind of food do you like?」，又再問一次「你喜歡什麼食物」，但回想題目不是才剛提出「喜歡美式食物」的嗎？實在不需要再問已經得知答案的問題，所以這個選項回應不適當。
- 選項 (B)「Right, American people are always direct.」內提到「Americans... direct」，提及「美國人很直接」，這個回應與題目提及的食物話題無關，所以不能選為答案。
- 選項 (C)「Me too. I especially love steaks.」內的關鍵點很明顯是「Me too.」，言外之意是「你喜歡美式食物，我也是呀」，很明顯地可以看出這個選項有針對問題回應，故為最佳答案。

題目陷阱 此題提到「喜歡美式食物」，很多時候會聽到選項中有出現與題目重複的字眼，例如：food，卻沒有針對「喜歡美式食物」回應，就不可能是答案。以下將列舉出常見的陷阱選項，以利各位避免選到錯誤的答案：

➡ Yeah, that <u>food</u> is a bit dry.（是呀，那份食物有點乾。）

　　這一個回應內重複唸了關鍵字與題目相同的「food」，要點卻是在「dry」上面，整句話的意思是「食物很乾」，回應也與題目句子產生矛盾之意，也沒有針對「美式食物」的要點訊息回應，故為陷阱選項。

➡ I often go to <u>America</u>.（我常去美國。）

　　此回應陷阱之處在於：提到與「American」音相近的「America」，這個回應與題目完全沒有關聯性，完全沒有回答到與美式食物相關的訊息，所以是一個相似音的陷阱選項。

討論到食物，在英文用語中也有不少是與食物相關的慣用語，不僅在聽力中可能會被提及，在日常生活中更是常見。以下列舉幾個慣用語：

❶ as easy as apple pie　極為簡單

　　➡ The English test I took this morning was <u>as easy as apple pie</u>.
　　（我早上考的英文考試相單簡單。）

❷ icing on the cake　錦上添花

　　➡ Wow, free software installed in my new laptop. That's really <u>icing on the cake</u>.
　　（哇，我的新電腦內還裝免費軟體，真是錦上添花呀！）

❸ everything from soup to nuts　應有盡有、一應俱全

　　➡ I've packaged <u>everything from soup to nuts</u> into my luggage.
　　（我已將所有大大小小的物品都包進行李內了。）

❹ have a sweet tooth　嗜吃甜食

　　➡ My mother <u>has a sweet tooth</u> and she loves candies.
　　（我媽媽愛吃甜食，尤其喜歡吃糖果。）

❺ sell like hotcakes（商品）熱賣

　　➡ Our new cars have been <u>selling like hotcakes</u>.
　　（我們的新車超級熱賣。）

關鍵字彙

direct [də`rɛkt] a 直接的
especially [ə`spɛʃəlɪ] ad 尤其
steak [stek] n 排餐、牛排

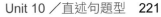

Mark your answer on your answer sheet.

(A)　　(B)　　(C)

解題分析

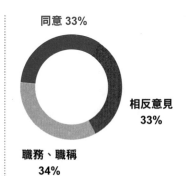

同意 33%

相反意見 33%

職務、職稱 34%

■ 同意 33%

■ 相反意見 33%

■ 職務、職稱 34%

本題也是一個直述句的題目，主要是在講述 Ms. Hart 這個人是個能力很強的經理，那麼有可能的回應方向，其中一個就是表「贊同意見」。

聽見句子是在表達 Ms. Hart 是個能力很強的經理，除了表示贊成外，也可以持相反意見，只要回答與題目的關鍵 competent manager 相符，應該沒有什麼太大的問題。

雖然本題的回答不外乎就是「贊同」、「反對」兩種方向，但是如果表達了贊同反對的意思，答案選項卻出現跟經理無關的敘述或是職務內容，就不是正確答案，考生也要多記單字，以免考試的時候被誤導。

聽稿

（AU / Ⓦ）

Ms. Hart seems like a competent manager.

(A) Yes, she certainly is.

(B) Yes, Ms. Hart will retire soon.

(C) Yes, she is a real spender.

中譯

（澳 / 女）

哈特小姐看來是能力很強的經理。（答案：**A**）

(A) 是的，她的確是。

(B) 是的，哈特小姐很快要退休了。

(C) 是的，她真的揮金如土。

解題技巧

聽到題目的同時，便應將注意力集中到聽問題關鍵點上，才有可能快狠準地選取正確答案。此題直述句是「Ms. Hart seems like a competent manager.」，那麼可判斷是講者在描述對 Ms. Hart 的觀感，認為她是個能力很強的經理人。由此看來，答案可能會出現同意、或持相反意見等方向。而此句中的關鍵之處會以加強重音來強調：「Ms. Hart **seems like a** competent manager.」

各選項解析

- 選項 (A)「Yes, she certainly is.」內關鍵點「She certainly is」，便是表示「同意哈特小姐真的是能力強的經理」之意味，的確有針對講者的意見回應，故為最佳答案。
- 選項 (B)「Yes, Ms. Hart will retire soon.」內提到「will retire」，意即「要退休了」。但請回想一下題目句，其中並沒有提及任何退休之事，所以可以刪除。
- 選項 (C)「Yes, she is a real spender.」內的重要訊息「spender」是「揮金如土的人」的意思，但這也與題目所討論的「competent manager」無直接關係，所以也不能選為答案。

此直述句是在描述 Ms. Hart 是個能力強的經理，因此若不是在回應與此句相關的選項，或僅是重複關鍵字，卻與題目牛頭不對馬嘴的選項，都不會是答案喔！比方說：

➡ Yes, Howard is very competitive. He always wants to win.

（是的，哈維很愛競爭，他一心只想要贏。）

此句內陷阱是以發音相似字「Howard」來混淆「Ms. Hart」。另外，「competitive」一字是「愛競爭」之意，也是用來混淆題目中的「competent」一字。以這兩點來看，這個回應並非在討論與題目同一人或同一件事，故不會是最佳的回應。

➡ Well, I can't stand this seagull manager at all.

（我簡直無法忍受這個狀況外的老闆。）

此句刻意重複「manager」一字，卻是以「seagull manager（海鷗經理）」的字來呈現。這個字的意思是指「不了解事務卻亂下決策，把爛攤子留給他人處理的經理」。此為在商業中頗有趣的慣用語，但沒有針對問題回應，故也是陷阱。

此題出現的「competent manager」是形容能力夠、稱職的經理，不論是在商場上、或是多益考題中都常常出現。如果要形容有領導能力的老闆之用語，還有以下說法：

❶ all-round 多才多藝的、全能的

➡ She is a fantastic all-round leader.（她是個了不起的全能領袖。）

❷ know the ropes 對細節瞭若指掌

➡ Jane really knows the ropes of teaching.（珍對教學瞭若指掌。）

❸ know ins and outs 全盤了解

➡ Terry knows ins and outs of reparing printers.

（泰瑞對修印表機再熟悉不過了。）

❹ pay one's dues 吃苦、花精力、盡責

➡ Mr. Smith paid his dues and reached his goals.

（他歷盡苦楚並達成了目標。）

❺ seasoned 經驗豐富的、老練的

➡ Ms. Chen is a seasoned supervisor.（陳先生是個老練的領班。）

關鍵字彙

competent [ˋkɑmpətənt] a 能力強的、能勝任的
certainly [ˋsɝtənlɪ] ad 的確、當然
retire [rɪˋtaɪr] v 退休
spender [ˋspɛndɚ] n 花錢如流水之人

綜合練習

Mark your answer on your answer sheet.

(A)　　(B)　　(C)

聽稿
（UK / M）

Who is your favorite singer?
(A) Jerry Palo, of course.
(B) Tina Johnson is my best friend.
(C) When in doubt, I sing.

中譯
（英 / 男）

你最喜歡的歌手是誰？（答案：A）
(A) 當然就是傑瑞‧保羅了。
(B) 提娜‧強森是我最好的朋友。
(C) 當我不知該怎麼辦時，我就唱歌。

解析

當聽到問題「Who is your favorite singer?」時，便可將注意力放在關鍵點在：首字「Who」和「singer」之上。因為首字是和人物相關的「Who」，所以在心中設想要聽到「歌手、人名」的答案才可當作答案。

各選項解析

- 選項 (A)「Jerry Palo, of course.」內關鍵人名「Jerry Palo」便可判斷是在針對題目回答，因此為正確答案。
- 選項 (B)「Tina Johnson is my best friend.」內雖然也有提到人名「Tina Johnson」，但因為其後的「best friend」，可以知道這個選項並非是題目所問的歌手，故不選。
- 選項 (C)「When in doubt, I sing.」提到了唱歌，但僅是為了和題目中的「singer」一字混淆罷了，完全沒有針對題目問的「人物」來回答，所以也不會是正確答案。

關鍵字彙

favorite [ˋfevərɪt] a 最喜歡的
singer [ˋsɪŋɚ] n 歌手
in doubt 存疑的、不肯定的

練習 2 │ 以 Where 為首的題型

Mark your answer on your answer sheet.

(A)　　(B)　　(C)

聽稿
（UK / **M**）

Where will the computer expo be held this year?
(A) Let's get some tickets in advance.
(B) At the Taipei Convention Center, I guess.
(C) I'm interested in attending some seminars.

中譯
（英 / **男**）

今年的電腦展會在哪裡舉辦？（答案：B）
(A) 我們事先買票吧。
(B) 我猜是在台北會議中心吧。
(C) 我有興趣聽些講座。

解析

在聽到題目「Where will the computer expo be held this year?」的同時，就要可以判斷出問題要點在這幾個關鍵字上：「Where will the computer expo be held this year?」。因此，根據關鍵字，在心中設定要聽到有關「展覽舉辦地點」的選項才能選。

各選項解析

- 選項 (A)「Let's get some tickets in advance.」中的關鍵訊息是要事先買票，但沒回答到此題問「地點」的問題，所以不能選。
- 選項 (B)「At the Taipei Convention Center, I guess.」內關鍵點是「Taipei Convention Center」可說明是電腦展舉辦之地點，所以有針對問題回答到，因此為正確答案。
- 選項 (C)「I'm interested in attending some seminars.」提到想參加研討會，但和選項 (A) 一樣沒說明到題目需要的「地點」關鍵字，所以也不選。

關鍵字彙

expo (= exposition) [ˈɛkspə] **n** 展覽會、展銷會
ticket [ˈtɪkɪt] **n** 門票、入場券
in advance **ph** 事先、在先前
convention [kənˈvɛnʃən] **n** 會議
seminar [ˈsɛməˌnɑr] **n** 研討會、講座

Mark your answer on your answer sheet.

(A)　　(B)　　(C)

聽稿
（US /**W**）

When are customers expected to arrive?
(A) Maybe in 2017.
(B) They'll arrive in ten minutes.
(C) Yes, they're our long-term customers.

中譯
（美 /**女**）

客戶大約會幾點到呢？（答案：B）
(A) 可能是二〇一七年吧。
(B) 他們再十分鐘會到。
(C) 是的，他們是我們的長期客戶。

解析

此題問的是「When are customers expected to arrive?」，那就需要將注意力集中在聽關鍵字：「When **are** customers expected to arrive?」。心裡有底之後，應很快地在腦中設定好要聽到「客戶到的時間」，再來聽選項，會比較有效率。

各選項解析

- 選項 (A)「Maybe in 2017.」內雖有關時間的年分，但對題目來說，這樣的時間範圍太大，無法精準地回答客戶到達的時間點，所以以並非正確答案。
- 選項 (B)「They'll arrive in ten minutes.」內關鍵點是「in ten minutes」，意味著「再十分鐘後會到」，有適當地回應問題，所以為正確答案。
- 選項 (C)「Yes, they're our long-term customers.」提到客戶是長期客戶，但沒提到「何時抵達」，沒有回應題目，因此不能選。

關鍵字彙

customer [ˋkʌstəmɚ] n 客戶
expect [ɪkˋspɛkt] v 預期
long-term [ˋlɔŋ ˋtɝm] a 長期的、歷久的

練習 4 | 以 What 為首的題型

Mark your answer on your answer sheet.

(A) (B) (C)

聽稿
(AU / W)

What's the point of that long sales meeting?
(A) It takes time, but you'll see the difference.
(B) What do you mean by that?
(C) The management wants us to generate more leads.

中譯
(澳 / 女)

那個冗長的業務會議要點是什麼？（答案：C）
(A) 那要花時間，但你會看到差異的。
(B) 你那是什麼意思？
(C) 管理階層想要我們多開發些客戶名單。

解析

題目問的是「What's the point of that long sales meeting?」，根據之前教的解題技巧，你順利找到問題的關鍵點了嗎？這一題的關鍵點是落在「What's the point of that long sales meeting?」上面喔！既然是問「會議的要點」，那麼便可預期要聽到關於「意義、目的」相關答案才可回答問題。

各選項解析

- 選項 (A)「It takes time, but you'll see the difference.」僅提到要花時間，之後會看到差異。但這並沒有回答到「會議的要點」，故不選。
- 選項 (B)「What do you mean by that?」提出反問，雖然在對話中，有可能反問他人提出的問題，但這樣的回應並不是最合適的答案。
- 選項 (C)「The management wants us to generate more leads.」有回答到題目所問「開會討論的內容」，故選為最佳答案。

關鍵字彙

difference [ˋdɪfərəns] n 不同、差異
generate [ˋdʒɛnəˏret] v 產生、產出
leads [lidz] n 客戶名單（生意來源）

Mark your answer on your answer sheet.

(A)　　(B)　　(C)

聽稿

（CA / **M**）

Why don't we take a short break?

(A) Haven't you had enough?

(B) How much is it?

(C) All right. Let's be back at 2 sharp.

中譯

（加 / **男**）

我們何不休息一下呢？（答案：C）

(A) 你還沒受夠嗎？

(B) 那要多少錢？

(C) 好的，我們就兩點整回來。

解析

聽到此題目「Why don't we take a short break?」的同時，應該要馬上判斷此為提議、建議的句型，且要點在於：「Why don't we take a short break?」。之後便可以在心裡馬上預設要聽到「Yes」或「No」等答案可能性。

各選項解析

- 選項 (A)「Haven't you had enough?」的意思是「還沒受夠嗎」，與題目問的「可否休息一下」無關，無法回應題目所問，所以不是正確答案。
- 選項 (B)「How much is it?」反問價格，但與題目所問完全無關，所以不能選。
- 選項 (C)「All right. Let's be back at 2 sharp.」內容提到「休息一下可以」，且後續還說「兩點整回來」，的確符合對話的情境，故為正確答案。

關鍵字彙

take a break 片 暫停、休息一下
sharp [ʃɑrp] ad 準時地

練習 6 ｜ 以 How 為首的題型

Mark your answer on your answer sheet.

(A)　　(B)　　(C)

聽稿
（AU / Ⓦ）

How do you usually go to work?
(A) I take the subway, but sometimes I drive.
(B) My office is located on 5ᵗʰ Street.
(C) I carpool with Jerry.

中譯
（澳 / 女）

你都怎麼去上班呀？（答案：A）
(A) 我都搭地鐵，有時候會開車。
(B) 我公司位於第五街上。
(C) 我跟傑瑞共乘。

解析

此題問到「How do you usually go to work?」，聽到問題的同時，心中應也可判斷關鍵點在哪裡：「How do you usually go to work?」。既然是以 how 開頭詢問「前往公司之方式」，那麼在心中可設定好要聽到如何前往公司的方式，以便回答 how 的題目。

各選項解析

- 選項 (A)「I take the subway, but sometimes I drive.」內有回應到去上班的方式，由搭乘交通工具「subway」和「drive」，可以知道回答者是搭地鐵或開車去上班，有針對問題回答，故為正確答案。
- 選項 (B)「My office is located on 5ᵗʰ Street.」是在說明公司的位置，但題目並非問「where」，而是在問「how」。此回應的關鍵點與題目的不符，故不選。
- 選項 (C)「I carpool with Jerry.」提到與傑瑞共乘，雖然和題目問的都有相關交通的訊息，但這個選項並沒有正面回應題目所問，所以也不是適合的答案。

關鍵字彙

usually [`juʒʊəlɪ] ad 經常、常常
subway [`sʌb͵we] n 地鐵
locate [lo`ket] v 位於、位置在～
carpool n 汽車共乘

Mark your answer on your answer sheet.

(A)　　(B)　　(C)

聽稿

（CA / **M**）

Are you still working at TDI Company?

(A) Yes, TDI is an international company.

(B) No, I prefer to live in rural areas.

(C) No, I joined IO-Tech last month.

中譯

（加 / **男**）

你還在 TDI 公司上班嗎？（答案：C）

(A) 是的，TDI 是間跨國公司。

(B) 不，我喜歡住鄉下。

(C) 不，我上個月就加入 IO-Tech 公司了。

解析

聽到此問題「Are you still working at TDI Company?」的同時，應立即將注意力集中到關鍵問題點上，也就是：「Are you **still working** at TDI Company?」。既然題目問的是「是否還在 TDI」，那麼可預期的答案就會有「還在 TDI」或「不在 TDI」等可能性。

各選項解析

- 選項 (A)「Yes, TDI is an international company.」，提到了 TDI 公司的性質，但沒回答到是否還在那上班一事，沒有針對問題回答，故為錯誤答案。
- 選項 (B)「No, I prefer to live in rural area.」內關鍵點提到喜歡住鄉下地區，但是要注意的是題目並非問 where 的問題，此選項無法回答問題，所以不能選。
- 選項 (C)「No, I joined IO-Tech last month.」內有先說關鍵點「No」，意味著已不在 TDI 公司上班了；且其後又說「I joined IO-Tech last month.」可聽出回答的人是上個月換去新公司了。可以知道此選項有針對問題回答，故選為最佳答案。

關鍵字彙

international [ˌɪntəˈnæʃənl] a 國際的

rural [ˈrʊrəl] a 鄉下的

練習 8 ｜附加問句題型

Mark your answer on your answer sheet.

(A)　　(B)　　(C)

聽稿
（US／Ｗ）

Mr. Chen's speech is really inspiring, isn't it?
(A) Yes, exactly. I love it.
(B) Okay, tell me more.
(C) No, actually the speech was about sales strategies.

中譯
（美／女）

陳先生的演講很激勵人心，對吧？（答案：A）
(A) 是的，的確，我喜歡那場演講。
(B) 好的，告訴我多點資訊。
(C) 不，事實上那演講是關於業務策略。

解析

根據此題問「Mr. Chen's speech is really inspiring, isn't it?」，可聽出問者的關鍵點是：「Mr. Chen's speech is really inspiring, isn't it?」。若是要根據問題回應的話，可能的答案會有「Yes... inspiring」，或是「No, not that inspiring.」等可能性。

各選項解析

- 選項 (A)「Yes, exactly. I love it.」可聽出回答者也是認為那場演講很棒的，有針對問題做出適當的回應，故正確。
- 選項 (B)「Okay, tell me more.」提到要了解更多，但沒針對問題回答演講是否激勵人心一事，沒有回答問題的選項絕不會是正確答案，故不選。
- 選項 (C)「No, actually the speech was about sales strategies.」提到演講是關於業務策略，雖然有提到演講，但也沒針對問題回答演講是否激勵人心一事，回應的方向與題目不同，所以不會是適合的答案。

關鍵字彙

speech [spitʃ] n 演講、演説
inspiring [ɪnˈspaɪrɪŋ] a 激勵的、鼓舞的
exactly [ɪɡˈzæktlɪ] ad 確實地、的確
strategy [ˈstrætədʒɪ] n 策略

Mark your answer on your answer sheet.

(A)　　(B)　　(C)

聽稿
（UK / **M**）

Would you like to park your car inside or outside the garage?
(A) Maybe inside.
(B) I don't like outdoor activities.
(C) It's raining, so stay inside.

中譯
（英 / **男**）

你想將車停在車庫內還是外面？（答案：A）
(A) 可能要停車庫內。
(B) 我不喜歡戶外活動。
(C) 外面在下雨，待在室內不要出去。

解析

聽到此問題「Would you like to park your car inside or outside the garage?」的同時，應該立刻判斷問句的關鍵點在哪裡。此問題的關鍵點在於：「Would you like to park your car inside or outside the garage?」。抓到問題的關鍵點之後，想要正確答題，就要聽到包含停車停「裡面」或「外面」的選項才可當答案。

各選項解析

- 選項 (A)「Maybe inside.」，馬上就可以判斷內有可回答問題關鍵點「inside」，非常明確地回應了題目，所以選為正確答案。
- 選項 (B)「I don't like outdoor activities.」提到不喜歡戶外活動，是故意使用與題目關鍵字「outside」相似的「outdoor」一字來混淆考生。儘管如此，此選項並沒有回答到問題，所以不選。
- 選項 (C)「It's raining, so stay inside.」提到因為外面下雨，所以不要外出。這個選項也只是故意以與題目相同的關鍵字「inside」一字來混淆考生，同樣地也沒有回應此問題，故不選。

關鍵字彙

park [pɑrk] ᵥ 停車
garage [gəˋrɑʒ] ⁿ 車庫
outdoor [ˋaʊt͵dor] ₐ 戶外的
activity [ækˋtɪvətɪ] ⁿ 活動

練習 10 | 直述句題型

Mark your answer on your answer sheet.

(A)　　(B)　　(C)

聽稿
（AU / **W**）

I think Ms. Wilson is a demanding supervisor.
(A) I think the theory is still questionable.
(B) I totally agree with you.
(C) I actually don't know Ms. Chen that well.

中譯
（澳 / **女**）

我認為威爾森小姐是個嚴苛的老闆。（答案：B）
(A) 我認為那理論還有待商榷。
(B) 我完全同意你的說法。
(C) 我其實和陳小姐不太熟。

解析

此題目「I think Ms. Wilson is a demanding supervisor.」為直述句，所以不能採取聽首字的技巧，而此題的要點在於：「I think Ms. Wilson **is a demanding supervisor**.」。聽完題目之後，可判斷要點在「威爾森小姐要求高」上面。因此預期可能的回應有「同意，說得對」、「的確是」或是「不同意，並非這樣」的可能性。

各選項解析

- 選項 (A)「I think the theory is still questionable.」內主要的訊息為「theory」和「questionable」，這個選項的意思是「對這個理論存疑」。但沒針對原句 Ms. Wilson 在討論，所以不能選。
- 選項 (B)「I totally agree with you.」可聽出答者同意題目所敘述的事，同樣也認為 Ms. Wilson 是個要求高、很嚴苛的老闆。此回應有針對問題回應，故正確。
- 選項 (C)「I actually don't know Ms. Chen that well.」提到「和陳小姐不熟」，不但和原句所討論的人不一致，也沒有針對題目陳述內容回應，因此就不會是正確答案囉！

關鍵字彙

demanding [dɪ`mændɪŋ] a 苛求的、嚴苛的
supervisor [ˌsupɚ`vaɪzɚ] n 領班、上司、總管
theory [`θiərɪ] n 理論
questionable [`kwɛstʃənəbl] a 存疑的、還有疑慮的
totally [`totlɪ] ad 完全地
agree with ph 同意
actually [`æktʃʊəlɪ] ad 事實上

應試策略總整理

為了讓考生在準備多益考試時，同時也培養可應用在日常生活與辦公環境的英語實力，聽力試題會增加各國口音。因此，訓練自己聽懂各國口音是絕對必要的。口音方面的訓練，並非靠短期做做模考試題就可以熟練，而是必須長期地多接觸各國英文的演講或廣播，才有可能日漸地熟練。建議同學多聽 BBC（英國口音）或 VOA（美國口音）的廣播節目，或聽有各國口音的 TED 演講。

Part 2 應答問題的題目通常不會很長，也僅是日常生活、社交、會議、機場、餐飲等場合的基本對話。但主要問題就在於：題目不長，且僅播放出一次，若沒有立即抓到問題的「關鍵點」，如何選出正確的回應呢？我們應該集中所有注意力在單一關鍵點上。以下，我們就列出幾個最常考的「應答問題關鍵點」，以便大家在準備考試時有個基礎可循。

❶ 聽到以「what」開頭的問句，可預期答案應有「事物、主題」的可能性。

　　Q: Under will you do this weekend?（你週末要做什麼？）

　　A: I'm going shopping with my friends.（我要跟朋友去逛街。）

❷ 聽到以「when」開頭可預期要聽到「日期、時間」的相關答案較為合理。

　　Q: When will the meeting be held?（會議何時召開？）

　　A: The meeting will be held at 2 this afternoon.（今天下午兩點要開會。）

❸ 聽到以「where」開頭的句子，可預期要聽到「地點、位置」等相關回答。

　　Q: Where are you from?（你從哪來的？）

　　A: I'm from Japan.（我來自日本。）

❹ 聽到以「who」開頭的句子，可預期要聽到「人名、職稱、關係」來回答。

　　Q: Who is that woman standing by the door?（那位站在門邊的女子是誰？）

　　A: That's my supervisor, Ms. Smith.（那是我的老闆史密斯小姐。）

❺ 聽到以「why」開頭，可預期要選「原因、理由」的回答較為合理。

　　Q: Why are you so tired?（你怎麼這麼累？）

　　A: I didn't sleep well last night.（我昨晚沒睡好。）

❻ 聽到以「how」開頭的問題，便預期要聽到「以～方式」的回應較為合理。

　　Q: How do you usually go to work?（你如何去上班？）

　　A: I go to work by bus.（我搭公車去上班。）

不管問題點如何變化，最重要的是考生自己要能夠集中注意力在題目關鍵字上，專心地聽相對應的答案即可。

LISTENING

PART

3

簡短對話
Conversations

Introduction

聽對話時，應將注意力放在以重音強調的主要資訊，並利用對話未播放前的三到五秒，將題目掃過一遍，知道題目的方向後，試著聽到至少三個關鍵點來判斷答案。

分類解析

綜合練習

攻略 1 | 公事上的會面

Q1. What does the woman want to do?

(A) Talk to Linda right away
(B) Meet with Ms. Jackins
(C) Make an appointment with the man
(D) Borrow some money from Linda

Q2. Who most likely is the man?

(A) An accountant
(B) A professor
(C) A receptionist
(D) A software designer

Q3. What does the man need to do first?

(A) Call Ms. Jackins directly and ask her to get down right away
(B) Check with Linda to see if Ms. Jackins is available
(C) Give the woman an application to fill out
(D) Ask Ms. Jackins to provide a password for the woman to use

解題分析

動作 64%
身分、職位 36%

■ 動作 64% 人物的動作、即將要去做的事、已經做過的事都是對話題最愛考的細節,只要抓到動作的「動詞」,就能順利答題。

■ 身分、職位 36% 由於此題的情境是在工作環境中,所以常考對話者的身分、職位;而在對話中,身分不會明講,只要透過了解大部分對話內容就能選到正確的答案。

聽稿

（US / W）Hello, my name is Sherry Taylor. I have an appointment with Ms. Jackins of Marketing at four. But I am a bit early today. I wonder if she is available now.

（UK / M）I see. It's okay. Let me check with her assistant first. Sorry, what's your name again? And which company are you from please?

（US / W）Oh, I am Sherry Taylor from Lead-A Software.

（UK / M）Okay, let me check with Linda at extension 117... Right, Ms. Taylor, Ms. Jackins just finished a meeting early, and she will be down and right with you shortly. Please take a seat there.

中譯　（美／**女**）你好，我是雪莉・泰勒。我與行銷部的傑金斯小姐約四點會面，我提早到了，不知道她現在有空嗎？

（英／**男**）我了解，沒關係，我先跟她的祕書詢問看看。不好意思，可以再跟我講一次您的姓名嗎？還有，您公司名稱是？

（美／**女**）我是雪莉・泰勒，領導軟體公司。

（英／**男**）好的，我先跟分機 117 的琳達聯絡看看。好的，泰勒小姐，傑金斯小姐剛好提早開完會了，她一會兒會下來與您碰面，請在那稍坐一下。

Q1. 女子想做什麼？（答案：**B**）

(A) 直接跟琳達談話　　　　　　　　　(B) 與傑金斯小姐會面

(C) 跟男子約個會議　　　　　　　　　(D) 跟琳達借點錢

Q2. 男子最有可能是誰？（答案：**C**）

(A) 會計師　　　　　　　　　　　　　(B) 教授

(C) 接待員　　　　　　　　　　　　　(D) 軟體設計師

Q3. 男子先要做什麼事？（答案：**B**）

(A) 直接打電話給傑金斯小姐並要她馬上下樓來

(B) 詢問琳達傑金斯小姐是否有空

(C) 請女子填寫申請書

(D) 請傑金斯小姐提供一組密碼給女子使用

解題技巧　相較於聽力第一與第二部分的短句，第三部分長篇的對話便比較難精準地預測兩名對話者會講的內容；且改制後的多益聽力測驗又刻意地加入英國、澳洲、加拿大等各地口音，因此考生會直覺地認為較難聽得懂內容。但無論是哪一國的口音，要聽懂對話的要點其實是在於「抓到重音」。以此對話為例，重音可能落在以下標示之處：

> （US／**W**）Hello, my name is Sherry Taylor. I have an appointment with Ms. Jackins of Marketing at four. But I am a bit early today. I wonder if she is available now.
>
> （UK／**M**）I see. It's okay. Let me check with her assistant first. Sorry, what's your name again? And which company are you from please?
>
> （US／**W**）Oh, I am Sherry Taylor from Lead-A Software.
>
> （UK／**M**）Okay, let me check with Linda at extension 117... Right, Ms. Taylor, Ms. Jackins just finished a meeting early, and she will be down and right with you shortly. Please take a seat there.

如此一來，聽得懂對話內的「關鍵點」，確實比試圖想聽到「每個字」來得有效率多了。正式考試時，在播放對話之前，通常會有兩到三秒的時間，可以利用此空檔很快地掃一下題本內所列出之題目，以便預期可聽到什麼樣的「內容」和需要專注聽什麼「類型」的答案。

第一題

此題先看到題目問的是「What does the woman want to do?（女子來此之目的是想做什麼）」。
那麼聽到女子所講的首句關鍵句「I have an appointment with Ms. Jackins at four.」，便可判斷女子到這裡是與傑金斯小姐有約，故選 (B)「Meet with Ms. Jackins」為答案。

各選項解析

- 選項 (A)「Talk to Linda right away.」，但是根據男子提供的資訊，Linda 是 Ms. Jackins 的祕書，而女子並沒有提到要找 Ms. Jackins 的祕書 Linda，故不選。
- 選項 (C)「Make an appointment with the man.」不能選。因為根據對話內容，男子可能是接待員，女子並非說跟男子有約，故不選。
- 選項 (D)「Borrow some money from Linda.」中的「borrow money」是「借錢」之意，完全沒在對話中出現，所以也不能選。

第二題

把握題目播放前一兩秒的時間先瀏覽題目「Who most likely is the man?」，問的是男子的身分。
既然男子是在幫女子聯絡 Ms. Jackins 及其助理，那麼最有可能是櫃台接待人員，故選 (C) 的「A receptionist」為最佳答案。

各選項解析

- 選項 (A)「An accountant」、選項 (B)「A professor」與選項 (D)「A software designer」都不是會在公司櫃台扮演接待訪客之角色，所以都可以先刪除。

第三題

先掃過題目「What does the man need to do first?」，問的是男子要先做之事。那麼根據男子所提及的關鍵句「Let me check with her assistant first.」可判斷他是要跟 Ms. Jackins 的助理確認 Ms. Jackins 是否有空，其後一句「Let me check with Linda...」，又可判斷出助理名字叫做 Linda，故選 (B)「Check with Linda to see if Ms. Jackins is available」為最佳答案。

各選項解析

- 選項 (A)「Call Ms. Jackins directly and ask her to get down right away.」男子是要透過 Linda 詢問，並非直接問 Ms. Jackins，故不選。
- 選項 (C)「Give the woman an application to fill out.」，根據對話內容女子並非去申請工作的，且對話中並無 application 字眼出現，所以也不選。
- 選項 (D)「Ask Ms. Jackins to provide a password for the woman to use.」錯誤，根據對話內容，女子並非要登入電腦，對話中也沒 password 字眼出現，故不選。

關鍵字彙

appointment [ə`pɔɪntmənt] n 會議
wonder [`wʌndɚ] v 想知道
available [ə`veləbl] a 有空的、可用的
assistant [ə`sɪstənt] n 助理
extension [ɪk`stɛnʃən] n 分機
shortly [`ʃɔrtlɪ] ad 立刻、馬上

Q1. Where is the conversation probably taking place?

 (A) In the park   (B) On the stage

 (C) In the office   (D) In a shopping mall

Q2. What are the speakers talking about?

 (A) The woman's trip to The National Museum

 (B) The man's impression of Taipei

 (C) The woman's resignation

 (D) The business environment in Hong Kong

Q3. What does the man think of Taipei?

 (A) He doesn't like the city at all   (B) Taipei residents are impersonal

 (C) The weather in Taipei is too hot   (D) He enjoys visiting Taipei

---

解題分析

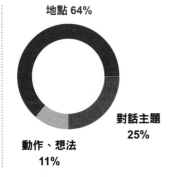

地點 64%

對話主題 25%

動作、想法 11%

■ 地點 64%

對話在哪裡發生是多益考試的一大考點，主要是測驗考生是否能透過對話內容以及對話者的身分，來推測出對話發生地點，例如：點餐的對話會發生在餐廳內、退換貨會發生在商店裡。

■ 對話主題 25%

與詢問對話發生地點的題目類似，若看到詢問有關對話主旨的題目，不需要背下整篇的對話，了解七成的內容、掌握對話者的身分，就能知道主題。

■ 動作、想法 11%

說話者對於對話主題的態度常常也是對話題的考試重點，可以透過對話者的語氣推測其態度或是看法如何。

聽稿

（US / W）Thank you for flying all the way from Chicago to discuss this project. So Jack, tell me... is this your first time in Taipei?

（UK / M）Well, it's not. I've been here many times actually. I used to work at a consulting firm and we did a lot of business with companies in Taipei, so I visited clients in Taipei pretty often.

（US / W）Oh really? It sounds cool. Then how do you like this city?

（UK / M）Yeah, I think Taipei is a fantastic city though. I'm especially impressed by the National Palace Museum. Oh, and best of all, people in Taipei are very friendly.

（美 / 女）謝謝你大老遠從芝加哥飛過來討論此專案之事。那麼，傑克，這是你第一次來台北嗎？

（英 / 男）不是。事實上我已經來過不少次了。我曾經在一間顧問公司工作，他們與台北的企業有許多生意上的往來，所以我常來台北拜訪客戶。

（美 / 女）真的嗎？聽起來不賴呢。你喜歡台北這個城市嗎？

（英 / 男）嗯，我覺得台北是一個令人驚豔的都市。尤其故宮博物院讓我印象深刻。而且最棒的一點是，台北人都非常地友善。

Q1. 此對話最有可能發生在何處？（答案：C）

    (A) 在公園　　　　　　　　　　　　　(B) 在舞台上

    (C) 在辦公室　　　　　　　　　　　　(D) 在購物中心

Q2. 兩位講者在討論什麼？（答案：B）

    (A) 女子去國家博物館的行程　　　　　(B) 男子對台北的印象

    (C) 女子離職事宜　　　　　　　　　　(D) 香港的產業環境

Q3. 男子覺得台北如何？（答案：D）

    (A) 他完全不喜歡此都市　　　　　　　(B) 台北居民都很冷漠

    (C) 台北天氣過熱　　　　　　　　　　(D) 他喜歡到台北旅遊

解題技巧

由於對話題的篇幅開始有點長了，不能像是照片題或應答問題一般，僅聽一兩句就好。考生不免會因為試圖想聽到每個字，卻又辦不到，因而心生挫折感。殊不知對話內每個字的重要性並非都一樣，我們僅需將注意力放在聽重點、關鍵要點上即可；而這些關鍵點通常會以加強重音來呈現。以此對話為例，其關鍵要點可能會是：

（US / W）Thank you for flying all the way from Chicago to discuss this project. So Jack, tell me... is this your first time in Taipei?

（UK / M）Well, it's not. I've been here many times actually. I used to work at a consulting firm and we did a lot of business with companies in Taipei, so I visited clients in Taipei pretty often.

（US / W）Oh really? It sounds cool. Then how do you like this city?

（UK / M）Yeah, I think Taipei is a fantastic city though. I'm especially impressed by the National Palace Museum. Oh, and best of all, people in Taipei are very friendly.

由幾個要點便可大約了解對話者的關係、在討論些什麼和男子對台北的觀感……等資訊了。通常考生可以聽到三到五個關鍵點，就大概可以了解百分之八十的對話內容了。

第一題

在聽到對話之前最好可以將題目掃過一遍，如此一來心中就能先有個底，也知道要將注意力放在聽什麼內容上。此題問的是「Where is the conversation probably taking place?」，便可判斷要將注意力放在聽地點、位置的資訊上。那麼根據此關鍵句「Thank you for flying all the way from Chicago to discuss this project.」可聽出是兩個商務人士在討論專案事宜，那麼最有可能應是在辦公室內的談話較為合理，故選 (C)「In the office」為最佳答案。

各選項解析

- 選項 (A)「In the park」、選項 (B)「On the stage」與選項 (D)「In a shopping mall」都不是商務人士討論生意之處,故不選。

第二題

先看到題目問的是「What are the speakers talking about?」那麼要將焦點放在「對話主題」上以便回答。那麼根據對話中已標出的加強重音關鍵字,可聽出 Jack 來台北拜訪很多次,並提到「Taipei is a fantastic city though... and best of all, people in Taipei are very friendly.」,由此可聽出男子是在講他來台北的經驗和對台北的印象,故選 (B)「The man's impression of Taipei」為最佳答案。

各選項解析

- 選項 (A)「The woman's trip to The National Museum」、選項 (C)「The woman's resignation」與選項 (D)「The business environment in Hong Kong」都沒在對話中被討論到,故不選。

第三題

先看題目問的是「What does the man think of Taipei?」,那麼要將注意力放在聽「男子對台北的印象」的要點上,那麼根據男子說的「I think Taipei is a fantastic city though. I'm especially impressed by the National Palace Museum. Oh, and best of all, people in Taipei are very friendly.」,可以聽出他喜歡到台北參訪,因此選 (D)「He enjoys visiting Taipei.」為最佳答案。

各選項解析

- 選項 (A)「He doesn't like the city at all.」、選項 (B)「Taipei residents are impersonal.」與選項 (C)「The weather in Taipei is too hot.」都沒在對話中被提及,故不選。

關鍵字彙

actually [ˋæktʃʊəlɪ] ad 事實上地、實際上地
consulting [kənˋsʌltɪŋ] a 顧問的
firm [fɝm] n 公司
client [ˋklaɪənt] n 客戶、顧客
fantastic [fænˋtæstɪk] a 令人驚豔的
impressed [ɪmˋprɛst] a 令人印象深刻的

新 Q1. What are the speakers talking about?

(A) The environmental problems 　　(B) The major theme of a conference

(C) Ways to handle difficult customers (D) The effectiveness of the long speech

新 Q2. Who are most likely the speakers?

(A) Neighbors 　　　　　　　　　(B) Relatives

(C) Close friends 　　　　　　　　(D) Conference attendees

新 Q3. What will happen in the afternoon?

(A) The man will deliver a speech 　(B) More meeting sessions will be held

(C) All three of them will go home 　(D) The man needs to leave for the airport

---

解題分析

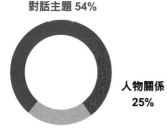

對話主題 54%

人物關係 25%

未來將發生的事 21%

■ 對話主題 54%

■ 人物關係 25%

■ 未來將發生的事 21%

對話題最常考的就是對話主題，通常會在說話者的言詞之中帶到主題，而其他對話參與者針對該主題表達贊成或是反對的意見。

對話者之間的關係可以透過談話內容來推測。在工作場合發生的對話，很有可能出現：同事、上司與下屬、客戶與廠商……等關係。

考題也很喜歡出現要考生推測對話者的下一步，這時候就可以抓住整篇對話的最後一句話，因為最後一句通常會暗示對話者接下來要做什麼。

聽稿

（US / Ⓦ）Excuse me, do you guys mind if I join you please? I'm Jessica Jensen.

（UK / Ⓜ）Not at all. I'm Jason Aden, and this is my colleague, Sarah.

（AU / Ⓦ）Hello, nice to meet you, Jessica.

（US / Ⓦ）Nice to meet you guys too. So this is a great conference, isn't it? I really enjoyed the keynote speech by Mr. Hart this morning.

（UK / Ⓜ）Yeah, I think so too. Mr. Hart really made a point. You know, big data has become a big game changer in most types of modern industries.

（AU / Ⓦ）Exactly. That's why we are here to learn more about the new trend. I'm looking forward to attending more sessions this afternoon.

中譯

（美／**女**）不好意思，請問，我能夠加入你們嗎？我叫潔西卡‧詹森。

（英／**男**）當然歡迎。我是傑森‧艾敦。這位是我的同事莎拉。

（澳／**女**）妳好，潔西卡，很高興認識妳。

（美／**女**）我也很高興認識你們。這是場頗盛大的會議，對吧？我很欣賞哈特先生今早的主題演說。

（英／**男**）是啊，我也認為他蠻令人敬佩的。哈特先生言之有理。妳們想想，大數據早已成為多數現代企業中一個顛覆遊戲規則的重要角色了。

（澳／**女**）千真萬確。所以我們才更該來此學習新的趨勢呀。我很期待今天下午的講習活動呢。

新 **Q1.** 講者在討論些什麼？（答案：**B**）

    (A) 環保問題   (B) 研討會主題

    (C) 處理難纏客戶的方式   (D) 冗長演講的成效

新 **Q2.** 講者可能是誰？（答案：**D**）

    (A) 鄰居   (B) 親戚

    (C) 很熟的朋友   (D) 會議參與者

新 **Q3.** 下午會有什麼活動？（答案：**B**）

    (A) 男子會講一場演說   (B) 會舉行更多研討會

    (C) 三人會回家去   (D) 男子要出發去機場

解題技巧

全新制多益增加了三人對話，目的是要符合實際上商業的狀況，一般辦公環境內本來就不會一直僅兩人在談話，反而很多機會是多於兩人以上在討論事情的，因此對這種題目不應排斥，反而要更加熟悉。三人對話的訣竅也是差不多，就是要將注意力放在聽有加強重音的關鍵點上。另外，就是因為有三個人在對話，那麼更要分辨出「誰是誰」、「誰講什麼」等，否則會很容易混淆內容。三人對話除了以性別來區分之外，也會以不同口音來區別。考生在聽內容時，可以同時在腦中想像三人對話的情景，以幫助記憶和了解。

針對此段對話的要點可能會是：

（US／**W**）Excuse me, do you guys mind if I join you please? I'm Jessica Jensen.

（UK／**M**）Not at all. I'm Jason Aden, and this is my colleague, Sarah.

（AU／**W**）Hello, nice to meet you, Jessica.

（US／**W**）Nice to meet you guys too. So this is a great conference, isn't it? I really enjoyed the keynote speech by Mr. Hart this morning.

（UK／**M**）Yeah, I think so too. Mr. Hart really made a point. You know, big data has become a big game changer in most types of modern industries.

（AU／**W**）Exactly. That's why we are here to learn more about the new trend. I'm looking forward to attending more sessions this afternoon.

聽到關鍵點後，便約略可以得知這篇對話六七成的大意了。大致上是在說三個人在研討會會場上認識，並稍微討論到研討會的內容與對下午場的期待。

新 第一題

在聽對話內容前最好是可以先掃描題目，以便得知要將注意力放在聽什麼要點上。 此題問的是「What are the speakers talking about?」，詢問關於對話的主題，那麼根據女子説的關鍵句「So this is a great conference, isn't it? I really enjoyed the keynote speech...」，以及男子的回應「You know, big data has become a big game changer in most types of modern industries.」，可聽出他們在討論此研討會的「big data」主題，所以選擇 (B)「The major theme of a conference」為最佳答案。

各選項解析

- 選項 (A)「The environmental problems」、選項 (C)「Ways to handle difficult customers」與選項 (D)「The effectiveness of the long speech」都沒在對話中被提及，所以都不會是正確答案。

新 第二題

此題問的是「Who are most likely the speakers?」，主要詢問對話者之間的關係，那麼根據對話一開頭的關鍵句「Excuse me, do you guys mind if I join you please?」與「Nice to meet you guys too. So this is a great conference, isn't it?」，很明顯地可以聽出三人都是在研討會會場，並互相介紹自己。故選擇 (D)「Conference attendees」為最佳答案。

各選項解析

- 選項 (A)「Neighbors」、選項 (B)「Relatives」與選項 (D)「Close friends」都不是會「向對方自我介紹」的關係，故不選。

新 第三題

這一小題問「What will happen in the afternoon?」，那麼便應將注意力放在聽「下午活動」的要點上。根據此關鍵句「That's why we are here to learn more about the new trend. I'm looking forward to attending more sessions this afternoon.」，可聽出下午有更多演講場次，故選擇 (B)「More meeting sessions will be held.」為最佳答案。

各選項解析

- 選項 (A)「The man will deliver a speech.」、選項 (C)「All three of them will go home.」與選項 (D)「The man needs to leave for the airport.」都沒在對話中出現，故不選。

關鍵字彙

colleague [ˋkɑlig] n 同事
conference [ˋkɑnfərəns] n 會議
keynote [ˋkiˌnot] n 主題
speech [spitʃ] n 演講
modern [ˋmɑdən] a 現代的
industry [ˋɪndəstrɪ] n 產業
trend [trɛnd] n 趨勢
attend [əˋtɛnd] v 出席
session [ˋsɛʃən] n 演講、講習課

Unit 2 業務績效類

攻略 1 │ 業務安排

Q1. Who is most likely the woman?

(A) The man's best friend   (B) A sales representative

(C) A scientist   (D) An English teacher

Q2. What does the man suggest the woman do?

(A) Call and discuss further the next day   (B) Come to his office immediately

(C) Meet Sherry in person this afternoon   (D) Send an e-mail to the CEO

Q3. What will they discuss tomorrow?

(A) Pay schedule only   (B) Delivery date

(C) Training issues   (D) Payment and training issues

解題分析

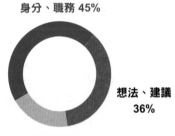

身分、職務 45%

想法、建議 36%

未來將發生的事 19%

■ 身分、職務 45%

由於此篇對話是打電話安排會議，所以在對話的開頭，一定會聽到說話者自我介紹，如此一來就能得知其身分或是職務。

■ 想法、建議 36%

當看到題目詢問其中一對話者的建議或是想法時，可以透過對話裡人物的談話內容，推敲出其態度，並搭配選項以選出最合適的答案。

■ 未來將發生的事 19%

遇到詢問對話者的下一步或是將去做何事時，我們可以將焦點放在對話的最後面，因為最後一句話常是對話者下一步的關鍵所在。

聽稿

（US / Ⓦ）Hello, this is Wendy Wu calling from Net-Tech. I'm calling to confirm that I've received your software order by e-mail. Also, we need to discuss the software training schedule.

（UK / Ⓜ）Well, is it okay if I get back to you about training? The person, Sherry, who is in charge of training is not in today.

（US / Ⓦ）I see. All right, I'll call again tomorrow. By the way, we also need to discuss the payment schedule.

（UK / Ⓜ）Sure. How about this? I will arrange a conference call with Sherry and you, so we three could discuss both the payment schedule and training issues tomorrow. I'll send you a con-call invitation later.

（美 / 女）您好，我是網路科技的吳溫蒂。想跟您確認：我已透過電郵收到您寄來的軟體訂單。而我也需要跟您討論該軟體的訓練課程進度。

（英 / 男）您好，我是否能晚點再向您確認有關訓練事宜？因為訓練事宜的負責人雪莉今日剛好外出。

（美 / 女）我了解，不然我明日再撥電話給您好了。對了，我們也需要討論付款流程。

（英 / 男）沒問題。您看這樣如何？我明天來安排一場電話會議，讓您、雪莉和我，三人共同參與以便討論這些付款流程和訓練事宜。我等等再發一封電話會議的邀請函給您。

Q1. 女子最有可能是誰？（答案：**B**）

(A) 男子的最好朋友　　　　　　　　　(B) 業務代表

(C) 科學家　　　　　　　　　　　　　(D) 英文老師

Q2. 男子建議女子做什麼？（答案：**A**）

(A) 第二天打電話討論細節　　　　　　(B) 馬上到他辦公室

(C) 下午親自與雪莉見面　　　　　　　(D) 寄封電郵給執行長

Q3. 他們明天會討論什麼？（答案：**D**）

(A) 僅討論付款流程　　　　　　　　　(B) 出貨日期

(C) 訓練事宜　　　　　　　　　　　　(D) 付款和訓練事宜

解題技巧

要了解一篇對話的大意，與其想要將每個字都聽到並聽懂，倒不如僅將注意力放在聽會影響理解力的關鍵要點上就好。所幸講者在提到想要聽者注意的關鍵要點時，通常會以「加強重音」的處理方式，來引起聽者的注意。此組對話的關鍵要點便可能是：

> （US / W）Hello, this is Wendy Wu calling from Net-Tech. I'm calling to confirm that I've received your software order by e-mail. Also, we need to discuss the software training schedule.
>
> （UK / M）Well, is it okay if I get back to you about training? The person, Sherry, who is in charge of training is not in today.
>
> （US / W）I see. All right, I'll call again tomorrow. By the way, we also need to discuss the payment schedule.
>
> （UK / M）Sure. How about this? I will arrange a conference call with Sherry and you, so we three could discuss both the payment schedule and training issues tomorrow. I'll send you a con-call invitation later.

了解此對話的關鍵要點之後，便可能大約了解：兩講者是在討論訂單處理，誰會負責交貨後的訓練，與付款方式等，還打算約個電話會議一併討論。大約了解一下對話內容，便比想要逐字聽懂並翻譯來得有效多了。

第一題

若在對話內容被播放出來之前，可以先快速將題目掃過一遍，便可知要將注意力放在聽什麼要點上了。此題「Who is most likely the woman?」，既然是問女子的角色，那麼我們便應專注在聽女子所提的內容上，根據此關鍵句「I'm calling to confirm that I've received your software order by e-mail. Also, we need to discuss the software training schedule.」，哪種角色的人會負責處理訂單，和安排後續的訓練呢？應是「業務代表」較為合理，故選 (B)「A sales representative」為最佳答案。

各選項解析

• 選項 (A)「The man's best friend」、選項 (C)「A scientist」或選項 (D)「An English teacher」都不是會負責處理訂單之人，故不選。

第二題

此題問的是「What does the man suggest the woman do?」，那麼便可判斷要聽到男子給女子的建議內容以便回答。根據男子說的此關鍵句「The person, Sherry, who is in charge of training is not in today.」，提及負責人今天不在，隨後女子回應說「I see. All right, I'll call again tomorrow.」，可聽出是要第二天再打來詢問，故選 (A)「Call and discuss further the next day」為最佳答案；其中「tomorrow」還替換為「the next day」，是典型的以換字表達、換句話說的方式來處理答案選項。

各選項解析

• 選項 (B)「Come to his office immediately」、選項 (C)「Meet Sherry in person this afternoon」與選項 (D)「Send an e-mail to the CEO」都沒有在對話中被提及，所以不選。

第三題

先掃描到題目問的是「What will they discuss tomorrow?」，可判斷要聽出「明天討論的內容」以便回答。根據此關鍵句「We three could discuss both the payment schedule and training issues tomorrow.」便可聽出是要討論付款與訓練之事，故選 (D)「Payment and training issues」為最佳答案。

各選項解析

• 選項 (A)「Pay schedule only」、選項 (B)「Delivery date」與選項 (C)「Training issues」雖然都有提到一點題目的關鍵字，但是所給予的訊息都不完整，因此都不會是合適的答案。

關鍵字彙

confirm [kən`fɝm] ☑ 確認
receive [rɪ`siv] ☑ 接收、收到
in charge of ☐ 負責、擔任
payment [`pemənt] ☐ 付款
arrange [ə`rendʒ] ☑ 安排
invitation [ˌɪnvə`teʃən] ☐ 邀請函

Q1. Who are the two speakers most likely?

(A) Tourists   (B) Government officials

(C) Company employees   (D) University professors

Q2. What are the speakers talking about?

(A) Meeting subjects   (B) Ways to expand new markets

(C) Budget proposals   (D) Employment opportunities

Q3. What does the man plan to do next month?

(A) Visit prospects in Asia   (B) Start his own business

(C) Take a vacation   (D) Learn Chinese and Japanese

解題分析

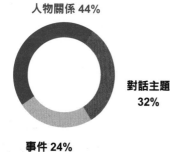

人物關係 44%

對話主題 32%

事件 24%

■ 人物關係 44% — 因為第一題詢問了對話者之間的關係，由於此篇對話是關於業務上的討論，所以可以大膽預測有可能會是同事、競爭對手、上司與下屬……等關係。

■ 對話主題 32% — 想要知道對話的主題不必每個字都聽懂，掌握對話中重複出現的字詞或是同義字，就可以猜出對話主題。

■ 事件 24% — 對話者接下來要做的事，有時候會出現在對話內容之中，這時要懂得搭配選項一起看，因為選項有時候只是將重點字換成同義字，所以平時也要補充字彙量喔！

聽稿

(US / W) So Jackson, what plans do you have for next quarter? I think we need to come up with some good plans to increase profits.

(CA / M) Well, I'm thinking to find new markets and new customers. We could expand the business into new areas, like China, Japan, and Korea.

(US / W) Yeah, that sounds like an excellent idea. I read an article the other day indicating that consumers in Asia buy nearly half of the world's luxury products.

(CA / M) Exactly. So here is what I'm gonna do next. I'm gonna pay a visit to China and Japan next month, talk to some local customers, and find out their real demands.

中譯（美／女）那麼傑克森，對於下一季的營運發展你有什麼規劃？我認為我們需要擬出能夠增加利潤的完善計劃。

（加／男）關於這點，我想我們可以試著開創新的市場與客群。我們應該要在新的地區開拓商機，比如說中國、日本，和韓國。

（美／女）我同意，這聽起來倒是個不錯的主意。我前幾天看到一篇文章，上面指出有關全世界奢侈品的消費，亞洲客源就占了快一半。

（加／男）完全正確，我正打算朝這個方向邁進。我下個月會去中國和日本一趟，先與當地的客戶們聊聊，找出他們的實質需求。

Q1. 兩位講者最有可能是何種關係？（答案：C）

(A) 遊客　　　　　　　　　　　　　(B) 政府官員

(C) 公司員工　　　　　　　　　　　(D) 大學教授

Q2. 兩位講者在討論什麼？（答案：B）

(A) 會議講題　　　　　　　　　　　(B) 拓展新市場的方式

(C) 預算提案　　　　　　　　　　　(D) 工作機會

Q3. 男子下個月計劃做什麼？（答案：A）

(A) 拜訪亞洲客戶　　　　　　　　　(B) 自己創業

(C) 去度假　　　　　　　　　　　　(D) 學中文和日文

解題技巧 聽對話時大家通常會有「想聽懂全部卻無法做到」的挫折感，但事實上在時間很緊迫，又要處理資訊，又要分辨口音的狀況下，最佳的策略是將注意力專注在聽「有需要聽的關鍵點」上比較有效率。而這些講者想要聽者注意的關鍵點，通常會以加強重音來強調。此對話的關鍵要點處可能會是：

（US／W）So Jackson, what plans do you have for next quarter? I think we need to come up with some good plans to increase profits.

（CA／M）Well, I'm thinking to find new markets and new customers. We could expand the business into new areas, like China, Japan, and Korea.

（US／W）Yeah, that sounds like an excellent idea. I read an article the other day indicating that consumers in Asia buy nearly half of the world's luxury products.

（CA／M）Exactly. So here is what I'm gonna do next. I'm gonna pay a visit to China and Japan next month, talk to some local customers, and find out their real demands.

聽出關鍵點之後便可對對話內容有個初步的了解了：兩人在討論下一季的業務策略以增加營收，兩人打算要找新客戶，拓展亞洲市場，在那之前要先去中國與日本走一趟，了解客戶的需求。由此可發現，要了解對話的大概內容，並不用將每個字都聽到或聽懂，僅靠幾個關鍵字一樣可以得到真正有效的效果呢！

若在聽對話之前可以將題目先掃描一下是再好不過了，因如此便可判斷要將注意力放在聽什麼要點上，此題問的是「Who are the two speakers most likely?」，可判斷要了解兩對話者的關係。根據首句關鍵點「So Jackson, what plans do you have for next quarter? I think we need to come up with some good plans to increase profits.」，可聽出會一起討論增加業績的辦法之人應是公司同事才合理，故選 (C)「Company employees」為最佳答案。

各選項解析

• 選項 (A)「Tourists」、選項 (B)「Government officials」與選項 (D)「University professors」都不會是「討論增加業績」的角色故不選。

第二題

此題問的是「What are the speakers talking about?」，那麼可判斷要聽出「討論主要內容」以便回答。根據男子所說的此兩個關鍵句「I'm thinking to find new markets and new customers. We could expand the business into new areas, like China, Japan, and Korea.」，與「I'm gonna pay a visit to China and Japan next month... and find out their real demands.」，可聽出是在討論「拓展亞洲市場」的點子與準備工作，故選 (B)「Ways to expand new markets」為最佳答案。

各選項解析

• 選項 (A)「Meeting subjects」、選項 (C)「Budget proposals」與選項 (D)「Employment opportunities」都沒在對話中出現，故不選。

第三題

此題問的是「What does the man plan to do next month?」，很明顯是問男子下個月所做之事，那麼根據此關鍵句「I'm gonna pay a visit to China and Japan next month, talk to some local customers, and find out their real demands.」，可聽出他是要去中國與日本，並與客戶談談需求。所以選 (A)「Visit prospects in Asia」為最佳答案。

各選項解析

• 選項 (B)「Start his own business」、選項 (C)「Take a vacation」與選項 (D)「Learn Chinese and Japanese」都沒在對話中被討論到，故不選。

關鍵字彙

quarter [ˋkwɔrtɚ] n 季度
profit [ˋprɑfɪt] n 盈收
expand [ɪkˋspænd] v 擴大
indicate [ˋɪndəˌket] v 指出、意指
consumer [kənˋsjumɚ] n 客戶、消費者
luxury goods [ˋlʌkʃərɪ ˋgʊdz] n 奢侈品
exactly [ɪgˋzæktlɪ] ad 的確
local [ˋlokl̩] a 地方上的
demand [dɪˋmænd] n 需求

攻略 3 ｜ 業務協商

Q1. What's the main purpose of this conversation?

(A) To schedule a meeting   (B) To negotiate prices

(C) To place an order   (D) To arrange a conference

Q2. What does the woman request?

(A) More sales leads   (B) Extra budgets

(C) Some training   (D) More discount

Q3. What does the man plan to do next?

(A) Consult with his supervisor first   (B) Place a larger order

(C) Invite Ms. Terry to attend a party   (D) Ask his competitors

解題分析

對話主題 64%

事件 36%

■ 對話主題 64%

■ 事件 36%

由於第一小題是問對話的主題，所以大致聽懂對話即可。又加上抓住重複出現的字詞，對話主題就會很清楚。

看到題目詢問對話者的下一步或是要求時，一定要記得在對話播放的同時也搭配選項一起看，這樣就可以立即刪去不合適的選項。

聽稿

（US / Ｗ）All right, Mr. Smith. So what kind of discount could you give on a large order?

（UK / Ｍ）Well, that really depends on how many units are we talking about, Ms. Terry.

（US / Ｗ）For this particular project, I would say... something in the ballpark of 8,000 IC chipsets. Also we've got other projects coming up, so we probably will have more demands.

（UK / Ｍ）I see, Ms. Terry. In this case, I can give you a 10% discount off the list price, if you order over 10,000 chipsets at one time.

（US / Ｗ）You know what, Mr. Smith? Actually, my boss is evaluating other suppliers, and I'm hoping for a little more help from you. Do you know what I mean?

（UK / Ｍ）Yes, absolutely. Uh... how about this, let me check with my head office, and I'll let you know afterwards, okay?

（美／女）好吧，史密斯先生，談談你們對於較大筆的訂單能給予何種優惠或折扣？

（英／男）這個嘛，泰利小姐，依照該訂單不同的數量，會有不同的方案。

（美／女）那麼請針對我們現在這一個專案來做試算。初步估計⋯⋯約略是八千個 IC 晶片組。
另外我們還有其他的案子要進行，所以可能還會有更多的需求。

（英／男）我明白了，泰利小姐，倘若您單筆訂購超過一萬個 IC 晶片組，我便能提供您九折的
優惠價格。

（美／女）這樣說吧，史密斯先生，其實我的老闆也正在向其他的供應商議價，我倒希望您這邊
能多幫些忙？您應該懂我的意思？

（英／男）是的，完全理解。嗯⋯⋯不然這樣吧，您讓我先跟總部回報，做個確認，我再告訴您
其他後續的消息，如何？

Q1. 此對話的主要目的為何？（答案：**B**）

(A) 為約個會議   (B) 為協商價格

(C) 為下訂單   (D) 為安排研討會

Q2. 女子要求什麼？（答案：**D**）

(A) 更多的潛在客戶   (B) 額外的預算

(C) 教育訓練   (D) 更多折扣

Q3. 男子接下來打算做什麼？（答案：**A**）

(A) 先跟他的上司確認   (B) 下個大訂單

(C) 邀請泰利小姐去參加派對   (D) 跟他的競爭對手詢問

解題技巧　2018 年改制後的多益有維持兩人對話的形式，但內容加得更長了！正是因為內容加得更長，想
要逐字聽到或全部聽懂將變得更加困難。如此一來，更應該將注意力放在聽有效且真正該聽的要
點上就好。而這些講者想要聽者聽到的關鍵點，也通常會被加以重音來處理，此篇加長對話的要
點可能如以下：

（US／W）All right, Mr. Smith. So what kind of discount could you give on a large
order?

（UK／M）Well, that really depends on how many units are we talking about, Ms.
Terry.

（US／W）For this particular project, I would say... something in the ballpark of
8,000 IC chipsets. Also we've got other projects coming up, so we
probably will have more demands.

（UK／M）I see, Ms. Terry. In this case, I can give you a 10% discount off the list
price, if you order over 10,000 chipsets at one time.

（US／W）You know what, Mr. Smith? Actually, my boss is evaluating other
suppliers, and I'm hoping for a little more help from you. Do you know
what I mean?

（UK／M）Yes, absolutely. Uh... how about this, let me check with my head office,
and I'll let you know afterwards, okay?

如此只要聽到幾個有效的關鍵點，也可大概得知：兩人在討論價格與折扣之事，客戶在要求更多折扣優惠，還說有可能會找其他廠商報價，業務便提議要回去問高層以做後續決定。僅聽到幾個關鍵點便可判斷內容大意，無需逐字聽懂！因此建議大家在處理長篇聽力時，不要將焦點分散到「每個字」上頭，而要將注意放在「有效的關鍵點上」即可。

第一題

先看到題目才知要將注意力放在聽什麼要點上，此題問的是「What is the main purpose of this conversation?」。那麼根據女子的此要點句「So what kind of discount could you give on a large order?」，以及男子的回應「Well, that really depends on how many units are we talking about.」，可聽出是在討論訂單價格與折扣之事，故選 (B)「To negotiate prices」為最佳答案。

各選項解析

• 選項 (A)「To schedule a meeting」、選項 (C)「To place an order」與選項 (D)「To arrange a conference」都不是此對話的要點，故不選。

第二題

看到此題問的是「What does the woman request?」，便可以知道要將注意力放在聽「女子的要求」上以便回答。根據男子提可以打九折，但女子似乎不滿意；接著女子所提的此關鍵句「You know what, Mr. Smith? Actually, my boss is evaluating other suppliers, and I'm hoping for a little more help from you. Do you know what I mean?」，她提到有其他廠商也在接洽中，意味著要求更高的折扣。所以正確答案要選擇 (D)「More discount」為最佳答案。

各選項解析

• 選項 (A)「More sales leads」、選項 (B)「Extra budgets」與選項 (C)「Some training」都沒有在對話中提及，故不選。

第三題

在題目播放之前，先掃過題目，發現問的是「What does the man plan to do next?」，便可判斷要聽到男子後續行動的關鍵點以便回答。則根據男子講的此關鍵句「... how about this, let me check with my head office, and I'll let you know afterwards, okay?」，可聽出他是要先去問老闆才可後續決定，故選 (A)「Consult with his supervisor first」為最佳答案。

各選項解析

• 選項 (B)「Place a larger order」、選項 (C)「Invite Ms. Terry to attend a party」與選項 (D)「Ask his competitors」都沒有在對話中提及，所以都不會是正確的答案喔！

關鍵字彙

discount [`dɪskaʊnt] n 打折、優惠折扣
particular [pɚ`tɪkjəlɚ] a 特別的、特殊的
project [`prɑdʒɛkt] n 專案、案子
ballpark [`bɔlpɑrk] n 約略的數目
evaluate [ɪ`væljuˌet] v 評估
supplier [sə`plaɪɚ] n 供應商
absolutely [`æbsəˌlutlɪ] ad 絕對地、完全地
afterwards [`æftɚwɚdz] ad 之後、後來

攻略 1 | 與客戶協商

Q1. What are the speakers talking about?

(A) The outcome of a negotiation

(B) A new employee

(C) Feedback from customers

(D) Pricing strategies

Q2. When does the conversation probably take place?

(A) In an English class

(B) In a meeting with clients

(C) During the weekend

(D) After the negotiation with the client

Q3. What does the man suggest?

(A) Providing more case studies

(B) Emphasizing product's selling points

(C) Keeping lowering the price

(D) Finding more customers

解題分析

對話主題 44%

意見、看法 24%

對話時間點 32%

■ 對話主題 44%　想要知道對話的主題不必每個字都聽懂，掌握此對話中重複出現的字詞或是同義字，例如：price、agree，就能知道對話的主題。

■ 對話時間點 32%　第二題主要是考對話發生的時間點，首先要知道對話的主題，再來是找尋對話中是否有出現時間的相關字眼。

■ 意見、看法 24%　由於第三題是問男子的建議，所以記得將注意力放在男子所說的話上面，就能聽到一些蛛絲馬跡。

聽稿

（US / W）Hey, Harry. How did the negotiation go with your client?

（UK / M）At first, we couldn't agree on anything. But after a lot of discussion, we finally reached an agreement.

（US / W）Sounds good. But did you have to lower the price much?

（UK / M）Well, price was one of that client's major concerns, that's true. But we kept emphasizing the value of our solutions and the benefits they're gonna get. Eventually, the client agreed on the price.

中譯　（美／**女**）嘿，哈利，你跟客戶協商得如何？

（英／**男**）起初，我們處於意見極度不合的狀態。但經過多次協商之後，我們雙方終於達成了共識。

（美／**女**）那就好。不過有需要把價錢降得很低嗎？

（英／**男**）關於這點，由於價格確實是客戶的主要考量，但我們持續強調我們解決方案的價值以及他們所得到的好處。最終客戶還是同意了所開出的價碼。

Q1. 兩位講者在討論什麼？（答案：**A**）

(A) 一場協商的結果　　　　　　　　　(B) 一個新員工

(C) 客戶意見回饋　　　　　　　　　　(D) 價格策略

Q2. 此對話有可能在何時發生？（答案：**D**）

(A) 在英文課中　　　　　　　　　　　(B) 在與客戶的會議中

(C) 在週末　　　　　　　　　　　　　(D) 在與客戶的協商會之後

Q3. 男子建議什麼事？（答案：**B**）

(A) 提供更多案例研究　　　　　　　　(B) 強調產品賣點

(C) 持續降低價格　　　　　　　　　　(D) 找到更多客戶

解題技巧　聽長篇對話時要有一個心理準備，若是將專注力放在每個單字上，那聽不到一兩句便會精神衰弱無法持續了。但是，若是將注意力分散到對話中不同階段的要點上，並且隨著一句話的語調起伏來判斷主要關鍵點與次要資訊的分別，便可僅將焦點放在聽懂主要關鍵點上。而通常主要關鍵點是以重音強調之處，以便提醒聽者要點之處。此對話所會強調的主要資訊可能會是：

> （US／**W**）Hey, Harry. How did the negotiation go with your client?
>
> （UK／**M**）At first, we couldn't agree on anything. But after a lot of discussion, we finally reached an agreement.
>
> （US／**W**）Sounds good. But did you have to lower the price much?
>
> （UK／**M**）Well, price was one of that client's major concerns, that's true. But we kept emphasizing the value of our solutions and the benefits they're gonna get. Eventually, the client agreed on the price.

如此將焦點放在幾個關鍵點上，便可以得知大概內容為：兩人在討論與客戶的協商結果，原本沒共識，但經過討論，並將要點放在好處上，而非放在價格上，最後便產生了不用放低價格的共識了。由此可知，僅注意幾個會發揮作用的焦點之處，比將一整段對話翻譯完來得有效喔！

第一題

若在對話播放出來之前可以先掃一下題目那是最好，如此一來才能得知要聽什麼焦點。此題問的是「What are the speakers talking about?」，便可判斷要聽對話主題。根據此關鍵句「How did the negotiation go with your client?」，可聽出是在問協商的結果如何，故選擇 (A)「The outcome of a negotiation」為最佳答案。

• 選項 (B)「A new employee」、選項 (C)「Feedback from customers」與選項 (D)「Pricing strategies」在對話中完全都沒有被提及，所以都不能選。

第二題

此題問的是「When does the conversation probably take place?」，那麼將要點放在時間點上以便回答。根據此關鍵句「At first, we couldn't agree on anything. But after a lot of discussion, we finally reached an agreement.」，可聽出應是協商結束之後才會有這樣的對話。所以要選擇 (D)「After the negotiation with the client」為最佳答案。

• 選項 (A)「In an English class」、選項 (B)「In a meeting with clients」與選項 (C)「During the weekend」都與對話內容的時間點沒有搭配到，因此都不會是正確答案喔！

第三題

一看到題目問的是「What does the man suggest?」，那麼要將焦點放在男子所提的事情上以便回答。根據男子所說的此關鍵句「But we kept emphasizing the value of our solutions and the benefits they're gonna get.」，可聽出他是一直強調產品優勢與客戶用了之後的好處，而非一直繞在價格上周旋的。所以在四個選項中選擇最為合適的 (B)「Emphasizing product's selling points」為最佳答案。

• 選項 (A)「Providing more case studies」、選項 (C)「Keeping lowering the price」與選項 (D)「Finding more customers」都沒有在對話中提及，故不選。

關鍵字彙

negotiation [nɪˌgoʃɪˋeʃən] n 協商、談判
discussion [dɪˋskʌʃən] n 討論
finally [ˋfaɪnl̩ɪ] adv 最後地
reach [ritʃ] v 達成
agreement [əˋgrimənt] n 同意、共識
major [ˋmedʒɚ] a 主要的、重大的
concern [kənˋsɝn] n 憂慮、擔憂之事
emphasize [ˋɛmfəˌsaɪz] v 強調
solution [səˋluʃən] n 解決方案
benefit [ˋbɛnəfɪt] n 好處
eventually [ɪˋvɛntʃʊəlɪ] adv 最終地

攻略 2 | 會議中場休息

Q1. When is the conversation taking place?

(A) Before lunch   (B) On Sunday

(C) After work   (D) During a meeting break

Q2. What is the man's concern?

(A) Being late for next meeting

(B) Buying coffee for meeting attendees

(C) Convincing managers to accept his proposal

(D) Collecting more marketing information

Q3. What does the woman suggest the man do?

(A) Arrange another meeting   (B) Take a good rest

(C) Be more confident   (D) Talk to more clients

解題分析

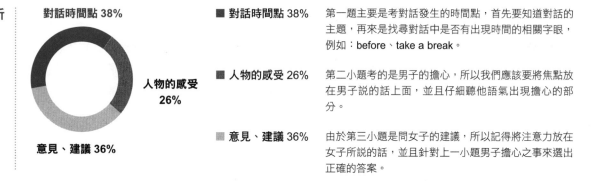

對話時間點 38%

人物的感受 26%

意見、建議 36%

■ 對話時間點 38% — 第一題主要是考對話發生的時間點，首先要知道對話的主題，再來是找尋對話中是否有出現時間的相關字眼，例如：before、take a break。

■ 人物的感受 26% — 第二小題考的是男子的擔心，所以我們應該要將焦點放在男子說的話上面，並且仔細聽他語氣出現擔心的部分。

■ 意見、建議 36% — 由於第三小題是問女子的建議，所以記得將注意力放在女子所說的話，並且針對上一小題男子擔心之事來選出正確的答案。

聽稿

（AU / W）Before we move on to the next item on the agenda, why don't we take a break?

（CA / M）Sure, good idea. Uh... Linda, let's get a cup of coffee downstairs and I need to talk to you about something. Well, it's about my budget proposal, really. I hope I can convince the managers.

（AU / W）All right, Sam. I think you should just communicate your absolute confidence in the proposal, and they will be more likely to buy your ideas.

（CA / M）Okay, good. I'll also use some statistics to back up my viewpoints.

（澳／女）在我們開始討論下一項議程之前，大家先暫時休息一下吧。

（加／男）好的，沒問題。嗯……琳達，我有事情要告訴妳，我們一起去樓下喝杯咖啡吧？其實是有關預算提案的事情，我希望能夠說服主管們同意。

（澳／女）好的，山姆。我覺得你只需要拿出充分的自信去和經理們溝通提案，他們會比較容易信服的。

（加／男）這樣啊，好吧。我會試著用些數據來輔助我提出的觀點。

Q1. 此對話最有可能是何時發生？（答案：D）

(A) 午餐前 　　　　　　　　　　　(B) 週日

(C) 下班後 　　　　　　　　　　　(D) 會議休息時

Q2. 男子擔心之事為何？（答案：C）

(A) 下一場會議會遲到 　　　　　　(B) 幫與會者買咖啡

(C) 說服經理們接受他的提案 　　　(D) 收集更多市場資訊

Q3. 女子建議男子做什麼？（答案：C）

(A) 安排另一個會議 　　　　　　　(B) 好好休息一下

(C) 更有自信 　　　　　　　　　　(D) 跟更多客戶談談

解題技巧

一段長篇對話內的句子並非每個字的重要性都一樣，而是會隨著說話者的語調起伏、速度快慢來分出哪些地方是講者想強調的要點，哪些則不是。因此，大家也應將注意力放在聽講者想強調的「關鍵點」上，這些關鍵資訊之處，通常會加以重音來強調，比方說此組對話，要點內容可能會是以下：

（AU／W）Before we move on to the next item on the agenda, why don't we take a break?

（CA／M）Sure, good idea. Uh... Linda, let's get a cup of coffee downstairs and I need to talk to you about something. Well, it's about my budget proposal, really. I hope I can convince the managers.

（AU／W）All right, Sam. I think you should just communicate your absolute confidence in the proposal, and they will be more likely to buy your ideas.

（CA／M）Okay, good. I'll also use some statistics to back up my viewpoints.

在了解幾個關鍵點之後，便可以大約了解此對話是在開會休息間所討論到的，兩人要去買咖啡的當中，順便討論了如何讓老闆接受預算提議之事。如此看來，真的要了解對話的大概，並不用每個字都翻譯，而要了解幾個關鍵字便可達到效果。

第一題

在聽對話題之前，若行有餘力，你可以將題目都看過一遍，以便知道要將注意力放在聽什麼要點上。此題問的是「When is the conversation taking place?」，那麼可得知要聽到「時間點」相關答案以便回答。根據此關鍵句「Before we move on to the next item on the agenda, why don't we take a break?」，可以得知是在會議的中場休息間的對話，故選 (D)「During a meeting break」為最佳答案。

各選項解析

- 選項 (A)「Before lunch」、選項 (B)「On Sunday」與選項 (C)「After work」都與對話發生的情景不合，也與原句的「take a break（休息一下）」不太有邏輯上的關聯性，故都不選。

第二題

此題問的是「What is the man's concern?」，那麼心中打定主意要聽到男子擔憂之事以便回答。接著，根據男子說的此關鍵句「Well, it's about my budget proposal, really. I hope I can convince the managers.」，可聽出他是想說服經理們接受他的預算提案的，故選 (C)「Convincing managers to accept his proposal」為最佳答案。

各選項解析

- 選 項 (A)「Being late for next meeting」、選 項 (B)「Buying coffee for meeting attendees」 與 選 項 (D)「Collecting more marketing information」，三個選項都沒有在對話中被討論到，故不選。

第三題

先看到題目問的是「What does the woman suggest the man do?」，那麼要聽到「女子對男子的建議」內容以便回答，根據此關鍵句「I think you should just communicate your absolute confidence in the proposal, and they will be more likely to buy your ideas.」可聽出女子是建議男子要有自信地跟老闆報告此事，故選 (C) Be more confident 為最佳答案。

各選項解析

- 選項 (A)「Arrange another meeting」、選項 (B)「Take a good rest」與選項 (D)「Talk to more clients」都沒有在對話中被提及，故不選。

關鍵字彙

item [ˈaɪtəm] n 項目
agenda [əˈdʒɛndə] n 議程
downstairs [ˌdaʊnˈstɛrz] ad 在樓下
budget [ˈbʌdʒɪt] n 預算
proposal [prəˈpozl̩] n 提議、提案
convince [kənˈvɪns] v 說服
communicate [kəˈmjunəˌket] v 溝通
absolute [ˈæbsəˌlut] a 確切的、完全的
confidence [ˈkɑnfədəns] n 信心
statistics [stəˈtɪstɪks] n 統計數據
viewpoint [ˈvjuˌpɔɪnt] n 觀點、看法

Meeting room	Time	Owner / Purposes
5A	9 a.m. - 11:30 a.m.	Sherry Liang
7B	10 a.m. - 1 p.m.	Mike Smith
12T	1 p.m. - 3 p.m.	Director of HR
1S	9 a.m. - 5 p.m.	Interview sessions

Q1. **What are the speakers talking about?**

(A) An upcoming meeting　　　　(B) New market trends

(C) Their chief rivals　　　　(D) Sales strategies

Q2. **What is the woman planning to do tomorrow afternoon?**

(A) Arrange a conference　　　　(B) Pick up her kids early

(C) Visit some customers　　　　(D) Chair the meeting

新 **Q3.** **Look at the table. Which meeting room will the speakers have the meeting in?**

(A) 7B　　　　(B) 5A

(C) 1S　　　　(D) 12T

解題分析

對話主題 43%

對話者身分 37%

對話細節 20%

■ 對話主題 43%　多益聽力考試中，最常考的是對話、獨白中的主題，主要是為了考大家有沒有聽懂或讀懂大概的內容，對於內容的主題有初步的理解即可。

■ 對話者身分 37%　由於是兩個人的對話，所以也會很常出現詢問其中一名對話者的職業、年紀等。只要根據對話內容，對話者的身分便可以輕鬆得知。

■ 對話細節 20%　對話細節有時也會在多益的聽力考試中出現，像是對話者提到的時間、藉由對話內容推測對話者的下一步等。

聽稿

（US / Ⓦ）Mark, the manager just called a meeting tomorrow, do you know what the meeting is about at all?

（CA / Ⓜ）Yeah, I do. Uh, the manager wants all team members to brainstorm creative ideas for better marketing strategies.

（US / Ⓦ）Well, then I guess it's essential for all marketing specialists to attend. Actually, I am planning to visit some clients tomorrow afternoon.

（CA / Ⓜ）You know what? I think the length of the meeting will be less than 2 hours. If the meeting ends by noon, you still have time for clients in the afternoon.

中譯

（美／**女**）馬克，經理剛宣布明天要開會，你知道會議是要談論什麼嗎？

（加／**男**）我知道。經理希望能透過團隊的集思廣益，腦力激盪出一些富有創意的行銷策略。

（美／**女**）若是如此，那所有行銷專員更應該參加。事實上，我原本計劃明天下午要去拜訪些客戶。

（加／**男**）照理來說，明日的會議應該在兩個小時以內就可以結束了。如果中午結束的話，妳下午依然能有多餘的時間去拜訪客戶的。

會議室	時間	負責人／目的
5A	早上九點～早上十一點半	梁雪莉
7B	早上十點～下午一點	麥可・史密斯
12T	下午一點～下午三點	人資經理
1S	早上九點～下午五點	面談

Q1. 兩位講者在討論什麼？（答案：**A**）

(A) 即將到來的會議　　　　　　(B) 新的市場趨勢
(C) 他們的主要敵手　　　　　　(D) 業務策略

Q2. 女子計劃明天下午要做什麼？（答案：**C**）

(A) 安排一場研討會　　　　　　(B) 提早去接小孩
(C) 拜訪一些客戶　　　　　　　(D) 主持會議

新 **Q3.** 請看表格，講者將會在哪間會議室內開會？（答案：**B**）

(A) 7B　　　　　　　　　　　　(B) 5A
(C) 1S　　　　　　　　　　　　(D) 12T

解題技巧

聽對話的同時應了解對話中並非每個字重要性都一樣，而是會有要點之處，講者在講這些要點訊息時，通常會以加強重音的方式來呈現，以提醒聽者注意。那麼此對話內可能的要點之處，便標如以下：

（US／**W**）Mark, the manager just called a meeting tomorrow, do you know what the meeting is about at all?

（CA／**M**）Yeah, I do. Uh, the manager wants all team members to brainstorm creative ideas for better marketing strategies.

（US／**W**）Well, then I guess it's essential for all marketing specialists to attend. Actually, I am planning to visit some clients tomorrow afternoon.

（CA／**M**）You know what? I think the length of the meeting will be less than 2 hours. If the meeting ends by noon, you still have time for clients in the afternoon.

了解幾個對話的要點之後，便可知道對話的大概方向，即是在討論會議內容與拜訪客戶之間的時間調配了。

在真正對話內容被播放出來之前,應把握時間先將題目看過,以便預設應將注意力放在聽什麼資訊上。此題問的是「What are the speakers talking about?」,兩人討論之主題為何。那麼根據女子所講的此關鍵句「Mark, the manager just called a meeting tomorrow, do you know what the meeting is about at all?」,可聽出是在討論明天的會議一事,故選 (A)「An upcoming meeting」為最佳答案。

各選項解析

- 選項 (B)「New market trends」說是在討論市場趨勢,但此主題並沒在對話中被提及,故不選。
- 選項 (C)「Their chief rivals」提到他們的主要競爭對手,但也沒在對話中聽到,不可當答案。
- 選項 (D)「Sales strategies」說要討論業務策略,是為了和男子所講的「marketing strategies(行銷策略)」混淆,故不選。

第二題

先掃過題目,看到此題問的是「What is the woman planning to do tomorrow afternoon?」。在聽到對話中,女子所提的此關鍵句「Actually, I am planning to visit some clients tomorrow afternoon.」,可聽出是要去拜訪客戶,那麼,選項 (C)「Visit some customers」就是最佳答案了。提醒大家一點,在選項 (C) 中,「clients」可與「customers」做替換。

各選項解析

- 選項 (A)「Arrange a conference」、選項 (B)「Pick up her kids early」和選項 (D)「Chair the meeting」都沒在對話中被提及,自然也不會是答案。

新 **第三題**

在對話播放之前,應該要先大致讀一下印在題本上的題目。這一題可看到是搭配表格的題目,這時就要在心中先做好準備,表格要搭配對話中的線索才可回答。此題問的是「Which meeting room will the speakers have the meeting in?」,主要考大家閱讀表格的能力,要查看在哪間會議室開會。

根據對話中男子最後一句「I think the length of the meeting will be less than 2 hours. If the meeting ends by noon...」的內容,可以得知會議有可能在中午前結束;再來根據會議室的登記表,就能得出此會議最有可能是在 5A 會議室舉辦的答案,故選 (B) 5A 為最佳答案。其他的會議都是在下午舉辦,或不是在中午前結束的會議,都不能選。

關鍵字彙

brainstorm [ˈbrenˌstɔrm] 🆅 腦力激盪、集思廣益
creative [krɪˈetɪv] 🅰 有創意的
strategy [ˈstrætədʒɪ] 🅽 策略
essential [ɪˈsɛnʃəl] 🅰 重要的、關鍵的
specialist [ˈspɛʃəlɪst] 🅽 專員
length [lɛŋθ] 🅽 長度

Unit 4 問題解決類

攻略 1 | 策略討論

Q1. What are the speakers discussing?

(A) Effective advertising strategies   (B) Budgets for advertising campaigns

(C) Hiring more ad designers   (D) Functions of a new product

Q2. What department do the speakers probably work in?

(A) Administration   (B) Accounting

(C) Engineering   (D) Marketing

Q3. What does the man suggest?

(A) Making more cold calls   (B) Sending out eDMs

(C) Place an ad in the newspapers   (D) Promoting products on TV

解題分析

對話主題 53%

對話細節 47%

■ 對話主題 53%

多益考試中，最常考的是對話、獨白中的主題，主要是為了考大家有沒有聽懂大概的內容，對於內容的主題有初步的理解即可。

■ 對話細節 47%

對話細節有時也會在多益的聽力考試中出現，像是對話者提到的部門、對話者的建議……等。

聽稿

（US / W）We need to create a powerful advertisement for our product that will really attract customers.

（UK / M）I'm thinking about it too. So what do you have in mind?

（US / W）Maybe we can place an advertisement in all the newspapers.

（UK / M）Well, I think we should broadcast a series of TV advertisements. You know, something so memorable that people will start talking about our products.

中譯

（美／女）我們需要為本產品製作一支具有強烈穿透力、能夠真正吸引顧客目光的廣告。

（英／男）英雄所見略同。妳有什麼想法？

（美／女）或許我們可以先從所有報紙上的平面廣告開始嘗試。

（英／男）嗯，我倒覺得一整套系列的電視廣告是比較可行的。妳知道的，好比加深觀眾的印象，讓產品成為他們生活中的熱門話題等等。

Q1. 兩位講者在討論什麼？（答案：A）

(A) 有效的廣告策略　　　　　　　　(B) 廣告活動的預算

(C) 僱用更多廣告設計者　　　　　　(D) 一個新產品的功能

Q2. 兩位講者可能在哪個部門工作？（答案：D）

(A) 行政部　　　　　　　　　　　　(B) 會計部

(C) 工程部　　　　　　　　　　　　(D) 行銷部

Q3. 男子建議什麼事？（答案：D）

(A) 打更多電話開發客戶　　　　　　(B) 寄發電子廣告

(C) 登報紙廣告　　　　　　　　　　(D) 透過電視廣告宣傳產品

解題技巧

聽長篇聽力時不比像照片或簡答題，只要聽一兩句，就可以試圖將整句聽懂，而是應養成習慣，可以判斷對話中的主要資訊和次要細節資訊。主要的關鍵資訊才是講者所想要強調的，也正因為如此，這些主要資訊才是題目會想問的。比方說此對話內有幾個主要資訊像是：

> （US／W）We need to create a powerful advertisement for our product that will really attract customers.
>
> （UK／M）I'm thinking about it too. So what do you have in mind?
>
> （US／W）Maybe we can place an advertisement in all the newspapers.
>
> （UK／M）Well, I think we should broadcast a series of TV advertisements. You know, something so memorable that people will start talking about our products.

如此看來，根據幾個關鍵要點，便可以聽出對話中的兩人在討論要做什麼廣告以吸引客戶。女同事想要在報紙上登廣告，男同事想要做的是電視廣告。依據對話關鍵點就可以知道對話內容了。是不是比一個字、一個字地翻譯來得更有效率呢？

第一題

事先查看問題的好處是，可以判斷要將焦點放在聽什麼資訊上。在對話正式播出之前，先看到此題問的是「What are the speakers discussing?」，便打定主意要聽到討論主題的選項以便回答。根據此句關鍵句「We need to create a powerful advertisement for our product that will really attract customers.」，便可以聽出討論內容與有影響力的廣告有關，故選 (A)「Effective advertising strategies」為最佳答案。

各選項解析

- 選項 (B)「Budgets for advertising campaigns」、選項 (C)「Hiring more ad designers」與選項 (D)「Functions of a new product」都沒有在對話中提到，故不選。

第二題

先瞄到此題問的是「What department do the speakers probably work in?」，既然是在問講者所工作的部門，隨即將焦點放在聽工作內容、工作部門的資訊上。根據關鍵句「Maybe we can place an advertisement in all the newspapers.」可以推斷，哪一個部門是處理刊登廣告之事呢？應是「行銷部」較為合理，故選 (D)「Marketing」為最佳答案。

各選項解析

- 選項 (A)「Administration」、選項 (B)「Accounting」與選項 (C)「Engineering」都不會是處理刊登廣告事宜的部門，所以都不會是正確答案喔！

第三題

先看到題目「What does the man suggest?」，問的是男子的建議，那麼便應將注意力放在聽男子說的內容上。根據此關鍵句「Well, I think we should broadcast a series of TV advertisements.」，可聽出男子是想在電視上做廣告的，故選 (D)「Promoting products on TV」為正確。

各選項解析

- 選項 (A)「Making more cold calls」、選項 (B)「Sending out eDMs」與選項 (C)「Place an ad in the newspapers」都沒有在男子所說的話中出現，故不選。

關鍵字彙

> powerful [`paʊɚfəl] a 有影響力的
> advertisement [ˌædvɚ`taɪzmənt] n 廣告
> attract [ə`trækt] v 吸引
> broadcast [`brɔdˌkæst] v 廣播、播送
> a series of ph 一系列
> memorable [`mɛmərəbl] a 令人難忘的

Q1. **Who most likely are the speakers?**

(A) Neighbors　　　　　　　　(B) Classmates

(C) Co-workers　　　　　　　(D) Shoppers

Q2. **What does the woman suggest they do?**

(A) Call all customers by themselves

(B) Hire a market research company to do the job

(C) Talk to their supervisor tomorrow

(D) Invite more friends to the party

Q3. **What will the man probably do next?**

(A) Write a proposal to his boss　　(B) Survey market research firms

(C) Discuss with the woman's brother　　(D) Talk to his consultant friend

解題分析

對話者身分 55%

對話細節 45%

■ 對話者身分 55%

■ 對話細節 45%

多益考試中，最常考的是對話、獨白中的主角身分，主要是為了考大家能不能從對話中找出關鍵點，例如：對話者的職位、公司名稱……等。

對話細節很常會在多益的聽力考試中出現，像是對話者提到的時間、藉由對話內容推測對話者的下一步……等。

聽稿

（AU / Ⓦ）I really think we should try more creative marketing strategies, otherwise we'll never improve our marketing performance.

（CA / Ⓜ）You are definitely right, Judy. Why don't we start with conducting some market research? We need to find out what customers really want first, don't we?

（AU / Ⓦ）Yes, we do. That's exactly what I am planning to do. I am thinking to work with a market research firm in order to save some time. Do you think it's workable?

（CA / Ⓜ）Yeah, that's a brilliant idea. One of my friends is working as a marketing consultant and I'm gonna check with him and see how he can collaborate with us.

中譯　（澳／女）我真的認為我們應該要開發些有創意的點子，否則將難以改善我們的績效。

（加／男）茱蒂，妳說得很有道理。我們何不從市場調查這塊著手？我們總要先知道消費者的真正需求是什麼，對吧？

（澳／女）那是當然。這正是我下一步的打算。或許該先從與其他市調公司協同合作這方面來進行切入，以便節省時間。你認為這樣是可行的嗎？

（加／男）嗯，這是很棒的主意。我有個朋友在當行銷顧問，我來問問看他是否有意願要跟我們合作。

Q1. 兩位講者最有可能是？（答案：C）

(A) 鄰居　　　　　　　　　　　　　　(B) 同學

(C) 同事　　　　　　　　　　　　　　(D) 購物者

Q2. 女子建議他們要做什麼？（答案：B）

(A) 親自打電話給所有客戶　　　　　　(B) 找個市場調查公司做市調

(C) 明天跟他們上司談談　　　　　　　(D) 邀請更多朋友參加派對

Q3. 男子接下來可能會做什麼？（答案：D）

(A) 寫個提議案給老闆　　　　　　　　(B) 比較市場調查公司

(C) 跟女子的哥哥討論一下　　　　　　(D) 跟他的顧問朋友談談

解題技巧　大家在準備聽力時通常會發下宏願，希望可以將所有字詞都聽到，最好還可以同時在腦中翻譯以聽懂每句意思。但事實上，這些對話內容都是虛構的，不會是需要逐字聽懂的實用知識。相反地，考試的目的僅要大家「回答問題」，為了要回答問題，便應該將注意力放在「可以回答問題」的要點上就好。而這些要點也會加以加強重音來處理，以吸引到聽者的注意，此對話的要點便可能是：

> （AU／W）I really think we should try more creative marketing strategies, otherwise we'll never improve our marketing performance.
>
> （CA／M）You are definitely right, Judy. Why don't we start with conducting some market research? We need to find out what customers really want first, don't we?
>
> （AU／W）Yes, we do. That's exactly what I am planning to do. I am thinking to work with a market research firm in order to save some time. Do you think it's workable?
>
> （CA／M）Yeah, that's a brilliant idea. One of my friends is working as a marketing consultant and I'm gonna check with him and see how he can collaborate with us.

如此聽到幾個關鍵點後，還可以歸納出對話的大意內容：兩人在討論行銷策略，想要做市場調查以了解客戶要什麼，故要跟市調公司合作，後續要先與一個在市調公司上班的朋友聯絡看看。可見得將注意力放在「聽關鍵點」上的重要性。

第一題

在聽對話之前務必要先將題目掃過一次，以便得知會被問到什麼方向的問題，和要找什麼答案。此題問的是「Who most likely are the speakers?」，那麼根據此關鍵句「I really think we should try more creative marketing strategies, otherwise we'll never improve our marketing performance.」，可以判斷會要共同討論行銷策略的人，應是公司同事較為合理，故選 (C)「Co-workers」為最佳答案。

各選項解析

• 選項 (A)「Neighbors」、選項 (B)「Classmates」與選項 (D)「Shoppers」都不會是要討論行銷策略之人，故不選。

第二題

此題問的是「What does the woman suggest they do?」，既然是問女子的建議，便應將注意力放在聽女子所提之建議上。根據女子所說的此關鍵句「I am thinking to work with a market research firm in order to save some time.」，可聽出她是傾向請市調公司做市調的，以節省時間。故選 (B)「Hire a market research company to do the job」為最佳答案。

各選項解析

• 選項 (A)「Call all customers by themselves」、選項 (C)「Talk to their supervisor tomorrow」與選項 (D)「Invite more friends to the party」都沒有在對話中被提及，故不選。

第三題

先看到題目問的是「What will the man probably do next?」，那麼便要注意聽男子所提的行動以便回答。根據男子所說的此關鍵句「One of my friends is working as marketing consultant and I'm gonna check with him and see how he can collaborate with us.」，他是打算要打電話給在市調公司工作的朋友，故選 (D)「Talk to his consultant friend」為最佳答案。

各選項解析

• 選項 (A)「Write a proposal to his boss」、選項 (B)「Survey market research firms」與選項 (C)「Discuss with the woman's brother」都沒有在對話中出現，故不選。

關鍵字彙

> otherwise [ˋʌðɚˌwaɪz] ad 否則、不然
> improve [ɪmˋpruv] v 進步、精進
> performance [pɚˋfɔrməns] n 表演、表現
> definitely [ˋdɛfənɪtlɪ] ad 真正地、的確
> conduct [kənˋdʌkt] v 處理、發起
> research [rɪˋsɝtʃ] n 調查
> brilliant [ˋbrɪljənt] a 聰明的
> workable [ˋwɝkəbl] a 可行的
> consultant [kənˋsʌltənt] n 顧問
> collaborate [kəˋlæbəˌret] v 協同合作

攻略 3 | 解決設備問題（三人對話）

新 Q1. Where is the conversation probably taking place?

(A) On the golf course   (B) On the campus

(C) In the office   (D) At the airport

新 Q2. What does the man offer to do?

(A) Buy both women some snacks   (B) Fix the copy machine problem

(C) Lend some money to the woman   (D) Buy a new copy machine

新 Q3. What does the man imply about the company?

(A) Some employees will be laid off

(B) All office equipment will be upgraded

(C) The management will increase budget soon

(D) The sales outcome is not good enough

解題分析

對話地點 52%

對話細節 48%

■ 對話地點 52%

■ 對話細節 48%

若在多益考試中出現詢問對話發生地點的題目，就像聽對話主題一樣，大家可以透過大致的內容，猜出對話發生的地點；例如：同事聊公事會在辦公室內發生。

對話細節有時也會在多益的聽力考試中出現，像是對話者提到的時間、藉由對話內容推測對話者的下一步等。

聽稿

（US / W）Oh, no. The copy machine is jammed again. This is the third time today.

（UK / M）Well, let me help you with that, Liz. First of all, we need to inspect the paper path and remove the jammed paper. Like this, okay? Now, it's working fine.

（AU / W）I'm just wondering why the management don't want to replace this old machine with a new one.

（US / W）Well, the management always want to cut expenses, don't they?

（UK / M）I guess Liz is right. Our sales this quarter is not as good as expected, so no wonder managers are less willing to invest budget in replacing equipment.

（AU / W）I see what you mean. Well, then we'd better treat this old copy machine more gently.

中譯　（美 / 女）噢，不，影印機又卡紙了。今天已經是第三次了。

（英 / 男）嗯，我來幫妳吧，麗茲。首先，我們要先檢查紙張傳送的途徑，把卡住的紙張先抽起來。像這樣，會了嗎？這樣就恢復正常了。

（澳 / 女）為何主管們不乾脆將這台舊的替換成新的呢？

（美 / 女）嗯，主管們總是無所不用其極地要節省開支，難道不是嗎？

（英 / 男）麗茲言之有理。我們這一季的銷售額不如預期中來得要好，難怪主管們不願花更多的預算投資在更換設備上。

（澳 / 女）我明白你的意思。好吧，那我們更該友善對待這台影印機了。

新 **Q1.** 此對話可能發生在何處？（答案：C）

(A) 在高爾夫球場上　　　　　　　　　(B) 在校園內

(C) 在辦公室　　　　　　　　　　　　(D) 在機場

新 **Q2.** 男子提供什麼樣的協助？（答案：B）

(A) 幫兩位女子買點心　　　　　　　　(B) 解決影印機的問題

(C) 借點錢給女子　　　　　　　　　　(D) 買台新的影印機

新 **Q3.** 男子暗示關於公司的什麼事？（答案：D）

(A) 一些員工要被資遣了　　　　　　　(B) 所有的公司設備都會更新

(C) 管理階層的人很快會增加預算　　　(D) 業績成果不夠理想

解題技巧　與其想將對話都聽懂，不如將有限的注意力放在聽關鍵要點上面，以針對題目問的來判斷答案。對話中的關鍵要點是講者要聽者注意的，自然也會想辦法引起聽者的注意力，最直接的就是在要點之處加強重音了。此組聽力是三人的對話，大家可能一聽到是三個人在講話時就慌了，但事實上不管是兩人還是三人，策略都是將注意力擺在聽關鍵字詞上即可。頂多在腦中想像一下三人對話的畫面，以增加臨場感，但最好還是可以聽出關鍵要點之處。此組對話的要點可能以重音強調如以下：

（US / W）Oh, no. The copy machine is jammed again. This is the third time today.

（UK / M）Well, let me help you with that, Liz. First of all, we need to inspect the paper path and remove the jammed paper. Like this, okay? Now, it's working fine.

（AU / W）I'm just wondering why the management don't want to replace this old machine with a new one.

（US / W）Well, the management always want to cut expenses, don't they?

（UK / M）I guess Liz is right. Our sales this quarter is not as good as expected, so no wonder managers are less willing to invest budget in replacing equipment.

（AU / W）I see what you mean. Well, then we'd better treat this old copy machine more gently.

有感覺到了嗎？我們將焦點放在有加強重音的要點上，也是可以非常清楚地了解對話內容。針對此對話便可歸納出幾個要點：「由於印表機卡紙，讓三人討論起公司為何不更新設備，原因是業

績不如預期，公司想節省成本，故不想更新設備。」，在有限時間內也能聽出個大概的內容，並不需要逐字聽到才可達成！

新 第一題

若在聽力播放出來之前可以先掃一遍題目，便可以判斷要聽什麼樣的答案以回答。此題問的是「Where is the conversation probably taking place?」，那麼要聽到地點相關資訊才會是答案。根據此關鍵句的內容「Oh, no. The copy machine is jammed again. This is the third time today.」，提到了印表機卡紙。那麼，哪裡才會是有印表機的地方呢？看了一下四個選項，應該是辦公室內才合理，故選 (C)「In the office」為最佳答案。

各選項解析

- 選項 (A)「On the golf course」、選項 (B)「On the campus」或選項 (D)「At the airport」，依據題目，並自我判斷，這三個都不會是有印表機的地方，故不選。

新 第二題

此題問的是「What does the man offer to do?」，既然是問男子的事情，就應將注意力放在男子所說的話上，根據男子此關鍵句內容「Well, let me help you with that, Liz. First of all, we need to inspect the paper path and remove the jammed paper. Like this, okay? Now, it's working fine.」，可聽出男子是要幫女子解釋印表機卡紙的問題，所以要選 (B)「Fix the copy machine problem」才合理。

各選項解析

- 選項 (A)「Buy both women some snacks」、選項 (C)「Lend some money to the woman」與選項 (D)「Buy a new copy machine」都沒有在對話內出現，故不選。

新 第三題

此題問的是「What does the man imply about the company?」，問到男子提及公司相關之事，便應將注意力放在聽男子所說的話上。根據此關鍵句「Our sales this quarter is not as good as expected, so no wonder managers are less willing to invest budget in replacing equipment.」，可判斷男子認為公司業績不如預期中的好，因此選 (D)「The sales outcome is not good enough.」為最佳答案。

各選項解析

- 選項 (A)「Some employees will be laid off.」、選項 (B)「All office equipment will be upgraded.」或選項 (C)「The management will increase budget soon.」都沒有在對話中被提及，故不選。

關鍵字彙

machine [mə`ʃin] n 機器	expense [ɪk`spɛns] n 花費
jam [dʒæm] v 使卡住	invest [ɪn`vɛst] v 投資
inspect [ɪn`spɛkt] v 檢查、檢視	equipment [ɪ`kwɪpmənt] n 設備
remove [rɪ`muv] v 移出、排除	treat [trit] v 對待
wonder [`wʌndɚ] v 想知道	gently [`dʒɛntlɪ] ad 溫柔地、輕輕地
replace [rɪ`ples] v 取代	

Q1. Why does the woman want to update her CV?

(A) To show her boss what she can do

(B) To look for new job opportunities

(C) To impress the man

(D) To transfer to other branches

Q2. What is the woman's major concern?

(A) Her old-fashioned supervisor

(B) Her stressful working environment

(C) Her children's education

(D) Her sales performance

Q3. What does the man suggest the woman do?

(A) To find a headhunter to help her

(B) To leave the company as soon as possible

(C) To start a high-tech company

(D) To find a more flexible company

解題分析

對話主題 52%

對話細節 48%

■ **對話主題** 52%　多益考試中，最常考的是對話、獨白中的主題，主要是為了考大家有沒有聽懂大概的內容，對於內容的主題有初步的理解即可。

■ **對話細節** 48%　這一個題組考了許多對話細節，像是對話者的建議、對話者的擔心……等，這些細節其實也不用太擔心，只要在對話播放時，搭配選項一起看，就能找到合適的答案。

聽稿

（US / Ⓦ）I'm thinking to update my resume.

（UK / Ⓜ）Why? Are you planning to change jobs?

（US / Ⓦ）Yeah, kind of. My current boss is a bit traditionally-minded. Like, he asks me to work on this outdated personal computer and expects me to deliver a high-level of performance.

（UK / Ⓜ）Well, I understand what you mean. Maybe you should work for an Internet company. Most high-tech companies are more flexible and have fun corporate culture. Oh, I've heard that they allow employees to wear casual clothes. They always need new employees with fresh ideas. You can give it a try.

中譯　（美 / 女）我打算來更新我的履歷表。

（英 / 男）為什麼？妳想找新工作了？

（美 / 女）嗯，是有點想。我現在的老闆作風有些太過傳統了。比方說，他一直要求我用這台早已過時的個人電腦做令人驚豔的高水準成果。

（英 / 男）嗯，我完全理解妳的處境。或許妳該找一間網際網路公司。大部分的高科技公司都比較有彈性空間，而且都會有較有趣的企業文化。我甚至還聽說過他們准許員工穿著便服去上班呢。他們總需要擁有新奇構想的新員工，妳可以往這個方向去嘗試。

Q1. 女子為何想要更新個人履歷表？（答案：**B**）

(A) 展現給老闆看她會什麼　　　　　　　(B) 找新的工作機會

(C) 讓男子驚豔　　　　　　　　　　　　(D) 調到其他分公司

Q2. 女子的主要顧慮為何？（答案：**A**）

(A) 她那老派的老闆　　　　　　　　　　(B) 她充滿壓力的工作環境

(C) 她孩子的教育問題　　　　　　　　　(D) 她的業績表現

Q3. 男子建議女子做什麼？（答案：**D**）

(A) 找個獵人頭公司來幫她　　　　　　　(B) 儘速離開公司

(C) 創辦一間高科技公司　　　　　　　　(D) 找間較有彈性的公司

解題技巧　要了解一組對話的大概內容，其實只要靠聽到幾個關鍵點就可以辦到了。若是想要靠逐字聽的方式，那麼就會發生聽了一句還沒消化完又想聽下一句的情形，更何況有時候根本就來不及聽呢！因此，在作答時，一定要將注意力放在聽有加強重音的關鍵點上，大概就可以了解六七成的內容了。比方說此組對話，要點可能是：

（US / **W**）I'm thinking to update my resume.

（UK / **M**）Why? Are you planning to change jobs?

（US / **W**）Yeah, kind of. My current boss is a bit traditionally-minded. Like, he asks me to work on this outdated personal computer and expects me to deliver a high-level of performance.

（UK / **M**）Well, I understand what you mean. Maybe you should work for an Internet company. Most high-tech companies are more flexible and have fun corporate culture. Oh, I've heard that they allow employees to wear casual clothes. They always need new employees with fresh ideas. You can give it a try.

聽到上述幾個關鍵點，如：resume、change jobs 與 work for an Internet company 等，大約也可以了解兩人是在討論換工作，女子因為不想在傳統的環境下工作，男子便建議她去找新興的網路工作較有彈性。這樣一來，不是僅靠幾個關鍵點就可聽出了嗎？不一定要試圖了解聽力內的所有字詞才可聽懂喔！

第一題

先很快地掃描到題目，問的是「Why does the woman want to update her CV?」，那麼便可先預期要聽到原因、理由的關鍵點以便回答。根據男子問的「Are you planning to change jobs?」，以及女子的回應「Yeah, kind of.」，可聽出女子修改履歷表是因為想換工作，故選 (B)「To look for new job opportunities」為最佳答案。

各選項解析

• 選項 (A)「To show her boss what she can do」、選項 (C)「To impress the man」與選項 (D)「To transfer to other branches」都沒有在文章中被討論到，故不選。

第二題

此題問「What is the woman's major concern?」，可在心中預期要聽到女子主要顧慮之事以便回答。根據女子所說的此關鍵句「My current boss is a bit traditionally-minded. Like, he asks me to work on this outdated personal computer and expects me to deliver a high-level of performance.」，可聽出女子對老闆行事作風傳統一事不是很滿意，故選 (A)「Her old-fashioned supervisor」為最佳答案。

各選項解析

• 選項 (B)「Her stressful working environment」、選項 (C)「Her children's education」與選項 (D)「Her sales performance」都沒有在女子所說的話中出現，故不選。

第三題

先掃描到題目問的是「What does the man suggest the woman do?」，心中便有個底，要聽到提到男子給女子的建議以便回答。根據男子說的「Maybe you should work for an Internet company. Most high-tech companies are more flexible and have fun corporate culture.」，可聽出男子建議女子去找個較有彈性的網路公司上班，因此選擇 (D)「To find a more flexible company」為最佳答案。

各選項解析

• 選項 (A)「To find a headhunter to help her」、選項 (B)「To leave the company as soon as possible」與選項 (C)「To start a high-tech company」都沒有在男子的談話中被提到，故不選。

關鍵字彙

update [ʌpˋdet] v 更新
resume [͵rɛzjuˋme] n 履歷表
current [ˋkɝənt] a 現有的、目前的
traditionally [trəˋdɪʃənl̩ɪ] ad 傳統地
outdated [͵autˋdetɪd] a 舊有的、過時的
expect [ɪkˋspɛkt] v 預期
deliver [dɪˋlɪvɚ] v 寄送、投遞；履行
performance [pɚˋfɔrməns] n 表現
flexible [ˋflɛksəbl̩] a 有彈性的
corporate culture [ˋkɔrpərɪt ˋkʌltʃɚ] n 企業文化
casual [ˋkæʒuəl] a 輕鬆的、不拘的

攻略 2 | 面試會談

Q1. Who is the man most likely?

(A) A tourist   (B) A job applicant

(C) An English professor   (D) A sales representative

Q2. When is the conversation taking place?

(A) During a family gathering   (B) During a sports competition

(C) During an interview   (D) During a business luncheon

Q3. What quality does the man think a leader should possess?

(A) Negotiation skills   (B) Interpersonal skills

(C) Programming skills   (D) Presentation skills

解題分析

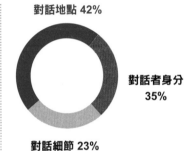

對話地點 42%

對話者身分 35%

對話細節 23%

■ 對話地點 42%　　多益考試中，對話發生的地點和對話主題一樣，大家主要對於內容的主題有初步的理解即可。

■ 對話者身分 35%　　由於是兩個人的對話，所以也會很常出現詢問其中一名對話者的職業、年紀等。只要根據對話內容，對話者的身分便可以輕鬆得知。

■ 對話細節 23%　　對話細節有時也會在多益的聽力考試中出現，像是對話者提到的時間、藉由對話內容推測對話者的下一步等。

聽稿

（US / W）All right, Mr. Thompson. So tell me, what do you consider to be your greatest accomplishment?

（CA / M）I think one of my greatest achievements is completing the wireless network project for the Springfield city government. I worked as the project manager and it took me and the whole team more than two years to implement.

（US / W）Sounds impressive, Mr. Thompson. Well, this position requires the person to lead five members. So what are some essential qualities of a good project leader? What are your thoughts?

（CA / M）Well, based on my experience, I would say to have strong interpersonal skills is absolutely important. I had to work with vendors, government officials, and other project partners. I really needed to have the ability to communicate with different types of people, and to integrate constructive criticism into my approach.

（美／女）好，湯普遜先生，你可以跟我分享你覺得自身最出色的成就為何嗎？

（加／男）我覺得我最有成就的其中一件事，就是幫助春田市政府完成他們無線網路的專案。當時我擔任專案經理一職，帶領整個團隊，花了超過兩年的時間使計劃得以順利實行。

（美／女）確實令人欽佩，湯普遜先生。此職位要求要帶領五個成員，那麼，一位好的專案經理要有什麼重要特質呢？您認為呢？

（加／男）嗯，根據我的經驗來看，我認為能擅長與人際互動的技能是非常重要的。我常常也要和廠商、政府官員、其他專案的夥伴們合作。我真的很需要能夠妥善地與形形色色的人們溝通的能力，並且在其中巧妙地融入建設性的討論。

Q1. 男子最有可能是誰？（答案：B）

(A) 遊客　　　　　　　　　　　　　　(B) 工作申請者

(C) 英文教授　　　　　　　　　　　　(D) 業務代表

Q2. 此對話在何時發生？（答案：C）

(A) 在家庭聚會時　　　　　　　　　　(B) 在運動比賽時

(C) 在面談時　　　　　　　　　　　　(D) 在商業午餐時

Q3. 男子認為領導者要有什麼特質？（答案：B）

(A) 談判能力　　　　　　　　　　　　(B) 人際處理能力

(C) 寫程式技能　　　　　　　　　　　(D) 簡報能力

解題技巧　此組對話雖也是兩人問答，卻也有加長的內容。愈是有加長的內容，愈是不可能想將所有資訊都聽到並聽懂，而是僅要將注意力放在聽會影響答題的關鍵點上面就好。所幸這些關鍵點通常會經過加以重音強調的處理方式，來引起聽者的注意力。此篇對話的要點便可能會是：

（US／W）All right, Mr. Thompson. So tell me, what do you consider to be your greatest accomplishment?

（CA／M）I think one of my greatest achievements is completing the wireless network project for the Springfield city government. I worked as the project manager and it took me and the whole team more than two years to implement.

（US／W）Sounds impressive, Mr. Thompson. Well, this position requires the person to lead five members. So what are some essential qualities of a good project leader? What are your thoughts?

（CA／M）Well, based on my experience, I would say to have strong interpersonal skills is absolutely important. I had to work with vendors, government officials, and other project partners. I really needed to have the ability to communicate with different types of people, and to integrate constructive criticism into my approach.

由此上的關鍵點便可聽出，兩人一問一答，是在討論男子過去的成就與男子對當專案經理的看法。抓出幾個關鍵點，便可大致了解七成的對話內容了。至於其他的細節，便要靠先看題目來決定所需關注的內容。

第一題

此題先看題目問的是「Who is the man most likely?」，那麼便要將注意力放在聽男子的身分上以便回答。根據此女子關鍵句所問「最大的成就為何」時，男子的回應是「I think one of my greatest achievements is completing the wireless network project for the Springfield city government. I worked as the project manager and it took me and the whole team more than two years to implement.」。既然是在講個人過去的成就，便最有可能是在面談時介紹自己經驗的談話，故男子最有可能是要申請工作者，故選 (B)「A job applicant」為最佳答案。

各選項解析

• 選項 (A)「A tourist」、選項 (C)「An English professor」或是選項 (D)「A sales representative」都不是會向詢問者說明自己過往經驗與成就之人，故不選。

第二題

先掃描到此問題問的是「When is the conversation taking place?」，那麼便可打定主意要聽到「時機、時間」等相關的資訊以便回答。接著，根據此關鍵句「Well, this position requires the person to lead five members. So what are some essential qualities of a good project leader?」，可聽出兩人是在討論工作職缺之事，可見是在面談的情境較為合理，故選 (C)「During an interview」為最佳答案。

各選項解析

• 選項 (A)「During a family gathering」、選項 (B)「During a sports competition」與選項 (D)「During a business luncheon」都不是討論工作職缺的時機，故不選。

第三題

先把握時間將題目掃過一遍，此題問的是「What quality does the man think a leader should possess?」，那麼便可判斷要聽到男子認為的領導才能才可回答。根據男子所講的關鍵句「I would say to have strong interpersonal skills is absolutely important.」，可聽出他認為知道與人相處的技巧很重要，所以最合適的答案要選 (B)「Interpersonal skills」喔！

各選項解析

• 選項 (A)「Negotiation skills」、選項 (C)「Programming skills」與選項 (D)「Presentation skills」都沒有在對談中的男子應答出現，故不選。

關鍵字彙

consider [kənˋsɪdɚ] ✔ 視為、考慮
accomplishment [əˋkɑmplɪʃmənt] ⋒ 成就
complete [kəmˋplit] ✔ 完成
government [ˋgʌvɚnmənt] ⋒ 政府
implement [ˋɪmpləmənt] ✔ 執行
impressive [ɪmˋprɛsɪv] ⓐ 令人印象深的
essential [ɪˋsɛnʃəl] ⓐ 重要的、關鍵的
quality [ˋkwɑlətɪ] ⋒ 特性、特質

interpersonal [ˌɪntɚˋpɝsən!] ⓐ 人際的
vendor [ˋvɛndɚ] ⋒ 廠商
official [əˋfɪʃəl] ⋒ 公務員、官員
integrate [ˋɪntəˌgret] ✔ 整合
constructive [kənˋstrʌktɪv] ⓐ 有建設性的
criticism [ˋkrɪtəˌsɪzəm] ⋒ 批評
approach [əˋprotʃ] ⋒ 方法、途徑

Q1. **What is the woman doing?**

(A) Interviewing the man　　　　(B) Presenting to a client

(C) Giving a speech　　　　　　(D) Negotiating prices

Q2. **What does the man use the Internet for?**

(A) Purchasing books

(B) Chatting with friends living overseas

(C) Searching for business related information

(D) Playing online games

Q3. **How would the man like to communicate with people?**

(A) In person　　　　　　　　(B) Via e-mail

(C) Using social media　　　　(D) Writing letters

解題分析

對話主題 53%

對話細節 47%

■ 對話主題 53%

■ 對話細節 47%

多益考試中，最常考的是對話的主題。此題組的第一題是換了個方式詢問對話的主題，所以只要抓住大方向以及關鍵字之後，就能選到正確的主題囉！

對話細節有時也會在多益的聽力考試中出現，像是對話者提到的時間、藉由對話內容推測對話者的下一步等。

聽稿

（US / Ⓦ）So, what's a typical day for you, Mr. Potter?

（UK / Ⓜ）Well, I divide my day up into two major sections. I make at least 30 cold calls before noon. In the afternoon, I either reply e-mails or participate in meetings.

（US / Ⓦ）Okay, and how much time per day are you on the Internet would you say? A couple of hours?

（UK / Ⓜ）Oh, averagely I spend two to three hours on the Internet searching for feedback from customers and even news from our competitors.

（US / Ⓦ）Right, I see. Do you usually communicate with clients via e-mail or in person?

（UK / Ⓜ）That's a good question. Well, you know, e-mails are good and convenient, but I still prefer to talk to clients in person. I think that things don't really come alive until I actually speak to people face to face.

中譯

（美／**女**）那麼波特先生，你平常工作日都做些什麼？

（英／**男**）這個嘛，照慣例我會把一天分為兩個主要部分。中午之前我會先撥出至少三十通以上的電話訪問；然後通常下午的時間收發電子郵件或參加會議。

（美／**女**）好的，那你一天大概花多少時間在使用網際網路上？幾個小時嗎？

（英／**男**）我大約會花二到三小時在網路上搜尋有關顧客的心得感想，甚至是競爭對手的相關消息。

（美／**女**）好的，我了解了。你通常都親自拜訪客戶，還是用電子郵件跟他們聯繫？

（英／**男**）這是個好問題。普遍來說，電子郵件確實是一個很方便的途徑，不過我個人依舊偏好親自跟客戶對談。我認為透過面對面的談話，才能夠使很多東西變得活靈活現。

Q1. 女子在做什麼？（答案：**A**）

(A) 與男子面談　　　　　　　　　　　(B) 跟客戶做簡報

(C) 發表一場演說　　　　　　　　　　(D) 談判價格

Q2. 男子用網路來做什麼？（答案：**C**）

(A) 買書　　　　　　　　　　　　　　(B) 跟住在海外的朋友聊天

(C) 尋找業務相關的資訊　　　　　　　(D) 玩線上遊戲

Q3. 男子喜歡如何跟人溝通？（答案：**A**）

(A) 面對面　　　　　　　　　　　　　(B) 透過電郵

(C) 使用社交媒體　　　　　　　　　　(D) 寫信

解題技巧

此組對話也是屬於加長內容型的，與其給自己「將所有對話內容都了解」這樣的困難任務，倒不如將注意力放在聽「真正的關鍵點」上即可。關鍵點的所在便是三題題目所問的問題，而且，答案出現的位置也通常會是講者加強重音之處。此篇對話的關鍵點便可能會是：

（US／**W**）So, what's a typical day for you, Mr. Potter?

（UK／**M**）Well, I divide my day up into two major sections. I make at least 30 cold calls before noon. In the afternoon, I either reply e-mails or participate in meetings.

（US／**W**）Okay, and how much time per day are you on the Internet would you say? A couple of hours?

（UK／**M**）Oh, averagely I spend two to three hours on the Internet searching for feedback from customers and even news from our competitors.

（US／**W**）Right, I see. Do you usually communicate with clients via e-mail or in person?

（UK／**M**）That's a good question. Well, you know, e-mails are good and convenient, but I still prefer to talk to clients in person. I think that things don't really come alive until I actually speak to people face to face.

由以上幾個關鍵點，不難聽出兩人是在討論「男子一天內時間的分配」、「使用網路的目的」與「偏好的溝通方式」等主題。由此可看出，抓住了大方向的主題，想要了解大概的對話內容並不一定只能將每一個字聽懂，而要抓到關鍵點才是最重要的。

此題問的是「What is the woman doing?」，可根據題目判斷要聽到「女子做什麼」的資訊以便回答。根據女子所說的「So, what's a typical day for you, Mr. Potter?」，她是在向男子提問，男子回答完之後她又提出第二個問題：「Okay, and how much time per day are you on the Internet would you say?」，由此可見，她是在與男子面談，並且向男子提問，故選 (A)「Interviewing the man」為最佳答案。

各選項解析

• 選項 (B)「Presenting to a client」、選項 (C)「Giving a speech」與選項 (D)「Negotiating prices」都不像是女子提問題的目的，故不選。

第二題

先大略地看題目以便確認要聽的答案之方向，此題問的是「What does the man use the Internet for?」，看到題目之後，心中便有底要聽到與「男子使用網路的作用」這類相關答案以便回答。

根據此關鍵句「Oh, averagely I spend two to three hours on the Internet searching for feedback from customers and even news from our competitors.」，可聽出他是在網路上搜尋客戶意見與競爭對手的消息，故選 (C)「Searching for business related information」為最佳答案。

各選項解析

• 選項 (A)「Purchasing books」、選項 (B)「Chatting with friends living overseas」與選項 (D)「Playing online games」都沒有在男子的對話中出現，故不選。

第三題

對話播放之前，首先看到此題問的是「How would the man like to communicate with people?」，可以先在心裡預設要聽到「男子所喜歡與人溝通之方式」以便回答。根據男子所說的此關鍵句「Well you know, e-mails are good and convenient, but I still prefer to talk to clients in person.」，可以得出男子喜歡與人面對面溝通的結論，所以選擇 (A)「In person」為最佳答案。

各選項解析

• 選項 (B)「Via e-mail」、選項 (C)「Using social media」與選項 (D)「Writing letters」都不是男子所提及他喜歡溝通的方式，故不選。

關鍵字彙

typical [ˈtɪpɪkl] a 典型的、一貫的
divide [dəˈvaɪd] v 區分、隔開
section [ˈsɛkʃən] n 部分、區隔
reply [rɪˈplaɪ] v 回應
participate [pɑrˈtɪsəˌpet] v 參與
averagely [ˈævərɪdʒlɪ] ad 平均地
feedback [ˈfidˌbæk] n 回饋意見
competitor [kəmˈpɛtətə] n 競爭對手
convenient [kənˈvinjənt] a 方便的
alive [əˈlaɪv] a 有生氣的

Unit 6 出差商旅類

攻略 1 │ 購買機票

Q1. Where is the conversation most likely taking place?

(A) At the airport

(B) In the classroom

(C) In the library

(D) In a restaurant

Q2. Where is the woman going?

(A) To the airport

(B) To New York

(C) To his office

(D) To Chicago

Q3. Which flight does the woman prefer?

(A) The next day flight

(B) The 2:50 p.m. flight

(C) The overnight flight

(D) The 3 p.m. flight

解題分析

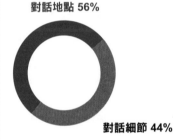

對話地點 56%

對話細節 44%

■ **對話地點 56%** 多益考試中，對話發生的地點和對話主題一樣，大家主要對於內容的主題有初步的理解即可。

■ **對話細節 44%** 對話細節有時也會在多益的聽力考試中出現，像是這一題組裡問到的對話者可能搭的班機、對話者的目的地……等。

聽稿

（US / Ⓦ）I need to reserve a flight to New York right away. I'd like a round-trip ticket and a window seat please. I have only one carry-on.

（UK / Ⓜ）Sure, ma'am. Let me check please. All right, no problem, ma'am. We've got an overnight flight available if you don't mind having jet lag.

（US / Ⓦ）Well, I'm not too sure about that. Taking a red-eye flight would be pretty tiring. Do you have other flights available?

（UK / Ⓜ）All right, here is an alternative. You can fly on the 3 p.m. flight, but you'll have to make a connection with an one-hour stop in Chicago. You can board the plane at 2:30 p.m. at gate 534.

（美／女）我需要立即訂一張飛到紐約的機票。麻煩您，我要一組靠窗邊的來回票。我只有一件隨身行李。

（英／男）好的，女士，我先幫您查查。我找到了，沒問題，女士，若您不介意時差問題的話，我們目前尚有一班過夜的航班。

（美／女）這個嘛，我不太確定是否能接受。搭乘一班需要熬夜的班機，聽起來蠻累人的。還有其他的航班有空位嗎？

（英／男）這樣啊，不然還有一個替代方案。您可以搭乘下午三點的班機，但中途需要停留一個小時在芝加哥轉機。下午兩點半開始於五三四號登機門登機。

Q1. 此對話最有可能發生在何處？（答案：A）

(A) 在機場　　　　　　　　　　　　(B) 在教室

(C) 在圖書館　　　　　　　　　　　(D) 在餐廳

Q2. 女子要去哪裡？（答案：B）

(A) 機場　　　　　　　　　　　　　(B) 紐約

(C) 他的辦公室　　　　　　　　　　(D) 芝加哥

Q3. 女子想搭哪一個班機？（答案：D）

(A) 第二天的班機　　　　　　　　　(B) 下午兩點五十分的班機

(C) 過夜的班機　　　　　　　　　　(D) 下午三點的班機

解題技巧

在聽力播放出來之前就要有認知，我們聽取內容的目的不是為了聽到每句內的每個字詞，而是為了聽到關鍵之處以便回答一整個題組內的三個問題。因此，大家應該將注意力放在聽取關鍵要點處即可，有需要聽的關鍵要點處自然就是三題題目所點出的問題點，且通常在對話之內這些關鍵處會被加強重音以便強調。此對話中的要點處便可能會是：

（US／W）I need to reserve a flight to New York right away. I'd like a round-trip ticket and a window seat please. I have only one carry-on.

（UK／M）Sure, ma'am. Let me check please. All right, no problem, ma'am. We've got an overnight flight available if you don't mind having jet lag.

（US／W）Well, I'm not too sure about that. Taking a red-eye flight would be pretty tiring. Do you have other flights available?

（UK／M）All right, here is an alternative. You can fly on the 3 p.m. flight, but you'll have to make a connection with an one-hour stop in Chicago. You can board the plane at 2:30 p.m. at gate 534.

如此一來，在作答這類題型時，我們可以不用聽到全部的資訊，僅是將焦點放在上述強調的幾處關鍵點上，便可歸納出要點了。這篇對話的要點是：兩講者在討論的是班機行程，女子提了不同的班機時刻給男子，男子可依需求來選擇要搭哪一班機。的確，僅聽到關鍵要點，便可以猜出對話的大概內容囉！

第一題

題目問的是「Where is the conversation most likely taking place?」，那麼便打定主意要聽到可以判斷地點、位置的相關資訊以便回答。根據此關鍵句「I need to reserve a flight to New York right away. I'd like a round-trip ticket and a window seat please. I have only one carry-on.」，可以聽出女子要買票飛往紐約，可以依據這樣的回應來判斷對話地點應是在機場較為合理，故選 (A)「At the airport」為最佳答案。

各選項解析

- 選項 (B)「In the classroom」、選項 (C)「In the library」與選項 (D)「In a restaurant」都不會是要購買機票飛往紐約之處，故不選。

第二題

此題問的是「Where is the woman going?」，判斷出要聽到女子要前往之地點以便回答。根據「I need to reserve a flight to New York right away.」，可明顯地聽出她是要飛往紐約，故選 (B)「To New York」為正確答案。

各選項解析

- 選項 (A)「To the airport」、選項 (C)「To his office」與選項 (D)「To Chicago」都不是女子說她要前往之處，所以都不會是正確答案。

第三題

題目問的是「Which flight does the woman prefer?」，那麼可判斷對話中可能有提到幾個班機的選擇，我們要聽到女子所想搭的一班來回答。根據男子所說的此關鍵句「Taking a red-eye flight would be pretty tiring. Do you have other flights available?」，和男子的回應「All right, here is an alternative. You can fly on the 3 p.m. flight...」，可以聽出女子不想搭紅眼班機，故男子給她其他的選擇是下午三點的班次，便會選後者，故選 (D)「The 3 p.m. flight」為最佳答案。

各選項解析

- 選項 (A)「The next day flight」、選項 (B)「The 2:50 p.m. flight」與選項 (C)「The overnight flight」都不是女子提到她想搭的班次，故不選。

關鍵字彙

reserve [rɪˋzɜv] Ⓥ 預留、預訂
flight [flaɪt] Ⓝ 班機
round-trip [ˋraʊndˏtrɪp] ⓐ 來回的
carry-on [ˋkærɪˏɑn] Ⓝ 手提的、可隨身攜帶的行李
overnight [ˋovəˋnaɪt] ⓐ 一整夜的
available [əˋveləbl̩] ⓐ 可獲得的
jet lag ⓟⁿ 時差
red eye flight [ˋrɛd ˏaɪ ˋflaɪt] Ⓝ 紅眼班機
tiring [ˋtaɪərɪŋ] ⓐ 疲憊的
alternative [ɔlˋtɜnətɪv] Ⓝ 其他選擇
connection [kəˋnɛkʃən] Ⓝ 轉機；接駁
board [bord] Ⓥ 登上、搭、乘

Q1. What are the speakers talking about?

(A) Musical events

(B) Business trips

(C) Vacation plans

(D) Sales performance

Q2. Where does the man want to go?

(A) Desert

(B) City

(C) Beach

(D) Mountain

Q3. What does the woman suggest the man do?

(A) Search for vacation destinations online

(B) Visit the Philippines

(C) Go to New York

(D) Stay home and relax

解題分析

對話主題 60%

對話細節 40%

■ 對話主題 60%　在長篇對話中，對於內容的主題只要有初步的理解即可，聽到關鍵字或是特別加強語氣的字，可以自己想像該對話的情境。

■ 對話細節 40%　對話細節有時也會在多益的聽力考試中出現，細節部分可以在題目播放時，搭配選項一起看，這樣就能及時找到正確答案。

聽稿

（AU / W）Hey, Derek. Where are you taking a vacation this summer?

（CA / M）Well, I don't know yet. Maybe just go on a beach holiday somewhere as usual. So Tiff, do you have any good suggestions?

（AU / W）Right, if you would like to enjoy sunshine, why don't you visit the Philippines? My family and I went to Subic Beach in Sorsogon, and it was one of the most fantastic vacations we've ever taken. I'm sure you're gonna love it as well.

（CA / M）Sounds pretty cool, Tiff. All right, I'm gonna do some research on the Internet this evening. Thank you for such a great idea.

中譯

（澳／女）嘿，德瑞克，這個暑假打算上哪兒去度假呀？

（加／男）說到這個，我還沒確定呢。可能會像往常一樣找個海邊去吧。所以媞芙妳有什麼好建議？

（澳／女）這個嘛，如果你喜歡曬太陽的話，何不考慮去菲律賓旅行呢？我曾經跟我的家人一同前往索索貢省的蘇比克灣，那是我們去過最棒的旅程之一呢！你一定也會愛上那裡的。

（加／男）媞芙，聽起來蠻不賴的。那好，我今晚先上網找尋一些相關資料吧。謝謝妳提供這麼棒的主意。

Q1. 講者在討論什麼？（答案：C）

(A) 音樂活動   (B) 商旅出差

(C) 度假計畫   (D) 業績表現

Q2. 男子想要去哪裡？（答案：C）

(A) 沙漠   (B) 都市

(C) 海灘   (D) 山上

Q3. 女子建議男子做什麼？（答案：B）

(A) 線上查詢度假聖地   (B) 去菲律賓玩

(C) 去紐約   (D) 在家放鬆

解題技巧

長篇對話不會是死板地講句子就好，而是會有快有慢，有輕音重音的韻律感。如同音樂一般，也可能有重音的拍子。而大家在處理長篇對話時，便應將焦點放在聽有加強重音的關鍵點上，以便了解大概的內容。此組對話的大概要點標示如以下：

> （AU／W）Hey, Derek. Where are you taking a vacation this summer?
>
> （CA／M）Well, I don't know yet. Maybe just go on a beach holiday somewhere as usual. So Tiff, do you have any good suggestions?
>
> （AU／W）Right, if you would like to enjoy sunshine, why don't you visit the Philippines? My family and I went to Subic Beach in Sorsogon, and it was one of the most fantastic vacations we've ever taken. I'm sure you're gonna love it as well.
>
> （CA／M）Sounds pretty cool, Tiff. All right, I'm gonna do some research on the Internet this evening. Thank you for such a great idea.

事實上，只要聽到幾個真的會發揮作用的關鍵點，便可以大概得知此對話是在討論假期規劃。男子說喜歡去海邊，女子便建議可以去菲律賓的海灘看看。由此可知，想試圖了解每字每句，還試圖想在心中想翻譯成中文是什麼意思，這是沒有必要的。將注意力放兩成在聽出重要的關鍵點上才是上策。

先大致看過題目才可判斷要聽什麼方向的答案以便回答。此題問的是「What are the speakers talking about?」，便可以判斷要聽到對話者討論之主題相關資訊才行。根據此句「Hey, Derek. Where are you taking a vacation this summer?」，可聽出兩人是在討論度假的計畫，故選 (C)「Vacation plans」為最佳答案。

各選項解析

- 選項 (A)「Musical events」、選項 (B)「Business trips」與選項 (D)「Sales performance」都沒有在對話中出現，不會是對話的主要討論內容，故不選。

第二題

此題詢問「Where does the man want to go?」，便可判斷要聽到男子想去度假的地點以便回答。那麼根據男子所說的此關鍵句「Maybe just go on a beach holiday somewhere as usual. So Tiff, do you have any good suggestions?」，可聽出他是想去海邊的，所以在四個選項中選擇 (C)「Beach」為最佳答案。

各選項解析

- 選項 (A)「Desert」、選項 (B)「City」與選項 (D)「Mountain」都沒有在對話中提及，故不選。

第三題

在對話播放前，先看到此題問的是「What does the woman suggest the man do?」，便可判斷要聽到女子給男子的建議相關資訊以便回答。根據此女子所說的「If you would like to enjoy sunshine, why don't you visit the Philippines? My family and I went to Subic Beach in Sorsogon... I'm sure you're gonna love it as well.」，可聽出女子建議男子去菲律賓海灘度假，故選 (B)「Visit the Philippines」為最佳答案。

各選項解析

- 選項 (A)「Search for vacation destinations online」、選項 (C)「Go to New York」與選項 (D)「Stay home and relax」都沒有在女子的對話中出現，故不選。

關鍵字彙

beach [bitʃ] n 海灘
suggestion [sə`dʒɛstʃən] n 建議
sunshine [`sʌn͵ʃaɪn] n 陽光
fantastic [fæn`tæstɪk] a 極棒的
vacation [ve`keʃən] n 度假

攻略 3 | 登機說明

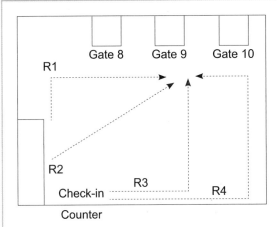

Q1. Where is this conversation most likely taking place?

(A) In a travel agency   (B) On the street

(C) At the airport   (D) In the hotel

Q2. What time will the man probably arrive at Gate 9?

(A) 10:50 a.m.   (B) 11:10 a.m.

(C) 11:00 p.m.   (D) 10:35 p.m.

新 **Q3. Look at the map. What is the best route for the man to get to Gate 9?**

(A) Route 1   (B) Route 2

(C) Route 3   (D) Route 4

解題分析

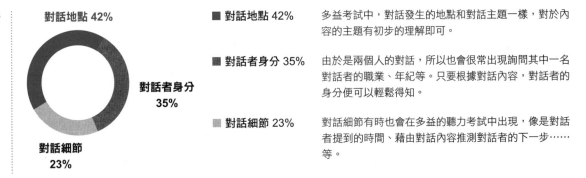

■ 對話地點 42%　多益考試中，對話發生的地點和對話主題一樣，對於內容的主題有初步的理解即可。

■ 對話者身分 35%　由於是兩個人的對話，所以也會很常出現詢問其中一名對話者的職業、年紀等。只要根據對話內容，對話者的身分便可以輕鬆得知。

■ 對話細節 23%　對話細節有時也會在多益的聽力考試中出現，像是對話者提到的時間、藉由對話內容推測對話者的下一步……等。

聽稿

（US / Ⓦ）Good morning, sir. Are you flying to Barcelona today? I need to see your ticket and passport please.

（UK / Ⓜ）Sure, here is my passport. Well, do you want to check my e-ticket? It's saved in my smart-phone device. Uh... let me show you here. This is the part you need, right?

（US / Ⓦ）Yes, exactly. All right, Mr. Wilson, here is your boarding pass. Be at Gate 9 prior to 11 a.m. please. Our flight crew will announce some safety instructions for take-off and landing.

（UK / Ⓜ）I see. One more thing, please. Do you have an outline of this airport, so that I know where to find Gate 9 please?

中譯　（美 / 女）先生，早安。您是搭飛往巴塞隆納的班機嗎？麻煩給我看一下您的機票和護照，謝謝。

（英 / 男）沒問題，這是我的護照。您需要檢視我的電子機票嗎？我儲存在我的智慧型手機裝置裡。呃……請您稍等我一會兒，讓我找找。這部分是您需要驗證的，對嗎？

（美 / 女）沒錯，正是。謝謝您，威爾森先生，這是您的登機證。麻煩請於上午十一點前抵達九號登機門。我們的機組人員會宣導飛機起降時的相關安全事項。

（英 / 男）我明白了。再請教您一個問題，您是否有這座機場的導覽圖？我才知道要如何前往九號登機門。

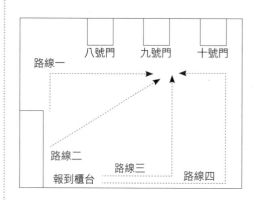

Q1. 此對話最有可能在何處發生？（答案：C）

(A) 在旅行社　　　　　　　　　　　　(B) 在街上

(C) 在機場　　　　　　　　　　　　　(D) 在飯店

Q2. 男子可能在幾點到達九號登機門？（答案：A）

(A) 早上十點五十分　　　　　　　　　(B) 早上十一點十分

(C) 晚上十一點　　　　　　　　　　　(D) 晚上十點三十五分

新 Q3. 請看地圖，何者是男子前往九號登機門最佳路線？（答案：B）

(A) 路線一　　　　　　　　　　　　　(B) 路線二

(C) 路線三　　　　　　　　　　　　　(D) 路線四

解題技巧　大家對於長篇對話的沒自信，通常來自想將所有對話內容都聽懂。但事實上，這些對話內容也是虛構的，在我們日常生活中，有必要將對話一字不漏地全部聽懂嗎？而且，一個題組也才問三個問題而已，何不將注意力放在聽會考的關鍵點上呢？如此才好回答問題呢？因此，若大家可能將分散的注意力集中，僅專心地聽有以重音強調的要點上，回答問題的自信心便可增加了。此篇的重音之處可能會是：

> （US / W）Good morning, sir. Are you flying to Barcelona today? I need to see your ticket and passport please.
>
> （UK / M）Sure, here is my passport. Well, do you want to check my e-ticket? It's saved in my smart-phone device. Uh... let me show you here. This is the part you need, right?
>
> （US / W）Yes, exactly. All right, Mr. Wilson, here is your boarding pass. Be at Gate 9 prior to 11 a.m. please. Our flight crew will announce some safety instructions for take-off and landing.
>
> （UK / M）I see. One more thing, please. Do you have an outline of this airport, so that I know where to find Gate 9 please?

由這些重音之處可以聽出，兩人是在機場討論班機之事，男子辦理登機準備，女子在檢查相關證件，並告知登機地點與時間。透過這些大略的要點，並不需要靠「逐字翻譯對話內容」來得知呀！因此，請大家有信心地選擇聽關鍵點就好了！

第一題

唯有先掃過一次問題才可判斷聽對話時要將注意力放在聽什麼要點上，此題問的是「Where is this conversation most likely taking place?」，那麼可判斷要聽到地點、位置等相關資訊以便回答。根據此句「Good morning, sir. Are you flying to Barcelona today? I need to see your ticket and passport please.」，便可明顯地聽出是在機場的對話，故選 (C)「At the airport」為最佳答案。

各選項解析

• 選項 (A)「In a travel agency」、選項 (B)「On the street」或選項 (D)「In the hotel」都不是會討論「飛去哪」、「要看機票與護照」的地點，都不能選。

第二題

先看到題目問的是「What time will the man probably arrive at Gate 9?」，那麼便可判斷要聽到「抵達登機門的時間」相關資訊以便回答這一題。根據此關鍵句「All right, Mr. Wilson, here is your boarding pass. Be at Gate 9 prior to 11 a.m. please.」，可判斷要在早上十一點之前抵達九號登機口，所有選項中僅 10:50 a.m. 是在早上十一點之前的時間，故選 (A)「10:50 a.m.」為最佳答案。

各選項解析

• 項 (B)「11:10 a.m.」、選項 (C)「11:00 p.m.」與選項 (D)「10:35 p.m.」都不是早上十一點之前的時間，故不選。

新 第三題

此題需要對照表格來回答，也一樣要先看題目，以便判斷要聽什麼方向的答案。 此題問的是「What is the best route for the man to get to Gate 9?」，那麼在男子提問「Do you have an outline of this airport, so that I know where to find Gate 9 please?」，再對照圖片內的路線之後，可判斷男子在「Check-in Counter（報到櫃台）」的位置，要前往 Gate 9，最直接的方式就是走 Route 2 了，故選 (B)「Route 2」為最佳答案。

各選項解析

• 選項 (A)「Route 1」、選項 (C)「Route 3」與選項 (D)「Route 4」，由圖中看來，都不是前往 Gate 9 最直接的路線，所以都不會是最佳答案。

關鍵字彙

device [dɪˋvaɪs] n 設備、工具
crew [kru] n 機組人員
announce [əˋnaʊns] v 宣布、公告
safety [ˋseftɪ] n 安全性

instruction [ɪnˋstrʌkʃən] n 指導
take-off [ˋtekˏɔf] n 起飛
landing [ˋlændɪŋ] n 登陸、著陸
outline [ˋaʊtˏlaɪn] n 草圖、輪廓

攻略 1 | 購買衣服

Q1. What is the woman doing?

(A) Ordering food
(B) Shopping for clothes
(C) Inviting the man to a meeting
(D) Requesting a refund

Q2. What does the man say about those sweaters?

(A) They are the latest style
(B) They are on sale
(C) They are for children
(D) They are very expensive

Q3. Where will the woman probably go next?

(A) To the restroom
(B) To the airport
(C) To the counter
(D) To the fitting room

解題分析

對話主題 52%

對話細節 48%

■ **對話主題** 52% 　如果遇到詢問對話主題的題目，可以透過聽關鍵字或是重複出現的字來選出適合的主題。

■ **對話細節** 48% 　對話細節像是對話者提到的時間、藉由對話內容推測對話者的下一步……等，可以透過看選項搭配播放內容來選出符合題意的答案。

聽稿

（AU / W）Excuse me, please. Do you have a small sweater which is not too expensive?

（UK / M）Please look at our sale items right down this aisle. These sweaters are much cheaper, but some sizes may be out of stock.

（AU / W）Okay, I see. Oh, this red sweater looks nice and it's cheap as well. The label shows it's only $5.99. Can I try this on please?

（UK / M）Sure, you can try clothes in the fitting cubicle. Oh, by the way, if you have the Loyalty Card, you can receive an additional 10% off.

中譯

（澳 / 女）不好意思，您們有沒有比較平價的小尺寸毛線衣？

（英 / 男）您可以參考位於這條走道的產品櫃。這些毛線衣價格比較低，但有些尺寸可能已經沒貨了。

（澳 / 女）這樣啊，我了解了。噢，這件紅色的毛線衣看起來蠻漂亮的，而且價錢也便宜。標價上寫著它只需要美金五元九十九分，方便讓人試穿嗎？

（英 / 男）當然可以，您可以去我們的試衣間試穿。對了，如果您持有我們的會員卡，商品還可以再打九折。

Q1. 女子在做什麼？（答案：B）
(A) 點餐
(B) 選購衣物
(C) 邀請男子去參加個會議
(D) 要求退款

Q2. 男子提及關於毛衣的何事？（答案：B）
(A) 它們都是最新款式
(B) 它們在特價
(C) 它們是給小孩穿的
(D) 它們很貴

Q3. 女子接下來可能去哪？（答案：D）
(A) 洗手間
(B) 機場
(C) 櫃台
(D) 試衣間

解題技巧

根據傳統的聽力教學方式，若不是將聽力內每個句子都翻譯好，我們就會感到沒安全感，好像沒聽懂似的。但若依照這種舊有的方式來聽多益聽力，就會產生又要處理單字和句子，還要聽懂口音，更要在心中翻譯，而導致根本聽了下句就忘了上句的窘境。多益對話聽力是有題組的，每對話組問三題題目，那麼我們為何不將注意力放在聽那三題題目會考的關鍵點上就好了呢？當然，這就可以用「先把握時間看題目」和「仔細聽對話中加強重音之處」來達成了。此組對話的要點可能會是：

（AU / W）Excuse me, please. Do you have a small sweater which is not too expensive?

（UK / M）Please look at our sale items right down this aisle. These sweaters are much cheaper, but some sizes may be out of stock.

（AU / W）Okay, I see. Oh, this red sweater looks nice and it's cheap as well. The label shows it's only $5.99. Can I try this on please?

（UK / M）Sure, you can try clothes in the fitting cubicle. Oh, by the way, if you have the Loyalty Card, you can receive an additional 10% off.

由這些關鍵點可以聽出，女子想買便宜的毛衣並想試穿，男子店員在協助她，並告知折扣優惠。如此，靠聽到一些關鍵點便可了解對話內容的大概了，是否簡單得多呢？

在對話內容播放出來前,建議務必要先將題目看一遍,以便了解要聽的關鍵點為何。此題問的是「What is the woman doing?」,便可判斷要聽到「女子做什麼」的相關答案以便回答。那麼根據此關鍵句的內容:「Excuse me, please. Do you have a small sweater which is not too expensive?」,可聽出女子是在購買毛衣,想找小號的,故選 (B)「Shopping for clothes」為最佳答案。

各選項解析

• 選項 (A)「Ordering food」、選項 (C)「Inviting the man to a meeting」與選項 (D)「Requesting a refund」都沒有在女子的對話中出現,故不選。

第二題

先看到題目問的是「What does the man say about those sweaters?」,那麼可判斷要聽到男子提到「關於毛衣之何事」的相關內容以便回答,根據男子所說的此關鍵句「Please look at our sale items right down this aisle. These sweaters are much cheaper...」,可聽出毛衣在特價中,所以選擇 (B)「They are on sale.」。

各選項解析

• 選項 (A)「They are the latest style.」、選項 (C)「They are for children.」與選項 (D)「They are very expensive.」都沒有在男子的對話中出現,故不能選。

第三題

先很快地看過題目,問的是「Where will the woman probably go next?」,那麼便可判斷要聽到「女子要走往何處」相關資訊以便回答。那麼女子問了「Can I try this on please?」,女子說要試穿之後,根據男子所回應的此關鍵句「Sure, you can try clothes in the fitting cubicle.」,可判斷男子請女子去試衣間試穿,那麼女子接下來應會走到試衣間較為合理,故選 (D)「To the fitting room」為最佳答案。

各選項解析

• 選項 (A)「To the restroom」、選項 (B)「To the airport」與選項 (C)「To the counter」都沒有在對話中出現,故不選。

關鍵字彙

sweater [ˋswɛtɚ] n 毛衣
expensive [ɪkˋspɛnsɪv] a 昂貴的
aisle [aɪl] n 走道
out of stock ph 無庫存
label [ˋlebl] n 標籤、商標
fitting cubicle [ˋfɪtɪŋ ˏkjubɪkl] n 試衣隔間
additional [əˋdɪʃənl] a 額外的、多出的

攻略 2 ｜購買電子產品

Q1. Where is the conversation most likely taking place?

(A) In a classroom   (B) In a fashion show

(C) In an electronic store   (D) In a chemistry lab

Q2. What is the woman's major concern?

(A) Her budget   (B) Functions of the device

(C) Payment terms   (D) Music selections

Q3. What does the man suggest the woman do?

(A) Save money for a rainy day   (B) Use a discount coupon

(C) Pay in installments   (D) Pay by cash

解題分析

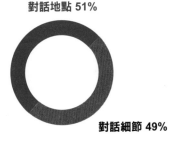

對話地點 51%

對話細節 49%

■ 對話地點 51%

■ 對話細節 49%

多益考試中，對話發生的地點和對話主題一樣，大家主要對於內容的主題有初步的理解即可。

對話細節有時也會在多益的聽力考試中出現，像是對話者主要的想法、藉由對話內容推測對話者的下一步……等。

聽稿

（US / Ⓦ）Hi, do you work here? Uh, I'm looking for a new smart-phone, and wonder if you could give me some suggestions.

（UK / Ⓜ）Okay, let me show you our latest model. This one here, T883, has a lot of fancy features, including camera, a video recorder, instant messaging tools, and you can even download music you like.

（US / Ⓦ）It does look fantastic. But is it expensive? I'm still a student, and you know, I don't have a huge budget for this.

（UK / Ⓜ）Don't worry. This one is on sale and costs only $59.99, and you can choose to pay in installments.

中譯

（美 / **女**）嗨，您是這裡的店員嗎？我想找一款新的智慧型手機，不知道您能否提供相關的建議呢？

（英 / **男**）好的，給您看看我們最新的款式。這一支 T883 擁有許多別緻的特色，像是相機、攝影、即時通訊工具，也可以下載您喜愛的音樂來聽。

（美 / **女**）它看起來是挺厲害的，不過價格會不會相對地較高？我還只是個學生，您知道的，我沒有太多的預算。

（英 / **男**）您不用擔心，這是支特價的手機，價格落在美金五十九元九十九分，您可以選擇分期付款。

Q1. 此對話最有可能在何處發生？（答案：**C**）

(A) 教室　　　　　　　　　　　　(B) 時尚秀場
(C) 電子商品店　　　　　　　　　(D) 化學實驗室

Q2. 女子的主要考量為何？（答案：**A**）

(A) 她的預算　　　　　　　　　　(B) 設備的功能
(C) 付款方式　　　　　　　　　　(D) 音樂選擇

Q3. 男子建議女子做什麼？（答案：**C**）

(A) 存錢以防萬一　　　　　　　　(B) 使用折扣券
(C) 分期付款　　　　　　　　　　(D) 以現金付款

解題技巧

筆者教學時常將聽力比喻為人生，我們人生的時間與精力都有限，不可能什麼事都想做，而是要經過選擇，將寶貴的時間聚焦到真正有用的事情上。長篇對話也不例外，在僅有五六秒得時間可以思考答案的情況下，自然是應該將注意力放在聽「真的會發揮作用又可以回答問題」的資訊上才是，而非什麼大大小小的資訊都想要去了解。此組對話內容的焦點便有可能是：

（US / **W**）Hi, do you work here? Uh, I'm looking for a new smart-phone, and wonder if you could give me some suggestions.

（UK / **M**）Okay, let me show you our latest model. This one here, T883, has a lot of fancy features, including camera, a video recorder, instant messaging tools, and you can even download music you like.

（US / **W**）It does look fantastic. But is it expensive? I'm still a student, and you know, I don't have a huge budget for this.

（UK / **M**）Don't worry. This one is on sale and costs only $59.99, and you can choose to pay in installments.

如此僅將注意力放在聽關鍵點上的好處便是：不用逐字翻譯；我們也可大略歸納出此對話內容是：客戶要買智慧手機，且考量到預算有限，男店員在幫她介紹，並說價格方面可以分期付款。透過抓關鍵訊息來協助我們理解內容，是不是比一個字一個字慢慢地翻譯來得有效率得多呢？

第一題

先把握時間將題目很快地看過，以便有把握接下來要將注意力放在聽何種關鍵點上。此題問的是「Where is the conversation most likely taking place?」，可判斷要聽到對話中出現相關地點的內容以便回答。那麼根據此關鍵句「Uh, I'm looking for a new smart-phone, and wonder if you could give me some suggestions.」，可聽出女子要買手機，便應該是在電子產品店內較為合理，故選 (C)「In an electronic store」為最佳答案。

各選項解析

- 選項 (A)「In a classroom」、選項 (B)「In a fashion show」與選項 (D)「In a chemistry lab」都不會是有賣手機之處，故不選。

第二題

先把握時間掃過題目以得知要將焦點放在聽什麼資訊上。此題問的是「What is the woman's major concern?」，那麼可判斷要注意聽的是女子的顧慮相關答案以便回答。根據女子所說的此關鍵句「It does look fantastic. But is it expensive? I'm still a student, and you know, I don't have a huge budget for this.」，可聽出她主要是擔心價格、預算方面的問題，故選 (A)「Her budget」為最佳答案。

各選項解析

- 選項 (B)「Functions of the device」、選項 (C)「Payment terms」與選項 (D)「Music selections」內容都沒有在對話中被提及，故不選。

第三題

先看到題目問的是「What does the man suggest the woman do?」，可以判斷要聽到「男子給女子的建議」這樣的相關資訊以便回答。根據男子說的此關鍵句「Don't worry. This one is on sale and costs only $59.99, and you can choose to pay in installments.」，可聽出男子是說可以分期付款的，故選 (C)「Pay in installments」為最佳答案。

各選項解析

- 選項 (A)「Save money for a rainy day」、選項 (B)「Use a discount coupon」與選項 (D)「Pay by cash」都沒有在男子的對話中被提及，所以都不選。

關鍵字彙

latest [ˋletɪst] ⓐ 最新的、最近的
model [ˋmɑdl̩] ⓝ 型號
fancy [ˋfænsɪ] ⓐ 奇特的
feature [fitʃɚ] ⓝ 特性、功能
download [ˋdaʊnˏlod] ⓥ 下載
installment [ɪnˋstɔlmənt] ⓝ 分期付款

新 Q1. **Where is the conversation most likely taking place?**

    (A) In a train station   (B) In a shopping mall

    (C) In a movie theater   (D) In a restaurant

新 Q2. **Who is most likely the man?**

    (A) A janitor   (B) An accountant

    (C) The store owner   (D) A sales clerk

新 Q3. **What's the final solution to the woman's problem?**

    (A) Call the police   (B) Return the jacket

    (C) Provide a discount voucher   (D) Exchange for a larger size

---

解題分析

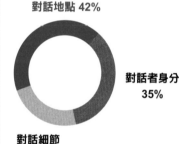

對話地點 42%

對話者身分 35%

對話細節 23%

■ 對話地點 42%   多益考試中，對話發生的地點可以藉由聽大概的對話內容，推敲出符合對話情境的地點。

■ 對話者身分 35%   在三人對話中也很常出現詢問其中一名對話者的職業、年紀等。只要根據對話內容或是情境，對話者的身分便可以輕鬆得知。

■ 對話細節 23%   對話細節有時也會在多益的聽力考試中出現，像是事情最後的解決方法、藉由對話內容推測對話者的下一步……等。

聽稿

（US / Ⓦ） Hello, I'd like to return this jacket, please.

（UK / Ⓜ） Please speak to my supervisor here. She is in charge of returns.

（AU / Ⓦ） Let me help you here. Is there anything wrong with the jacket?

（US / Ⓦ） Well, the thing is that it's a bit too tight for me.

（UK / Ⓜ） In that case, maybe you can just exchange for a bigger one. Here is the size 8. See, it fits you perfectly.

（US / Ⓦ） All right, that's good. I'll just exchange for this one.

（AU / Ⓦ） Let me remove the security tag for you. And here is the receipt for your exchange. Have a nice day.

中譯

（美／**女**）您好，我要將這件夾克辦理退貨，謝謝。

（英／**男**）請您找我的管理人員談，她會負責處理退貨的部分。

（澳／**女**）讓我來為您服務吧，這件夾克有什麼問題嗎？

（美／**女**）它穿起來太緊了。

（英／**男**）若是這樣的情況，您可以辦理換貨，選一件較大尺寸的夾克。這裡有件八號尺寸的。您穿上去剛剛好。

（美／**女**）嗯，這樣也好。我就直接換成這件好了。

（澳／**女**）我先幫您把安全標籤拿掉。這是您換貨的收據。祝您有美好的一天。

新 Q1. 此對話最有可能在何處發生？（答案：**B**）

(A) 火車站 　　　　　　　　　　(B) 購物中心

(C) 電影院 　　　　　　　　　　(D) 餐廳

新 Q2. 男子最有可能是什麼身分？（答案：**D**）

(A) 清潔工 　　　　　　　　　　(B) 會計師

(C) 店經理 　　　　　　　　　　(D) 銷售人員

新 Q3. 針對女子的問題，最終解決辦法為何？（答案：**D**）

(A) 打電話叫警察 　　　　　　　(B) 將夾克退回

(C) 提供折扣優惠券 　　　　　　(D) 換件尺碼大一點的夾克

解題技巧

先不論對話內容是哪個主題的，大家若有辦法練習到將注意力聚焦到真正的關鍵訊息上，不管內容是講什麼都難不倒我們了。再者，不管對話內容的主題為何，其內容都不是真正需要我們去了解或背下的，實在無需將注意力分散到所有資訊上。大家所應做的事，只有將焦點放在聽「題目有問到以及可以回答題目」的重要訊息上即可。此組對話的內容要點可能如以下：

（US／**W**）Hello, I'd like to return this jacket, please.

（UK／**M**）Please speak to my supervisor here. She is in charge of returns.

（AU／**W**）Let me help you here. Is there anything wrong with the jacket?

（US／**W**）Well, the thing is that it's a bit too tight for me.

（UK／**M**）In that case, maybe you can just exchange for a bigger one. Here is the size 8. See, it fits you perfectly.

（US／**W**）All right, that's good. I'll just exchange for this one.

（AU／**W**）Let me remove the security tag for you. And here is the receipt for your exchange. Have a nice day.

根據以上所標出的幾個關鍵便可以大略得知：三人在討論要將夾克退貨之事，客戶認為夾克過小，後來店員建議換大一點的尺碼即可，客戶也同意了。如此一來便可以了解大約的內容了。若可以搭配上先很快地看過題目，便可更精準地預測出要聽什麼方向的答案了。

聽到對話之前務必先看題目以確認聽要點的方向，此題問的是「Where is the conversation most likely taking place?」，便可判斷要將焦點放在聽地點、位置相關資訊上以便回答。根據此關鍵句內容「Hello, I'd like to return this jacket, please.」，可判斷要退夾克一事應是在購物中心或是百貨公司內較為合理，故選 (B)「In a shopping mall」為最佳答案。

各選項解析

- 選項 (A)「In a train station」、選項 (C)「In a movie theater」或選項 (D)「In a restaurant」都不是可以將夾克退貨的地方，故不選。

先掃描到題目問的是「Who is most likely the man?」，那麼便判斷要聽到男子的身分相關訊息以便回答。在女客戶要求要將夾克退貨之後，男子回應了此關鍵句「Please speak to my supervisor here. She is in charge of returns.」，可判斷男子本身也只是一位銷售員，上面還有領班，故選 (D)「A slaes clerk」為最佳答案。

各選項解析

- 選項 (A)「A janitor」、選項 (B)「An accountant」與選項 (C)「The store owner」都不會是在賣場接待客戶之人，故不選。

先掃描到題目問的是「What's the final solution to the woman's problem?」，可以知道要聽到最終解決方法的資訊才可回答。根據男子說的「In that case, maybe you can just exchange for a bigger one. Here is the size 8. See, it fits you perfectly.」，再來看女客戶的回應「All right, that's good. I'll just exchange for this one.」，可聽出最終是要以換貨來取代退貨了，所以選擇 (D)「Exchange for a larger size」為最佳答案。

各選項解析

- 選項 (A)「Call the police」、選項 (B)「Return the jacket」與選項 (C)「Provide a discount voucher」都不是雙方皆認同的解決方式，故不選。

關鍵字彙

return [rɪ`tɝn] v 退貨
supervisor [ˌsupɚ`vaɪzɚ] n 管理人
tight [taɪt] a 緊的
exchange [ɪks`tʃendʒ] v 交換
fit [fɪt] v 適合
perfectly [`pɝfɪktlɪ] ad 完美地
remove [rɪ`muv] v 移除、除去
security tag [sɪ`kjurətɪ ˌtæg] n 安全標籤
receipt [rɪ`sit] n 發票

Unit 8 客戶抱怨類

攻略 1 詢問訂單問題

Q1. Why is the woman calling the man?

(A) To place an order   (B) To trace her order

(C) To thank the man   (D) To return the books she bought

Q2. How does the woman feel about the incident?

(A) Eye-opening   (B) Exciting

(C) Impatient   (D) Delighted

Q3. When will the woman receive her books most likely?

(A) Next month   (B) Within two days

(C) By the end of the year   (D) This afternoon

解題分析

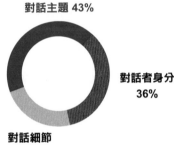

對話主題 43%

對話者身分 36%

對話細節 21%

■ 對話主題 43%　　此題組的第一小題即是換了個方式詢問對話的主題，通常主題會在對話的第一或是第二句就講出，所以試著將注意力集中在前面幾句，就能夠知道對話的主題。

■ 對話者身分 36%　　由於是兩個人的對話，所以也會很常出現詢問其中一名對話者的職業、年紀等。只要根據對話一直重複的字以及心中猜測的對話地點，對話者的身分便可以輕鬆得知。

■ 對話細節 21%　　對話細節要同時間注意播放內容以及選項，還要特別注意問題的首字，這樣才不會選到錯誤的答案。

聽稿

（AU / W）Hello. I'm Vicky Grand. I called three days ago to inform you that I hadn't received my book order and I'm calling again to let you know it still hasn't arrived.

（UK / M）Let me check the record for you please, Ms. Vicky Grand. Well, you ordered 4 books, and one book didn't arrive yet, so I couldn't send the whole package out until we'd received all four books.

（AU / W）Come on, how many more days do I need to wait anyway?

（UK / M）I'm truly sorry about this, Ms. Grand. I'll try my best to send all four books out to you within two days.

（澳／**女**）您好，我是薇琪・葛登。我三天前有打過電話，是通知您關於我所訂購的書籍一直沒有到貨一事，而今日我又再次打來告知商品仍舊尚未到貨。

（英／**男**）薇琪・葛登小姐，請您稍待片刻，讓我為您查詢一下相關資料。您總共訂購了四本書籍，其中的一本尚未完成進貨，因此我們必須等到四本書都到齊之後才有辦法為您寄出整批商品。

（澳／**女**）拜託，我到底還需要再等多久啊？

（英／**男**）我真的感到萬分抱歉，葛登小姐。我會盡量在兩天內把您的四本書都寄送給您。

Q1. 女子為何打電話給男子？（答案：B）

(A) 為下訂單　　　　　　　　　　　　(B) 為追蹤她的貨
(C) 為謝謝男子　　　　　　　　　　　(D) 為退她所買的書

Q2. 女子針對此事件的感覺如何？（答案：C）

(A) 開眼界了　　　　　　　　　　　　(B) 興奮
(C) 失去耐性　　　　　　　　　　　　(D) 愉悅

Q3. 女子最有可能何時會收到書？（答案：B）

(A) 下個月　　　　　　　　　　　　　(B) 兩天內
(C) 年底前　　　　　　　　　　　　　(D) 當日下午

解題技巧

在長篇對話播放出之前，應先做好心理準備，就是不要試圖處理對話中的所有資訊，而是應該先看過題目，了解題目方向，再將焦點放在聽「可以回答到題目的關鍵點上」即可。這些會發揮作用的關鍵點，通常會以加強重音來強調並引起聽者的注意。此組對話的關鍵點可能會是：

（AU／**W**）Hello. I'm Vicky Grand. I called three days ago to inform you that I hadn't received my book order and I'm calling again to let you know it still hasn't arrived.

（UK／**M**）Let me check the record for you please, Ms. Vicky Grand. Well, you ordered 4 books, and one book didn't arrive yet, so I couldn't send the whole package out until we'd received all four books.

（AU／**W**）Come on, how many more days do I need to wait anyway?

（UK／**M**）I'm truly sorry about this, Ms. Grand. I'll try my best to send all four books out to you within two days.

在聽出幾處的關鍵點之後，便可以判斷此對話的大概內容了：女客戶要查書的訂單，男子說要等貨到齊了再一起寄出，並承諾兩日內會處理好。有發現了嗎？就算是冗長的對話，也能只靠幾個關鍵點就可得知全篇對話的主要訊息，根本不需要花精力與時間去逐字處理。因此，在此要再次強烈地建議大家在聆聽多益考試的對話題時，要練習到「聚焦到可以回答問題的關鍵點」喔！

第一題

先掃描到題目所問的是「Why is the woman calling the man?」，那麼可判斷要聽到女子打電話的原因或理由相關資訊以便回答。根據女子所說的此關鍵句「I called three days ago to inform you that I hadn't received my book order and I'm calling again to let you know it still hasn't arrived.」，自然可以聽出她是要問書的訂單事宜，故選 (B)「To trace her order」為最佳答案。

各選項解析

- 選項 (A)「To place an order」、選項 (C)「To thank the man」與選項 (D)「To return the books she bought」都不是女子打此電話的目的，故不選。

第二題

先掃描題目以便判斷要將注意力放在聽什麼資訊上。此題問的是「How does the woman feel about the incident?」，那麼可判斷要聽到選項中有出現女子的感受、態度以便回答。根據女子所說的此關鍵句「Come on, how many more days do I need to wait anyway?」，可聽出她的語氣是有點不耐煩地問「拜託！我到底還要等幾天呀？」，故選 (C)「Impatient」為最佳答案。

各選項解析

- 選項 (A)「Eye-opening」、選項 (B)「Exciting」與選項 (D)「Delighted」都與女子談話中的感覺不符，都不是最適合的答案。

第三題

此題問的是「When will the woman receive her books most likely?」，那麼便可以在心裡打定主意要聽到收到書的時間點相關資訊才可回答。根據男子的此句「I'll try my best to send all four books out to you within two days.」，可聽出最有可能是兩天以內，故選 (B)「Within two days」為最佳答案。

各選項解析

- 選項 (A)「Next month」、選項 (C)「By the end of the year」或選項 (D)「This afternoon」都沒有在男子的談話中出現，故不會是答案。

關鍵字彙

inform [ɪn`fɔrm] v 通知
record [`rɛkɚd] n 紀錄
package [`pækɪdʒ] n 包裹
truly [`trulɪ] ad 真正地

Q1. Where is the conversation most likely taking place?

(A) In a supermarket　　　　　　　(B) In a bank

(C) In a cinema　　　　　　　　　(D) In a university

Q2. What does the woman want to do?

(A) Cancel all her accounts　　　　(B) Withdraw all her money from the bank

(C) Apply for a new credit card　　(D) Cancel one account

Q3. What does the man want from the woman?

(A) Her signature　　　　　　　　(B) Her money

(C) Her credit history　　　　　　(D) Her identification

解題分析

對話地點 53%

對話細節 47%

■ **對話地點** 53%　　第一小題詢問對話發生的地點，我們在對話中可以聽到重複出現的 account、transfer money，便可以大膽假設對話發生的地點即有可能在銀行或是郵局。

■ **對話細節** 47%　　對話細節要同時間注意播放內容以及選項，還要特別注意問題的首字、以及詢問哪一個對話者的相關問題。

聽稿

（US / Ⓦ）Hi, my name is Diane Brown. I need to cancel my checking account. Can you help me with that?

（CA / Ⓜ）Ms. Brown, hi. Um... do you have a problem with your checking account?

（US / Ⓦ）Well, I don't need two different accounts actually. I'd also like to transfer the money to my savings account.

（CA / Ⓜ）All right, Ms. Brown. Please sign here and it'll take me around ten minutes to process your money transfer and account cancellation.

中譯

（美／女）您好，我叫黛安・布朗。我想要取消我的提款帳戶。能麻煩您幫我這個忙嗎？

（加／男）布朗小姐您好。請問您遇上了哪方面的問題呢？

（美／女）這個嘛，我不需要兩種不同的帳戶。另外我還需要轉帳到我的存款帳戶裡。

（加／男）我明白了，布朗小姐，請您在這個地方簽名，隨後我需要花大約十分鐘的時間來幫您完成轉帳和取消戶頭的動作。

Q1. 此對話最有可能發生在何處？（答案：**B**）

(A) 超市   (B) 銀行

(C) 電影院   (D) 大學

Q2. 女子想做什麼？（答案：**D**）

(A) 取消她所有帳戶   (B) 將她所有錢都提出來

(C) 申請新的信用卡   (D) 取消一個帳號

Q3. 男子想要女子的什麼？（答案：**A**）

(A) 簽名   (B) 錢

(C) 信用狀況   (D) 身分證

解題技巧

聽到對話內容播放出來之前，可先把握時間將題目看一下，以便判斷要聽的關鍵訊息方向。在聽對話內容的同時，也不用想逐字處理意思，而是要練習將注意力聚焦，打定主意聽「可以回答到題目」的相關資訊即可。此組對話的關鍵訊息經過加以重音強調之後，便可能是：

> （US／W）Hi, my name is Diane Brown. I need to cancel my checking account. Can you help me with that?
>
> （CA／M）Ms. Brown, hi. Um... do you have a problem with your checking account?
>
> （US／W）Well, I don't need two different accounts actually. I'd also like to transfer the money to my savings account.
>
> （CA／M）All right, Ms. Brown. Please sign here and it'll take me around ten minutes to process your money transfer and account cancellation.

如此便可歸納出此對話的幾個方向了：女子想要取消銀行帳號，還想要將錢轉去另一戶頭，男子在幫她處理。聽懂此篇對話的重要資訊後，就可以歸納出對話要點，確實會是較有效率的聽力策略。

第一題

先看一遍題目以便預期要將焦點放在聽什麼樣的資訊上以便回答。此題問的是「Where is the conversation most likely taking place?」，由於是以 where 為首的問句，那麼便可判斷要聽到地點、位置等相關資訊以便回答。根據此關鍵句的內容「I need to cancel my checking account. Can you help me with that?」，可以判斷出要取消銀行帳戶的地點在銀行較為合理，故選 (B)「In a bank」為最佳答案。

- 選項 (A)「In a supermarket」、選項 (C)「In a cinema」與選項 (D)「In a university」都不會是取消銀行帳號的地點,故不選。

第二題

先看過題目以便預測答題的方向,此題問的是「What does the woman want to do?」,所以可以知道這題的答案要聽到女子想做之事以便回答。根據女子所提及的此關鍵句「Well, I don't need two different accounts actually. I'd also like to transfer the money to my savings account.」,可以聽出她沒有要取消所有帳號,僅想取消一個帳號,並把錢都轉到另一個帳戶中,故選 (D)「Cancel one account」為最佳答案。

- 選項 (A)「Cancel all her accounts」、選項 (B)「Withdraw all her money from the bank」與選項 (C)「Apply for a new credit card」不是與對話內容衝突了,就是在對話中沒有被提及,故不選。

第三題

此題問的是「What does the man want from the woman?」,那麼可判斷要聽到男子說出有關女子所要之物品的資訊以便回答。接著,根據男子所提的此關鍵句「Please sign here and it'll take me around ten minutes to process your money transfer and account cancellation.」,可聽出他是要請女子簽名,所以選擇選項 (A)「Her signature」為最佳答案。

- 選項 (B)「Her money」、選項 (C)「Her credit history」與選項 (D)「Her identification」都沒有在男子的談話中被提及,故不選。

關鍵字彙

cancel [ˋkænsl] ⓥ 取消
checking account [tʃɛkɪŋ əˋkaʊnt] ⓝ 支票帳戶
transfer [trænsˋfɝ] ⓥ 轉移
savings account [ˋsevɪŋz əˋkaʊnt] ⓝ 存款帳戶
process [ˋprɑsɛs] ⓥ 處理、辦理

攻略 3 │ 電子產品問題

Q1. **Who is the woman most likely?**

(A) An unsatisfied customer   (B) A sales representative

(C) A company CEO   (D) A store owner

Q2. **What does the woman ask the man to do?**

(A) Install some applications for her   (B) Replace her computer

(C) Return her money   (D) Call a technician

Q3. **What will the man do next most likely?**

(A) Uninstall some applications from the computer

(B) Give the woman a brand new computer

(C) Ask a technician to check the laptop

(D) Return the money to the woman

解題分析

對話細節 59%

■ 對話細節 59%

■ 對話者身分 41%

對話細節一定要記得搭配選項一起看，也要注意問題是詢問哪一方的對話者，專注在其講的話上面，加上關鍵字，就能夠選到適合的答案。

由於是兩個人的對話，所以也會很常出現詢問其中一名對話者的職業、年紀等。只要根據對話一直重複的關鍵字以及心中猜測的對話地點，對話者的身分便可以輕鬆得知。

聽稿

（US / W ）Hi, there. I purchased this laptop from this store last week. I'm not satisfied with this laptop at all.

（CA / M ）I'm sorry to hear that, madam. What seems to be the problem?

（US / W ）Well, this laptop crashes whenever I try to run my work-processing applications. I'd like a replacement.

（CA / M ）Let me clarify something first, madam. Did you install any software applications by yourself?

（US / W ）No, I didn't. Actually, I bought this laptop with all software applications pre-loaded.

（CA / M ）All right. Once again I'm sorry that you're not satisfied with this laptop. I promise you our technicians will check the settings of everything and get back to you immediately.

（美 / 女）嗨，您好。我上星期從您們這裡買了一台筆記型電腦。坦白說我對它不是很滿意。

（加 / 男）小姐，我真的很抱歉，是哪裡出了問題嗎？

（美 / 女）每一次只要我一開啟工作上的應用程式，它就馬上處於當機的狀態。我希望能夠換一台新的。

（加 / 男）小姐，請容許我先進一步了解更詳細的情況。您是否有自行安裝任何應用程式軟體呢？

（美 / 女）完全沒有。事實上，我買這台筆電的時候，所有的應用程式軟體都是已經內建好的了。

（加 / 男）我明白了。對於這台電腦無法滿足您的需求，我再次向您說聲抱歉。我向您保證我們的技師一定會在短時間內替您做好所有後續的檢查與維修處理。

Q1. 女子最有可能是誰？（答案：A）

(A) 不滿意的客戶　　　　　　　　　　(B) 銷售人員

(C) 公司執行長　　　　　　　　　　　(D) 商店老闆

Q2. 女子要求男子做什麼？（答案：B）

(A) 幫她安裝些應用程式　　　　　　　(B) 換台新電腦給她

(C) 退錢給她　　　　　　　　　　　　(D) 打電話給技術人員

Q3. 男子接下來最有可能做什麼？（答案：C）

(A) 解除安裝電腦中的一些程式　　　　(B) 拿一台全新電腦給女子

(C) 請技術人員檢查一下筆電　　　　　(D) 將錢退還給女子

2018 年改制的多益考試，其中一個新的考點是將對話加長。大家一聽到這種變化便慌了手腳，內心想說短的對話要聽懂都覺得有點吃力了，那長對話不就更難處理嗎？但請各位大家靜心想想，就算對話加長，題目也還是維持在三題呀！

那麼對話加長的部分正是要使大家分心之處呢！若我們可以將自己的注意力都放在「那三道題目」上，僅想聽有用的資訊來回答問題，便不一定要受到加長的內容影響呀！可見「僅將焦點放在聽關鍵點」的策略是相當重要的。關於此篇對話的關鍵點可能如以下所示：

（US / W）Hi, there. I purchased this laptop from this store last week. I'm not satisfied with this laptop at all.

（CA / M）I'm sorry to hear that, madam. What seems to be the problem?

（US / W）Well, this laptop crashes whenever I try to run my work-processing applications. I'd like a replacement.

（CA / M）Let me clarify something first, madam. Did you install any software applications by yourself?

（US / W）No, I didn't. Actually, I bought this laptop with all software applications pre-loaded.

（CA / M）All right. Once again I'm sorry that you're not satisfied with this laptop. I promise you our technicians will check the settings of everything and get back to you immediately.

由所標出的關鍵點可得知出，此對話是女客戶買了電腦後感到不滿意，因為電腦操作上似乎有問題，男子處理並承諾會請技術人員檢查看看。

第一題

先掃描到題目以便判斷要將注意力放在聽什麼資訊上。此題問的是「Who is the woman most likely?」，那麼可判斷要聽到女子的身分、角色相關資訊以便回答這一題。根據女子所說的「I purchased this laptop from this store last week. I'm not satisfied with this laptop at all.」，可以聽出女子不滿意自己所買的商品，故選 (A)「An unsatisfied customer」為最佳答案。

各選項解析

• 選項 (B)「A sales representative」、選項 (C)「A company CEO」與選項 (D)「A store owner」都不會是說出「買了電腦，卻不是很滿意」的人，故不選。

第二題

此題問的是「What does the woman ask the man to do?」，那麼可判斷要聽到「女子要求男子做之事」相關答案以便回答。根據女子所說的此關鍵句「Well, this laptop crashes whenever I try to run my work-processing applications. I'd like a replacement.」，可聽出她是想要換貨的，因此，(B)「Replace her computer」為最佳答案。

各選項解析

• 選項 (A)「Install some applications for her」、選項 (C)「Return her money」與選項 (D)「Call a technician」都沒有在女子的對話中出現。

第三題

先掃描到題目以便判斷要將焦點放在聽什麼樣的資訊上。此題問的是「What will the man do next most likely?」，那麼便可判斷要聽到「男子接下來會做什麼」的相關資訊以便回答。根據男子所說的此關鍵句「I promise you our technicians will check the settings of everything and get back to you immediately.」，可聽出他是會請技術人員看電腦的問題出在哪裡，再給女子回應。故選 (C)「Ask a technician to check the laptop」為最佳答案。

各選項解析

• 選項 (A)「Uninstall some applications from the computer」、選項 (B)「Give the woman a brand new computer」與選項 (D)「Return the money to the woman」都沒有在男子的談話中出現，故不選。

關鍵字彙

purchase [ˋpɝtʃəs] v 購買	madam [ˋmædəm] n 女士、小姐
satisfied [ˋsætɪsˌfaɪd] a 滿意的	install [ɪnˋstɔl] v 安裝
laptop [ˋlæptɑp] n 筆記型電腦	promise [ˋprɑmɪs] v 答應、承諾
crash [kræʃ] v 當機	technician [tɛkˋnɪʃən] n 技術人員
application [ˌæpləˋkeʃən] n 應用程式	setting [ˋsɛtɪŋ] n 設定
replacement [rɪˋplesmənt] n 取代（物品）	immediately [ɪˋmidɪɪtlɪ] ad 立即地、馬上地
clarify [ˋklærəˌfaɪ] v 澄清、闡明	

攻略 1 | 問路

Q1. What is the woman doing?

(A) Working in a gas station

(B) Asking for directions

(C) Looking for a church

(D) Attending a training course

Q2. Where is the woman most likely?

(A) On the plane

(B) On a bike

(C) Inside her car

(D) On the bus

Q3. After seeing a church, what should the woman do?

(A) Make a U-Turn

(B) Turn right

(C) Go straight

(D) Turn left

解題分析

對話主題 43%

對話地點 36%

對話細節 21%

■ 對話主題 43%　此題組的第一小題即是換了個方式詢問對話的主題，通常主題會在對話的第一或是第二句就講出，所以試著將注意力集中在前面幾句，就能夠知道對話的主題。

■ 對話地點 36%　對話發生地點可以根據對話關鍵字以及情境，便可以輕鬆解題、拿分。像這個對話裡，一開始出現的就是「gas station」，再依據選項來選出符合題意的答案。

■ 對話細節 21%　對話細節要同時間注意播放內容以及選項，還要特別注意問題的首字，這樣才不會選到錯誤的答案。

聽稿

（US / Ⓦ）Excuse me. Can you please point me to the nearest gas station?

（CA / Ⓜ）Well, it's a bit far from here. You can take a left at the next traffic light. And then drive for maybe five minutes, you'll see a church on your right hand side. After you pass the church, turn right at the next street.

（US / Ⓦ）Sorry, wait... Did you say that I need to turn right or left after passing the church?

（CA / Ⓜ）Turn right after you see the church, okay? And immediately take a left. You'll then see a gas station on your right.

中譯　　（美／女）打擾了，請問離這裡最近的加油站在哪裡？

（加／男）嗯，離這裡會有一小段距離。妳在下一個紅綠燈左轉之後，繼續往前開大約五分鐘，在右手邊的方向會看到一座教堂。看到教堂以後，就在下一條街口右轉。

（美／女）不好意思，等等，你剛是説經過教堂後要右轉還是左轉？

（加／男）看到教堂後右轉，知道嗎？然後再馬上左轉，妳就會看到右手邊的加油站了。

Q1. 女子在做什麼？（答案：B）

(A) 在加油站上班　　　　　　　　　　(B) 問路

(C) 找教堂　　　　　　　　　　　　　(D) 上訓練課程

Q2. 女子最有可能在哪裡？（答案：C）

(A) 飛機上　　　　　　　　　　　　　(B) 單車上

(C) 她車內　　　　　　　　　　　　　(D) 公車上

Q3. 看到教堂之後，女子應該做什麼？（答案：B）

(A) 迴轉　　　　　　　　　　　　　　(B) 右轉

(C) 直走　　　　　　　　　　　　　　(D) 左轉

解題技巧　　多益改制的要點其中一項是增加不同口音的比重，但事實上不同口音在舊有的多益考試內便已存在，不應該被拿來當「聽不懂」新制題型的藉口。想要熟悉不同口音可靠平常就多聽新聞來練習。在熟悉口音之後，還是要回歸到最基本的策略，將焦點放在聽問題所問的關鍵點上即可。此對話的關鍵點可能是：

（US／W）Excuse me. Can you please point me to the nearest gas station?

（CA／M）Well, it's a bit far from here. You can take a left at the next traffic light. And then drive for maybe five minutes, you'll see a church on your right hand side. After you pass the church, turn right at the next street.

（US／W）Sorry, wait... Did you say that I need to turn right or left after passing the church?

（CA／M）Turn right after you see the church, okay? And immediately take a left. You'll then see a gas station on your right.

由以上的關鍵點可聽出，此對話大概是問路的狀況，女子在找加油站，男子告知她如何前往。在這篇對話內，大家所要了解的主要內容也僅限於此，其他的細節就是題目有問到的話，才需特別去聽答案。

第一題

此題問的是「What is the woman doing?」，那麼可判斷要將注意力放在「女子做什麼事」相關資訊上以便回答。根據女子所說的「Excuse me. Can you please point me to the nearest gas station?」，我們可以得知她是在向人問路，想問加油站的所在位置，故選 (B)「Asking for directions」為最佳答案。

- 選項 (A)「Working in a gas station」、選項 (C)「Looking for a church」與選項 (D)「Attending a training course」都與女子所講的句子內容不符,故不選。

第二題

此題問的是「Where is the woman most likely?」,女子身處何處,那麼便可判斷要聽到與女子所在的位置有關的資訊以便回答。在聽了女子的首句話得知她是在問路之後,再根據男子所回答的此關鍵句「Well, it's a bit far from here. You can take a left at the next traffic light. And then drive for maybe five minutes, you'll see a church on your right hand side.」,可聽出女子是開車問路,所以會是在車內。由此可知,答案要選 (C)「Inside her car」。

- 選項 (A)「On the plane」、選項 (B)「On a bike」與選項 (D)「On the bus」都與關鍵字「drive」無關,故不選。

第三題

此題問的是「After seeing a church, what should the woman do?」,可判斷要聽到「遇到教堂之後要做什麼」相關的資訊,以便回答。根據男子說的此關鍵句「... you'll see a church on your right hand side. After you pass the church, turn right at the next street.」,可以得知遇到教堂之後是要右轉的,故選 (B)「Turn right」為最佳答案。

- 選項 (A)「Make a U-Turn」、選項 (C)「Go straight」與選項 (D)「Turn left」都與對話內容不相符,故不選。

關鍵字彙

traffic light [ˋtræfɪk ˏlaɪt] n 紅綠燈、交通號誌
church [tʃɝtʃ] n 教堂

攻略 2 ｜迷路指引

Q1. What is the woman's problem?

(A) She thinks the city is too noisy　　(B) She doesn't know where the bank is

(C) She can't find her child　　(D) Her car is running out of gas

Q2. Who is most likely the man?

(A) A resident in Springfield　　(B) The woman's best friend

(C) A bank clerk　　(D) The mayor of the city

Q3. When did the man move to Springfield?

(A) In March　　(B) Last year

(C) Eight months ago　　(D) Last week

解題分析

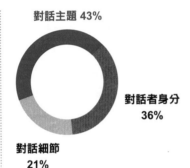

對話主題 43%

對話者身分 36%

對話細節 21%

■ **對話主題** 43% 　此題組的第一小題即是換了個方式詢問對話的主題，通常主題會在對話的第一或是第二句就講出，所以試著將注意力集中在前面幾句，就能夠知道對話的主題。

■ **對話者身分** 36% 　由於是兩個人的對話，所以也會很常出現詢問其中一名對話者的職業、關係等。只要根據對話裡加強重音的字，以及心中猜測的對話地點，對話者的身分便可以輕鬆得知。

■ **對話細節** 21% 　對話細節要同時間注意播放內容以及選項，還要特別注意問題的首字，例如第三小題是問「when」，所以在聽對話時，可以將注意力集中在聽對話者說的時間。

聽稿

（US／Ⓦ）Excuse me. I'm sorry to trouble you. I'm looking for Summit Bank. I thought it was around this corner.

（UK／Ⓜ）Well, it's actually that direction, okay? Keep walking this way then after you pass a gas station, you have to go across the street. The Summit Bank will be on your left. You cannot miss it.

（US／Ⓦ）Thank you very much, sir. I just moved to Springfield last week, so I'm trying to be familiar with the area.

（UK／Ⓜ）Don't worry. I understand the feeling. My family also moved here around eight months ago, and we still have trouble finding some certain places. Well, Springfield is a big city anyway.

中譯　（美 / 女）不好意思，抱歉打擾了。我在找瑞豐銀行，我以為它是在這個街角。

（英 / 男）其實它是在那一個方向耶。妳從這邊繼續走，經過加油站之後，過馬路到另一邊，就會在左邊看到瑞豐銀行了。妳不太可能會錯過的。

（美 / 女）先生，真的很感謝你。我上星期才剛搬到春田市，還需要點時間熟悉地方環境。

（英 / 男）別放在心上，我能體會妳的感受。我和我家人也才剛搬來八個月，依然有許多會讓我們迷路的地點，春田市畢竟是個大都市嘛。

Q1. 女子所遇到的問題為何？（答案：**B**）

(A) 她認為都市太吵了　　　　　　　　　(B) 她不知道銀行在哪裡

(C) 她找不到小孩　　　　　　　　　　　(D) 她的車快沒油了

Q2. 男子最有可能是？（答案：**A**）

(A) 春田市的居民　　　　　　　　　　　(B) 女子的最好朋友

(C) 銀行行員　　　　　　　　　　　　　(D) 那都市的市長

Q3. 男子何時搬到春田市？（答案：**C**）

(A) 三月　　　　　　　　　　　　　　　(B) 去年

(C) 八個月前　　　　　　　　　　　　　(D) 上週

解題技巧　相信練習到此，大家應該都有一個認知，那就是不要想逐字去翻譯或了解對話的所有內容，而是要有信心地將注意力放在先看題目，再聽可回答題目的關鍵點上。而通常這些關鍵點會被說話者以加強重音來處理，以吸引聽者的注意。此組對話的要點便可能是：

> （US / W）Excuse me. I'm sorry to trouble you. I'm looking for Summit Bank. I thought it was around this corner.
>
> （UK / M）Well, it's actually that direction, okay? Keep walking this way then after you pass a gas station, you have to go across the street. The Summit Bank will be on your left. You cannot miss it.
>
> （US / W）Thank you very much, sir. I just moved to Springfield last week, so I'm trying to be familiar with the area.
>
> （UK / M）Don't worry. I understand the feeling. My family also moved here around eight months ago, and we still have trouble finding some certain places. Well, Springfield is a big city anyway.

由以上關鍵點便不難得知，此對話主要是女子在問銀行位置，男子告知她，並小聊了一下自己也是剛搬到此市，有不熟悉之處是正常的！

第一題

在聽到對話之前先將題目看過一遍的好處是：可以預期應聽到什麼樣的答案方向以便回答。此題問的是「What is the woman's problem?」，便可以判斷出要聽到「女子所遭遇之問題」相關資訊以便回答。女子找不到銀行，因為她所說的此關鍵句「Excuse me. I'm sorry to trouble you. I'm looking for Summit Bank. I thought it was around this corner.」，所以她想問銀行的方位。所以這一題的答案就是 (B)「She doesn't know where the bank is.」。

各選項解析

- 選項 (A)「She thinks the city is too noisy.」、選項 (C)「She can't find her child.」與選項 (D)「Her car is running out of gas.」都沒有在女子的對話中被提及，故不選。

第二題

在對話播放之前，首先留意各小題，此題問的是「Who is most likely the man?」，想要正確回答此題，就要聽到相關男子的角色、身分等資訊。根據男子所說的此關鍵句「I understand the feeling. My family also moved here around eight months ago...」，可判斷男子是搬到此都市的居民，故選 (A)「A resident in Springfield」為最佳答案。

各選項解析

- 選項 (B)「The woman's best friend」可以從對話的氛圍得知這是錯的。選項 (C)「A bank clerk」與選項 (D)「The mayor of the city」都與對話中內容不符，故不選。

第三題

此題問的是「When did the man move to Springfield?」，那麼便可判斷要將注意力放在聽男子搬到此都市之時間點相關資訊以便回答。根據男子所說的此關鍵句「My family also moved here around eight months ago...」可明顯地聽出他與家人是八個月前搬來的，故選 (C)「Eight months ago」為最佳答案。

各選項解析

- 選項 (A)「In March」、選項 (B)「Last year」與選項 (D)「Last week」都沒有在對話中被提及，所以都可以刪除。

關鍵字彙

> trouble [ˋtrʌbl] **v** 麻煩、打擾
> corner [ˋkɔrnɚ] **n** 角落
> direction [dəˋrɛkʃən] **n** 方向、方位
> be familiar with **ph** 對～熟悉
> certain [ˋsɝtən] **a** 特定的

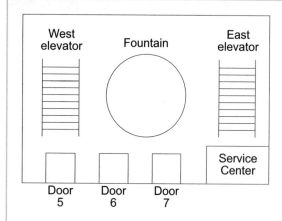

Q1. What is the woman looking for?

(A) Scooter   (B) Shuttle bus

(C) Taxi   (D) Airplane

Q2. What does the woman need to do before boarding the bus?

(A) Buy a cup of coffee   (B) Retrieve her luggage

(C) Prepare some changes   (D) Get a boarding pass

新 Q3. Look at the map. What's the quickest way for the woman to get to the Service Center?

(A) Take the East elevator   (B) Go through Door 5

(C) Take the West elevator   (D) Go over the fountain

解題分析

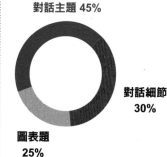

■ 對話主題 45%

■ 對話細節 30%

■ 圖表題 25%

此題組的第一小題即是換了個方式詢問對話的主題，第一小題詢問女子在找何種東西，我們試著將注意力集中在前面幾句，就能夠知道對話的主題。

對話細節要同時間注意播放內容以及選項，還要特別注意問題的首字，這樣才不會選到錯誤的答案。

新制題型新增的圖表題，只要搭配對話內容以及選項，就可以從圖表中選到正確答案。第三小題的解題祕訣是要先從對話內容中判斷出對話者的位置。

聽稿

（AU / W）Hello, sir. I'm wondering if there is an airport bus to the city.

（UK / M）Yes, of course. The airport bus is parked downstairs and it will take you to the City Hall. Please wait at Door 7. Oh, it costs $10.5, so you'd better prepare changes in advance.

（AU / W）Right, okay. But is there a place I can break this 50-dollar note?

（UK / M）Yeah, you can do that at the Service Center, which is also downstairs.

中譯

（澳／**女**）先生，您好，我想請教這裡是否有開往都市的機場接駁車？

（英／**男**）當然有。機場接駁車就在樓下搭乘，它會直接載您到市政府。請您在七號門口處稍待。對了，車資是美金十元五分，所以您可能需要提早準備些零錢。

（澳／**女**）好的，我知道了。有沒有哪個地方能換掉這張五十元紙鈔？

（英／**男**）有的，您可以直接去服務中心，它就在樓下。

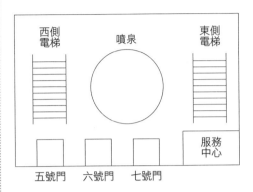

Q1. 女子在找什麼？（答案：**B**）

(A) 機車　　　　　　　　　　　(B) 接駁車

(C) 計程車　　　　　　　　　　(D) 飛機

Q2. 女子上公車之前應先做什麼？（答案：**C**）

(A) 買杯咖啡　　　　　　　　　(B) 取回行李

(C) 準備零錢　　　　　　　　　(D) 拿到登機證

新 Q3. 請看地圖。何者為女子可以到達服務中心的最快方式？（答案：**A**）

(A) 搭東側電梯　　　　　　　　(B) 穿過五號門

(C) 搭西側電梯　　　　　　　　(D) 越過噴泉

解題技巧

聽對話內容時，與其想將逐字聽懂還想一邊翻譯，倒不如將精神放在聽可以回答問題的有用資訊上。要知道哪些資訊是需要聽的，就要先把握時間大略看過題目，且仔細地聽有經過重音處理的關鍵字上。而此對話內容的關鍵點可能會是：

（AU／**W**）Hello, sir. I'm wondering if there is an airport bus to the city.

（UK／**M**）Yes, of course. The airport bus is parked downstairs and it will take you to the City Hall. Please wait at Door 7. Oh, it costs $10.5, so you'd better prepare changes in advance.

（AU／**W**）Right, okay. But is there a place I can break this 50-dollar note?

（UK／**M**）Yeah, you can do that at the Service Center, which is also downstairs.

聽到經過強調的關鍵點之後，便可聽出此對話的大概內容了。女子詢問機場到市區接駁車的訊息，男子告知她搭接駁車的位置，和所需的價格。這樣就可以了解對話百分之八十的內容，的確比翻譯來得輕鬆多了。

在聽對話之前最好可以先看一下題目，才不會抓不到答案的方向。這一題問的是「**What is the woman looking for?**」，那麼便可判斷要將注意力放在聽女子在找的事物上。根據女子所說的「**Hello, sir. I'm wondering if there is an airport bus to the city.**」，可聽出她是在討論接駁公車，故選 (B)「Shuttle bus」為最佳答案。

各選項解析

• 選項 (A)「Scooter」、選項 (C)「Taxi」與選項 (D)「Airplane」都沒有在女子所說的關鍵句內出現，故不選。

第二題

先看到題目問的是「**What does the woman need to do before boarding the bus?**」，那麼可判斷要仔細聽到女子上公車之前所應採取的行動以便回答問題。根據男子所說的此關鍵句「**Oh, it costs $10.5, so you'd better prepare changes in advance.**」，可判斷搭接駁車前要先換零錢，故選 (C)「Prepare some changes」為最佳答案。

各選項解析

• 選項 (A)「Buy a cup of coffee」、選項 (B)「Retrieve her luggage」與選項 (D)「Get a boarding pass」都沒在對話中出現，故不選。

新 第三題

此題要搭配地圖查看。題目問的是「**What is the quickest way for the woman to get to the Service Center?**」，依據男子所說「**You can do that at the Service Center, which is also downstairs.**」，可聽出 Service Center 在樓下，也是要搭電梯下來的，再搭配地圖內容，Service Center 較接近 East elevator，故可判斷最快的方式是搭 East elevator 下來，就可以看到服務中心了。所以這一題的答案選 (A)「Take the East elevator」。

各選項解析

• 對照地圖看來，選項 (B)「Go through Door 5」、選項 (C)「Take the West elevator」與選項 (D)「Go over the fountain」，都不會是最方便且最快速到達 Service Center 的路線。

關鍵字彙

change [tʃendʒ] n 零錢

Unit 10 金融交易類

攻略 1 | 投資討論

Q1. What are the speakers talking about?

(A) Their vacations   (B) Their investments

(C) Their family members   (D) Their supervisors

Q2. What does the woman say about John?

(A) He works in an investment firm   (B) He's lost a couple of cases

(C) He's recently made a bundle   (D) He is a demanding manager

Q3. What kind of person does the man say he himself is?

(A) Attractive   (B) Bold

(C) Impartial   (D) Not too extreme

解題分析

對話主題 59%

對話細節 41%

■ 對話主題 59%

此題組的第一小題即是換了個方式詢問對話的主題，通常主題會在對話的第一或是第二句就講出，所以試著將注意力集中在前面幾句，就能夠知道對話的主題。出現的關鍵字有：stock market。

■ 對話細節 41%

對話細節要同時間注意播放內容以及選項，還要特別注意問題的首字，如此一來便可以避開陷阱選項。

聽稿

（AU / Ⓦ）Did you hear about John? He's been following stock market prices and trends and just made a fortune when his stock split.

（UK / Ⓜ）Sounds great. But I'm a more conservative person and don't want to gamble like that.

（AU / Ⓦ）I totally understand. I'm more like you. I'd rather buy a stock and keep it until its price increases.

（UK / Ⓜ）Yeah, I'd also buy stocks of well-established companies. I don't want to spend my entire savings on anything high risk.

中譯

（澳 / 女）你有聽說約翰的事了嗎？他有在注意股價的動向，而且才剛透過股票交易賺了一筆呢。

（英 / 男）聽起來蠻厲害的。但我是個比較保守的人，不太喜歡賭太大。

（澳 / 女）我懂你的意思，我也跟你一樣。我寧願買一支股票然後一直放到它漲價為止。

（英 / 男）是呀，而且我也只會買績優股吧。我可不想把所有的存款都放進同一個高風險投資的籃子裡。

Q1. 對話者們在討論什麼？（答案：B）

(A) 他們的假期　　　　　　　　　　(B) 他們的投資

(C) 他們的家人　　　　　　　　　　(D) 他們的老闆

Q2. 女子提到關於約翰的何事？（答案：C）

(A) 他在投資公司上班　　　　　　　(B) 他剛失掉兩個案子

(C) 他最近賺很多錢　　　　　　　　(D) 他是個苛刻的經理

Q3. 男子自認為是怎樣的人？（答案：D）

(A) 吸引人的　　　　　　　　　　　(B) 進取的

(C) 中立的、不偏的　　　　　　　　(D) 不會太極端的

解題技巧

我們平日與人對話也是一樣的，就算是打電話給朋友聊天也要有「主題」，而非天南地北地亂聊吧！那個「主題」也正是我們在聽多益對話題時要聽出的資訊。要得知對話的大約主題內容，不用了解每個字才能達成，而是聽到關鍵點就可完成；這些關鍵點通常就是講者加強重音之處，此對話內容的關鍵點可能會是：

> （AU / W）Did you hear about John? He's been following stock market prices and trends and just made a fortune when his stock split.
>
> （UK / M）Sounds great. But I'm a more conservative person and don't want to gamble like that.
>
> （AU / W）I totally understand. I'm more like you. I'd rather buy a stock and keep it until its price increases.
>
> （UK / M）Yeah, I'd also buy stocks of well-established companies. I don't want to spend my entire savings on anything high risk.

由這些標出的關鍵資訊可以聽出，此對話是兩位說話者在討論 John 股票賺錢一事，而這兩位說話者都是屬於較保守的人，不喜歡高風險投資。

第一題

此題問的是「What are the speakers talking about?」，可判斷要聽到討論主題相關資訊以便回答。根據首句關鍵句「He's been following stock market prices and trends and just made a fortune when his stock split.」，與男子的回應「Sounds great. But I'm a more conservative person and don't want to gamble like that.」，可輕鬆聽出他們是在討論股票投資之事，選 (B)「Their investments」為最佳答案。

- 選項 (A)「Their vacations」、選項 (C)「Their family members」與選項 (D)「Their supervisors」都沒有在兩人對話內被討論到,是用來混淆視聽的錯誤選項,故不選。

第二題

「What does the woman say about John」是這一題詢問的問題,想要找出答案,那麼可判斷應將注意力放在聽「女子提及約翰之事」等相關資訊以便回答。根據女子所講的「He's been following stock market prices and trends and just made a fortune when his stock split.」,可以知道約翰近日因股票賺了不少錢,與「make a bundle」意思一致,也是「賺很多錢、進帳不少」之意,所以 (C)「He's recently made a bundle.」為最佳答案。

- 選項 (A)「He works in an investment firm.」、選項 (B)「He's lost a couple of cases.」與選項 (D)「He is a demanding manager.」都沒有在對話中提及,故不選。

第三題

此題問的是「What kind of person does the man say he himself is?」,找答案的焦點應放在聽「男子提及自己個性」的相關要點資訊上。根據男子所說的此句「I'd also buy stocks of well-established companies. I don't want to spend my entire savings on anything high risk.」,能夠聽出他是不喜歡高風險的投資,故選 (D)「Not too extreme」為最佳答案。

- 選項 (A)「Attractive」、選項 (B)「Bold」與選項 (C)「Impartial」都與男子個性的描述不相符,故不選。

關鍵字彙

stock market ['stɑk ˌmarkɪt] n 股票市場
make a fortune ph 大賺一筆
split [splɪt] v 分開、割
conservative [kən'sɜvətɪv] a 保守的
gamble ['gæmbl] v 賭博
well-established ['wɛləs'tæblɪʃt] a 非常確實的
entire [ɪn'taɪr] a 所有的
risk [rɪsk] n 風險

Q1. Who is most likely the man?

(A) A bank clerk   (B) A professor

(C) A pilot   (D) A client

Q2. What would the woman like to do later?

(A) Close her bank account   (B) Prepare lunch

(C) Deposit some money   (D) Change a new driver's license

新 Q3. What does the man mean when he says "Everything is set-up."?

(A) Your driver's license is valid

(B) Please wait a bit longer

(C) Your account has been opened successfully

(D) Dinner is ready

解題分析

對話者身分 45%

對話細節 45%

句子的意思 10%

■ **對話者身分 45%**   由於是兩個人的對話,所以也會很常出現詢問其中一名對話者的職業、年紀等。只要根據對話一直重複的字(bank),以及心中猜測的對話地點,對話者的身分便可以輕鬆得知。

■ **對話細節 45%**   對話細節要同時間注意播放內容以及選項,還要特別注意問題的首字,這樣才不會選到錯誤的選項。

■ **句子的意思 10%**   如果在聽力對話題看到要選句子意思的題目,只要事先看題目,對話播放時注意前後文,就能理解說這個句子的語氣以及涵義。

聽稿

（US / Ⓦ） Good morning. Uh, can I open a bank account with the Summit Bank please?

（CA / Ⓜ） Of course, madam. Please fill in these application forms and show me your identification, like a valid passport or driver's license.

（US / Ⓦ） Sure, here is my driver's license. I'd also like to deposit some money into my new account today, is it okay?

（CA / Ⓜ） Certainly. When the savings account is opened, you can deposit money straight away. Give me another three minutes to process your account. All right, now everything is set-up. Here is your card. You can use this card to access the tellers to deposit or withdraw your money.

中譯

（美／女）早安，我想要開一個瑞豐銀行的帳戶。

（加／男）沒問題，小姐。麻煩您先填寫好這些表格，並且把您的身分證件交給我。有效護照或駕照都可以。

（美／女）好的，這是我的駕照。我今天可以馬上存一些錢到新帳戶嗎？應該沒問題吧？

（加／男）那是當然，您的存款帳戶一開立好，您就能馬上做後續存款作業。請您稍等我三分鐘為您完成開戶作業。好了，程序都已經完成。這是您的提款卡，您能夠使用它向任何出納員辦理存款或提款的相關動作。

Q1. 男子最有可能是？（答案：A）

(A) 銀行行員　　　　　　　　　　　　(B) 教授
(C) 飛行員　　　　　　　　　　　　　(D) 客戶

Q2. 女子稍後想要做什麼？（答案：C）

(A) 關閉銀行帳戶　　　　　　　　　　(B) 準備午餐
(C) 存點錢進戶頭　　　　　　　　　　(D) 換一張新的駕照

新 Q3. 當男子說「Everything is set-up.」時，他是什麼意思？（答案：C）

(A) 妳的駕照是有效的　　　　　　　　(B) 請再等一下
(C) 妳的帳戶已成功開通　　　　　　　(D) 晚餐準備好了

解題技巧

若是大家擺脫不了舊有逐字翻譯的聽力處理方式，可試著在聽到加強重音的關鍵點後，用自己的話將對話的大約內容描述一次，看自己的理解是否與對話內一樣。如此一來便可訓練並半強迫自己將注意力轉移到「聽有用的資訊上」，而非將注意力都分散到每個單獨的字詞上。此組對話內的關鍵點可能會是：

> （US／W）Good morning. Uh, can I open a bank account with the Summit Bank please?
>
> （CA／M）Of course, madam. Please fill in these application forms and show me your identification, like a valid passport or driver's license.
>
> （US／W）Sure, here is my driver's license. I'd also like to deposit some money into my new account today, is it okay?
>
> （CA／M）Certainly. When the savings account is opened, you can deposit money straight away. Give me another three minutes to process your account. All right, now everything is set-up. Here is your card. You can use this card to access the tellers to deposit or withdraw your money.

在聽到關鍵點後，我們便可將內容做個整體的描述：女子要在銀行開戶，男子要她填表格和看身分證，之後便可處理開戶之事。由此可知，單靠關鍵點是可以了解對話大致的內容，不一定要靠翻譯每個字才可處理喔！

此題問的是「Who is most likely the man?」，心中便有底要聽到「男子的角色、身分」相關資訊以便回答。根據女子說的首句「Can I open a bank account with the Summit Bank please?」，以及男子的回答「Of course, madam. Please fill in these application forms and show me your identification...」，可判斷男子是在銀行工作的人，選項中只有 (A)「A bank clerk」為最佳答案。

各選項解析

• 選項 (B)「A professor」、選項 (C)「A pilot」或選項 (D)「A client」都不會是在銀行幫客戶辦理開戶的角色，故不選。

第二題

先大略看過題目的好處是可以預測應該要聽的焦點內容之方向。此題問的是「What would the woman like to do later?」，根據題目，我們可以判斷要聽到有關「女子想做什麼」的訊息以便回答。根據女子所提的此關鍵句「I'd also like to deposit some money into my new account today, is it okay?」，我們能知道她想存些錢到帳戶內，所以選 (C)「Deposit some money」為最佳答案。

各選項解析

• 選項 (A)「Close her bank account」、選項 (B)「Prepare lunch」或選項 (D)「Change a new driver's license」都沒有在女子的對話中出現。

新 第三題

這一題問「What does the man mean when he says "Everything is set-up."?」，首先來理解「Everything is set-up.」的意思，這個短語的意思是「所有事情都處理妥當了」。再對照此對話，我們可以知道這裡指的事情「Your account has been opened successfully」為最佳答案。

各選項解析

• 選項 (A)「Your driver's license is valid.」、選項 (B)「Please wait a bit longer.」與選項 (D)「Dinner is ready.」都與對話內容不相符，不會是男子提及「Everything is set-up.」內之事情，所以都不能選。

關鍵字彙

bank account [ˋbæŋk əˋkaʊnt] n 銀行帳戶
application form [ˌæpləˋkeʃən ˌfɔrm] n 申請表
identification [aɪˌdɛntəfəˋkeʃən] n 識別
valid [ˋvælɪd] a 有效的
deposit [dɪˋpɑzɪt] v 寄存
certainly [ˋsɝtənlɪ] ad 的確
access [ˋæksɛs] v 存取
teller [ˋtɛlɚ] n 出納員
withdraw [wɪðˋdrɔ] v 提出、領款

攻略 3 ｜ 轉職討論（三人對話）

新 Q1. Who are most likely the speakers?

(A) Classmates   (B) Customers

(C) Colleagues   (D) Competitors

新 Q2. What does the man say about the company?

(A) The company is expanding its product line

(B) The company is hiring more people

(C) The company is doing a roaring trade

(D) The company is suffering losses

新 Q3. What will Susan do next most likely?

(A) Hunt for new job opportunities   (B) Ask her supervisor for assistance

(C) Open a new bank account   (D) Write a reference letter for the man

---

解題分析

對話者身分 53%

對話細節 47%

■ **對話者身分 53%**　由於是兩個人的對話，所以也會很常出現詢問對話者的職業、關係等。只要根據對話一直重複的字以及心中猜測的對話地點，對話者的身分便可以輕鬆得知。

■ **對話細節 47%**　第二小題和第三小題都是詢問對話中的細節，大家同時間注意播放內容以及選項，看到不符合對話敘述的選項就可以刪除。

聽稿

（US / Ⓦ）I can't believe this. The company is laying off 10 employees, and I'm one of them.

（UK / Ⓜ）Oh, no. I'm really sorry to hear that, Susan. It seems like the company is losing its ground.

（AU / Ⓦ）Well, you know what, Susan? What I urge you to do now is to join those networking groups online immediately.

（US / Ⓦ）Thanks, Sherry. But what are networking groups? I haven't tried those before.

（UK / Ⓜ）They are groups of people who are also hunting for jobs. They help each other find new opportunities, right?

（AU / Ⓦ）Yeah, exactly. You join networking groups online, Susan, describe your capabilities, personal attributes, and work experience. They'll share with you some suitable job opportunities.

（美 / 女）這簡直不可置信，公司要解僱十名員工，而我竟然是其中的一位。

（英 / 男）噢，天哪，蘇珊，我真的感到萬分遺憾。看來公司的運作已岌岌可危了。

（澳 / 女）蘇珊，妳知道嗎？我建議妳趕緊加入網路人脈社群。

（美 / 女）謝了，雪莉。不過人脈社群是什麼東西？我以前從沒接觸過。

（英 / 男）他們是一群正在尋找工作的人。應該說他們互相幫忙彼此搜索新的工作機會，對吧？

（澳 / 女）完全正確。妳加入網路人脈社群，蘇珊，填上個人的專長技能、人格特質、和工作經驗，他們會跟妳分享適合妳的工作機會。

新 Q1. 講者的關係最有可能是？（答案：C）

(A) 同學　　　　　　　　　　　　(B) 客戶

(C) 同事　　　　　　　　　　　　(D) 競爭者

新 Q2. 男子提到關於公司的什麼事？（答案：D）

(A) 公司要拓展產品線　　　　　　(B) 公司要請更多員工

(C) 公司業績做得很好　　　　　　(D) 公司業務虧損

新 Q3. 蘇珊接下來最有可能做什麼？（答案：A）

(A) 找尋更多工作機會　　　　　　(B) 請她老闆提供協助

(C) 開一個新的銀行帳號　　　　　(D) 幫男子寫封推薦信

解題技巧

此組三人對話的內容，處理上與一般原則無異，都是要將注意力放在聽關鍵點上，只是因為有三個人在交談，更要特別注意聽哪一句話是誰說的。通常對話中會搭配姓名，比方說：Mark、Sherry、Kevin……等，可以使用這些名字來做區分。若行有餘力的話，可以在腦中想像一下三人對話的狀況、他們的位置以及所搭配的表情等，以幫助自己了解三人的關係。而此組對話的關鍵訊息可能會是：

（US / W）I can't believe this. The company is laying off 10 employees, and I'm one of them.

（UK / M）Oh, no. I'm really sorry to hear that, Susan. It seems like the company is losing its ground.

（AU / W）Well, you know what, Susan? What I urge you to do now is to join those networking groups online immediately.

（US / W）Thanks, Sherry. But what are networking groups? I haven't tried those before.

（UK / M）They are groups of people who are also hunting for jobs. They help each other find new opportunities, right?

（AU / W）Yeah, exactly. You join networking groups online, Susan, describe your capabilities, personal attributes, and work experience. They'll share with you some suitable job opportunities.

由以上的關鍵點便可聽出，此三人對話內容是在討論其中一個女子被公司裁員，而男子說是因為公司營運不佳的關係，另一個女子建議趕緊加入線上社團找其他工作。由此可知道，無論是幾人的對話，想要了解大致的對話內容，還是要抓住「關鍵訊息」才是最有效的喔！

新 第一題

此題問的是「Who are most likely the speakers?」，根據題目，可以預期要聽到有關「三個人的關係、角色」的資訊以便回答。從對話中的「I can't believe this. The company is laying off 10 employees, and I'm one of them.」，與回應此句的「Oh, no. I'm really sorry to hear that, Susan. It seems like the company is losing its ground.」，我們可以聽出他們是在討論公司狀況，那麼應是同事間的對話較為合理，故選 (C)「Colleagues」為最佳答案。

各選項解析

- 選項 (A)「Classmates」同學間、選項 (B)「Customers」客戶之間或選項 (D)「Competitors」競爭者等都不會是討論公司裁員與公司現況的關係，所以都不能選。

新 第二題

先看到題目才有機會判斷所要聽的關鍵點之方向。此題問的是「What does the man say about the company?」，我們可預期要聽到男子提及「公司狀況如何」來回答。根據男子所說的此要點句「It seems like the company is losing its ground.」，可聽出公司榮景不再，表現不是很理想的狀況。所有選項中，只有 (D)「The company is suffering losses.」為最佳答案。

各選項解析

- 選項 (A)「The company is expanding its product line.」、選項 (B)「The company is hiring more people.」與選項 (C)「The company is doing a roaring trade.」都與「The company is losing its ground.」的描述不相符，故不選。

新 第三題

先看過題目以便確認要聽到關鍵要點的方向為何。此題問的是「What will Susan do next most likely?」，便可判斷要聽到「蘇珊的下一步行動」相關資訊以便回答。根據 Sherry 所說的此關鍵句「You join networking groups online, Susan, describe your capabilities, personal attributes, and work experience. They'll share with you some suitable job opportunities.」，可聽出 Sherry 建議 Susan 去參加網路上的人才互助圈，並找新的工作機會，故選 (A)「Hunt for new job opportunities」為最佳答案。

各選項解析

- 選項 (B)「Ask her supervisor for assistance」、選項 (C)「Open a new bank account」與選項 (D)「Write a reference letter for the man」都沒有在對話中被提及，所以都不是正確答案喔！

關鍵字彙

lay off ph 解僱、遣散
lose ground ph 退步、沒發展
immediately [ɪˋmidɪɪtlɪ] ad 立即地、馬上地
hunt for ph 尋找
opportunity [ˌɑpɚˋtjunətɪ] n 機會
describe [dɪˋskraɪb] v 描述
capability [ˌkepəˋbɪlətɪ] n 能力
attribute [ˋætrəˌbjut] n 特質、屬性
suitable [ˋsutəbl̩] a 適合的

Unit 10／金融交易類　325

攻略 1 | 討論工作

Q1. **What is the woman's problem?**

(A) She just lost a couple of important cases

(B) She thought she doesn't perform well enough

(C) She has too many projects on hand

(D) She couldn't communicate effectively with her boss

Q2. **What does the woman say about her job?**

(A) Demanding   (B) Effortless

(C) Annoying   (D) Dull

Q3. **What does the man suggest the woman do?**

(A) Ask her supervisor to promote her   (B) Drink more water

(C) Keep going forward   (D) Go home and relax

解題分析

對話主題 55%

■ 對話主題 55%

■ 對話細節 45%

此題組的第一小題即是換了個方式詢問對話的主題，通常主題會在對話的第一或是第二句就講出，所以試著將注意力集中在前面幾句，就能夠知道對話的主題。

對話細節 45%

對話細節要同時間注意播放內容以及選項，還要特別注意問題的首字，這樣才不會選到錯誤的答案。若是遇到詢問對話者的心情，可以看著選項並找出對話中的關鍵字，例如：challenging。

聽稿

（AU / **W**）I can't become proficient at this new job. I feel frustrated.

（CA / **M**）Well, what happened? I thought you enjoy your new job.

（AU / **W**）Yeah, I do. I think my new job is challenging yet fun. My supervisor told me what to do and I keep thinking about it carefully, but I just don't see any concrete achievement.

（CA / **M**）Well, don't worry, it takes time. The only and the best advice I could provide is to keep trying and don't give up, okay?

中譯

（澳／**女**）我無法對這份新工作得心應手，我感到精疲力竭了。

（加／**男**）發生了什麼事？我以為妳熱愛妳的新工作呢。

（澳／**女**）我蠻喜歡的，我覺得這份工作不但有趣又充滿挑戰。我照著主管的指示去做，在過程中也深思熟慮，可就是看不到任何具體的成果。

（加／**男**）嗯，妳別往心裡去，這需要點時間。我唯一能提供妳最好的建議就是堅持到底、不放棄，好嗎？

Q1. 女子遇到什麼問題？（答案：B）

    (A) 她剛丟掉兩個重要案子   (B) 她認為她工作表現不夠好

    (C) 她手上案子過多了   (D) 她無法跟老闆有效溝通

Q2. 女子認為她的工作如何？（答案：A）

    (A) 要求很高   (B) 不需費力

    (C) 令人厭煩   (D) 了無生氣

Q3. 男子建議女子做什麼事？（答案：C）

    (A) 請她主管讓她升遷   (B) 多喝點水

    (C) 持續向前努力   (D) 回家放鬆

解題技巧

要了解對話內容不可以靠蠻力，想將每個字都聽懂來處理；而是要有效率地將有限的精力與時間放在聽「可回答題目的關鍵點」上。那麼這些會發揮影響力的關鍵點，自然會被說話者以加強重音來強調，以顯示出其重要性。比方說此組對話的關鍵點可能會落在：

（AU／**W**）I can't become proficient at this new job. I feel frustrated.

（CA／**M**）Well, what happened? I thought you enjoy your new job.

（AU／**W**）Yeah, I do. I think my new job is challenging yet fun. My supervisor told me what to do and I keep thinking about it carefully, but I just don't see any concrete achievement.

（CA／**M**）Well, don't worry, it takes time. The only and the best advice I could provide is to keep trying and don't give up, okay?

由這些關鍵點可聽出，女子工作上力不從心，但男子鼓勵她要慢慢來，應該繼續努力不要放棄。憑藉這幾個關鍵點就可以了解大概對話內容，的確是省事多了呢！

第一題

在對話播放之前，若可利用那短暫的時間將題本內的題目先瞄一下，便有機會可以正確判斷要將注意力放在聽哪些要點上。此題問的是「What is the woman's problem?」，可判斷要聽到「女子所遇到的困擾」的訊息以便回答此題。根據關鍵句「I can't become proficient at this new job. I feel frustrated.」，可以聽出女子是認為自己在工作上的表現不夠好，因而感到沮喪。所以要選 (B)「She thought she doesn't perform well enough.」為最佳答案。

- 選項 (A)「She just lost a couple of important cases.」，女子並沒有提到她失去幾個案子，因此可以刪除。
- 選項 (C)「She has too many projects on hand.」也沒有在對話中被提到，也可以刪去。
- 選項 (D)「She couldn't communicate effectively with her boss.」的內容也一樣沒有在對話中討論到，故不選。

第二題

第一小題作答完之後，先看到第二小題所問的是「What does the woman say about her job?」，那麼可判斷要聽到「女子認為她的工作如何」相關訊息以便回答。根據女子所說的此關鍵句「I think my new job is challenging yet fun.」，可聽出她認為她的工作是很有挑戰性的，這與選項 (A)「Demanding」同義，都是要求很高的意思，所以選擇 (A) 為最佳答案。

各選項解析

- 選項 (B)「Effortless」、選項 (C)「Annoying」與選項 (D)「Dull」都與女子說的「challenging」不同義，所以都可以刪除。

第三題

此題問的是「What does the man suggest the woman do?」，便可判斷要聽到「男子所提的建議」相關資訊以便回答。根據男子所說的此關鍵句「Well, don't worry, it takes time. The only and the best advice I could provide is to keep trying and don't give up, okay?」，可聽出他是建議女子要繼續努力，不要放棄，故選 (C)「Keep going forward」為最佳答案。

各選項解析

- 選項 (A)「Ask her supervisor to promote her」、選項 (B)「Drink more water」與選項 (D)「Go home and relax」都沒有在對話中被討論到，故不選。

關鍵字彙

proficient [prə`fɪʃənt] a 精通的、熟練的
frustrated [`frʌstretɪd] a 沮喪的
challenging [`tʃælɪndʒɪŋ] a 具挑戰性的
supervisor [ˌsupəˋvaɪzə] n 管理人
concrete [`kɑnkrit] a 具體的
achievement [əˋtʃivmənt] n 成就
advice [ədˋvaɪs] n 忠告
give up ph 放棄

攻略 2 | 討論度假

Q1. What are the speakers mainly talking about?

    (A) Sports competitions   (B) Vacation plans

    (C) Project outline   (D) Sales performance

Q2. How does the woman feel about her stay in Florida?

    (A) Expensive   (B) Troublesome

    (C) Exceptional   (D) Lifeless

Q3. What will the man do next most likely?

    (A) Hire a diving coach

    (B) Plan his trip to Asia with the woman

    (C) Purchase a flight ticket to Florida

    (D) Search for more information about Mexico

解題分析

對話主題 57%

對話細節 43%

■ 對話主題 57%

■ 對話細節 43%

通常主題會在對話的第一或是第二句就講出，所以試著將注意力集中在前面幾句，就能夠知道對話的主題。所以可以知道此題組的關鍵字為 vacation。

對話細節—推測對話者下一步、對話者感受……等，大家要同時間注意播放內容以及選項，還要特別注意問題的首字，這樣才不會選到錯誤的答案。

聽稿

（US / Ⓦ）The last time we had a vacation, my husband and I went diving in Florida.

（CA / Ⓜ）Really? I never tried diving before. How was it? Fun?

（US / Ⓦ）It was such a marvelous experience. It was a completely different world out there. There was peace and silence, and the only sound I could hear was the sound of my breath. Anyway, it was just an experience of a lifetime.

（CA / Ⓜ）Wow, it really sounds fantastic. I'm gonna plan my next trip this evening and I would very much like to visit Cancun, Mexico. I heard that the sea is crystal clear there.

中譯

（美 / **女**）上一次度假，我跟我老公跑去佛羅里達潛水。

（加 / **男**）真的嗎？我從來沒有去潛水過。結果如何？好玩嗎？

（美 / **女**）那是一段不可思議的旅程，水底下簡直就是另一個世界。既寧靜又祥和，除了自己的呼吸聲之外，其他什麼都聽不到。總之，絕對是一場千載難逢的體驗。

（加 / **男**）聽起來真的很美妙。我決定今晚要開始來規劃下一趟去墨西哥坎昆的度假旅程了。聽說那裡的海水可是清澈見底呢。

Q1. 講者主要在討論什麼？（答案：B）

(A) 運動賽事　　　　　　　　　　　　(B) 度假計畫

(C) 專案綱要　　　　　　　　　　　　(D) 業績表現

Q2. 女子認為她在佛羅里達過得如何？（答案：C）

(A) 很貴　　　　　　　　　　　　　　(B) 很麻煩

(C) 很特別　　　　　　　　　　　　　(D) 很無趣

Q3. 男子接下來最有可能做什麼？（答案：D）

(A) 僱用潛水教練　　　　　　　　　　(B) 規劃他跟女子去亞洲的行程

(C) 買張去佛羅里達的機票　　　　　　(D) 找尋更多關於墨西哥的資訊

解題技巧

曾經遇過有同學說他聽力特別好，不僅每個字都聽懂，還可默寫出來。這樣的能力是很不錯，但針對多益的聽力，只是要大家正確地回答到問題就好，並不用默寫內容！因此若非是有特殊能力要默寫內容，還不如將注意力放在做「可以回答到問題」的有意義之事就好。這些可以回答到問題的關鍵點，有可能就是以加強重音之處，比方說此對話的要點可能是：

（US / **W**）The last time we had a vacation, my husband and I went diving in Florida.

（CA / **M**）Really? I never tried diving before. How was it? Fun?

（US / **W**）It was such a marvelous experience. It was a completely different world out there. There was peace and silence, and the only sound I could hear was the sound of my breath. Anyway, it was just an experience of a lifetime.

（CA / **M**）Wow, it really sounds fantastic. I'm gonna plan my next trip this evening and I would very much like to visit Cancun, Mexico. I heard that the sea is crystal clear there.

根據此上的關鍵點可以聽出，此對話內容大致是：兩人在討論度假的規畫，女子說去佛羅里達州潛水，男子聽後也決定要去墨西哥海邊玩。如此大致了解一下對話內容，比起默寫整個對話有用多囉！

第一題

先看一下題目以便對於所要聽的關鍵點有個底。此題問的是「What are the speakers mainly talking about?」，那麼可判斷要聽到講者討論的主題相關資訊以便回答。根據此首句關鍵句「The last time we had a vacation, my husband and I went diving in Florida.」，可判斷兩人是在討論度假之事，故選 (B)「Vacation plans」為最佳答案。

各選項解析

- 選項 (A)「Sports competitions」、選項 (C)「Project outline」與選項 (D)「Sales performance」都沒有在文章中被提及，故不選。

第二題

此題問的是「How does the woman feel about her stay in Flordia?」，那麼便可判斷要聽到「女子在佛羅里達州度假的感受」相關資訊以便回答。根據女子所提的此關鍵句「It was such a marvelous experience... Anyway, it was just an experience of a lifetime.」，可以聽出女子認為在佛羅里達州的度假是很特別的經驗，所以選擇 (C)「Exceptional」為最佳答案。

各選項解析

- 選項 (A)「Expensive」、選項 (B)「Troublesome」與選項 (D)「Lifeless」都沒有在女子的對話中被提及，故不選。

第三題

先找到機會在對話播放前注意題目，以便預期對話開始播放後，應該聽之要點的方向。此題問的是「What will the man do next most likely?」，既然是問男子接下來的行動，便要將注意力放在聽「男子提及的行動」相關資訊上以便回答。根據男子所提到的此關鍵句「I'm gonna plan my next trip this evening and I would very much like to visit Cancun, Mexico.」，可聽出男子想要規劃去墨西哥的假期，所以選擇 (D)「Search for more information about Mexico」為最佳答案。

各選項解析

- 選項 (A)「Hire a diving coach」、選項 (B)「Plan his trip to Asia with the woman」與選項 (C)「Purchase a flight ticket to Florida」都沒有在對話中被提及，所以都不選。

關鍵字彙

vacation [ve`keʃən] n 度假
diving [`daɪvɪŋ] n 潛水
marvelous [`mɑrvələs] a 極棒的、極佳的
completely [kəm`plitlɪ] ad 完全地
silence [`saɪləns] n 安靜
breath [brɛθ] n 呼吸
fantastic [fæn`tæstɪk] a 美好的、令人讚嘆的
crystal clear ph 透明的、清楚的

Q1. **What is the man's problem?**

(A) He wears too many hats in the company

(B) He doesn't feel well

(C) His stay in India was unpleasant

(D) He just lost a big case

Q2. **What happened to the woman when she was in India?**

(A) She got food poisoning

(B) She lost all her money.

(C) She caught a cold

(D) Her flight was delayed for five hours

Q3. **What does the man suggest the woman do?**

(A) Schedule an appointment with her doctor

(B) Travel less frequently

(C) Try different prescriptions

(D) Try to take good care of herself

解題分析

對話主題 58%

對話細節 42%

■ 對話主題 58%

■ 對話細節 42%

此題組的第一小題即是換了個方式詢問對話的主題，由於是詢問男子的狀況，可以將注意力放在男子所說的話，就能夠知道對話的主題。

對話細節一定要同時間注意播放內容以及選項，還要特別注意問題的首字，這樣才不會選到錯誤的答案。特別的是，通常第二小題關鍵字會出現在對話的中段，第三小題的則出現在對話的末段。

聽稿

（US / W） John, are you all right? You look tired.

（UK / M） Well, I just came back from a business trip to Japan. It's easy for me to catch cold from flying.

（US / W） I totally understand. During my last business trip to India, I got food poisoning.

（UK / M） Oh, no. That must be terrible! Are you sure it wasn't just an upset stomach?

（US / W） No, according to the doctor, it was food poisoning. Luckily, the doctor gave me a prescription that really worked well.

（UK / M） Well, I guess we as frequent travelers should really strengthen our immune systems.

中譯　　（美／女）你還好吧，約翰？你看起來疲憊不堪。

（英／男）我剛從日本出差回來，我很容易坐一趟飛機就感冒一次。

（美／女）我完全理解。我上回去印度出差的時候，還搞到食物中毒了。

（英／男）噢，我的天，那真的糟透了！妳確定不單單只是拉肚子嗎？

（美／女）不，經過醫生的檢查，確定是食物中毒。幸好醫生開給我的處方籤還蠻有效。

（英／男）嗯，我覺得我們這種常出差的空中飛人真應該好好提升自己的免疫力。

Q1. 男子遇到什麼問題？（答案：B）

(A) 他在公司身兼數職　　　　　　　(B) 他感覺不舒服

(C) 他的印度之旅感受不佳　　　　　(D) 他剛輸掉一個大案子

Q2. 女子在印度時發生何事？（答案：A）

(A) 她食物中毒　　　　　　　　　　(B) 她丟了錢

(C) 她感冒　　　　　　　　　　　　(D) 她班機延誤五小時

Q3. 男子建議女子做什麼事？（答案：D）

(A) 跟她醫生約看診　　　　　　　　(B) 少去旅遊

(C) 試不同的藥方　　　　　　　　　(D) 試著照顧好自己

解題技巧　在準備對話聽力時應有一個認知，就是大家的目的要正確地回答題目就好，而不是想將注意力分散到其他不相關的資訊上。如此說來，題目有問到的才是大家應注意聽的資訊。若在聽力內容播放出來之前，可以把握時間先將題目看過一遍，是最好不過了，便可得知應將注意力放在聽什麼要點上。此組對話的要點內容可能會是：

（US／W）John, are you all right? You look tired.

（UK／M）Well, I just came back from a business trip to Japan. It's easy for me to catch cold from flying.

（US／W）I totally understand. During my last business trip to India, I got food poisoning.

（UK／M）Oh, no. That must be terrible! Are you sure it wasn't just an upset stomach?

（US／W）No, according to the doctor, it was food poisoning. Luckily, the doctor gave me a prescription that really worked well.

（UK／M）Well, I guess we as frequent travelers should really strengthen our immune systems.

得知這些關鍵要點之後可以歸納出，此對話主要是在討論出差後身體不適的經驗，男子最後結論是出門在外還是要提升自己免疫力才重要。

第一題

先看題目問什麼，才有機會知道要將注意力放在聽什麼關鍵點上。此題問的是「What is the man's problem?」，那麼便可判斷要聽到「男人所遇到的困擾」相關資訊以便回答。根據男子所說的此關鍵句「I just came back from a business trip to Japan. It's easy for me to catch cold from flying.」，可以知道他出差後身體不適，所以選擇和身體狀況有關的 (B)「He doesn't feel well.」為最佳答案。

各選項解析

• 選項 (A)「He wears too many hats in the company.」、選項 (C)「His stay in India was unpleasant.」與選項 (D)「He just lost a big case.」，都沒有在對話中被提及，因此都不會是這一題需要的答案。

第二題

先看到題目問的是「What happened to the woman when she was in India?」，既然是問女子在印度所發生之事，那我們應該將焦點都轉移到聽「女子提到印度之事」上以便回答。從對話中找答案，我們可以根據女子所說的「During my last business trip to India, I got food poisoning.」，明顯聽出她食物中毒了，所以在四個選項中，選擇 (A)「She got food poisoning.」為最佳答案。

各選項解析

• 選項 (B)「She lost all her money.」、選項 (C)「She caught a cold.」與選項 (D)「Her flight was delayed for five hours.」都沒有在女子的對話中提到，故不選。

第三題

此題問的是「What does the man suggest the woman do?」，所以我們知道要聽到與「男子給女子的建議」有關的選項來當作答案。根據男子所說的此句「I guess we as frequent travelers should really strengthen our immune systems.」，可以聽出男子就是認為要照顧好自己，並加強自己的免疫系統，選 (D)「Try to take good care of herself」最為合適。

各選項解析

• 選項 (A)「Schedule an appointment with her doctor」、選項 (B)「Travel less frequently」與選項 (C)「Try different prescriptions」都沒有在男子的對話中出現，所以都不選。

關鍵字彙

catch a cold ph. 感冒
food poisoning [fud `pɔɪznɪŋ] n. 食物中毒
terrible [`tɛrəbl] a. 很糟的
upset stomach ph. 肚子痛
luckily [`lʌkɪlɪ] ad. 幸運地
prescription [prɪ`skrɪpʃən] n. 藥方、處方
frequent [`frikwənt] a. 經常的
strengthen [`strɛŋθən] v. 加強
immune system [ɪ`mjun ˌsɪstəm] n. 免疫系統

Unit 12 餐飲服務類

攻略 1 | 訂單錯誤

Q1. Why is the woman calling?

(A) To check why her order hasn't arrived yet

(B) To return the product she bought two days ago

(C) To ask the man to reschedule their meeting

(D) To reserve a table for Sunday evening

Q2. According to the man, what seems to be the problem?

(A) The woman doesn't want to accept the man's apology

(B) The man doesn't know what to order

(C) The woman's credit card has been declined

(D) The order system is not working properly

Q3. What will the woman most likely do next?

(A) Place her order all over again   (B) Go to the man's store directly

(C) Ask the man to return her money   (D) Pick up the goods by herself

---

解題分析

對話主題 60%

對話細節 40%

■ 對話主題 60%

■ 對話細節 40%

此題組的第一小題即是換了個方式詢問對話的主題，通常主題會在對話的第一或是第二句就講出。加上聽到一些重要資訊，例如：order、wait、so long……等。

對話細節要同時間注意播放內容以及選項，還要特別注意問題的首字，這樣才不會選到錯誤的答案。也要試著抓出關鍵訊息：your order was never recorded、order once again 等。

聽稿

（AU / W） Is this Tasty-Ham? My name is Judy Bush, and I ordered some burgers, salads, and beverages over an hour ago, and I've been waiting for so long.

（UK / M） Ms. Judy Bush, hold on please. I'm really sorry, Ms. Bush, but it seems like I can't find your order on our delivery system. There might be an error, and your order was never recorded.

（AU / W） What? I really can't believe this.

（UK / M） I apologize for that, Ms. Bush. Please let me know what you would like to order once again and I'll deliver your meals to your house immediately. I'm sorry for the inconvenience.

（澳／女）請問是美味火腿專賣店嗎？我是茱蒂‧布希，在一個小時前向您訂了幾個漢堡、沙拉和飲料，我已經等非常久了。

（英／男）茱蒂‧布希小姐，請您稍待片刻。我很抱歉，布希小姐，我無法從點餐系統上找出您的訂單資料。可能是哪裡出了差錯，您的訂單並沒有成立。

（澳／女）您說什麼？太扯了吧。

（英／男）我向您說聲抱歉，布希小姐。請您再告訴我一次您的訂購內容，我馬上將您的餐點外送至您的住所。抱歉造成您的不便。

Q1. 女子打電話的目的為何？（答案：A）

    (A) 查看為何她訂的東西尚未送達　　　　(B) 將她兩天前買的產品退貨

    (C) 請男子將她們的會議改期　　　　　　(D) 訂一個週日晚上的桌位

Q2. 根據男子的描述，問題點為何？（答案：D）

    (A) 女子不想接受男子的道歉　　　　　　(B) 男子不知要點些什麼才好

    (C) 女子的信用卡被拒刷了　　　　　　　(D) 訂餐系統發生異常

Q3. 女子接下來最有可能做什麼？（答案：A）

    (A) 重新點一次餐點　　　　　　　　　　(B) 直接前往男子的店家

    (C) 要求男子退錢　　　　　　　　　　　(D) 親自前往領取商品

解題技巧　與其將自己的注意力分散到所有資訊上，不如聚焦聽有用的，可以回答問題的重要關鍵訊息上就好。而這些想引起聽者注意的要點，說話者通常會以加強重音來加以強調。此組對話的關鍵內容有可能會是：

> （AU／W）Is this Tasty-Ham? My name is Judy Bush, and I ordered some burgers, salads, and beverages over an hour ago, and I've been waiting for so long.
>
> （UK／M）Ms. Judy Bush, hold on please. I'm really sorry, Ms. Bush, but it seems like I can't find your order on our delivery system. There might be an error, and your order was never recorded.
>
> （AU／W）What? I really can't believe this.
>
> （UK／M）I apologize for that, Ms. Bush. Please let me know what you would like to order once again and I'll deliver your meals to your house immediately. I'm sorry for the inconvenience.

由以上的幾個關鍵點，我們就可以拼湊出此對話的約略內容了。也就是女子要確認她的餐點狀況，但是男子似乎因系統問題沒看到訂單，於是男子便要重新接一次訂單，並承諾馬上送達。聽力部分在作答時，要時時刻刻記得抓住幾個有效的關鍵點來判斷對話的主要內容，才是大家應該練習的。

第一題

首先把握時間看題目，才可得知要聽什麼方向的要點。此題問的是「Why is the woman calling?」，那麼便可預期要將要點放在聽「女子打電話的原因」以便回答。根據女子所說的此關鍵句「My name is Judy Bush, and I ordered some burgers, salads, and beverages over an hour ago, and I've been waiting for so long.」，可聽出女子是客戶，訂了餐點卻一直沒送達，所以才要打電話來確認。所以最好的答案是選項 (A)「To check why her order hasn't arrived yet」。

各選項解析

• 選項 (B)「To return the product she bought two days ago」、選項 (C)「To ask the man to reschedule their meeting」與選項 (D)「To reserve a table for Sunday evening」都沒有在對話中被討論到，故不選。

第二題

此題問的是「According to the man, what seems to be the problem?」，那麼便可得知要將焦點放在聽「男子所說的問題點」上以便回答。根據男子所說的此關鍵句「Ms. Bush, but it seems like I can't find your order on our delivery system. There might be an error, and your order was never recorded.」，可聽出他沒看到女子的點餐訂單，可能是系統有問題，故選 (D)「The order system is not working properly.」為最佳答案。

各選項解析

• 選項 (A)「The woman doesn't want to accept the man's apology.」、選項 (B)「The man doesn't know what to order.」與選項 (C)「The woman's credit card has been declined.」都沒有在男子的對話中出現，故不選。

第三題

聽到對話之前可把握時間先看題目，以便得知要將焦點放在聽什麼資訊上。此題問的是「What will the woman most likely do next?」，我們就能知道要將注意力放在聽「女子接下來的行動」上以便回答。對話中，男子所說的此關鍵句「Please let me know what you would like to order once again and I'll deliver your meals to your house immediately.」，可聽出男子請女子將她要點的餐點再說一次，好為她準備並送餐。所以我們可推斷女子接下來應會「將想點的餐點品項再講一次」，故選 (A)「Place her order all over again」為最佳答案。

各選項解析

• 選項 (B)「Go to the man's store directly」、選項 (C)「Ask the man to return her money」與選項 (D)「Pick up the goods by herself」都沒在對話中討論到，故不選。

關鍵字彙

beverage [`bɛvərɪdʒ] n 飲料
delivery [dɪ`lɪvərɪ] n 寄送、遞送
error [`ɛrɚ] n 錯誤、過失
apologize [ə`pɑləˌdʒaɪz] v 道歉
immediately [ɪ`midɪɪtlɪ] ad 立即地、馬上地
inconvenience [ˌɪnkən`vinjəns] n 不便之處

Q1. **Where is the conversation probably taking place?**

(A) In the office

(B) In the woman's house

(C) In a restaurant

(D) In the library

Q2. **Why didn't the man try the pork?**

(A) He thought it was spicy

(B) He was too full to try it

(C) He didn't like the dish at all

(D) He wanted to leave it for the woman

Q3. **What will the speakers most likely do next?**

(A) Pay by credit card

(B) Order desserts and drinks

(C) Split the bill

(D) Order some more food

解題分析

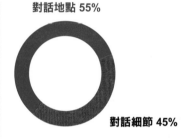

對話地點 55%

對話細節 45%

■ **對話地點** 55%　對話的地點可以透過對話主要內容以及自己猜想的情境下去作答,而此對話發生地點可以由 meal、order 來看出。

■ **對話細節** 45%　對話細節要同時間注意播放內容以及選項,還要特別注意問題的首字,這樣才不會選到錯誤的答案,以 why 開頭就要知道要聽原因、理由。

聽稿

(US / **W**) How do you like your meal, Jack?

(CA / **M**) It's wonderful. All the food is delicious. My favorites are the stuffed eggplant and beef steak.

(US / **W**) The grilled chicken is also very tasty. Well, I noticed you didn't try the pork. Don't you like pork?

(CA / **M**) Well, that pork dish looked a bit spicy. Okay, now let's order desserts. I'd like to have a cup of coffee. And you, Linda?

中譯

（美／女）你還喜歡你的餐點嗎，傑克？

（加／男）這裡太棒了。它的食物非常好吃，我最愛的是鑲茄子和牛排。

（美／女）它的炙燒雞也非常美味。咦，我注意到你沒有試試豬肉，你不吃豬肉嗎？

（加／男）嗯……那道豬肉料理看起來有點辛辣。好啦，我們來點些甜點吃吧。我想喝杯咖啡。妳呢，琳達？

Q1. 此對話可能是在何處聽到？（答案：C）

   (A) 辦公室　　　　　　　　　　(B) 女子家中

   (C) 餐廳　　　　　　　　　　　(D) 圖書館

Q2. 男子為何不試試豬肉？（答案：A）

   (A) 他覺得那有點辣　　　　　　(B) 他太飽了吃不下

   (C) 他完全不喜歡那道餐點　　　(D) 他想將它留給女子吃

Q3. 講者接下來最有可能做什麼？（答案：B）

   (A) 以信用卡付款　　　　　　　(B) 點甜點和飲料

   (C) 分開付帳　　　　　　　　　(D) 點更多食物

解題技巧

一般人聽到一句英文，就會有習慣將此句話在腦中翻譯成中文，才會有「聽懂」了這句話的感覺。但一再強調的是，多益對話聽力內容沒有要大家全數聽懂，僅要求大家了解內容大約在講什麼，並且可以正確地「回答三題問題」即可。因此，大家在準備時應多練習聽可以回答問題的關鍵點即可，而非想將所有對話內容翻譯完並聽懂。此組對話的關鍵內容可能會是：

> （US／W）How do you like your meal, Jack?
>
> （CA／M）It's wonderful. All the food is delicious. My favorites are the stuffed eggplant and beef steak.
>
> （US／W）The grilled chicken is also very tasty. Well, I noticed you didn't try the pork. Don't you like pork?
>
> （CA／M）Well, that pork dish looked a bit spicy. Okay, now let's order desserts. I'd like to have a cup of coffee. And you, Linda?

由這些關鍵內容便可得知八成的大概了，兩人在討論餐點好不好吃，接著就要點甜點與飲料了。

第一題

聽到對話之前最好先將題目看一下，以便得知要聽的答案方向為何。此題問的是「Where is the conversation probably taking place?」，由於是 where 開頭的問句，可判斷要聽的是對話可能發生地的相關資訊以便回答。根據女子說的此句「How do you like your meal, Jack?」，與男子的回應「It's wonderful. All the food is delicious.」，可以聽出兩人是在討論餐點好不好吃，最有可能是在餐廳較為合理，故選 (C)「In a restaurant」為最佳答案。

各選項解析

- 選項 (A)「In the office（辦公室）」、選項 (B)「In the woman's house（在女子的家裡）」與選項 (D)「In the library（圖書館）」，以上三個地點都不會是「討論餐點好不好吃」最合適的地點。

先很快地將題目看一遍，可以看到題目問的是「Why didn't the man try the pork?」，便應將焦點放在聽「男子沒吃豬肉料理的原因」相關資訊以便回答。根據男子說的此關鍵句「Well, that pork dish looked a bit spicy.」，可聽出男子是認為豬肉料理看起來很辣，所以選 (A)「He thought it was spicy.」為最佳答案。

各選項解析

• 選項 (B)「He was too full to try it.」、選項 (C)「He didn't like the dish at all.」與選項 (D)「He wanted to leave it for the woman.」都沒有在對話內被討論，所以都可以刪除。

第三題

這一題詢問「What will the speakers most likely do next?」，在知道題目要問什麼之後，我們就可以先預設要將注意力放在聽「兩人接下來的行動」等相關資訊上以便回答。根據此關鍵句「Okay, now let's order desserts. I'd like to have a cup of coffee. And you, Linda?」，可聽出兩人吃完主餐，接下來要點甜點了，故選 (B)「Order desserts and drinks」為最佳答案。

各選項解析

• 選項 (A)「Pay by credit card」、選項 (C)「Split the bill」與選項 (D)「Order some more food」都沒有在對話中出現，故不選。

關鍵字彙

delicious [dɪ`lɪʃəs] a 美味的
favorite [`fevərɪt] a 最喜歡的
stuffed [stʌft] a 塞滿的
eggplant [`ɛɡ͵plænt] n 茄子
grilled [ɡrɪld] a 燒烤的
tasty [`testɪ] a 美味的
notice [`notɪs] v 察覺、意識到
spicy [`spaɪsɪ] a 辣的

攻略 3 ｜ 餐廳用餐

Q1. **Where is the conversation most likely taking place?**

(A) In an office   (B) In a restaurant

(C) In the train station   (D) In a church

Q2. **Who is the man most likely?**

(A) A chef   (B) A waiter

(C) A cashier   (D) A customer

Q3. **What will the woman most likely do next?**

(A) File a complaint to the restaurant manager

(B) Pay by cash and go home

(C) Order desserts

(D) Look at the menu and decide what to order

解題分析

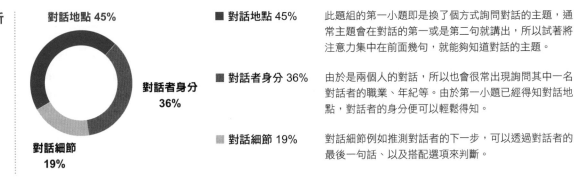

■ 對話地點 45%　　此題組的第一小題即是換了個方式詢問對話的主題，通常主題會在對話的第一或是第二句就講出，所以試著將注意力集中在前面幾句，就能夠知道對話的主題。

■ 對話者身分 36%　　由於是兩個人的對話，所以也會很常出現詢問其中一名對話者的職業、年紀等。由於第一小題已經得知對話地點，對話者的身分便可以輕鬆得知。

■ 對話細節 19%　　對話細節例如推測對話者的下一步，可以透過對話者的最後一句話、以及搭配選項來判斷。

聽稿

（US /Ⓦ）Hi. I rang up yesterday and reserved a table for four at 7. My name is Liz Jones.

（UK /Ⓜ）Let's see. Yes, Ms. Jones, this way please. We've reserved a table for four by the window. Here are menus. So can I get you anything to drink?

（US /Ⓦ）Four beers please. And may we get an order of BBQ wings as an appetizer?

（UK /Ⓜ）Sure, no problem. I'll just leave the menus with you. Please call me when you're ready to place the rest of your order.

（美／女）您好，我昨天打電話來訂了七點的四人位置。我的名字是麗茲·瓊斯。

（英／男）我看看。有的，麗茲小姐，這邊請。我們為您保留了靠窗邊的四人桌。這是我們的菜單。請問要喝點什麼嗎？

（美／女）四罐啤酒，謝謝。前菜的部分可以給我們來份燒烤雞翅嗎？

（英／男）當然可以，沒問題。我先留菜單給您們參考。決定好其他餐點後再招我過來就行了。

Q1. 此對話最有可能在何處聽到？（答案：B）

(A) 辦公室 　　　　　　　　　　(B) 餐廳

(C) 火車站 　　　　　　　　　　(D) 教堂

Q2. 男子最有可能是誰？（答案：B）

(A) 主廚 　　　　　　　　　　　(B) 服務生

(C) 收銀員 　　　　　　　　　　(D) 客戶

Q3. 女子接下來最有可能做什麼？（答案：D）

(A) 跟餐廳經理抱怨 　　　　　　(B) 以現金付款並回家去

(C) 點甜點 　　　　　　　　　　(D) 看菜單並決定要點什麼

練習到最後，大家應有感覺到了，不管題目如何變化，是加口音的、不同主題的、還是篇幅加長的對話，我們所需要做的最重要的聽力策略僅有一個：要專注在題目所問的要點上，以便可以將注意力放在聽可以回答題目的關鍵點即可。所幸這些關鍵點也不會是難以聽出的，因為講者為了要強調要點，會在要點上加強重音，讓聽者明確地聽出。此對話的要點內容可能會是：

（US／W）Hi. I rang up yesterday and reserved a table for four at 7. My name is Liz Jones.

（UK／M）Let's see. Yes, Ms. Jones, this way please. We've reserved a table for four by the window. Here are menus. So can I get you anything to drink?

（US／W）Four beers please. And may we get an order of BBQ wings as an appetizer?

（UK／M）Sure, no problem. I'll just leave the menus with you. Please call me when you're ready to place the rest of your order.

由以上這些關鍵點可聽出，此對話內容大約是在發生在餐廳內。女子有訂位，男子帶賓客就座後便提供菜單。要得知大約的概念，只要有焦點就行了，不需要逐字翻譯對話內容喔！

第一題

在對話內容播放出來之前，務必先把握時間看一下題目，以便判斷要聽何種方向的資訊以便回答。這一題問「Where is the conversation most likely taking place?」，可判斷要聽到對話發生之地點、位置才可回答到問題。從「Hi. I rang up yesterday and reserved a table for four at 7.」，可以聽出女子是顧客，並且訂了七點的座位。那麼就可以推論對話地點應該會是在餐廳較為合理，所以選 (B)「In a restaurant」為最佳答案。

• 選項 (A)「In an office」、選項 (C)「In the train station」或選項 (D)「In a church」都不會是需要訂七點座位的地方,故不選。

第二題

此題問的是「Who is the man most likely?」,那麼便應將焦點放在聽「男子的角色、身分」上以便回答。根據男子所說的此關鍵句「We've reserved a table for four by the window. Here are menus. So can I get you anything to drink?」,可聽出男子的身分是服務生,才會引領顧客去位子上,也提供菜單。所以在四個選項中,(B)「A waiter」為最佳答案。

• 選項 (A)「A chef」、選項 (C)「A cashier」或選項 (D)「A customer」都不太像是男子的身分、角色,所以都可以刪除。

第三題

此題問的是「What will the woman most likely do next?」,既然是問女子接下來的行動,那麼我們便應將焦點放在聽「女子所要做之事」上以便回答。根據男子所說的此關鍵句「I'll just leave the menus with you. Please call me when you're ready to place the rest of your order.」,可以聽出男子是將菜單留著給女子看,若女子決定好要點什麼才會再請男子過來,故可判斷接下來女子應會先看菜單內容較為合理,選項 (D)「Look at the menu and decide what to order」為最適合的答案。

• 選項 (A)「File a complaint to the restaurant manager」、選項 (B)「Pay by cash and go home」與選項 (C)「Order desserts」都沒有在對話中提及,故不選。

關鍵字彙

ring up 打電話
reserve [rɪˋzɝv] v 預約、預訂
menu [ˋmɛnju] n 菜單
appetizer [ˋæpəˌtaɪzɚ] n 開胃菜

練習 1 │ 會議協商類

Q1. What are the speakers doing?

(A) Discussing environmental problems

(B) Writing e-mails to Mr. Chen

(C) Getting ready for a couple of meetings

(D) Preparing for an upcoming party

Q2. What will happen on Wednesday?

(A) All rales reps will meet

(B) Mr. Chen will leave for New York

(C) The man will visit a customer

(D) A new employee will join the team

Q3. What should the woman prepare for Friday's meeting?

(A) Product brochures

(B) Quarterly sales reports

(C) Some wine

(D) Some innovative ideas

聽稿

（US / Ⓦ）All right, John. Let me quickly go over our schedule for this week. The sales meeting on Tuesday has been moved to Wednesday at 10, right?

（UK / Ⓜ）Yes, exactly. This is because Mr. Chen is away and won't be back until Wednesday. Well, all sales reps will meet in conference room 8A at 10 on Wednesday.

（US / Ⓦ）Okay, I see. One more thing please. What are we supposed to prepare for the brainstorming meeting on Friday? I mean should we come up with ideas in advance or something?

（UK / Ⓜ）Well, the brainstorm meeting is really about how to increase customer satisfaction, so you may want to think about what else we can do to make customers happy.

中譯

（美 / 女）那麼，約翰，讓我快速地跟你對照一下這星期的行程進度。銷售會議從原本的星期二改到星期三早上十點了，是嗎？

（英 / 男）對的，正確無誤。這是因為陳先生星期三才會回來。另外，所有的銷售代表會於星期三早上十點在 8A 會議室集合。

（美 / 女）好，我知道了。還有一件事，有關星期五的那場腦力激盪會議，我們應該要準備些什麼？我的意思是說，我們需要事前先想出些點子或其他什麼嗎？

（英 / 男）嗯，星期五的腦力激盪會議主要是探討如何增加顧客滿意度，或許妳可以先思考我們還能怎麼做才能讓顧客心滿意足。

Q1. 講者在做什麼？（答案：C）

(A) 討論環境議題

(B) 寫電郵給陳先生

(C) 為幾個會議做準備

(D) 準備即將來臨的派對

Q2. 有什麼事情會在週三發生？（答案：**A**）

(A) 所有業務代表會開會   (B) 陳先生會出發去紐約

(C) 男子會去拜訪客戶   (D) 一位新員工會加入團隊

Q3. 女子應為週五的會議準備什麼？（答案：**D**）

(A) 產品目錄   (B) 每季業務報告

(C) 一些酒   (D) 一些有創意的點子

解析

第一題

先看到題目問的是「What are the speakers doing?」，我們可以知道應將焦點放在聽「他們在做什麼事」上面。根據此關鍵句「Let me quickly go over our schedule for this week. The sales meeting on Tuesday has been moved to Wednesday at 10, right?」可聽出他們是在對本週內會議的時程，故選 (C)「Getting ready for a couple of meetings」為答案。

各選項解析

- 選項 (A)「Discussing environmental problems」、選項 (B)「Writing e-mails to Mr. Chen」與選項 (D)「Preparing for an upcoming party」都沒在對話中被提及，故不選。

第二題

此題問「What will happen on Wednesday?」，既然是問週三會發生之事，自然是要將注意力放在聽週三的關鍵點上。根據「Well, all sales reps will meet in conference room 8A at 10 on Wednesday.」，可聽出是所有業務代表要開會，選項 (A)「All sales reps will meet.」即為最佳答案。

各選項解析

- 選項 (B)「Mr. Chen will leave for New York.」、選項 (C)「The man will visit a customer.」與選項 (D)「A new employee will join the team.」都沒在對話中被提及，故不選。

第三題

此題問的是「What should the woman prepare for Friday's meeting?」，自然要將焦點放在「女子週五做準備」的相關資訊上面。根據女子問的此關鍵句「What are we supposed to prepare for the brainstorming meeting on Friday?」，以及男子的回答「Well, the brainstorm meeting is really about how to increase customer satisfaction, so you may want to think about what else we can do to make customers happy.」，可以聽出是要先寫一些關於客服的點子，故選 (D)「Some innovative ideas」為最佳答案。

各選項解析

- 選項 (A)「Product brochures」、選項 (B)「Quarterly sales reports」與選項 (C)「Some wine」都沒在對話中提及，所以可以刪除喔！

關鍵字彙

exactly [ɪgˋzæktlɪ] ad 一點也沒錯

sales reps [ˋselz ͵rɛps] n 業務代表

suppose [səˋpoz] v 料想、認定

prepare [prɪˋpɛr] v 準備

brainstorm [ˋbren͵stɔrm] v 腦力激盪

satisfaction [͵sætɪsˋfækʃən] n 滿意度

customer [ˋkʌstəmɚ] n 客戶、主顧

Q1. What is the woman concerned about?

(A) How to quickly expand Japanese market

(B) How to interact with international clients properly

(C) How to master Japanese within three months

(D) How the weather condition can affect her trip to Japan

Q2. What does the man suggest the woman do when talking to clients?

(A) Provide some trophies

(B) Ask clients to sign an agreement

(C) Start with small talks

(D) Get right into business issues

Q3. What does the man say about Mr. Toyota?

(A) He speaks good English

(B) He's a pretty serious person

(C) He's been to the US before

(D) He'll place a big order

聽稿　　（AU / W） You know what, Jason? I'm worried about calling Mr. Toyota in Japan. I'm not good at dealing with international clients. I heard that Japanese clients tend to be more serious.

（CA / M） Well, Linda, it's always good to start with small talk before you get down to business. Maybe you can start with talking about weather or news.

（AU / W） Right, I see your point. We respect directness, but Japanese clients may not. That's why I'd better start with small talk. Okay, but what about if I don't understand his accent.

（CA / M） You don't need to worry about it, Linda. I've talked to Mr. Toyota several times before, and I think he speaks very clear and fluent English. If you need anything, just ask him to repeat or clarify.

中譯　　（澳 / 女） 傑森，你知道嗎？我不太敢打電話給日本的豐田先生。我不擅長與國際客戶洽商，尤其又聽說日本客戶都是非常正經八百的。

（加 / 男） 這樣啊，琳達，要不要試著在切入公事之前先來個閒話家常？或許話題能先從天氣、新聞等等開始。

（澳 / 女） 嗯，我理解你的重點。我們尊重直接性的談話，但或許日本客人不吃這一套。先從一般大眾的話題切入會是比較妥當的選擇。好吧，可是如果我聽不懂對方的口音呢？

（加 / 男） 這妳就更無須擔心了，琳達。我跟豐田先生講過蠻多次話的，他的英文口語還算清晰流暢呢。倘若妳有需要，可以請他再重複一遍、或描述地再清楚些。

Q1. 女子主要擔心什麼事？（答案：B）

(A) 如何快速地拓展日本市場

(B) 如何適當地與國際客戶互動

(C) 如何在三個月內精通日文

(D) 天氣狀況如何影響她的日本行程

Q2. 男子建議女子在與客戶談話時要注意什麼？（答案：C）

    (A) 給一些獎品   (B) 請客戶簽個合約

    (C) 先從寒暄開始   (D) 立即切入商業主題

Q3. 男子提到關於豐田先生的何事？（答案：A）

    (A) 他英文講得不錯   (B) 他是個頗嚴肅的人

    (C) 他之前去過美國   (D) 他會下個大訂單

解析

第一題

先掃描題目才有機會得知要聽什麼關鍵內容，此題問的是「What is the woman concerned about?」，那麼便要聽到關於女子擔憂之事以回應。根據此關鍵句「I'm worried about calling Mr. Toyota in Japan. I'm not good at dealing with international clients. I heard that Japanese clients tend to be more serious.」，可聽出她是擔心與外國客戶談話之事，故選 (B)「How to interact with international clients properly」為最佳答案。

各選項解析

• 選項 (A)「How to quickly expand Japanese market」、選項 (C)「How to master Japanese within three months」與選項 (D)「How the weather condition can affect her trip to Japan」都僅是故意將對話中的「Japan / Japanese」重唸一次而已，但不是女子主要擔心之事，故不選。

第二題

此題問的是「What does the man suggest the woman do when talking to clients?」，那麼可判斷要聽到男子的建議以便回答。根據男子的此關鍵句「Well, Linda, it's always good to start with small talk before you get down to business.」，可聽出男子是建議要先聊些輕鬆的話題，故選 (C)「Start with small talks」為最佳答案。

各選項解析

• 選項 (A)「Provide some trophies」、選項 (B)「Ask clients to sign an agreement」與選項 (D)「Get right into business issues」都非「start with small talks」的替換說法，故不選。

第三題

此題問的是「What does the man say about Mr. Toyota?」，那麼便可判斷要聽到男子提到關於 Toyota 先生的事才可回答。根據此關鍵句「I've talked to Mr. Toyota several times before, and I think he speaks very clear and fluent English.」，可聽出男子認為 Toyota 先生的英文講得不錯，故選 (A)「He speaks good English.」為最佳答案。

各選項解析

• 選項 (B)「He's a pretty serious person.」、選項 (C)「He's been to the U.S. before.」與選項 (D)「He'll place a big order.」都沒在對話中被提及，故不選。

關鍵字彙

deal with 處理、交涉	accent [ˈæksɛnt] 口音
small talk [ˈsmɔl ˌtɔk] 寒暄	fluent [ˈfluənt] 流利的
respect [rɪˈspɛkt] 尊重	repeat [rɪˈpit] 重複
directness [dəˈrɛktnɪs] 坦白、直率	clarify [ˈklærəˌfaɪ] 闡明、澄清

新 Q1. **What are the speakers talking about?**

(A) Their family problems   (B) Their sales performance

(C) Their leisure activities   (D) Their retirement plans

新 Q2. **When is the conversation most likely taking place?**

(A) Sunday   (B) Monday

(C) Friday   (D) Tuesday

新 Q3. **What does the woman say about swimming?**

(A) She only swims during summer time

(B) She doesn't like swimming

(C) She just watches swimming competitions on TV

(D) She thinks swimming helps her stay healthy

聽稿

（US / W）So, guys. How do you spend your free time?

（UK / M）Well, most weekends, my wife and I work around the house or just go shopping. Like... tomorrow we'll go to the Grand Mall, and probably just stay at home on Sunday.

（CA / M）I simply enjoy tennis. Sometimes I invite my friends to play at the tennis courts by my house. So how about you, Sherry?

（US / W）Well, I go swimming whenever I have time. It helps me keep in good shape.

（UK / M）Oh, since you love swimming, did you watch the MAX Swimming Competition on TV?

（US / W）No, I didn't. I don't really care much for watching it on TV.

（CA / M）Yeah, I understand. I love tennis, but I can't stand watching the game on TV, either.

中譯

（美 / 女）欸，夥伴們，你們平常都從事哪些消遣娛樂呀？

（英 / 男）這個嘛，通常在週末的時候，我都會和太太整理房子或者去購物。像是明天我們會去格蘭購物中心，週日的話可能就待在家裡。

（加 / 男）我純粹只喜歡打網球。有時會邀請朋友一起去我家附近的網球場練習。那妳呢，雪莉？

（美 / 女）嗯，只要我一有空，我就會跑去游泳。游泳幫助我維持好身材。

（英 / 男）噢，既然妳那麼愛游泳，妳有沒有在看電視播的 MAX 游泳大賽節目？

（美 / 女）沒有，我對於電視上的游泳比賽並沒有太大的興趣。

（加 / 男）嗯，我能理解。我雖然熱愛網球，但我也不喜歡在電視上看它的相關賽事。

新 Q1. 對話者在討論些什麼？（答案：C）

(A) 他們的家庭問題　　　　　　　　(B) 他們的業績表現

(C) 他們的休閒活動　　　　　　　　(D) 他們的退休計畫

新 Q2. 此對話最有可能在何時聽到？（答案：C）

(A) 週日　　　　　　　　　　　　　(B) 週一

(C) 週五　　　　　　　　　　　　　(D) 週二

新 Q3. 女子提到關於游泳的何事？（答案：D）

(A) 她只有在夏季游泳　　　　　　　(B) 她不喜歡游泳

(C) 她僅看電視上的游泳比賽　　　　(D) 她認為游泳可讓身體健康

解析 新 第一題

先掃描到問題「What are the speakers talking about?」，那麼心中預期要聽到對話主題相關資訊以便回應。根據此首句關鍵句「So, guys. How do you spend your free time?」，可聽出三人是在討論休閒時做的活動，故選 (C)「Their leisure activities」為最佳答案。

各選項解析

• 選項 (A)「Their family problems」、選項 (B)「Their sales performance」與選項 (D)「Their retirement plans」都沒有在對話中提及，故不選。

新 第二題

此題問的是「When is the conversation most likely taking place?」，那麼便預期要聽到關於時間點的資訊以便回答。根據此關鍵句「Well, most weekends, my wife and I work around the house or just go shopping. Like... tomorrow we'll go to the Grand Mall...」，可聽出男子說「週末通常會去購物，像是明天就會去……」，如此一來便可判斷明天是週末，那麼三人在討論的時間最有可能是週五。所以選 (C)「Friday」為最佳答案。

新 第三題

此題問的是「What does the woman say about swimming?」，那麼心中有底要聽到女子所提及游泳相關資訊以便回答。根據此關鍵句「Well, I go swimming whenever I have time. It helps me keep in good shape.」，可聽出她認為游泳可以讓身體健康，故選 (D)「She thinks swimming helps her stay healthy.」為最佳答案。

各選項解析

• 選項 (A)「She only swims during summer time.」、選項 (B)「She doesn't like swimming.」與選項 (C)「She just watches swimming competitions on TV.」內容都與對話內容不符，故不選。

關鍵字彙

simply [ˈsɪmplɪ] ad 僅是、簡單地

invite [ɪnˈvaɪt] v 邀請

competition [ˌkɑmpəˈtɪʃən] n 競爭

Q1. **Who are the speakers most likely?**

(A) Patients (B) Colleagues

(C) Neighbors (D) Strangers

Q2. **What is the man doing?**

(A) Going over the slides with the woman

(B) Modifying the sales report for the woman

(C) Cooking dinner for his family

(D) Presenting a project outline to the whole team

Q3. **What will the woman most likely do next?**

(A) Revise the slides and talk to the man again

(B) Ask another colleague for opinions

(C) Present to the man immediately

(D) Take a day off and relax

聽稿

（US / Ⓦ）Joe, have you have the chance to review the powerpoint slides for my presentation?

（CA / Ⓜ）Yes, Sherry. Actually I just finished looking over these slides and was about to talk to you about it. There might be some problems about the content.

（US / Ⓦ）Really? Then it's a good thing I consult your opinions in advance. So what are the problems, Joe?

（CA / Ⓜ）Well, the two charts here are way too complicated and may be too much to explain in the allotted time for this presentation. Also the example on page 10 is not that relevant to the theme of the presentation. Anyway, after you've made proper modifications, you can practice in front of me.

中譯

（美 / 女）喬，你有時間幫我檢查簡報稿件嗎？

（加 / 男）有的，雪莉。其實我才剛剛看完妳的簡報內容，正打算找妳來討論一下。有些部分可能會有點問題。

（美 / 女）真的嗎？還好我在報告之前就先向你尋求意見了。那是出了些什麼樣的問題呢，喬？

（加 / 男）嗯，這兩個表格的細節太過繁複了，妳可能不會有足夠的時間把它們解釋完全。還有第十頁的舉例跟這份簡報的主題並沒有什麼關聯性。總之，等妳調整好之後，妳可以演練一遍給我看。

Q1. 對話者最有可能是？（答案：B）

(A) 病人 (B) 同事

(C) 鄰居 (D) 陌生人

Q2. 男子在做什麼？（答案：**A**）

(A) 與女子共同看簡報檔案   (B) 幫女子修改業務報告

(C) 為家人煮晚餐   (D) 向整個團隊報告專案綱要

Q3. 女子接下來最有可能做什麼？（答案：**A**）

(A) 修改簡報檔並再與男子討論   (B) 去問另一位同事的意見

(C) 馬上簡報給男子聽   (D) 請假一天並放鬆

解析

第一題

先很快地掃描題目，問的是「Who are the speakers most likely?」，根據此首句關鍵句「Joe, have you have the chance to review the powerpoint slides for my presentation?」，可判斷會一起討論簡報檔案的人應是公司同事較為合理，故選 (B)「Colleagues」為最佳答案。

各選項解析

• 選項 (A)「Patients」、選項 (C)「Neighbors」與選項 (D)「Strangers」都不會是討論簡報檔案之人，故不選。

第二題

此題問的是「What is the man doing?」，那麼預期要聽到男子的行動相關資訊以便回答。聽到「Actually I just finished looking over these slides and was about to talk to you about it. There might be some problems about the content.」，可以知道男子在幫女子看簡報檔並挑出錯誤，故選 (A)「Going over the slides with the woman」為最佳答案。

各選項解析

• 選項 (B)「Modifying the sales report for the woman」、選項 (C)「Cooking dinner for his family」與選項 (D)「Presenting a project outline to the whole team」都沒在對話中提到，故不選。

第三題

先掃描題目問的是「What will the woman most likely do next?」可判斷要聽到「女子接下來會做之事」相關資訊才可回答。又根據男子跟她講的此關鍵句「Anyway, after you've made proper modifications, you can practice in front of me.」，可聽出女子會將錯誤都改好之後，再練習講給男子聽，所以最合適的答案是 (A)「Revise the slides and talk to the man again」為最佳答案。

各選項解析

• 選項 (B)「Ask another colleague for opinions」、選項 (C)「Present to the man immediately」與選項 (D)「Take a day off and relax」都沒在文中提及。

關鍵字彙

review [rɪ`vju] v 檢視、檢查      explain [ɪk`splen] v 解釋

content [`kɑntɛnt] n 內容      allotted [ə`lɑtɪd] a 指定的、撥出的

consult [kən`sʌlt] v 諮詢、商議      relevant [`rɛləvənt] a 有關的、相關的

in advance ph 事先、事前   theme [θim] n 主題

chart [tʃɑrt] n 圖表   proper [`prɑpɚ] a 適當的

complicated [`kɑmplə͵ketɪd] a 複雜的      modification [͵mɑdəfə`keʃən] n 修改、修正

Q1. What is the woman trying to do?

(A) Asking permission to leave early

(B) Requesting the man to repeat what he'd said

(C) Providing answers to a question

(D) Interrupting the man's presentation

Q2. According to the man, what subject will he cover afterwards?

(A) Generating sales leads

(B) Organizing customer feedback

(C) Promoting products

(D) Arranging marketing campaigns

Q3. When does the man prefer to answer the audience's questions?

(A) During the break

(B) Before tomorrow's meeting

(C) After his presentation

(D) Anytime during his presentation

聽稿

（AU / W）Sorry, David, can I interrupt here? I wonder if you use any system to organize and share customer feedback. I mean I've collected a lot of customer opinions and now I need an effective system to organize these ideas so I could share with other colleagues.

（CA / M）That's a great question, Mary. I also plan to cover that topic later. How about let me finish the whole presentation, then I'll come back to your questions, okay?

（AU / W）Sure, no problem. Please go ahead.

（CA / M）All right, now I would like to return to how the rate of customer satisfaction can influence our sales revenue.

中譯

（澳 / 女）不好意思，大衛，可以讓我插個話嗎？我想知道你是否會透過任何系統進行顧客反饋意見的整理或分享。因為我收集了大量的顧客意見調查，如今需要一個有效率的系統幫我整理這些資料，以便分享給其他的同事。

（加 / 男）這是個好問題，瑪莉。我本也打算等會兒要討論一樣的東西呢。不然妳先讓我講完這個簡報，我再幫忙妳解決妳的問題，好嗎？

（澳 / 女）當然沒問題，你先講完吧。

（加 / 男）好了，現在回到剛探討的主題，來看看顧客滿意度是如何影響銷售的收入。

Q1. 女子試著要做什麼事？（答案：D）

(A) 請求允許她早點離開

(B) 請男子重覆一次他所說的

(C) 針對問題提出回答

(D) 打斷男子的簡報

Q2. 根據男子所言，接下來他會討論到什麼主題？（答案：B）

(A) 產生客戶名單

(B) 整理客戶意見回饋

(C) 推廣產品

(D) 安排行銷活動

Q3. 男子想要在何時回答聽眾的問題？（答案：C）

    (A) 休息時間   (B) 明天會議之前

    (C) 他簡報完之後   (D) 他在做簡報中的任何時間

解析

第一題

此題問「What is the woman trying to do?」，我們可以預設要聽到女子想做之事以便回答。根據女子所提的此關鍵句「Sorry, David, can I interrupt here?」，可聽出她是在男子談話當中想插話並提出問題，所以選擇 (D)「Interrupting the man's presentation」為最佳答案。

各選項解析

• 選項 (A)「Asking permission to leave early」、選項 (B)「Requesting the man to repeat what he'd said」與選項 (C)「Providing answer to a question」都不是女子的本意，故不選。

第二題

先掃描題目問的是「What subject will he cover afterwards?」，那麼便預期要聽到男子他會講什麼主題的資訊以便回答。首先女子問到此句「I wonder if you use any system to organize and share customer feedback.」，接著男子回答說「That's a great question, Mary. I also plan to cover that topic later.」，意味著男子隨後會討論此主題的。故選 (B)「Organizing customer feedback」為最佳答案。

各選項解析

• 選項 (A)「Generating sales leads」、選項 (C)「Promoting products」與選項 (D)「Arranging marketing campaigns」都沒有在對話中出現，故不選。

第三題

此題問到「When does the man prefer to answer the audience's questions?」，那麼要聽到有關時間之資訊以便回答。根據男子所說的此關鍵句「How about let me finish the whole presentation, then I'll come back to your questions, okay?」，可聽出他想在簡報都講完之後再討論問題，故選 (C)「After his presentation」為最佳答案。

各選項解析

• 選項 (A)「During the break」、選項 (B)「Before tomorrow's meeting」與選項 (D)「Anytime during his presentation」都沒有在對話中被提及，故不選。

關鍵字彙

interrupt [ˌɪntəˈrʌpt] ⓥ 打斷、中斷
wonder [ˈwʌndɚ] ⓥ 想知道
organize [ˈɔrgəˌnaɪz] ⓥ 規劃、安排
collect [kəˈlɛkt] ⓥ 收集
effective [ɪˈfɛktɪv] ⓐ 有效的
colleague [ˈkɑlig] ⓝ 同事
cover [ˈkʌvɚ] ⓥ 含括、包含
satisfaction [ˌsætɪsˈfækʃən] ⓝ 滿意
influence [ˈɪnfluəns] ⓥ 影響

Q1. What are the speakers mainly talking about?

(A) New technologies

(B) Environmental problems worldwide

(C) Sales trends of the company

(D) Market situations in Japan

Q2. According to the man, what happened two years ago?

(A) Customers reacted positively to their products

(B) Sales performance was terrible

(C) Several new products were launched

(D) Some new sales reps were hired

Q3. What is the man's attitude toward next year?

(A) Optimistic

(B) Pitiful

(C) Pessimistic

(D) Skeptical

聽稿

（AU / W）Okay, the next slide we're gonna look at shows that our sales doubled over the past two years.

（CA / M）Wow! Two years ago we hit quite a low point. It's a good thing that sales increase steadily now.

（AU / W）Yes, exactly. From this graph we can see that they dropped slightly in the beginning of this year, but then made a quick recovery in the second quarter.

（CA / M）The good news is that the economy is going strong now and we can expect even better results next year.

中譯

（澳 / 女）好了，現在我們要從下一張投影片來看看過去兩年銷售雙倍成長的業績。

（加 / 男）天哪！我們兩年前的業績怎麼會那麼低，還好現在已經持續平穩地成長了。

（澳 / 女）是的，沒錯。從這個圖表我們可以看出今年初的一小段滑落，不過在第二季又隨即攀升了。

（加 / 男）好消息是，現在經濟的狀況也愈來愈好，我們能期待明年會有更好的成績。

Q1. 對話者主要在討論什麼？（答案：C）

(A) 新科技

(B) 世界的環境問題

(C) 公司業務趨勢

(D) 日本的市場狀況

Q2. 根據男子所言，兩年前發生何事？（答案：B）

(A) 客戶對他們的產品反應熱烈

(B) 業務表現不佳

(C) 推出很多新產品

(D) 一些新業務代表受聘進公司

Q3. 男子對下一年抱持何種態度？（答案：A）

(A) 樂觀的

(B) 遺憾的

(C) 悲觀的

(D) 懷疑的

解析

第一題

先掃描到題目問的是「What are the speakers mainly talking about?」，可得知是問對話主題。再來根據此關鍵句「... the next slide we're gonna look at shows that our sales doubled over the past two years.」，可聽出是在討論公司業績，故選 (C)「Sales trends of the company」為最佳答案。

各選項解析

- 選項 (A)「New technologies」、選項 (B)「Environmental problems worldwide」與選項 (D)「Market situations in Japan」都沒有在對話中提到，故都可以先刪除。

第二題

題目問的是「What happened two years ago?」，便預期要聽到兩年前所發生之事以便回答。再來依據男子所説的此關鍵句「Two years ago we hit quite a low point. It's a good thing that sales increase steadily now.」，可聽出兩年前業績達到低點，現在又回升，故選 (B)「Sales performance was terrible.」為最佳答案。

各選項解析

- 選項 (A)「Customers reacted positively to their products.」、選項 (C)「Several new products were launched.」與選項 (D)「Some new sales reps were hired.」都沒在對話中提及，故不選。

第三題

此題問「What is the man's attitude toward next year?」，那麼打定主意要聽到男子的態度以便回答。根據此關鍵句「The good news is that the economy is going strong now and we can expect even better results next year.」，可聽出男子很看好明年的發展，故選 (A)「Optimistic」為最佳答案。

各選項解析

- 選項 (B)「Pitiful」、選項 (C)「Pessimistic」與選項 (D)「Skeptical」都不是「going strong」或「even better」的替換字，所以可以先刪除。

關鍵字彙

slide [slaɪd] n 投影片
double [`dʌbl] v 雙倍、變兩倍
steadily [`stɛdəlɪ] ad 穩定地
drop [drɑp] v 下滑、下跌
slightly [`slaɪtlɪ] ad 輕微地、些許地
recovery [rɪ`kʌvərɪ] n 恢復、回升
economy [ɪ`kɑnəmɪ] n 經濟
expect [ɪk`spɛkt] v 預期
result [rɪ`zʌlt] n 結果

Q1. When is the conversation probably taking place?

(A) After work

(B) During a break

(C) In an international conference

(D) At a family gathering

Q2. Who is the man most likely?

(A) A client

(B) A newly hired employee

(C) A senior lawyer

(D) One of the woman's friends

Q3. What kind of experience did the man have previously?

(A) Teaching children English

(B) Writing technical documents

(C) Arranging trip itineraries

(D) Coordinating international conferences

聽稿

（US / W）Well, we've been discussing issues all afternoon. Let's take a short break and go out for coffee. One of the most popular coffee shops in town is right downstairs.

（UK / M）It sounds like a good idea.

（US / W）So, Jack told me that you just joined the company last month?

（UK / M）That's right. My hometown is in Utah, and I came to New York to work last month.

（US / W）What did you do in Utah then?

（UK / M）Well, I worked in a travel agency in Salt Lake City. I assisted customers to arrange a family vacation, honeymoon cruise, or escorted tour.

中譯

（美 / 女）我們整個下午都在談論這些議題，不如先暫停一下，大家出去喝杯咖啡吧。樓下正好有間全鎮最熱門的咖啡店。

（英 / 男）聽起來是個好主意。

（美 / 女）傑克跟我說你是上個月才剛加入公司的新人？

（英 / 男）沒有錯。我的老家在猶他州，我上個月才來到紐約求職。

（美 / 女）你之前在猶他州是從事哪一行的？

（英 / 男）我在鹽湖城的一間旅行社工作。我專門幫助顧客安排他們的家庭旅遊、蜜月旅行、或是團體旅遊等。

Q1. 此對話可能是在何處發生？（答案：B）

(A) 下班後

(B) 休息時間

(C) 國際會議間

(D) 家庭聚餐

Q2. 男子最有可能是？（答案：B）

(A) 客戶

(B) 新進員工

(C) 資深律師

(D) 女子的一個朋友

Q3. 男子之前有過什麼樣的經驗？（答案：C）

(A) 教小孩英文　　　　　　　　　　(B) 寫技術文件

(C) 安排旅遊行程　　　　　　　　　(D) 協調國際會議

解析

第一題

先掃描到題目所問的「When is the conversation probably taking place?」，可判斷是要聽出對話的時間點。那麼根據此關鍵句「... we've been discussing issues all afternoon. Let's take a short break and go out for coffee.」，聽出是在會議中休息時間的對話，故選 (B) 為最佳答案。

各選項解析

- 選項 (A)「After work」、選項 (C)「In an international conference」與選項 (D)「At a family gathering」都沒在對話中出現，故不選。

第二題

此題問的是「Who is the man most likely?」，既然是問男子的身分，那麼便要聽到相關關鍵點以便回答。根據女子對男子說的此關鍵句「Jack told me that you just joined the company last month?」，可聽出男子上個月才加入公司，男子應是一位「A newly hired employee」較為合理，選 (B)。

各選項解析

- 選項 (A)「A client」、選項 (C)「A senior lawyer」與選項 (D)「One of the woman's friends」都不會是「just joined the company last month」的替換說法，故不選。

第三題

先看到題目問的是「What kind of experience did the man have previously?」，那麼預期要聽到男子提及自己之前的經驗以便回答。根據男子所說的「I worked in a travel agency in Salt Lake City. I assisted customers to arrange a family vacation, honeymoon cruise, or escorted tour.」，可聽出他之前是在旅行社幫客戶安排行程，故選 (C)「Arranging trip itineraries」為最佳答案。

各選項解析

- 選項 (A)「Teaching children English」、選項 (B)「Writing technical documents」與選項 (D)「Coordinating international conferences」都沒在對話中被提及，故不選。

關鍵字彙

issue [ˈɪʃju] n 議題、事件
popular [ˈpɑpjələ] a 流行的、熱門的
hometown [ˈhomˈtaʊn] n 家鄉、故鄉
travel agency [ˈtrævl̩ ˌedʒənsɪ] n 旅行社
assist [əˈsɪst] v 協助、幫助
arrange [əˈrendʒ] v 安排
honeymoon [ˈhʌnɪˌmun] n 蜜月
cruise [kruz] n 航遊、航行
escort [ˈɛskɔrt] v 護送、陪同

Q1. What is the purpose of the conversation?

(A) To conduct a training session

(B) To set up a conference call

(C) To arrange a sales seminar

(D) To schedule a meeting

Q2. When does the woman prefer to meet?

(A) Monday

(B) Tuesday

(C) Thursday

(D) Saturday

Q3. Where will the speakers meet on Tuesday?

(A) In the employee lounge

(B) In a meeting room

(C) At the airport

(D) On the street

聽稿

（US / **W**）When would you like to schedule our meeting, Paul? We need to discuss details of the upcoming fund-raising event.

（UK / **M**）Yeah, it's one of the major events for this year. Well, I'm available this week, so when would be best for you?

（US / **W**）I'm free on Tuesday and Friday. Let me see... How about Tuesday afternoon at 2? Is that day ideal for you?

（UK / **M**）Well, let me check my planner. Yes, 2 p.m. on Tuesday is convenient for me. Let's meet at Conference room 4B then.

中譯

（美 / **女**）保羅，你何時有空能安排開會？我們需要討論一下即將到來的募款活動和細節。

（英 / **男**）嗯，那是今年主要的大型活動之一。我這個星期都有空檔，妳是什麼時候比較有空呢？

（美 / **女**）我星期二和星期五都可以。我瞧瞧……星期二下午兩點可以嗎？對你來說方不方便？

（英 / **男**）我看一下我的計畫表。嗯，星期二下午兩點沒問題。我們就去 4B 會議室討論吧。

Q1. 此對話的目的為何？（答案：D）

(A) 安排訓練課程

(B) 安排電話會議

(C) 安排業務研討會

(D) 安排會議

Q2. 女子想要在何時開會？（答案：B）

(A) 週一

(B) 週二

(C) 週四

(D) 週六

Q3. 對話者週二會在哪裡碰面？（答案：B）

(A) 員工休息室

(B) 會議室

(C) 機場

(D) 大街上

解析 | **第一題**

先掃描題目問的是「What is the purpose of the conversation?」,那麼便預期要聽到此對話大方向的目的以便回答。根據此首關鍵句「When would you like to schedule our meeting, Paul? We need to discuss details of the upcoming fund-raising event.」,可判斷是要約會議時間以討論活動細節,故選 (D)「To schedule a meeting」為最佳答案。

各選項解析

• 選項 (A)「To conduct a training session」、選項 (B)「To set up a conference call」與選項 (C)「To arrange a sales seminar」都沒在對話中提及,故不選。

第二題

先看到題目問的是「When does the woman prefer to meet?」,那麼預期要聽到女子所提的時間點以便回答。根據此關鍵句「I'm free on Tuesday and Friday. Let me see... How about Tuesday afternoon at 2?」,可聽出女子偏好在週二下午開會,故選 (B) 為最佳答案。

第三題

先掃描到題目問的是「Where will the speakers meet on Tuesday?」,那麼就是要聽到地點類型的答案才能回答此題。根據男子所説的此關鍵句「Yes, 2 p.m. on Tuesday is convenient for me. Let's meet at Conference room 4B then.」,可聽出會是在 4B 會議室內開會,故選 (B)「In a meeting room」為最佳答案。

各選項解析

• 選項 (A)「In the employee lounge」、選項 (C)「At the airport」與選項 (D)「On the street」都沒有在對話中提及,所以可以先刪除。

關鍵字彙

upcoming [`ʌpˌkʌmɪŋ] a 將至的、接近的
fund-raising [`fʌndˌrezɪŋ] n 募款
ideal [aɪˋdiəl] a 理想的
planner [`plænɚ] n 規畫文件;記事本
convenient [kənˋvinjənt] a 方便的、便捷的

Q1. Why is the woman calling?

(A) To return the product

(B) To check the order process

(C) To invite the man to a seminar

(D) To indicate problems on the invoice

Q2. What position most likely does the man have?

(A) Sales representative

(B) Technician

(C) Janitor

(D) Vice President

Q3. What will the two speakers do afterwards?

(A) Listen to a presentation

(B) Arrange a conference call

(C) Meet each other

(D) Go over the invoice

聽稿

（AU / Ⓦ）Hi, Frank. This is Jessie. I'm calling to check and see if our furniture order has been shipped.

（CA / Ⓜ）You mean Order#547, right? Let's see here... Yes, according to the record on my computer. Your order was shipped yesterday.

（AU / Ⓦ）Oh, that's great. And then I'll need to check the invoice issue later.

（CA / Ⓜ）Well, Jessie. I can go over the invoice with you, if you're available to talk about it now.

中譯

（澳 / 女）嗨，法蘭克，我是潔西。我想確認我們訂的家具是否已經出貨了？

（加 / 男）您是指訂單五四七號嗎？我查查看……有的，根據我們的電腦紀錄，您的貨昨天已經送出了。

（澳 / 女）噢，太好了。那我等等就可以著手處理發票的相關事宜了。

（加 / 男）嗯，潔西，若您方便的話，我現在就可以跟您一起討論發票的相關事務。

Q1. 女子打電話目的為何？（答案：B）

(A) 為退貨

(B) 為查詢訂貨進度

(C) 為邀請男子參加研討會

(D) 為告知發票上的問題

Q2. 男子可能是什麼職位？（答案：A）

(A) 業務代表

(B) 工程人員

(C) 清潔工

(D) 副總

Q3. 兩位對話者之後可能會做什麼？（答案：D）

(A) 聽一場簡報

(B) 安排電話會議

(C) 見一面

(D) 討論發票事宜

解析

第一題

先掃描到題目問的是「Why is the woman calling?」，可聽出是在問女子打電話的目的，那麼心中期望要聽到女子所提的關鍵句以便回答。接著聽到女子說「I'm calling to check and see if our furniture order has been shipped.」，可聽出她是要查詢訂貨狀況，故選 (B)「To check the order process」為最佳答案。

各選項解析

• 選項 (A)「To return the product」、選項 (C)「To invite the man to a seminar」與選項 (D)「To indicate problems on the invoice」相關字眼都沒在對話中出現，故不選。

第二題

此題問「What position most likely does the man have?」，問及男子的職位，那麼根據男子所提到的此兩個關鍵句「Your order was shipped yesterday.」與「I can go over the invoice with you...」可判斷出適合的答案，他會處理客戶訂單，還會跟客戶對帳單細節的人，應是業務代表較為合理。所以選擇 (A)「Sales representative」為最佳答案。

各選項解析

• 選項 (B)「Technician」、選項 (C)「Janitor」與選項 (D)「Vice President」都不會是負責處理客戶訂單的人，所以都可以刪除。

第三題

先看到題目「What will the two speakers do afterwards?」，心中便有底要聽到之後可能會做之事的資訊以便回答。我們可以聽到女子講的關鍵句「I'll need to check the invoice issue later.」，以及男子的回應「I can go over the invoice with you, if you're available to talk about it now.」，可聽出兩人接下來有可能會討論帳單發票事宜，故選 (D)「Go over the invoice」為最佳答案。

各選項解析

• 選項 (A)「Listen to a presentation」、選項 (B)「Arrange a conference call」與選項 (D)「Meet each other」都沒在對話中提及，故不是答案。

關鍵字彙

furniture [ˋfɝnɪtʃɚ] n 傢俱
ship [ʃɪp] v 寄送、遞送
according to ph 根據～
invoice [ˋɪnvɔɪs] n 發票
available [əˋveləbl] a 可獲得的、有空的

Time	Topic
1 p.m. - 2 p.m.	Customer Service
2 p.m. - 3 p.m.	International Marketing Strategy
3:10 p.m. - 4:10 p.m.	Socializing With Clients
4:10 p.m. - 5:10 p.m.	Sales Performance Review

Q1. What are the speakers talking about?

(A) Company policies

(C) Jason's family issues

(B) The woman's presentation

(D) The man's promotion

Q2. What does the man say about the woman's presentation?

(A) Tedious

(C) Boring

(B) Engrossing

(D) Serious

新 Q3. Look at the table. What was the woman's presentation topic most likely?

(A) Customer Service

(C) Socializing With Clients

(B) International Marketing Strategy

(D) Sales Performance Review

聽稿

（US / Ⓦ）Mark, what did you think of my presentation?

（CA / Ⓜ）Tiffany, hey. I think the way you opened your presentation was really brilliant and that really caught people's attention.

（US / Ⓦ）Well, it's good to hear that. I just want everyone to feel relaxed, you know.

（CA / Ⓜ）Yeah, I understand. Especially your session is right after Jason's. His presentation subject was a bit too serious.

中譯

（美 / 女）馬克，你覺得我的報告表現得如何？

（加 / 男）媞芙妮，嗨。妳用的開場方式真的是太有才了，完全吸引住眾人的目光。

（美 / 女）嗯，聽你這樣說我就放心了。我只希望大夥兒都能輕鬆點，你懂的。

（加 / 男）嗯，我明白。尤其妳的講習部分又是接在傑森之後，他的報告主題比較嚴肅。

時間	主題
下午一點～兩點	客戶服務
下午兩點～三點	國際行銷策略
下午三點十分～四點十分	與客戶社交
下午四點十分～五點十分	業績檢討

Q1. 對話者們在討論什麼？（答案：B）

(A) 公司政策

(C) 傑森的家庭問題

(B) 女子的簡報

(D) 男子的升遷

Q2. 男子覺得女子的簡報如何？（答案：B）

(A) 冗長乏味的   (B) 引人入勝的

(C) 無趣的   (D) 嚴肅的

新 Q3. 請看表格。女子的簡報主題最有可能為何？（答案：C）

(A) 客戶服務   (B) 國際行銷策略

(C) 與客戶社交   (D) 業績檢討

解析

第一題

先掃描題目「What are the speakers talking about?」，可得知是在考對話主題，那麼便預期要聽到大方向的主題。接著聽到女子所說的此關鍵句「Mark, what did you think of my presentation?」，與男子的回應「I think the way you opened your presentation was really brilliant...」，可聽出兩人是在討論女子的簡報表現，故選 (B)「The woman's presentation」為最佳答案。

各選項解析

- 選項 (A)「Company policies」、選項 (C)「Jason's family issues」與選項 (D)「The man's promotion」都沒有在對話中出現，故不會是答案。

第二題

先掃描題目問的是「What does the man say about the woman's presentation?」，可得知是在問男子認為女子簡報做得如何；那麼便要將注意力放在聽男子所提的意見上。男子回應說「I think the way you opened your presentation... really caught people's attention.」，可知道男子認為女子簡報方式可以吸引到聽眾的注意力，故選 (B) 為最佳答案。

各選項解析

- 選項 (A)「Tedious」、選項 (C)「Boring」與選項 (D)「Serious」都不會是「catch people's attention（吸引眾人注意）」的替換字。

新 第三題

此題要搭配表格，首先掃描到題目問的是「What was the woman's presentation topic most likely?」，那麼就要對照對話內容和表格資訊，以推斷出女子簡報主題可能為何。接著根據男子所說的「Especially your session is right after Jason's. His presentation subject was a bit too serious.」可得知：女子簡報是在 Jason 之後，且 Jason 的主題又很嚴肅，那麼對照表格內的四個主題，當中較為嚴肅的話題是「International Marketing Strategy」；且也說了女子在其之後，所以判斷最有可能是較為輕鬆的主題「Socializing With Clients」。所以選 (C)。

各選項解析

- 選項 (A)「Customer service」、選項 (B)「International Marketing Strategy」與選項 (D)「Sales Performance Review」都沒在對話中被提到，所以都可以刪除。

關鍵字彙

presentation [ˌprizɛnˋteʃən] n 簡報	especially [əˋspɛʃəlɪ] ad 尤其是
catch someone's attention ph 吸引某人的注意力	subject [ˋsʌbdʒɪkt] n 主題、科目
relaxed [rɪˋlækst] a 放鬆的	serious [ˋsɪrɪəs] a 嚴肅的、嚴重的

Part 3

應試策略總整理

我們要有一個體認，一個長篇對話中的內容並不是每個字的重要性都一樣，一句話中會有主要資訊，通常會被加以重音強調；有主要資訊，也有次要資訊，通常就會被很快地帶過，不會是對話句中的要點。所以大家在聽對話時，應將注意力放在聽「有以重音強調的主要資訊」上，而非想要將每個字都聽到、且聽懂。而這些「加以重音強調的主要資訊」，自然是考題喜歡問的所在點了。

為了要更精準地得知應該聽什麼「關鍵點」，大家應利用在對話尚未播放出來之前的三到五秒的時間，將題目很快地掃過一遍，以便判斷應該要聆聽的焦點方向。唯有如此，才能預期我們接下來應該要注意聽哪部分和哪些關鍵字上。比方說，題目是問「where」題型，要聽到「地點相關」的資訊以便回答。若看到題目問「why」題型，知道要聽到講述「原因、理由」的相關資訊以便回答。若在快速掃過題目的同時，最好也帶到四個答案選項；但若時間太趕而沒看到選項也無妨，至少一定要先看到題目。

知道題目的方向之後，可以試著聽到至少三個關鍵點來判斷。比方說聽「flight」、「passport」和「Gate 8」三個關鍵字，判斷出題目有可能是在「機場」內的情境了。又例如聽到「sales strategies」、「meeting schedule」與「products」等字，大概也可以判斷是「同事」在「辦公室」內的對話了。

值得注意的是，這些會影響到我們對對話內容理解力的關鍵部分，通常會經過「語調」不同的處理。舉例來說，我們可以藉著語調來了解對話者是快樂、悲傷、煩惱、還是輕鬆的。最後要再強調的是，通常句子中加強重音的地方便會是考試的重點。

若是行有餘力的話，可以一邊聽對話一邊「想像」對話的真實情境。以「想像」和「真實情境」聯想起來，就比較容易在腦中描繪出對話的圖像，也容易記憶。比方說，聽到可能是餐廳內點餐的情境對話便可在腦中想像餐廳內客人坐著點餐，服務生站著介紹的情景。這樣的想像有助於理解對話中的真實情景，並進一步了解對話內容要點喔！

LISTENING

PART

4

TOEIC LISTENING

簡短獨白
Talks

Introduction

先了解問題點，再仔細聽答案是得分的關鍵。在「語調」方面，獨白並不是使用單一語調，而是有上揚、下降，或有強有弱之語調變化的。同時「想像」所唸的真實情境，則更可以理解獨白內容。

攻略 1 | 學術人士介紹

Q1. Where does the speaker most likely work?

(A) At the airport

(B) At a university

(C) At a software company

(D) At a restaurant

Q2. Who are most likely listening to the talk?

(A) The general public

(B) University students

(C) Young kids

(D) Senior citizens

Q3. What will happen next most likely?

(A) Dr. Law will go on stage and speak

(B) The speaker will assign homework

(C) Listeners will leave and go home

(D) Students will take an exam

解題分析

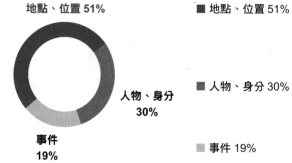

地點、位置 51%

人物、身分 30%

事件 19%

■ 地點、位置 51%　第一個問題是 where 開頭，看到這樣的問句就可以知道是在問某個地點，而另一個關鍵詞 work 則是清楚將範圍縮小成「工作的地點」，故獨白題中出現的工作場所，必須特別留意。

■ 人物、身分 30%　第二個問題是 who 開頭，因此要特別注意聽到的人物或說話對象的身分，像本題問的是「聽演講的對象」，可以根據場合或是人物的關係找到答案。

■ 事件 19%　第三題為 what 開頭，搭配關鍵字 happen 可以清楚抓到題目的主旨是問「接下來發生的事」，根據相關內容回答。

聽稿

（US / W）Dear students, it's my pleasure to announce that Dr. Morgan Law has joined Roman School of International Affairs as a visiting professor. Dr. Law is an expert on international economics and trade policy and he will teach graduate students and work with faculty members on a range of public-policy issues. Dr. Law is delighted to have the opportunity to share his experience with talented young people who aspire to engage in the world of public policy and international affairs. Dr. Law had experience working as the Chief Operating Officer of Summit Bank and Executive Vice President of Springfield University, where he was also a professor of public administration. Now, let's welcome Dr. Morgan Law.

中譯　（美／**女**）親愛的同學們，很榮幸能為各位宣布，摩根・洛爾博士來到了羅曼國際事務學院擔任我們的客座教授。洛爾博士是研究國際經濟與貿易政策的專家，他將會和本校教職員合作教導大學同學有關公共政策等的相關議題。洛爾博士很開心能夠與那些對於公共政策領域和國際事務抱有高度熱忱的才華洋溢之青年們一同分享他的個人經驗。洛爾博士曾經在瑞豐銀行擔任過營運長，並於春田大學擔任執行副校長的同時，教授公共行政學此一科目。現在，就讓我們歡迎摩根・洛爾博士。

Q1. 講者最有可能在何處工作？（答案：B）
(A) 機場 　　　　　　　　　　　(B) 大學
(C) 軟體公司 　　　　　　　　　(D) 餐廳

Q2. 此獨白的聽眾最有可能是誰？（答案：B）
(A) 一般大眾 　　　　　　　　　(B) 大學生
(C) 小孩子 　　　　　　　　　　(D) 年長的市民

Q3. 接下來最有可能發生何事？（答案：A）
(A) 洛爾博士會上台演講 　　　　(B) 講者會指派回家功課
(C) 聽眾會回家去 　　　　　　　(D) 學生會考個試

解題技巧　與其想要將所有內容都聽懂，還不如將注意力放在「聽關鍵要點」即可，而這些講者想強調的關鍵要點，通常不會很快地帶過，而是會以講慢一點，或加強重音來強調：

（US／**W**）Dear students, it's my pleasure to announce that Dr. Morgan Law has joined Roman School of International Affairs as a visiting professor. Dr. Law is an expert on international economics and trade policy and he will teach graduate students and work with faculty members on a range of public-policy issues. Dr. Law is delighted to have the opportunity to share his experience with talented young people who aspire to engage in the world of public policy and international affairs. Dr. Law had experience working as the Chief Operating Officer of Summit Bank and Executive Vice President of Springfield University, where he was also a professor of public administration. Now, let's welcome Dr. Morgan Law.

如此，僅專注在聽有強調重音的關鍵點上，便可以了解獨白的大意了，包括：講者跟同學介紹一位客座教授，他的專長、經歷、與今後會教的課程等，之後這位教授會講話發言。如此可以聽出，其實不用聽懂每個字，不用想翻譯每一句，僅專注在關鍵點上，還是可以了解八成以上的內容的。

利用獨白播放出來之前的幾秒空檔，很快地將題目先掃描一下，以便預期可能的獨白內容與要將注意力放在聽什麼要點上。

先掃描到題目問的是「Where does the speaker most likely work?」那麼便打定主意要聽到講者工作之「地點」相關答案以便回答問題。根據獨白中的此要點句「It's my pleasure to announce that Dr. Morgan Law has joined Roman School of International Affairs as a visiting professor.」可聽出，會幫學生介紹客座教授的人，本身應也是在「大學內」工作的人較為合理，故講者工作之地點應為 (B)「At a university」。

各選項解析

- 選項 (A)「At the airport」、選項 (C)「At a software company」與選項 (D)「At a restaurant」都沒在獨白中提及，故不選。

第二題

先掃描到題目問的是「Who are most likely listening to the talk?」那麼可預期要聽到「聽眾身分」的要點以便回答。根據此首句關鍵點「Dear students,」可聽出聽眾是學生，故選 (B)「University students」為正確。

各選項解析

- 選項 (A)「The general public」、選項 (C)「Young kids」與選項 (D)「Senior citizens」都非「students」的替換字，故不選。

第三題

先掃描到此題問的是「What will happen next most likely?」便可判斷要聽到「接下來會發生何事」相關答案以便回答。根據此關鍵句「Now, let's welcome Dr. Morgan Law.」可聽出講者要介紹洛爾博士出場了，接下來便應該是洛爾博士要演講較為合理，故選 (A)「Dr. Law will go on stage and speak.」為最佳答案。

各選項解析

- 選項 (B)「The speaker will assign homework.」、選項 (C)「Listeners will leave and go home.」與選項 (D)「Students will take an exam.」都沒在獨白中提到，故不選。

關鍵字彙

pleasure [ˈplɛʒɚ] n 榮幸
announce [əˈnaʊns] v 宣布
expert [ˈɛkspɚt] n 專家
graduate student [ˈɡrædʒʊɪt] [ˈstjudṇt] n 研究所學生
faculty [ˈfækḷtɪ] n 教員
delighted [dɪˈlaɪtɪd] a 愉悅的、高興的
aspire [əˈspaɪr] v 刺激、鼓舞
engage [ɪnˈɡedʒ] v 從事
executive [ɪɡˈzɛkjʊtɪv] n 執行者

攻略2 | 演講者自我介紹

Q1. What is the main purpose of this talk?

(A) To promote new products   (B) To motivate people

(C) To explain some theories   (D) To sell insurance plans

Q2. What is the speaker's current position?

(A) A university professor   (B) A motivational speaker

(C) A company manager   (D) A math tutor

Q3. What will the speaker probably talk about next?

(A) Some success stories   (B) Some R&D plans

(C) Some tourist attractions   (D) Some sales strategies

解題分析

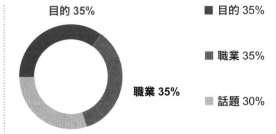

■ 目的 35%

■ 職業 35%

■ 話題 30%

第一題的關鍵放在「main purpose」上,是在問整段獨白的主要目的,可以依聽到的關鍵字來判斷。

第二個問題關鍵在於「current position」,可了解到是在問講者的「職業」,因此要把握聽到的工作相關內容。

第三題的重點在詢問接下來講者會講些什麼,也就是「話題」,因此預測會聽到跟「討論的話題」相關的內容。

聽稿

（UK / M）Thank you, ladies and gentlemen, thank you very much for attending my speech. I'm Mark Lewis. Well, when I left school at the age of seventeen, I, like many young people, did not have a clear idea of what I really wanted to do. However, on my first overseas trip to Asia, I fell in love with travel. In order to maintain my passion, I have joined the travel industry and worked my way up to Manager at Best Travel Agency, where I now manage six agents and also design holidays for individuals and families. Well, today you, all my audience, see me standing here as living proof that if you set your goals and following them with perseverance, you can achieve big dreams. All right, in today's speech I'm gonna share more with you how some people from humble beginnings can eventually rise rapidly in the world.

（英／男）感謝各位先生小姐，非常感謝各位前來參加我此次的演講。我是馬克·路易斯。當我十七歲離開學生生涯的時候，就如同大多數的年輕人一樣，對於自己的未來感到一片茫然。然而，在我第一次踏上亞洲的土地時，我便愛上了旅行。為了延續我的熱情，我選擇加入了旅遊這個行業，並鍥而不捨地一路爬到了「最佳旅行社」的經理位置，我現在有六名部下，為個人和家庭客戶設計規劃種種度假旅程。今日，台下所有的觀眾，站在你們眼前的是一個活生生的實例，只要你們能為自己訂下目標、堅持不懈，心想事成的一刻將指日可待。今天的演說，我將與各位分享一些有關真人真事的故事，看看他們是如何從毫不起眼的小人物，迅速竄成明日之星。

Q1. 此談話的主要目的為何？（答案：**B**）

(A) 為宣傳新產品   (B) 為激勵人們

(C) 為解釋理論   (D) 為賣保險

Q2. 講者目前工作為何？（答案：**C**）

(A) 大學教授   (B) 激勵講師

(C) 公司經理   (D) 數學家教

Q3. 講者接下來可能會討論什麼？（答案：**A**）

(A) 成功故事   (B) 研發計劃

(C) 旅遊勝地   (D) 業務策略

解題技巧

在聽獨白前，考生多半有想聽懂每個字，會翻每句話的憧憬。但事實上有限的時間並不允許我們這麼做。最重要的應是「全心全意地聽關鍵點」以期了解主要內容即可，而這些關鍵點可能就是「有加強重音強調」之處：

（UK／**M**）Thank you, ladies and gentlemen, thank you very much for attending my speech. I'm Mark Lewis. Well, when I left school at the age of seventeen, I, like many young people, did not have a clear idea of what I really wanted to do. However, on my first overseas trip to Asia, I fell in love with travel. In order to maintain my passion, I have joined the travel industry and worked my way up to Manager at Best Travel Agency, where I now manage six agents and also design holidays for individuals and families. Well, today you, all my audience, see me standing here as living proof that if you set your goals and following them with perseverance, you can achieve big dreams. All right, in today's speech I'm gonna share more with you how some people from humble beginnings can eventually rise rapidly in the world.

如此聽到幾個關鍵點，便也可大約聽出此獨白的約略內容了，包括：講者針對他的求學經驗做簡報分享，他到亞洲後愛上旅遊，故成為旅行社經理並規劃旅遊行程，他也相信設定好目標，努力以赴之後會成功。如此，僅注意聽幾個關鍵字還是有可能了解獨白之大意的喔！

利用獨白播放出來之前的幾秒空檔，很快地將題目先掃描一下，以便預期可能的獨白內容與要將注意力放在聽什麼要點上。

第一題

先掃描到題目問的是「What is the main purpose of this talk?」那麼便判斷要聽到此獨白的「主要目的」以便回答。根據此兩處關鍵點「Thank you very much for attending my speech.」與「Well, today you, all my audience, see me standing here as living proof that if you set your goals and following them with perseverance, you can achieve big dreams.」，可聽出講者是在一演講會場上講自己的故事，並鼓勵他人朝自己目標前進，故選 (B)「To motivate people」為最佳答案。

各選項解析

• 選項 (A)「To promote new products」、選項 (C)「To explain some theories」與選項 (D)「To sell insurance plans」都沒在獨白中被討論到，故不選。

第二題

此題問的是「What is the speaker's current position?」，那麼便應聽到講者目前的「職業」以便回答。根據此關鍵句「I have joined the travel industry and worked my way up to Manager at Best Travel Agency, where I now manage six agents and also design holidays...」可聽出他現在是在旅行社當經理，故選 (C)「A company manager」為最佳答案。

各選項解析

• 選項 (A)「A university professor」、選項 (B)「A motivational speaker」與選項 (D)「A math tutor」都沒在獨白中被提及，故不選。

第三題

先掃描到此題問的是「What will the speaker probably talk about next?」，那麼便判斷要聽到講者接下來會討論的「話題」以便回答。根據此關鍵句「All right, in today's speech I'm gonna share more with you how some people from humble beginnings can eventually rise rapidly in the world.」，可聽出他要討論出身低的人也可以成功的故事，故選 (A)「Some success stories」為最佳答案。

各選項解析

• 選項 (B)「Some R&D plans」、選項 (C)「Some tourist attractions」與選項 (D)「Some sales strategies」都沒被討論到，故不選。

關鍵字彙

overseas [`ovɚ`siz] a 國外的、海外的
maintain [men`ten] v 保持、維持
passion [`pæʃən] n 熱情
industry [`ɪndəstrɪ] n 產業
individual [ˌɪndə`vɪdʒʊəl] n 個人、個體
audience [`ɔdɪəns] n 聽眾
proof [pruf] n 證明、證據
perseverance [ˌpɝsə`vɪrəns] n 毅力
humble beginning ph 出身卑微
eventually [ɪ`vɛntʃʊəlɪ] ad 最終地、最後地
rapidly [`ræpɪdlɪ] ad 快速地

Q1. Who is Jason Well most likely?

    (A) An angry customer   (B) An English teacher

    (C) A senior consultant   (D) A newly hired employee

Q2. Where is the talk probably taking place?

    (A) In a meeting room   (B) In a classroom

    (C) In a cubicle   (D) In a restaurant

Q3. What will happen on Friday?

    (A) The CEO will deliver a speech   (B) A launch event will take place

    (C) A party will be held   (D) Some workers will be fired

解題分析

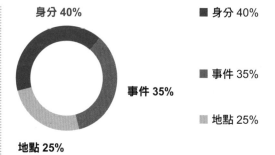

身分 40%

事件 35%

地點 25%

■ 身分 40%

■ 事件 35%

■ 地點 25%

第一題開頭是 who，可以判斷是在問「Jason Well」這個人的「身分」，所以在接下來的獨白中要把握此人的背景、職業等有關的資訊。

第三題主要在詢問星期五會發生「什麼事」，所以聽的時候要留意即將發生的事件或活動，有很大的機會是正解。

第二個問題首先看到 where，便可以知道重點在於說話者所在的「地點」，聽的時候要特別注意提到的地點，或是根據相關線索判斷正確答案。

聽稿

（AU / **W**）All right, all team members. Before our meeting, I'm happy to let you know that Jason Well will join our team as an account manager starting today. We're convinced that he'll add another layer of success to our sales efforts. Jason's degree is in business administration from the Roman University, and he has worked in sales management since graduating from college eleven years ago. Well, he is a big fan of traveling the world looking for new experiences and perspectives. Jason's cubicle will be right next to Mark's. We'll host a welcome party this Friday at 4 p.m. All team members are invited to attend as appetizers, snacks and iced tea will be served. Right, now let's start our weekly brainstorming meeting.

中譯　（澳／**女**）好了，各位同事們，在會議開始之前，很高興在這裡告訴你們：傑森・威爾將以客戶經理的身分加入我們的團隊，並於今日開始正式上班。我們相信他會帶領我們邁向飛黃騰達的銷售成果。傑森在十一年前取得羅曼大學企業管理的文憑之後，便開始從事營銷管理方面的工作。他是一位旅行愛好者，熱衷於探索新的體驗與觀點。傑森的座位就在馬克的隔壁。我們將於這星期五下午四點舉行迎新派對，提供開胃小菜、點心、和冰茶等飲品，誠摯邀請所有的團隊成員一同參與。好了，現在我們就開始每週的腦力激盪會議吧！

Q1. 傑森・威爾最有可能是誰？（答案：**D**）
(A) 生氣的客戶　　　　　　　　　　(B) 英文老師
(C) 資深顧問　　　　　　　　　　　(D) 新進員工

Q2. 此獨白最有可能在何處聽到？（答案：**A**）
(A) 會議室　　　　　　　　　　　　(B) 教室
(C) 座位隔間　　　　　　　　　　　(D) 餐廳

Q3. 週五會有何事發生？（答案：**C**）
(A) 執行長會演講　　　　　　　　　(B) 會有上市發表活動
(C) 將舉行派對　　　　　　　　　　(D) 有些員工會被資遣

解題技巧　在聽之前要有心理準備，不要想聽懂所有內容，而是可以僅專注聽「關鍵資訊」，以便可以了解獨白的大意，而這些關鍵資訊自然有可能是會考的要點，並且比重音強調，以引起聽者的注意：

（AU／**W**）All right, all team members. Before our meeting, I'm happy to let you know that Jason Well will join our team as an account manager starting today. We're convinced that he'll add another layer of success to our sales efforts. Jason's degree is in business administration from the Roman University, and he has worked in sales management since graduating from college eleven years ago. Well, he is a big fan of traveling the world looking for new experiences and perspectives. Jason's cubicle will be right next to Mark's. We'll host a welcome party this Friday at 4 p.m. All team members are invited to attend as appetizers, snacks and iced tea will be served. Right, now let's start our weekly brainstorming meeting.

由這些關鍵處可聽出，的確只要專注在幾個關鍵點上，就可以了解八成的內容了，包括：此講者在跟同仁介紹新進員工，提到他的學歷背景、工作經驗，和提醒大家週五的歡迎派對訊息。由此可聽出，幾個有用的關鍵資訊，真的比起想全盤了解細節要來得重要多了喔！

利用獨白播放出來之前的幾秒空檔，很快地將題目先掃描一下，以便預期可能的獨白內容與要將注意力放在聽什麼要點上。

先掃描到此題問的是「Who is Jason Well most likely?」，那麼便可判斷要聽到可能得知 Jason Well 之「身分」的相關資訊以便回答。根據此關鍵句「I'm happy to let you know that Jason Well will join our team **as an account manager** starting today.」可聽出 Jason 是今日第一天上班的員工，故選 (D)「A newly hired employee」為最佳答案。

各選項解析

- 選項 (A)「An angry customer」、選項 (B)「An English teacher」與選項 (C)「A senior consultant」都沒在獨白中出現，故不選。

第二題

此題問的是「Where is the talk probably taking place?」便可判斷要聽到此獨白可能發生的「地點」相關資訊以便回答。根據此關鍵句「All right, all team members. Before our meeting, I'm happy to let you know...」可聽出講者是在會議之前對所有同仁做報告，那麼應該是在「會議室」內的談話較為合理，故選 (A)「In a meeting room」為最佳答案。

各選項解析

- 選項 (B)「In a classroom」、選項 (C)「In a cubicle」與選項 (D)「In a restaurant」都不是會聽到此會議前討論的地點，故不選。

第三題

此題問的是「What will happen on Friday?」那麼便應該要聽出週五所會發生「什麼事」相關資訊以便回答。根據此關鍵句「We'll host a welcome party this Friday at 4 p.m. All team members are invited to attend...」可聽出是會有一個「迎新派對」在週五舉辦，故選 (C)「A party will be held.」為最佳答案。

各選項解析

- 選項 (A)「The CEO will deliver a speech.」、選項 (B)「A launch event will take place.」與選項 (D)「Some workers will be fired.」都沒有在獨白中提及，故不選。

關鍵字彙

convince [kən'vɪns] ⓥ 使信服
effort ['ɛfət] ⓝ 努力、嘗試
perspective [pə'spɛktɪv] ⓝ 角度、洞察
cubicle ['kjubɪkl] ⓝ 隔間、空間
appetizer ['æpə،taɪzə] ⓝ 開胃菜
snack [snæk] ⓝ 點心
serve [sɜv] ⓥ 服務

Unit 2 電話留言類

攻略 1 │ 業務報價留言

Q1. Who is the speaker most likely?

(A) A support engineer   (B) An English teacher

(C) A janitor   (D) A sales representative

Q2. What type of product does the speaker provide?

(A) Software   (B) Stationery

(C) Shoes   (D) Food

Q3. What will the listener probably do next?

(A) Schedule a meeting   (B) Answer some questions

(C) Install the software   (D) Check his e-mail

解題分析

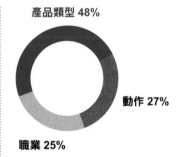

產品類型 48%

動作 27%

職業 25%

■ **產品類型** 48%　從第二題 what type of product 判斷出本題是在問講者的公司推出哪種「產品」，因此在聽的時候可特別留意講者公司的類型以及公司產品的訊息，很有可能就是線索。

■ **動作** 27%　第三題很明確是在詢問「聽者接下來會做的事」，所以很有可能接下來會聽到此人將要執行的動作，或是被指派的工作內容等等。

■ **職業** 25%　看到第一題首先抓到 who 這個字，告訴我們這題的關鍵跟人物相關，而看到此題的選項，便能猜測出接下來會聽到「職業」的相關敘述，是在問講者的工作是什麼。

聽稿

（CA / M）Hello, this message is for Mr. David Smith. Mr. Smith, my name is Carl Chen with Best Software Company. You had inquired a Quick-Do software quotation for your database needs. I've sent an e-mail with our software function sheets, application whitepapers, and a quotation to your smith@ mail.com account. As your company is our existing client, I provide a 15% off discount for your purchase this time, and a 5-hour free training session. If you have more questions, I'd be happy to answer them. Please feel free to call my cell at 0912-345-678. Thank you for your business, and have a nice day.

（加／男）你好，這是給大衛‧史密斯先生的留言。史密斯先生，我是陳卡爾，從最佳軟體公司打電話來的。你有資料庫的需求並詢問我們速成軟體的報價，我已寄電郵到您的 smith@mail.com 信箱了，並附上我們軟體的功能表、應用白皮書，和報價單。因您是現有客戶，我針對您此次購買幫您打八五折優惠，並送五小時的免費訓練課程。若您還有其他問題，我樂意為您服務，請隨時聯絡我，手機號碼是 0912-345-678。謝謝您的惠顧，祝您有美好的一天。

Q1. 講者最有可能是誰？（答案：D）
    (A) 支援工程師   (B) 英文老師
    (C) 清潔人員   (D) 業務代表

Q2. 講者提供何種產品？（答案：A）
    (A) 軟體   (B) 文具
    (C) 鞋子   (D) 食物

Q3. 聽者接下來可能會做什麼？（答案：D）
    (A) 安排一個會議   (B) 回答些問題
    (C) 安裝軟體   (D) 查看他的電子郵件

解題技巧

長篇獨白因內容長，講的速度快，又有口音影響，導致考生會覺得難以掌握重要訊息。與其試圖想要聽到聽懂每個字，倒不如將焦點放在「重要的關鍵點」上。這些「關鍵點」是講者想要強調的訊息，故極有可能會「加強重音」。

（CA／M）Hello, this message is for Mr. David Smith. Mr. Smith, my name is Carl Chen with Best Software Company. You had inquired a Quick-Do software quotation for your database needs. I've sent an e-mail with our software function sheets, application whitepapers, and a quotation to your smith@mail.com account. As your company is our existing client, I provide a 15% off discount for your purchase this time, and a 5-hour free training session. If you have more questions, I'd be happy to answer them. Please feel free to call my cell at 0912-345-678. Thank you for your business, and have a nice day.

以「僅專注在聽關鍵要點」的方式聽取重要資訊，便可很快抓出此獨白的要點，而這些要點也有可能是題組內會考出的題目，包括：此電話留言是軟體公司業務幫客戶提供報價單，打八五折優惠，還提供五小時免費訓練課程等。聽到關鍵資訊便可了解獨白的大概內容，的確比聽懂每個字重要多了。

利用獨白播放出來之前的幾秒空檔，很快地將題目先掃描一下，以便預期可能的獨白內容與要將注意力放在聽什麼要點上。

第一題

此題「Who is the speaker most likely?」問的是留言的講者是誰,那麼根據留言的關鍵句(也就是講者講獨白時所加強重音之字詞)「... my name is Carl Chen with Best Software Company. You had inquired a Quick-Do software quotation...」,可判斷在軟體公司上班,且會提供客戶報價單,應是業務人員較為合理,故選 (D)「A sales representative」為答案。

各選項解析

- 選項 (A)「A support engineer」、選項 (B)「An English teacher」與選項 (C)「A janitor」都不是會給客戶報價的角色,故不選。

第二題

此題「What type of product does the speaker provide?」問的是講者公司的產品為何,那麼根據此首句「... my name is Carol Chen with Best Software Company.」可聽出講者是在軟體公司上班,公司應是銷售軟體,故選 (A)「Software」為正確。

各選項解析

- 選項 (B)「Stationery」、選項 (C)「Shoes」和選項 (D)「Food」都沒有在獨白中被提及,故不選。

第三題

此題「What will the listener probably do next?」問的是聽者接著可能會做什麼,那麼根據講者所提的此句「I've sent an e-mail with our software function sheets, application whitepapers, and a quotation to your smith@mail.com account.」可聽出講者已經將客戶 David Smith 要的報價單寄到他的電郵信箱了,之後 David Smith 應要去查電子信箱較為合理,故選 (D)「Check his e-mail」為最佳答案。

各選項解析

- 選項 (A)「Schedule a meeting」說要安排會議,但電話留言中並無提到 meeting、conference、appointment 等會議相關字眼,故不選。
- 選項 (B)「Answer some questions」說要回答一些問題,但獨白中是提到說是「可以提出問題」,並非「回答問題」,故不選。
- 選項 (C)「Install the software」提到要安裝軟體,但根據獨白內容應是還在「軟體採購」階段而已,尚未購買也還尚未安裝,故不選。

關鍵字彙

message [ˈmɛsɪdʒ] n 訊息
inquire [ɪnˈkwaɪr] v 詢問
quotation [kwoˈteʃən] n 報價單
whitepaper [hwaɪtˈpepɚ] n 白皮書
existing [ɪgˈzɪstɪŋ] a 現有的
discount [ˈdɪskaʊnt] n 優惠、打折
purchase [ˈpɝtʃəs] n 購買
training session [ˈtrenɪŋ ˌsɛʃən] n 訓練、講習

Q1. Why is Vivian calling?

(A) To talk to Ms. Linda James   (B) To confirm a meeting schedule

(C) To file a complaint   (D) To invite Mark to a party

Q2. Where does Vivian want to meet?

(A) On the bus   (B) In her own office

(C) In Mark Jones' office   (D) In a coffee shop

Q3. What will Mark Jones probably do next?

(A) Make more cold calls   (B) Hold a meeting with his boss

(C) Return Vivian's call   (D) Write an e-mail to Linda

解題分析

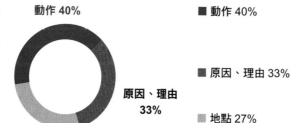

動作 40%

原因、理由 33%

地點 27%

■ 動作 40%

第三題目的在詢問一位名叫 Mark Jones 的人「接下來會做的事」，所以預期會聽到他即將進行的「動作」，要注意這個動作的主詞必須是 Mark 才行。

■ 原因、理由 33%

第一題的題目開頭是 why，要聽到的內容很有可能與「原因、理由」相關，並且與 Vivian 這個人物有關聯。

■ 地點 27%

第二題的關鍵為開頭的 Where，搭配後面的 meet 可知道題目是在詢問 Vivian 希望會面的「地點」，因此必須留意獨白中與地點、位置相關的訊息。

聽稿

（US / W）Hello. Uh... this is Vivian Jackson calling for Mr. Mark Jones please. Mr. Jones, I'm calling about the planned project meeting. Last week you asked me if July 7th would be all right for me, and I just wanted to confirm with you it is convenient for me. So Ms. Linda James, our project manager, and I will go to your office at 10 in the morning on July 7th. You may want to confirm the date and time with members in your team, and get back to me as soon as you're able. I think you have my number already. In case you don't, here it is again. My cell phone number is 039-483-4839. Hope to speak to you soon. Bye now.

中譯

（美／女）您好，麻煩請找馬克‧瓊斯先生，我是薇薇安‧傑克森。瓊斯先生，我是要和您討論有關專案的會議時程。由於上個星期您問我七月七日是否可行，而我現在便是想跟您確定我那天是有空檔的。我們的專案經理琳達‧詹姆斯小姐會和我一起於七月七日早上十點到您的辦公室找您。等您向您的團隊成員確認日期和時間後，再請您於方便時給我答覆。您應該有我的電話，以防有什麼閃失，我再留一次電話號碼給您。我的手機是 039-483-4839，期望能盡快得到您的消息。再見。

Q1. 薇薇安打電話的目的為何？（答案：B）

(A) 為與琳達‧詹姆士小姐談話　　　　(B) 為確認會議時間

(C) 為提出抱怨　　　　　　　　　　(D) 為邀請馬克參加派對

Q2. 薇薇安想在哪裡開會？（答案：C）

(A) 公車上　　　　　　　　　　　　(B) 她的辦公室

(C) 馬克‧瓊斯的辦公室　　　　　　(D) 咖啡廳

Q3. 馬克‧瓊斯接下來可能會做什麼？（答案：C）

(A) 打更多開發客戶的電話　　　　　(B) 跟老闆約個會議

(C) 回薇薇安的電話　　　　　　　　(D) 寫電郵給琳達

解題技巧

獨白內容頗長，又包括各國口音，速度也頗快，想要將所有資訊都聽到並了解，其實是沒必要的，考生應該做的是先掃描題目，了解此獨白想考的要點，並專注在聽這些關鍵點上即可。而這些講者想強調的關鍵之處，通常會以「加強重音」來強調：

（US／W）Hello. Uh... this is Vivian Jackson calling for Mr. Mark Jones please. Mr. Jones, I'm calling about the planned project meeting. Last week you asked me if July 7th would be all right for me, and I just wanted to confirm with you it is convenient for me. So Ms. Linda James, our project manager, and I will go to your office at 10 in the morning on July 7th. You may want to confirm the date and time with members in your team, and get back to me as soon as you're able. I think you have my number already. In case you don't, here it is again. My cell phone number is 039-483-4839. Hope to speak to you soon. Bye now.

由這些關鍵點，我們可整理出此獨白的幾個要點，包括：此留言是為了跟 Mark Jones 確認會議時間、日期、與開會地點等訊息，且講者希望 Mark Jones 可以回電確認。如此，先了解幾個「關鍵點」的確比想聽懂全數內容重要多了喔！

利用獨白播放出來之前的幾秒空檔，很快地將題目先掃描一下，以便預期可能的獨白內容與要將注意力放在聽什麼要點上。

第一題

此題問的是「Why is Vivian calling?」那麼便可判斷要聽出 Vivian 打電話的「原因、理由」以便回答。根據此關鍵句「Mr. Jones, I'm calling about the planned project meeting. Last week you asked me if July 7th would be all right for me, and I just wanted to confirm with you it is convenient for me.」，可聽出她要確認會議時間，故選 (B)「To confirm a meeting schedule」為最佳答案。

各選項解析

• 選項 (A)「To talk to Ms. Linda James」、選項 (C)「To file a complaint」與選項 (D)「To invite Mark to a party」都沒在留言中被提及，故不選。

第二題

此題問的是「Where does Vivian want to meet?」那麼便可判斷要聽到 Vivian 想會面之「地點、位置」相關資訊以便回答。根據此關鍵句「So Ms. Linda James, our project manager, and I will go to your office at 10 in the morning on July 7th.」可聽出她是想在「your office」、也就是在 Mr. Mark Jones 的辦公室內討論，故選 (C)「In Mark Jones' office」為最佳答案。

各選項解析

• 選項 (A) On the bus、選項 (B) In her own office 與選項 (D) In a coffee shop 都沒在留言中提及，故不選。

第三題

此題問的是「What will Mark Jones probably do next?」，那麼便打定主意要聽到 Mark Jones 接下來可能「做什麼事」相關訊息以便回答。根據此關鍵句「You may want to confirm the date and time with members in your team, and get back to me as soon as you're able.」可聽出 Vivian 是希望 Mark 可以回電確認，故 Mark 接下應是會回電給 Vivian 較為合理，故選 (C)「Return Vivian's call」為最佳答案。

各選項解析

• 選項 (A)「Make more cold calls」、選項 (B)「Hold a meeting with his boss」與選項 (D)「Write an e-mail to Linda」都沒在留言中提及，故不選。

關鍵字彙

project [`prɑdʒɛkt] n 專案、案子
confirm [kən`fɝm] v 確認
convenient [kən`vinjənt] a 方便的
member [`mɛmbɚ] n 同仁、隊員

攻略 3 ┃ 推銷留言

Q1. Who is the caller most likely?

(A) A software developer   (B) A tourist

(C) A real estate agent   (D) A university student

Q2. What is Ms. Martha Well looking for most likely?

(A) A decent job   (B) An English tutor

(C) A good graduate school   (D) A nice place to live

Q3. What is suggested about the house?

(A) It's extremely expensive   (B) It has a large garage

(C) It's a 30-year-old house   (D) It's currently occupied

解題分析

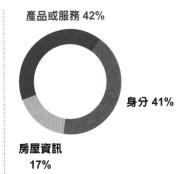

產品或服務 42%

身分 41%

房屋資訊 17%

■ 產品或服務 42%

第二題的關鍵在於開頭的 what 及 looking for，搭配選項可以推測會聽到 Ms. Martha 正在尋找的某樣產品或服務。

■ 身分 41%

本段獨白的第一題是 who 開頭，因為是電話，弄清楚來電者跟要找的對象是很重要的，這題就是在問打電話的人的「身分」，因為答案選項都是與職業相關，所以可能會聽到職業或業務等等。

■ 房屋資訊 17%

第三題很明確的在詢問房屋建案的相關資訊，因此只要聽到與選項符合的內容很可能就是答案。

聽稿

（UK / **M**）Hello, this is the message for Ms. Martha Well, please. This is George Lin calling from Marina Real Estate. Ms. Well, I thought you might be interested in a great house in Parkview Garden. It's located in Parkview County and has 360-degree panoramic views of the Taylor mountain range. The house is near quality schools, abundant shopping, recreational opportunities, community services, and is also in close proximity to freeway access for ease of commute. And garage side yards are large enough to accommodate most RVs or boats. All right, so if you're interested in making appointment and checking the environment, please call me at 593-4838. Again this is George Lin from Marina Real Estate.

（英 / 男）您好，這是要給瑪莎・威爾小姐的留言。我是瑪利納房地產公司的林喬治。威爾小姐，我這裡有一個郊野公園房屋案件，是一座位於郊野縣的大宅，能夠遠眺三百六十度的泰勒山脈全景，或許您會有興趣想看看。房屋鄰近優質的學區、購物中心與休閒活動等設施、社區服務、還有便於通勤的高速公路交流道。車庫的大小可以容納停駐一台休旅車或小船。倘若您有興趣看屋和其周遭環境，請您撥打預約電話 593-4838。這是瑪利納房地產公司的林喬治。

Q1. 打電話者有可能是誰？（答案：**C**）

(A) 軟體開發人員　　　　　　　　　(B) 遊客
(C) 房屋仲介　　　　　　　　　　　(D) 大學生

Q2. 瑪莎・威爾最有可能是在找什麼？（答案：**D**）

(A) 像樣的工作　　　　　　　　　　(B) 英文家教
(C) 優秀的研究所　　　　　　　　　(D) 良好的居所

Q3. 講者提到關於房子的何事？（答案：**B**）

(A) 它相當昂貴　　　　　　　　　　(B) 它有很大的車庫
(C) 它是間三十年的老房屋　　　　　(D) 它目前有人住

解題技巧

與其想要聽懂所有細節，還想在心中翻譯成中文意思，還不如將有限的時間和精力放在聽「會考的關鍵點上」就好。獨白內的關鍵點，很可能被講者以「加強重音」來強調，以突顯其重要性：

（UK / **M**）Hello, this is the message for Ms. Martha Well, please. This is George Lin calling from Marina Real Estate. Ms. Well, I thought you might be interested in a great house in Parkview Garden. It's located in Parkview County and has 360-degree panoramic views of the Taylor mountain range. The house is near quality schools, abundant shopping, recreational opportunities, community services, and is also in close proximity to freeway access for ease of commute. And garage side yards are large enough to accommodate most RVs or boats. All right, so if you're interested in making appointment and checking the environment, please call me at 593-4838. Again this is George Lin from Marina Real Estate.

聽了幾個關鍵處之後，便可抓出關於此獨白的大約內容了，包括：此講者是不動產公司之人，打電話給某客戶介紹新的建案，提到了數個關於新建案的優點，並邀請客戶約時間來鑑賞。如此可知，要了解大部分內容，不用靠聽懂每個字，僅要抓到關鍵點，一樣可以辦到的喔！

利用獨白播放出來之前的幾秒空檔，很快地將題目先掃描一下，以便預期可能的獨白內容與要將注意力放在聽什麼要點上。

第一題

此題問的是「Who is the caller most likely?」那麼便可判斷要聽到打電話留言者之「身分」以便回答問題。根據此關鍵句「This is George Lin calling from Marina Real Estate. Ms. Well, I thought you might be interested in a great house in Parkview Garden.」可聽出電話留言者是在不動產公司上班，且打電話給客戶介紹建案，故此人應是房屋仲介較為合理，故選 (C)「A real estate agent」為最佳答案。

各選項解析

- 選項 (A)「A software developer」、選項 (B)「A tourist」與選項 (D)「A university student」都不會是在「Real Estate」上班之人，故不選。

第二題

此題問的是「What is Ms. Martha Well looking for most likely?」那麼可判斷要聽到 Martha 要找「什麼」（產品或服務）相關資訊以便回答。根據此關鍵句「... great house in Parkview Garden. It's located in Parkview County and has 360-degree panoramic views of the Taylor mountain range. The house is near quality schools...」可聽出，George 打電給 Martha 介紹房子建案，可見得 Martha 應是在找住所較為合理，故選 (D)「A nice place to live」為最佳答案。

各選項解析

- 選項 (A)「A decent job」、選項 (B)「An English tutor」或選項 (C)「A good graduate school」都不是 Martha 在找的，因為此留言內容都沒提及這些：工作、家教老師、或研究所等產品或服務資訊，故不選。

第三題

此題問的是「What is suggested about the house?」既然問的是關於此房屋建案的相關資訊，便判斷應該要聽到相關資訊以便回答。根據此關鍵句「And garage side yards are large enough to accommodate most RVs or boats.」可聽出此房子有大到可以停得下休旅車與船的車庫，故選 (B)「It has a large garage.」為最佳答案。

各選項解析

- 選項 (A)「It's extremely expensive.」、選項 (C)「It's a 30-year-old house.」與選項 (D)「It's currently occupied.」都沒在此留言中聽到，故不選。

關鍵字彙

message [ˋmɛsɪdʒ] n 訊息
panoramic [ˌpænəˋræmɪk] a 全景的、全貌的
quality [ˋkwɑlətɪ] a 品質好的、高品質的
abundant [əˋbʌndənt] a 數量多的、大量的
recreational [ˌrɛkrɪˋeʃən] a 娛樂的
community [kəˋmjunətɪ] n 社區
proximity [prɑkˋsɪmətɪ] n 鄰近、鄰邊
commute [kəˋmjut] n 通勤
accommodate [əˋkɑməˌdet] v 容納
appointment [əˋpɔɪntmənt] n 約定、會議、約會

攻略 1 | 行銷會議開場

Q1. Who are most likely the listeners of the talk?

(A) Company investors   (B) Tourists

(C) Conference attendees   (D) High school students

Q2. What is the main theme of the conference?

(A) Customer service   (B) Marketing strategies

(C) Foreign affairs   (D) Advanced technologies

Q3. What will happen next most likely?

(A) A singer will sing a song   (B) The meeting will adjourn

(C) One of the attendees will go on stage   (D) Mr. Jones Lin will speak

解題分析

主題 44%

身分 30%

事件 26%

■ 主題 44%   本題的關鍵在 main theme 這個詞，詢問的是本次會議的「主題」，注意聽與研討會主題相關的字詞即可找出答案。

■ 身分 30%   第一題是 who 開頭的問句，可以很快速的判斷本題與人物相關，是在問聽者的「身分」，因此預計要聽到足以判別其身分的內容。

■ 事件 26%   第三題主要在詢問接下來會發生什麼事，因此聽獨白時可將注意力放聽在即將發生的「事件」上。

聽稿   （AU / W） All of our guests, welcome. We're delighted to have you here to participate in the 2018 Annual Marketing Conference hosted by New-Era Association. Thank you all for coming. That many of attendees travel long distances serves to remind us all how important marketing is. Indeed, the heart of your business success lies in its marketing. The overall marketing umbrella covers products, pricing strategies, distribution channels and fulfilling customers' demands. Without marketing, none of our potential customer would know about what outstanding products or services we're offering them. So today in this conference, you will be learning more about what and how effective marketing strategies can contribute to your business success. Before I handover to our first speaker, Mr. Jones Lin, I want to say once more, welcome.

中譯　（澳／女）歡迎各位貴賓。我們很高興各位來參加二〇一八年由新世代協會所舉辦的年度行銷會議。感謝您們撥空前來。有許多嘉賓甚至遠渡重洋來參加，提醒了我們行銷的重要性。事實上，行銷方法不外乎是一項生意成功的關鍵。行銷的全面性涵蓋了產品、定價策略、銷路管道、和顧客滿意度等的各個層面。少了行銷手段，便不會有任何一位潛在客戶能夠順利地得知我們所銷售的產品，或所提供之服務的優點或長處。所以今天的這場會議，我們將與各位分享有效的行銷策略是如何為企業帶來後續的成功。在我把麥克風交予主講者林瓊斯先生之前，讓我再次地歡迎各位的蒞臨。

Q1. 誰最有可能在聽此獨白？（答案：C）
    (A) 公司投資人　　　　　　　　　　　　(B) 遊客
    (C) 會議出席者　　　　　　　　　　　　(D) 高中學生

Q2. 此會議主題為何？（答案：B）
    (A) 客戶服務　　　　　　　　　　　　　(B) 行銷策略
    (C) 外交事務　　　　　　　　　　　　　(D) 高科技

Q3. 接下來最有可能發生何事？（答案：D）
    (A) 歌手會唱首歌　　　　　　　　　　　(B) 會議結束
    (C) 一位與會者會上台　　　　　　　　　(D) 林瓊斯先生會演講

解題技巧　考生通常會給自己一個不可能的任務，就是想聽懂全部的獨白細節。但仔細想想，一篇很長的獨白，也才考三題題組，真的需要聽的是那三題會考的「要點」就好，有需要了解全部的內容嗎？其實是不必要的。讓我們僅將注意力放在聽「有加強重音」的要點上即可：

> （AU／W）All of our guests, welcome. We're delighted to have you here to participate in the 2018 Annual Marketing Conference hosted by New-Era Association. Thank you all for coming. That many of attendees travel long distances serves to remind us all how important marketing is. Indeed, the heart of your business success lies in its marketing. The overall marketing umbrella covers products, pricing strategies, distribution channels and fulfilling customers' demands. Without marketing, none of our potential customer would know about what outstanding products or services we're offering them. So today in this conference, you will be learning more about what and how effective marketing strategies can contribute to your business success. Before I handover to our first speaker, Mr. Jones Lin, I want to say once more, welcome.

由這些要點可以聽出，此獨白的關鍵點包括：講者在歡迎與會者參與研討會，並介紹了行銷的策略與其重要性，並且要介紹第一位演講者來簡報了。如此也可以了解八成的內容，實在無需逐字翻譯喔！

利用獨白播放出來之前的幾秒空檔，很快地將題目先掃描一下，以便預期可能的獨白內容與要將注意力放在聽什麼要點上。

第一題

此題問的是「Who are most likely the listeners of the talk?」那麼可判斷要聽到可以推斷出此獨白之「聽眾會是誰」相關訊息以便回答。根據此關鍵句「All of our guests, welcome. We're delighted to have you here to participate in the 2018 Annual Marketing Conference...」可聽出聽眾應是出席研討會的人較為合理,故選 (C)「Conference attendees」為最佳答案。

各選項解析

- 選項 (A)「Company investors」、選項 (B)「Tourists」與選項 (D)「High school students」都不像會是要聽「年度行銷會議」的人,故不選。

第二題

此題問的是「What is the main theme of the conference?」那麼便專注在聽研討會的「主題」即可回答。根據此關鍵句「... serves to remind us all how important marketing is. Indeed, the heart of your business success lies in its marketing.」,可聽出主題會是行銷,因此介紹講者一直強調其重要性,故選 (B)「Marketing strategies」為最佳答案。

各選項解析

- 選項 (A)「Customer service」、選項 (C)「Foreign affairs」與選項 (D)「Advanced technologies」都沒有在獨白中被提及,故不選。

第三題

此題問的是「What will happen next most likely?」那麼便要聽到接下來會發生「什麼事」相關資訊以便回答。根據此關鍵句「Before I handover to our first speaker, Mr. Jones Lin, I want to say once more, welcome.」可聽出接下來是 Mr. Jones Lin 要上台演講了,故選 (D)「Mr. Jones Lin will speak.」為最佳答案。

各選項解析

- 選項 (A)「A singer will sing a song.」、選項 (B)「The meeting will adjourn.」與選項 (C)「One of the attendees will go on stage.」都沒在獨白中聽到,故不選。

關鍵字彙

participate [par`tɪsəˌpet] v 參與
host [host] v 主辦、做東
attendee [ə`tɛndi] n 與會者
remind [rɪ`maɪnd] v 提醒
marketing [`markɪtɪŋ] n 行銷
indeed [ɪn`did] ad 當然、的確
strategy [`strætədʒɪ] n 策略
distribution [ˌdɪstrə`bjuʃən] n 分配、分發、散播
channel [`tʃænl] n 頻道、管道
fulfill [fʊl`fɪl] v 滿足、實現、達成
demand [dɪ`mænd] n 需求
potential [pə`tɛnʃəl] a 潛在的、有潛力的
effective [ɪ`fɛktɪv] a 有效的
contribute [kən`trɪbjut] v 貢獻
handover [`hændˌovə] v 交接、轉移

攻略 2 ｜ 會議總結

Q1. **Where is the talk probably taking place?**

(A) At a business meeting   (B) On the TV talk show

(C) Inside an aircraft   (D) In a classroom

Q2. **What is the main purpose of this talk?**

(A) To launch a new product   (B) To summarize some action items

(C) To welcome new employees   (D) To announce bad news

Q3. **When will the next meeting be held?**

(A) Tomorrow morning   (B) Monday afternoon

(C) Wednesday morning   (D) Friday at noon

解題分析

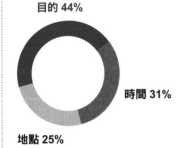

目的 44%

時間 31%

地點 25%

■ 目的 44%　第二題是在問這段獨白的主要「目的」，因此可以判斷要將注意力放在相關的訊息上。

■ 時間 31%　第三題是以 when 為開頭，搭配題目的其他關鍵字，可判斷接下來要聽到的是下一場會議舉行的「時間」。

■ 地點 25%　看見第一題的開頭 where，可以推測題目是在問此段獨白的「地點」，所以聽的時候要特別注意是否有出現地點或場合的關鍵字。

聽稿

（CA / **M**）All right, everybody. Let's wrap things up here. Good job, everyone. Before we adjourn the meeting, let me just go over what we've discussed and decided this morning. Okay, so... we've decided to outsource the network management rather than hiring our own IT manager. As we agreed, it'll be better to leave the job to the professionals. Mike will contact two or three IT firms and ask them to give quotations for managing our network systems. Mike's going to investigate that for us. Now, let's fix a time for our next meeting, okay? Is next Wednesday at 10 a.m. convenient for everyone? Yes? Wonderful. Well, and that concludes our meeting for today. Thank you for all your active participation this morning. I think it's a pretty productive meeting.

中譯　（加 / 男）好吧，各位。讓我們來做個總結吧。大家表現得很好。在此次的會議結束之前，請容我再重複一次今天早上討論的內容和所做出的決定。好了，與其聘請另一位新的資訊經理，我們決議將網路管理這一部分外包給其他廠商。如我們達成的共識，把此項任務交由專業的人員來處理。麥克會試著跟二至三間資訊公司聯絡討論網路系統的相關事宜，並請對方報價。麥克會完成調查工作。現在，讓我們來訂定下一次會議的時間，好嗎？不知各位同仁下個星期三早上十點是否方便？都可以嗎？太好了。那麼今天會議就到此為止，謝謝你們今日早晨的熱情參與，這是個收穫良多的會議。

Q1. 此獨白有可能是在何處聽到？（答案：A）

(A) 在商業會議中 　　　　　　　　　　(B) 在電視談話節目中

(C) 在飛機內 　　　　　　　　　　　　(D) 在教室

Q2. 此獨白的主要目的為何？（答案：B）

(A) 推出新產品 　　　　　　　　　　　(B) 歸納一些決議事項

(C) 歡迎新進員工 　　　　　　　　　　(D) 宣布壞消息

Q3. 下一次會議會在何時舉行？（答案：C）

(A) 明天早上 　　　　　　　　　　　　(B) 週一下午

(C) 週三早上 　　　　　　　　　　　　(D) 週五中午

解題技巧　想要了解獨白內部的大意，不一定要靠每個字都聽到，或每個字都會翻譯才可達成。時間非常有限的情況之下，其實僅需要聽到一些關鍵點就可以了解長篇獨白的大意了。而這些要點之處正是講者想要強調之處，故有可能會以「加強重音」來強調：

（CA / M）All right, everybody. Let's wrap things up here. Good job, everyone. Before we adjourn the meeting, let me just go over what we've discussed and decided this morning. Okay, so... we've decided to outsource the network management rather than hiring our own IT manager. As we agreed, it'll be better to leave the job to the professionals. Mike will contact two or three IT firms and ask them to give quotations for managing our network systems. Mike's going to investigate that for us. Now, let's fix a time for our next meeting, okay? Is next Wednesday at 10 a.m. convenient for everyone? Yes? Wonderful. Well, and that concludes our meeting for today. Thank you for all your active participation this morning. I think it's a pretty productive meeting.

聽了這些關鍵點之後，可以大致了解此獨白的大意：講者要為會議做個結論了，他提及一些代辦事項，還敲定了下次會議的時間，講者認為會議效率高且效果好。如此可了解，聽到幾個關鍵點便可了解大概內容了。而這些要點便可能會是出題之處。

利用獨白播放出來之前的幾秒空檔，很快地將題目先掃描一下，以便預期可能的獨白內容與要將注意力放在聽什麼要點上。

第一題

此題問的是「Where is the talk probably taking place?」那麼便應該聽出可以判斷此獨白會在「何處、何場合」聽到的相關資訊以便回答。根據此關鍵句「All right, everybody. Let's wrap things up here. Good job, everyone. Before we adjourn the meeting, let me...」可聽出講者是要在會議結束之前做總結了,那麼應該是在商業會議中會聽到的談話較為合理,故選 (A)「At a business meeting」為最佳答案。

各選項解析

• 選項 (B)「On the TV talk show」、選項 (C)「Inside an aircraft」與選項 (D)「In a classroom 都不會是聽到「會議要結束」相關訊息之場合,故不選。

第二題

此題問的是「What is the main purpose of this talk?」那麼便可判斷要將注意力放在聽此談話的「主要目的」上以便回答。根據此關鍵句「Before we adjourn the meeting, let me just go over what we've discussed and decided this morning.」,可聽出講者是要針對早上的會議做些總結了,故選 (B)「To summarize some action items」為最佳答案。

各選項解析

• 選項 (A)「To launch a new product」、選項 (C)「To welcome new employees」與選項 (D)「To announce bad news」都沒有在獨白中被提及,故不選。

第三題

此題問的是「When will the next meeting be held?」那麼便應該將注意力放在聽下一次會議的「時間點」資訊上以便回答。根據此關鍵句「Now, let's fix a time for our next meeting, okay? Is next Wednesday at 10 a.m. convenient for everyone? Yes? Wonderful.」可聽出下次會議是在週三早上十點,故選 (C)「Wednesday morning」為最佳答案。

各選項解析

• 選項 (A)「Tomorrow morning」、選項 (B)「Monday afternoon」與選項 (D)「Friday at noon」都沒在談話中被提及,故不選。

關鍵字彙

wrap up 四 完成、結束
adjourn [ə`dʒɜn] ⅴ 閉會、結束會議
outsource [`aut͵sɔrsɪ] ⅴ 外包
hire [haɪr] ⅴ 僱用
professional [prə`fɛʃən] ⓐ 專業的
contact [kən`tækt] ⅴ 聯絡
quotation [kwo`teʃən] ⓝ 報價
investigate [ɪn`vɛstə͵get] ⅴ 檢視、調查
conclude [kən`klud] ⅴ 下結論
active [`æktɪv] ⓐ 活動的、活躍的
productive [prə`dʌktɪv] ⓐ 生產力高的

1:30 p.m. - 2 p.m.	Registration
2 p.m. - 3:30 p.m.	Session I
3:40 p.m. - 4:40 p.m.	Session II
4:40 p.m. - 5 p.m.	Q / A Discussion

Q1. Who is the speaker most likely?

(A) A researcher

(B) A patient

(C) An attendee

(D) An event coordinator

Q2. What is the speaker discussing most likely?

(A) Who are more likely to gain weight

(B) Where to buy fresh fruit

(C) How human metabolism works

(D) Why children need to exercise

新 **Q3. Look at the agenda. What time will the speaker probably answer audience's questions?**

(A) 2:15 p.m.

(B) 1:45 p.m.

(C) 4:20 p.m.

(D) 4:45 p.m.

解題分析

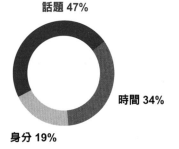

話題 47%

時間 34%

身分 19%

■ 話題 47% 第二題問的是講者討論的「話題是什麼」，因此在聽獨白的時候必須抓出談話的主題，才是正確答案。

■ 時間 34% 第三題問句的開頭是 what time，可得知是在問講者回答問題的「時間」，但因為本題有搭配表格，所以可以依據聽到的活動階段來判斷正確答案是什麼時間。

■ 身分 19% 第一題是以 who 為句首，可以很快速判斷聽的時候要鎖定的是講者的「身分」，可能會聽到與工作內容有關的敘述。

聽稿

（UK / M）Welcome all attendees. I'm Dr. Marry Worth. I'm pleased to be here today to explain my research on weight loss and metabolism. Well, first of all, I'd like to say that there is an evolutionary reason for obesity. Early humans were subjected to frequent periods of poor access to nutrition. Those who were best at storing fat calories when food was available, and conserving them when it wasn't, were most likely to survive and reproduce. Now in the modern world, people are richly endowed with traits that defend the storage of calories as fat. Therefore, after losing weight, our metabolism is probably slower and our appetite is probably greater. Yes, a lady back there just raised her hand. Do you have a question? All right, I'd be happy to answer your questions after I finish this part, okay? So now let me get back to where I was.

中譯 （英/男）歡迎所有的參與者。我是瑪力·沃斯博士，很高興能夠來此向大家說明我最新完成的減重與新陳代謝之研究結果。首先，我要來說說有關肥胖的演進成因。早期的人們由於常常處於營養不易取得的狀態，導致於能夠存活並繁衍後代的，往往皆是懂得在物資豐足時於體內儲存脂肪熱量，並在物資缺乏時妥善保存的那一群。如今來到了現代，人們天生便具有了豐富的特徵，即是把熱量轉化成脂肪的保護機制。因此，當我們嘗試減重之後，反而會發現我們的新陳代謝變慢了，但胃口卻變得更好了。是的，那位坐在後頭舉起手的女子，請問您有什麼疑問嗎？這樣吧，等我完成這部分的說明之後，再開放時間給各位自由提問，好嗎？請先容許我言歸正傳。

下午一點半～兩點	報到
下午兩點～三點半	第一場演講
下午三點四十分～四點四十分	第二場演講
下午四點四十分～五點	問題討論

Q1. 講者最有可能是誰？（答案：A）
(A) 研究員
(B) 病人
(C) 與會者
(D) 活動規劃人員

Q2. 講者主要在討論什麼？（答案：C）
(A) 哪種人最可能變胖
(B) 哪裡可以買到新鮮水果
(C) 人體新陳代謝是如何運作的
(D) 為何小孩應多運動

新 Q3. 請看議程，講者最有可能在幾點時回答聽眾的問題？（答案：D）
(A) 下午兩點十五分
(B) 下午一點四十五分
(C) 下午四點二十分
(D) 下午四點四十五分

解題技巧 獨白類的題目，唸得很長資訊又多，與其想將所有資訊都聽到聽懂，不如將注意力放在聽「關鍵點」上。根據英文母語使用者的習慣，通常會在重要關鍵之處以「加強重音」的方式來呈現，目的也是在提醒聽者要注意此資訊。此獨白內有加強重音的要點可能會是：

（UK/M）Welcome all attendees. I'm Dr. Marry Worth. I'm pleased to be here today to explain my research on weight loss and metabolism. Well, first of all, I'd like to say that there is an evolutionary reason for obesity. Early humans were subjected to frequent periods of poor access to nutrition. Those who were best at storing fat calories when food was available, and conserving them when it wasn't, were most likely to survive and reproduce. Now in the modern world, people are richly endowed with traits that defend the storage of calories as fat. Therefore, after losing weight, our metabolism is probably slower and our appetite is probably greater. Yes, a lady back there just raised her hand. Do you have a question? All right, I'd be happy to answer your questions after I finish this part, okay? So now let me get back to where I was.

在聽出講者以「加強重音」方式表示所想強調的重點之後，便比較有可能將焦點放在要點上，而非讓思緒分散掉。而此獨白的要點可能包括：講者在報告他研究瘦身的成果，與新陳代謝的關係，並告知聽眾若有問題討論可等到演講完再討論……等相關資訊。

在播放出獨白聽力內容之前總會有三四秒的時間可以利用，便可很快地將題目大略掃描一下，以便得知大概是問什麼問題，也才有機會知道要將注意力放在聽什麼樣的資訊上。

第一題

首先很快地掃描題目，問的是「Who is the speaker most likely?」那麼根據講者開場的此要點句「I'm Dr. Marry Worth. I'm pleased to be here today to explain my research on weight loss and metabolism.」可聽出他要報告研究成果，那最有可能是位研究員才合理。故選 (A)「A researcher」為最佳答案。

各選項解析

- 選項 (B)「A patient」、選項 (C)「An attendee」和選項 (D)「An event coordinator」都不會是「做完研究之後，將研究結果簡報給眾人聽」的角色，故不選。

第二題

先把握時間很快地掃描題目，可得知此題問的是「What is the speaker discussing most likely?」那麼既然是問演講主題，根據此關鍵句「Therefore, after losing weight, our metabolism is probably slower and our appetite is probably greater.」可聽出，講者是在討論人體卡路里消耗，與新陳代謝等主題。故選 (C)「How human metabolism works」為最佳答案。

各選項解析

- 選項 (A)「Who are more likely to gain weight」內的關鍵字「gain weight」似乎有在獨白中提及，但並沒針對「who」也就是「較易肥胖的族群」來討論，故不選。
- 選項 (B)「Where to buy fresh fruit」提到「在哪裡可以買到新鮮水果」，這些字眼完全沒出現在獨白中，故也不會是答案。
- 選項 (D)「Why children need to exercise」提到「小孩應多運動」，但獨白中講者並沒有特別針對「小孩運動」一事做討論，故也不會是演講的主題。

新 第三題

此題搭配表格，那麼就是要根據獨白內容，再搭配上表格內資訊來判斷答案。題目問的是「What time will the speaker probably answer audience's questions?」那麼就要查表找出講者會回答問題的時間。根據講者內容的關鍵句「Yes, a lady back there just raised her hand. Do you have a question? All right, I'd be happy to answer your questions after I finish this part, okay?」可聽出講者並沒打算中斷演講，隨時停下來回答問題的，而是想在演講完之後再一起回答。那麼查議程後看到，回答問題與討論時間是在 4:40 p.m. - 5 p.m. 之間，因此選項 (D)「4:45 p.m.」在此時間內，是最佳答案。

各選項解析

- 其他選項內所提及的時間都是講者還在演講的時段，不是回答問題的討論時段，故不選。

關鍵字彙

explain [ɪkˋsplen] ⅴ 解釋	conserve [kənˋsɜv] ⅴ 保育、保存
research [rɪˋsɝtʃ] ⋒ 研究	survive [səˋvaɪv] ⅴ 存活
metabolism [mɛˋtæbḷͺɪzəm] ⋒ 新陳代謝	reproduce [ͺriprəˋdjus] ⅴ 繁殖
evolutionary [ͺɛvəˋluʃənͺɛrɪ] ⓐ 革新的、革新性的	endow [ɪnˋdau] ⅴ 授予、給予
obesity [oˋbisətɪ] ⋒ 肥胖	trait [tret] ⋒ 特性、優點
nutrition [njuˋtrɪʃən] ⋒ 營養、養分	defend [dɪˋfɛnd] ⅴ 保護、保衛
calorie [ˋkælərɪ] ⋒ 卡路里、熱量	

Unit 4 廣告促銷類

攻略 1 | 房地產廣告

Q1. Who is the intended audience of this commercial message?

(A) Workers who plan to change jobs

(B) Mothers who would like to work part-time

(C) People who are searching for a new house

(D) Students who wish to study abroad

Q2. What is the purpose of this talk?

(A) To hire new real estate agents　　(B) To introduce a new condominium

(C) To announce a seminar　　(D) To release a new policy

Q3. What does the speaker ask listeners to do?

(A) To schedule a visit　　(B) To remodel their houses

(C) To write to him　　(D) To make a personal website

解題分析

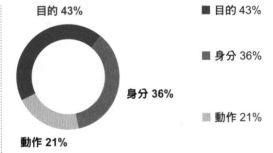

目的 43%
身分 36%
動作 21%

■ 目的 43%　第二題的關鍵字很明顯為 purpose，在詢問講述此段獨白的「目的」，聽的時候必須抓住這個重點。

■ 身分 36%　第一題是 who 開頭，可以知道是在問某個人的身分，根據其他關鍵詞 intended audience 判斷，發問重點為本則廣告「主要聽眾」的身分，因此在聽的時候要特別留意相關資訊。

■ 動作 21%　第三題是在詢問講者要求聽眾「做什麼事」，聽的時候就要注意講者有無特別提到相關的「動作」指令，根據這些資訊來回答。

聽稿

（UK / **M**）Home shoppers, are you looking for a place to live in the Corte City area? Why not consider the brand new Flower Garden condominium? In this newly built condominium, residents can enjoy state-of-the-art community amenities, including 1/2-acre private landscaped park complete with heated pool, spa, BBQs and outdoor fireplaces. For residents who love to exercise, we've got fully equipped Fitness Center, Yoga Retreat and resident lounge for you. One and two bedroom apartments as well as three bedroom town homes with private garages are available. So why wait? Call us at 858-483-382 immediately to schedule a visit. Please call 858-483-382 now.

PART 1
PART 2
PART 3
PART 4

中譯　（英 / 男）各位在找好房子的朋友們，您正在尋找柯爾特城市附近的優質住宅嗎？何不考慮全新的花園大廈？這是一棟剛落成的大廈建築，居民們可以享受最先進的社區福利設施，包括由二分之一英畝的私人景觀公園組成的熱水泡湯池、水療設備、戶外燒烤活動、和露天壁爐。為了喜愛運動的居民們，我們有設備齊全的健身中心、瑜伽教室和會客廳等等。一房、兩房、甚至是三房的車庫住宅，我們皆有出售。心動不如馬上心動。預約看屋專線 858-483-382 馬上為您安排參觀。請立刻撥打 858-483-382。

Q1. 此廣告的主要聽眾會是誰？（答案：C）

(A) 想換工作的上班族　　　　　　　　　(B) 想找兼職工作的媽媽

(C) 想找房子的民眾　　　　　　　　　　(D) 想出國留學的學生

Q2. 此獨白的主旨為何？（答案：B）

(A) 為招募新的不動產銷售員　　　　　　(B) 為介紹新的房屋建案

(C) 為宣布研討會訊息　　　　　　　　　(D) 為公告新政策

Q3. 講者請聽眾做什麼？（答案：A）

(A) 安排拜訪　　　　　　　　　　　　　(B) 將房屋翻修一下

(C) 寫信給他　　　　　　　　　　　　　(D) 建立自己的網站

解題技巧　考生應捨棄想將所有內容聽到並聽懂的堅持，而僅將有限的注意力放在「關鍵要點上」，事實上大致了解關鍵點，也可以了解獨白的八成內容了。而這些關鍵點也可能是以「加強重音」來呈現：

（UK / M）Home shoppers, are you looking for a place to live in the Corte City area? Why not consider the brand new Flower Garden condominium? In this newly built condominium, residents can enjoy state-of-the-art community amenities, including 1/2-acre private landscaped park complete with heated pool, spa, BBQs and outdoor fireplaces. For residents who love to exercise, we've got fully equipped Fitness Center, Yoga Retreat and resident lounge for you. One and two bedroom apartments as well as three bedroom town homes with private garages are available. So why wait? Call us at 858-483-382 immediately to schedule a visit. Please call 858-483-382 now.

由此可聽出，此獨白的要點包括：在跟想買房子的人介紹建案，講者描述了一些設施，講了建案住家的格局，並邀請有興趣的人預約看屋。如此了解大致的內容比想要逐字翻譯來得有效率多了哩！

利用獨白播放出來之前的幾秒空檔，很快地將題目先掃描一下，以便預期可能的獨白內容與要將注意力放在聽什麼要點上。

第一題

此題問的是「Who is the intended audience of this commercial message?」那麼便可判斷要聽到此廣告的「目標聽眾」相關資訊以便回答。根據此關鍵句「Home shoppers, are you looking for a place to live in the Corte City area? Why not consider the brand new Flower Garden condominium?」可聽出此廣告的目標聽眾是有意要買屋換屋的人，故選 (C)「People who are searching for a new house」為最佳答案。

各選項解析

- 選項 (A)「Workers who plan to change jobs」、選項 (B)「Mothers who would like to work part-time」與選項 (D)「Students who wish to study abroad」都不會是「介紹房屋建案」廣告的客群，故不選。

第二題

此題問的是「What is the purpose of this talk?」那麼便要聽出此獨白的「目的」以便回答。根據此關鍵句「In this newly built condominium, residents can enjoy state-of-the-art community amenities...」可聽出此廣告是在介紹「Flower Garden」這個新屋建案與其有的設施，故選 (B)「To introduce a new condominium」為最佳答案。

各選項解析

- 選項 (A)「To hire new real estate agents」、選項 (C)「To announce a seminar」與選項 (D)「To release a new policy」都沒有在獨白中提及，故不選。

第三題

此題問的是「What does the speaker ask listeners to do?」那麼便應將注意力放在聽講者要聽眾「做什麼」的相關資訊上以便回答。根據此關鍵句「So why wait? Call us at 858-483-382 immediately to schedule a visit. Please call 858-483-382 now.」可聽出講者邀請聽眾馬上打電話預約看房，故選 (A)「To schedule a visit」為最佳答案。

各選項解析

- 選項 (B)「To remodel their houses」、選項 (C)「To write to him」與選項 (D)「To make a personal website」都沒有在獨白中提及，故不選。

關鍵字彙

consider [kənˋsɪdə] ☑ 考量、思量
condominium [ˏkɑndəˋmɪnɪəm] ⊓ 公寓、大廈
resident [ˋrɛzədənt] ⊓ 居民
state-of-the-art [ˋstetəvðiˋɑrt] ⊞ 先進的、跟得上科技的
amenity [əˋmɪnətɪ] ⊓ 舒適、適意；便利設施
landscape [ˋlændˏskep] ⊓ 景觀、風景
lounge [laʊndʒ] ⊓ 休息室
garage [gəˋrɑʒ] ⊓ 車庫
immediately [ɪˋmidɪɪtlɪ] ⊞ 立即地、馬上

Q1. What is the purpose of this announcement?

(A) To welcome people to join the meeting

(B) To invite people to attend an information session

(C) To inform employees of a new company policy

(D) To remind students of the midterm test

Q2. Who is the intended audience of this message?

(A) Young children   (B) Seasoned teachers

(C) Potential MBA students   (D) Senior engineers

Q3. Where will the event be held?

(A) In a hotel   (B) In a private company

(C) In a college   (D) In a restaurant

解題分析

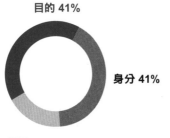

目的 41%

身分 41%

地點 18%

■ 目的 41%　第一個問題的重點在於 purpose 這個詞，因此可以判斷接下來要聽到的是這段公告的「目的」。

■ 身分 41%　第二題是 who 開頭的問句，看到這個關鍵字就可以清楚知道是跟人物相關的問題，搭配選項得知接下來聽到的資訊，必須能夠說明觀眾的「身分」。

■ 地點 18%　第三題是 where 為首的句子，很明確的是在問某個活動舉行的「地點」，可以預測接下來會聽到跟地點有關的訊息。

聽稿

（AU / Ⓦ）The Superb Forum is designed for outstanding business people considering an MBA, college students planning for the future, or professionals ready to take your careers to the next level. This Superb Forum, a free event unlike any other, will empower you with information about an MBA's value, leading business schools, and financing your degree. This is a great opportunity for participants to make critical connections with representatives, alumni, and students of top business schools in the U.S. Successful business people representing diverse industries and career stages will also share how their MBAs help them make a huge difference. The forum will be held on May 25th at 3 p.m. at Grand Hotel in Chicago. For more information or to register, please call 458-4883 or visit our website at www.mbaforum.com.

中譯　（澳／**女**）頂級研討會是專門為了傑出的企業管理人、正在規劃自己未來的大學生、或想要進修的專業職人而設計的。頂級研討會是一場舉世無雙的免費活動，它能夠幫助你釐清企業管理碩士的附加價值，了解頂尖商館學院的資訊，及領取獎學金的途徑。這是一個難能可貴的機會，參與者將能夠與各界代表、校友、和就讀於美國一流管理大學的菁英們近距離接觸。各式各樣不同領域、不同層級的成功商業人士代表，將會分享企業管理碩士課程是如何使他們在職涯上與眾不同。這場研討會將在五月二十五日下午三點，於芝加哥的格蘭飯店舉行。預約報名或欲知其他詳情，請撥 458-4883 與我們聯繫，或上 www.mbaforum.com 網站查詢。

Q1. 此公告的主旨為何？（答案：B）
　　(A) 歡迎大家來參與會議　　　　　　(B) 邀請大家參與說明會
　　(C) 通知員工關於新的公司政策　　　(D) 提醒學生期中考事宜

Q2. 誰是此訊息的主要聽眾？（答案：C）
　　(A) 年輕孩童　　　　　　　　　　　(B) 有經驗的老師
　　(C) 想讀企業管理碩士的學員　　　　(D) 資深工程師

Q3. 活動會在哪裡舉辦？（答案：A）
　　(A) 在飯店　　　　　　　　　　　　(B) 在私人公司
　　(C) 在大學　　　　　　　　　　　　(D) 在餐廳

解題技巧　討論到聽力，考生通常會直接想到「想將所有內容都聽懂」才算完成，但事實上，最後一部分獨白題，內容長、速度快，若想每個字都聽，無疑是給自己不必要的麻煩。考生所做的應該是將有限的時間與精神放在聽「會考的關鍵點」上才是，而這些關鍵點極有可能會以「加強重音」來強調：

（AU／**W**）The Superb Forum is designed for outstanding business people considering an MBA, college students planning for the future, or professionals ready to take your careers to the next level. This Superb Forum, a free event unlike any other, will empower you with information about an MBA's value, leading business schools, and financing your degree. This is a great opportunity for participants to make critical connections with representatives, alumni, and students of top business schools in the U.S. Successful business people representing diverse industries and career stages will also share how their MBAs help them make a huge difference. The forum will be held on May 25th at 3 p.m. at Grand Hotel in Chicago. For more information or to register, please call 458-4883 or visit our website at www.mbaforum.com.

如此將注意力放在聽「關鍵要點」上，便可得知此獨白的八成內容了，包括「講者在說明進修 MBA 的好處與價值」，且在說明會內可以跟相關人士交流意見，並說了頂級研討會所舉辦的日期，時間與地點。如此可得知，聽到關鍵字便可了解大概內容喔！

利用獨白播放出來之前的幾秒空檔，很快地將題目先掃描一下，以便預期可能的獨白內容與要將注意力放在聽什麼要點上。

第一題

先掃描到題目問的是「What is the purpose of this announcement?」那麼便判斷要聽到此公告之「目的」以便回答。根據此關鍵句「The Superb Forum is designed for outstanding business people considering an MBA, college students planning for the future, or professionals ready to take your careers to the next level.」，可聽出是在介紹一個研討會、說明會，期望有興趣的人可以參加，故選 (B)「To invite people to attend an information session」為最佳答案。

各選項解析

- 選項 (A)「To welcome people to join the meeting」、選項 (C)「To inform employees of a new company policy」與選項 (D)「To remind students of the midterm test」都沒有在獨白中被提及，故不選。

第二題

此題問的是「Who is the intended audience of this message?」那麼可判斷要聽到「聽眾」可能會是誰的相關資訊以便回答。根據此關鍵句「This Superb Forum, a free event unlike any other, will empower you with information about an MBA's value, leading business schools, and financing your degree.」可聽出是要吸引「想讀 MBA 的學員」而舉辦的研討會，故選 (C)「Potential MBA students」為最佳答案。

各選項解析

- 選項 (A)「Young children」、選項 (B)「Seasoned teachers」與選項 (D)「Senior engineers」都不是在此獨白中提到會想進修 MBA 的學員族群，故不選。

第三題

此題目問的是「Where will the event be held?」活動會在哪裡舉辦，那麼便可判斷應要聽到活動舉辦的「場所」相關資訊以便回答。根據此關鍵句「The forum will be held on May 25th at 3 p.m. at Grand Hotel in Chicago.」可聽出是在 Grand Hotel 舉辦，故選 (A)「In a hotel」為最佳答案。

各選項解析

- 選項 (B)「In a private company」、選項 (C)「In a college」與選項 (D)「In a restaurant」都沒有在獨白中聽到，故不選。

關鍵字彙

forum [`forəm] n 論壇、討論區
outstanding [`aut`stændɪŋ] a 突出的、傑出的
career [kə`rɪr] n 職業
empower [ɪm`pauɚ] v 授權、准許
finance [faɪ`næns] v 為～提供資金
critical [`krɪtɪkl] a 關鍵的、重要的
connection [kə`nɛkʃən] n 連結、關連
alumni [ə`lʌmnaɪ] n 校友
represent [ˌrɛprɪ`zɛnt] v 代表
diverse [daɪ`vɝs] a 不同的、互異的
register [`rɛdʒɪstɚ] v 登記、註冊

攻略 3 ｜鞋店廣告

Q1. What is being advertised?

(A) Athletic footwear   (B) Business suits

(C) Software packages   (D) Online games

Q2. Who is the intended audience?

(A) Musicians   (B) Women

(C) Children   (D) Doctors

Q3. How can listeners get a list of stores?

(A) Ask the personal trainer   (B) Write to the brand manager

(C) Call the store owner   (D) Check the company website

解題分析

產品 40%

身分 37%

方法 23%

■ 產品 40%

可明確看出第一題是在問這段獨白在「廣告什麼」，也就是預期接下來會聽到某一段「產品」相關的描述，可以依據這些線索找到正確答案。

■ 身分 37%

第二題是 who 開頭的問句，加上後面的重點 intended audience，可預期接下來會聽到的訊息跟觀眾的「身分」有關聯。

■ 方法 23%

第三題的開頭是 how，可得知本題在詢問「如何」取得商店觀眾的名單，因此，在接下來的獨白中最有可能聽到的是取得名單的「方法、方式」。

聽稿

（UK / M）Ladies, nothing sets your style off like a fresh pair of sneakers. If you're looking for that perfect pair of women's shoes, then please do come to Sneaker Town. Sneaker Town brings you the most complete selection around with all major brands. Whether you need some new Jump running shoes or a casual pair of New Balance, we've got you covered. Look at your best and play even better when you have a new pair of running shoes from your favorite brand. With the perfect pair of women's sneakers on your feet, nothing will stand in your way at all. Come to the Sneaker Town nearest you, and shop for the perfect pair of women's shoes for yourself. Visit our website at www.sneakertown.net for store locations.

（英／男）女士們，沒有什麼會比擁有一雙充滿活力的球鞋能使妳看起來更有型。如果妳在尋找一雙完美的女用鞋款，請妳務必前來球鞋城鎮走一趟。球鞋城鎮提供各大品牌最完整的系列款式，不論妳需要的是將門的慢跑鞋或是紐巴倫的休閒鞋，都能在我們這裡找到。當妳在最愛的品牌之中尋得一雙全新的慢跑鞋之後，不但使妳看起來更美、更可以讓妳一展長才。擁有一雙完美的球鞋，就不會有任何障礙能阻擋妳的前進。快到離妳最近的球鞋城鎮，選購一雙妳個人最完美無瑕的女鞋吧。請上官網 www.sneakertown.net 查詢鄰近的門市地點。

Q1. 此獨白在廣告什麼產品？（答案：**A**）

(A) 運動鞋   (B) 商業套裝

(C) 軟體產品   (D) 線上遊戲

Q2. 此廣告的聽眾會是誰？（答案：**B**）

(A) 音樂家   (B) 女子

(C) 小孩   (D) 醫生

Q3. 聽眾要如何取得商店名單？（答案：**D**）

(A) 問私人教練   (B) 寫信給品牌經理

(C) 打電話給店長   (D) 上公司網站查詢

在準備聽力時應有一個體認，就是不要試圖將所有資訊聽懂，而是要打定主意僅聽「關鍵點」之處即可。而這些講者想強調的關鍵點，通常會以「加強重音」來強調，以便引起聽者的注意：

> （UK／M）Ladies, nothing sets your style off like a fresh pair of sneakers. If you're looking for that perfect pair of women's shoes, then please do come to Sneaker Town. Sneaker Town brings you the most complete selection around with all major brands. Whether you need some new Jump running shoes or a casual pair of New Balance, we've got you covered. Look at your best and play even better when you have a new pair of running shoes from your favorite brand. With the perfect pair of women's sneakers on your feet, nothing will stand in your way at all. Come to the Sneaker Town nearest you, and shop for the perfect pair of women's shoes for yourself. Visit our website at www.sneakertown.net for store locations.

將此獨白的關鍵點抓出之後，自然也可以了解大約八成的內容了，比方說：此廣告是介紹女性運動鞋，講者強調了店內有各種品牌以供女性挑選，並邀請大家就近到經銷店參觀選購。有了這樣的認知，回答問題起來也得心應手多了。

利用獨白播放出來之前的幾秒空檔，很快地將題目先掃描一下，以便預期可能的獨白內容與要將注意力放在聽什麼要點上。

第一題

先掃描描題目問的是「What is being advertised?」那麼便可判斷要聽到「廣告什麼產品」相關資訊以便回答。根據此關鍵句「Ladies, nothing sets your style off like a fresh pair of sneakers.」可聽出是在廣告女性運動鞋產品，故選 (A)「Athletic footwear」為最佳答案。

各選項解析

- 選項 (B)「Business suits」、選項 (C)「Software packages」與選項 (D)「Online games」都沒有在獨白中被提及，故不選。

第二題

此題目問的是「Who is the intended audience?」那麼便要判斷此廣告的「目標聽眾」會是誰以便回答。根據此關鍵句「If you're looking for that perfect pair of women's shoes, then please do come to Sneaker Town.」可聽出此女性運動鞋廣告之目標客群應是針對「女子」較為合理，故選 (B)「Women」為最佳答案。

各選項解析

- 選項 (A)「Musicians」、選項 (C)「Children」與選項 (D)「Doctors」都沒在獨白中提及，故不選。

第三題

此題問的是「How can listeners get a list of stores?」那麼便判斷要聽到「如何」取得商店名單之「方式」，根據此關鍵句「Visit our website at www.sneakertown.net for store locations.」可聽出要得知哪些店家有販售，可以上網查詢，故選 (D)「Check the company website」為最佳答案。

各選項解析

- 選項 (A)「Ask the personal trainer」、選項 (B)「Write to the brand manager」與選項 (C)「Call the store owner」等方式都沒有在獨白中提到，故不選。

關鍵字彙

sneakers [ˋsnikɚs] n. 運動鞋
complete [kəmˋplit] a. 完整的、完全的
selection [səˋlɛkʃən] n. 選項、選擇
casual [ˋkæʒuəl] a. 休閒的
favorite [ˋfevərɪt] a. 最喜愛的

攻略 1 ｜ 面試者說明工作內容

Q1. Who is most likely the speaker?

(A) A product vendor   (B) An interviewer

(C) A job applicant   (D) A headhunter

Q2. Where is the speaker located?

(A) New York   (B) Singapore

(C) Barcelona   (D) Perth

Q3. What will the listener most likely do next?

(A) Take a personality test

(B) Propose some sales strategies

(C) Talk about her capabilities and experience

(D) Sign an offer letter

解題分析

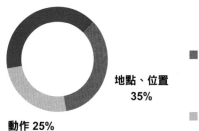

身分 40%

地點、位置 35%

動作 25%

■ 身分 40%　第一個問題是 who 開頭，很明顯是在問講者的「身分」，聽的時候要將注意力集中在能夠判斷身分的線索。

■ 地點、位置 35%　第二題是 where 開頭的問句，後面也出現 located 這個字，很明顯都跟「地點、位置」有關，可預期接下來會聽到講者所在地的資訊。

■ 動作 25%　很明顯的，第三題的重點是在詢問聽者接下來會「做什麼」，因此預測接下來會聽到聽者即將進行的「動作」。

聽稿

（AU / W）Thank you very much for coming today, Ms. Wilson. As you're applying for our Product Marketer position, I'd like to explain the job responsibilities a bit. As a product expert, you'll need to coordinate and contribute to the creation of product-related information on our www.datasoft.com website, and to support our sales team. You'll closely work with sales reps to figure out what our clients' demands really are. This position reports into the Director of R&D and is based here New York. Some of the tasks you'll be doing include: to support product launch campaigns, monitor and respond to questions and comments on our online community, and most importantly perform competitive analysis. Okay, now I'd like to learn more about your background and skills. So what were you involved in the previous company?

中譯 （澳／女）威爾森小姐，非常感謝您今日抽空前來。既然您是要應徵我們產品經銷專員一職，我便大概向您說明一下此工作的主要職責。身為一位產品專家，您需要貢獻一己之力於創造並規劃我們網頁 www.datasoft.com 上的產品相關資訊，並與我們的銷售團隊互相合作。您將需要與業務代表密切合作以便了解客戶們的真正需求。此項職務是歸屬研究開發部的經理管轄，而此一辦公部門就正好設置於紐約這裡。您需要完成的工作包含協助產品發表活動、控管並回覆我們網路社群上的意見評論和疑難雜症，還有最重要的是彙整競爭分析。好了，現在讓我們來談談您的個人背景和專業技能吧！您上一份工作是從事何種的作業內容呢？

Q1. 講者最有可能是誰？（答案：B）
    (A) 產品經銷商   (B) 面試者
    (C) 工作申請者   (D) 工作仲介

Q2. 講者身處何地工作？（答案：A）
    (A) 紐約   (B) 新加坡
    (C) 巴塞隆納   (D) 柏斯

Q3. 聽者接下來最有可能做什麼？（答案：C）
    (A) 接受人格測驗   (B) 提出一些業務策略
    (C) 談論她的能力與經驗   (D) 簽署聘用信

解題技巧 處理長篇的獨白題，將全部的內容都聽懂是不必要的，題組僅問三題，因此要點應放在先掃描三題題目，再將要點放在聽「可以回答題目的關鍵點」上即可。而講者想要聽者注意的要點通常會加以「重音」強調，以便讓聽者知道那是重要之處，比方說此獨白：

（AU／W）Thank you very much for coming today, Ms. Wilson. As you're applying for our Product Marketer position, I'd like to explain the job responsibilities a bit. As a product expert, you'll need to coordinate and contribute to the creation of product-related information on our www.datasoft.com website, and to support our sales team. You'll closely work with sales reps to figure out what our clients' demands really are. This position reports into the Director of R&D and is based here New York. Some of the tasks you'll be doing include: to support product launch campaigns, monitor and respond to questions and comments on our online community, and most importantly perform competitive analysis. Okay, now I'd like to learn more about your background and skills. So what were you involved in the previous company?

如此僅專注在聽關鍵點的好處便是，僅以少量的資訊便可以得知八成的大概內容了。此獨白的幾個要點包括：面試官向申請者解釋職缺的內容、此職位的人要做的任務有哪些、老闆是誰、和工作地點等。這些要點也可能是會出題目之處。

利用獨白播放出來之前的幾秒空檔，很快地將題目先掃描一下，以便預期可能的獨白內容與要將注意力放在聽什麼要點上。

第一題

此題問的是「Who is most likely the speaker?」那麼便可判斷要聽到講者「身分」相關訊息以便回答。根據此關鍵句「Thank you very much for coming today, Ms. Wilson. As you're applying for our Product Marketer position, I'd like to explain the job responsibilities a bit.」可聽出，會歡迎面試者且還先解釋工作內容的人，應該是「面試者」較為合理，故選 (B)「An interviewer」為最佳答案。

各選項解析

- 選項 (A)「A product vendor」、選項 (C)「A job applicant」或選項 (D)「A headhunter」都不是會解釋工作內容與需求的人，故不選。

第二題

此題問的是「Where is the speaker located?」那麼便要聽出可判斷講者身處「何地」的相關資訊以便回答。根據此關鍵句「This position reports into the Director of R&D and is based here New York.」可聽出講者也是身在紐約辦公室，故選 (A)「New York」為最佳答案。

各選項解析

- 選項 (B)「Singapore」、選項 (C)「Barcelona」與選項 (D)「Perth」都沒有在獨白內被提及，故不選。

第三題

此題問的是「What will the listener most likely do next?」那麼便可判斷要聽到講者接下來會「做什麼」相關資訊以便回答。根據此關鍵句「Okay, now I'd like to learn more about your background and skills. So what were you involved in the previous company?」可聽出講者是希望聽者可做個自我介紹，故選 (C)「Talk about her capabilities and experience」為最佳答案。

各選項解析

- 選項 (A)「Take a personality test」、選項 (B)「Propose some sales strategies」與選項 (D)「Sign an offer letter」都沒有在獨白中被提及，故不選。

關鍵字彙

apply for ph 申請
position [pə`zɪʃən] n 職位
responsibility [rɪˌspɑnsə`bɪlətɪ] n 責任
coordinate [ko`ɔrdn̩et] v 協調、整合
creation [krɪ`eʃən] n 發明物
launch [lɔntʃ] v 上市
campaign [kæm`pen] n 活動、戰役
comment [`kɑmɛnt] n 意見
perform [pɚ`fɔrm] v 表現、呈現
competitive [kəm`pɛtətɪv] a 競爭的
analysis [ə`næləsɪs] n 分析
involve [ɪn`vɑlv] v 從事、涉及

攻略 2 ｜ 業務經驗分享

Q1. **What is the speaker talking about?**

(A) Learning approaches

(B) Environmental crises

(C) His experience as a leader

(D) Market trends

Q2. **How does the speaker want his members to react when encountering problems?**

(A) Wait for assistance

(B) Feel panic

(C) Ask others to provide solutions

(D) Find answers independently

Q3. **What important skill does the speaker want workers to develop?**

(A) Strategic thinking skill

(B) English skill

(C) Negotiation skill

(D) Problem-solving skill

解題分析

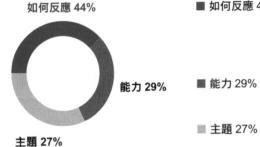

如何反應 44%

能力 29%

主題 27%

■ 如何反應 44%

第二題的題目較長，但可以從開頭的 how 快速抓出題問的是某種「方式」，根據句子後面的 react，得知整句的重點為面對困難時要「如何反應」，並預期接下來會聽到選項中所列出的反應。

■ 能力 29%

第三題的重點是在詢問講者想要工作者培養什麼樣的「能力」，可判斷接下來會聽到與選項中能力相關的訊息。

■ 主題 27%

第一題主要是詢問講者在説什麼，因此在聽的時候要集中注意力在講者説話的「主題」上。

聽稿

（CA/ **M**）Yes, let me share with you some of my past experience. In my past position, I was part of a software project team. I was the project leader and worked with the other ten members to plan and manage the schedule and budget of software development projects. Of course, from time to time my team members came to me and asked all sorts of problems. Well, at first I thought it was tempting to give them the answers to their problems. But eventually I realized that when I gave my team members answers, I made them dependent on me, not dependent on themselves. So afterwards instead of solving problems for them, I encouraged them to develop their own problem skills simply because I didn't want to take away their power.

中譯（加 / 男）是的，讓我來跟各位分享我過去的一些經驗。在我以往的職務中，我曾擔任過軟體專案的團隊成員。我是專案的負責人，與另外十位同事一起規劃並管理軟體發展專案的進度和預算。起初，針對夥伴們所遇到的各式疑難雜症，我認為直接給予答案是最恰當的選擇。但最終卻體會到反而在那樣的過程中，造就了團員們對我的依賴性，致使他們無法以獨立思考的模式運作。於是，與其直接幫他們解決問題，我決定鼓勵他們培養獨自應對的能力，好讓自己不再繼續剝奪夥伴們發展潛能的機會。

Q1. 講者在講些什麼？（答案：C）

(A) 學習方式   (B) 環境隱憂

(C) 他的領導經驗   (D) 市場趨勢

Q2. 當遇到問題時，講者想要他的同仁如何應對？（答案：D）

(A) 等待協助   (B) 感到驚慌

(C) 請他人提供解決辦法   (D) 獨立找出答案

Q3. 講者想要同仁具備什麼重要的能力？（答案：D）

(A) 策略思考能力   (B) 英文能力

(C) 談判能力   (D) 問題解決能力

解題技巧準備要聽獨白之前要先有的體認是，不要想了解全部的內容，因這些內容也不見得是真的，考試的目的僅是要測驗考生是否有專注力，可以專注在「回答問題」即可。因此若考生可以先很快地將三道題目掃描一下，知道要聽的「關鍵點」有哪些，專心地聽可以回答題目的關鍵點就好，自然有較高的機會可以正確地答題。而這些會考的重要資訊，自然也可能會是「加強重音」來強調：

（CA / M）Yes, let me share with you some of my past experience. In my past position, I was part of a software project team. I was the project leader and worked with the other ten members to plan and manage the schedule and budget of software development projects. Of course, from time to time my team members came to me and asked all sorts of problems. Well, at first I thought it was tempting to give them the answers to their problems. But eventually I realized that when I gave my team members answers, I made them dependent on me, not dependent on themselves. So afterwards instead of solving problems for them, I encouraged them to develop their own problem skills simply because I didn't want to take away their power.

聽取了幾個要點之後，便可以了解關於此獨白的八成要點了，包括：講者在介紹自己的經驗，之前當過專案經理，若部屬遇到問題就由他來解決的話，部屬便沒機會練習解決問題之能力，因此講者希望問題是由部屬自己想辦法解決。由此可知，要了解大概內容只要專心地聽關鍵點即可喔！

利用獨白播放出來之前的幾秒空檔，很快地將題目先掃描一下，以便預期可能的獨白內容與要將注意力放在聽什麼要點上。

第一題

此題問的是「What is the speaker talking about?」那麼便可判斷要聽到講者在講的「主題」相關資訊以便回答。根據此關鍵句「Yes, let me share with you some of my past experience. In my past position, I was part of a software project team. I was the project leader...」可聽出他是要分享他的過去經驗，而過去經驗是當過專案經理，故選 (C)「His experience as a leader」為最佳答案。

各選項解析

• 選項 (A)「Learning approaches」、選項 (B)「Environmental crises」與選項 (D)「Market trends」都沒有在獨白中被提及，故不選。

第二題

此題問的是「How does the speaker want his members to react when encountering problems?」那麼便可判斷要聽到講者希望同仁遇到問題要「如何反應」相關訊息以便回答。根據此關係句「I realized that when I gave my team members answers, I made them dependent on me, not dependent on themselves.」可聽出，講者其實是不想要同仁遇到問題就靠他來解決，而是希望他們靠自己解決問題，故選 (D)「Find answers independently」為最佳答案。

各選項解析

• 選項 (A)「Wait for assistance」、選項 (B)「Feel panic」和選項 (C)「Ask others to provide solutions」都不是講者期望同仁做的事，故不選。

第三題

此題問的是「What important skill does the speaker want workers to develop?」那麼便可判斷要聽到講者想要員工培養的「能力」為何，以便回答。根據此關鍵句「So afterwards instead of solving problems for them, I encouraged them to develop their own problem skills...」可聽出講者是希望員工培養「解決問題」的能力，故選 (D)「Problem-solving skill」為最佳答案。

各選項解析

• 選項 (A)「Strategic thinking skill」、選項 (B)「English skill」與選項 (C)「Negotiation skill」都沒在獨白中被提及，故不選。

關鍵字彙

project [ˈprɑdʒɛkt] n 專案
manage [ˈmænɪdʒ] v 掌管、管控
budget [ˈbʌdʒɪt] n 預算
development [dɪˈvɛləpmənt] n 開發、發展
eventually [ɪˈvɛntʃuəlɪ] ad 最後地
dependent [dɪˈpɛndənt] a 依賴的
encourage [ɪnˈkɝɪdʒ] v 鼓勵
simply [ˈsɪmplɪ] ad 僅是、簡單地

Q1. Who is most likely the caller?

(A) A retired employee   (B) A job candidate

(C) A customer   (D) A freelancer

Q2. What is the purpose of Vivian's call?

(A) To state her interest in the job position   (B) To ask for a promotion

(C) To reschedule an appointment   (D) To turn down a job offer

Q3. What would the speaker like to work as?

(A) Assistant   (B) Accountant

(C) Chief editor   (D) Waiter

解題分析

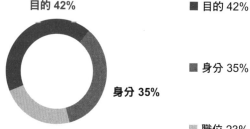

目的 42%

身分 35%

職位 23%

■ 目的 42%　第二個問題的關鍵在 purpose 這個字，詢問的是一位名叫 Vivian 的人打電話來的「目的」，因此聽的時候要特別注意是否有表明這樣的內容。

■ 身分 35%　第一題為 who 開頭問句，問來電者是什麼人，也就是說接下來很有可能在獨白中聽到對方的「身分」或是可以幫助判斷的相關資訊。

■ 職位 23%　第三題的意思是詢問講者想要做什麼樣的工作，根據題目的四個選項判斷，可以猜測接下來在獨白中可以聽到講者所想要擔任的「職位」。

聽稿

（AU / Ⓦ）This message is for Mr. Thompson please. Hello, Mr. Thompson, this is Vivian Kelly. We had a discussion about the chief editor position last Wednesday and I'm calling to check if I could provide any further information to help you decide. Well, I'd like to emphasize that with my ten years of experience working in both online and print publishing, I do know how to save you thousands of dollars by working effectively with freelancers. Also just as I mentioned in our discussion, I'm able to stay focused in stressful situations. I'm passionate about editing and confident that I'll be the best candidate for this chief editor position. I can be reached at 483-5837 at any time and I'm looking forward to your reply. Thank you once again, Mr. Thompson.

中譯

（澳／女）此通留言是要轉給湯普遜先生的，謝謝。您好，湯普遜先生，我是薇薇安‧凱莉。上個星期三我們討論了有關總編輯的職缺，而我打來是想詢問您是否還需要我提供任何更進一步的詳細資料。我依然要向您強調，以過去十年我所擁有的線上和印刷出版業的相關經歷，我知道要如何有效地透過與自由接案者們合作，幫助您節省幾千元以上的成本開銷。另外就如同我在面談時提到的，我是個抗壓性與專注力都高的人才，對於編輯這一途不只有足夠的熱忱，更有足夠的信心，相信自己會是所有應徵者裡最適合擔任總編輯的不二人選。我的電話號碼為 483-5837，請於任何您方便的時段與我聯繫，我會靜候您的回覆。再次感謝您給予機會，湯普遜先生。

Q1. 打電話者可能是誰？（答案：**B**）

(A) 退休員工   (B) 應徵工作者

(C) 客戶   (D) 自由工作者

Q2. 薇薇安打電話的目的為何？（答案：**A**）

(A) 說明她對工作職缺的興趣   (B) 要求升遷

(C) 改會議日期   (D) 拒絕工作機會

Q3. 講者想做什麼工作？（答案：**C**）

(A) 助理   (B) 會計師

(C) 總編輯   (D) 服務生

解題技巧

與其想將獨白內的每個字都聽懂，還想將每句都翻譯一下，還不如將注意力放在僅聽「可以回答問題的關鍵點」上即可。而這些可以回答問題的關鍵點，也通常會以「加強重音」來強調：

（AU／W）This message is for Mr. Thompson please. Hello, Mr. Thompson, this is Vivian Kelly. We had a discussion about the chief editor position last Wednesday and I'm calling to check if I could provide any further information to help you decide. Well, I'd like to emphasize that with my ten years of experience working in both online and print publishing, I do know how to save you thousands of dollars by working effectively with freelancers. Also just as I mentioned in our discussion, I'm able to stay focused in stressful situations. I'm passionate about editing and confident that I'll be the best candidate for this chief editor position. I can be reached at 483-5837 at any time and I'm looking forward to your reply. Thank you once again, Mr. Thompson.

聽了幾個關鍵點之後，便可判斷此電話留言的八成內容了，包括：講者重申她對總編輯職缺的興趣，並有能力可以幫公司省錢，並再次強調她會是最佳人選的原因，並希望 Thompson 先生可以回應。由此可聽出，將焦點放在聽「關鍵點」上，比想逐字翻譯更可以抓到整篇的大意喔！

利用獨白播放出來之前的幾秒空檔，很快地將題目先掃描一下，以便預期可能的獨白內容與要將注意力放在聽什麼要點上。

第一題

此題問的是「Who is most likely the caller?」，那麼便判斷要聽出打電話留言者「會是誰」之相關資訊以便回答。根據此關鍵句「Hello, Mr. Thompson, this is Vivian Kelly. We had a discussion about the chief editor position last Wednesday and I'm calling to check if I could provide any further information to help you decide.」可聽出講者是打電話追蹤面談之後續進度的，故應是一位「求職者」較為合理，故選 (B)「A job candidate」為最佳答案。

各選項解析

• 選項 (A)「A retired employee」、選項 (C)「A customer」與選項 (D)「A freelancer」都不會是追蹤面談後續之人，故不選。

第二題

此題問的是「What is the purpose of Vivian's call?」，可判斷要聽出 Vivian 打此電話的「目的」相關資訊以便回答。根據此關鍵句「I'd like to emphasize that with my ten years of experience working in both online and print publishing, I do know how to save you thousands of dollars by working effectively with freelancers.」，可聽出講者是要強調她有相關經驗與能力可以做好這份工作，並讓公司獲利，故選 (A)「To state her interest in the job position」為最佳答案。

各選項解析

• 選項 (B)「To ask for a promotion」、選項 (C)「To reschedule an appointment」與選項 (D)「To turn down a job offer」都沒有在獨白中被提及，故不選。

第三題

此題問的是「What would the speaker like to work as?」，那麼便可判斷要聽到講者想做的「職位」相關資訊以便回答。根據此關鍵句「I'm passionate about editing and confident that I'll be the best candidate for this chief editor position.」可聽出她是想擔任「總編輯」的職務，故選 (C)「Chief editor」為最佳答案。

各選項解析

• 選項 (A)「Assistant」、選項 (B)「Accountant」與選項 (D)「Waiter」都沒有在留言獨白中被提及，故不選。

關鍵字彙

discussion [dɪˋskʌʃən] n 討論
chief editor [tʃif ˋɛdɪtɚ] n 總編輯
emphasize [ˋɛmfəˌsaɪz] v 強調
effectively [ɪˋfɛktɪvlɪ] ad 有效地
freelancer [ˋfriˌlænsɚ] n 自由職業者
mention [ˋmɛnʃən] v 提及
stressful [ˋstrɛsfəl] a 有壓力的
passionate [ˋpæʃənɪt] a 熱心的、有熱忱的
candidate [ˋkændədet] n 候選人

Unit 6 機場廣播類

Q1. **Where is this talk most likely taking place?**

(A) In a conference room   (B) On an airplane

(C) In a classroom   (D) On the street

Q2. **Where are the listeners going?**

(A) Montreal   (B) Taipei

(C) Tokyo   (D) Houston

Q3. **What will probably happen in ten minutes?**

(A) Another flight attendant will talk   (B) Passengers will change a flight

(C) Snacks and drinks will be served   (D) Duty free shops will be closed

解題分析

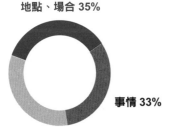

地點、場合 35%

事情 33%

目的地 32%

■ 地點、場合 35%   第一題首字為 where，很明確是在詢問此段獨白發生的「地點」，推測可以在獨白中聽到地點相關線索。

■ 事情 33%   第三個問題主要是在詢問接下來的十分鐘以內會「發生什麼事」，也就是要將注意力集中在聽即將發生的「事情」上。

■ 目的地 32%   第二題也是 where 開頭，問的是聽者要前往的「地點」，預期接下來會聽到選項中出現的地名。

聽稿

（UK / Ⓜ）Good evening passengers. This is Captain Jones speaking. On behalf of Sky Airline, I'd like to welcome all passengers on Flight SA487 flying from Tokyo to Houston. We're cruising at an altitude of 20,000 feet. The weather looks nice. We're expecting to land in Houston at five in the morning local time, which is approximately twenty minutes ahead of schedule. The weather in Houston is clear and sunny. Our cabin crew will be coming around in ten minutes to offer you a light snack and beverage. I'll talk to you again before we reach our destination. Until then, please sit back, relax and enjoy the rest of the flight. Once again, thank you for flying with Sky Airline.

中譯 （英 / **男**）各位乘客晚安。我是機長瓊斯，僅代表所有天空航空的機組成員，歡迎大家搭乘 SA487 由東京飛往休士頓的班機。我們正飛行於兩萬英呎的高度，外面天氣宜人。我們將於當地時間早上五點抵達休士頓，比原先預計的飛行時間提早了二十分鐘。休士頓的天氣是萬里無雲的晴天。我們的機艙人員會在十分鐘後提供各位一些簡單的點心和飲品。我會於快要抵達目的地時再次通知各位。在這段期間，請各位繼續輕鬆地享受接下來的飛行時光。再次感謝您搭乘天空航空。

Q1. 此獨白最有可能在何處聽到？（答案：**B**）

(A) 會議室　　　　　　　　　　　　　　(B) 飛機上

(C) 教室內　　　　　　　　　　　　　　(D) 街上

Q2. 聽眾要前往哪裡？（答案：**D**）

(A) 蒙特婁　　　　　　　　　　　　　　(B) 台北

(C) 東京　　　　　　　　　　　　　　　(D) 休士頓

Q3. 十分鐘之後可能發生何事？（答案：**C**）

(A) 另一位空姐會講話　　　　　　　　　(B) 旅客會換班機

(C) 點心和飲料會被送上　　　　　　　　(D) 免稅商店會關起來

解題技巧 心裡有準備要聽「關鍵點」即可，而非想要每字每句都聽懂。因這些關鍵點才是真正題組會想出題之處，也因此若可能的話，在聽到獨白前可先將三道題目掃描一下，以便知道要聽的「關鍵點」有哪些。另外，為了強調並讓聽者容易抓到要點，講者想傳遞的主要訊息自然可能以「加強重音」的方式呈現：

（UK / **M**）Good evening passengers. This is Captain Jones speaking. On behalf of Sky Airline, I'd like to welcome all passengers on Flight SA487 flying from Tokyo to Houston. We're cruising at an altitude of 20,000 feet. The weather looks nice. We're expecting to land in Houston at five in the morning local time, which is approximately twenty minutes ahead of schedule. The weather in Houston is clear and sunny. Our cabin crew will be coming around in ten minutes to offer you a light snack and beverage. I'll talk to you again before we reach our destination. Until then, please sit back, relax and enjoy the rest of the flight. Once again, thank you for flying with Sky Airline.

抓出此獨白的幾個要點後，便可歸納以下幾個摘要了：機長在歡迎乘客，並報告要飛往休士頓班機的狀況，如抵達時間、在機上的活動等，並希望乘客有個愉快的旅程。這樣的主要資訊並不需要逐字聽懂就可以抓出了，因此，考生應培養的是「將專注力放在聽關鍵點上」的能力喔！

利用獨白播放出來之前的幾秒空檔，很快地將題目先掃描一下，以便預期可能的獨白內容與要將注意力放在聽什麼要點上。

第一題

此題問的是「Where is this talk most likely taking place?」，便可判斷要聽到此獨白可能聽到之「地點、場合」相關資訊以便回答。根據此關鍵句「Good evening passengers. This is Captain Jones speaking.」可聽出此獨白是機長在報告，因此地點應該是在「飛機上」較為合理，故選 (B)「On an airplane」為最佳答案。

各選項解析

• 選項 (A)「In a conference room」、選項 (C)「In a classroom」與選項 (D)「On the street」都不會是有機長報告之處，故不選。

第二題

此題問的是「Where are the listeners going?」，那麼便可判斷要聽到聽眾正要前往「何處、地點」相關資訊以便回答。根據此關鍵句「I'd like to welcome all passengers on Flight SA487 flying from Tokyo to Houston.」可聽出此班機上的乘客是要自東京飛往休士頓，故選 (D)「Houston」為最佳答案。

各選項解析

• 選項 (A)「Montreal」、選項 (B)「Taipei」與選項 (C)「Tokyo」都不是此班機要飛往之處，故不選。

第三題

此題問的是「What will probably happen in ten minutes?」，那麼便可判斷要聽到十分鐘後可能會發生之「事情」之相關資訊以便回答。根據此關鍵句「Our cabin crew will be coming around in ten minutes to offer you a light snack and beverage.」可聽出會有小點心和飲料。故選 (C) 為最佳答案。

關鍵字彙

captain [ˈkæptɪn] n 機長
on behalf of ph 代表
cruise [kruz] v 航行、行駛
altitude [ˈæltəˌtjud] n 高度
expect [ɪkˈspɛkt] v 預期
approximately [əˈprɑksəmɪtlɪ] ad 大約地、約略
beverage [ˈbɛvərɪdʒ] n 飲料
destination [ˌdɛstəˈneʃən] n 目的地

Q1. Who is most likely the speaker?

(A) A passenger

(B) A cabin crew

(C) A doctor

(D) An officer

Q2. What is being announced?

(A) Company history

(B) Movie options

(C) Weather conditions

(D) Security equipment on the plane

Q3. What is most likely going to happen next?

(A) The plane will take off

(B) The pilot will give a speech

(C) A band will play music

(D) Passengers will go home

解題分析

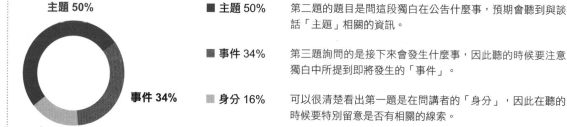

主題 50%

第二題的題目是問這段獨白在公告什麼事，預期會聽到與談話「主題」相關的資訊。

事件 34%

第三題詢問的是接下來會發生什麼事，因此聽的時候要注意獨白中所提到即將發生的「事件」。

身分 16%

可以很清楚看出第一題是在問講者的「身分」，因此在聽的時候要特別留意是否有相關的線索。

聽稿

（AU / Ⓦ）Attention please, all passengers. Please now direct your attention to the monitors in front of your seats as we review the emergency procedures. There are six emergency exits on this plane. The nearest exit may be behind you, so please take a minute to locate the exit closest to you. If the cabin experiences sudden pressure loss, please stay calm. Oxygen masks will drop down from your seats. If you're traveling with children, make sure that your own mask is on before assisting your children. May we ask you to make sure that all carry-on luggage is stowed away safely during the flight. Now we're waiting for take-off, and please take a moment to review the safety information card in the seat pocket in front of you. Thank you and wish you have a safe and pleasant journey.

中譯　（澳／女）所有旅客請注意，請注意您前方座椅上的螢幕顯示，我們將再次宣導緊急安全程序。這架飛機總共有六個逃生門，離您座位最近的逃生門有可能位於您的後方，請各位稍微查看一下離您最近的逃生門所在位置。倘若機艙突然出現瞬間壓力失衡的情形，請各位務必保持冷靜，您座位上方的氧氣罩將會自動掉下來。如果您身邊有孩童，請您先確保自己的氧氣罩已戴妥，隨後再為孩童掛上。請您於飛行期間確保您的隨身行李皆已妥善地放好。現在請您花點時間閱讀放置於您前方椅袋中的飛機安全資訊卡並稍待片刻，我們即將起飛。感謝您的搭乘，祝您旅途愉快。

Q1. 講者最有可能是誰？（答案：B）

(A) 旅客　　　　　　　　　　　　(B) 航班機組員

(C) 醫生　　　　　　　　　　　　(D) 警員

Q2. 此獨白公告何事？（答案：D）

(A) 公司歷史　　　　　　　　　　(B) 電影選擇

(C) 天氣狀況　　　　　　　　　　(D) 機上安全設備

Q3. 接下來可能發生何事？（答案：A）

(A) 班機會起飛　　　　　　　　　(B) 機長會演講

(C) 樂團會演奏音樂　　　　　　　(D) 旅客會回家去

解題技巧　心裡已有準備要將注意力集中到「聽該聽的要點」就好，不要分散到整個獨白的每個字句上！這些「該聽的關鍵點」便是有可能出試題之處呀。若考生可以事先將三個題目掃描一次，知道題目想問些什麼，便可以將專心聽「可以回答題目的要點」就好了。而這些要點處極有可能被「加強重音」來強調：

（AU／W）Attention please, all passengers. Please now direct your attention to the monitors in front of your seats as we review the emergency procedures. There are six emergency exits on this plane. The nearest exit may be behind you, so please take a minute to locate the exit closest to you. If the cabin experiences sudden pressure loss, please stay calm. Oxygen masks will drop down from your seats. If you're traveling with children, make sure that your own mask is on before assisting your children. May we ask you to make sure that all carry-on luggage is stowed away safely during the flight. Now we're waiting for take-off, and please take a moment to review the safety information card in the seat pocket in front of you. Thank you and wish you have a safe and pleasant journey.

大概抓出要點便可以整理出一些關於此獨白的摘要了，包括：此機上組員要跟乘客報告安全設施，像是安全門位置與氧氣面罩的使用等，飛機起降時行李要放固定位置。如此，聽「關鍵點」比翻譯完整篇，更可以對此獨白有個全面性的了解。

利用獨白播放出來之前的幾秒空檔，很快地將題目先掃描一下，以便預期可能的獨白內容與要將注意力放在聽什麼要點上。

第一題

此題問的是「Who is most likely the speaker?」，那麼便可判斷要聽到講者可能的「身分、職稱」等相關資訊以便回答。根據此關鍵句「Attention please, all passengers. Please now direct your attention to the monitors in front of your seats as we review the emergency procedures.」便可聽出，會報告機上安全規定的人，應是飛機上的「機組人員」較為合理，故選 (B)「A cabin crew」為最佳答案。

各選項解析

- 選項 (A)「A passenger」、選項 (C)「A doctor」與選項 (D)「An officer」都不會是報告飛機上安全規則之人，故不選。

第二題

此題問的是「What is being announced?」，我們便可判斷要聽到所報告的「主題」相關資訊以便回答。根據數個關鍵點「There are six emergency exits on this plane... If the cabin experiences sudden pressure loss, please stay calm. Oxygen masks will drop down from your seats...」可聽出講者在介紹最近的安全出口，氧氣面罩……等物，那麼便是在介紹機上的安全設備之位置與用法，故選 (D)「Security equipment on the plane」為最佳答案。

各選項解析

- 選項 (A)「Company history」、選項 (B)「Movie options」與選項 (C)「Weather conditions」都沒有在獨白中被提及，故不選。

第三題

此題問的是「What is most likely going to happen next?」，便可判斷要聽到接下來可能發生「什麼事」相關訊息以便回答。根據此關鍵句「Now we're waiting for take-off, and please take a moment to review the safety information card in the seat pocket in front of you.」可聽出接下來就是稍後要起飛了，故選 (A)「The plane will take off.」為最佳答案。

各選項解析

- 選項 (B)「The pilot will give a speech.」、選項 (C)「A band will play music.」與選項 (D)「Passengers will go home.」都沒有在獨白內被提及，故不選。

關鍵字彙

direct [dəˋrɛkt] v 導向
attention [əˋtɛnʃən] n 注意力
monitor [ˋmɑnətɚ] n 螢幕
emergency [ɪˋmɝdʒənsɪ] n 緊急事件
procedure [prəˋsidʒɚ] n 程序、步驟
locate [loˋket] v 位於
sudden [ˋsʌdn̩] a 突發的、突然的
pressure [ˋprɛʃɚ] n 壓力
calm [kɑm] a 穩定的
assist [əˋsɪst] v 協助
stow away ph 收藏
pleasant [ˋplɛzənt] a 高興的、愉悅的
journey [ˋdʒɝnɪ] n 旅途

攻略 3 | 到達目的地廣播

Airline	From	To	Exit
Sky Air	Chicago	Jersey City	7A
Fun Airline	Houston	Jersey City	9F
Bird Skyline	Tokyo	Jersey City	1Z
Blue Air	Barcelona	Jersey City	4X

Q1. Where is the talk probably taking place?

(A) On the airplane   (B) In a restaurant

(C) In a shopping mall   (D) At a coffee shop

Q2. What does the speaker ask listeners to do?

(A) Say goodbye to each other   (B) Grab their suitcases immediately

(C) Walk out directly   (D) Remain seated

新 **Q3. Look at the chart. Which exit will the passengers of this flight leave from?**

(A) 7A   (B) 9F

(C) 1Z   (D) 4X

解題分析

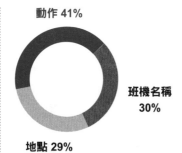

動作 41%

班機名稱 30%

地點 29%

■ 動作 41%   第二題詢問講者請聽者做什麼事，所以在聽的時候，可以特別留意獨白中提到的相關「動作」或是指令。

■ 班機名稱 30%   第三題的題目是在問某一班飛機的乘客要從哪一個出口離開，可以看到選項都是出口的編號，所以預期會在獨白中聽到「班機的名稱」，然後對應到表格的出口編號，找出答案。

■ 地點 29%   第一題的開頭是 where，詢問的是獨白的「地點」，因此預期可以在這段獨白中聽到跟地點有關的線索。

聽稿   （CA／M）Ladies and gentlemen, welcome to the Jersey International Airport. Local time in Jersey City is 5:05 p.m., and the temperature is 25 degree Celsius. For your safety, please remain seated with your seat belt fastened until the Captain turns off the "Fasten Seat Belt" sign. This will indicate that the plane has parked at the gate safely and it's then safe for passengers to stand up and move about. If you require special assistance, please inform our crew members. They will then be pleased to assist you. On behalf of the entire crew, I'd like to thank you for flying with Fun Airline on this trip and we're looking forward to seeing you on board again in the near future. Have a wonderful stay in Jersey City.

（加/**男**）各位先生小姐們，歡迎蒞臨澤西國際機場。澤西市目前的時間是下午五點零五分，氣溫是攝氏二十五度。為了您的安全，請您繼續待在座位上並繫好安全帶，直到機長將安全帶警示燈號解除；這代表飛機已經安全地停妥於登機門前，而乘客也能開始起身準備下機。倘若您需要其他的協助，請通知機組人員，他們會很樂意地為您服務。僅代表所有機艙組員，感謝您此次搭乘樂航空，希望很快能再次為您服務。祝大家在澤西市有個美好的旅程。

班機	來自	前往	出口
天空航空	芝加哥	澤西市	7A
樂航空	休士頓	澤西市	9F
翱翔航空	東京	澤西市	1Z
藍航空	巴塞隆納	澤西市	4X

Q1. 此獨白最有可能是在何處聽到？（答案：**A**）

(A) 飛機上　　　　　　　　　　　　(B) 餐廳

(C) 購物中心　　　　　　　　　　　(D) 咖啡廳

Q2. 講者要求聽眾做什麼？（答案：**D**）

(A) 互相道別　　　　　　　　　　　(B) 馬上拿取行李

(C) 直接走出去　　　　　　　　　　(D) 留在座位上

新 Q3. 請看表格。此班機旅客會由哪一個出口離開？（答案：**B**）

(A) 7A　　　　　　　　　　　　　　(B) 9F

(C) 1Z　　　　　　　　　　　　　　(D) 4X

解題技巧 不要試圖將每個單字都聽懂，或是想翻譯每個字。因為一篇獨白中不是每個字重要性都一樣的，且會英翻中也不等於抓得到要點以回答問題喔！考生應做的事是，將專注力放在聽「可以會答問題的關鍵點」上即可，幸運的是這些可能考出的關鍵要點通常會以「加強重音」來強調喔：

（CA / **M**）Ladies and gentlemen, welcome to the Jersey International Airport. Local time in Jersey City is 5:05 p.m., and the temperature is 25 degree Celsius. For your safety, please remain seated with your seat belt fastened until the Captain turns off the "Fasten Seat Belt" sign. This will indicate that the plane has parked at the gate safely and it's then safe for passengers to stand up and move about. If you require special assistance, please inform our crew members. They will then be pleased to assist you. On behalf of the entire crew, I'd like to thank you for flying with Fun Airline on this trip and we're looking forward to seeing you on board again in the near future. Have a wonderful stay in Jersey City.

從此獨白抓出關鍵點後，便可以了解大約八成的內容了，包括：機長在降落機場前的報告，提到請大家坐在座位上繫好安全帶，若有需要可通知空服員，最後感謝大家的搭乘。如此可看出要了解大意，其實只要聽出並抓住「關鍵點」就可以了，而非逐字翻譯喔！

利用獨白播放出來之前的幾秒空檔，很快地將題目先掃描一下，以便預期可能的獨白內容與要將注意力放在聽什麼要點上。

第一題

此題問的是「Where is the talk probably taking place?」，那麼便可判斷要聽到此獨白可能發生之「位置、地點」相關資訊以便回答。根據此關鍵句「Ladies and gentlemen, welcome to the Jersey International Airport. Local time in Jersey City is 5:05 p.m., and the temperature is 25 degree Celsius.」，可聽出是機長報告說已經抵達機場，並說明當地時間與溫度，這些應是機長在機上跟乘客所做的說明較為合理，故選 (A)「On the airplane」為最佳答案。

各選項解析

• 選項 (B)「In a restaurant」、選項 (C)「In a shopping mall」與選項 (D)「At a coffee shop」都不會是聽到此類報告之處，故不選。

第二題

此題問的是「What does the speaker ask listeners to do?」，那麼，我們可判斷要聽到講者要求聽眾「所做之事」相關資訊以便回答。根據此關鍵句「For your safety, please remain seated with your seat belt fastened until the Captain turns off the "Fasten Seat Belt" sign.」可聽出是要先留在座位上，故選 (D)「Remain seated」為最佳答案。

各選項解析

• 選項 (A)「Say goodbye to each other」、選項 (B)「Grab their suitcases immediately」與選項 (C)「Walk out directly」都沒有在獨白中被提及，故不選。

新 第三題

此題目要搭配表格，先看到題目問的是「Which exit will the passengers of this flight leave from?」，判斷要聽到此班機的公司名稱，才有辦法對照表格看此班機是要停靠在哪個出口。根據獨白中的此關鍵句「I'd like to thank you for flying with Fun Airline on this trip...」可聽出此班機是「Fun Airline」，那麼對照表格，Fun Airline 是停靠在 9F 出口，故乘客應也是會由 9F 出口出來較為合理，故選 (B)「9F」為最佳答案。

各選項解析

• 選項 (A)「7A」、選項 (C)「1Z」與選項 (D)「4X」都是其他班機的出口，故不選。

關鍵字彙

temperature [ˋtɛmprətʃɚ] n 溫度
remain [rɪˋmen] v 保持
indicate [ˋɪndəˌket] v 指出
safely [ˋseflɪ] ad 安全地
assistance [əˋsɪstəns] n 協助
inform [ɪnˋfɔrm] v 通知
entire [ɪnˋtaɪr] a 全部的
wonderful [ˋwʌndɚfəl] a 很棒的

攻略 1 | 訓練課程公告

Q1. Who are listening to this talk most likely?

(A) Pedestrians   (B) Clients

(C) Company employees   (D) High school students

Q2. What does the speaker emphasize in the talk?

(A) How to use e-mail systems correctly

(B) The ways to increase sales revenues

(C) Keeping good relationships with customers

(D) The importance of writing good e-mails

Q3. What does the speaker encourage listeners to do next?

(A) Write more e-mails   (B) Attend the training course

(C) Improve their English skills   (D) Take a good rest

解題分析

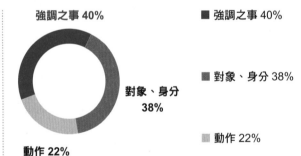

強調之事 40%

對象、身分 38%

動作 22%

■ 強調之事 40%

第二題的關鍵詞為 emphasize，問講者在這段獨白中「強調什麼事」，所以推測接下來會聽到特定內容被強調或是一再重複。

■ 對象、身分 38%

第一題問的是這一段獨白的聽眾是什麼人，也就是在問聽眾的「身分」，因此在聽的時候要特別留意相關資訊。

■ 動作 22%

第三題問的是講者鼓勵聽者做的事，因此可以猜測這段獨白裡會聽到講者提到某個「動作」，要聽眾去執行。

聽稿 （AU / W）Majority of people thought writing e-mails is just as easy as 123. They don't need to worry about spelling or punctuation. No need to check grammar. All they have to do is just type and send. That's it. Well, as a matter of fact, they are absolutely wrong. Our clients, vendors and business partners actually think that it really annoys them to receive e-mails with the wrong spelling and no punctuation. It seems as if the sender just doesn't care. No one wants to do business with a person who is sloppy and careless, right? All right, so that's why the company has decided to offer our employees a training course for e-mail writing next Friday afternoon. If you're interested in attending, please call Erin Well at extension 445 to enroll.

中譯

（澳／**女**）大多數的人們都認為寫電子郵件是一件輕而易舉的小事，因為他們不需要擔心錯別字和標點符號、也不需要檢查文法是否正確。他們只有打完內容並把信件傳送出去即可，就這麼簡單。事實上，這是一種錯誤的認知。對我們的客戶、供應商和商業夥伴來說，收到一封滿滿是錯別字和缺少標點符號的信件，會是一件極度惱人的事，就好像發信人對於此事不甚重視。沒有人會想跟粗枝大葉又敷衍了事的人合作，不是嗎？正因如此，所以本公司已決議於下週五下午為員工們開辦電子郵件書寫的訓練課程。若您有興趣參加，請直接聯絡艾琳‧威爾報名。她的分機是 445。

Q1. 誰最有可能在聽此獨白？（答案：**C**）
(A) 行人　　　　　　　　　　　　　(B) 客戶
(C) 公司員工　　　　　　　　　　(D) 高中生

Q2. 講者在談話中強調什麼？（答案：**D**）
(A) 如何正確地使用電郵系統　　　　(B) 增加業績的方式
(C) 與客戶保持良好關係　　　　　　(D) 寫好電子郵件的重要性

Q3. 講者鼓勵聽者要做什麼？（答案：**B**）
(A) 寫更多電郵　　　　　　　　　　(B) 參加訓練課程
(C) 增強英文能力　　　　　　　　　(D) 好好休息一下

解題技巧

考生通常會認為要聽到每個字，會翻譯每一句對聽力才有安全感，但事實上若將注意力分散到每個字上，還在腦中翻譯中文意思，反而會抓不到會考的要點呢！因此對應長篇聽力的策略應該是相反，不要分散注意力，而是要集中所有的精神專注在聽「會考的要點上」即可。可以先掃描題目、了解問題點，再專注在聽那三個問題的答案即可。而這些喜歡考的要點通常會特別以「加強重音」來強調：

（AU／**W**）Majority of people thought writing e-mails is just as easy as 123. They don't need to worry about spelling or punctuation. No need to check grammar. All they have to do is just type and send. That's it. Well, as a matter of fact, they are absolutely wrong. Our clients, vendors and business partners actually think that it really annoys them to receive e-mails with the wrong spelling and no punctuation. It seems as if the sender just doesn't care. No one wants to do business with a person who is sloppy and careless, right? All right, so that's why the company has decided to offer our employees a training course for e-mail writing next Friday afternoon. If you're interested in attending, please call Erin Well at extension 445 to enroll.

經過要點的擷取過程後，便可抓出幾個關於此獨白的幾個關鍵處了，包括：講者認為寫 e-mail 不非很簡單，大家不喜歡跟 e-mail 寫作很差的人做生意，因此辦了 e-mail 訓練課程，希望同仁來參與。如此可聽出，靠幾個「真正重要」的關鍵點，便可以了解大約八成的內容了，不用靠逐字翻譯也可達成呀！因此建議考生平時要多練習「聽出要點」的能力喔！

利用獨白播放出來之前的幾秒空檔，很快地將題目先掃描一下，以便預期可能的獨白內容與要將注意力放在聽什麼要點上。

此題問的是「Who are listening to this talk most likely?」，要聽到此獨白可能的「聽眾」會是誰相關資訊以便回答。根據此關鍵句「Our clients, vendors and business partners actually think that it really annoys them to receive e-mails with the wrong spelling and no punctuation.」，可聽出會寫電郵給客戶聯絡事情的人，應會是公司內部員工較為合理，故選 (C)「Company employees」為最佳答案。

各選項解析

- 選項 (A)「Pedestrians」、選項 (B)「Clients」與選項 (D)「High school students」都不會是在聽此「寫給客戶的電郵要專業」講題的人，故不選。

第二題

此題問的是「What does the speaker emphasize in the talk?」，那麼便可判斷要聽到講者所「強調之事」以便回答。根據此關鍵句「Majority of people thought writing e-mails is just as easy as 123... Well, as a matter of fact, they are absolutely wrong.」可聽出講者提出「認為寫電郵很簡單的人是大錯特錯」，意即「要將電郵寫好是很重要的」，故選 (D)「The importance of writing good e-mails」為最佳答案。

各選項解析

- 選項 (A)「How to use e-mail systems correctly」、選項 (B)「The ways to increase sales revenues」與選項 (C)「Keeping good relationships with customers」都沒有在獨白中提及，並非此講者強調之事，故不選。

第三題

此題問的是「What does the speaker encourage listeners to do next?」，判斷要聽到講者鼓勵聽眾「要做什麼事」之相關資訊以便回答。根據此關鍵句「... the company has decided to offer our employees a training course for e-mail writing next Friday afternoon. If you're interested..., please... to enroll.」，可聽出講者提及有電郵書寫相關訓練課程，要聽眾報名參加，故選 (B)「Attend the training course」為最佳答案。

各選項解析

- 選項 (A)「Write more e-mails」、選項 (C)「Improve their English skills」與選項 (D)「Take a good rest」都沒有在獨白中被提及，故不選。

關鍵字彙

majority [mə'dʒɔrətɪ] n 多數
punctuation [ˌpʌŋktʃu'eʃən] n 標點符號
absolutely ['æbsəˌlutlɪ] ad 絕對地、完全地
vendor ['vɛndɚ] n 廠商
annoy [ə'nɔɪ] v 惹惱、使厭煩
sloppy ['slɑpɪ] a 草率的
careless ['kɛrlɪs] a 粗心的
attend [ə'tɛnd] v 出席

攻略 2 ｜ 業務會議開場

Q1. **What is the purpose of this talk?**

    (A) To open a sales meeting   (B) To persuade clients

    (C) To announce a new policy   (D) To promote new products

Q2. **Who are listening to this talk most likely?**

    (A) Technical support engineers   (B) Sales and marketing personnel

    (C) Company investors   (D) Angry customers

Q3. **Who is Linda Smith most likely?**

    (A) A competitor   (B) A receptionist

    (C) A pre-sales engineer   (D) A marketing specialist

解題分析

身分、職稱 76%

目的 24%

■ 身分、職稱 76%

■ 目的 24%

第二題是 who 開頭，詢問聽眾是什麼人，也就是聽眾的「身分」，根據下方的選項可以得知，接下來聽到的內容要跟公司的職稱有關。

第三題也是 who 開頭的問句，在問一位名叫 Linda Smith 女子的「身分」，預期可能會在獨白中聽到跟此人職稱有關的訊息。

第一題的重點在於獨白的「目的」，因此接下來要聽到相關的內容，才能選擇答案。

聽稿

（CA／**M**）All right, guys. As I'd like to end the meeting by three, let's get started right away, okay? Well, you all know that our sales have been slower recently, right? We do need to take some proper actions to change this. And that's why we meet today to discuss our strategies for increasing sales. Linda Smith from marketing will be giving us an overview of what our major rivals are doing. After that, I'll present an analysis of some of the problems with our sales strategy at the moment. And finally, Peter Norman will lead the brainstorming session and hopefully we can come up with some constructive ideas. Also, we need to make some important decisions today. Okay, so now, let's get down to business.

（加 / 男）好了，各位。我希望能在三點以前把這場會議結束，所以我們何不直接開始吧？你們都知道我們近期的銷售處於頗為低靡的狀態，對吧？我們需要想些對策來突破此瓶頸。這就是為什麼我們今日在這裡舉行會議，討論如何提高銷售量的有效策略。行銷部門的琳達·史密斯會先提供本公司在市場上之主要競爭者的概述，然後我將開始分析我們當前行銷策略所碰上的問題。會議最後則有請彼得·諾曼帶領大家集思廣益，腦力激盪出一些有建設性的新見解，另外，我們必須在今日就做出一些重要的決定。那麼現在就讓我們直接進入正題吧。

Q1. 此獨白的主要目的為何？（答案：**A**）

(A) 為業務會議開場　　　　　　　　　　(B) 為說服客戶

(C) 為公布新政策　　　　　　　　　　　(D) 為推廣新產品

Q2. 誰最有可能是此獨白的聽眾？（答案：**B**）

(A) 技術支援工程師　　　　　　　　　　(B) 業務行銷人員

(C) 公司投資人　　　　　　　　　　　　(D) 生氣的客戶

Q3. 琳達·史密斯最有可能是誰？（答案：**D**）

(A) 競爭對手　　　　　　　　　　　　　(B) 接待人員

(C) 售前工程師　　　　　　　　　　　　(D) 行銷專員

解題技巧　與其想要將所有內容都聽懂，還不如將注意力放在「聽關鍵要點」即可，而這些講者想強調的關鍵要點，通常不會很快地帶過，而是會以講慢一點，或加強重音來強調：

（CA / **M**）All right, guys. As I'd like to end the meeting by three, let's get started right away, okay? Well, you all know that our sales have been slower recently, right? We do need to take some proper actions to change this. And that's why we meet today to discuss our strategies for increasing sales. Linda Smith from marketing will be giving us an overview of what our major rivals are doing. After that, I'll present an analysis of some of the problems with our sales strategy at the moment. And finally, Peter Norman will lead the brainstorming session and hopefully we can come up with some constructive ideas. Also, we need to make some important decisions today. Okay, so now, let's get down to business.

經過抓出上述的要點後，可以歸納出幾要關於此獨白的要點：講者在做會議開場，提到業績下滑所以請大家想策略來提升業績，接著會有不同人報告不同面向的議題，還會有腦力激盪的討論，最終希望可以做出些決定。如此要了解一篇獨白的約略內容，就是要靠「抓出關鍵點」的方式喔！

利用獨白播放出來之前的幾秒空檔，很快地將題目先掃描一下，以便預期可能的獨白內容與要將注意力放在聽什麼要點上。

第一題

此題目問的是「What is the purpose of this talk?」，那麼便可判斷要聽到此獨白的「目的」相關資訊以便回答。根據此關鍵句「As I'd like to end the meeting by three, let's get started right away, okay?」，可聽出講者說會議要三點前結束，因此要趕緊開始開會，便應是在會議前的「開場白」較為合理，故選 (A)「To open a sales meeting」為最佳答案。

各選項解析

- 選項 (B)「To persuade clients」、選項 (C)「To announce a new policy」與選項 (D)「To promote new products」都並非此獨白的目的，故不選。

第二題

此題問的是「Who are listening to this talk most likely?」，判斷要聽到此獨白的「聽眾」會是哪些人以便回答。根據此關鍵句「Well, you all know that our sales have been slower recently, right? We do need to take some proper actions to change this. And that's why we meet today to discuss our strategies for increasing sales.」可聽出要想辦法挽救業務下滑危機的人，應會是行銷與業務相關的人較為合理，故選 (B)「Sales and marketing personnel」為最佳答案。

各選項解析

- 選項 (A)「Technical support engineers」、選項 (C)「Company investors」與選項 (D)「Angry customers」都不是直接參與「業務銷售」之人，故不選。

第三題

此題問的是「Who is Linda Smith most likely?」，可判斷要聽到 Linda Smith 的「身分、職稱」相關資訊以便回答。根據此關鍵句「Linda Smith from marketing will be giving us an overview of what our major rivals are doing.」，可聽出 Linda 是行銷部門的人，那麼應該是「行銷人員」較為合理，故選 (D)「A marketing specialist」為最佳答案。

各選項解析

- 選項 (A)「A competitor」、選項 (B)「A receptionist」與選項 (C)「A pre-sales engineer」都不會是「在行銷部工作」之人，故不選。

關鍵字彙

recently [`risn̩tlɪ] ad 最近地
proper [`prɑpɚ] a 適當的、合適的
strategy [`strætədʒɪ] n 策略
overview [`ovɚˌvju] n 概觀
rival [`raɪvl̩] n 對手、敵手
present [`prɛzn̩t] a 當今的、現下的
analysis [ə`næləsɪs] n 分析
brainstorming [`brenˌstɔrmɪŋ] n 集體研討
constructive [kən`strʌktɪv] a 有建設性的
get down to business ph 切入主題

Q1. What is going to happen on Sunday?

(A) All workers need to participate in a conference

(B) A company event will be held

(C) Some senior employees will retire

(D) The CEO has scheduled a meeting on that day

Q2. According to the talk, what will listeners do in the event?

(A) Listen to sales presentations

(B) Cook by themselves

(C) Participate in a variety of activities

(D) Practice their English oral skills

Q3. Who is Sherry most likely?

(A) An event coordinator

(B) A presenter

(C) A chef

(D) An executive

解題分析

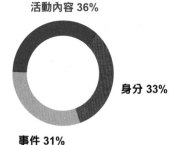

活動內容 36%

身分 33%

事件 31%

■ 活動內容 36% 第二題問的是聽眾在活動中要做什麼事，重點在「做什麼」，也就是要注意聽「活動的內容」，再判斷正確答案為何。

■ 身分 33% 第三題的關鍵字是 who，很明確可以了解題目在問的是 Sherry 這個人的「身分」，預測接下來可能會聽到職業或是工作內容相關的描述。

■ 事件 31% 第一個題目問的是星期天會發生什麼事，所以推測接下來要鎖定的重點是即將發生的「事件」，且時間還要符合星期天這個條件。

聽稿

（US / Ｗ）All colleagues. Please note that the annual Team Building Day will take place this upcoming Sunday. A Team Building Day is all about getting together with all colleagues for a wonderful shared experience as part of staff motivation and simply to celebrate company success together. All team members will have a great time on a wide range of activities, such as flying high on the giant bungee trampolines, and relaxing in the pamper zone. When you're ready to take a break, you can enjoy a refreshing fruit smoothie or a drink from the bar to accompany a sumptuous BBQ. The executives of the company will also join and have fun with all members. Aren't you excited about it? Well, get ready and see you guys in the Springfield Park this Sunday at 9 a.m. If you have any questions regarding this event, please feel free to contact Sherry at extension 889.

中譯 （美／女）各位同事們，請注意本年度團隊管理活動將於這星期日舉行。設置團隊管理日的目的，主要是集合所有的同仁，除藉由歡慶公司的優良事蹟激勵員工，同時給予大家相互交流經驗的機會。所有的團隊成員可於此日參加許多活動，例如：高空蹦床彈跳和休閒舒適懶人區。當你想要休息的時候，我們也供應清涼的水果冰沙、小酒吧的酒類飲品，搭配奢華的燒烤食物。公司的主管們也會一起與各位同樂。有沒有很令人期待呀？趕緊準備好，我們將於這星期日早上九點，在春田公園與你見面。如果你對於此次活動有任何疑問，歡迎隨時撥打雪莉的分機 889。

Q1. 週日會發生何事？（答案：B）
(A) 所有員工都要參加研討會　　　　(B) 會舉行一場公司活動
(C) 一些資深員工要退休了　　　　　(D) 執行長已在那天安排了個會議

Q2. 根據獨白內容，聽眾在活動中會做什麼？（答案：C）
(A) 聽業務簡報　　　　　　　　　　(B) 自己煮飯
(C) 參與各式活動　　　　　　　　　(D) 練習英文口語技巧

Q3. 雪莉最有可能是？（答案：A）
(A) 活動籌劃者　　　　　　　　　　(B) 簡報講者
(C) 廚師　　　　　　　　　　　　　(D) 管理人員

解題技巧 多數考生通常會「想將所有內容都聽懂」才算了解聽力內容，但事實上，針對內容長，唸的速度又快的獨白題，若想將每個字都聽懂，無疑是給自己找不必要的麻煩。建議考生應該做的事，是將有限的時間與精神放在聽「會考的關鍵點」上才是，而這些關鍵點極有可能會以「加強重音」來強調：

（US／W）All colleagues. Please note that the annual Team Building Day will take place this upcoming Sunday. A Team Building Day is all about getting together with all colleagues for a wonderful shared experience as part of staff motivation and simply to celebrate company success together. All team members will have a great time on a wide range of activities, such as flying high on the giant bungee trampolines, and relaxing in the pamper zone. When you're ready to take a break, you can enjoy a refreshing fruit smoothie or a drink from the bar to accompany a sumptuous BBQ. The executives of the company will also join and have fun with all members. Aren't you excited about it? Well, get ready and see you guys in the Springfield Park this Sunday at 9 a.m. If you have any questions regarding this event, please feel free to contact Sherry at extension 889.

經過擷取上述的要點後，便可以得知此獨白大概是在講什麼了，也就是：講者報告了在週日舉行的公司活動，希望大家可以全力參與各式活動，也可以享用美食，另報告了活動時間地點，與活動相關聯絡人的訊息。如此僅聽出幾個關鍵點，也是可以了解獨白大致內容的喔！

利用獨白播放出來之前的幾秒空檔，很快地將題目先掃描一下，以便預期可能的獨白內容與要將注意力放在聽什麼要點上。

此題問的是「What is going to happen on Sunday?」，可得知要聽到「週日所會發生之活動」相關訊息以便回答。根據此關鍵句「All colleagues. Please note that the annual Team Building Day will take place this upcoming Sunday.」，可聽出週日有一場公司的「Team Building Day」活動要舉辦，故選 (B)「A company event will be held.」為最佳答案。

各選項解析

- 選項 (A)「All workers need to participate in a conference.」、選項 (C)「Some senior employees will retire.」與選項 (D)「The CEO has scheduled a meeting on that day.」都沒有在獨白中被提及，故不選。

第二題

此題問的是「What will listeners do in the event?」，便可判斷要聽到聽眾在此活動中「要做什麼」之相關資訊以便回答。根據此關鍵句「All team members will have a great time on a wide range of activities, such as flying high on the giant bungee trampolines, and relaxing in the pamper zone.」可聽出員工在那個活動中會參與各式各樣的活動，故選 (C)「Participate in a variety of activities」為最佳答案。

各選項解析

- 選項 (A)「Listen to sales presentations」、選項 (B)「Cook by themselves」與選項 (D)「Practice their English oral skills」都沒有在獨白中提及，故不選。

第三題

此題目問的是「Who is Sherry most likely?」，我們便知道要聽到 Sherry 之「身分、職稱」之相關資訊以便回答。根據此關鍵句「If you have any questions regarding this event, please feel free to contact Sherry at extension 889.」，可聽出 Sherry 是處理活動相關問題之主要負責人，故選 (A)「An event coordinator」為最佳答案。

各選項解析

- 選項 (B)「A presenter」、選項 (C)「A chef」與選項 (D)「An executive」都不會是處理活動相關問題的人，故不選。

關鍵字彙

colleague [ˋkɑlig] n 同事
annual [ˋænjʊəl] a 每年的
upcoming [ˋʌpˏkʌmɪŋ] a 即將發生的
motivation [ˏmotəˋveʃən] n 激勵、刺激
celebrate [ˋsɛləˏbret] v 慶祝
trampoline [ˋtræmpəˏlɪn] n 彈跳床
pamper [ˋpæmpɚ] v 嬌養、放縱
refreshing [rɪˋfrɛʃɪŋ] a 提神的
smoothie [ˋsmuðɪ] n 冰沙
accompany [əˋkʌmpənɪ] v 陪同、伴隨
sumptuous [ˋsʌmptʃʊəs] a 奢華的
extension [ɪkˋstɛnʃən] n 分機

Unit 8 飯店餐飲類

攻略 1 │ 飯店介紹

Q1. Who is the speaker most likely?

　　(A) A waiter　　　　　　　　　　(B) An English professor

　　(C) A hotel manager　　　　　　 (D) The mayor of the city

Q2. Where is the hotel most likely located?

　　(A) Near the beach　　　　　　　(B) On the high mountain

　　(C) In Japan　　　　　　　　　　(D) In a crowded city

Q3. What are listeners going to do next most likely?

　　(A) Dress up for dinner　　　　　(B) Fly to Marco Island

　　(C) Head to the airport　　　　　(D) Place their luggage in a certain place

解題分析

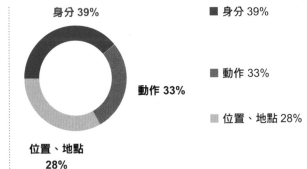

■ 身分 39%

■ 動作 33%

■ 位置、地點 28%

看到 who 開頭的問句，就可以推測要問的重點與人物的「身分」相關，因此在聽的時候，要特別注意身分跟職業有關係的資訊。

第三題主要是在問聽者接下來要做的事，所以必須留意獨白中所提到的「動作」是否符合題目的敘述。

第二題的關鍵字是 where，問旅館的「位置」，預測接下來要聽到的是「位置、地點」的內容。

聽稿　（UK / M）Welcome to Royal Hotel, all guests. Here in Royal Hotel, you can experience the tradition of afternoon tea in the parlor, dressing up for dinner, nightly dancing to the sound of the Royal Hotel orchestra, and sitting in a rocking chair with view of the beach. Family-owned for two generations, the Royal Hotel has always embraced its rich history, while keeping up with current times. Our guests enjoy modern amenities while the hotel's original architecture and charm have been tastefully preserved. Guests especially enjoy the relaxed atmosphere of Marco Island, where cars are not allowed and the horse and carriage and bicycle are favored modes of transportation. I'm sure you'll be surprised at every turn. All right, now please come this way and place your luggage here.

（英 / 男）歡迎您們光臨皇家飯店。在皇家飯店裡，您能在我們的接待室體驗傳統的下午茶點、盛裝打扮出席晚宴餐會、宵夜場有由飯店皇家交響樂團伴奏的舞蹈活動、坐在搖椅中欣賞絕美的海景。由於是傳承兩代的家庭企業，皇家飯店不但能擁有豐富的古老歷史，更追隨時代的腳步往前推移。在客人們享受極具現代感設施的同時，也能欣賞我們特別保留之原始建築的魅力。尤其最令人喜愛的，是馬可小島的舒適氛圍。搭乘馬車或騎腳踏車是此塊區域的主要交通方式，而汽車則是禁止隨意出入的，我確定您們一定會發現處處有許多令人意想不到的驚喜。那麼，現在請跟隨著我並移動您的腳步，並將您的行李留在原地即可。

Q1. 此講者最有可能是誰？（答案：C）

(A) 服務生　　　　　　　　　　　　　(B) 英文教授

(C) 飯店經理　　　　　　　　　　　　(D) 市長

Q2. 此飯店最有可能位於何處？（答案：A）

(A) 靠近海邊　　　　　　　　　　　　(B) 在高山上

(C) 在日本　　　　　　　　　　　　　(D) 在擁擠的都市

Q3. 聽眾接下來最有可能會做什麼？（答案：D）

(A) 盛裝打扮去吃晚餐　　　　　　　　(B) 飛往馬可小島

(C) 前往機場　　　　　　　　　　　　(D) 將行李放在特定之處

解題技巧

與其想將注意力放在聽每個字每一句話上，倒不如僅聽取「可能回答題目的關鍵點」即可。因此類考題的目的並非考英譯中，而是要測驗考生的答題與專注力呀，不是嗎？因此聽「要點處」比會英翻中重要多了。所幸這些要點關鍵處，通常會以「加強重音」來強調喔：

（UK / M）Welcome to Royal Hotel, all guests. Here in Royal Hotel, you can experience the tradition of afternoon tea in the parlor, dressing up for dinner, nightly dancing to the sound of the Royal Hotel orchestra, and sitting in a rocking chair with view of the beach. Family-owned for two generations, the Royal Hotel has always embraced its rich history, while keeping up with current times. Our guests enjoy modern amenities while the hotel's original architecture and charm have been tastefully preserved. Guests especially enjoy the relaxed atmosphere of Marco Island, where cars are not allowed and the horse and carriage and bicycle are favored modes of transportation. I'm sure you'll be surprised at every turn. All right, now please come this way and place your luggage here.

在聽到上述的關鍵點後，便可以大略地歸納出以下幾個要點了：講者歡迎聽眾到飯店，並介紹了一些飯店的設施與建築歷史，另外也介紹了飯店周邊的值得一遊的景點。如此可聽出，靠抓出幾個關鍵點，比逐字翻譯更可以了解獨白的大意內容喔！

利用獨白播放出來之前的幾秒空檔，很快地將題目先掃描一下，以便預期可能的獨白內容與要將注意力放在聽什麼要點上。

第一題

此題問的是「Who is the speaker most likely?」，那麼可判斷要聽到此獨白的「講者身分職稱」相關資訊以便回答。根據此關鍵句「Welcome to Royal Hotel, all guests. Here in Royal Hotel, you can experience the tradition of afternoon tea in the parlor...」，可聽出此講者在歡迎飯店賓客與介紹飯店設施，那麼應該是飯店經理較為合理，故選 (C)「A hotel manager」為最佳答案。

各選項解析

• 選項 (A)「A waiter」、選項 (B)「An English professor」與選項 (D)「The mayor of the city」都不像是會講此番話的人，故不選。

第二題

此題問的是「Where is the hotel most likely located?」，很明顯地，要聽到此飯店所在之「地點、位置」相關資訊以便回答。根據此關鍵句「... nightly dancing to the sound of the Royal Hotel orchestra, and sitting in a rocking chair with view of the beach.」，可聽出在此飯店可以看到海灘，故應是「在海灘附近」較為合理，故選 (A)「Near the beach」為最佳答案。

各選項解析

• 選項 (B)「On the high mountain」、選項 (C)「In Japan」或選項 (D)「In a crowded city」都沒有在獨白中被提及，故不選。

第三題

此題問的是「What are listeners going to do next most likely?」，那麼可判斷要聽到聽眾接下來「要做什麼事」相關資訊以便回答。根據此關鍵句「All right, now please come this way and place your luggage here.」，可聽出講者請聽眾「將他們的行李放在這裡」，故選 (D)「Place their luggage in a certain place」為最佳答案。

各選項解析

• 選項 (A)「Dress up for dinner」、選項 (B)「Fly to Marco Island」與選項 (C)「Head to the airport」都沒有在獨白中被提及，故不選。

關鍵字彙

guest [ɡɛst] ⋒ 賓客、客人
parlor [ˋpɑrlɚ] ⋒ 客廳、接待室
orchestra [ˋɔrkɪstrə] ⋒ 管弦樂隊
generation [ˌdʒɛnəˋreʃən] ⋒ 世代
embrace [ɪmˋbres] ⋓ 擁抱
preserve [prɪˋzɝv] ⋓ 保育、保存
atmosphere [ˋætməsˌfɪr] ⋒ 氣氛、氛圍
transportation [ˌtrænspɚˋteʃən] ⋒ 交通工具
luggage [ˋlʌɡɪdʒ] ⋒ 行李

Q1. **Who are the listeners most likely?**

(A) Newly hired service staff   (B) Hotel managers

(C) University professors   (D) Travel agents

Q2. **What is most likely Vivian Chen's position?**

(A) Schoolmaster   (B) Police officer

(C) Training manager   (D) Accountant

Q3. **What will the speaker most likely do next?**

(A) Prepare dinner   (B) Introduce another speaker

(C) Offer some tips   (D) Explain the topic in detail

解題分析

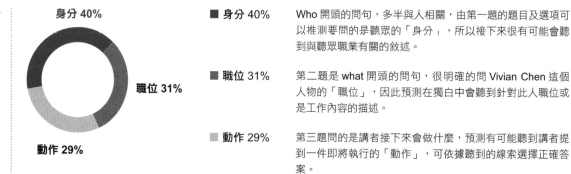

身分 40%　職位 31%　動作 29%

■ 身分 40% Who 開頭的問句，多半與人相關，由第一題的題目及選項可以推測要問的是聽眾的「身分」，所以接下來很有可能會聽到與聽眾職業有關的敘述。

■ 職位 31% 第二題是 what 開頭的問句，很明確的問 Vivian Chen 這個人物的「職位」，因此預測在獨白中會聽到針對此人職位或是工作內容的描述。

■ 動作 29% 第三題問的是講者接下來會做什麼，預測有可能聽到講者提到一件即將執行的「動作」，可依據聽到的線索選擇正確答案。

聽稿

（AU / Ⓦ）Hi, everybody. This is your first day working here, and this training session is required for all new waiters and waitresses. I'm Vivian Chen and I'm gonna share with you how to be more persuasive. Some of our waiters have found that they receive larger tips when they repeat their customers' orders back to them exactly as the customer verbalized it. Perhaps many of you have had the experience of a waiter taking your order and then passively saying "right." No surprise then we're left sitting at the table wondering whether the burger we ordered will arrive at our table reincarnated as a sandwich. In fact, waiters who match their customers' verbalization after receiving the order will increase their tip size. But why? Next let's discuss the reasons behind.

中譯　（澳／**女**）各位好，這是你們第一天開始在這裡上班，我們將進行所有新進服務人員的訓練課程。我是陳薇安，我會為你們示範要如何變得更有說服力。有些服務生發現，當他們正確地重複客人們口頭上所點的餐點給客人聽時，他們便有機會獲取更高額的小費。或許你們之中有很多人，曾經遇過在點餐時，服務生只是一昧被動地回答「好的」。這使我們通常會不自覺地想像：會不會我們剛剛所點的漢堡，送上來時會變成一份三明治呢。事實上，當服務生能夠重複客人們口頭上所點的餐點時，他們真的會得到更多小費。究竟是為什麼呢？我們來談談其背後的原因吧。

Q1. 聽眾最有可能是誰？（答案：**A**）

(A) 新進的服務生　　　　　　　　　　(B) 飯店經理

(C) 大學教授　　　　　　　　　　　　(D) 旅行社人員

Q2. 陳薇安的職位最有可能為何？（答案：**C**）

(A) 校長　　　　　　　　　　　　　　(B) 警察

(C) 培訓經理　　　　　　　　　　　　(D) 會計師

Q3. 講者接下來最有可能做什麼？（答案：**D**）

(A) 準備晚餐　　　　　　　　　　　　(B) 介紹另一講者

(C) 給些小費　　　　　　　　　　　　(D) 更詳細地解釋主題

解題技巧　處理長篇的獨白題，不用試圖將所有內容聽懂，而應該將注意力放在聽「關鍵點」上以便回答問題。也因此若可以事先掃描題目便再好不過了。先了解題目便可判斷應該要聽哪些關鍵點。講者想強調的關鍵處則通常會以「加強重音」來處理：

> （AU／**W**）Hi, everybody. This is your first day working here, and this training session is required for all new waiters and waitresses. I'm Vivian Chen and I'm gonna share with you how to be more persuasive. Some of our waiters have found that they receive larger tips when they repeat their customers' orders back to them exactly as the customer verbalized it. Perhaps many of you have had the experience of a waiter taking your order and then passively saying "right." No surprise then we're left sitting at the table wondering whether the burger we ordered will arrive at our table reincarnated as a sandwich. In fact, waiters who match their customers' verbalization after receiving the order will increase their tip size. But why? Next let's discuss the reasons behind.

大概抓一下此獨白的關鍵點，便可得知約略的內容了：講者在對第一天工作的服務生們講話，教導他們如何接待及回應客戶，這並與他們的小費多寡有關係。由此可聽出，少數幾個要點資訊比很多次要資訊更可以影響到我們對獨白的理解力喔！

利用獨白播放出來之前的幾秒空檔，很快地將題目先掃描一下，以便預期可能的獨白內容與要將注意力放在聽什麼要點上。

此題問的是「Who are the listeners most likely?」，那麼預期要聽到可以判斷此獨白之聽眾「身分、角色」之相關資訊以便回答。根據此關鍵句「Hi, everybody. This is your first day working here, and this training session is required for all new waiters and waitresses.」可聽出，既然是第一天上班的服務生，應是新被聘請的較為合理，故選 (A)「Newly hired service staff」為最佳答案。

各選項解析

- 選項 (B)「Hotel managers」、選項 (C)「University professors」與選項 (D)「Travel agents」都沒有在獨白中提及，故不選。

第二題

此題問的是「What is most likely Vivian Chen's position?」，那麼便可判斷要聽到 Vivian Chen 的「角色、職稱」相關資訊以便回答。根據此關鍵句「I'm Vivian Chen and I'm gonna share with you how to be more persuasive.」可聽出 Vivian 要訓練這批新進服務生，教他們如何更具說服力，那 Vivian 本身應是訓練人員較為合理，故選 (C)「Training manager」為最佳答案。

各選項解析

- 選項 (A)「Schoolmaster」、選項 (B)「Police officer」與選項 (D)「Accountant」都不是這方面的角色，故不選。

第三題

此題問的是「What will the speaker most likely do next?」，便要聽到講者接下來要「做什麼事情」相關資訊以便回答。根據此關鍵句「In fact, waiters who match their customers' verbalization after receiving the order will increase their tip size. But why? Next let's discuss the reasons behind.」可聽出講者先講個約略的概念，然後說要「討論背後的原因」，便是要討論一些細節了，故選 (D)「Explain the topic in detail」為最佳答案。

各選項解析

- 選項 (A)「Prepare dinner」、選項 (B)「Introduce another speaker」與選項 (C)「Offer some tips」都沒有在獨白中被提及，故不選。

關鍵字彙

persuasive [pɚˋswesɪv] a 具說服力的
repeat [rɪˋpit] v 重複
verbalize [ˋvɝbəˌlaɪz] v 以言語表述
passively [ˋpæsɪvlɪ] ad 被動地
reincarnate [ˌriɪnˋkɑrˌnet] v 化身為～、轉換
match [mætʃ] v 符合、搭配
tip [tɪp] n 小費

攻略 3 ｜ 績優頒獎

Q1. **On what occasion does the talk probably take place?**

(A) On the first day of school   (B) On an awards ceremony

(C) During an investors' meeting   (D) In an international conference

Q2. **Who are listening to this talk most likely?**

(A) The speaker's coworkers   (B) City officials

(C) International visitors   (D) Technicians

Q3. **According to the speaker, what makes him succeed most likely?**

(A) His talents in music   (B) His supervisor's encouragement

(C) His father's support   (D) His consideration for guests

解題分析

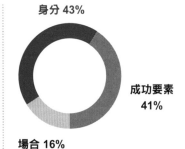

身分 43%

成功要素 41%

場合 16%

■ 身分 43%　第二題是 who 開頭，問這場獨白的聽眾是誰，因此推測很有可能聽到針對其「身分」的描述，或是根據説話者跟聽者的關係找出答案。

■ 成功要素 41%　第三題重點在於什麼是講者的「成功要素」，預測接下來會聽到他的成功要素，且與其中一個選項相符。

▨ 場合 16%　從第一題的 On what occasion 可以判斷本題問的是獨白發表的「場合」，接下來必須在獨白中找出與此相關的線索，才能得到解答。

聽稿　（CA / **M**）Well, it's my honor to be the Best Waiter of the month. As a matter of fact, I don't really have some so-called "tricks," but I just ensure all customers have a good dining experience. Once customers have reasonable requests about their meals, I always do my best to accommodate them. If I can't, then I offer an alternative. My purpose is to show customers that I care about their dining experience, and that I value their business and I want to make them satisfied. I anticipate customers' needs, rather than waiting to be asked for something. Well, once again thank you for naming me the Best Waiter of September. I hope my sharing today is helpful for you guys.

（加 / 男）能夠獲選本月最佳服務人員是我的榮幸。事實上，我並沒有什麼所謂的「獨門訣竅」，我只是單純地確保所有客人們都能夠有一個優質的用餐經驗。當客人們對於餐點提出合理的要求時，我總是盡心竭力地提供他們任何服務。若超乎我本人能力範圍以外的事物，我也會盡其所能地給予替代方案等協助。我的最終目的就是向客人們展現自身對於他們用餐的誠意和重視，希望他們能為此感到滿意。我也會預先考慮到客人們可能會有的需求，而不單只是被動地等待他們的指令或問題。我要再次感謝各位提名我為九月份的最佳服務生，希望今日的分享能夠帶給各位實質的幫助。

Q1. 此談話有可能是在何種場合聽到的？（答案：**B**）
　　(A) 開學第一天　　　　　　　　　　(B) 在頒獎典禮上
　　(C) 在投資客的會議上　　　　　　　(D) 在一場國際會議上

Q2. 誰最有可能是此獨白的聽眾？（答案：**A**）
　　(A) 講者的同事　　　　　　　　　　(B) 市府官員
　　(C) 國際賓客　　　　　　　　　　　(D) 技術人員

Q3. 根據講者所言，什麼最有可能是他成功的因素？（答案：**D**）
　　(A) 他的音樂才華　　　　　　　　　(B) 他老闆的鼓勵
　　(C) 他爸爸的支持　　　　　　　　　(D) 他對客人的用心

心中打定主意，要將專注力放在聽「會考的關鍵點」上即可，要達成這樣的目標，就要先掃描題目，先知道題目問哪方面的問題，再針對問題去聽「可以回答問題」的關鍵點，千萬不要將注意力分散到想聽每個字句上。通常講者想強調的要點會以「加強重音」來呈現，以吸引聽者的注意力：

（CA / **M**）Well, it's my honor to be the Best Waiter of the month. As a matter of fact, I don't really have some so-called "tricks," but I just ensure all customers have a good dining experience. Once customers have reasonable requests about their meals, I always do my best to accommodate them. If I can't, then I offer an alternative. My purpose is to show customers that I care about their dining experience, and that I value their business and I want to make them satisfied. I anticipate customers' needs, rather than waiting to be asked for something. Well, once again thank you for naming me the Best Waiter of September. I hope my sharing today is helpful for you guys.

聽到此獨白內的關鍵處之後，便可歸納一些要點了，包括：講者被選為本月最佳服務生，他便分享他在接待客戶時的訣竅，要用心去滿足客戶的需求等。由此可聽出，僅將焦點放在幾個要點上，更可以抓出獨白的精髓內容喔！

利用獨白播放出來之前的幾秒空檔，很快地將題目先掃描一下，以便預期可能的獨白內容與要將注意力放在聽什麼要點上。

第一題

此題問的是「On what occasion does the talk probably take place?」，那麼便可判斷要聽到此獨白可能發表的「場合」相關資訊以便回答。根據此關鍵句「It's my honor to be the Best Waiter of the month.」可聽出講者是在為被選為本月最佳服務生，並在發表感言，故此感言應是在頒獎典禮上所聽到的較為合理，故選 (B)「On an awards ceremony」為最佳答案。

各選項解析

- 選項 (A)「On the first day of school」、選項 (C)「During an investors' meeting」與選項 (D)「In an international conference」都不會是聽到此獨白的時機，故不選。

第二題

此題問的是「Who are listening to this talk most likely?」，藉由首字，我們要聽到此獨白「聽眾會是誰」相關資訊以便回答。根據此關鍵句「As a matter of fact, I don't really have some so-called "tricks," but I just ensure all customers have a good dining experience.」與此尾句「I hope my sharing today is helpful for you guys.」，可聽出講者在跟其他服務生分享他的客服經驗，故聽眾應是其他服務生，也是「講者的同事」較為合理，故選 (A)「The speaker's coworkers」為最佳答案。

各選項解析

- 選項 (B)「City officials」、選項 (C)「International visitors」與選項 (D)「Technicians」都不是此獨白的聽眾，故不選。

第三題

此題問的是「What makes the speaker succeed most likely?」，那麼便可判斷要聽出講者所提及之「他成功的要素」相關資訊以便回答。根據此關鍵句「Once customers have reasonable requests about their meals, I always do my best to accommodate them.」，可聽出講者是會「盡力滿足客戶需求」的，故選 (D)「His consideration for guests」為最佳答案。

各選項解析

- 選項 (A)「His talents in music」、選項 (B)「His supervisor's encouragement」與選項 (C)「His father's support」都沒有在獨白中被提及，故不選。

關鍵字彙

honor [ˈɑnɚ] n 榮譽、信用
ensure [ɪnˈʃur] v 確保
reasonable [ˈriznəbl] a 合理的
request [rɪˈkwɛst] n 要求
accommodate [əˈkɑməˌdet] v 給～方便、通融
alternative [ɔlˈtɝnətɪv] n 其他選擇
purpose [ˈpɝpəs] n 目的
anticipate [ænˈtɪsəˌpet] v 預期、預料
helpful [ˈhɛlpfəl] a 有幫助的

攻略 1 | 導遊介紹景點

Q1. Who are listening to this talk most likely?

(A) Tourists   (B) Athletes

(C) Children   (D) Investors

Q2. According to the talk, what is special about Spring City?

(A) Only farmers are living there

(B) It is near the beach

(C) It has both the traditional and modern sides

(D) It is one of the oldest cities in the world

Q3. What are the listeners going to do next?

(A) Interact with local people   (B) Enter a museum

(C) Go shopping   (D) Have lunch

解題分析

特別之處 52%

動作 32%

身分 16%

■ 特別之處 52%   第二題的重點是在問 Spring City 的「特別之處」是什麼，預測在獨白中會聽到與此相關的描述。

■ 動作 32%   第三題主要在詢問聽眾在說話者講完之後，接下來要做的事情，因此推測會聽到相關的「動作」敘述，或是講者的指令。

■ 身分 16%   第一題為 who 開頭的問句，問的是聽眾的「身分」，因此接下來要聽到聽者的身分才能回答。

聽稿   （US / **W**） Welcome all visitors. My name is Linda Terry, and I'll be your tour guide for today. Well, speaking of Spring City, it's quite known for the hustle and bustle of city life. Here in Spring City, you can see all kinds of art galleries, shops, and restaurants. Also heritage and history are imbedded in local people's DNA. Well, but while local people preserve tradition, the can-do gumption of their forebears continues to propel them forward. You'll find contemporary museums, modern art, vibrant cultural events in the city, along with farmers' markets, festivals and agricultural fairs. All right, so our first stop for this morning is the National Art Museum. Please line up here as we're preparing to enter.

中譯　（美 / **女**）歡迎所有來參觀的遊客。我是各位今天的導遊，名叫琳達・泰利。說到春日市，不免要提到它以熙來攘往的都市生活為名。在春日市裡，您可以看到形形色色的藝廊、商店和餐廳。歷史與文化的資產也根深蒂固地存於當地百姓的基因中。不過當市民盡力維護傳統的同時，老祖宗傳承下來的樂觀進取的魄力依舊驅動著他們不斷向前行。所以，您們也會看到當代博物館、現代美術館、生氣蓬勃的文化活動，還有其他農夫市集、慶典以及農業博覽會。好的，我們今日早晨的第一站是國立美術館。請各位排成一列準備依序進入參觀。

Q1. 此獨白的聽眾最有可能是誰？（答案：**A**）

(A) 旅客　　　　　　　　　　　　(B) 運動員

(C) 小孩　　　　　　　　　　　　(D) 投資者

Q2. 根據獨白內容，春日市特殊之處為何？（答案：**C**）

(A) 僅農夫住在此處　　　　　　　(B) 此市很靠近海邊

(C) 此市有著傳統和現代的風貌　　(D) 此市是世界上最古老的都市之一

Q3. 聽者接下來會做什麼？（答案：**B**）

(A) 跟當地人互動　　　　　　　　(B) 進入博物館

(C) 去購物　　　　　　　　　　　(D) 吃午餐

解題技巧　考生通常會想將聽力內每個字都聽懂，還可能在心底默默地翻譯中文內容，認為如此才可了解獨白內容，也才有安全感。但如此的作法在有限的時間下是不可行的，可能會上一句還沒翻完，就錯失掉下一句了。因此，考生應該練習將所有的精神集中到聽「關鍵點」上面，以便回答三題問題，而這些刻意引起聽眾注意的關鍵點，可能會以「加強重音」來處理：

（US / **W**）Welcome all visitors. My name is Linda Terry, and I'll be your tour guide for today. Well, speaking of Spring City, it's quite known for the hustle and bustle of city life. Here in Spring City, you can see all kinds of art galleries, shops, and restaurants. Also heritage and history are imbedded in local people's DNA. Well, but while local people preserve tradition, the can-do gumption of their forebears continues to propel them forward. You'll find contemporary museums, modern art, vibrant cultural events in the city, along with farmers' markets, festivals and agricultural fairs. All right, so our first stop for this morning is the National Art Museum. Please line up here as we're preparing to enter.

如此聽到幾個加強重音的關鍵點之後，便可歸納出關於此獨白的要點了，包括：此講者是導遊並在跟遊客介紹都市景點，還提到其歷史，接下來他們會去參觀美術博物館。如此專注在幾個要點上，比分散注意力去聽每個字來得有效率多了。

利用獨白播放出來之前的幾秒空檔，很快地將題目先掃描一下，以便預期可能的獨白內容與要將注意力放在聽什麼要點上。

第一題

此題問的是「Who are listening to this talk most likely?」，那麼可判斷要聽到「聽者身分」相關答案以便回答。根據此關鍵句「Welcome all visitors. My name is Linda Terry, and I'll be your tour guide for today.」可聽出是導遊在報告，那麼聽者應是「旅客」較為合理，故選 (A)「Tourists」為最佳答案。

各選項解析

- 選項 (B)「Athletes」、選項 (C)「Children」與選項 (D)「Investors」都不會是聽「導遊介紹」之人，故不選。

第二題

此題問的是「What is special about Spring City?」，要聽出關於 Spring City 的「特別之處」相關資訊以便回答。根據此關鍵句「Well, speaking of Spring City, it's quite known for the hustle and bustle of city life. Here in Spring City, you can see all kinds of art galleries, shops, and restaurants. Also heritage and history are imbedded in local people's DNA.」，可聽出此都市是繁榮的都市，同時也保有傳統，故選 (C)「It has both the traditional and modern sides.」為最佳答案。

各選項解析

- 選項 (A)「Only farmers are living there.」、選項 (B)「It is near the beach.」與選項 (D)「It is one of the oldest cities in the world.」都沒有在獨白中被提及，故不選。

第三題

此題問的是「What are the listeners going to do next?」，我們知道要聽出「聽眾接下來會做什麼事」相關資訊以便回答。根據此關鍵句「All right, so our first stop for this morning is the National Art Museum. Please line up here as we're preparing to enter.」，可聽出聽者接下來要排隊進入博物館參觀，故選 (B)「Enter a museum」為最佳答案。

各選項解析

- 選項 (A)「Interact with local people」、選項 (C)「Go shopping」與選項 (D)「Have lunch」都沒在獨白中聽到，故不選。

關鍵字彙

hustle and bustle ph 熙來攘往
gallery [ˈɡælərɪ] n 美術館、畫廊
heritage [ˈhɛrətɪdʒ] n 遺產
imbed [ɪmˈbɛd] v 埋藏
contemporary [kənˈtɛmpəˌrɛrɪ] a 現代的
vibrant [ˈvaɪbrənt] a 鮮明的、活躍的
festival [ˈfɛstəvl̩] n 節慶、慶典
agricultural [ˌæɡrɪˈkʌltʃərəl] a 農業的

攻略 2 │ 提供旅客安全建議

Q1. What is the main purpose of this talk?

(A) To provide some safety tips for listeners

(B) To warn listeners of the danger of living in big cities

(C) To explain the history of Newland City

(D) To announce a schedule change

Q2. What does the speaker suggest listeners do when paying for goods?

(A) Don't get too close to strangers

(B) Use credit cards instead of cash

(C) Pay attention to short-changing

(D) Always pay by travelers check

Q3. What is Ada Jones going to do next most likely?

(A) Lead listeners to tour the city

(B) Invite the speaker for dinner

(C) Apply for a credit card

(D) Prepare lunch for guests

解題分析

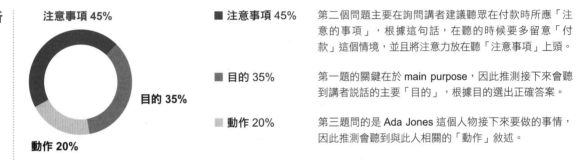

注意事項 45%

目的 35%

動作 20%

■ 注意事項 45%

第二個問題主要在詢問講者建議聽眾在付款時所應「注意的事項」，根據這句話，在聽的時候要多留意「付款」這個情境，並且將注意力放在聽「注意事項」上頭。

■ 目的 35%

第一題的關鍵在於 main purpose，因此推測接下來會聽到講者說話的主要「目的」，根據目的選出正確答案。

■ 動作 20%

第三題問的是 Ada Jones 這個人物接下來要做的事情，因此推測會聽到與此人相關的「動作」敘述。

聽稿

（CA / **M**）All right, everybody. Please pay attention to me here. Right, my name is Mark Hill and I'm a staff member from Happy Travel Agency. Before you go on a tour in Newland City, I'd like to offer you some tips about how to avoid trouble. Well, first of all, to guard against pickpockets, please carry your valuables under your clothes if possible and keep your eyes open for people who get unnecessarily close to you in the street. Also when paying for goods, or a meal or whatever, keep an eye on the notes you hand over and then count your change carefully. Short-changing is another form of theft. Everybody should keep that in mind, okay? Now, please follow your guide, Ms. Ada Jones. Have a nice day.

中譯　（加 / 男）好了，各位，麻煩請注意我這邊一會兒，我是快樂旅行社的工作人員馬克・希爾。在我們開始新地城的都市巡禮之前，我要先告知各位幾項能幫助您避開麻煩的小提醒。首先，請各位看管好自己的貴重物品，最好將它們藏於衣服內側，並隨時留意街上是否有陌生人向您靠近，以防扒手竊取您的隨身行李。再者，當您在買東西、用餐或購物時，務必清楚地看好您手中紙鈔上的面額，同時仔細地計算找回的零錢數目。少找零錢也是偷竊的一種型態。大家一定要記得這些事項，好嗎？現在請跟隨導遊艾達・瓊斯小姐啟程，祝您們有愉快的一天。

Q1. 此獨白的主要目的為何？（答案：A）
(A) 提供一些安全建議給聽眾
(B) 警告聽眾住在此都市的危險性
(C) 解釋新地城都市的歷史
(D) 公告行程的改變

Q2. 講者建議聽眾在買東西付款時要做什麼？（答案：C）
(A) 不要太靠近陌生人
(B) 使用信用卡而非現金
(C) 注意看是否少找零錢
(D) 都使用旅行支票付款

Q3. 艾達・瓊斯接下來最有可能會做什麼？（答案：A）
(A) 引領聽眾遊覽都市
(B) 邀請講者吃晚餐
(C) 申請信用卡
(D) 幫賓客準備午餐

解題技巧　與其想逐字聽到並聽懂每個字，還不如將注意力集中到聽「題目有問的關鍵點上」即可。先了解題目問的，再根據方向去聽對應的答案，這樣才是事半功倍的作法。而通常講者希望聽者會特別注意之要點，不會輕輕地帶過，反而會以加強重音來加以強調：

（CA / M）All right, everybody. Please pay attention to me here. Right, my name is Mark Hill and I'm a staff member from Happy Travel Agency. Before you go on a tour in Newland City, I'd like to offer you some tips about how to avoid trouble. Well, first of all, to guard against pickpockets, please carry your valuables under your clothes if possible and keep your eyes open for people who get unnecessarily close to you in the street. Also when paying for goods, or a meal or whatever, keep an eye on the notes you hand over and then count your change carefully. Short-changing is another form of theft. Everybody should keep that in mind, okay? Now, please follow your guide, Ms. Ada Jones. Have a nice day.

如此將專注力放在聽關鍵點上的好處便是可以更有效率聽到要點，此獨白要點包括：講者是旅行社員工，在跟旅客提醒避免旅遊麻煩的方式，包括財物要收好，注意有沒少找零等，接下來旅遊就開始跟導遊開始進行參觀了。如此僅專注在幾個要點上，反而更可以聽出大意喔！

利用獨白播放出來之前的幾秒空檔，很快地將題目先掃描一下，以便預期可能的獨白內容與要將注意力放在聽什麼要點上。

第一題

此題目問的是「What is the main purpose of this talk?」，那麼便可判斷要聽到此獨白的「主要目的」相關內容以便回答。根據此關鍵句「I'm a staff member from Happy Travel Agency. Before you go on a tour in Newland City, I'd like to offer you some tips about how to avoid trouble.」，可聽出是旅行社的人提醒旅客在都市內應注意的安全事項，故選 (A)「To provide some safety tips for listeners」為最佳答案。

各選項解析

- 選項 (B)「To warn listeners of the danger of living in big cities」、選項 (C)「To explain the history of Newland City」與選項 (D)「To announce a schedule change」都沒在獨白中提到，故不選。

第二題

此題問的是「What does the speaker suggest listeners do when paying for goods?」，可判斷要聽到講者建議聽眾在付款時所應「注意的事項」為何。根據此關鍵句「Also when paying for goods, or a meal or whatever, keep an eye on the notes you hand over and then count your change carefully. Short-changing is another form of theft.」，可知道是要注意是否有少找錢的情況，故選 (C)「Pay attention to short-changing」為最佳答案。

各選項解析

- 選項 (A)「Don't get too close to strangers」、選項 (B)「Use credit cards instead of cash」與選項 (D)「Always pay by travelers check」都不是講者強調之要點，故不選。

第三題

此題問的是「What is Ada Jones going to do next most likely?」，要聽到 Ada 這人接下來要「做什麼事情」相關答案以便回答。根據此關鍵句「Now, please follow your guide, Ms. Ada Jones. Have a nice day.」可聽出講者要大家去跟著導遊 Ada Jones 一起走，故可判斷 Ada 會引領遊客開始去遊覽，故選 (A)「Lead listeners to tour the city」為最佳答案。

各選項解析

- 選項 (B)「Invite the speaker for dinner」、選項 (C)「Apply for a credit card」與選項 (D)「Prepare lunch for guests」都不是 Ada 接下來會做之事，故不選。

關鍵字彙

attention [ə`tɛnʃən] n 注意力
tour [tur] n 旅遊、巡視
avoid [ə`vɔɪd] v 避免
guard [gɑrd] v 保護
pickpocket [`pɪk͵pɑkɪt] n 扒手
carry [`kærɪ] v 背著
valuable [`væljuəbl] n 貴重物品
goods [gudz] n 商品

Artist	Painting	Room
Carel Fabritius	The Goldfinch	7A
Mario Nuzzi	Composizione con vaso di fiori	7F
Carel Fabritius	Young Man in a Fur Cap	7C
Guido Ren	Self-Portrait	6A

Q1. **Where is the talk most likely taking place?**

(A) On campus (B) In an art gallery

(C) On the street (D) At the airport

Q2. **Who is most likely the speaker?**

(A) A government official (B) A math teacher

(C) A visitor (D) A professional docent

新 **Q3.** **Please look at the chart. Which room will the listeners go to next most likely?**

(A) 7A (B) 7F

(C) 7C (D) 6A

解題分析

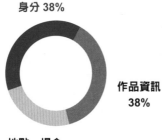

身分 38%

作品資訊 38%

作品資訊 38%

地點、場合 24%

地點、場合 24%

第二題的重點是 who，詢問講者的「身分」，因此接下來要聽到的很有可能與講者的職業或背景相關。

第三題需要搭配圖表解答，從圖表可以看到藝術家、作品、展館等資訊。問題的關鍵在於 Which room，詢問聽眾等一下會到「哪一間展館」，但本題要搭配表格，因此推斷會先聽到獨白提到畫作或畫家等「作品的資訊」，再與展館編號配對，選出正確答案。

第一題是 where 為首的問句，很清楚可以知道題目在問的是本段獨白出現的「地點、場合」，猜測講者有可能會提到地點或說出相關的線索，讓考生判斷正確答案。

聽稿 （AU / W） All right, visitors. Please step forward as we're looking at this painting "The Goldfinch" painted by Carel Fabritius in 1654. As you can see, a goldfinch is sitting on its feeder, chained by its foot. Goldfinches were popular pets, as they were intelligent birds thus could be taught tricks. They could also sing beautifully, especially the males. That's why goldfinches appear in 17th Century paintings occasionally. Well, this "The Goldfinch" painting is one of the few works we know by Fabritius. And now, please come this way and take a look at another painting called "Young Man in a Fur Cap" also by Carel Fabritius. This painting is generally considered to be a self-portrait.

中譯

（澳 / 女）各位旅客，請您往前移動腳步，我們要來看看這幅出自卡萊爾‧法布里契亞於一六五四年手繪的《金翅雀》作品。如同您們看到的，有一隻金翅雀正站在牠的餵食箱上，足上扣著條鍊子。由於金翅雀擁有高等智商能學會各式各樣不同的把戲，在當時是挺受歡迎的寵物。牠們的歌聲也很悅耳動聽，尤其是雄鳥。這也是為什麼在十七世紀的時候，金翅雀很常被拿來當作畫作的主題。這幅《金翅雀》是卡萊爾‧法布里契亞幾幅眾所皆知的名畫中的一幅。現在請各位轉到這邊來，我們接下來要瞧瞧另一幅同樣由卡萊爾‧法布里契亞所繪的肖像畫《戴毛帽的青年》。這幅畫普遍被視為是一幅卡萊爾‧法布里契亞的自畫像。

畫家	畫作	展廳
卡萊爾‧法布里契亞	金翅雀	7A
馬里奧‧努齊	花籃	7F
卡萊爾‧法布里契亞	戴毛帽的青年	7C
圭多‧雷尼	自畫像	6A

Q1. 此獨白最有可能在哪裡聽到？（答案：B）

(A) 校園內　　　　　　　　　　(B) 美術館內

(C) 街上　　　　　　　　　　　(D) 機場

Q2. 講者最有可能是誰？（答案：D）

(A) 政府官員　　　　　　　　　(B) 數學老師

(C) 訪客　　　　　　　　　　　(D) 專業解說員

新 Q3. 請看表格。聽眾接下來會前往哪一個展廳？（答案：C）

(A) 7A　　　　　　　　　　　　(B) 7F

(C) 7C　　　　　　　　　　　　(D) 6A

解題技巧

先打定主意要將注意力放在要聽「關鍵點」即可，而非分散到每個字或句子上，若碰到單字可能還會卡住，便會失去往下聽的動力呢！因此，最佳策略應是先掃描題目看是問些什麼，再根據題目問的來聽答案就好。而這些可以回答題目的關鍵點，通常也會被「加強重音」喔：

（AU / W）All right, visitors. Please step forward as we're looking at this painting "The Goldfinch" painted by Carel Fabritius in 1654. As you can see, a goldfinch is sitting on its feeder, chained by its foot. Goldfinches were popular pets, as they were intelligent birds thus could be taught tricks. They could also sing beautifully, especially the males. That's why goldfinches appear in 17th Century paintings occasionally. Well, this "The Goldfinch" painting is one of the few works we know by Fabritius. And now, please come this way and take a look at another painting called "Young Man in a Fur Cap" also by Carel Fabritius. This painting is generally considered to be a self-portrait.

聽到幾個關鍵點之後，便可歸納關於此獨白的以下要點了，包括：講者在帶領遊客欣賞畫作，講解畫作內容與歷史，接著便要繼續去看同一畫家的另一自畫像了。如此了解一下獨白的約略內容，比想每句每句地翻譯來得有效多囉！

利用獨白播放出來之前的幾秒空檔，很快地將題目先掃描一下，以便預期可能的獨白內容與要將注意力放在聽什麼要點上。

第一題

先看到此題目問的是「Where is the talk most likely taking place?」，要聽到此獨白可能出現「地點、場合」相關資訊以便回答。根據此關鍵句「All right, visitors. Please step forward as we're looking at this painting "The Goldfinch" painted by Carel Fabritius in 1654.」，可判斷講者是在討論某名畫，那應該是在美術館較為合理，故選 (B)「In an art gallery」為最佳答案。

各選項解析

- 選項 (A)「On campus」、選項 (C)「On the street」與選項 (D)「At the airport」都不會是討論「名畫」的地方，故不選。

第二題

此題目問的是「Who is most likely the speaker?」，那麼便可判斷要聽到講者的「身分、職稱」相關資訊以便回答。根據此關鍵句「Please step forward as we're looking at this painting "The Goldfinch" painted by Carel Fabritius in 1654. As you can see, a goldfinch is sitting on its feeder, chained by its foot.」，可聽出講者在介紹名畫內容，會了解這些名畫細節且要會介紹的人，應是專業的解說員較為合理，故選 (D)「A professional docent」為最佳答案。

各選項解析

- 選項 (A)「A government official」、選項 (B)「A math teacher」與選項 (C)「A visitor」都不是會很深入了解名畫內容之人，故不選。

新 第三題

先看到此題目要搭配表格內容，此題問的是「Which room will the listeners go to next most likely?」，知道要先聽到聽眾接下來要去看哪幅畫，再比對表格內容看會前往哪一個展館。根據此關鍵句「And now, please come this way and take a look at another painting called "Young Man in a Fur Cap" also by Carel Fabritius.」，可聽出接下來要去看「Young Man in a Fur Cap」這幅畫，再看表格內容，此畫是在 7C 展館，故選 (C)「7C」為最佳答案。

各選項解析

- 選項 (A)「7A」、選項 (B)「7F」與選項 (D)「6A」都不是展「Young Man in a Fur Cap」畫作之處，故不選。

關鍵字彙

goldfinch [ˋgoldˌfɪntʃ] n 金翅雀
feeder [ˋfidə] n 飼料箱
chain [tʃen] v 鏈住、以鏈圈住
intelligent [ɪnˋtɛlədʒənt] a 聰明的
trick [trɪk] n 花招
occasionally [əˋkeʒənḷɪ] ad 偶爾、間或
generally [ˋdʒɛnərəlɪ] ad 一般地
consider [kənˋsɪdə] v 視為、認為
self-portrait [ˋsɛlfˋportret] n 自畫像

Unit 10 廣播訊息類

攻略 1 │ 生物工程廣播

Q1. Who is the speaker most likely?

(A) A software engineer   (B) A high school student

(C) A host for the radio program   (D) A father of two girls

Q2. Who is Ms. Cheryl Anderson most likely?

(A) An expert in the bioengineering field

(B) The author of the "Love from future" novel

(C) A D.J. in the radio station

(D) A medical doctor

Q3. What is going to happen next most likely?

(A) A professor will present   (B) A radio listener will join the program

(C) The speaker will go home   (D) Ms. Anderson will talk

解題分析

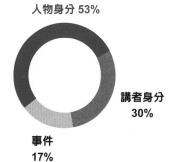

人物身分 53%

講者身分 30%

事件 17%

■ 人物身分 53% 第二題也是 who 為首的問句，不過這次問的人物為 Ms. Cheryl Anderson，很有可能會聽到此人的職稱或是工作內容等能夠判別「身分」的描述。

■ 講者身分 30% 第一題是 who 開頭的問句，很明確是在詢問講者的「身分」，推測接下來要聽到的是與講者的背景或職稱相關的內容。

■ 事件 17% 第三個問題重點在於接下來會「發生什麼事」，也就是說必須從這段獨白中找到即將發生「事件」的線索。

聽稿

（CA / **M**）Good morning Americans. This is Bird's Eye, Paul Jackins, bringing you the latest and most wanted knowledge and news. Now in the studio is our special guest for today, the author of a newly-published book "Our Future," Ms. Cheryl Anderson. As we know technological interventions that can transform the body and mind beyond its natural state have in recent years become commonplace. Bioengineering is largely being used to help patients suffering from disease, and Ms. Anderson thought "why not see how far we can push it?" Thus Ms. Anderson has consolidated her ideas and research in her new book "Our Future." Without further ado, let's welcome Ms. Cheryl Anderson and hopefully she can explain further about the concept and answer questions from our audience. Ms. Anderson, thank you for being here.

（加／男）早安，各位美國公民。這是節目鳥之眼，我是保羅·傑金斯，為您帶來最新的、最熱門的資訊與消息。今日邀請到近期出版《我們的未來》一書的作者謝里爾·安德森小姐來到錄音室。就如同眾所皆知的，科技媒介的介入致使身心靈轉化並超越本身的固有型態早已是司空見慣的事。生物工程學也被廣泛運用在醫學病理的治療上，而安德森小姐提出「為何不將之物盡其用、挑戰其極限潛能呢？」。因此，安德森小姐整合了所有觀點和研究，完成了此部《我們的未來》作品。我的淺見便言盡於此，讓我們誠摯地歡迎謝里爾·安德森小姐來為各位聽眾描述更詳細的概念，並為大家解答所有的困惑吧！安德森小姐，非常感謝您的到來。

Q1. 此獨白的講者最有可能是誰？（答案：C）

(A) 軟體工程師　　　　　　　　　　　(B) 高中生

(C) 廣播節目主持人　　　　　　　　　(D) 兩個女孩的爸爸

Q2. 謝里爾·安德森小姐最有可能是誰？（答案：A）

(A) 在生物工程領域的專家　　　　　　(B)《未來的愛》小說作者

(C) 廣播電台的 D.J.　　　　　　　　　(D) 一位醫生

Q3. 接下來最有可能發生何事？（答案：D）

(A) 一個教授會演講　　　　　　　　　(B) 一位聽眾會加入節目

(C) 講者會回家去　　　　　　　　　　(D) 安德森小姐會講話

解題技巧

考生在處理聽力獨白題時，應先有「專注在聽關鍵點以便回答問題」的體認，而非想以將「所有內容都聽到」將成目標。因此重要的是可先掃描題目，了解題目是在問什麼，再針對題目問的去聽「關鍵點」即可，所幸這些講者想強調的關鍵之處，通常會被加強重音：

（CA／M）Good morning Americans. This is Bird's Eye, Paul Jackins, bringing you the latest and most wanted knowledge and news. Now in the studio is our special guest for today, the author of a newly-published book "Our Future," Ms. Cheryl Anderson. As we know technological interventions that can transform the body and mind beyond its natural state have in recent years become commonplace. Bioengineering is largely being used to help patients suffering from disease, and Ms. Anderson thought "why not see how far we can push it?" Thus Ms. Anderson has consolidated her ideas and research in her new book "Our Future." Without further ado, let's welcome Ms. Cheryl Anderson and hopefully she can explain further about the concept and answer questions from our audience. Ms. Anderson, thank you for being here.

聽出此獨白的幾個關鍵點，便可了解整篇的大概了，要點包括：講者是廣播主持人，要介紹今天的來賓是「Our Future」一書的作者，此專家主要研究生物工程並將概念與研究結合寫成此書，到節目中會討論相關問題！由此可聽出，抓到幾個關鍵點的確是可以了解全篇獨白的要義的喔！

利用獨白播放出來之前的幾秒空檔，很快地將題目先掃描一下，以便預期可能的獨白內容與要將注意力放在聽什麼要點上。

第一題

此題目問的是「Who is the speaker most likely?」，那麼便可判斷要聽出講者可能的「身分、職稱」以便回答。根據此關鍵句「Good morning Americans. This is Bird's Eye, Paul Jackins, bringing you the latest and most wanted knowledge and news. Now in the studio is our special guest for today...」，可聽出講者可能是廣播主持人，且在介紹來賓，故選 (C)「A host for the radio program」為最佳答案。

各選項解析

- 選項 (A)「A software engineer」、選項 (B)「A high school student」或選項 (D)「A father of two girls」都不會是在廣播節目上主持談話之人，故不選。

第二題

此題問的是「Who is Ms. Cheryl Anderson most likely?」，判斷要聽出 Cheryl Anderson 的「身分、職稱」相關資訊以便回答。根據此關鍵句「Bioengineering is largely being used..., and Ms. Anderson thought "why not see how far we can push it?" Thus Ms. Anderson has consolidated her ideas and research in her new book "Our Future."」，可聽出 Cheryl Anderson 是寫 bioengineering 相關領域書籍的人，那應該是那方面專家較為合理，故選 (A)「An expert in the bioengineering field」為最佳答案。

各選項解析

- 選項 (B)「The author of the "Love from future" novel」、選項 (C)「A D.J. in the radio station」與選項 (D)「A medical doctor」都不是 Ms. Anderson 的身分，故不選。

第三題

此題問的是「What is going to happen next most likely?」，接著在內心預設聽到接下來會「發生何事」相關資訊以便回答。根據此關鍵句「... let's welcome Ms. Cheryl Anderson and hopefully she can explain further about the concept and answer questions from our audience. Ms. Anderson, thank you for being here.」，可聽出講者要介紹 Ms. Anderson 出場，接下來應該是 Ms. Anderson 會講話較為合理，故選 (D)「Ms. Anderson will talk.」為最佳答案。

各選項解析

- 選項 (A)「A professor will present」、選項 (B)「A radio listener will join the program」與選項 (C)「The speaker will go home」都不是在獨白中提及接下來會發生之事，故不選。

關鍵字彙

technological [tɛknəˋlɑdʒɪk!] a 科技的
intervention [͵ɪntəˋvɛnʃən] n 介入、干預
transform [trænsˋfɔrm] v 轉變
commonplace [ˋkɑmən͵ples] a 司空見慣的
bioengineering [͵baɪo͵ɛndʒəˋnɪrɪŋ] n 生物工程
patient [ˋpeʃənt] n 病人
disease [dɪˋziz] n 疾病
consolidate [kənˋsɑlə͵det] v 合併、聯合
concept [ˋkɑnsɛpt] n 概念

Q1. When is the talk taking place most likely?

(A) After midnight   (B) In the morning

(C) In the afternoon   (D) In the evening

Q2. What is the main topic of the program?

(A) How to boost team members' confidence

(B) Why children always want to play games

(C) How team spirit influences children's performance

(D) How to help children to score high on math

Q3. Who will probably speak next?

(A) A professor from the University of Norman

(B) Mr. Oliver Jackson

(C) Ms. Sandra Jones

(D) A child

解題分析

主題 57%

時間 22%

人物 21%

■ **主題 57%** 第二題的關鍵在於 main topic，也就是在問這段廣播想表達的「主題」為何，因此聽的時候要特別注意與此相符的內容。

■ **時間 22%** 第一題的開頭是 when，可以知道本題與「時間」有關，因此推測接下來要聽的重點為這段獨白發表的「時間、時機點」。

■ **人物 21%** 第三個問題是以 who 為開頭，問下一個說話的人是哪位，由此推敲在獨白中會聽到某位即將登場的「人物」。

聽稿

（US / Ⓦ）Hello, listeners. This is Sandra Jones. Thank you for listening to our "Max Health" program this morning. Today we're going to talk about how team players make better students, all right? So a new study of the University of Norman found that children who participated in regular, structured team sports early on performed better in the classroom. According to the study, children who were involved in team sport in kindergarten were markedly better at following instructions and staying focused in school by the time they reached fifth grade. The researchers believed the sense of belonging to a team with a common goal appears to help children understand the importance of following rules and living up to responsibilities. Well, guess what? We're lucky to have one of the researchers to be here today with us and talk further about this. Let's now welcome Mr. Oliver Jackson please.

中譯

（美／女）各位聽眾大家好，我是珊卓・瓊斯。感謝您們收聽今早的「極致健康」廣播節目。今天我們要談論關於團隊合作如何提升莘莘學子的技能。一篇諾曼大學的研究報告發現：凡定期參與有組織性的團隊運動之孩童，都能夠在課堂上有較傑出的表現。該研究指出，那些於幼稚園時期便參加團隊運動的孩童，在讀到國小五年級的時候，明顯地比其他同學有著更高的紀律和專注力。學者們相信培養團隊歸屬感與向心力，處於為了同一個目標奮戰的情況下，孩子們能更深刻地了解遵守規則與責任感的重要性。各位知道嗎？我們很幸運能邀請到其中一位研究者來到節目現場，為大家做更進一步的說明。讓我們一同歡迎奧利弗・傑克森先生。

Q1. 此獨白最有可能在何時聽到？（答案：B）
(A) 午夜後　　　　　　　　　　　　　(B) 早上
(C) 下午　　　　　　　　　　　　　　(D) 晚上

Q2. 此節目主要討論的話題為何？（答案：C）
(A) 如何增加同仁的自信　　　　　　　(B) 為何小朋友都喜歡玩遊戲
(C) 團隊精神如何影響小孩的表現　　　(D) 如何協助小孩數學考高分

Q3. 接下來誰會說話？（答案：B）
(A) 諾曼大學的教授　　　　　　　　　(B) 奧利弗・傑克森先生
(C) 珊卓・瓊斯小姐　　　　　　　　　(D) 一個兒童

解題技巧

考生有時會認為：對獨白內所說的內容之背景不了解，因此聽不懂導致答對機率降低！但所考的三道題組真的是在問「專業內容」嗎？！並不是吧！三道題目也多是在問關於「獨白本身」的相關問題罷了，像是「誰在講話」、「聽到此獨白的時機」等，並不會問到「專業內容」，故不一定要聽懂所有內容；而是應專注在「回答題目」即可！先看題目再針對題目問的聽相對應答案，這才是有效的策略。而通常講者想強調的要點也會被加以重音來呈現：

（US／W）Hello, listeners. This is Sandra Jones. Thank you for listening to our "Max Health" program this morning. Today we're going to talk about how team players make better students, all right? So a new study of the University of Norman found that children who participated in regular, structured team sports early on performed better in the classroom. According to the study, children who were involved in team sport in kindergarten were markedly better at following instructions and staying focused in school by the time they reached fifth grade. The researchers believed the sense of belonging to a team with a common goal appears to help children understand the importance of following rules and living up to responsibilities. Well, guess what? We're lucky to have one of the researchers to be here today with us and talk further about this. Let's now welcome Mr. Oliver Jackson please.

抓到幾個要點後，便可大概了解此獨白的大意了，包括：講者在為廣播節目開場，主題是團隊合作對孩童表現的影響，若孩童有團體合作的經驗，則各方面表現較良好、也較有責任感，隨後講者會請專家 Oliver Jackson 來一同討論此主題。由上可知，僅聽到幾處關鍵點的確是可以對全篇獨白有個通盤了解的！

利用獨白播放出來之前的幾秒空檔，很快地將題目先掃描一下，以便預期可能的獨白內容與要將注意力放在聽什麼要點上。

第一題

此題問的是「When is the talk taking place most likely?」，那麼便可判斷要聽到此獨白可能發生之「時間、時機點」相關資訊以便回答。根據此關鍵句「Hello, listeners. This is Sandra Jones. Thank you for listening to our "Max Health" program this morning.」，既然講者是在介紹早上節目的主題，那應該是在「早上」聽到較為合理，故選 (B)「In the morning」為最佳答案。

各選項解析

- 選項 (A)「After midnight」、選項 (C)「In the afternoon」與選項 (D)「In the evening」都沒在獨白中提到，故不選。

第二題

此題問的是「What is the main topic of the program?」，我們便判斷要聽到此廣播的「主題」以便回答。根據此關鍵句「Today we're going to talk about how team players make better students, all right? So a new study... found that children who participated in regular, structured team sports early on performed better in the classroom.」，可聽出講者是在討論「團隊精神影響小孩表現」相關議題，故選 (C)「How team spirit influences children's performance」為最佳答案。

各選項解析

- 選項 (A)「How to boost team members' confidence」、選項 (B)「Why children always want to play games」與選項 (D)「How to help children to score high on math」都沒在獨白中被討論到，故不選。

第三題

先看到此題目問的是「Who will probably speak next?」，所以我們可以知道要聽到下一位講者「是誰」相關資訊以便回答。根據此關鍵句「We're lucky to have one of the researchers to be here today with us and talk further about this. Let's now welcome Mr. Oliver Jackson please.」，可聽出下一位講者是 Mr. Oliver Jackson，他會就此主題深入地討論，故選 (B)「Mr. Oliver Jackson」為最佳答案。

各選項解析

- 選項 (A)「A professor from the University of Norman」、選項 (C)「Ms. Sandra Jones 與選項 (D)「A child」都不是講者介紹下一位要出場的講者，故不選。

關鍵字彙

regular [ˋrɛgjələ] a 正常的、規律的
markedly [ˋmɑrkɪdlɪ] ad 顯著地
belonging [bəˋlɔŋɪŋ] n 親密安全關係
researcher [riˋsɝtʃə] n 研究員

攻略 3 │ 音樂節目廣播

Q1. Who are the listeners most likely?

(A) Parents who would like to know how to control kids

(B) People who enjoy listening to light music in the evening

(C) Students who are eager to enter the best universities

(D) Managers who plan to expand international markets

Q2. What does the speaker suggest interested listeners do?

(A) Attend a classic music event

(B) Discuss with more friends

(C) Do some market research

(D) Learn to play the piano

Q3. What will listeners hear next?

(A) Some English songs

(B) A long presentation

(C) Jazz music

(D) Commercial message

解題分析

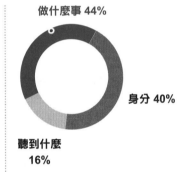

做什麼事 44%

身分 40%

聽到什麼 16%

■ 做什麼事 44% 第二題的重點是問講者建議有興趣的聽眾「做什麼事」，因此聽的時候要特別注意相關資訊。

■ 身分 40% 第一題的開頭是 who，表示本題要聽的重點與「人物」有關，且根據選項可以判斷本題所問的是聽眾的「身分」，很有可能是某個特定的族群。

■ 聽到什麼 16% 第三個問題是問聽眾接下來會「聽到什麼」，所以預測接下來的獨白中會提到選項中出現的內容。

聽稿

（UK / **M**）Dear listeners, this is Keven Jones. Welcome to the 9 p.m. Classic Music program. Well, some friends have been asking me where to begin listening to and appreciate classic music. In today's program, let me just provide all listeners with some tips, okay? So first of all, you can begin with what you already know. You may hear a piece of classic music in a restaurant, a shopping mall, or in the movies. It can be very easy to find on the Internet. Well, and then perhaps you like to listen to and research popular composers such as Beethoven, and Bach. Or if you are interested, attending a classical music performance would be a wonderful idea. All right, next we're gonna talk about some famous and popular classical music albums later. We'll be right back after these commercial messages.

（英／男）親愛的聽眾們，我是凱文‧瓊斯，歡迎收聽晚上九點的古典音樂節目。有一些朋友們曾問過我該從哪方面著手進入古典音樂之欣賞和聆聽的領域。今日的節目我決定分享各位聽眾一些獨到的小祕訣。首先，你可以從你已知的角度去切入。或許你曾經在某間餐廳、購物中心、或電影院裡聽到了某段古典音樂的樂章，這些資料在網路上的搜尋引擎都是唾手可得的。或者你可能喜歡聆聽一些較為有名之音樂家的作品，好比貝多芬、巴哈等人，也可以針對他們的音樂進行尋找。再不然，如果你有興趣，直接參加一場古典音樂的演奏會絕對是個不錯的選擇。好的，接著我們要來聊聊一些有名且熱門的古典音樂，讓我們先進段廣告，馬上回來。

Q1. 聽眾最有可能是誰？（答案：B）

(A) 想了解如何控制小孩的家長

(B) 喜歡在晚上聽點輕音樂的人

(C) 想進最佳大學的學生

(D) 想擴大國際市場的經理人

Q2. 講者建議有興趣的聽眾可以做什麼？（答案：A）

(A) 參與一場古典音樂活動

(B) 跟更多朋友討論

(C) 做些市場調查

(D) 學彈鋼琴

Q3. 聽眾接下來會聽到什麼？（答案：D）

(A) 一些英文歌曲

(B) 冗長的報告

(C) 爵士樂

(D) 廣告訊息

在處理長篇的獨白，考生可能會想先將獨白全盤聽懂之後，再來回答三道題組的策略，但事實上這樣的作法並非最有效！較佳的策略應是相反，先看三道題目問什麼，再根據所問的去聽「可回答題目的關鍵句」即可。而這些講者想要強調的關鍵句，自然會以「加強重音」來處理，以便吸引到聽眾的注意：

（UK／M）Dear listeners, this is Keven Jones. Welcome to the 9 p.m. Classic Music program. Well, some friends have been asking me where to begin listening to and appreciate classic music. In today's program, let me just provide all listeners with some tips, okay? So first of all, you can begin with what you already know. You may hear a piece of classic music in a restaurant, a shopping mall, or in the movies. It can be very easy to find on the Internet. Well, and then perhaps you like to listen to and research popular composers such as Beethoven, and Bach. Or if you are interested, attending a classical music performance would be a wonderful idea. All right, next we're gonna talk about some famous and popular classical music albums later. We'll be right back after these commercial messages.

此篇獨白不經過逐字翻譯，而是僅聽幾個關鍵點，便可歸納出一些大意了，包括：講者是為音樂廣播節目開場，在討論如何進入欣賞古典音樂的領域，有興趣的人可以去聽場古典音樂的演奏會，廣告後回來他便會討論一些古典音樂專輯。如此專注在幾個關鍵點，便可了解全篇的八成內容了。

利用獨白播放出來之前的幾秒空檔，很快地將題目先掃描一下，以便預期可能的獨白內容與要將注意力放在聽什麼要點上。

第一題

先很快地看到此題目問的是「Who are the listeners most likely?」，那麼便可判斷要聽到聽眾可能的「身分」相關資訊以便回答。根據此關鍵句「Dear listeners, this is Keven Jones. Welcome to the 9 p.m. Classic Music program.」，可聽出講者是在為晚間的古典音樂廣播節目開場，會聽此頻道的會是「喜歡在晚上聽點古典音樂之人」較為合理，故選 (B)「People who enjoy listening to light music in the evening」為最佳答案。

各選項解析

• 選項 (A)「Parents who would like to know how to control kids」、選項 (C)「Students who are eager to enter the best universities」與選項 (D)「Managers who plan to expand international markets」都無法從獨白中推論出，故不選。

第二題

此題問的是「What does the speaker suggest interested listeners do?」，可判斷要聽到講者建議有興趣的聽眾「做什麼事」相關資訊以便回答。根據此關鍵句「Or if you are interested, attending a classical music performance would be a wonderful idea.」，可聽出講者建議可以聽場音樂會，故選 (A)「Attend a classic music event」為最佳答案。

各選項解析

• 選項 (B)「Discuss with more friends」、選項 (C)「Do some market research」與選項 (D)「Learn to play the piano」都沒在獨白中被提及，故不選。

第三題

先看到題目問的是説「What will listeners hear next?」，我們可以知道要聽到聽眾接下來會「聽到什麼」相關資訊以便回答。根據此關鍵句「We'll be right back after these commercial messages.」，可聽出講者講完此段話，就要進廣告了，因此接下來可能會聽到一段廣告，故選 (D)「Commercial message」為最佳答案。

各選項解析

• 選項 (A)「Some English songs」、選項 (B)「A long presentation」與選項 (C)「Jazz music」都沒有在獨白中被提及，故不選。

關鍵字彙

welcome [ˈwɛlkəm] v 歡迎
appreciate [əˈpriʃˌɛt] v 感激、讚賞
classic music ph 古典音樂
tip [tɪp] n 訣竅
perhaps [pəˈhæps] ad 大概、可能
composer [kəmˈpozə] n 作曲家
famous [ˈfeməs] a 有名的
album [ˈælbəm] n 專輯
commercial [kəˈmɝʃəl] a 商業的

攻略 1 | 今日天氣預報

Q1. When is the talk most likely taking place?

(A) In the evening   (B) In the morning

(C) At midnight   (D) In the afternoon

Q2. According to the speaker, what are the weather conditions in Taipei?

(A) Rainy   (B) Snowy

(C) Sunny   (D) Extremely hot

Q3. What is the weather like in the south of Taiwan?

(A) Sunny   (B) Cold

(C) Cool   (D) Snowy

解題分析

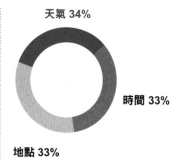

- 天氣 34%
- 時間 33%
- 地點 33%

■ 天氣 34% 第二題的關鍵詞為 weather condition，可以清楚看出題目在問的是台北的「天氣」，所以要注意聽接下來有關天氣的敘述。

第三個問題也有出現 weather，本題很清楚的是在詢問南台灣的「天氣」，預計在接下來的獨白中會聽到與此地區相符的天氣狀況。

■ 時間 33% 第一題是 when 開頭的問題，很明顯地與「時間」相關，問的是講者說話的時間點，預測在獨白中要聽到足以判定時間的線索。

■ 地點 33% 由於後兩題的問題中都有出現「地點」，因此在聽的時候要仔細分辨獨白中的地點和天氣是否跟題目相符。

聽稿

（US / W）Hello, all listeners. This is Lily Anna with your 9 a.m. weather report. Well, we've still got some heavy showers rumbling around in Taipei area. And for the next two days, there is a chance of some rain too, so be sure to bring an umbrella with you all the time. The temperature is around twenty degree Celsius. In the east, it's also rainy all day today. There may be a thunderstorm in the afternoon. The good news is in the west and middle of Taiwan, fewer showers and more in the way of sunshine. The south of Taiwan has the best weather conditions today. It's cloudy this morning but sunny this afternoon. The current temperature is around 27 degree Celsius.

中譯　（美／女）各位聽眾好，我是早上九點鐘負責氣象報導的莉莉‧安娜。今天的大台北地區依然會有豪大陣雨，而接下來的兩天，則可能都會有持續降雨的機率。請各位務必隨身攜帶雨具出門。今日的氣溫大約在攝氏二十度上下。東半部會出現一整天的降雨情形，午後可能會有雷陣雨。好消息是西半部和中部地區，零星的降雨機率將伴隨陽光普照的美好晴天。南台灣則能沐浴在萬里無雲的好天氣裡。今日白天普遍為多雲的陰天，下半天則逐漸豔陽高照。此時的氣溫約略在攝氏二十七度左右。

Q1. 此獨白最有可能在何時聽到？（答案：**B**）

(A) 晚上　　　　　　　　　　　　(B) 早上

(C) 午夜　　　　　　　　　　　　(D) 下午

Q2. 根據講者所言，台北天候狀況如何？（答案：**A**）

(A) 雨天　　　　　　　　　　　　(B) 下雪

(C) 晴天　　　　　　　　　　　　(D) 極熱

Q3. 台灣南部天氣如何？（答案：**A**）

(A) 晴天　　　　　　　　　　　　(B) 很冷

(C) 涼爽　　　　　　　　　　　　(D) 下雪

解題技巧　考生若有「不聽懂全部內容會不安心」的觀念，應盡早修正。獨白的內容設計不是要以將考生考倒為目的，而是為了測驗考生的專注力，和是否有準確地回答到問題。因此較有效的策略應是先掃描問題，了解問題的方向，才知道要聽什麼要點。聽力播出時便應將注意力放在聽「關鍵點」上即可，而這些要點通常會被講者「加強重音」以突顯其重要性：

> （US／W）Hello, all listeners. This is Lily Anna with your 9 a.m. weather report. Well, we've still got some heavy showers rumbling around in Taipei area. And for the next two days, there is a chance of some rain too, so be sure to bring an umbrella with you all the time. The temperature is around twenty degree Celsius. In the east, it's also rainy all day today. There may be a thunderstorm in the afternoon. The good news is in the west and middle of Taiwan, fewer showers and more in the way of sunshine. The south of Taiwan has the best weather conditions today. It's cloudy this morning but sunny this afternoon. The current temperature is around 27 degree Celsius.

聽到幾個關於此獨白的關鍵點之後，便可了解個大概內容了，包括：此講者是在報氣象狀況，台北下雨、中西部有出太陽、南部天氣晴朗……等。如此聽到幾個要點，便可以掌握獨白的八成內容了，並不一定要逐字了解翻譯才可做到呀！因此，建議考生要多訓練「專注在關鍵點」的能力喔！

利用獨白播放出來之前的幾秒空檔，很快地將題目先掃描一下，以便預期可能的獨白內容與要將注意力放在聽什麼要點上。

此題問的是「When is the talk most likely taking place?」，那麼可判斷要聽到此獨白可能發生之「時間點、時機」相關訊息以便回答。根據此關鍵句「Hello, all listeners. This is Lily Anna with your 9 a.m. weather report.」可聽出是「早上九點」，故選 (B)「In the morning」為最適合的答案。

各選項解析

• 選項 (A)「In the evening」、選項 (C)「At mid night」與選項 (D)「In the afternoon」都不是會聽到此獨白的時間，故不選。

第二題

此題問的是「What are the weather conditions in Taipei?」，判斷要聽到「台北天氣狀況」以便回答問題。根據此關鍵句「Well, we've still got some heavy showers rumbling around in Taipei area. And for the next two days, there is a chance of some rain too...」可聽出台北會下雨，故選 (A)「Rainy」為最佳答案。

各選項解析

• 選項 (B)「Snowy」、選項 (C)「Sunny」與選項 (D)「Extremely hot」都沒在文中被提及是台北的狀況，故不選。

第三題

此題問的是「What is the weather like in the south of Taiwan?」，我們要聽出「台灣南部氣候」狀況以便回答。根據此關鍵句「The south of Taiwan has the best weather conditions today. It's cloudy this morning but sunny this afternoon.」，可聽出南部是好天氣，故選 (A)「Sunny」為最佳答案。

各選項解析

• 選項 (B)「Cold」、選項 (C)「Cool」與選項 (D)「Snowy」都並非獨白中提及的南部天氣狀況，故不選。

關鍵字彙

thunderstorm [ˋθʌndɚˌstɔrm] n 雷雨
sunshine [ˋsʌnˌʃaɪn] n 陽光
condition [kənˋdɪʃən] n 狀況
cloudy [ˋklaʊdɪ] a 多雲的

Q1. What are the listeners most likely learning about?

(A) World history   (B) English reading skills

(C) Knowledge about typhoons   (D) Math

Q2. According to the talk, what are storms called in the Atlantic Ocean?

(A) Hurricane   (B) Typhoon

(C) Tropical Cyclone   (D) Heavy Storm

Q3. What would the listeners like to do next?

(A) Go home and find their parents   (B) Learn more about storms

(C) Take a break   (D) Play online games

解題分析

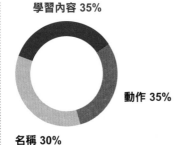

學習內容 35%

動作 35%

名稱 30%

■ 學習內容 35% 　第一題重點在於問聽眾在「學習什麼」，因此可以推斷接下來要聽到的與「學習的內容」有關。

■ 動作 35% 　第三個問題是在問聽眾等一下要做什麼，因此聽的時候要將注意力放在聽眾即將做出的「動作」上，即可判斷答案。

■ 名稱 30% 　第二題主要是問暴風這個天氣現象，在大西洋地區是什麼「名稱」，預測接下來要聽到與此相符的內容。

聽稿

（CA / **M**）Hello, all my little friends. My name is Jerry, and I'm happy to be here in Class 304. Here in Taiwan, we encounter typhoons especially during summer time, right? So do you all know what a typhoon is? Well, not really? All right, so today I'm gonna tell you what a typhoon really is. A typhoon is a type of large storm system with heavy rain and violent winds. And you know what? There are different names for such storms, like "typhoon" is the name of these storms that occur in the Western Pacific. And let us take a look at the map here. In the Indian Ocean, they are called "tropical cyclones." In Atlantic Ocean, they are called "hurricane." All right, now raise your hands if you'd like to learn more about "super storms." Wonderful, you're all good students. Now let's talk about the "eye" of typhoons.

（加 / **男**）各位小朋友你們好。我的名字是傑利，很高興能夠加入 304 班的行列。大家都知道在台灣，我們常常會在夏季時遇到不少颱風，對吧？那麼你們知道什麼是颱風嗎？咦？不是很了解嗎？沒關係，今天我就來告訴你們什麼是颱風。颱風是一種很強大的暴風雨系統，它夾帶著大量的雨水和猛烈的風力。你們知道嗎？類似這種暴風雨的氣候型態其實有著不同的名稱，在西太平洋形成的我們稱之為颱風。大家一起來看看地圖上的這一區塊。在印度洋這裡，我們稱之為熱帶氣旋。在大西洋這邊，它們則叫颶風。好了，如果還想學習更多有關這些超級暴風雨的知識的小朋友們，請舉起你們的手。太好了，你們都是認真的學生。那麼就讓我們繼續來講關於颱風眼的常識吧。

Q1. 聽眾最有可能是在學些什麼？（答案：**C**）

(A) 世界歷史   (B) 英文閱讀技巧

(C) 關於颱風的知識   (D) 數學

Q2. 根據獨白內容，暴風在大西洋地區的名稱為何？（答案：**A**）

(A) 颶風   (B) 颱風

(C) 熱帶氣旋   (D) 大暴風雨

Q3. 聽眾接下來想做什麼？（答案：**B**）

(A) 回家找爸媽   (B) 了解更多關於暴風之事

(C) 休息一下   (D) 玩線上遊戲

解題技巧

若是僅唸一兩句的題目，還有可能想每個字都聽到並聽懂，但面對長篇的獨白，便無法也沒必要將每字每句都加以了解。考生的目標應是「正確地回答到問題」即可，因此聽獨白時大可以捨棄次要資訊，將專注在聽「有問的要點」即可。先掃描題目會是個好的開始，接著再聽題目有問的資訊上，所幸這些會考的要點也通常是講者想強調之處，可能會以「加強重音」來突顯：

（CA / **M**）Hello, all my little friends. My name is Jerry, and I'm happy to be here in Class 304. Here in Taiwan, we encounter typhoons especially during summer time, right? So do you all know what a typhoon is? Well, not really? All right, so today I'm gonna tell you what a typhoon really is. A typhoon is a type of large storm system with heavy rain and violent winds. And you know what? There are different names for such storms, like "typhoon" is the name of these storms that occur in the Western Pacific. And let us take a look at the map here. In the Indian Ocean, they are called "tropical cyclones." In Atlantic Ocean, they are called "hurricane." All right, now raise your hands if you'd like to learn more about "super storms." Wonderful, you're all good students. Now let's talk about the "eye" of typhoons.

經過抓出幾個要點後，便可歸納關於此獨白的大意了，包括：此講者在對小朋友介紹颱風相關知識，討論到在不同地區，颱風便有不同名稱，接下來還會討論到「颱風眼」其他相關知識。如此便可有效地了解大約內容了，千萬不要一邊聽一邊在心裡翻譯句子喔！

利用獨白播放出來之前的幾秒空檔，很快地將題目先掃描一下，以便預期可能的獨白內容與要將注意力放在聽什麼要點上。

第一題

此題問的是「What are the listeners most likely learning about?」，那麼便可判斷要聽到聽眾所在「學習什麼新知」相關資訊以便回答。根據此關鍵句「So do you all know what a typhoon is? Well, not really? All right, so today I'm gonna tell you what a typhoon really is.」，可聽出講者是在介紹關於颱風的知識，故選 (C)「Knowledge about typhoons」為最佳答案。

各選項解析

• 選項 (A)「World history」、選項 (B)「English reading skills」與選項 (D)「Math」都沒有在獨白中提及，故不選。

第二題

此題問的是「What are storms called in the Atlantic Ocean?」，判斷要聽到暴風在 Atlantic Ocean 地區的「名稱」相關資訊以便回答。根據此關鍵句「In Atlantic Ocean, they are called "hurricane."」，可聽出是稱為「Hurricane」，故選 (A)「Hurricane」為最佳答案。

各選項解析

• 選項 (B)「Typhoon」、選項 (C)「Tropical Cyclone」與選項 (D)「Heavy Storm」都不是在 Atlantic Ocean 地區對暴風的稱呼，故不選。

第三題

此題問的是「What would the listeners like to do next?」，知道要聽到聽眾接下來「想做什麼」相關資訊以便回答。根據此關鍵句「All right, now raise your hands if you'd like to learn more about "super storms." Wonderful, you're all good students. Now let's talk about the "eye" of typhoons.」，可聽出他們是想多了解颱風相關的知識，故選 (B)「Learn more about storms」為最佳答案。

各選項解析

• 選項 (A)「Go home and find their parents」、選項 (C)「Take a break」與選項 (D)「Play online games」都沒在獨白中被提及，故不選。

關鍵字彙

encounter [ɪnˋkaʊntɚ] ⓥ 遭受、遭遇
typhoon [taɪˋfun] ⓝ 颱風
storm [stɔrm] ⓝ 暴風
violent [ˋvaɪələnt] ⓐ 激烈的
tropical [ˋtrɑpɪkl] ⓐ 熱帶的
cyclone [ˋsaɪklon] ⓝ 旋風、氣旋
hurricane [ˋhɝɪˏken] ⓝ 颶風

Q1. Who is most likely the speaker?

(A) A foreign visitor   (B) A professor

(C) A news reporter   (D) An Indian actor

Q2. According to the talk, what happened to the people in India?

(A) Winter is coming

(B) Some people died because of the heat

(C) More Indian students choose to study in the U.S.

(D) Citizens are all required to learn English

Q3. What will the speaker talk about afterwards most likely?

(A) A famous American singer   (B) Education issues in Asia

(C) Weather conditions in India   (D) News from other countries

---

解題分析

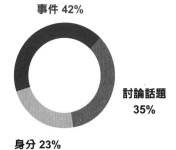

事件 42%

討論話題 35%

身分 23%

■ 事件 42%　第二個題目重點在於印度「發生了什麼事」，因此聽的時候要特別留意說話者提到的「事件」，找出跟題目符合的敘述。

■ 討論話題 35%　第三題詢問的是接下來講者會討論什麼事，可以推測會聽到的資訊與稍後「討論的話題」有關，必須特別注意。

■ 身分 23%　第一題是 who 開頭的句子，很明顯是要問說話者的「身分」，預計接下來要聽到的是有關其身分與職稱的敘述。

聽稿

（US / Ⓦ）All listeners. Now let's find out what is happening around the world. India is facing a record hot and deadly summer this year. In July, scores of people died as they were struck by high temperatures more than 51 degrees Celsius, which is equivalent to 124 degrees Fahrenheit. The Indian Meteorological Department predicts that New Delhi, India's capital, will hit 50 degrees Celsius again tomorrow. Indians are doing whatever they can to stay cool during a brutal heat wave that has killed more than a thousand people. Heat waves will become more intense, and that's one of the most obvious outcomes of the global warming. Please stay tuned as we'll be back with more international news right after these messages.

中譯　（美／女）所有聽眾，我們來探索其他世界上發生的大事吧。印度今年夏天正面臨著前所未有的致命性高溫。七月時已經有許多人死於攝氏五十一度以上的高溫，相當於華氏一百二十四度的氣溫。印度的氣象局預測，印度的首都新德里可能會在明日又達到攝氏五十度左右的高溫。由於該國家已經有超過一千人死亡的紀錄，印度居民正無所不用其極地想盡辦法讓自己在殘酷的熱浪中保持涼爽。熱浪將會愈演愈烈，這其實正是全球暖化其中一項明顯的後果。請繼續收聽接下來的節目，廣告後我們將為您報導其他的國際新聞。

Q1. 講者最有可能是誰？（答案：C）
(A) 國外訪客 　　　　　　　　　　(B) 教授
(C) 新聞播報員 　　　　　　　　　(D) 印度演員

Q2. 根據獨白所言，在印度的人遭受何事？（答案：B）
(A) 冬天快到了 　　　　　　　　　(B) 一些人因酷暑而死了
(C) 更多印度學生想去美國讀書 　　(D) 人民都被要求學英文

Q3. 接下來講者最有可能會討論什麼？（答案：D）
(A) 一位有名的美國歌手 　　　　　(B) 亞洲的教育議題
(C) 印度的天候狀況 　　　　　　　(D) 其他國家的新聞

解題技巧　考生常在聽獨白的同時將眼睛閉上，想要專心地聽內容，但眼睛閉上的話要如何同時掃描題目和比對答案呢？這是頗危險的作法。較安全有效的作法應該是，聽獨白之前馬上先掃描題目，知道題目問的方向，聽獨白時僅聽到「可以回答題目的資訊」即可，最好是還可以一邊比對四個答案選項。若無法判斷「關鍵點」之處，可以試著將注意力放在聽「講者有加強重音」之處，因這些要點才有可能是講者想強調的地方呀：

> （US／W）All listeners. Now let's find out what is happening around the world. India is facing a record hot and deadly summer this year. In July, scores of people died as they were struck by high temperatures more than 51 degrees Celsius, which is equivalent to 124 degrees Fahrenheit. The Indian Meteorological Department predicts that New Delhi, India's capital, will hit 50 degrees Celsius again tomorrow. Indians are doing whatever they can to stay cool during a brutal heat wave that has killed more than a thousand people. Heat waves will become more intense, and that's one of the most obvious outcomes of the global warming. Please stay tuned as we'll be back with more international news right after these messages.

了解幾處關鍵點之後，便可聽出約略的大意了，也就是：講者在報告世界新聞，在印度因熱浪來襲，便造成很多人死亡，人們想辦法在大熱天保持涼爽，而此熱浪也可能是氣候暖化的結果，接下來講者還會報告其他國際消息。由此可聽出，我們並沒有一字一句地翻譯，而是僅專注在幾個關鍵點上而已，一樣可以了解大意喔！

利用獨白播放出來之前的幾秒空檔，很快地將題目先掃描一下，以便預期可能的獨白內容與要將注意力放在聽什麼要點上。

此題問的「Who is most likely the speaker?」，那麼便可判斷要聽到講者可能之「身分、職稱」等相關資訊以便回答。根據此關鍵句「All listeners. Now let's find out what is happening around the world.」，可聽出要跟聽眾報告「世界上發生什麼事」的人應是「新聞播報員」較為合理，故選 (C)「A news reporter」為最佳答案。

各選項解析

- 選項 (A)「A foreign visitor」、選項 (B)「A professor」或選項 (D)「An Indian actor」都不會是播報新聞之人，故不選。

第二題

此題問的是「What happened to the people in India?」，判斷要聽到在印度「發生什麼事」相關資訊以便回答。根據此關鍵句「India is facing a record hot and deadly summer this year. In July, scores of people died as they were struck by high temperatures more than 51 degrees Celsius...」，可聽出是天氣太熱導致印度很多人熱死，故選 (B)「Some people died because of the heat.」為最佳答案。

各選項解析

- 選項 (A)「Winter is coming.」、選項 (C)「More Indian students choose to study in the U.S.」與選項 (D)「Citizens are required to learn English.」都沒在獨白中被討論到，故不選。

第三題

先看到題目問的是「What will the speaker talk about afterwards most likely?」，我們知道要聽出講者「接下來討論何事」相關資訊以便回答。根據此關鍵句「Please stay tuned as we'll be back with more international news right after these messages.」可聽出講者接下來是要講發生在其他國家的新聞，故選 (D)「News from other countries」為最佳答案。

各選項解析

- 選項 (A)「A famous American singer」、選項 (B)「Education issues in Asia」與選項 (C)「Weather conditions in India」都不是講者說接下來要討論之事，故不選。

關鍵字彙

deadly [ˈdɛdlɪ] a 致命的
equivalent [ɪˈkwɪvələnt] n 相等物
predict [prɪˈdɪkt] v 預測
brutal [ˈbrutl̩] a 嚴苛的、粗暴的
intense [ɪnˈtɛns] a 激烈的
obvious [ˈɑbvɪəs] a 明顯的
outcome [ˈautˌkʌm] n 結果
global warming [ˈglobl̩ ˌwɔrmɪŋ] n 全球暖化

Unit 12 表演會場類

攻略 1 | 發表會開場

Q1. What is the purpose of this talk?

(A) To announce new policies   (B) To thank teachers

(C) To open a dancing event   (D) To invite singers

Q2. According to the talk, who will perform next?

(A) Parents   (B) Students

(C) Teachers   (D) Schoolmasters

Q3. Who will introduce the first dance?

(A) Ms. Lily Lee   (B) Ms. Kelly Jones

(C) A teacher   (D) A performer

解題分析

人物 68%

目的 32%

■ 人物 68%　第二題的關鍵是 who，所以接下來預計要聽到的是下一個表演的「人物」，也因為有 perform 這個字，推測等一下的獨白是發生在表演場合。

第三題也是跟「人物」有關的問題，詢問誰會介紹下一支舞，因此聽的時候要特別注意有無出現跟這個動作相關的對象。

■ 目的 32%　第一題的關鍵在於 purpose 這個字，很明顯是問這段獨白的主要「目的」，因此推測要聽到關於說話者目的的訊息。

聽稿

（US / Ⓦ）Good evening and welcome to the 1st performance of Lily's Dancing School. I'm Kelly Jones the head teacher, and it's been my pleasure to work with all students and other teachers for the past four months. The students have made great strides in a very short time. Most of them had never learned any kind of dancing before May. They've learned not only how to dance elegantly, but how to work with others as a group, and most of all proper etiquette and discipline. I'm sure you'll be impressed with their wonderful performance. At this time it's my pleasure to introduce the director of Lily's Dancing School, Ms. Lily Lee, who is also going to introduce the first dance being performed.

（美 / 女）各位晚安，歡迎蒞臨莉莉舞蹈學院第一屆成果發表會，我是指導老師凱莉‧瓊斯。很榮幸能和學生及老師們一起合作參與過去四個月的演練。學生們在短時間內進步神速，甚至有很多同學在五月以前完全沒有任何舞蹈基礎。他們不只學會了優雅的舞步，也學習到如何與他人進行團體合作，最重要的是養成了他們的禮儀和素養。相信各位將會對他們的表演留下深刻的印象。現在就讓我邀請莉莉舞蹈學院的大家長李莉莉出場，同時請她為我們介紹第一支舞蹈的表演節目。

Q1. 此獨白的主旨為何？（答案：C）

(A) 為公告新的政策

(B) 為感謝老師

(C) 為舞蹈表演活動開場

(D) 為邀請歌手

Q2. 根據獨白內容，接下來誰會表演？（答案：B）

(A) 家長

(B) 學生

(C) 老師

(D) 校長

Q3. 誰會介紹第一支舞？（答案：A）

(A) 李莉莉小姐

(B) 凱莉‧瓊斯小姐

(C) 老師

(D) 表演者

解題技巧　與其想要將所有內容全盤了解，不如將有限的精神發揮在「聽可以回答問題」的關鍵點上即可。要達成這樣的目標，便可先掃描題目，再聽題目問及的相關資訊以便回答。考生也不用太擔心會聽不到要點，通常講者想要強調的關鍵點會經過「加強重音」的處理，以便引起聽者的注意：

（US / W）Good evening and welcome to the 1st performance of Lily's Dancing School. I'm Kelly Jones the head teacher, and it's been my pleasure to work with all students and other teachers for the past four months. The students have made great strides in a very short time. Most of them had never learned any kind of dancing before May. They've learned not only how to dance elegantly, but how to work with others as a group, and most of all proper etiquette and discipline. I'm sure you'll be impressed with their wonderful performance. At this time it's my pleasure to introduce the director of Lily's Dancing School, Ms. Lily Lee, who is also going to introduce the first dance being performed.

如此聽到幾個關鍵點，便可得之此講者是在為舞蹈表演做開場，講者讚賞表演學生很努力練習，不但學到優雅舞姿，還學到團隊合作，接下來會由 Lily Lee 來介紹第一支舞蹈表演。如此專注在要點上，的確是可以了解全篇獨白的大意的！

利用獨白播放出來之前的幾秒空檔，很快地將題目先掃描一下，以便預期可能的獨白內容與要將注意力放在聽什麼要點上。

第一題

先掃描到題目問的是「What is the purpose of this talk?」，那麼便判斷要聽到此獨白的「目的」以便回答。根據此關鍵句的內容「Good evening and welcome to the 1st performance of Lily's Dancing School.」，可聽出講者是在介紹舞蹈表演的開場，故選 (C)「To open a dancing event」為最佳答案。

各選項解析

- 選項 (A)「To announce new policies」、選項 (B)「To thank teachers」或選項 (D)「To invite singers」都與開場關鍵句無直接關係，故不選。

第二題

先看到此問題問的是「Who will perform next?」，既然是問接下來會表演的「是誰」，便可判斷要聽到「人物」相關資訊以便回答。根據此關鍵句「... it's been my pleasure to work with all students and other teachers for the past four months. The students have made great strides in a very short time.」，可聽出講者是在說「學生」為了此表演花了很多精力與時間準備，故要表演的應該是學生較為合理，故選 (B)「Students」為最佳答案。

各選項解析

- 選項 (A)「Parents」、選項 (C)「Teachers」與選項 (D)「Schoolmasters」都不是講者口中說要表演的人，故不選。

第三題

先看到題目問的是「Who will introduce the first dance?」，那麼便可判斷要聽到介紹首場表演之「人物」以便回答。根據此關鍵句「... it's my pleasure to introduce the director of Lily's Dancing School, Ms. Lily Lee, who is also going to introduce the first dance being performed.」，可聽出是「Ms. Lily Lee」要介紹，故選 (A)「Ms. Lily Lee」為答案。

各選項解析

- 選項 (B)「Ms. Kelly Jones」、選項 (C)「A teacher」與選項 (D)「A performer」都不是獨白內容提到要介紹舞曲之人，故不選。

關鍵字彙

pleasure [ˈplɛʒɚ] n 榮幸
stride [straɪd] n 步姿、步幅
elegantly [ˈɛləgəntlɪ] ad 優雅地
etiquette [ˈɛtɪkɛt] n 禮儀、禮節
discipline [ˈdɪsəplɪn] n 紀律、教養
impress [ɪmˈprɛs] v 印象深刻、留下深刻印象
director [dəˈrɛktɚ] n 領導人、導演

7:00 p.m. - 7:10 p.m.	Opening
7:10 p.m. - 8:20 p.m.	Act one
8:20 p.m. - 8:40 p.m.	Intermission
8:40 p.m. - 9:50 p.m.	Act two

Q1. **When is the talk most likely taking place?**

(A) Before a ballet performance   (B) During a company meeting

(C) In an English class   (D) Before a flight takes off

Q2. **What does the speaker ask listeners to do?**

(A) Donate some money   (B) Go on stage and perform

(C) Turn off cell phones   (D) Record the entire performance

新 Q3. **Look at the chart. What time are the audience members allowed to use a cell phone?**

(A) Between 8:20 p.m. and 8:40 p.m.   (B) After 7 p.m.

(C) Between 7:30 p.m. and 8:00 p.m.   (D) Anytime before 9:30 p.m.

解題分析

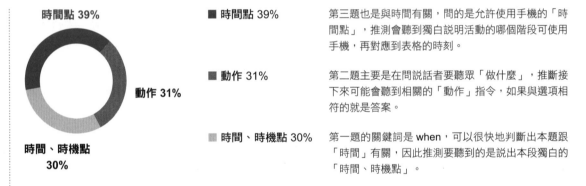

■ 時間點 39%

■ 動作 31%

■ 時間、時機點 30%

第三題也是與時間有關，問的是允許使用手機的「時間點」，推測會聽到獨白說明活動的哪個階段可使用手機，再對應到表格的時刻。

第二題主要是在問說話者要聽眾「做什麼」，推斷接下來可能會聽到相關的「動作」指令，如果與選項相符的就是答案。

第一題的關鍵詞是 when，可以很快地判斷出本題跟「時間」有關，因此推測要聽到的是說出本段獨白的「時間、時機點」。

聽稿

（US / ）Good evening, ladies and gentlemen. Welcome to tonight's performance of "Loving Ballet." The performance will begin in five minutes. Please note that any recording of this performance is strictly prohibited. We would also like to remind all of you that mobile phones should be turned off for the entire performance. There will be a twenty-minute intermission between act one and two. Should you be required to be contactable, please take advantage of the interval between acts. Thank you, and we hope you enjoy tonight's performance of "Loving Ballet."

中譯　（美／女）各位先生小姐晚安，歡迎蒞臨今晚「愛戀芭蕾」的表演現場。表演將於五分鐘後開始，過程中均嚴格禁止從事任何錄音、錄影的活動。敬請各位觀眾將行動電話關機，直至演出結束為止。在第一幕表演銜接第二幕的時候，我們會有二十分鐘的中場休息時間，若您有重要事務需要聯絡處理，請您妥善利用這段時間做安排。感謝您的配合，希望您盡情地享受今晚的「愛戀芭蕾」。

晚上七點～七點十分	開場
晚上七點十分～八點二十分	第一場表演
晚上八點二十分～八點四十分	中場休息
晚上八點四十分～九點五十分	第二場表演

Q1. 此獨白最有可能在何時聽到？（答案：A）

(A) 在芭蕾舞表演之前　　　　　　　(B) 在公司會議當中
(C) 在英文課上　　　　　　　　　　(D) 在班機起飛之前

Q2. 講者要求聽眾做什麼？（答案：C）

(A) 捐款　　　　　　　　　　　　　(B) 到台上表演
(C) 將手機關機　　　　　　　　　　(D) 將整場比賽錄下來

新 **Q3. 請看表格。觀眾在何時可以使用手機？（答案：A）**

(A) 晚上八點二十分到八點四十分　　(B) 晚上七點過後
(C) 晚上七點半到八點　　　　　　　(D) 晚上九點半前的任何時間

解題技巧　首先設定好策略便是要將注意力放在聽「可以回答問題的關鍵點」上頭，因此若可以先掃描題本上的題目是最好不過了，也只有先知道題目問什麼，才可針對問題去聽答案呀！所幸這些問題所專注的關鍵點，通常為被加以重音強調，讓聽者不致錯失資訊才是：

> （US／W）Good evening, ladies and gentlemen. Welcome to tonight's performance of "Loving Ballet." The performance will begin in five minutes. Please note that any recording of this performance is strictly prohibited. We would also like to remind all of you that mobile phones should be turned off for the entire performance. There will be a twenty-minute intermission between act one and two. Should you be required to be contactable, please take advantage of the interval between acts. Thank you, and we hope you enjoy tonight's performance of "Loving Ballet."

了解幾個關鍵之處，便可以歸納全篇獨白要點了：此講者在為舞蹈表演做開場，並提醒觀眾不要錄影、要關手機，要講電話應利用中場休息時間，最後希望觀眾喜歡此表演。抓到幾個關鍵點，對得知獨白大意有很大的幫助的喔！

利用獨白播放出來之前的幾秒空檔，很快地將題目先掃描一下，以便預期可能的獨白內容與要將注意力放在聽什麼要點上。

先掃描到此題問的是「When is the talk most likely taking place?」，那麼便可判斷要聽到此獨白可能講出的「時間、時機點」以便回答。根據此關鍵句「Good evening, ladies and gentlemen. Welcome to tonight's performance of "Loving Ballet."」，可聽出講者是在介紹芭蕾舞表演，那麼應該是在「表演之前」的開場白較為合理，故選 (A)「Before a ballet performance」為最佳答案。

各選項解析

• 選項 (B)「During a company meeting」、選項 (C)「In an English class」與選項 (D)「Before a flight takes off」都不像是此獨白會聽到的場合，故不選。

第二題

此題問的是「What does the speaker ask listeners to do?」，判斷要聽到講者要求聽眾「所做之事」相關資訊以便回答。根據此關鍵句「We would also like to remind all of you that mobile phones should be turned off for the entire performance.」，可聽出是要大家將手機關閉，故選 (C)「Turn off cell phones」為最佳答案。

各選項解析

• 選項 (A)「Donate some money」、選項 (B)「Go on stage and perform」與選項 (D)「Record the entire performance」都沒有在獨白中被提及，故不選。

新 第三題

先看到此題是有需要配合表格內容的，那麼應該將題目與表格內容先掃描一下。此題目問的是「What time are the audience members allowed to use a cell phone?」，既然問的是可以使用手機的「時間點」，也要搭配節目單內的時間點來判斷。根據此關鍵句「There will be a twenty-minute intermission between act one and two. Should you be required to be contactable, please take advantage of the interval between acts.」，可聽出要使用手機要在兩場表演之間的休息時間，再對照表格內的時間，中場休息是晚上八點二十分～八點四十分，故選 (A)「Between 8:20 p.m. and 8:40 p.m.」為最佳答案。

各選項解析

• 選項 (B)「After 7 p.m.」、選項 (C)「Between 7:30 p.m. and 8:00 p.m.」與選項 (D)「Anytime before 9:30 p.m.」都不是獨白中提到的「中場休息時間」，故不選。

關鍵字彙

performance [pɚˋfɔrməns] n 表演
strictly [ˋstrɪktlɪ] ad 嚴格地
prohibit [prəˋhɪbɪt] v 禁止
remind [rɪˋmaɪnd] v 提醒
intermission [ˌɪntɚˋmɪʃən] n 中場休息
contactable [ˋkɑntæktəbl̩] a 可聯繫到的
interval [ˋɪntɚvl̩] n 間隔、空檔

攻略 3 │ 運動會開場

Q1. Who is the speaker most likely?

(A) A sales representative
(B) A basketball player
(C) An HR specialist
(D) A basketball coach

Q2. What does the speaker encourage all listeners to do?

(A) Finish reports as early as possible
(B) Do their best in the event
(C) Drink more water
(D) Generate more sales leads

Q3. What will happen next most likely?

(A) All listeners will sing a song
(B) Some drinks will be served
(C) Competitions will begin
(D) The general manager will talk

解題分析

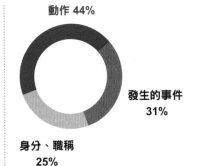

動作 44%
發生的事件 31%
身分、職稱 25%

■ 動作 44%

■ 發生的事件 31%

▨ 身分、職稱 25%

第二題的重點在於講者鼓勵聽眾「做什麼事」，因此可能會聽到獨白中提到相關的「動作」。

第三題詢問的是接下來會「發生什麼事」，預測會聽到的內容與「發生的事件」有關。

第一題是 who 開頭的問句，問說話者「是誰」，根據選項可預測接下來會聽到的是與其「身分、職稱」相關的描述。

聽稿　（UK / M ）Dear colleagues, it's our company's 23rd Annual Sports Day. I'm Tim from HR. Well, I'm sure all of you know me already. I would like to take this opportunity to extend a warm welcome to all participants. This company event speaks for the commitment that all colleagues hold for the sport. Do your best and compete in the spirit of sportsmanship and fair play, and take this opportunity to come closer to each other. Before we kick start the competition, and the General Manager, Ms. Julie Cambridge, would like to say a few words. Now let's welcome Ms. Cambridge please.

（英／男）親愛的同仁們，今天是本公司第二十三屆的年度運動大會，我是人資部的提姆，相信大家對我都不陌生。我要藉此機會表達對所有參與者的熱烈歡迎。此項活動代表著所有同仁對於運動的堅持與責任心。期望各位都能以公平競爭的方式、全力以赴地落實運動家精神，並藉由此次活動拉近彼此的距離。在比賽正式開始前，有請我們的總經理朱莉·康橋小姐來為大家勉勵幾句。讓我們歡迎康橋小姐。

Q1. 講者最有可能是誰？（答案：C）

(A) 業務代表　　　　　　　　　　　(B) 籃球員

(C) 人資專員　　　　　　　　　　　(D) 籃球教練

Q2. 講者鼓勵所有聽眾要做什麼？（答案：B）

(A) 儘早完成報告　　　　　　　　　(B) 在活動中全力以赴

(C) 多喝點水　　　　　　　　　　　(D) 開發更多生意機會

Q3. 接下來最有可能發生何事？（答案：D）

(A) 所有聽眾會唱首歌　　　　　　　(B) 會上飲料

(C) 比賽會開始　　　　　　　　　　(D) 總經理會上台講話

要精準地回答到三個題組，重要的是可以先掃描題目，了解題目方向之後再針對題目問的去聽「關鍵點」以便回答。千萬不要將思緒分散到每個字每句話上面，還試圖在心底將句子都翻譯成中文意思，如此對答題幫助是不大的。有效的策略是應將專注力放在聽「關鍵點」處，也就是有經過「加強重音」處理的地方：

（UK／M）Dear colleagues, it's our company's 23rd Annual Sports Day. I'm Tim from HR. Well, I'm sure all of you know me already. I would like to take this opportunity to extend a warm welcome to all participants. This company event speaks for the commitment that all colleagues hold for the sport. Do your best and compete in the spirit of sportsmanship and fair play, and take this opportunity to come closer to each other. Before we kick start the competition, and the General Manager, Ms. Julie Cambridge, would like to say a few words. Now let's welcome Ms. Cambridge please.

聽到以上幾個關鍵點，便可得知此獨白的大概內容了：此講者歡迎同事參加年度體育日活動，期望大家盡力參與並展現運動家精神，接下來請總經理上台致詞。如此抓到幾個要點便可得知大意了，可見得主要關鍵資訊，是比次要細節資訊來得重要多了喔！

利用獨白播放出來之前的幾秒空檔，很快地將題目先掃描一下，以便預期可能的獨白內容與要將注意力放在聽什麼要點上。

第一題

先看到題目問的是「Who is the speaker most likely?」，那麼便可判斷要聽出講者「身分、職稱」等相關資訊以便回答。根據此關鍵句「Dear colleagues, it's our company's 23rd Annual Sports Day. I'm Tim from HR. Well, I'm sure all of you know me already.」，可聽出講者說他是在「HR」部門上班，便應該是「人資專員」較為合理，故選 (C)「An HR specialist」為最佳答案。

各選項解析

- 選項 (A)「A sales representative」、選項 (B)「A basketball player」與選項 (D)「A basketball coach」都不會是在「HR」部門工作之人，故不選。

第二題

此題問的是「What does the speaker encourage all listeners to do?」，判斷要聽到講者鼓勵聽眾要「做什麼事情」以便回答。根據此關鍵句「Do your best and compete in the spirit of sportsmanship and fair play, and take this opportunity to come closer to each other.」，可聽出講者是要大家盡力參與活動，故選 (B)「Do their best in the event」為最佳答案。

各選項解析

- 選項 (A)「Finish reports as early as possible」、選項 (C)「Drink more water」與選項 (D)「Generate more sales leads」都沒有在獨白中提及，故不選。

第三題

此題問的是「What will happen next most likely?」，我們知道要聽到接下來所會「發生之事」以便回答。根據此關鍵句「Before we kick start the competition, and the General Manager, Ms. Julie Cambridge, would like to say a few words. Now let's welcome Ms. Cambridge please.」，可聽出在開始運動日之前，總經理會先談話，故選 (D)「The general manager will talk.」為最佳答案。

各選項解析

- 選項 (A)「All listeners will sing a song.」、選項 (B)「Some drinks will be served.」或選項 (C)「Competitions will begin.」都沒有在獨白中提及，故不選。

關鍵字彙

extend [ɪkˋstɛnd] v 給予
participant [parˋtɪsəpənt] n 參與者
commitment [kəˋmɪtmənt] n 承諾
compete [kəmˋpit] v 競爭
spirit [ˋspɪrɪt] n 精神
sportsmanship [ˋsportsmənˏʃɪp] n 運動家精神
kick start ph 開始

綜合練習

Q1. Where is the introduction probably taking place?

(A) At a business meeting

(B) At a radio program

(C) At a beach resort

(D) At a baseball game

Q2. According to the talk, who is Michael Brooks?

(A) A pupil

(B) An actor

(C) A linguist

(D) A Chinese

Q3. What most likely will Michael Brooks do next?

(A) Talk about his experience in China

(B) Give a presentation in Chinese

(C) Introduce a Chinese friend

(D) Analyze why Chinese is difficult to learn

聽稿　（US / Ⓦ）All right, my audience. I'm Jessie Goodwill. In tonight's program, we'll be interviewing the famous actor Michael Brooks. Michael went to China with his parents when he was 13 years old and persuaded the Beijing Art School to take him as their pupil. At that time, Michael was twice the age of the other students and hardly spoke Chinese. In the class, he took his little English-Chinese dictionary all the time as he really would like to show the teachers how determined he was. At first, Michael and the teachers were making signs at each other and misunderstanding. He just remained patient and kept learning. Eventually, he could now communicate with people in Chinese without any difficulties! Now I'm gonna let Michael share with us more of his valuable learning experience in China! Welcome!

中譯　（美 / 女）您好，各位觀眾，我是潔西・古威爾。在今晚的節目當中，我們將與赫赫有名的麥克・布魯克斯進行座談。麥克在十三歲的時候便與他的父母親前往中國，進入當地的北京藝術學院就讀。當時麥克的年齡比其他同學多了兩倍，而他幾乎不會說中文。課堂上，他總是隨身攜帶中英對照的小字典，只為了向師長們證明他學習的決心。剛開始麥克和老師們只能靠比手畫腳來溝通，也常常造成了許多的誤解，但他仍舊保有極大的耐心，鍥而不捨地學習。最後他終於能夠用流利的中文與人群互動溝通，應付自如。現在有請麥克來跟我們分享更多關於他在中國求學的寶貴經驗，歡迎！

Q1. 此簡介可能在何處聽到？（答案：**B**）

    (A) 商業會議   (B) 廣播節目

    (C) 海灘飯店   (D) 棒球比賽

Q2. 根據獨白內容，麥克‧布魯克斯是誰？（答案：**B**）

    (A) 學生   (B) 演員

    (C) 語言學家   (D) 中國人

Q3. 麥克‧布魯克斯接下來可能會做什麼？（答案：**A**）

    (A) 講述他在中國的經驗   (B) 用中文做簡報

    (C) 介紹一位中國朋友   (D) 分析中文很難學的原因

解析

第一題

此題問的是「Where is the introduction probably taking place?」，那麼便可判斷要聽到此獨白可能出現之「地點場合」以便回答。根據此關鍵句「All right, my audience. I'm Jessie Goodwill. In tonight's program...」，可聽出這應是廣播節目中主持人的開場白，在介紹節目主題，故選 (B)「At a radio program」為最佳答案。

各選項解析

- 選項 (A)「At a business meeting」、選項 (C)「At a beach resort」與選項 (D)「At a baseball game」場合都不會是歡迎聽眾的場合，故不選。

第二題

此題問的是「Who is Michael Brooks?」，那麼便要聽到 Michael Brooks 是誰，他的「身分」相關資訊以便回答。根據此關鍵句「... we'll be interviewing the famous actor Michael Brooks.」，可聽出 Michael Brooks 是一位演員，故選 (B)「An actor」為最佳答案。

各選項解析

- 選項 (A)「A pupil」、選項 (C)「A linguist」或選項 (D)「A Chinese」都不是 Michael Brooks 的身分，故不選。

第三題

此題問的「What most likely will Michael Brooks do next?」，那麼便應該要聽到 Michael Brooks 接下來會做的事以便回答。根據此關鍵句「Now I'm gonna let Michael share with us more of his valuable learning experience in China!」，可聽出接下來主持人介紹 Michael 出場後，他會講在中國的學習經驗，故選 (A)「Talk about his experience in China」為最佳答案。

各選項解析

- 選項 (B)「Give a presentation in Chinese」、選項 (C)「Introduce a Chinese friend」與選項 (D)「Analyze why Chinese is difficult to learn」都沒在獨白中被提及，故不選。

關鍵字彙

audience [ˈɔdɪəns] n 聽眾	determined [dɪˈtɜmɪnd] a 決心的
interview [ˈɪntɚˌvju] v 訪問	misunderstand [ˈmɪsʌndɚˈstænd] v 誤解
persuade [pɚˈswed] v 說服、勸說	remain [rɪˈmen] v 保持、保有
pupil [ˈpjupl̩] n 學生	communicate [kəˈmjunəˌket] v 溝通

Q1. What is the purpose of the message?

(A) To cancel an order

(B) To inform a new policy

(C) To change the meeting time

(D) To question a proposal

Q2. When will Anny call Mark most likely?

(A) Friday at 5 p.m.

(B) Wednesday at 11 a.m.

(C) Monday at 8 p.m.

(D) Tuesday at noon

Q3. What does Mark need to do on Friday?

(A) Meet Anny

(B) Visit a client

(C) Call his boss

(D) Fly to Japan

聽稿　（CA / **M**）Hi Anny. This is Mark. Well, I'm calling to tell you that we've got an appointment this Friday, right? Well, I'm afraid I can't make it, as I was just assigned by my boss to visit an important client on Friday. Could you call me tomorrow to set up another time please? Uh, wait a second, no... not tomorrow, I'll be in Chicago. Can you call me on Wednesday instead? I'm available after ten in the morning. Any time after then will be fine with me. My number is 583-4893. Thank you very much, and sorry about Friday. Bye for now.

中譯　（加 / **男**）您好，安妮，我是馬克。我打來告訴您關於這個星期五我們有約在先的事，由於老闆派我於該日去拜訪一位重要的客戶，恐怕不能如期跟您見面了。能不能麻煩您於明日撥通電話給我，以便敲定另一個時段呢？呃，等等，不……明天也不行，我明天要出差去芝加哥。能否麻煩您星期三再打電話過來給我呢？我早上十點過後都會在，那之後的任何時間我都方便。我的號碼是 583-4893。非常感謝您的體諒，週五的事很抱歉，再見。

Q1. 此訊息的主要目的為何？（答案：**C**）

(A) 取消訂單

(B) 通知新政策

(C) 改會議時間

(D) 質疑提議案

Q2. 安妮最有可能在何時打電話給馬克？（答案：**B**）

(A) 週五下午五點

(B) 週三上午十一點

(C) 週一晚上八點

(D) 週二中午十二點

Q3. 馬克週五要做什麼？（答案：**B**）

(A) 跟安妮會面

(B) 拜訪客戶

(C) 打電話給老闆

(D) 飛去日本

解析

第一題

先掃描題目問的是「What is the purpose of the message?」，便預期要聽到留言的「目的」以便回答。根據此關鍵句「This is Mark. Well, I'm calling to tell you that we've got an appointment this Friday, right? Well, I'm afraid I can't make it...」，可聽出 Mark 電話留言的目的是為了「無法參與原先約好的會議，並要改時間」，故選 (C)「To change the meeting time」為最佳答案。

各選項解析

• 選項 (A)「To cancel an order」、選項 (B)「To inform a new policy」與選項 (D)「To question a proposal」都沒在文中被提及，故不選。

第二題

先掃描到題目問的是「When will Anny call Mark most likely?」，要聽到 Anny 回電給 Mark 的「時間點」資訊以便回答。根據此關鍵句「Can you call me on Wednesday instead? I'm available after ten in the morning. Any time after then will be fine with me.」，可聽出 Mark 要週三早上十點之後才方便接電話，故選 (B)「Wednesday at 11 a.m.」為最佳答案。

各選項解析

• 選項 (A)「Friday at 5 p.m.」、選項 (C)「Monday at 8 p.m.」與選項 (D)「Tuesday at noon」都沒有在獨白中被提及，故不選。

第三題

先掃描到題目問的是「What does Mark need to do on Friday?」，我們要聽到 Mark 週五應「做什麼事」相關答案以回答。根據此關鍵句「I was just assigned by my boss to visit an important client on Friday.」，可聽出週五他要去拜訪客戶，故選 (B)「Visit a client」為最佳答案。

各選項解析

• 選項 (A)「Meet Anny」、選項 (C)「Call his boss」與選項 (D)「Fly to Japan」都沒有在獨白中提及，故不選。

關鍵字彙

appointment [ə`pɔɪntmənt] n 約會、會議
available [ə`veləbl] a 有空的、可獲得的

Q1. What is Linda's duty in the company most likely?

(A) Designing new products　　　　　(B) Making cold calls

(C) Training new employees　　　　　(D) Arranging activities

Q2. According to the talk, what is special about the T5000 model?

(A) It's housewives' favorite　　　　　(B) It's the best-selling model

(C) It's very expensive　　　　　(D) It's designed for commercial users

Q3. What will be discussed next most likely?

(A) Customer feedback　　　　　(B) Sales channels

(C) Pricing　　　　　(D) Marketing

聽稿　（AU / W）Good afternoon, everyone. I'm Linda Jones from R&D. Today I'd like to introduce you to the newly developed product – a new version of our vacuum cleaner – the T5000. Well, we all know that the previous T4000 model was very successful last year. It's popular with the domestic users, but it didn't sell within the commercial sector of the market. This new T5000 model is specifically designed for commercial users. This vacuum cleaner is perfect for cleaning carpets. It also features a floor adjustment feature and can change between carpet and hardwood floors with an effortless flick of a switch. Best of all, it's very lightweight at only 9 pounds and is quite easy to steer. All right, now Marco from Marketing will talk about the pricing structure of this new product. Marco please.

中譯　（澳 / 女）大家午安，我是研發部的琳達・瓊斯。今天我要向各位介紹一項新的研發產品，本公司一款新型的吸塵器——型號 T5000。我們都知道去年上市的 T4000 款式在市場上的銷量非常傑出，尤其在家庭使用者方面造成了一股轟動，不過在商用這一區塊的購買量卻稍顯不足。這款 T5000 正是針對商業用途而設計的。這台吸塵器是清理地毯的最佳選擇。它也強調對於不同材質之地板的調整功能，只要輕輕按個鍵，便馬上能在地毯與硬質的木板地間做轉換。最厲害的是，它只有九磅的重量，輕盈的設計使它操作起來更為方便。我就暫且介紹到這邊，現在請我們行銷部門的馬可來繼續為各位說明此項新產品的價格，有請馬可。

Q1. 琳達在公司最有可能是負責什麼？（答案：A）

(A) 研發新產品　　　　　(B) 打推銷電話

(C) 訓練新進員工　　　　　(D) 安排活動

Q2. 根據獨白內容，T5000 型號特別之處為何？（答案：D）

(A) 那是家庭主婦的最愛　　　　　(B) 那是賣最好的型號

(C) 那款非常貴　　　　　(D) 那是為商業用戶設計的

Q3. 接下來最有可能會討論什麼？（答案：C）

(A) 客戶意見   (B) 銷售管道

(C) 價格   (D) 行銷

解析

第一題

先看到此題目問的是「What is Linda's duty in the company most likely?」，那麼可判斷要聽到 Linda 在公司的「職責、任務」相關資訊以便回答。根據此關鍵句「Good afternoon, everyone. I'm Linda Jones from R&D.」，可聽出她是在 R&D 部門工作，也就是產品研究發展部門，會在此部門工作的人自然就是要研發設計新產品較為合理了，故選 (A)「Designing new products」為最佳答案。

各選項解析

• 選項 (B)「Making cold calls」、選項 (C)「Training new employees」與選項 (D)「Arranging activities」都不會是「R&D」部門的人職責，故不選。

第二題

先掃描到此題問的是「What is special about the T5000 model?」，判斷要聽到關於 T5000 型號產品的「特殊之處」以便回答，根據此關鍵句「This new T5000 model is specifically designed for commercial users.」，可聽出此型號是設計給企業用戶，故選 (D)「It's designed for commercial users」為最佳答案。

各選項解析

• 選項 (A)「It's housewives' favorite」、選項 (B)「It's the best-selling model」與選項 (C)「It's very expensive」都沒在獨白中被提及，故不選。

第三題

此題問的是「What will be discussed next most likely?」，我們預期要聽到接下來會討論到的「主題」以便回答。根據此關鍵句「All right, now Marco from Marketing will talk about the pricing structure of this new product. Marco please.」可聽出接下來是要討論價格，故選 (C)「Pricing」為最佳答案。

各選項解析

• 選項 (A)「Customer feedback」、選項 (B)「Sales channels」與選項 (D)「Marketing」都沒有在獨白中提到，故不選。

關鍵字彙

introduce [ˌɪntrəˈdjus] **v** 介紹	adjustment [əˈdʒʌstmənt] **n** 調整
previous [ˈpriviəs] **a** 之前的	effortless [ˈɛfɚtlɪs] **a** 不費力的
domestic [dəˈmɛstɪk] **a** 家庭的	flick [flɪk] **n** 輕彈
commercial [kəˈmɝʃəl] **a** 商業的	lightweight [ˈlaɪtˈwet] **a** 輕量的
specifically [spɪˈsɪfɪkl̩ɪ] **ad** 特定地、特別地	steer [stɪr] **v** 掌控
carpet [ˈkɑrpɪt] **n** 地毯	structure [ˈstrʌktʃɚ] **n** 結構

Time	Topic	Speaker
9:30 a.m. - 10:30 a.m.	Business plans	George Golden
10:30 a.m. - 11:15 a.m.	Market conditions	George Golden
11:15 a.m. - 12 p.m.	Financial plans	Liz Jones
12 p.m. - 12:15 p.m.	Q / A discuss	Golden / Jones

Q1. Where is the meeting being held?

(A) At a hotel

(B) In a restaurant

(C) At the airport

(D) In a shopping mall

Q2. What will the speaker talk about first?

(A) Market research results

(B) Budget plans

(C) Product types

(D) Business vision

新 Q3. Look at the agenda. What time is proper for listeners to raise questions?

(A) Before 10 a.m.

(B) After 11 a.m.

(C) After 12 p.m.

(D) At 10:30 a.m.

聽稿　（CA / **M**）Good morning, and welcome to the Ritz Hotel. Thank you all so much for coming. Let me introduce myself: my name is George Golden and this is my partner, Liz Jones. The purpose of this presentation is to explain our business plans to you and hopefully to get you interested in investing in our AI Express company. I've divided my presentation into three major parts. First of all, I'll give you a short summary of our main business idea. After that I'll share with you the findings of the market research that we've been conducting, and finally I'll outline our financial requirements and plans. If you have any questions, I'll be happy to answer them in the end of my presentation please. All right, now let's start with my first point: our main business idea.

中譯　（加 / **男**）早安，歡迎來到麗絲飯店。非常感謝各位的蒞臨。先讓我做個簡單的自我介紹，我的名字是喬治‧高登，而這位是我的工作夥伴麗茲‧瓊斯。這場簡報說明會的主旨是要向各位說明我們最新的營運規劃，同時希望能爭取到各位投資我們 AI 快捷公司。我將我們簡報分成三個部分。首先我會先簡單敘述本公司的主要經營理念，接著分享本公司已著手進行的市場調查之結果，最後則會提出我們財務需求的大綱和計畫給各位做參考。倘若您有任何疑問，我很樂意在說明完畢後為各位逐一解答。那麼現在開始我的第一項重點主題：關於本公司的營運理念。

時間	主題	講者
早上九點半～十點半	商業計劃	喬治‧高登
早上十點半～十一點十五分	市場狀況	喬治‧高登
早上十一點十五分～十二點	財務計劃	麗茲‧瓊斯
下午十二點～十二點十五分	問題討論	高登、瓊斯

Q1. 此會議在何處舉辦？（答案：**A**）

　　(A) 飯店　　　　　　(B) 餐廳　　　　　　(C) 機場　　　　　(D) 購物中心

Q2. 講者會先討論什麼？（答案：**D**）

　　(A) 市場研究結果　　(B) 預算規劃　　　　(C) 產品類型　　　(D) 商業遠景

新 **Q3.** 請看議程。幾點是聽眾適合提出問題的時間？（答案：**C**）

　　(A) 早上十點前　　　(B) 早上十一點後　　(C) 中午十二點後　(D) 早上十點半

解析

第一題

很快地掃描題目問的是「Where is the meeting being held?」，那麼便可判斷要聽到會議所舉辦的「地點」相關資訊以便回答。根據此關鍵句「Good morning, and welcome to the Ritz Hotel. Thank you all so much for coming.」，可聽出是在飯店內舉行，故選 (A)「At a hotel」為最佳答案。

各選項解析

・選項 (B)「In a restaurant」、選項 (C)「At the airport」與選項 (D)「In a shopping mall」都沒有在獨白中被提及，故不選。

第二題

先掃描到此題問的是「What will the speaker talk about first?」，判斷要聽到講者會先討論的「主題」相關資訊以便回答。根據此關鍵句「I've divided my presentation into three major parts. First of all, I'll give you a short summary of our main business idea.」，可聽出講者會先討論的是 summary of main business idea，故選 (D)「Business vision」為最佳答案。

各選項解析

・選項 (A)「Market research results」、選項 (B)「Budget plans」與選項 (C)「Product types」都不是講者首先會討論的，故不選。

新 第三題

先掃描到題目，此題是要搭配表格內容回答的。此題問的是「What time is proper for listeners to raise questions?」，那麼便可判斷要聽講者希望聽眾可以提問的「時間點」，再來搭配表格內容。根據此關鍵句「If you have any questions, I'll be happy to answer them in the end of my presentation please.」，可聽出講者是希望大家在演講結束後再一起提問討論，查詢表格內時間之後可看出演講結束後可以問題討論的時間為中午十二點～十二點十五分之間，故選 (C)「After 12 p.m.」為最佳答案。

各選項解析

・選項 (A)「Before 10 a.m.」、選項 (B)「After 11 a.m.」或選項 (D)「At 10:30 a.m.」都不是可以提問的時段，故不選。

關鍵字彙

explain [ɪk`splen] v 解釋	finding [`faɪndɪŋ] n 發現
hopefully [`hopfəlɪ] ad 期望地、抱著希望地	conduct [kən`dʌkt] v 處理
invest [ɪn`vɛst] v 投資	outline [`aʊtͺlaɪn] v 列出大綱
divide [də`vaɪd] v 分隔、分開	financial [faɪ`nænʃəl] a 財務的、財政的
summary [`sʌmərɪ] n 結論	

Q1. Who are listening to this talk most likely?

(A) Investors of a private university

(B) Employees of a high-tech company

(C) Residents of Roman City

(D) Visitors from the U.S.

Q2. What is Mr. Legg's current position?

(A) Sales Director

(B) Vice President

(C) Professor

(D) Chief Executive Officer

Q3. What is suggested about Mr. Kevin Legg?

(A) He's an experienced language trainer

(B) He's a seasoned business leader

(C) He's going to reschedule his presentation

(D) He's talking about the pollution problem

聽稿　（US / Ⓦ）Attention please, guys. All right, so our quarterly briefing will begin in a minute. It's my pleasure to introduce our guest speaker for today, Mr. Kevin Legg. Mr. Legg has worked in the mobile and software technology industry for over 10 years. He is currently working at UPA as a Vice President. Prior to UPA, he was Founder and Chief Executive Officer of Max-Info Technologies, a renowned network management company. Mr. Legg has an MBA from Dickenson Business School, and a Bachelor's degree in Engineering from Roman College. Mr. Legg has spent a decade in the mobile and software field with a primary focus on enterprise solutions. I'm sure he's gonna give all of us a very special insight by sharing his experience. Now let's welcome Mr. Kevin Legg.

中譯　（美 / Ⓦ）大家請注意，我們的季度簡報馬上要開始了。很高興能為各位介紹今日的主講人——凱文・雷格先生。雷格先生已經在手機軟體系統科技這行待超過十年，現於 UPA 擔任副總一職。在任職於 UPA 之前，他曾是馬克思資訊科技公司的創辦人兼執行長，這是一間名聞遐邇的網路管理公司。雷格先生擁有狄更生管理學院的企業管理碩士學位，和羅曼學院的工程學士學位。他花了十年的時間耕耘手機軟體系統的領域，主要負責各項企業解決方案。我相信他將會透過自身經驗分享來給予大家獨特的見解。現在就讓我們歡迎凱文・雷格先生。

Q1. 此獨白的聽眾可能是誰？（答案：B）

(A) 私立大學的投資者

(B) 高科技公司的員工

(C) 羅曼市的居民

(D) 美國來的遊客

Q2. 雷格先生目前的職位為何？（答案：B）

(A) 業務總監

(B) 副總

(C) 教授

(D) 執行長

Q3. 獨白中提到關於凱文，雷格的什麼事？（答案：**B**）

(A) 他是個有經驗的語言講師　　　　　(B) 他是個身經百戰的商業經理人

(C) 他的簡報要改期了　　　　　　　　(D) 他要討論污染的問題

解析

第一題

此題問的是「Who are listening to this talk most likely?」，那麼便判斷要聽出可以得知「聽眾群」的相關資訊以便回答。根據此關鍵句「Attention please, guys. All right, so our quarterly briefing will begin in a minute. It's my pleasure to introduce our guest speaker for today...」，可聽出講者是歡迎大家參與每季的簡報，還請外來客座的講者來演講，故聽眾應是公司同仁較為合理，故選 (B)「Employees of a high-tech company」為最佳答案。

各選項解析

• 選項 (A)「Investors of a private university」、選項 (C)「Residents of Roman City」與選項 (D)「Visitors from the U.S.」都不會是要參加公司「季度報告」的人，故不選。

第二題

此題問的是「What is Mr. Legg's current position?」，應留意聽到 Mr. Legg 的「職稱」相關資訊以便回答。根據此關鍵句「Mr. Legg has worked in the mobile and software technology industry for over 10 years. He is currently working at UPA as a Vice President.」，可明顯聽出是「Vice President」，故選 (B)「Vice President」為最佳答案。

各選項解析

• 選項 (A)「Sales Director」、選項 (C)「Professor」與選項 (D)「Chief Executive Officer」都沒在獨白中被提及，故不選。

第三題

此題問的是「What is suggested about Mr. Kevin Legg?」，因此要聽到關於 Kevin Legg 先生之資訊以便推論，根據此關鍵句「Mr. Legg has spent a decade in the mobile and software field with a primary focus on enterprise solutions.」，可推斷 Mr. Legg 是管理階層之人，且在產業也服務超過十年了，應是有經驗的經理人較為合理，故選 (B)「He's a seasoned business leader」為最佳答案。

各選項解析

• 選項 (A)「He's an experienced language trainer」、選項 (C)「He's going to reschedule his presentation」與選項 (D)「He's talking about the pollution problem」都沒在獨白中討論到，故不選。

關鍵字彙

attention [əˋtɛnʃən] **n** 注意力	renowned [rɪˋnaʊnd] **a** 知名的
quarterly [ˋkwɔrtəlɪ] **ad** 每季地	decade [ˋdɛked] **n** 十年
briefing [ˋbrifɪŋ] **n** 簡報	primary [ˋpraɪˏmɛrɪ] **a** 主要的
introduce [ˏɪntrəˋdjus] **v** 介紹	enterprise [ˋɛntəˏpraɪz] **n** 企業
currently [ˋkɜntlɪ] **ad** 目前地	insight [ˋɪnˏsaɪt] **n** 見解

Q1. When is the talk most likely taking place?

(A) Before a training session   (B) After a serious discussion

(C) In the middle of a meeting   (D) Prior to a ceremony

Q2. What does the speaker say about customer service?

(A) Reps should try to avoid difficult customers

(B) It has a lot to do with company reputation

(C) It's not as important as sales revenue

(D) Only sales reps should know about it

Q3. Who is most likely Vicky Jones?

(A) A famous professor   (B) An excellent customer

(C) A senior vice president   (D) An expert in customer service field

聽稿

（CA / **M**）All right, all customer service representatives. Thank you for attending today's training session. As you know, word of mouth is one of the most economical and most effective ways of marketing our business and extending our customer base. If we don't treat our customers the right way, well, we could lose both business opportunities and company reputation. And that's why we emphasize the importance of this training course. This course is designed for customer service representatives who want to know how to eliminate customer dissatisfaction and learn how to handle awkward customers appropriately. All right, now let's welcome the trainer, Ms. Vicky Jones.

中譯

（加 / **男**）好的，所有客服人員的代表們，感謝您們參加今天的訓練講座。如您們所知，口耳相傳對於市場行銷和擴大我們的客戶來源是最簡單且有效的方法之一。如果我們以不正確的方式對待客戶，公司的信譽和商機則將付之一炬。這便是為什麼我們要特別強調這次訓練課程的重要性。這堂課是專門為那些想要知道如何降低客訴、並學習如何適當地應付難纏客戶的客服代表們而設計。那麼就讓我們歡迎今天的指導人——薇琪・瓊斯小姐。

Q1. 此獨白最有可能在何時聽到？（答案：**A**）

(A) 訓練講座開始之前   (B) 嚴肅的討論之後

(C) 會議進行當中   (D) 慶典之前

Q2. 講者提到關於客服的什麼事？（答案：**B**）

(A) 客服代表應避免接觸難纏的客戶   (B) 客服跟公司聲譽有很大的關係

(C) 客服不比業績重要   (D) 只有業務代表需要知道

Q3. 薇琪・瓊斯小姐最有可能是誰？（答案：**D**）

(A) 有名的教授   (B) 優良客戶

(C) 資深副總   (D) 客服領域的專家

解析

第一題

此題問的是「When is the talk most likely taking place?」，便可判斷要聽到可能推論會聽到此獨白的「時機點」相關資訊以便回答。根據此關鍵句「All right, all customer service representatives. Thank you for attending today's training session.」，可聽出講者是訓練課程之前，先歡迎大家來參加訓練的開場詞，故選 (A)「Before a training session」為最佳答案。

各選項解析

• 選項 (B)「After a serious discussion」、選項 (C)「In the middle of a meeting」與選項 (D)「Prior to a ceremony」都不是會聽到此開場白的時間點，故不選。

第二題

先掃描題目看到此題問的是「What does the speaker say about customer service?」，判斷要聽到講者提供「客戶服務」之相關資訊以便回答。根據此關鍵「If we don't treat our customers the right way, well, we could lose both business opportunities and company reputation.」，可聽出，若不做好客戶服務，可能會失去公司的好名聲，如此可推斷「客戶服務和公司名聲是息息相關」，故選 (B)「It has a lot to do with company reputation」為最佳答案。

各選項解析

• 選項 (A)「Reps should try to avoid difficult customers」、選項 (C)「It's not as important as sales revenue」與選項 (D)「Only sales reps should know about it」都沒有在獨白中提及，故不選。

第三題

此題問的是「Who is most likely Vicky Jones?」，我們要聽到可能得知 Vicky Jones 的「身分」之相關資訊以便回答。根據此關鍵句「All right, now let's welcome the trainer, Ms. Vicky Jones.」可聽出，要有辦法提供客服相關訓練的人，應是客服方面的專家才較合理，故選 (D)「An expert in customer service field」為佳答案。

各選項解析

• 選項 (A)「A famous professor」、選項 (B)「An excellent customer」與選項 (C)「A senior vice president」都不是會提供「客戶服務訓練」的人，故不選。

關鍵字彙

session [ˈsɛʃən] n. 講習
word of mouth ph. 口耳相傳
economical [ˌikəˈnɑmɪkl̩] a. 經濟的、節約的
extend [ɪkˈstɛnd] v. 擴大、給予
reputation [ˌrɛpjəˈteʃən] n. 名聲、名譽
emphasize [ˈɛmfəˌsaɪz] v. 強調
eliminate [ɪˈlɪməˌnet] v. 消除、排除
dissatisfaction [ˌdɪssætɪsˈfækʃən] n. 不滿意
awkward [ˈɔkwɚd] a. 棘手的
appropriately [əˈproprɪˌetlɪ] ad. 恰當地、適當地
trainer [ˈtrenɚ] n. 訓練者、講師

Q1. **When is this talk most likely taking place?**

(A) In winter

(B) During a company meeting

(C) After dinner

(D) In a sports competition

Q2. **What issue is being discussed?**

(A) Customer satisfaction

(B) Sales performance

(C) Employee recruitment in Japan

(D) Japanese language training

Q3. **What will the speaker most likely do next?**

(A) Welcome the next speaker from Japan

(B) Encourage everybody to learn Japanese

(C) Ask each participant to input opinions

(D) Buy all members snacks and drinks

聽稿

（US / Ⓦ）Right, so the next item on our agenda is the new sales division in Japan. Well, as you may know already, we're going to establish a new sales office in Japan next year and so need to discuss recruitment please. Basically, I've got two alternatives in mind. I'm thinking either to take on new Japanese sales representatives and train them or to teach our Chinese sales representatives Japanese and transfer them to Japan. Well, of course there will be pros and cons to both proposals. I need all of you to provide inputs please. Let's start with Jack. So Jack, what's your view on this issue please?

中譯

（美 / 女）接著要討論我們議程的下一個事項——關於公司要在日本設置的新銷售分部。各位應該已經知道，我們將於明年在日本建立新的銷售處所，因而需要想想有關招募人才的議題。基本上，我想了兩種方案。其一是直接聘請日本當地的銷售代表駐點，給予他們教育訓練；或是教中國業務人員日語，然後再將他們送去日本任職。當然此兩種提案皆各有利弊，所以我需要請各位提供你們個人的意見，我們就從傑克開始吧。傑克，你對於這件事情有什麼樣的看法？

Q1. 此獨白最有可能發生在何時？（答案：B）

(A) 在冬天

(B) 在公司會議中

(C) 晚餐後

(D) 在運動比賽時

Q2. 此獨白在討論何議題？（答案：C）

(A) 客戶滿意度

(B) 業績表現

(C) 日本人力招募

(D) 日文訓練

Q3. 講者接下來最有可能做什麼？（答案：C）

(A) 歡迎下一位來自日本的講者

(B) 鼓勵大家學日文

(C) 請與會者提供意見

(D) 買點心和飲料請大家

解析

第一題

此題問的是「When is this talk most likely taking place?」，那麼便可判斷應聽到此獨白可能會被提及的「時間點」，根據此關鍵句「Right, so the next item on our agenda is the new sales division in Japan.」，可聽出會議中某個主題討論完了，接著要討論下個主題，那麼此獨白應該是在「會議當中」會講到的較為合理，故選 (B)「During a company meeting」為最佳答案。

各選項解析

• 選項 (A)「In winter」、選項 (C)「After dinner」與選項 (D)「In a sports competition」都非會聽到此談話的時機，故不選。

第二題

此題目問的是「What issue is being discussed?」，要聽到所討論的「主題」為何以便回答。根據此關鍵句「... we're going to establish a new sales office in Japan next year and so need to discuss recruitment please.」，可聽出是要討論在日本招募員工之事，故選 (C)「Employee recruitment in Japan」為最佳答案。

各選項解析

• 選項 (A)「Customer satisfaction」、選項 (B)「Sales performance」與選項 (D)「Japanese language training」都沒有在獨白中被提及，故不選。

第三題

此題問的是「What will the speaker most likely do next?」，應該要聽到講者接下來會「做什麼事」相關資訊以便回答。根據此關鍵句「I need all of you to provide inputs please. Let's start with Jack. So Jack, what's your view on this issue please?」，可聽出她是要每個與會者表達意見，故選 (C)「Ask each participant to input opinions」為最佳答案。

各選項解析

• 選項 (A)「Welcome the next speaker from Japan」、選項 (B)「Encourage everybody to learn Japanese」與選項 (D)「Buy all members snacks and drinks」都沒有在獨白中聽到，故不選。

關鍵字彙

agenda [ə`dʒɛndə] n 議程
division [də`vɪʒən] n 區域、部分
establish [ə`stæblɪʃ] v 建立、創辦
recruitment [rɪ`krutmənt] n 招募
alternative [ɔl`tɜnətɪv] n 其他選擇
transfer [træns`fɜ] v 轉移
proposal [prə`pozl] n 提議案
input [`ɪn‚put] n （意見）投入
issue [`ɪʃju] n 議題

Bookstore	Inventory
Stone Bookstore	> 13
First-rate Bookstore	= 8
Big-know Bookstore	< 5
Happy Bookstore	0

Q1. What is being advertised?

(A) A fashion store   (B) A new book

(C) A new service   (D) A fancy car

Q2. What does the speaker ask listeners to do?

(A) Develop communication skills   (B) Buy a copy of this book

(C) Write the author an e-mail   (D) Visit Canada in person

新 Q3. Look at the chart. If a client would like to order 12 copies of the book, which store does he need to contact?

(A) First-rate Bookstore   (B) Big-know Bookstore

(C) Stone Bookstore   (D) Happy Bookstore

聽稿　（UK / **M**）Are you low in self-esteem? Do you want to achieve more? "Take Actions, Now" is just the book right for you. Canada's best motivational author, Mary Worth shows you how to focus fully on your goals and achieve them. You deserve to be successful and this new book provides you with the right tools and techniques to attract that success. The author teaches you how to practice accepting compliment and grow your self-esteem, how to let go of past mistakes and soar above them, and even discover how to find your true purpose in life. "Take Actions, Now" is about becoming more focused on what you really wants to achieve in life. It's about not listening to noises around you and believing in your goals. This book is available in all major bookstores. Why not get a copy today and start to work toward success.

中譯　（英 / **男**）你是一個缺乏自信心的人嗎？你想要更多成就嗎？《即刻行動》正是一本最適合你的讀物，讓來自加拿大最能激勵人心的暢銷作者瑪莉・沃斯指導你如何堅持到底、完成目標。成功是你應得的寶物，而這本新書提供正確的工具和技巧去輔助你成功。作者教導你如何練習接受讚美、培養你的自信，如何放下過去的錯誤並超越、甚至協助找尋人生貨真價實的意義。《即刻行動》主要談論你如何專注於自己在生命中想要達成的目標，同時也教你堅信自己的夢想、不為周遭的種種雜音所動。這本書於各大書店皆有販售，何不今日就把它帶回家，並開始邁向成功的康莊大道呢？

書局	庫存
石頭書局	多於十三本
一流書局	八本
大知識書局	少於五本
快樂書局	零本

Q1. 此獨白是在介紹何種產品？（答案：**B**）

    (A) 流行商店   (B) 新書   (C) 新的服務   (D) 拉風的車

Q2. 講者請聽眾做什麼？（答案：**B**）

    (A) 培養溝通能力   (B) 買此新出版的書   (C) 寫電郵給作者   (D) 親自去加拿大一趟

新 Q3. 請看表格。若有個客戶想訂十二本此書，他應該要跟哪個書局聯絡？（答案：**C**）

    (A) 一流書局   (B) 大知識書局   (C) 石頭書局   (D) 快樂書局

解析

第一題

此題目問的是「What is being advertised?」，那麼便可判斷要聽到此獨白內所宣傳的「產品」為何以便回答。根據此關鍵句「Are you low in self-esteem? Do you want to achieve more? "Take Actions, Now" is just the book right for you.」，可聽出是在介紹新出的一本書，故選 (B)「A new book」為最佳答案。

各選項解析

- 選項 (A)「A fashion store」、選項 (C)「A new service」與選項 (D)「A fancy car」都沒有在獨白中被提及，故不選。

第二題

此題問的是「What does the speaker ask listeners to do?」，判斷要聽到講者要聽者「做什麼」相關資訊以便回答。根據此關鍵句「This book is available in all major bookstores. Why not get a copy today and start to work toward success.」，可聽出講者鼓勵聽眾去買本書來看，故選 (B)「Buy a copy of this book」為最佳答案。

各選項解析

- 選項 (A)「Develop communication skills」、選項 (C)「Write the author an e-mail」與選項 (D)「Visit Canada in person」都沒在獨白中被提到，故不選。

新 第三題

先掃描到此題目，是要對照圖表的。題目問的是「If a client would like to order 12 copies of the book, which store does he need to contact?」，因此我們知道要查看圖表，看哪間書店是有書的庫存多於十二本以上的。查看之後，Stone bookstore 的庫存是多於十三本，故選 (C)「Stone Bookstore」為最佳答案。

各選項解析

- 選項 (A)「First-rate Bookstore」、選項 (B)「Big-know Bookstore」與選項 (D)「Happy Bookstore」的庫存都不到十二本，故不選。

關鍵字彙

self-esteem [ˌsɛlfəsˈtim] n 自尊心
achieve [əˈtʃiv] v 達成
motivational [ˌmotəˈveʃənəl] a 激勵的
deserve [dɪˈzɝv] v 應受、該得
technique [tɛkˈnik] n 技巧

compliment [ˈkɑmpləmənt] n 讚美、恭維
soar [sor] v 飆飛、飆高
purpose [ˈpɝpəs] n 目的
available [əˈveləbl] a 可得的、有空的

Q1. Who is most likely the speaker?

(A) The security guard of the company   (B) The chair of the meeting

(C) A new employee   (D) A difficult customer

Q2. When is this talk most likely taking place?

(A) During the company outing   (B) After work

(C) During the break   (D) In the beginning of the meeting

Q3. What will A.J. be in charge of in the company?

(A) Arranging campaigns   (B) Hosting parties

(C) Taking meeting minutes   (D) Designing new products

聽稿

（AU / Ⓦ）All right, our weekly meeting is about to begin. Is everybody here? Ah, here comes James. Good morning James, please take a seat. Now, it's nice to see you guys here. Before we begin, I'd like to introduce a new colleague to you all: A.J. McHill. For those who don't already know, A.J. is our new event coordinator. He will be responsible for coordinating details of our conferences, calculating budgets, and scheduling speakers, vendors, and participants. Before joining our company, A.J. worked at an advertising agency handling major advertising campaigns. With his background and experience, I'm sure A.J. will be a great asset for our company. Welcome, A.J. All right, now let's take a look at the agenda for today's meeting.

中譯

（澳 / 女）那麼馬上要開始我們這週的例行會議。全員到齊了嗎？啊，詹姆斯來了。詹姆斯，早安，請找張椅子就座。很開心見到各位，在我們開始之前，我要先向各位介紹一位新的同事：A.J.・麥希爾。有些人可能還不知道，A.J. 是我們的活動策辦人，他會負責大大小小的會議細節、預算編列、還有規劃主講人、供應商、和參與者的事宜等等。在他加入公司之前，A.J. 曾在廣告公司負責策劃主要的廣告活動。擁有這種專業的背景和經驗，我相信 A.J. 會成為本公司舉足輕重的角色。歡迎你，A.J.。現在開始我們今日的例行會議流程吧。

Q1. 講者最有可能是誰？（答案：B）

(A) 公司警衛   (B) 會議主席

(C) 新進員工   (D) 難纏的客戶

Q2. 此獨白最有可能是在何時聽到？（答案：D）

(A) 在公司旅遊間   (B) 下班後

(C) 休息期間   (D) 會議開始時

Q3. A.J. 在公司將會負責什麼事務？（答案：A）

(A) 安排活動   (B) 主辦派對

(C) 做會議紀錄   (D) 設計新產品

解析

第一題

先掃描到題目問的是「Who is most likely the speaker?」，那麼便要專注聽到講者「身分」相關資訊以便回答。根據此關鍵句「All right, our weekly meeting is about to begin. Is everybody here? ... Now, it's nice to see you guys here.」，可聽出會在會議開始之前說話的人，應是「會議主席」較為合理，故選 (B)「The chair of the meeting」為最佳答案。

各選項解析

• 選項 (A)「The security guard of the company」、選項 (C)「A new employee」與選項 (D)「A difficult customer」都不會是在會議開始之前講話的人，故不選。

第二題

此題問的是「When is this talk most likely taking place?」，知道要聽到此獨白可能會聽到的「時機、時間點」以便回答。根據此關鍵句「Now, it's nice to see you guys here. Before we begin, I'd like to introduce a new colleague to you all...」，可聽出主席說要在會議真正開始之前先介紹新進員工，故選 (D)「In the beginning of the meeting」為最佳答案。

各選項解析

• 選項 (A)「During the company outing」、選項 (B)「After work」與選項 (C)「During the break」都不是此主席講話的時間點，故不選。

第三題

此題目問的是「What will A.J. be in charge of in the company?」，要聽到 A.J. 在公司負責什麼「業務、職責」以便回答。根據此關鍵句「For those who don't already know, A.J. is our new event coordinator. He will be responsible for coordinating details of our conferences...」，可聽出他是負責辦活動，故選 (A)「Arranging campaigns」為最佳答案。

各選項解析

• 選項 (B)「Hosting parties」、選項 (C)「Taking meeting minutes」與選項 (D)「Designing new products」都沒在獨白中被提及，故不選。

關鍵字彙

coordinator [ko`ɔrdn͵etɚ] n 協調者
responsible [rɪ`spɑnsəbl̩] a 負責任的
calculate [`kælkjə͵let] v 計算
advertising [`ædvɚ͵taɪzɪŋ] n 廣告
agency [`edʒənsɪ] n 代辦處
handle [`hændl̩] v 處理
background [`bæk͵graʊnd] n 背景
asset [`æsɛt] n 資產
agenda [ə`dʒɛndə] n 議程

Q1. What is being advertised?

(A) A high-tech car

(B) A software solution

(C) A new restaurant

(D) An e-mail writing course

Q2. Who is the intended audience?

(A) Students learning English

(B) Drivers using GPS systems

(C) Companies with e-mail systems

(D) Mothers with children

Q3. What should listeners do if they'd like to learn more?

(A) Buy a fax machine

(B) Check the company website

(C) Call the software developer

(D) Fill in an application form

聽稿 （UK / M）Are you receiving unwanted spam e-mails? Are you wondering if there is ever a way to stop it? Well, let our Anti-Spam system help. Our one-of-a-kind Anti-Spam system is a spam filter that can detect unwanted e-mails and delete them before they reach your network. The system scans your network for spam and viruses and offers complete e-mail security with no software to install and no changes on your e-mail clients. Additionally we use strong encryption technology to ensure that your sensitive e-mails are securely protected as they travel over the Internet. To find out more, please call Anti-Spam at 1-800-111-2222 or visit our website at www. antispam.net.

中譯 （英 / 男）您常常收到一大堆令人討厭的垃圾郵件嗎？您是否想知道有無任何方法可以阻止它們的出現？讓我們的垃圾郵件防制系統助您一臂之力吧。我們獨一無二的垃圾郵件防制系統運用過濾的原理去偵測無關緊要的信件，並在它們發送到您的網路之前便逐一刪除。在無需安裝任何軟體、也不影響您電子郵件上聯絡人資訊的情況下，系統能夠掃描您的網路是否存有多餘的垃圾郵件和病毒，對於您的信件有一定的保護作用。除此之外，我們還設置了強而有力的加密功能，以確保您的私人信件在遊歷網際網路的過程中是處於絕對安全的狀態。欲知詳情請撥 1-800-111-2222，或上我們垃圾郵件防制系統 www.antispam.net 的網站查詢。

Q1. 此獨白是在介紹何種產品？（答案：B）

(A) 高科技車

(B) 軟體解決方案

(C) 新餐廳

(D) 電郵寫作課程

Q2. 此獨白是針對何類聽眾？（答案：C）

(A) 學英文的學生

(B) 有導航系統的駕駛

(C) 有電郵系統的企業

(D) 有小孩的媽媽

Q3. 想了解更多的聽眾應做什麼？（答案：B）

(A) 買台傳真機

(B) 查詢公司網頁

(C) 打電話給軟體開發員

(D) 填寫申請表

解析 第一題

此題問的是「What is being advertised?」，那麼要聽到此獨白在廣告什麼「產品」相關資訊以便回答。根據此關鍵句「Are you receiving unwanted spam e-mails? Are you wondering if there is ever a way to stop it? Well, let our Anti-Spam system help.」，可聽出是在介紹「電郵過濾系統」，故選 (B)「A software solution」為最佳答案。

各選項解析

• 選項 (A)「A high-tech car」、選項 (C)「A new restaurant」與選項 (D)「An e-mail writing course」都沒在獨白中被提及，故不選。

第二題

先掃描到題目問的是「Who is the intended audience?」，那我們便應該要聽到可能的「聽眾群」相關資訊以便回答。根據此關鍵句「Our one-of-a-kind Anti-Spam system is a spam filter that can detect unwanted e-mails and delete them before they reach your network.」，可聽出是要有企業網路的公司才會使用此過濾系統，故選 (C)「Companies with e-mail systems」為最佳答案。

各選項解析

• 選項 (A)「Students learning English」、選項 (B)「Drivers using GPS systems」與選項 (D)「Mothers with children」都沒在獨白中被提及，故不選。

第三題

此題問的是「What should listeners do if they'd like to learn more?」，我們要聽到想了解更多資訊的客戶應「做什麼」相關資訊以便回答。根據此關鍵句「To find out more, please call Anti-Spam at 1-800-111-2222 or visit our website at www.antispam.net.」，可聽出是可以打電話詢問或查看公司網站，故選 (B)「Check the company website」為最佳答案。

各選項解析

• 選項 (A)「Buy a fax machine」、選項 (C)「Call the software developer」或選項 (D)「Fill in an application form」都沒有在獨白中被提到，故不選。

關鍵字彙

receive [rɪ`siv] v 接收	security [sɪ`kjurətɪ] n 安全性
spam [spæm] n 垃圾郵件	install [ɪn`stɔl] v 安裝
wonder [`wʌndɚ] v 想知道	additionally [ə`dɪʃənl̩ɪ] ad 另外地
filter [`fɪltɚ] n 過濾器	encryption [ɛn`krɪpʃən] n 加密
detect [dɪ`tɛkt] v 偵查到	technology [tɛk`nɑlədʒɪ] n 科技
scan [skæn] v 掃描	sensitive [`sɛnsətɪv] a 敏感的
virus [`vaɪrəs] n 病毒	protect [prə`tɛkt] v 保護

Part 4 應試策略總整理

聽力最後的 Part 4 簡短獨白與 Part 3 的簡短對話有點類似，都是以三小題一題組的方式呈現，不同點在於 Part 4 是一人講完聽力內容。而且，長篇獨白還包括：不同口音、內容加長、對照圖表資料……等。無疑是要求考生具備百分之兩百的專注力，與極快的資訊對應處理能力。

大家務必專注在會考的要點，講者會「加強重音」來加以強調，所以也應該要學會辨別英文聽力的語調、語氣，被輕聲帶過的弱音與被加強的重音各為何，也才可將注意力放在「真正重要且會考、又被加強重音強調的資訊上」，進而增加答對機率。

那麼，哪些資訊是應該注意聽的呢？自然是三道題目的題組呀！要克服 Part 4 簡短獨白，第一步要做的便是「務必先看題目」在問什麼。獨白題一篇固定搭配三道題目，這些題目所問的順序通常會以獨白短文中的順序來出題，獨白中的第一句會是重點，應該會考一題；中間細節的部分，再考一題；最後結尾的結論句也很重要，也考一題。

請考生先了解問題點，再仔細聽答案，這是得分的關鍵。以下將整理出出題頻率高的問題點。

❶「Who」開始之問句，則可預期要聽到有提到「人名」、「職位名稱」、或「與某人之關係」等關鍵字詞來回答。

❷「What」開始之問句，便打定主意要聽到「物件」、「主題」、或「活動名稱」等關鍵字以便回答問題。

❸「When」開始之問句，便可推斷要聽到「時間」、「星期幾」、「月分」、及「年分」等關鍵點才可回答。

❹「Where」開始之問句，便預期要聽到「地點」相關的答案。

❺「Why」開始之問句，便預期要聽到「原因」、及「理由」等相關答案。

另外，在「語調」方面，獨白內容時並不是使用單一語調，而是有上揚、下降，或有強有弱之語調變化的。同學也應該自己熟悉各種語調，並藉著語調來幫助你了解情境。

最後，要集中精神一邊對照題目一邊聽資訊之外，若可以同時「想像」所唸的真實情境」則更可以理解獨白內容，獨白內容只是反映真實的商務環境中的情況，所以將想像與真實情形聯想起來，也就容易理解和容易記憶。

國家圖書館出版品預行編目（CIP）資料

神猜解TOEIC多益聽力:「攻略」+「試題」+
「解析」一本搞定/ 薛詠文著. -- 初版. -- 臺北
市 : 我識, 2019.10　　面; 公分
ISBN 978-986-94501-5-7(平裝附光碟)

1.多益測驗

805.1895　　　　　　　　106010166

書名 / 神猜解TOEIC多益聽力:「攻略」+「試題」+「解析」一本搞定

作者 / 薛詠文

審訂 / 全新制多益解題小組

發行人 / 蔣敬祖

出版事業群總經理 / 廖晏婕

銷售暨流通事業群總經理 / 施宏

總編輯 / 劉俐伶

執行編輯 / 吳紹瑜

校對 / 劉婉瑀、紀珊、林意清

視覺指導 / 姜孟傑、鍾維恩

內文排版 / 張靜怡、黃莉庭

內文圖片 / www.shutterstock.com

法律顧問 / 北辰著作權事務所蕭雄淋律師

印製 / 金濬印刷事業有限公司

初版 / 2019年10月

出版 / 我識出版教育集團──我識出版社

電話 / (02) 2345-7222

傳真 / (02) 2345-5758

地址 / 台北市忠孝東路五段372巷27弄78-1號1樓

網址 / www.17buy.com.tw

E-mail / iam.group@17buy.com.tw

facebook網址 / www.facebook.com/ImPublishing

定價 / 新台幣699元 / 港幣233元

總經銷 / 我識出版社有限公司出版發行部

地址 / 新北市汐止區新台五路一段114號12樓

電話 / (02) 2696-1357　傳真 / (02) 2696-1359

地區經銷 / 易可數位行銷股份有限公司

地址 / 新北市新店區寶橋路235巷6弄3號5樓

港澳總經銷 / 和平圖書有限公司

地址 / 香港柴灣嘉業街12號百樂門大廈17樓

電話 / (852) 2804-6687　傳真 / (852) 2804-6409

2011 不求人文化

2009 懶鬼子英日語

I'm 我識出版集團
I'm Publishing Group
www.17buy.com.tw

2005 意識文化

2005 易富文化

2003 我識地球村

2001 我識出版社

2011 不求人文化

2009 懶鬼子英日語

I'm 我識出版集團
I'm Publishing Group
www.17buy.com.tw

2005 意識文化

2005 易富文化

2003 我識地球村

2001 我識出版社

2011 不求人文化

2009 懶鬼子英日語

I'm 我識出版集團
I'm Publishing Group
www.17buy.com.tw

2005 意識文化

2005 易富文化

2003 我識地球村

2001 我識出版社

2011 不求人文化

2009 懶鬼子英日語

I'm 我識出版集團
I'm Publishing Group
www.17buy.com.tw

2005 意識文化

2005 易富文化

2003 我識地球村

2001 我識出版社